Graham Masterton Omnibus

THE HYMN
NIGHT PLAGUE

Also by Graham Masterton

Graham Masterton Omnibus

THE HYMN
NIGHT PLAGUE

GRAHAM
MASTERTON

timewarner
paperbacks

A *Time Warner* Paperback

This omnibus edition first published in Great Britain
by Time Warner Paperbacks in 2003
Graham Masterton Omnibus Copyright © Graham Masterton 2003

Previously published separately:
The Hymn first published in Great Britain in
1991 by Macdonald & Co (Publishers) Ltd
Published by Warner Books in 1993
Reprinted 1995, 2000
Copyright © Graham Masterton 1991

Night Plague first published in Great Britain in 1991 by
Severn House Publishers Ltd by arrangement with
Macdonald & Co (Publishers) Ltd
Published by Warner Books in 1994
Reprinted 1994, 1995, 1998, 2001
Copyright © Graham Masterton 1991

A CIP catalogue record for this book is
available from the British Library.

ISBN 0 7515 35034 4

Printed and bound in Great Britain by
Clays Ltd, St Ives plc

Time Warner Paperbacks
An imprint of
Time Warner Books UK
Brettenham House
Lancaster Place
London WC2E 7EN

www.TimeWarnerBooks.co.uk

THE HYMN

The San Diego Opera Company
in association with Mander Promotions
extends a personal invitation to

---

to attend a Gala Evening of
Operatic Tributes To Richard Wagner

San Diego Civic Theater, Second Avenue at A Street
June 21, at 9 p.m.

Dress Formal

— ONE —

If Bob Tuggey had thought for an instant that the girl in the red-chequered cowboy shirt was carrying that bright yellow petrol can across the car-park with the intention of burning herself alive, he would immediately have thrown down his spatula, vaulted the counter and run out of the restaurant as fast as his cruiser-weight build could have taken him.

From where he was standing in the kitchen, he was probably the first person in the Rosecrans Avenue branch of McDonald's to catch sight of her. And – ironically – he was probably the only person who had the experience to realize what was wrong about the way she was walking, even though she was smiling and swinging the petrol can like a basketful of summer flowers.

In another time, in another life, Bob Tuggey had been a junior clerk for Deputy Chief of Mission William Trueheart in South Viet Nam; and one evening late in June, 1963, when he was driving back to the embassy after buying himself half a dozen new sports shirts from his Chinese tailor in Cholon, a Buddhist monk had walked across the road in front of him in just the same way, swinging a petrol can. *A-tisket, a-tasket ...*

Bob's Valiant had been brought to a halt a little further up the road by a long military convoy grinding past, and while he had sat smoking and listening to Peter, Paul and Mary, the monk had eased himself down on the pavement less than seventy feet away, splashed sparkling petrol all over his head, and set himself alight.

'*The answer, my friend, is blowin' in the wind ...*'

Bob had never forgotten the soft flaring noise of burning petrol, the whirl of ashes from burning robes, the stoical agony on the monk's gradually blackening face.

1

There had been shouting, arguing, bicycle bells ringing, but nobody had screamed. Bob had heaved himself out of the car, dragging his picnic-blanket after him with the intention of smothering the flames, but three more monks had pushed him away, persistently, with the heels of their bony hands, until their brother had fallen stiffly sideways, still burning, beyond the ministrations of anybody but Buddha.

Bob had doubled up by the side of the road, under that bronze smoky sky, and vomited churned-up chicken and tomatoes. Even today, 'Blowin' In The Wind' made his stomach tighten.

Maybe the smallest of small bells tinkled in Bob's memory as the girl came into view. But of course there was nothing about her that would have put him instantly in mind of a protesting Buddhist monk. She was petite and blonde, with bouncy brushed-back hair that reminded him of Doris Day. Her cowboy shirt was matched with a wide tan-leather belt, cinched tight, and well-fitting 501s.

'Four quarter-pounders down,' called Sally, the ginger-haired manageress. Bob peeled off the greaseproof paper, and pressed the burgers on to the hotplate. Outside the window, the girl was already halfway across the car-park, still swinging the can, her shrunken shadow dancing after her. The sunlight flashed for an instant off the yellow enamel paint.

Bob was balding and overweight and by far the oldest employee at McDonald's Rosecrans Avenue. When his left eye looked west, his right eye looked nor'-nor'-west. But all of the kids liked him, and called him 'Unca Tug'. He was fifty-one next week, a birthday he would have to celebrate on his own. After William Trueheart had left Saigon, Bob had drifted through one menial government clerkship after another, black coffee, brown offices. He had started to drink, a bottle of Ricard a day, often more. Days of milk-white clouds and aniseed. In France one rainy afternoon, in his small apartment in the Domaine de la Ronce, he had tried to commit suicide by gassing himself. What was the point of living, with no prospects, no money, and no companions but a brindled boxer with slobbery jowls that kept chewing the furniture?

All that had saved him was the stink of gas, which (with a stomachful of Ricard) had made him feel unbearably dizzy and sick. He had gone out for a breath of fresh air. Absurd, in the middle of killing himself, but he hadn't wanted to die nauseous. While he was out, the gas had blown up his kitchen, and deafened his dog. The *concierge* had been furious, and had followed him around for an hour, shouting at him.

'*Idiot*! You think it's a good joke, to blow up your apartment?'

'Pardon?' he had repeated, again and again. He, too, had been deafened, but only temporarily.

The girl kept walking towards the far side of the car-park. The hot shuddering air made it look as if she were walking through a crystal-clear lake. It was 95 degrees outside which, in San Diego, was exceptional for June. She was walking towards the far side of the car-park with what, by the slow way it swung, was obviously a full can of petrol. Yet where was she taking it? There were no cars parked on that side of the car-park, none at all, and no vehicles in sight on the road.

Bob turned the quarter-pounders over, and took two special orders for cheeseburger grills.

'Sally – fillets up!' called Gino, next to him, all Adam's apple and razored black sideburns. The girl outside stepped with her can over the scrubby row of bushes that separated one section of the car-park from the next.

'Unca Tug, where's those quarter-pounders?' Sally demanded. Bob glanced down. They were almost ready.

'Three chicken sandwiches down!' Marianne called.

'Big Macs up!' said Gino.

'Two cheeseburgers down!' said Doyle.

Bob looked up again and the girl was still walking. She was probably five hundred feet away from the restaurant now. He didn't know why he kept on watching her, but she was so far away from any parked vehicles now, with that can of petrol, and she was slowing down, looking around her, as if she were lost, or as if she had decided that *this* was the spot.

The sizzle of quarter-pounders distracted Bob for a second. He scooped them off the hotplate and shovelled them into their buns. 'Four Macs down!' called Sally.

Bob lifted the metal tray of quarter-pounders on to the counter and, as he did so, he saw the girl lowering herself crosslegged on to the concrete. He frowned, trying hard to focus. His eyes weren't so good at this kind of distance. He always wore his glasses when he went to the movies, or to San Diego Stadium to watch the Padres. But as the girl turned herself slightly to twist open the petrol can, he instantly interpreted the meaning of her gesture and it was *then*, in a thrill of total horror, that he connected the buoyant determined walk to nowhere in particular – *a-tisket, a-tasket* – with the yellow can swinging, and the dignified crosslegged posture, and the terrible composure with which she reached out to turn the screwtop.

His ears heard the spitting of cheeseburgers, and the chattering of Girl Scouts. But his eyes saw a burning Buddhist monk.

'Oh Christ,' he said.

'Unca Tug?' frowned Gino.

'Two fillets down!' called Sally.

He dropped his spatula. It rang on the hotplate, bounced to the floor. 'Hey, Unca *Tug* ...' Sally began.

But Bob was already shouldering his way past Gino and David, jarring his thigh on the edge of the worktop. They were shouting at him but their voices just sounded like a deep blur. '*Unnncccaaa Ttttuuggggg* ...' He hoisted the bright red fire-extinguisher off the wall. *For Fat Fires Only* – Jesus! Then his shoulder had collided with the emergency exit at the back of the kitchen and he was out in the heat, in his Mcdonald's hat and his flapping apron, carrying the fire-extinguisher like a quarterback heading for a touchdown.

He circled the restaurant, awkwardly hop-hurdling the

4

low chainlink fencing at the side. *Oh please God don't let her, oh please God don't let her.*

His sneakers slapped loudly on the hot tarmac. His vision jumbled. *Hunh*! he panted. Overweight, unfit. *Hunh! hunh! hunh!* He heard a soft explosion, scarcely audible, *pooofffff!* and a woman scream. He saw orange flame wagging in the breeze like a burning flag. His heart was bursting; the hot air scorched his lungs. But then he was crashing his way through the crackling dry bushes into the next section of the car-park and there she was, sitting right in front of him, on fire.

She was still crosslegged, but sitting rigidly upright. Her back was arched, her hands stiffly clenching her thighs. Her eyes were tightly shut; nobody had the will-power to burn with their eyes open. Her blonde hair was already blackened, a thousand ends glowing orange like a burning broom. Flames poured out of her face. She must have poured most of the petrol down her front, because her lap was a roaring nest of fire.

'*Hold on*!' Bob screamed at her, although he didn't know why. He banged the fire-extinguisher against the concrete, and it started to spurt out foam. He directed a jet of foam straight at her face, then at her legs, and kept on squirting foam at her until the last flame had been smothered. There was foam, steam and oily smoke, and an overwhelming smell of burned flesh.

Five or six people were running from the shopping mall toward him. Some children were crying, and a woman was screaming, 'Oh, God! Oh, God!'

'Call an ambulance!' Bob roared, almost hysterical. Spit flew from his mouth. 'Call a fucking ambulance!'

He turned back, off-balance, gasping, to look at the girl. She was still sitting upright, although all of her hair had burned off, and her face was corked black like a nigger minstrel's. She was shuddering with pain and shock. The skin on the back of her hands had burned through, and the bare bones were exposed.

'It's all right,' Bob told her. He knew better than to touch her. 'Just stay still, try not to move. The ambulance is coming.'

5

She opened her shrivelled eyelids, and stared at him with milked-over eyes.

'*You bastard,*' she whispered. '*You bastard. Why didn't you let me burn?*'

'It's all right,' he reassured her. 'You're going to be fine. Do you want to lie down?'

A curious and shuffling crowd was already gathering around them. Bob heard a teenage kid say, 'Shit man, just look at her.'

'Would you go away, please?' Bob demanded, with a stiff sweep of his arm. There were tears in his eyes. 'This woman's hurt. Would you please just go away?'

Nobody moved. Somebody even knelt down and started taking photographs. But when Bob looked back at the girl, she had stretched her cracked scarlet lips across her teeth. She was staring at him as if she could have damned him to hell.

'*Bastard,*' she repeated. Then she coughed, and coughed again, and suddenly vomited up a bibful of blood and blackened lung and unburnt petrol. She fell sideways, trembling, and then she lay still. Bob would never forget the sound of her hairless skull, knocking against the concrete.

With an odd genuflexion, he laid down his fire-extinguisher. *By the rivers of Babylon, I laid my fire-extinguisher down.* In the distance, he could hear the yelping of a siren. He didn't know what to do. He didn't know what made him feel worse: the fact that he had tried to save her, and failed; or the fact that he had tried to save her at all. Nobody had ever looked at him with such hostility before, nobody. If looks could have killed, he would have been lying beside her, burned to death, just like she was – and *his* soul, too, would have been blowing in the wind, like smoke.

— TWO —

'Did you ever cook grunion, Mr Denman?' asked Waldo.

Lloyd swallowed wine and looked up from his cluttered rolltop desk, 'Grunion? No, I never even *thought* about cooking them. Why?'

'Oh, nothing. It's just that grunion's in season right now. I was wondering whether I ought to take the kids grunion-catching. Trouble is, I don't know what you're supposed to do with grunion once you've caught them.'

'Did you ask Louis?'

'Louis said he didn't have a clue.'

Lloyd eased himself back in his captain's chair. 'Well ... you remember Charles Kuerbis? The realtor? He was always the first one down on the beach when the grunion started running. I asked him once how he cooked them. He said he didn't know: he gave them to his wife. Whatever it was she did to them, they were always excellent. So I asked his wife, and *she* said she fed them to the cat, and went out to the market and bought some decent fish.'

'Maybe I'll take them to Sea World instead,' Waldo suggested, in a defeated tone.

'Didn't you take them to Sea World last time?'

'Sure, and the time before that, and the time before that. I can't remember an access visit in three years when I haven't come back soaking wet. The kids always like to sit at the front. Did you ever smell a killer whale's *breath*, Mr Denman?'

'Sure, halibutosis,' joked Lloyd. He shuffled a heap of bills together and jammed them on to a spike. 'You're enough to put a guy off getting married, you know that?'

Waldo shook his head. 'Don't take no notice of me, Mr Denman. There's only one woman in the world as bad as my Tusha, and that's my Tusha. Celia's perfect for you, and you know it. Celia's bright, she's pretty, she's classy. She knows all about music. Not like Tusha. Tusha thinks that Pavarotti is some kind of cheese, you know, like ricotta. Besides, you never met her, she's hideous.'

'Why on earth did you marry her in the first place, if you think she's hideous?'

'Oh, no, don't get me wrong. On the outside, she looks great. Great eyes, great smile. Great gazongas. It's just on the inside she's hideous. A really hideous inside.'

Lloyd stood up, and carried his empty glass out of the office and through to the bar. He took a bottle of San Pasqual Chenin Blanc out of the icebox and poured himself a generous measure. He allowed himself only two glasses of wine during the afternoon: otherwise things would start getting a little unreal by the time the restaurant opened for the evening trade.

He checked his watch, the Corum Gold Coin watch that Celia had given him for his birthday last April. Waldo, the *maitre d'*, always came early, because he really had no place else to go. They talked usually, or shared a bottle of wine, or played draughts. The rest of the staff would be arriving in ones and twos within a half-hour, ready for their opening at six-thirty.

Lloyd walked through the twenty-six table restaurant, checking each place-setting individually. Fresh orchids, gleaming Lauffer cutlery, shell-pink linen napkins folded like chrysanthemums. Quite a few restaurants let their waiting staff leave for the afternoon without resetting the tables, but Lloyd insisted that when the staff returned for the evening shift, the place should look as entrancing to them as it did to their customers.

It was still magical for Lloyd. After eleven years as an insurance assessor for San Diego Marine Trust, working out how much rich men's boats were worth, this restaurant was everything he had always wanted. Freedom, independence, profitable hard work, fun. Denman's Original Fish Depot, an informal but stylish seafood restaurant with Victorian-tiled walls, oak parquet floor and mahogany ceiling-fans, and a balcony outside overlooking La Jolla Cove.

San Diego magazine had already complimented Lloyd on his north-west salmon steaks broiled over alderwood, his glazed *mahi-mahi*, and his trademark dish, the Denman's Original Fish Depot Delight, which was lobster chunks, shrimp, clams, crab legs and mushrooms, served with poured-over chowder in a hot French-style brioche.

He walked across to the sliding glass doors that led out on to the balcony, and opened them. A warm briny wind was blowing off the sea, and gulls were sloping and crying around the steep sandy-coloured cliffs. He leaned against the wooden rail and breathed in the evening air. This was it. This was the dream. It was all so ridiculously idyllic that sometimes it made him grin to himself in shameless self-satisfaction.

He had it all, or the best part of it, anyway. His own restaurant in a posh and profitable location; a talented and startling pretty girlfriend who loved him like crazy and wanted to marry him; a white 5-Series BMW with the personalized licence FISHEE, and a $568,000 house close to the University of California at San Diego with a hot tub and an olive tree and what his realtors had called 'a tantalizing peek' of the North Shore. A full peek would have cost him $30,000 more, and so far an actual view was financially out of the question.

But think of it: his father had been a mail-carrier, and his mother had taken in sewing, and here he was.

Lloyd didn't really look the part of a *restaurateur*. He was very lean and tall, with a mop of grey-streaked hair and a prominent bony nose which had led his mother to describe him as 'proud-looking' and his father to call him 'the yooman can-opener'. But now that his fortieth birthday was approaching, and he was lightly suntanned and psychologically well balanced and everything was well with the world, he had an air about him that was both distinguished and light-hearted. Celia always said that if Basil Rathbone had been both Californian and funny, then he would have been Lloyd Denman instead.

He turned around and watched Waldo setting up his reservations book on the oak lectern beside the front doors. Waldo had smoothed-back hair, a clipped Oliver Hardy moustache, and a wide dark green cummerbund that made him look like a ribbon-wrapped Easter egg. He spoke to the customers with an amazingly over-the-top French accent, '*Zees way, sair, see voo play – pardonnay mwuh, madarm*,' but in fact his name was Waldo Slonimsky and he was Lithuanian; the only survivor of his entire family. Sometimes Lloyd could look at his face and clearly see the plump lonely seven-year-old boy who had been brought over to America just before the war. Waldo had married, had kids, divorced, dated a few women the same shape as him. But Lloyd thought: when you've lost for ever the people you love the most, how can you ever stop being lonely?

'Waldo,' he called. 'Come on out here.'

Waldo stepped out on to the balcony, tugging his cummerbund straight. 'You want something, Mr Denman?'

Lloyd nodded. 'Yes, I do. I want you to drop everything for just a couple of minutes and come out here and take a look at the cove.'

Waldo kept his eyes on Lloyd; obviously tense, obviously thinking anxiously about everything he had to do. Check the menus, update the wine-lists, call for two replacement waitresses because Angie and Kay had both phoned in sick. Sick, my ass, excuse my Lithuanian, surfing more like.

Lloyd tried to encourage him, 'Relax, look around. What do you think of the cove this evening?'

Waldo glanced at it quickly. 'This evening, it's a nice cove.'

'Is that all? Just *nice*?'

Waldo contrived to look around some more. 'This evening, it's a *heck* of a nice cove.'

Llody laughed and clamped his arm around Waldo's shoulders. 'You know what your trouble is, Waldo?'

'What?' asked Waldo, uneasily. 'What's my trouble?'

'You never stop to think how lucky you are.'

Waldo plainly didn't understand what Lloyd was trying to say to him. He shrugged, twisted the napkin that he always used for polishing fingerprints from knives and forks. 'I do what I can, Mr Denman. You know that.'

'Sure, Waldo, I know that. But just close your eyes and take a breath of this good Pacific air and let your muscles loose. You may have had your troubles with Tusha, but you've got yourself two beautiful children, and your own apartment and a car that actually runs, and a whole lot of people who like you.'

'Well, that's nice, Mr Denman. Thank you very much.'

'Waldo . . .' Lloyd began, squeezing Waldo's arm. But he knew that it was no use pushing Waldo any further. He would simply embarrass him.

Waldo went to the rail and looked out over the sea. Now that the sun was setting, La Jolla and all its jostling restaurants and souvenir shops and colour-washed apartment buildings were thickly coated in a glutinous shellac of amber light. The gulls continued to wheel and scream, and Waldo lifted his double chin and watched them.

'My family used to live in Palanga, you know, on the Baltic,' he said. 'It seems very far from here now, very long ago. My grandfather used to take me for walks along the shore. It's funny, don't you think, Mr Denman? I can see him as clear now as I did then. He always used to wear a long grey wool coat, and an old-fashioned black felt hat.'

'That's not so funny,' smiled Lloyd. 'I can almost see him myself.'

Waldo slowly shook his head. 'Grandfather used to say to me that when we die, our souls become seagulls. They fly, they swoop. That is why seagulls always sound so sad. They are always looking for the people they left behind.'

Lloyd said, 'That's a cute little story.'

Waldo wiped his eyes with his fingers. 'I used to believe it. I think I *still* believe it. Maybe in the Baltic my grandfather still flies and swoops along the shoreline, looking for that boy that he once used to take for walks.'

He shrugged, and then he said, 'I'd better get back in

now. There's a whole lot to do.'

As he went in, however, Lloyd saw two men in budget-priced suits push their way in through the restaurant's oak-panelled front door, and stand uncertainly among the pot-plants. They certainly didn't look like the Fish Depot's usual type of customer, but then they didn't look like health inspectors, either. One of them was cavernous-cheeked and unshaven, with glittering eyes. The other was podgy and rumpled, with a surprised-looking face, and an uncontrollable quiff of fraying brown hair. Jackie Gleason meets James Belushi.

The unshaven one came up to Waldo and spoke to him. Waldo nodded, then shook his head. He said something else, and then he turned and pointed toward the balcony. The two men weaved their way between the tables with their hands in their pockets, and emerged out on the balcony.

'Mr Lloyd Denman?' the unshaven one asked him, with a slight catch in his throat.

'That's right. How can I help you?'

The man produced a gold badge. 'I'm Sergeant David Houk, sir, San Diego Police Department. This is Detective Ned Gable.'

'This doesn't concern unpaid parking tickets, does it?' asked Lloyd, mock-defensively. 'There's a whole bunch still in my glovebox. You know how it is. Busy, busy, busy.'

'Well, no, sir. We just wanted to ask you a couple of questions, sir.'

Lloyd could sense their disquiet. 'What is it?' he demanded. 'What's happened?'

Sergeant Houk cleared his throat, and then he said, 'There's been an accident, Mr Denman, on Rosecrans Avenue, downtown.'

'An accident? What kind of an accident?'

'Woman got fatally burned, sir. Right in front of Mc-Donald's restaurant.'

'Well, that's terrible.'

'Yes, sir.'

Lloyd waited. He didn't know what else to say. 'So, a

woman got burned. What does that have to do with me?'

'Do you know Ms Celia Williams, sir?' asked Detective Gable.

Lloyd was baffled. 'Sure I know Ms Celia Williams. She's my fiancée. But she's in San Francisco right now, giving a course of music lectures.'

'She's in San Francisco?' asked Houk, glancing at Gable with unconcealed surprise.

'Sure. She left at the weekend. I don't expect her back until Saturday afternoon. She called me last night ... I don't know – it must have been twelve, half after twelve.'

Sergeant Houk massaged his bony, unshaven jowls. 'Mr Denman ... I don't know how to start saying this, sir. But as far as we can tell, Ms Celia Williams was the woman who burned to death in front of McDonald's today.'

Lloyd stared at him, and then laughed. The idea that Celia had been outside McDonald's today, only six or seven miles away from La Jolla on Rosecrans Avenue, was so patently absurd that he wasn't even upset. 'Sergeant, that's impossible. That's totally impossible. Celia's in San Francisco. She was giving a lecture this afternoon at the Performing Arts Center.'

'Did you speak to her today?' asked Detective Gable, sniffing, and wiping his nose with the back of his hand.

'No, not yet. She usually calls me around midnight, when the restaurant's emptying out.'

'And you're expecting her to call tonight?'

'Of course I'm expecting her to call tonight. She's my fiancée. We're going to be married come September.'

Sergeant Houk reached into the pocket of his creased Sears suit and produced a transparent plastic envelope. He held it up, so that Lloyd could see what was in it. A white credit card wallet, badly charred at one end, and a gold charm bracelet.

'Mr Denman, do you recognize either of these two items?'

Lloyd stared at him. 'She's in San Francisco. If you doubt my word, you can try calling her. She's staying at the Miyako. Listen – do you want the number?'

A small spasm of panic. The wallet's clasp was curved and gold, in the shape of the Chinese symbol for yin and yang; just like the clasp of Celia's wallet. And although he hadn't looked closely at the charms, the charm bracelet looked startlingly like the one that he had given Celia when she had first moved in … and to which he had added a new charm each month. A treble clef, for the day she had graduated as a doctor of music; a house, for the day they had moved into 4884 North Torrey; a heart, for the day he had proposed to her.

'Mr Denman,' Sergeant Houk told him, with heart-breaking professional gentleness, 'do you want to sit down and take a look at these things? The wallet contains a social security card and credit cards belonging to Celia Jane Williams, as well as business cards from this restaurant, and two photographs of a man who I now recognize to be you.'

Lloyd looked mechanically around, and then dragged over a rattan chair, and sat down. Sergeant Houk handed him the wallet, and then the charm bracelet. Detective Gable coughed uncomfortably, and sniffed.

This can't be real, thought Lloyd. *Something's slipped, something's gone haywire. This is not me, this is some-body else. Or maybe I'm still asleep, and this is nothing but a dream. But I can feel the wind. I can hear the gulls crying. And there's Waldo, staring at me pale-faced through the tinted glass window, and Waldo wouldn't stare at me like that, so apprehensive and so sorrowful, if this weren't real.*

He opened the wallet. He stared inside. The embossed label said F. David, Del Mar. He knew it was hers. He had been with her at the Flower Hill Shopping Center when she had bought it. He didn't have to look at the credit cards, but he did. Sears, Exxon, American Express. *Don't leave home without it.*

'Where were these found?' he managed to say, his lips woolly and numb.

'They were found on the body of a white Caucasian female aged about twenty-nine, in the parking lot outside

14

McDonald's Restaurant, Rosecrans Avenue, at 11.30 a.m. this morning,' said Houk.

'She was blonde,' added Gable, trying to be helpful, trying hard to be sympathetic. 'She was pretty, by all accounts, with blue eyes. She wore a red chequered shirt and blue 501s.'

Lloyd didn't look up, but rubbed his thumb across the white leather wallet again and again, as if he were expecting a secret message to appear. 'Red chequered shirt?' he asked.

'That's right, sir. Red chequered shirt and 501s.'

'Outside McDonald's on Rosecrans?'

'That's correct, sir.'

'I don't understand,' said Lloyd, and he didn't. He was so sure that Celia was in San Francisco that he was prepared to call her now, at the Performing Arts Center, even though he knew she was right in the middle of a lecture on reading operatic scores. Just to call her and say, 'You're there, aren't you, in San Francisco?' And to hear her say, 'yes! of course I am!'

'And what did you say? *Fatally* burned? Dead?'

Sergeant Houk sucked in his cheeks even more cavernously. 'I'm sorry, Mr Denman, but it sure looks like it. I mean, there's still a possibility it *isn't* Ms Williams. Somebody could've stole your fiancée's wallet. But I wouldn't count on it.'

'What the hell are you talking about?' Lloyd protested. 'She flew out of here Sunday afternoon! I put her on the flight myself! She was giving five lectures on Wagner and operatic technique, and then she was coming directly back home! There's no conceivable reason why she should have come back to San Diego before Saturday, none at all. And I can't believe she wouldn't have called me.'

'Well, there must have been some motive,' Sergeant Houk said, gently. 'The only trouble is, we don't yet know what it was.'

Detective Gable said. 'She wasn't under any kind of strain, was she? Worried about this lecture tour, anything

15

like that? Some people crack up without any warning whatsoever, just crack up, and the next thing you know they've left their family and their friends behind and they're riding lettuce-trains all over the country.'

Lloyd slowly shook his head. *Lettuce-trains?* He couldn't make any sense of what they were telling him. It was totally unbelievable that Celia was dead. On Sunday morning they had lain side by side in bed together with fresh coffee and the Sunday paper and the sun striping the sheets. She had leaned on her elbow, one hand thrust into her tangled blonde hair, and said to him, 'We're going to have babies, aren't we?'

He had finished reading *Calvin & Hobbes* and then leaned forward and kissed her forehead. 'Sure we're going to have babies. A boy like me and a girl like you.'

She had smiled a distant smile. 'One will do.'

'Just one? I want a dynasty!'

'One's enough. If you have a baby, you know, you live for ever.'

But she hadn't had a baby, hadn't even had the chance to have a baby. Now she was dead, impossibly and unimaginably dead. No life everlasting, nothing.

The tears dripped down Lloyd's cheeks and he didn't even know that he was crying.

'When did this happen?' he asked, trying to remember if he had experienced any unusual feelings during the day. Any feeling of coldness, any sudden sense of loss. But lunchtime had been chaotically busy, and for most of the afternoon he had been writing up his accounts. He couldn't recall anything but frantic hard work and wondering how to keep laundry costs down. Ah Kim's had just put up their prices two cents a napkin.

Houk said, 'It seems like she poured petrol over herself. Kind of a ritual suicide. One of the cooks from McDonald's managed to reach her with a fire-extinguisher, but it was too late.'

'She *killed* herself?'

'I'm sorry, Mr Denman, it sure looks that way.'

'I don't even know what she was *doing* there,' Lloyd

16

protested. 'I mean – what in God's name was she *doing* there? She wasn't depressed, she wasn't upset.'

'I'm sorry, Mr Denman, we really don't know. We don't even know how she got there. There were no private vehicles anywhere in the vicinity left unaccounted for, and nobody saw a woman riding a bus with a petrol can.'

Lloyd dragged out his handkerchief and wiped his eyes. 'God, what a waste. God, what a terrible waste. I can't tell you how ...' he stopped, his throat was too tight, and his mouth didn't seem to work. *She had killed herself, burned herself to death, and she hadn't even tried to tell him what was wrong. That was what hurt. She hadn't even asked him for help.*

Sergent Houk waited for a long moment. Two of Lloyd's waitresses had arrived, and Lloyd could see them anxiously talking to Waldo, and glancing out at the balcony now and again. He gave them a hesitant wave, but they probably didn't understand what he was doing, or else they were too upset, because they didn't wave back.

Sergeant Houk glanced around at them, and then carefully took back the wallet and the charm bracelet. 'You'll have these back as soon as possible, Mr Denman. Meanwhile there's one thing I'm going to have to ask you to do. It won't be easy, but we do need somebody to come downtown to the mortuary tomorrow morning to identify Ms Williams' remains.'

Remains, thought Lloyd. *What a forlorn, contradictory word. When your soul has left your body, nothing remains. Only memories, only a scattering of objects. Clothes, photographs, a voice that speaks over and over again on video-recordings, an endlessly repeated smile.*

'We'll have to ask you a few more questions,' Sergeant Houk told him. 'We're going to have to piece together everything that happened.'

Lloyd nodded. 'All right, I understand.'

Detective Gable laid his hand consolingly on Lloyd's shoulder. 'You okay, sir? You want a ride home or anything?'

'No ... no thanks,' Lloyd replied. 'I have a restaurant to run.'

The two policemen left him out on the balcony, and went to have a word with Waldo. Essentially, it was 'keep an eye on him, he's already in shock'. Then they left. Lloyd sat alone for a long time, unaware that the restaurant wasn't filling up, that no customers were coming in. Waldo had put a hastily-chalked sign outside saying *Closed: Family Bereavement* and Suzie was calling up all the customers who had made reservations, cancelling them all apologetically, and offering them free Fish Depot cocktails the next time they came.

Lloyd stood up, and leaned against the rail of the balcony. The ocean lay below him like molten solder, with a gradually wrinkling skin. The seagulls turned and cried. Lloyd wondered if one of them were already Celia, circling around La Jolla Cove, looking for him.

Waldo came out and stood a little way behind him. 'You all right, Mr Denman?' he asked, at length. 'You want a drink, maybe?'

Lloyd shook his head. 'No thanks.'

'You want that I should drive you home?'

'I don't know. I don't feel real. I feel like I'm here, but at the same time I'm not here at all. Can you understand that?'

Waldo came up and clasped Lloyd's shoulder. 'It's a beautiful evening, Mr Denman. The cove is beautiful. Do you know what they say in Lithuania, when somebody dies on a day like this? They say that God loved them so much that he lit all the lamps of heaven to guide them on their way.'

— THREE —

A little after eight o'clock, Lloyd drove himself back to
North Torrey. He switched on the car radio but KFSD was
playing 'Un Bel Di Vedremo' from *Madame Butterfly* and
he couldn't bear it; it had always been Celia's favourite.
He drove the rest of the way home with tears running
down his cheeks.

As he turned into the driveway, a lantern was alight on
the front verandah, and the living-room lights were
shining, but only because they had been tripped by automatic timers. There was nobody waiting for him, and now
there never would be.

He parked his white BMW in the driveway and killed
the engine. He stayed behind the wheel for three or four
minutes, trying to decide if he really wanted to go inside.
She was dead, but all of her clothes would still be there,
her towel would still be hanging in the bathroom. Her
photograph would still be smiling at him from his night-
table. Most painful of all, he would still be able to *smell*
her. *Red*, by Giorgio of Beverly Hills.

He had opened the BMW's glovebox to find the
remote-control for opening the front gates, and her sunglasses and her lipstick had been lying inside, just where
she had last tossed them. He had opened the lipstick case.
Cantata Red.

The evening was growing shadowy. The air was thick
and warm, and there was a strong smell of eucalyptus and
pine. Up above him, it looked as if God had stirred boysenberry jelly into the sky, the way Lloyd's mother used to
stir boysenberry jelly into his milk when he was a kid. *I
prefer boysenberry to any ordinary jam*, somebody sang
in the back of his brain.

At last Lloyd climbed out of the car, slammed the door,

19

and walked up to the house with the terrible reluctance of true grief. The ocean gleamed knowingly through the ferns – that peek of the North Shore for which they had paid so much, and about which they had teased themselves so often. They had even considered renaming the house *Peek House*.

He opened the front door and went inside. The house seemed so pillow-silent that he was almost tempted to call out, 'Hello? Celia?'

His shoes barked across the hallway, which was floored in bleached and polished oak; but were silent across the living-room, which was thickly carpeted in cream-coloured wool. He walked right to the middle of the living-room and looked around, as if he hadn't been here for years. There was a strong smell of oak, and new rugs. *I prefer boysenberry to any ...*

The living-room was painted plain pottery white and furnished with tasteful sparseness. Celia had always preferred simple furniture, open spaces. If only Lloyd had known how complicated her mind was. There were two couches, upholstered in pink-and-blue glazed cotton; two French-style armchairs; and a coffee-table with a drift-wood sculpture on it, as well as a neatly marshalled stack of *Opera News* and *Musical America*.

On the walls hung vivid oil paintings by local artists. A view of the Presidio, domed, white-walled, in shimmering sunlight. Next to it, a portrait of a Mexican woman, standing by an open adobe, selling lemons from a basket. The portrait was entitled, *Who'll Buy My Lemons?*

But the centre of visual and emotional gravity in the living-room – in fact the centre of visual and emotional gravity in the whole house – was Celia's ice-white Yamaha grand piano, which Lloyd had given her when they first moved in. That piano had meant commitment, and permanence. A house of their own, a relationship which was going to last. 'After all,' Lloyd had told her, 'you can storm out of the door with an overnight bag, but you can't storm out of the door with a grand piano.'

Fatally burned.

Lloyd went over to the piano and picked out two or three plaintive notes. All those years that Celia had practised. All those years that she had dedicated to Wagner and Verdi and Puccini. Fingers flying across the keys. Eyes closed, voice uplifted. *Fatally burned.* He played the first three bars of 'Evergreen' because he could never play opera: *love, soft as an easy chair* ... then stopped, and closed the lid over the keyboard, turning the key. From now on, it was going to stay silent, unplayed. Nobody else was going to touch it.

On top of the piano, meticulously arranged, was Celia's collection of scrimshaw – whale-ivory carvings from Nantucket and Salem and the Barbary Coast. Some of them dated as far back as 1720, but her favourite had always been the fragment of twenty-thousand-year-old fossilized mammoth tusk, exquisitely carved by Bonnie Schulte, one of the most accomplished scrimshanders in America.

Lloyd had promised Celia another Bonnie Schulte piece for her birthday. But the only carving she needed now was her headstone.

It was so difficult for Lloyd to believe that their life together was all over, when it had scarcely started. Even worse, there was nobody that he could call. Celia's parents were both dead, and although she had mentioned an older sister in Denver, Colorado, Lloyd had no idea of where her sister lived, or what her married name was, or how to get in touch with her.

He poured himself a glassful of Wild Turkey from the heavy crystal decanter on the black-enamelled Spanish linen-chest which they had brought back from Baja. His hand was shaking, and the decanter clattered against the rim of the glass. He walked through to the bedroom with his drink in his hand and stared at the big oak bed. On the wall behind the headboard was a stylized painting of two California quail, touching beaks, and Celia had said that it was a painting of them, kissing, in another incarnation.

'You want to come back as a quail?' he had asked her.

She had smiled. 'Better to come back as a quail than not to come back at all.'

On impulse, he called the Miyako Hotel, in San Francisco.

'I want to speak to Ms Williams, please?'

A pause, and then politely, 'No Ms Williams registered here, sir.'

'Maybe she checked out. Was she there yesterday, or the day before?'

'No, sir. Nobody by the name of Williams.'

'How about Denman? Anybody by the name of Denman?'

'No, sir. Denbigh, but no Denman.'

Lloyd hung up, frowning. Celia had told him on the phone last night that she was calling from the Miyako, he was quite sure of it. She had even mentioned the Japanese meal she had ordered from room service, the teriyaki shrimp. But unless she had registered under a totally different name altogether, she hadn't been there at all.

Plainly, she had been deceiving him. But why?

He swallowed whisky, and thought to himself: *maybe the grand piano hadn't been enough to hold her back, after all. Maybe she had found herself a new lover.*

He paced around the living-room, his mind helter-skeltering. *A lover? It didn't make any sense. Celia had always told him the truth, even when it hurt. She wouldn't have fallen for another man without telling him. She couldn't.* Besides, she had seemed to be deliriously happy. Come September, they were going to be married: they had even talked about how many children they wanted, and what they were going to call them. Joseph for a boy, Tershia for a girl.

And, if she had fallen in love with another man – really fallen in love – why had she set herself alight?

He leafed through the telephone book, and found the number of Sylvia Cuddy, Celia's best friend from the San Diego Opera (designer glasses, sensual pink lips, wildly tangled hair). He jabbed the phone-buttons with his middle finger, then tucked the receiver under his chin and waited for Sylvia to answer.

'Sylvia? It's Lloyd.'

'Well, hello! This is a surprise! How can I help you?'

Lloyd found himself swallowing tightly. A throatful of burrs. 'Sylvia ... I'm afraid I have some really bad news.'

He heard himself telling Sylvia in a clogged-up voice that Celia was dead. He heard Sylvia denying it. He heard himself say that it was true. He was desperately sorry, but it was true. He didn't even know whether he believed it himself. Maybe he was making some kind of surrealistic mistake, like one of those films where you pick up the wrong suitcase and open it up and *voila!* no pyjamas, no dirty rolled-up socks, no shaver, only four million dollars' worth of pure heroin, in plastic bags.

'Sylvia ... I've been trying to find out who might have seen Celia last ... before she left San Francisco.'

A hesitant pause. 'San Francisco? What do you mean?'

'She was lecturing for the opera in San Francisco, wasn't she? A two-week engagement at the Performing Arts Center.'

'Well, she may have been lecturing, Lloyd, but it wasn't for us. She never told *me* anything about it.'

'When did you last talk to her?' asked Lloyd.

'Why, just yesterday morning. She told me she was calling from home.'

'You mean from here? From La Jolla? What did she say to you?'

'I don't know ...' Sylvia confessed. 'Nothing much, really. She gave me her recipe for veal tarantino, the one I was always nagging her about. Then she said something about how excited she was, looking forward to the future. Then she hung up.'

'She didn't say anything unusual? Anything that struck you as weird?'

Sylvia thought about it for a while. 'I'm not sure. I suppose the whole phone call was weird, in a way – just suddenly calling me out of the blue to give me that recipe. And the way she said, at the end, "Well, *goodbye*, Sylvia." It was so *final.* I said, "You sound as if you're going on a trip." But she didn't answer.'

Lloyd slowly replaced the receiver. The more he discovered about Celia's last moments, the more mysterious and unsettling they appeared to be. He had imagined that he and Celia had shared everything. Their friendship, their passion, their ambitions, their most inconsequential thoughts. Now he felt that a mask was slipping, and that a different Celia was coming into view, a Celia who had kept herself secret. A Celia who had told him lies, and lied to her best friend, too.

Through the open door to the bedroom, he could just see Celia's photograph laughing at him, the photograph he had taken in the courtyard at the Rancho Santa Fe. *What are you laughing at, my lady?* he thought. *What were you doing in that car-park today, dowsing yourself with petrol and setting yourself on fire?*

He walked through to the bedroom, picked up the photograph and stared at it closely, trying to see if her face gave anything away. *Most of all, Celia, why didn't you tell me what was worrying you? Why didn't you ask me to help?*

Maybe she had, he thought, but maybe he hadn't understood. The pain of that was almost more than he could bear, and he uttered a sob of grief that hurt his throat.

He drained the last of the Wild Turkey, holding the decanter upside-down until the last drop had fallen into his glass. *Plip*, the last drop. Then he struggled awkwardly out of his trousers, and bundled the Danish duck-down quilt around himself, and huffed and puffed, and made a determined effort to sleep.

She's dead, she's gone, but you have to sleep. If you don't sleep, you won't be able to cope with the restaurant, and Waldo, and everybody else who's depending on you.

Soon the quilt grew impossibly hot, so he untwisted himself, and lay spread-eagled across the bed, feeling drunker than he had ever felt in his life. The mattress tilted and swam as if it were adrift off Point Loma. His whole head seemed to be filled with potentially explosive whisky fumes.

'Celia?' he said, knowing that she wasn't there, but drunk enough to defy reality. 'Celia, I love you, for Chrissake! Don't you know that? Celia!'

Celia didn't answer, Celia was gone, burned in a carpark on Rosecrans Avenue. Tomorrow he would see her body for himself, and then maybe he would be able to accept it. He slept, with his mouth hanging open, and dreamed that he was arguing with his realtors. *You said there was a conversation pit. This isn't a conversation pit, it's a grave.* Then he dreamed about the restaurant kitchens. Louis was stirring the fish stock, oblivious to the giant lobsters that crawled and heaved and clattered around the floor, blue-black and glistening, slowly waving their claws at him. The swing doors swung. *Ee*-urk - *ee* - urk! There was somebody behind him, running away from him. He pushed his way into the corridor. The restaurant was blazing. All around him, naked women were running screaming in all directions, with their hair alight. *Eeeeeee-eeee!!!!*

He opened his eyes. He was still drunk, but he was conscious that he had heard a noise. He lay still, tense, listening. A creak, a rustle, a hollow-cheeked whisper like the draught of a door opened, and then closed. He listened even more intently.

Something dropped with a thud, and rolled. Then a drumming, tumbling noise. Lloyd swung his legs out of bed, and made his way unsteadily out of the bedroom door, jarring his shoulder painfully on the doorframe.

Shit, that hurts. He may have said it out loud. He stopped, swayed, almost lost his balance, listened.

The house was silent. But he was sure that he could *feel* something, feel somebody moving. He was sure that he could sense somebody breathing. He was supposed to be alone, wasn't he, now that Celia had gone, and yet he was sure that he wasn't.

His next-door neighbour, Hal Pinkerton, had always

25

nagged him about buying himself a gun. Now he wished very much that he had listened. He could imagine a six-foot sixteen-stone black junkie with sweaty muscles and a Rambo knife waiting for him in the living-room, next to the conversation-pit that was more like a grave.

He patted the wall, searching for the lightswitch. He found it, and switched it on. He stood blinking at an empty living-room. Nobody there. Only the painted face of the Mexican woman, with her unbought lemons. Only rugs and floors and furniture.

When he looked over toward the grand piano, however, he realized that something was different. All of the scrimshaw had disappeared. Twenty or thirty pieces of carved whale-ivory, which Celia had carefully and artistically arranged on the piano-lid. Now the top of the piano was completely bare.

Lloyd went up to the piano and laid his hands flat on the lid. Cool and shiny and white as death. The Chinese always said that death was white. He looked around, but nothing else seemed to be missing. Who the hell would risk breaking into a house for the sake of a couple of dozen pieces of scrimshaw?

He went through to the kitchen. The back door was wide open, and the cool night air was flowing in. He could smell the sea. Cautiously, he edged open one of the kitchen drawers and took out his largest Sabatier butcher-knife. He stepped out on to the back porch, bricks under bare feet, and strained his eyes in the darkness.

He thought he glimpsed something, out by the avocado trees beyond the patio. Something that flickered quick and pale.

There was no logical reason for it, but he was suddenly gripped with a terrible sense of dread.

Don't be ridiculous. Whoever it was, they've gone. Some spaced-out kid, most likely, looking for crack money.

He called out, 'Who's there?' But he didn't really expect a reply. What was a burglar going to say? 'It's me, don't worry. Just been doing a bit of burgling.'

He thought he heard a faint rustling in the under-growth by the back fence, but he couldn't be sure.

'You get this straight!' he shouted, harshly. 'You'd better not try breaking into this house again! Not if you want your goddamn head to stay on your goddamn shoulders! I've got the biggest goddamn shotgun you ever saw, and I'm not afraid to use it!'

He waited for almost a minute, but there were no further noises; no indication that anybody was hiding behind the avocado trees or crouching in the bushes. *Be serious, they're probably halfway to Leucadia by now.*

He stepped back into the kitchen and closed the door. He was shivering a little; but not from the cold alone. It was then, turning around, that he realized the intruder had entered the house without forcing the door. There were no broken panes of glass, no screwdriver marks. He opened the door again, and there, still in the lock, was the spare key.

The spare key which they always kept concealed deep in the soil of the Sicilian terracotta planter, on the oppo-site corner of the patio.

The spare key which only he and Celia had known about.

Christ, this is ridiculous. Somebody must have watched us putting it there. The Pinkertons' gardener, maybe. He was always up on his stepladder, pruning the creeper. The pool cleaner. Or anybody. Or maybe it was one of those hiding places that dumb innocent house-holders thought was totally unfindable, but which an expert thief could locate in a matter of minutes.

Celia was dead. Celia was never coming back. And in the morning, oh God, he would have to identify her body. He would have to confront her burned remains, and say, yes, this was the woman I loved. He had no idea what a burned body would look like, and he was terrified.

He closed the door and locked it, tugging at the handle to make doubly sure. Then he walked back into the living-room, feeling parched and hungover and nauseous. He went across to the Spanish bureau and splashed out a huge glass of club soda, half of which he swallowed in three breathless gulps.

While he was drinking, he happened to glance down at the floor behind one of the sofas. To his surprise, all of Celia's scrimshaw was lying scattered on the carpet. It had been hidden from sight when he had first crossed the living-room on his way to the kitchen. But here it was, all of it, twenty or thirty pieces. That must have been the tumbling noise he had heard. It looked exactly as if somebody had cleared the whole lot off the top of the piano with one impatient sweep of their arm.

Lloyd knelt down on the carpet and examined the pieces of ivory carefully, turning them over and over. Schooners, harbours, mermaids, storms at sea, all engraved in meticulous spidery detail. Why should anyone have wanted to throw all of this scrimshaw on to the floor? It didn't make any kind of sense. Not unless the intruder had been totally crazy, or out of his brain on crack, or angry because he hadn't been able to find anything particularly valuable – or at least anything that could be fenced for the price of a score.

Lloyd stood up again. This was nuts. This was completely nuts. Then he caught sight of Celia's most valuable piece, her 20,000-year-old piece of fossilized mammoth ivory, laid with obvious care on the seat of the couch.

He slowly picked it up. He couldn't understand this at all. What kind of housebreaker would have known that this one piece was worth twenty times the price of all the whale ivory arranged around it? How had he managed to pick it out from twenty or thirty others, in the dark? Even more to the point – if he had been able to pick it out, then he must have known what it was worth. *So why hadn't he slipped it into his pocket and taken it with him?*

Lloyd couldn't begin to think of a logical answer. He was too hungover, too shocked, and he really didn't want to think that the answer might not be logical at all.

He sipped the rest of his club soda. Then he switched

off the lights and stood in the dark for what seemed like an hour. Exhausted, haunted, and hopeless. *Celia*, he thought, or whispered, or both.

He heard the Italian clock in the hallway prissily chiming three. *Uno, duo, très.* He took a last reluctant look around him and then he made his way back to bed. He fell backwards on to the quilt as if he been shot. Celia had always hated the way he did that.

In his head he heard the words that Allen Ginsberg had written. *You're out, Death let you out, Death had the Mercy, you're done with your century, done with God, done with the path thru it – Done with yourself at last – Pure – Back to the Babe dark before your Father, before us all, before the world . . .*

There, rest. No more suffering for you. I know where you've gone, and it's good.

He thought that he wouldn't be able to sleep but, after half an hour, his eyes closed and his breathing grew deep and harsh, and he was slowly swallowed by the night.

He dreamed that there was a marble-grey face pressed close to his bedroom window, watching him for almost an hour with the strangest expression of bereavement and greed. It might have been real, he might not have dreamed it at all. But whatever it was, it faded when the night faded, and by the time that morning broke, there was nobody in the garden at all.

— FOUR —

They smelled burning on the wind from three to four miles away, long before the bus came into view. After a while, they began to run into occasional drifts of pale filthy smoke.

If they hadn't been so hungry, if they hadn't been so tired, they probably would have realized immediately that it was burning flesh.

But Ric wound down the patrol-car window and sniffed two or three times. He gave a nod of approval. 'Can you believe it?' he remarked. 'Somebody's having a cookout.'

'Oh, for sure,' growled Sergeant Jim Griglak, without taking the King Edward cigar from his mouth. 'A hundred-and-fifteen in the shade, in the middle of the desert, at twenty after three in the afternoon, and somebody's having a cookout?'

'No, come on, smell it, that's a cookout,' Ric assured him. 'Baby back ribs, charred on the outside, tender on the inside. A nice frosty jug of margaritas. Egg and avocado and green-onion salad, with crispy tacos, salsa, and a little sprinkling of cilantro.'

'Munoz, my friend, you're hallucinating,' retorted the sergeant. 'If that's barbecued anything, that's barbecued Goodyear.' He took the cigar out of his mouth and tapped the firm fedora-grey ash on to the floormat. 'Somebody's overheated, or blown out a tyre. Now, you want to shut that frigging window before we dry-fry?'

Ric wound up the window. 'It sure *smells* like a cookout,' he insisted.

Jim Griglak continued to drive at the same monotonous fifty-five, his mountainous shoulders hunched, his huge hands grasping the steering-wheel as if he were driving a tiny fairground bumper-car. All around them,

the scrubby off-white hills of the Anza Borrego Desert were
blinded with heat, hill after undulating hill, with the
highway running undeviatingly up and down them like the
dusty sloughed-off skin of a huge desert snake.

Up they went, and the next valley came into view.
Deserted and baking-hot, just like the valley before it, and
the valley before that. The sky was so blue it didn't seem
to fit together with the horizon properly, a badly printed
jigsaw. Down they went, and the previous valley disappeared from sight.

'This whole barbecue thing is a closed book to me,' Jim
Griglak sniffed. 'I can set fire to my food any time I feel
like it, no trouble. All it takes is a can of unleaded and a
match. Who needs mesquite wood at $7 a sack and a $15
apron with a picture of a whore's underwear on it?'

'It's not just a question of heat and meat,' Ric insisted.
'It's all in the marinades. You should try chilli-and-tomato
with your chicken, teriyaki with your pork. Maybe some
lime and yogurt with your lamb.'

Jim Griglak shook his head, and sucked hard at his
cigar, which, out of sheer cheapness, had decided to
extinguish itself. 'Munoz,' he said, 'you watch too many of
these faggy cookery shows. You should've come to Norm
Fox's barbecue last year. Norm was up to his bermudas in
fancy marinades, but what did we get? Coalburgers,
chicken à la coal, shrimp coaletti, coalfurters. Barbecue?
That was a frigging cremation.'

Ric didn't let Jim Griglak upset him. Jim was huge –
6' 3" in his conspicuously self-darned socks and probably
well over sixteen stone, if his bathroom scales had been
able to protest out loud. He was country-freckled and
slow and wise, and just a little sad, but he was one of the
best sergeants that Ric had ever worked with. Ric had
seen him shoot an armed crack-dealer between the eyes
so quick that it was all over before Ric had even un-
holstered his .357, and another time he had seen him
pursuing a fleeing wetback through a beanfield with all
the speed and majesty of a charging rhino. The Mexican
himself had stopped running just to watch the spectacle

31

of Jim Griglak thundering towards him, a whole lifetime of Pabst Blue Ribbons and cheese'n'baconburgers in undulating motion.

Ric was well aware that – in return – Jim considered him to be an irredeemable pantywaist – a law-enforcing yuppie. He was one of the new generation of well-groomed career-conscious highway patrolmen who always wore Reynolds Engineering sunglasses, drank Carta Blanca beer and went to *Space in Time* at La Jolla to have their hair cut and their little Magnum moustaches trimmed. In spite of that, Ric and Jim maintained a cautious truce between them, a truce that occasionally flirted with genuine affection. There was, after all, no real contest between them. By the time Ric came up for senior promotion, Jim would have handed in his badge and hung up his gun, and retired to his two-bedroomed chalet in the Cuyamaca forest, just him and his shaggy crossbreed dog Akron and his pale moonlike belly and the real moon and miles of fragrant manzanita.

Ric said, 'You know something, Sergeant? You should come round to my place. I'll show you how to barbecue. It's something in the blood, you know what I mean? No Yankee ever knew how to barbecue.'

'This smoke's goddamned thick,' Jim interrupted him. 'Goddamned what d'you call it?' He flapped his hand, trying to think of the word. '*Pungent.*' He was a halting but devoted reader of *It Pays To Increase Your Word Power.*

'Well, that's the whole key to a successful barbecue,' Ric told him. 'You have to keep on spraying the mesquite with ...'

He stopped as abruptly as a switched-off radio. They had topped another rise, and ahead of them lay just another valley, glaring and dusty. But two or three hundred feet north of the highway, amongst the thorn and the scrub and the prickly pear, smoked the blackened skeleton of a burned-out bus.

'Holy Cremona,' Jim breathed. He didn't have to say 'There's people in it ...' because they had both seen them

32

the instant that they crested the rise. Burned people, maybe a dozen of them, maybe more. And for the past three miles, they had been bantering each other about hamburgers and ribs and chicken kebabs. Because of the smell. Because of these people, burning.

'Oh, Mary Mother of God,' whispered Ric. 'Don't let this be.'

As they descended the hill, they could see that the ribcage structure of the bus was still blossoming with tiny orange flames, almost as if it had been decorated with marigolds, and that its tyres were still thickly smoldering.

The hot afternoon wind was blowing from the south-west, and it was hanging out the ragged brown smoke all across the valley.

'Oh, Mary Mother of God,' Ric repeated quietly. 'Don't let this be.'

Jim picked up his r/t microphone and said matter-of-factly, as if he were ordering dinner at a Korean take-out, 'One-four-six, this is one-four-six. Doris, this is Jim Griglak. I have a multiple traffic fatality here on Highway 78, just about fifteen miles due east of Borrego Springs. I'm going to need choppers and firetrucks and ambulances, make that at least ten ambulances, repeat ten – we have a considerable number of casualties here – and backup. I'll get back to you, okay?'

'Don't let this be,' Ric whispered, more to the Holy Virgin than to Jim as the patrol car jounced off the highway and sped across the scrub toward the burned-out bus, a plume of dust rising high behind it.

'It *be*, all right,' Jim assured him. He took a last suck on his extinguished cigar, and then tossed the butt out of the window. Fire department regulations forbade smoking at the scene of a blaze. 'You can pray all you like, Munoz, but it frigging well be.'

They swerved to a halt about thirty feet away from the bus, and climbed out. Ric wrestled out the fire-extinguisher, but Jim called across the roof of the car, 'Forget it, Munoz. They're all dead. Better to leave everything the way it is.'

Ric nodded, and gave him an oddly clogged-up 'Sure', obediently replacing the fire-extinguisher. He took off his sunglasses and followed Jim closer to the bus, glancing at it with hesitant up-and-down motions of his head, and swallowing, desperately wanting not to look, but knowing that he had to. He didn't know how Jim managed to stay so goddamned calm. Ric had been with the California Highway Patrol for six-and-a-half years and, like all patrolmen, he had seen some shockers. Bloody and scarcely recognizable children, jet-propelled through car windscreens because their parents hadn't bothered to buckle them up. Irrationally cheerful men, crushed flat as cardboard from the chest down, still joking and asking for a cigarette. Women lying in the road screaming, unable to get up, because they had both of their arms torn off.

He had seen people trapped behind brown smoked-up windows, burning alive, pleading with him, screaming at him, 'Save me! Save me!' but unreachable because of the heat. He had never seen anything like this.

Maybe it was the silence that affected him so much. Usually there were sirens and traffic and people shouting. Out here in the desert there was nothing but the warm soft fluffing of the breeze and the *ping-tikk-pinging* of slowly cooling metal. Occasionally one of the tyres flared up, but for the most part the fire was out now.

Maybe it was the dense charred-pork smell of burned human flesh. It saturated the air, so that every breath he took was greasy with it. *Oh Christ*, he thought to himself, *I'm breathing in dead people. I'm actually breathing them in.*

It looked like an ordinary bus, a ten-wheeler GMC. Most of its paint was burned off and what was left of its aluminium bodywork was darkly discoloured, but Ric could make out the words *Balboa Hi-Way Bus Ren* in brownish-red letters, on the side.

The blackened driver was still sitting in his seat; still grasping his carbonized steering-wheel. A rough head-count came up with twelve more passengers, men and women. They were all dead, no doubt about it, although

34

the fire had charred them unevenly. Those sitting on the left-hand side of the bus were burned into tiny crispy monkeys, their teeth grinning brown through their black flaking skin, their little fists raised in front of them as if they had all been drumming, their drumsticks suddenly confiscated.

Those sitting on the right-hand side, particularly those at the back, had been less devastatingly charred, and one Hispanic girl of about twenty-four years old looked almost untouched at first. It was only when Ric walked around the back of the bus that he saw that her black hair was all burned off down one side of her head, and her pretty floral-pink sundress had been incinerated from her left knee to her left shoulder. He could see her scorched white panties and it made him feel like a ghoul.

Ric and Jim met each other round on the far side of the bus. Ric took out his handkerchief, folded it into a triangle, and pressed it against his nose and mouth.

'Some cookout, hunh?' asked Jim, although he was far from laughing.

'What the hell do you think *happened* here?' Ric asked him, unsteadily. 'You think maybe the gas tank exploded, something like that?'

Jim grunted and hunkered down, and examined the underside of the bus. 'No *signs* of explosion. Nothing's ripped apart, no distortion. Gas tank's intact, luggage is burned but not blown apart. This baby just caught fire and that was that.'

He stood up, and wiped the perspiration from his forehead with his fat ginger arm. 'It can happen, I guess, especially with fuel injection. But you don't often see it with diesel.'

He squinted at the tyre-tracks that the bus had left in the dust between here and the highway. 'No signs of any other vehicle involved. The driver headed straight here, no swerving, no skids. It's hard to say for sure, but it doesn't look like he was panicking none.'

'His whole goddamned bus was on fire and he wasn't panicking? It doesn't make sense.'

Jim reached into his shirt pocket and took out a roll of wintergreen Life-Savers. He offered one to Ric but Ric shook his head. '*Nobody* was panicking,' he observed, tucking a Life-Saver into his cheek. 'Look at them, they're all sitting in their seats, no heaps of bodies next to the door, nobody anywhere near the emergency exits.'

Ric walked back along the side of the bus and stared up at the girl in the floral-pink sundress. The unburned side of her face was Spanish-looking and remarkably pretty, and her right eye was open and staring at him, or just past him, anyway. The extraordinary thing was that she looked like she was smiling. She looked *happy.*

You, young lady, you're a goddamned conundrum, you are, thought Ric. *How can you smile when your legs are on fire? I mean, Jesus – how much that must have hurt.*

Jim came up and stood beside him and stared at the girl, too.

'She's smiling,' said Ric, with a nervous laugh.

'Naw,' Jim's Life-Saver rattled between his teeth. 'It's the heat, shrinks the facial muscles, same way a steak curls up. Saw a guy burning in a truck once, trapped, couldn't get out. Looked like he was laughing his head off. I felt like calling out, what's the frigging joke?'

They walked back to the patrol car. Ric glanced back once or twice, and the girl was still staring at him with that single expressionless prune-brown eye.

Jim reached into the car and lifted out the radio microphone. 'Doris? Jim Griglak. Listen, tell the coroner we got thirteen of them. That's right, a baker's dozen. Yeah, that's right, baked pretty good, too.'

There was nothing else for them to do but wait. They stood leaning against their patrol car in the wavering afternoon heat, watching the bus tyres burn themselves down to criss-cross hoops of radial-ply steel, and the last few flames around the body framework gutter out. In the distance, from the west, they heard the echoing *flacker-flacker-flacker* of approaching helicopters.

'You know what we've got ourselves here, don't you,

Ric?' asked Jim, lifting his bulk away from the car. Jim had never called him 'Ric' before.

Ric shook his head, conscious that Jim was going to tell him something serious.

'We've got ourselves a massacre, that's what we got.'

'You think this was *deliberate*?'

'Come on, Munoz, use your grey matter. This was no traffic accident, for Christ's sake. You don't have to be Sherlock Holmes to see that. This is a massacre. A crack massacre, or a sect massacre, or maybe both. Santaria maybe. You know the kind of thing. Candles and beads and plaster madonnas and sacrificed chickens, and the kids with the Uzis will get you if the voodoo-dolls don't. Whoever it was, they were seriously less-than-amiable.'

He shook his head in exasperation. 'What I can't understand is why they all look so frigging happy about it.'

'It sure seems kind of unusual,' Ric agreed.

'Unusual? I'd call it frigging unreal. I mean, think about it. A busload of people get themselves driven out to the desert. Very nice, very scenic. Then they get burned to death with happy smiles on their faces and without making the *slightest* attempt to escape. That, my friend, is what I personally define as a problem I could do without. A question which may be susceptible to solution, but to which I don't care to know the answer.'

They were still waiting for the first helicopters to come into sight when Ric noticed something shifting at the top of the ridge, something tawny-brown, maybe a dog or a coyote. He nodded to Jim Griglak and said, 'Did you see that?'

Jim Griglak shaded his eyes with his hand.

'I can't see nothing.'

'Top of the ridge – there, to the left.'

They glimpsed something of what looked like a shoulder, then an arm. 'Goddamn it, there's somebody up there!' Jim Griglak exclaimed, and then yelled out, 'Hey! Hey up there! You come on down here! Do you hear me? You come right down here!'

A dark head bobbed just above the horizon, then ducked away.

'Goddamn it,' Jim cursed. 'Goddamn it to hell!' He hitched up his gunbelt, and began to trundle around the burned-out bus and up the slope. Ric started after him, but without turning his head, Jim waved him away. 'You stay there ... guard the bus. I'll get this bastard.'

Ric watched him as he scaled the dusty, heat-dazzled rocks. His arms pumped, his trousers flapped, his saddle-bags bounced with every stride, but he clambered up to the top of the ridge with awesome agility, and disappeared from view.

Ric turned his head. He could see the first helicopter now, its canopy reflecting a sharp star of sunlight as it came skimming low and fast over the desert hills.

Ric blinked, and grimaced, and looked around him in deep uncertainty. The helicopter was landing now, and lashing up smoke and dust and fragments of blackened fabric. The hair of the half-burned Hispanic girl flew up over her head like a fright-wig. She seemed to be laughing. A blizzard of ash suddenly burst from the busdriver's face, and was swept away in the downdraught.

As the helicopter's rotors were whip-whistling to a standstill, Jim reappeared on the crest of the ridge. At first he looked as if he were alone, but when he moved aside, Ric saw that he was prodding in front of him an Indian boy of about twelve. The boy came down the slope crab-wise, clutching at the rocks. He had long greasy black hair, circular grannie Ray-Bans and a red bandana around his forehead. He was dressed in a grubby Elvis Presley T-shirt and yellow-and-purple bermudas.

'Hey, Sergeant!' called Ric.

'Yeah, look what I found,' Jim called back. He nudged the boy down the slope and around the wreck of the bus.

Two lean young highway patrolmen climbed out of the helicopter and came walking slowly across toward them, staring at the bus in disbelief.

'Jesus,' said one of them, wiping the sweat from his face with his neckscarf. 'What the hell happened here?'

'I was hoping Geronimo here might be able to tell us,' Jim replied. 'What's your name, son? Were you here when this bus went up?'

The boy said, 'Sure, man, I was here.' He kept nodding, and turning his head around as if he were high.

'Did you see what happened?'

'No way, man. Didn't see nothing.'

'The bus was burning and you were here and you didn't see nothing?'

'That's what I said, man.'

Jim said harshly, 'Will you stop calling me "man", for Christ's sake.'

'Sorry, man.'

'What's your name, son?'

'Tony.' Again that odd distracted head-nodding.

'Tony who?'

'Tony Express.'

'*Tony Express*? Who the hell are you trying to kid?'

'I'm not trying to kid nobody, man. That's what everybody calls me. I guess it's kind of a joke. My Indian name is Child-Who-Looked-At-The-Sun.'

'Child-Who-Looked-At-The-Sun, hey?' asked Ric. 'That's some kind of fancy name.'

Jim said, 'Where do you live, Tony? And what the hell are you doing out here in any case?'

'I live here, man,' Tony told him. 'Well, just back over the ridge a'ways. My pa runs that Indian souvenir stand next to the 76 gas station.'

'And you were here when the bus burned?' asked one of the helicopter patrolmen, vigorously chewing sugar-free gum.

Tony nodded. 'Sure. I was right on top of the ridge.'

'So how come you didn't see nothing?' asked the patrolman.

Tony took off his Ray-Bans. Underneath, his eyes were milky and swivelling, and blind as marbles. 'I was born this way, man,' he explained. 'Child-Who-Looked-At-The-Sun, get it?'

'Oh, shit,' swore Jim Griglak. He stood with his fists on

39

his hips and shook his head over and over as if he were never going to stop. 'For Christ's sake. The luck of the frigging Griglaks.'

Ric said, 'Tony, listen, even if you couldn't see anything, maybe you *heard* something? Voices, footsteps? Anything at all?'

'Come on, Munoz, what's the frigging use?' Jim demanded.

'Hey, come on,' Ric told him. 'Blind people are supposed to have this really acute sense of hearing. Like they can hear dog-whistles and stuff.'

'Man, I didn't hear no dog-whistles, man,' Tony replied. He replaced his Ray-Bans and stood scratching the dry skin on his elbows and staring at nothing at all.

'What did I tell you?' Jim complained. 'The luck of the frigging Griglaks.'

Two more helicopters were circling, and it was hard to hear what anybody was saying. But Tony suddenly said, 'I heard the bus leaving the road, and coming this way. And I heard somebody talking, too.'

'You heard somebody talking? What did they say?'

'I was way back in the rocks, there. I couldn't hear too good.'

'Was it a man or a woman?' asked Ric.

'It was a guy. He sounded old, man, know what I mean? Kind of croaky. He was talking but I couldn't understand what he was saying.'

'You didn't catch anything at all?' asked Ric, raising his voice above the flackering of helicopters.

Tony said, 'Unh-hunh. Only one thing, maybe. He kept saying, "You knew us". Real loud. "You knew us".'

'"You knew us"? Any idea what he meant?'

'I don't know, man. Some old guy stands in the desert saying, "you knew us", how am I supposed to know what he means?'

'Was this before or after the bus burned?' asked the gum-chewing patrolman.

'It was before, and it was during, too. Like, while it was burning, he kept saying it, "you knew us".'

'How come he didn't see you, this old guy?' Jim wanted to know.

'I was in the rocks, man, way back there, over there. My pa wanted me to mind the store, see, but I didn't want to mind the store, so I came out to listen to my Walkman, man, and have a smoke. When I first heard the bus, I thought maybe I should come out. Sometimes the marks give you money to have your picture took.'

'But you didn't come out?' Ric asked him.

Tony Express hesitated. Then he said, 'No.'

'Why?' Ric coaxed him. 'Was it something you heard? Something somebody said?'

'I don't know, man. I just had this weird feeling that something weird was going down.'

'Jesus, the frigging articulate youth of today,' said Jim. Then, 'Okay, Tony, that'll do it for now. Somebody'll want to talk to you later. You live right by the gas station, that it?'

'Indian Jack's Genuine Pechanga Souvenirs.'

'Sure, made in Taiwan.'

'You need any help getting back?' asked Ric.

Tony Express shook his head. 'I may be blind, man, but I'm not stupid.'

'I bet you fall ass over tit down the first arroyo you come to,' Jim Griglak retaliated.

But they all knew that he wouldn't. They watched him climb without hesitation back up the ridge again, and disappear from sight. A weaving black silhouette, then nothing but ink-blue sky.

'Look at him go,' said one of the patrolmen, impressed. 'He's *blind* and look at him go.'

'They're all the same,' Jim answered, aggressively. 'The deaf and the dumb, the blind and the lame. They all think they're God's gift. If only they knew what a pain in the ass they really are.'

The highway patrolmen exchanged a quick, encyclopaedic glance. Everybody on the force knew that Jim Griglak was awkward and prejudiced and mean as a sackful of polecats. They also knew that it wasn't worth

41

arguing with him, not unless you wanted months and months of aggression and sarcasm and practical jokes. He was a paradox, but maybe you had to be a paradox to be a really good policeman. Maybe a mild variety of fascism was one of the basic requirements for the job.

One of the patrolmen turned around to the burned-out bus and said, 'So what do you think went down here, Jim? You have to admit that it's pretty weird.'

'How the hell should I know what happened?' Jim snapped at him. 'But something sure stinks around here, and it ain't just these human hamburgers.'

They shuffled their boots in the white uncompromising Anza Borrego dust, and waited for the far-off scribbling of sirens.

— FIVE —

At almost the same moment that the first highway patrol helicopter landed next to the burned-out bus, Lloyd stepped out of the mortuary at San Diego police head-quarters. He turned momentarily toward his BMW, parked alongside three blue-and-white patrol cars with *To Serve And Protect* emblazoned on their doors, but decided against it. He was too shaken to think about driving. He had to walk. Under a furnace-like blue sky, he crossed the street, and started threading his way northward along the Embarcadero, his shirt sticking to his back, his eyes stung with sweat and tears.

He had never seen a dead body before. Not even a peaceful, unmarked, cosmetically prepared dead body. Celia's had been horrendous, blackened and reeking of petrol, raw. Her tendons had been tightened by the heat of her immolation, and she had been crouched in her grey-green body-bag like some terrible huge incinerated embryo. But he had known as soon as the zipper began to slide down that it was her. He had recognized her, he had recognized her. He had nodded desperately, swallowed, turned away, blinked back tears, while his mouth had suddenly filled up with hot orange-juice, regurgitated from breakfast. Sergeant Houk had taken him by the elbow and steered him out into the corridor.

'I just want you to know that we're all real sorry about this, Mr Denman.'

Lloyd had been unable to speak. *Sorry?* How could a word like 'sorry' apply to such an horrific invasion of his whole existence, his happiness, his sanity, everything that he had invested in the future? He felt as if all he could do was to walk and walk and walk under the grilling mid-morning sun, until he finally collapsed from exhaustion

43

and grief, and lay on the ground, where he wouldn't have to focus on anything larger than a few grains of earth.

As usual on a summer's morning, the harbourside was crowded with sightseers. Lloyd walked through them as if he were a half-drowned man walking up a beach. He jarred his shoulder against a fat woman in a pink T-shirt emblazoned with a cartoon drawing of three macho surfers and the legend *San Diego – No Wimps*. 'Well, pardon *me*,' she snarled at him.

He passed the dark wooden hull of the *Star of India*, one of the historic old sailing-ships moored along the Embarcadero. There was a strong aroma on the breeze of old timber, coconut Coppertone and cotton candy. He side-stepped a crowd of Japanese tourists who were clustered around the gangplank, endlessly taking each other's photographs. It was then that he heard somebody calling his name.

Lloyd! Lloyd! A voice as small as a hornet in a sealed glass jar. Tiny, desperate.

He looked around him; then up at the sides of the ship. Tourists filed around the upper decks, talking and pointing and staring around them in a way that suddenly struck Lloyd as particularly odd, as if they were expecting something momentous to appear. But what? A magnetic storm? A sea-serpent? A flying saucer from outer space?

There was a strange tightness in the air. He couldn't understand it. Maybe it was just him. He was reminded of the atmosphere in those 1950s science-fiction movies, *Them* and *This Island Earth*.

He was about to carry on walking along the Embarcadero when he glimpsed a girl high up on deck, close to the *Star of India*'s bow. She was wearing a yellow-silk headscarf and dark upswept sunglasses, and a white raincoat with the collar turned up. Lloyd's attention wasn't only caught by the incongruity of the girl's clothing, on a hot June day. There was something else, too. Something disturbingly familiar about her. Something in the way she turned her head that reminded him of Celia.

He hesitated. Of course it couldn't be Celia. He had just

seen Celia lying raw-burned-dead in the San Diego police mortuary. But at the same time he couldn't carry on walking without taking a closer look at her. Just to make absolutely sure.

Absolutely sure of what, Lloyd? That you're not hallucinating? That you're not going out of your mind? Or absolutely sure that things couldn't conceivably be different; that life couldn't possibly have different endings, different manifestations, different destinies?

He remembered his grandfather telling him, after his grandmother's funeral: 'It isn't the dead that haunt the world, it's the people they leave behind.'

Apologetically shoving his way through the crowd, he made his way up the *Star of India*'s gangplank. He paid for a tour and waited impatiently while a simulated salt in a Popeye's-pappy hat gave him a ticket and told him to have a good day. 'And don't forget to look at the whaling exhibition. Harpoons and scrimshaw.'

Scrimshaw. Like the superstitious baseball player, Turkey Mike Donlin, Lloyd felt that he had seen the barrels. He hurried forward, through light and shade, through the criss-cross pattern of rigging.

The foredeck was deserted, except for a family of father, mother and daughter, all wearing mirror sunglasses. They turned away from the rail and stared at Lloyd as he approached them, and Lloyd saw himself cross to the other side of the deck six times over, in miniature, in their bright and meaningless lenses.

He returned to the shadows. A sandy-haired man passed him by, telling his wife, 'It's no damned good, you know. It never was any damned good and it never will be any damned good.'

Ahead of him, around the side of the *Star of India*'s wheelhouse, he thought he glimpsed the skirts of a white raincoat. He pushed his way more urgently along the crowded deck. The planking echoed under his white leather-soled Gucci loafers.

Lloyd, he heard her whisper. *Lloyd.* Or maybe it was nothing but the kerfuffle of wind in the rigging, or the slap of water on the hull of a passing motorboat, or a gull mewling as it turned its feathers to the morning sun.

He searched twice around the upper deck, but the girl in the yellow-silk headscarf had gone. He hesitated for a while, looking this way and that, biting his lip. Then he went slowly down the companionway to the lower deck, where it was gloomier and cooler. In illuminated glass cabinets, charts and knots and compasses were neatly displayed, along with antique carvings and scrimshaw. The lower deck was almost as crowded as the upper, and Lloyd had to edge his way through the tourists with a repetitious litany of 'Pardon me, thank you; pardon me, thank you ...' until he reached the souvenir counter.

There he stopped, and stretched himself up so that he could see better, and meticulously scanned everybody around him. The girl behind the counter watched him for a while. She was freckled and blonde and busty, with a striped nautical-style T-shirt and a peaked cap with a gilt *Star of India* badge.

'May I help you, sir?' she asked him.

He turned around. 'I was looking for a girl.'

'Any special girl or will any girl do?'

Lloyd was too abstracted to understand. 'She was wearing a white raincoat and a headscarf and dark glasses.'

The girl behind the counter widened her eyes. 'She was wearing a *raincoat*?'

Lloyd kept on looking around. 'A white raincoat and a yellow headscarf.'

The girl watched him for a little longer. 'You sure you're okay?'

'I'm fine, I'm okay.'

'Well, if you don't mind my saying so, you look pretty upset.'

Lloyd frowned at her. He didn't quite know what to say. 'Look,' he said, reaching into his back trouser pocket, and taking out his wallet, 'Here's my card ... if you ever see a girl looking like that ... if she buys anything here ... maybe you could let me know. Maybe note down her name from her credit card.'

The girl peered at Lloyd's restaurant card. 'I can't see too well without my glasses.'

'Denman's Original Fish Depot, up at La Jolla.'

'Oh, sure, we drove past it once,' the girl nodded, with Betty Boopish enthusiasm. 'And that's you? You're the Original Fish Depot?'

'I'm Denman.'

'Hi, I'm Lawreign. That's "law" like *LA Law* and "reign" like *queen.*'

'Nice name,' said Lloyd, still looking around for any sign of the girl who had looked so much like Celia. 'Unusual spelling.'

'Oh, my daddy never went past third grade. Neither did I. I didn't want to make him feel that I was like superior or something.'

'You're a big-hearted young lady.'

'Well, thank you, noble sir. Compliment accepted.'

At that instant, however, Lloyd thought he saw that yellow headscarf, a flicker as bright and as fleeting as a gale-blown sunflower behind a yard fence. Immediately he pushed his way through the crowds around the souvenir counter, and made for the exit.

Damn it, there she is again! That scarf, that raincoat, halfway down the ramp!

'Hey-y-y!' called Lawreign.

He struggled past the huge hard unyielding belly of a black Marine, then found himself scrambling through a bespectacled and camera-thrusting crowd of chattering Japanese. He had almost made the top of the gangplank when a frail old woman in a straw hat and a flowery dress stepped out in front of him, her sun-measled hand reaching for the rail and obstructing his pursuit as effectively as a three-car roadblock. He was powerless to do anything but follow behind her as she made her slow and painful progress down the gangplank, and the girl who had looked so much like Celia disappeared into the throng of tourists on the Embarcadero below.

He thought he had lost her completely. But then he glimpsed that sunflower scarf flashing through the crowd.

She had reached the kerb, and was just about to cross the road.

'Celia!' he yelled at her. 'Celia!' Even though it *couldn't* be Celia, even though all of this running after her was total madness. It was nothing but exhaustion, and hysteria, and devastating grief.

But just before she crossed the street, she turned, and stared at him, and even though she was wearing those black upswept sunglasses he was *convinced* with a shiver that stopped him right where he was, unable to remember how to run, unable to remember which foot to lift or how his ankles worked. He was convinced that she was Celia.

'Celia,' he said, out loud. People bumped and jostled against him, laughing, as if they were all in on the joke and he wasn't. *C-E-L-I-A* he shouted, so loudly that he stunned himself. Faces turned, somebody said, 'What, is he crazy or something?' Then he was quarterbacking across the sidewalk, colliding, bumping, and all the time that flicker of yellow danced in front of him, just out of reach.

He started to cross the street, but stepped right in front of a Federal Express van, which bucked to a halt, both sliding doors slamming shut. Its bespectacled black driver indignantly blared the horn at him.

'What the hell are you trying to do, asshole, meet your goddamned Maker?'

Lloyd lifted both hands in apology. The van drove off, but by the time it had passed in front of him, there was no sign of that tantalizing glimpse of yellow. He searched quickly left and right, taking two steps hesitantly forward when he caught sight of a dancing lick of yellow amidst the crowds. But the dancing lick of yellow turned out to be a child's balloon, and the girl in the raincoat had gone.

He felt as if he could drop to his knees on the sidewalk, struck deaf and dumb by sheer illogicality. He was so sure that the girl in the raincoat had been Celia. But how could it, when Celia was dead and burned in the San Diego police mortuary?

He was still standing on the kerb when a dusty saddle-brown Buick drew up in front of him, and parked. Sergeant Houk climbed out, wearing a sweaty-looking drip-dry shirt and a narrow brown necktie.

'Mr Denman? I was hoping I'd catch up with you. Don't forget that fancy automobile of yours. Our captain's been giving it the eye all morning. Reckons it's his kind of car.'

Lloyd unhooked his sunglasses. 'I'm sorry. I was going right back to collect it. I just had to take a walk, that's all. Breath of fresh air.'

'Sure, I understand,' said Sergeant Houk, sniffing. 'What you had to do today – well, I wouldn't ever try to pretend that there's anything easy about it.'

Lloyd said, 'You know something ... Celia loved life so much. She enjoyed everything she did, from morning till night. She was so damned *happy.* I can't think of one single reason why she should have ...'

Sergeant Houk sniffed again, and looked around him. 'There's no grass here, no pollen. I'm seriously beginning to think that I must be allergic to tourists.'

Lloyd said, 'I called the Miyako. She never even checked in. So far as I can make out, the lecture tour was all a lie.'

'We know that,' Sergeant Houk nodded. 'What we don't yet know is when she came back to San Diego from San Francisco, and how or why. She didn't use the return half of her airline ticket, we know that much.'

He squinted at Lloyd against the sunshine. 'You'll pardon me for asking, maybe it's a bad time, but she wouldn't have had any close men-friends? What I mean is, apart from you?'

Lloyd shook his head, and let out a funny blurting noise that was nearly a laugh. 'No,' he mouthed. 'She didn't have any close man-friends. That's if you mean by close what I *think* you mean by close.'

'How about you? Did you have any extra-curricular friendships? Anything which might have upset her? You see, you'll forgive me for asking, but these self-immolations, they're almost invariably motivated either by wacky political grievances, like the U.S. invasion of Outer

49

Weirdolia or saving the purple-spotted parakeet, or else they're about personal relationships.'

He paused, and cleared his throat, and then continued, 'People who torch themselves ... well, I've seen people on fire, and that ain't the way that *I* want to go. No, sir. But I was talking to our psychologist this morning and she was saying that they do it to kind of *purify* themselves. Almost like they're disinfecting themselves of all the infections they think the rest of us are crawling with.'

'I'm not too sure I understand that,' Lloyd admitted, although he was only half listening.

'Well, I wanted you to think about it, Mr Denman, because any kind of clue to your fiancée's state of mind could possibly be helpful.'

'All right, I'll try to think of something.'

Sergeant Houk gave him an unshaven, cavernous grin. 'How about a ride back to headquarters? I just had my air-conditioning fixed. It's like sitting in a goddamned igloo.'

Numbly, Lloyd accepted his invitation. Inside, Sergeant Houk's car smelled of pine air-freshener and stale cigarettes, and there was a sticker on the dash which said *No Farting Zone*. The rubbery beige upholstery was penetrated with dozens of cigarette burns. A naked plastic dolly with scarlet-painted nipples swung from the rearview mirror. A souvenir from Tijuana. Sergeant Houk thrust his arm out of the window and illegally U-turned on squittering tyres.

He was right about the air-conditioning. The interior of the Riviera was penetratingly cold, cold as the morgue in which Celia's body had been rolled out in front of him. So cold that Lloyd began to tremble.

Sergeant Houk drove with his wrist draped casually on top of the steering-wheel. 'It's a funny thing, with suicides. Most of the time they leave a note. But even if they don't, the nearest and dearest almost always come up with the answer. Once that first shock has worn off, they start to think about their loved ones the way they really were, and they start to *analyze*. And suddenly, *po-zah!* they understand what happened, and why. At the

50

beginning, though, it's pretty hard to accept that somebody you were in love with didn't love you enough to want to stay around. I mean, not even in the *world*. Packing your bags and going home to momma is one thing. Setting fire to yourself, well, that's something else altogether.'

'Yes, it is,' Lloyd agreed, dully.

They drove for a minute or two without talking. Then Sergeant Houk started to say, 'In my view, you know...' when he was interrupted by his radio.

'*Three-niner, three-niner.*'

He picked up his r/t mike, which had been lying loose on the seat, under an untidy loose heap of newspapers and Snickers wrappers and folded-up warrants. 'Three-niner, gotcha.'

There was a crackle as somebody else was patched through. Then, 'Dave? Lieutenant Pratt. Listen, we just received an urgent bulletin from the State Police out in the Anza Borrego State Park.'

'Oh, yeah?' asked Sergeant Houk. 'What are they squawking about now?'

'Two Highway Patrol officers located a burned-out bus, about a half-hour ago, fifteen miles east of Borrego Springs.'

Sergeant Houk didn't reply, but turned to Lloyd, and said, 'This is typical, you know? A burnt-out bus in the middle of the desert, and they're telling *me*? You can bet your ass to a beef burrito, this is going to turn out to be some chore so menial you wouldn't let your dog do it.'

Almost as if he could hear him, Lieutenant Pratt said, 'The State Police have requested assistance in checking the bus rental company. Balboa Hi-Way Bus Rental, 2339 Mark Street.'

'I know them,' replied Sergeant Houk, dispassionately. 'Run by a guy called Dan Browder. Just opposite the Playa Hotel.'

'They're also asking for assistance in checking the identities of the casualties.'

'Casualties? How many casualties?'

'Thirteen, no survivors.'

'Thirteen? Jesus.'

There was a long pause. They waited at a pedestrian crossing while a long crocodile of chattering Mexican children crossed in front of them. Sergeant Houk sniffed, then sneezed. 'What did I tell you? Tourists! I'm allergic.'

The voice on the radio said, 'Sergeant? Are you still there?'

'Still here, Lieutenant.'

'I want you to check out the bus rental, then I want you to drive out to Borrego Springs and liaise with the Highway Patrol and the State Police and see what you can do to assist. Ask for a Sergeant Jim Griglak.'

Sergeant Houk sniffed. 'Can't you get Rollins to do it? I'm up to my duff.'

Lieutenant Pratt ignored him. 'Dave, I want us to keep in touch with this one. We haven't had the full details yet, but there are two possible explanations for what happened here, and both of them are potentially explosive. All the casualties were burned alive, and the first indications are that it wasn't an accident. Either this was a crack massacre, some kind of major revenge killing … Colombia comes to Southern California. But judging from the way the bodies were found, there's an even stronger possibility that it could have been a mass suicide.'

'Hey, come on, Lieutenant,' Sergeant Houk replied, shaking his head in disbelief. 'A massacre I can swallow. But thirteen people torch themselves deliberately?'

'I'm not sure, Sergeant. As of now that's all we know. They were all burned to death and the circumstances seem to point to the probability that we're dealing with mass homicide or mass suicide. I'll give more information as and when.'

'Okay, I'm coming in now anyway.'

Sergeant Houk tossed the r/t mike back on to the seat. 'Jesus. How about a chorus of "I Don't Want To Set The World On Fire"?'

He looked across at Lloyd and suddenly realized what he had said. 'I'm sorry. That was very tasteless. I'm sorry. I apologize.'

Lloyd's mouth was dry, and he was shaking with cold and tiredness. 'Do you think there might be some connection?'

'What do you mean?'

'Do you think there might be some connection between Celia's death and these people on the bus?'

Sergeant Houk wiped his nose with a tiny screwed-up Kleenex. 'I'll tell you something, Mr Denman, from now on, every time you switch on your TV or every time you pick up a newspaper you're going to see a report about somebody burning themselves to death. It's happening all the time, it's just that you didn't notice it before. There's a certain type of suicide who feels that burning themselves to death is the way they have to do it. Who really knows why? There's no connection. It's happening all the time.'

He turned into police headquarters and parked at an angle next to the steps. 'About six weeks ago, I investigated a suicide that was exactly similar to your fiancée's, out in Florida Canyon. Yellow petrol can, everything the same. The only difference was that nobody got to *that* suicide with a fire-extinguisher. There was nothing left but ashes, believe me. It took us two weeks to identify the victim. A store assistant from Sears. No connection with your fiancée whatsoever, apart from the mode of demise.'

Lloyd climbed shakily out of the freezing-cold car into the grilling heat of the downtown sun.

'Take it easy,' Sergeant Houk told him, leaning across the front seat. 'Throw yourself into your work, maybe. A lot of people find that helps.'

'Thanks for the tip,' Lloyd replied, though Sergeant Houk didn't hear the sarcasm in his voice.

'And if anything occurs to you ... any conceivable reason why Ms Williams might have wanted to take her own life ... even if it was nothing more than premenstrual tension, well, you'll call me, yes?'

'For sure,' Lloyd told him.

He crossed the dazzling white car-park. He was conscious that Sergeant Houk was watching him as he went. He unlocked his BMW and climbed in, and sat for a

53

while with his eyes closed, and repeated the words of Allen Ginsberg's *Kaddish*:

There, rest. No more suffering for you. I know where you've gone, and it's good.

He didn't see the girl in the raincoat standing on the opposite side of Broadway, staring at him, unmoving, her yellow scarf flapping in the warm harbour wind, her upswept sunglasses reflecting two dazzling points of light.

— SIX —

When he arrived back at North Torrey, he was surprised and annoyed to find a metallic red Lincoln Continental parked in his driveway. He drew into the kerb, climbed out of his BMW, and cautiously approached the Lincoln across the lawn, jingling his car-keys in his hand.

As he came closer, he saw that a balding man of about sixty-five was sitting in the driver's seat, and next to him was sitting a white-rinsed woman in a purple-and-white blouse and more gold necklaces and bangles and brooches than Nefertiti. Lloyd tapped with his knuckle on the window, and both of them beamed at him.

'Hi there! You must be Otto,' the white-haired man greeted him, letting down his window. He held out his hand, still beaming.

Lloyd said. 'I'm sorry, sir. I think you have the wrong house. This is 4884 North Torrey.'

The man frowned, and unfolded a pair of heavy-rimmed spectacles. He fished a well-folded letter out of his shirt pocket, and examined it closely. 'That's right. That's the address I'm looking for. 4884 North Torrey.'

'Well, I'm afraid there's no Otto here,' Lloyd told him. 'Never has been, to my knowledge.'

'Oh, I'm sorry,' the man answered. 'We weren't actually looking for Otto. We were looking for Celia – Celia Williams?'

'You're friends of hers?' asked Lloyd.

The man laughed, and the woman joined in. 'You could say that. Do you happen to know where we might find her? We've driven all the way from San Clemente this morning, and we've been waiting here for almost an hour.'

Lloyd rubbed the back of his neck. 'I'm afraid I have some pretty bad news for you.'

'Don't tell me she's gone off on one of her lecture tours?' said the woman. 'Oh, *Wayne* ... I told you to call first.'

'What kind of surprise would it have been if I'd called first?' the man demanded.

'It would have saved us two hours on the freeway, for goodness' sake.'

The woman gave Lloyd a fixed grin, and asked, 'Do you happen to know if she's going to be away for very long?'

'Ma'am,' said Lloyd, and he couldn't stop his throat from tightening nor the tears from prickling his eyes. 'I'm sorry to tell you that Celia died yesterday.'

The man and the woman stared at him with their mouths open. At last, the man managed to blurt out, 'She *died*?'

'How could she *die*?' the woman asked.

Lloyd took out his handkerchief and wiped his eyes. 'I'm sorry. There was an accident, she was burned. Nobody really knows what happened.'

'Oh my God,' said the woman. Her hair was white, her face was white. 'Oh my God, tell me it's not true.'

The man climbed out of the car and stood next to Lloyd. He was short, bulky-chested and large-headed, but still quite handsome for his age.

'Sir,' he said, 'I don't even know who you are. It seems like Celia hasn't been giving us the whole picture. I'm sorry.'

Lloyd shook his head. 'Lloyd Denman. Celia and I were going to be married. This house here ... well, we *were* joint owners.'

'This is quite a shock,' the man replied. 'We didn't even know that Celia was seeing anybody, let alone planning to marry. Oh, by the way, I'm Wayne ... this is Vela.'

'Do you want to come in?' Lloyd asked them. 'I've just been down to the mortuary. I could use a drink.'

'Thank you,' said Wayne. He walked around the car and opened the passenger door so that Vela could climb out. 'Burned, you say? How did that happen? Was it an auto accident?'

'Come on inside, and I'll tell you,' said Lloyd.

He led them into the house. The two of them jostled against each other as they looked around the white-painted living-room, as if they were out-of-town tourists in a smart La Jolla art gallery.

'The lemon picture,' said Vela, suddenly. 'That used to be mine, the lemon picture. *Who'll Buy My Lemons?*'

'Please, have a seat,' Lloyd told them. 'Do you want a drink? Or coffee maybe?'

'Do you have a diet soda of any kind?' asked Wayne.

'Nothing for me, thank you,' said Vela.

'Please, sit down,' Lloyd insisted, as he walked through to the kitchen, but still they wouldn't sit.

'We'd really like to know what happened,' said Wayne.

Lloyd came back with a can of diet 7-Up, popped the top, filled a heavy-bottomed Boda glass, and handed it over to Wayne. Then he poured himself a large Wild Turkey.

'It seems that she took her own life,' he said.

'*What?*' said Vela.

'It seems that she committed suicide.'

'But *why?* She was so happy! I never knew her so happy! Her career at the opera was going so well ... she had so many friends. And she was going to be married, which we didn't even know. Why, in heaven's name, should she commit suicide?'

Lloyd stared at the carpet. 'I'm sorry. I don't have any idea.'

'She didn't leave a note?' asked Wayne, his voice trembling.

'Nothing. No clues at all. The police have asked me to try and think of some reason why she might have done it, but I can't.'

Vela was shaking her head and sobbing, her wrinkled red-fingernailed hands slowly clawing at each other in anguish.

'I can't believe it, I can't believe it. I just can't believe it.'

Lloyd said, 'Maybe you can think of some reason. You obviously knew her pretty well.'

Wayne's crumpled-up expression unfolded like origami in reverse. 'Pardon me? Of course we knew her pretty well. I thought you understood. We're her parents.'

Lloyd stared at Wayne, then at Vela, and then back at Wayne. 'You're her *parents*? Her real parents? She told me that both her parents were dead.'

Wayne at last sat down, and laid his arm around Vela's shaking shoulders. 'Lloyd,' he said, 'I don't know what the blazes has been going on here. But whatever it is, I think Vela could use a doctor right now. Her heart's not too good, and this is just about as much shock as she can take.'

Lloyd nodded. 'I'll call Dr Meyer. He's one of the university doctors. He can usually come out directly.'

'Oh, my darling, my little darling,' Vela wept. 'Oh, Wayne, what are we going to do?'

Dr Meyer arrived in his Porsche sunglasses and his golfing shoes and gave Vela a light sedative. 'I'll call by tomorrow morning, just to check she's okay,' he assured Lloyd, climbing into his gleaming charcoal Seville. 'If you want me this afternoon, I'm out at Whispering Palms, playing with Bill Manzo. Ball therapy.' He showed his teeth.

Vela slept in the spare bedroom for most of the afternoon. Lloyd and Wayne stayed in the living-room and talked.

Most of the life-story that Celia had told Lloyd turned out to be true, but there were occasional inexplicable discrepancies, not the least of which was her almost fanatical interest in religion and life after death. She had never spoken to Lloyd about religion, and when he had asked her if she believed in God, she had laughed and answered, 'Whose God? Not mine, my darling!'

Since Vela was far too shocked and distraught to be driven back to San Clemente tonight, Wayne graduated from diet 7-up to Four Roses. He lit a cigar, too, and took off his shoes. Usually, Lloyd found cigar-smoking offensive, not to mention old men's sports socks, but tonight he didn't object at all. At least he wouldn't have to spend the evening here in the house alone, with nobody for company but Celia's haunting, incommunicative photograph.

Wayne said, 'Celia started getting serious about religion when her grandma died. That was when Celia was … oh, I don't know, fifteen or sixteen. Sixteen I think. She adored her grandma. They were so close, those two, such affection, such understanding. Peas in a pod. Vela used to be jealous sometimes, although there was never any need. But Celia was hit real hard when her grandma finally went. I don't think that she could believe it, you know? She used to say, "Why couldn't grandma live for ever?" She said that over and over, and she used to say, "I'm going to live for ever. I'm going to live for ever and ever." I used to tease her about it, she said it so often. But she always sounded totally serious, wouldn't be teased. I used to call her The Immortal Celia, or The Everlasting Girl. She used to smile and say nothing.'

He paused, and lowered his head. Then he took a large swallow of whisky, and mouthwashed it around his teeth. 'That's why it's so hard to believe that she could have taken her own life.'

Lloyd suggested, 'I guess she could have come to believe that death is a way of living forever. You know … "*they shall grow not old, as we who are left grow old.*" '

Wayne set down his empty glass. 'I don't know. It doesn't make any kind of sense at all. Particularly the way she told you that she didn't have any parents. I mean – she was going to *marry* you and not invite us?'

'I don't know, Mr Williams. I can't figure it out.'

They sat in depressed silence for five or ten minutes, and then Lloyd asked, 'You said that she was obsessed with religion. Do you happen to know what kind of religion? She wasn't in with a cult or anything, was she? Like the Moonies, maybe? Or the Bhagwan?'

Wayne made a face. 'I'm not sure. She started off at the Episcopalian church at San Clemente. She went to Bible meetings and church socials and all that kind of thing. Then about three months after they gave her a place with the San Diego Opera, she met this guy Otto – the guy I thought was you. She always talked about Otto like the sun shone out of his – well, like she thought a whole lot of him, you know? Otto had this group that was all into communicating with the world beyond, all that crap, if you'll excuse my French.'

'Oh, sure.' Lloyd got up and poured both of them another large drink. 'You don't happen to know the name of this group? Where they hang out? What they're into?'

Wayne shook his head. 'All Celia ever talked about was how much she enjoyed the group, the group was brilliant, and Otto was brilliant, she thought Otto was wonderful. God, practically.'

'You never met Otto?'

'We only came down to see the opera once. Personally I can take it or leave it, opera. I don't know where Celia got her interest from. Especially that goddamned Wagner. After she met Otto, it was Wagner this and Wagner that, and when she came home weekends she played this real loud heavy stuff with screaming women. I used to take the dog for a walk. That Wagner music, Jesus. It sounded like somebody dropping an A-bomb on an afternoon session of weight-watchers.'

Wayne paused, cleared his throat, and then continued, 'Barbershop, that's more my style. "In The Good Old Summertime".' There were tears in his eyes.

Lloyd sank back into the sofa and toyed with his glass. Wayne puffed at his cigar and blew smoke-rings up to the ceiling. He was quite drunk now, which was probably just as well. The full impact of his daughter's death wouldn't hit him until he woke up tomorrow morning with a cement-truck hangover.

Twenty minutes later, Wayne's eyes drooped and he dozed off. Lloyd gave him a moment or two to fall more heavily asleep. Then he walked softly across and removed the half-burned cigar from Wayne's lifeless fingers.

He went through to the kitchen, picked up the telephone and dialled Sylvia Cuddy's number. While he waited for Sylvia to answer, he switched on the portable television next to the spice-rack, and watched a Wrigley's Doublemint commercial with the sound turned down to gnat-in-a-jam-jar level.

Sylvia answered. There was opera in the background, Verdi, played at devastating volume.

'Sylvia? This is Lloyd.'

'Oh, Lloyd! I've been waiting for your call! I was just about to go out.'

'Don't let me keep you.'

'Oh, not at all. Wait, just let me turn this down. I can't hear myself think. Leonard Katzmann's taking me to Mario's for dinner, as if I haven't had enough opera for one day. Or enough of Leonard, come to that. How are you, my dear? Was it terrible today?'

Terrible? How could he possibly put into words the sheer grisly horror of those gaping Lon Chaney nostrils, those stretched-back lips, that incinerated hair? That beautiful face that had been turned into a grinning blackened voodoo death-mask?

'Well,' he said, trying to sound matter-of-fact, 'it was pretty difficult, to be honest with you. It was just about the worst thing I've ever had to do in the whole of my life.'

'Lloyd, my love, I'm so sorry. You don't know how badly everybody feels for you.'

'Thanks, Sylvia. Listen ... I'll talk to you tomorrow about the funeral and all that kind of thing. The medical examiner hasn't released her body to the morticians yet. Apparently it's a rule that they always have to carry out an autopsy after a suicide.'

'Take your time, Lloyd. I'll call around tomorrow, if you like.'

'Sure, I'd like that. There's just one thing I wanted to ask you.'

'Anything. Go ahead.'

'Well ... do you happen to know anybody at the opera called Otto?'

There was a pause. 'Otto? Not that I know of. Do you

61

happen to know his second name?'

'Otto, that's all I've got. Maybe he's not exactly a member of the opera company, but just knows some of the people there. He's involved with some kind of religious study group.'

'I can't say that I've ever *heard* of any Otto. But I'll ask around, if you like. Maybe Don knows him.'

She hesitated, and then she said, 'Is it something you want for yourself? I know a marvellous priest you could talk to, Father Bernard.'

'No, no, it's just ... just somebody that Celia happened to mention. I guessed I ought to tell him what happened.'

'Oh, sure. Well, I'll ask. You don't know anything else about him?'

'Just that Celia thought he was something between Jesus Christ and Robert Redford.'

'Did she? Well, knowing how critical Celia was, he sounds like just the kind of man I'd like to get my hands on. I'll ask around, okay? Goodnight, Lloyd, and take care of yourself.'

Lloyd recradled the receiver. As he did so, the seven o'clock news came on to the television. Immediately, he saw the unsteady hand-held image of a blackened, burned-out bus, out in the desert. The same bus that Sergeant Houk had been sent to investigate. Lloyd pressed the remote-control, and caught the reporter in mid-sentence.

'... this afternoon by two Highway Patrol officers on a routine journey through the Anza Borrego State Park ...'

Lloyd watched as the TV news cameras circled around the skeletal wreck of the bus.

'... only known witness was a blind Indian boy who claims to have heard voices in the vicinity of the bus immediately prior to its burning, but ...'

The camera pulled back to show three ambulances parked on the edge of the highway, and a row of body bags lying on the ground. The reporter said, 'Only two of the victims have so far been positively identified. One was Mr Ronald Korshaw, a carpet salesman from Escondido.

The other was Ms Marianna Gomes, a scenic designer for the San Diego Opera Company ...'

Lloyd stared at the television with a tight feeling of fright and elation. *So there's no connection between the deaths of all of these people in a burned-out bus in the Anza Borrego State Park and Celia's suicide on Rosecrans Avenue, is there, Sergeant Houk? But what do you think are the odds that two girls from the San Diego Opera Company should burn themselves to death on successive days? A zillion to one?*

Lloyd had once met Marianna Gomes. He remembered a vivacious, dark-skinned girl in a flouncy red blouse. Red lips, black eyes, hips that swayed to a silent salsa. Hardly the suicidal type – any more than Celia had been.

He recalled Celia talking to him about Marianna, too. 'She's so bright and so talented, and she has the craziest sense of humour.' Several times, when Celia had returned home late, she had told him that she and Marianna had been 'working on something' together, and that they had 'lost track of time'.

Was this what they had both been working on? Their mutual suicide by fire?

Lloyd swallowed the rest of his drink. His mind was clamorous with images, possibilities, snatches of remembered conversation.

'Marianna and I have been working on this idea together ... I guess we just got carried away ...'

He could picture her now, in her sheepskin jacket, turning around as she closed the front door.

'We were talking about what you could do if you had all the time in the world.'

When had she said that? He could distinctly remember her saying it: '... all the time in the world'.

Maybe both Celia and Marianna had been attending religious discussions with this mysterious Otto character? Maybe they had been working out their self-immolation with him? Because – think about it – how had Celia managed to get to Rosecrans Avenue with that yellow petrol can, if she hadn't had somebody to take her there?

She hadn't been seen on the bus, no taxi-driver had reported taking her, and there were no vehicles in the area that were unaccounted for.

Lloyd picked up the phone again, and redialled Sylvia's number, but Sylvia must have left for her dinner at Mario's. He went back into the living-room, collecting the Wild Turkey bottle from the table. He hadn't bothered to refill the decanter. Wayne was still dozing, his head thrown back and his mouth open, purring deep like a cat.

Lloyd opened his desk-drawer, and lifted out a thick yellow legal pad. Writing in firm italics, in dark purple ink, he set down the title *CELIA JANE WILLIAMS* and then underneath he wrote *June 15*, the day of her death.

He had no real evidence; nothing to go on but speculation and fear. But he was sure now that Celia's decision to set herself alight hadn't been done spontaneously or rashly, nor had she done it in a moment of irrationality. She had planned it, maybe for weeks, maybe for months.

Whether Otto and his religious study group had anything to do with it, he didn't yet know. But he was determined to find out.

OTTO, he wrote on his pad, and then filled in the two Os with two eyes and a smile. Have a nice day.

He hadn't been brought up as a fighter, not in the physical sense, anyway. His father had always said that it was crazy people who demanded an eye for an eye. Survival was more dignified than trying to do to others what they had done unto you. But now Lloyd found himself consumed with a feeling of revenge that was like nothing he had ever experienced in his life. It was almost like being on fire himself. He couldn't sit still, he could scarcely breathe. He was going to find out who had taken Celia away from him, no matter how long it took, no matter how much it cost, and he would get even.

— SEVEN —

La Jolla was masked in a pearl-grey Pacific fog the following morning, as Lloyd drove down to Denman's Original Fish Depot. Waldo's light-blue Cutlass Supreme was already parked outside, and behind the Victorian-style frontage, with its parlour palms and its art nouveau window-frames, Lloyd could see the lights inside the main restaurant. He unlocked the door and went straight in.

'Waldo?'

Waldo was sitting at one of the dining-tables, writing menus. Outside the window, La Jolla Cove was invisible, as if the world ended just beyond the balcony.

'Mr Denman, how are you? You didn't have to come in to the restaurant yet. Everything is fine. Everything is running smooth.'

He stood up, and they embraced each other, a little awkwardly because of Waldo's intervening pot-belly and his insistence on proper protocol. Lloyd would never be 'Lloyd' to Waldo, not even if they were still running the Fish Depot together when they were nonagenarians. Waldo's first law of industrial relations was that if a man gave you a job, then you respected that man. If you couldn't respect him, you should find another job.

'You went to the mortuary?' asked Waldo, gently. 'You saw her?'

Lloyd nodded. 'Yes. I've met her parents, too.'

Waldo frowned at him. 'Didn't you say she didn't have no parents?'

'Well, yes, that's what she said, but it turns out she does. They came down from San Celemente last night and stayed over. I saw them off about a half an hour ago. They're very broken up about it.'

'Everybody is broke up, Mr Denman. Everybody is broke up real bad.'

Lloyd went through to the kitchens. A huge copper saucepan of fish stock was simmering on the hob. He lifted the lid and sniffed it. 'Smells good. Louis is going to be giving Marcel Perrin a run for his money one of these days. Did he manage to buy any bluefish?'

'He's gone down to the dock to fetch some now. He wanted more abalone too.'

Lloyd looked around, and then he said, 'I'm going to need some time off, Waldo. I want you to take charge of things for a while.'

'Sure, Mr Denman. You can count on me. How long do you think you're going to need?'

'I don't know, it could be a couple of days, it could be a week. There's a problem I have to take care of. I'll try to keep in touch, but if you get into any kind of trouble you can always call my lawyer, Dan Tabares. He's in the phone-book, Tabares Oldenkamp Tabares.'

Waldo watched Lloyd uneasily. 'You want to tell me what's wrong, Mr Denman? Maybe there's something I can do.'

Lloyd squeezed Waldo's hard, podgy arm. 'Not this time, amigo. This is one that I have to sort out on my own. I'll pay you two hundred dollars a week more, okay? And you'll have full authority to sign cheques.'

'Mr Denman, it wasn't for the extra money that I offered to help.'

'Of course you didn't. But you're going to have extra responsibilities now, and extra responsibilities means extra pay. Okay?'

'Well, okay, Mr Denman, if that's what you want.'

Lloyd went through to his office. He collected his Filofax, his spare set of keys, and the cassette from his answering-machine. Then he went across to the small table where he kept his business cheque books. Some-body had crowded the top of it with about a dozen of the old salt-and-pepper pots they used to use, before Lloyd had bought a complete new service from Villeroy &

Boche. He unlocked the desk, and eased the lid up only a quarter of an inch so that he could retrieve a cheque book without dislodging any of the salt-and-pepper pots.

He had managed to tweak one cheque book between two fingers when the salt-and-pepper pots suddenly slid, and scattered all over the floor.

'God damn it,' he cursed.

'Everything okay, Mr Denman?' asked Waldo, peering around the door.

'Oh, sure, fine – I just ...'

He looked down at the scattered salt-and-pepper pots and they suddenly reminded him of something. *Celia's scrimshaw, scattered across the carpet.* And why had the scrimshaw scattered like that? Not because somebody had swept it all off the top of the piano with their arm. If somebody had done that, the scrimshaw would have been sprayed over a much wider area. No – it had all slid off the piano-top together, in the same tumbled cluster as these salt-and-pepper pots. Because somebody had done what he had just done with this desk. Lifted the lid, to retrieve something that was inside.

He gave Waldo a last quick list of instructions, and then he left the Original Fish Depot and stepped quickly out into the cool, moist fog. He wanted to go home and see what it was that his late-night visitor had been looking for.

The house seemed even quieter and emptier during the day than it did at night. He carried all his office papers inside, and left them on the kitchen counter. Then he went into the living-room and across to the piano.

He listened. Nothing but the sound of insects in the yard, and the whispering of lawn-sprinklers. Nothing but the measured dripping of a bathroom tap.

It was like a life, dripping away, *drip, drip, drip,* down the drain.

Carefully, he took all of the pieces of scrimshaw off the piano-lid, and laid them out on the cushions of one of the sofas. He was conscious as he did so that the photograph of Celia was watching him from the open bedroom door. *Come, my Celia, let us prove ... while we can, the sports of love.*

The telephone rang and made his skin tingle with shock. He took off the last two pieces of scrimshaw, and went to answer it.

'Lloyd? It's Sylvia.'

'Oh hi, Sylvia. I guess you heard about Marianna.'

'Wasn't that terrible? I was devastated. And the day after Celia, too.'

'She was a really terrific girl.'

Sylvia said, 'I came back from Mario's and saw it on the late-night news. I was just devastated. You don't think there's any connection, do you?'

'That's what I asked the police, but they really didn't know. I think there's a pretty strong chance that there *is* a connection. It seems like far too much of a coincidence, two girls from the same opera company burning to death two days apart.'

'I don't know, Lloyd. It's not as if Marianna killed herself on her own. You know, not as if she was following Celia's example. She had twelve other people with her, and none of *them* had anything to do with the San Diego Opera.'

'Well, I guess the police will come up with something,' Lloyd told her, guardedly.

'I guess so,' Sylvia agreed. 'It's such a terrible waste of life.'

'I really have to go now,' Lloyd told her, eyeing the bare white lid of the piano. 'Did you say you were coming around today?'

'For sure ... that's if you still want me to.'

'Why don't we go out for drinks? I could use somebody to talk to. I'll pick you up at six-thirty.'

'I'd like that.'

Lloyd put down the phone and returned to the piano. Gently, he eased up the lid, and peered into the shadowy interior. Pianos always smelled the same inside, of wax and resin and felt dampers, almost like church. He lifted the lid right up, and propped it open.

At first glance, there didn't appear to be anything inside it. The trouble was, he didn't know what he was supposed to be looking for. A key, maybe? A wad of dollar-bills? A message? A chamois-leather bag, crammed with diamonds?

Nor did he know if his nocturnal visitor had managed to find what he was looking for. It was quite possible that he had already taken it – in which case, Lloyd would *never* find out what it was.

And there was still the question of who had hidden it, and why, and how come a burglar had known what to look for, and where it was?

As he peered around inside the piano, he came up with all kinds of random, half-developed, kaleidoscopic theories. Maybe some drugs dealer had been using the piano store as a front for selling crack, and had stashed some of it inside the piano he least expected to sell. Maybe the piano-frame had been cast out of solid gold by the Brinks Mat gang, as a way of smuggling it out of Europe. Maybe some spy had been using the piano as a drop for information stolen from the US Navy base.

Maybe ...

He inclined his head sideways and caught sight of a pale brown envelope sellotaped to the inside of the piano. He carefully picked off the tape, and lifted the envelope out, making sure he held it right by the very corner. After all, it might have some Russian agent's fingerprints all over it, and what would the FBI say if he smudged them? He had seen enough episodes of *Mission Impossible* to know the correct procedure. *This message will self-destruct in ten seconds.*

He laid the envelope on his writing-desk, and opened it. Inside, there was a sheaf of yellowed papers. He slid them out on to his blotter, and carefully fanned them out. He wouldn't have known what they were before he had met Celia, but he recognized them immediately as an operatic libretto. It must have been a pretty major opera, too, since the pages were numbered from 125 to 137.

There were also some pages of music manuscript,

written with a spidery, splotchy pen, and heavily crossed-out and corrected. On the very last page there was a pencil note: *Wagner 'Junius', January 1883*.

Lloyd sat back in his chair and stared at all these discoloured sheets of paper in perplexity. They looked as if they could be Wagner's original score – although Lloyd had no idea what Wagner's writing had been like. If they were, they were probably quite valuable. But why had Celia hidden them inside her piano? Why hadn't she locked them up at the bank? And who had known, apart from Celia, that they were hidden there?

He leafed through the libretto again and again. He couldn't understand it, because it was all in German, and written in a handwriting that he could scarcely decipher anyway.

Maybe he should show it to the police. Celia had never mentioned it to him. Maybe her big secret was that she had stolen it. He knew what a nut she had always been for Wagner memorabilia. Maybe its rightful owner had killed her out of revenge. Despite what several eye-witnesses had said on the local televison news, Lloyd still found it difficult to believe that Celia had actually poured petrol all over herself and set herself alight. Maybe somebody had forced her to do it – at gunpoint, perhaps. Somebody who had been standing sufficiently far away not to be noticed when the petrol went up.

Wagner 'Junius', January 1883. He left his desk, and went across to the bookshelf, taking out *Richard Wagner* by Hans von Kiel. Licking his finger, he leafed through it until he reached the index of Wagner's operas: *Die Feen, The Flying Dutchman, Tannhäuser, The Twilight of the Gods, Lohengrin* and, lastly, *Parsifal*, which had been written in 1882, the year before Wagner died of a heart attack. No mention of an opera called *Junius*.

Lloyd looked through the list of overtures and pieces for chorus and orchestra. The *Siegfried Idyll*, the *Faust Overture*, but no *Junius*. He closed the book and sat with his mouth covering his hand, deep in thought.

Was it possible that Celia had *faked* this opera – either

70

as a wicked joke or as a way of making herself some extra money, and that somebody who resented that kind of fraud had found her out? She had been brilliant at improvising Wagneresque music. At parties, she had been able to sing great bursts of pretence verses from *The Ring*. She had even invented a Wagnerian operatic character of her own, Bulkhilde, and she had once discussed Bulkhilde with the San Diego Opera's artistic director, Tito Caporosso, for over twenty minutes before he realized he was being leg-pulled.

He had heard of homicides in the art world, after forgers had tried to con dealers and auctioneers out of millions of dollars. But was there a music mafia, too? People who would burn you alive because you sold them a fake opera? It didn't seem particularly likely. In fact it seemed almost laughable.

Lloyd found a spare plastic record sleeve, and slipped the pages of music manuscript into it. His first step would be to take them to Sylvia's tonight. Sylvia was an expert when it came to long-lost music manuscripts, and her knowledge of Wagner was almost as encyclopaedic as Celia's had been. In 1972, Sylvia had found nine previously undiscovered piano suites written by Debussy after his visit to the Bayreuth Festival in 1889 – compositions that were strongly influenced by Wagner.

If anybody would know about *Junius*, it would be Sylvia.

Lloyd was beginning to feel hungry. He hadn't been able to eat properly since he had first heard about Celia, and despite the horror of having to identify her body, or even because of it, his stomach had started to growl. He decided to go down to Michelangelo's Italian restaurant on Rosecrans and treat himself to a plate of their *spaghettini alla vongole*.

There was another reason why he wanted to go to Rosecrans: he wanted to see for himself the place where Celia had died.

He called Waldo to check how the Original Fish Depot was faring. 'You don't worry about nothing, Mr Denman.

71

All booked up this lunchtime, all booked up tonight. No problems.'

Lloyd was still talking to Waldo when he thought he glimpsed a shadow moving silently across the kitchen floor. He paused in his conversation for a second, keeping his eyes on the open kitchen doorway. Then he said, 'Okay, Waldo, thanks a lot. I'll check in later, okay?'

'You got it, Mr Denman.'

Lloyd gently replaced the telephone receiver, and waited. He thought he heard the back doorhandle eased on its spring. Somebody trying to turn it. Somebody with infinite patience, trying to open the back door without him hearing. This time, however, they wouldn't have any luck. He had not only locked the door, he had shot the bolts, too, top and bottom. Nobody would be able to break into the kitchen without kicking the door out of its frame.

He softly crossed the living-room until he reached the kitchen door. He hesitated for a moment, his chest tight with anticipation.

Suppose somebody's standing outside the back door, trying to force their way in? Even worse, supposing it's . . .

He let out a long, controlled breath. *Don't be so goddamned ridiculous. Celia's dead. You saw her body, you saw it for yourself. They gave you back her charm bracelet, and they gave you back her purse.*

He stepped into the kitchen, and turned immediately toward the back door. For a fraction of a second, he thought he glimpsed a pale fawn figure, ducking down. He heard footsteps brush quickly on the brickwork outside.

'Come here!' he shouted. 'If you run, I'm going to call the cops!'

Furiously, he twisted the key in the back door, and cursed as he forced back the bolts. He hardly ever used them, and they were so stiff that he chipped the heel of his hand on the edge of the metal. He hurled open the door, knowing how foolish it was, knowing that it was madness, but he was convinced that he had glimpsed a fleeting triangle of bright yellow, and a pale blur that could easily have been a raincoat.

He rushed out into his back yard, alarming a brace of California quail. There was nobody there. No yellow scarf, no raincoat. What was more, the sprinkler was glittering in the middle of the lawn, and if anybody had run away through the garden they would have had to pass directly through the spray.

There were no tracks across the silvery moisture-beaded grass, no sign that anybody had run that way. But sidling toward the fence was a cloud of slowly frag-menting smoke, like a ghost that was coming apart at the seams. Eventually, it rose in the breeze and was abruptly whirled away. No – not smoke, but *steam*, as if somebody had run through the sprinkler whirling a red-hot poker around their head.

— EIGHT —

His appetite wasn't as hearty as he had imagined it would be, and he left most of the pasta pushed to the side of his plate. Gino was hurt, and came out of the kitchen and stared at him with cow-like eyes.

'There's something wrong? Maybe I should cook you some of my *rognoncini di agnello saltati con cipolla.*'

'You've got to be joking,' Lloyd responded. 'Gino, that was brilliant. *Spaghettini* like they make in heaven. But I guess my eyes were bigger than my stomach.'

'Aren't you the man who said to me, "to waste food is to waste life itself …"?' Gino demanded.

'Sure, but I'm also the man who said, "never eat anything you can't lift".'

Gino sat down at the table with him and snapped his fingers for the waiter to bring them two glasses of verdicchio. 'You tease me, Lloyd, you make fun,' he said, laying a hand on Lloyd's arm. 'But you must miss her so much. Such a lady. Such elegance.'

'Yes, well,' said Lloyd, and lowered his eyes. He was trying very hard not to think about the Celia that he could remember, but to concentrate on the Celia that he had obviously never known. The secret Celia, the Celia who had pretended that she had no parents. The Celia who had believed so obsessively in living for ever. The Celia who had gone to Otto's religious study group, and who had burned herself alive not five blocks from where he was sitting now.

'What are you going to do?' Gino asked him. 'Maybe you should take some time off?'

Lloyd nodded. 'Two or three days, maybe. But I can't keep away from the job too long. You know what it's like. You take too much time off, you lose your edge.'

'Hey … if you get bored, come back down here, and I will show you how to make *insalatina tenera con la pancetta.*'

'What the hell is that? It sounds like a street direction to the Vatican.'

Gino swallowed wine and shook his head. 'Lettuce, fried. It's wonderful. But I can't explain how to do it, I have to show you.'

Just then, Gino was called back to the kitchen to whip up some *coste di biete saltate,* and Lloyd was left to finish his wine on his own. He was glad of the chance to be silent. He was summoning up all of the courage he possibly could, so that he would have the strength to visit the place where Celia had died. He had to go. It was not just an investigation, it was a pilgrimage. He had to know exactly where it was before he could begin to visualize it, and then to understand. He couldn't imagine what pain had been suffered by wives in wartime, to learn that their husbands had been killed, but never to know exactly *where.* It seemed to him then that the place where somebody dies is even more important than where they were born.

He stood in the car-park opposite McDonald's with his hands by his sides, staring at the smoke-stained kerb. Some of the bushes had been scorched, too, so Lloyd could judge how fierce the fire must have been. He wished he had brought some flowers. Lilies had always been Celia's favourite.

What a place to die. Barren and public, noisy with traffic. He couldn't imagine why she had chosen such a dreary location.

He tried to say a prayer. He hoped that her soul was at rest. He hoped that she hadn't suffered. He hoped that she would forgive him, for not understanding that she was suffering so much that she wanted to die.

'And one day we'll meet again, for sure. Amen.'

He was walking back to his car when one of the chefs came out of the side entrance of the McDonald's restaurant and began to walk hurriedly toward him. A bulky man, with a startling wide-apart cast in his eyes.

'Pardon me!' he called. 'Sir!'

Lloyd waited for him to reach him. He was in his fifties, grey-haired and sweating. He smelled strongly of hamburgers.

'I'm sorry to bother you, sir,' he said, wiping the palms of his hands on his apron. 'But I couldn't help noticing you standing over there.'

Lloyd said, 'I'm not one of your sensation-seekers, if that's what you think. The girl who was burned ... well, she was my fiancée.'

'I figured something like that. Well, I saw the BMW. Your average ghoul doesn't usually turn up to gawp in a BMW.'

He held out his hand. 'Bob Tuggey. Most people call me Unca Tug.'

'Lloyd Denman.'

Bob said, 'I was here when it happened. I tried to stop her. It was terrible.'

'You were the one with the fire-extinguisher?'

Bob lowered his eyes, and nodded. 'I tried, believe me, but I just wasn't fast enough. Fifteen seconds sooner, and I could have saved her.'

Lloyd looked back toward the burned bushes. 'I appreciate what you did.'

'I saw her walking across the car-park, swinging this yellow can. I should have guessed right away what she was planning on doing.'

Lloyd shook his head. 'I don't think anybody could have guessed what she was planning on doing.'

'I was in Saigon,' Bob told him. 'I saw one of those monks setting himself alight. Your young lady sat right down, crosslegged, exactly the same way that monk did, and then I knew for sure what she was going to do. I just wasn't fast enough.'

'Well, thanks anyway,' Lloyd told him.

'Hey, listen ...' said Bob, reaching into the breast pocket of his shirt. 'I found something afterwards, in the

76

bushes. I was going to take it to the police yesterday but I didn't have the time. It must've been hers, so I guess the best person to give it to is you.'

Between finger and thumb, he held up a small gold charm, discoloured by heat. Its link was broken, as if it had been tugged from a chain or a bracelet. But Lloyd had never noticed it on Celia's bracelet. Certainly he hadn't given it to her, and she had never mentioned buying it.

'I don't recognize it,' he frowned, holding it flat on the palm of his hand. 'It must be somebody else's.'

The charm was a circle, and inside the circle was a lizard, with its head bent sideways and its legs and its tail bent sideways, too.

'You're sure?' asked Bob. 'I found it right where it happened, the same afternoon. I kept meaning to take it in.'

'I could show it to her mother, see if *she* recognizes it.'

'Okay,' Bob agreed.

'Do you want a receipt for it?' asked Lloyd.

Bob gave him a smile. 'Don't worry about it. You're not going to get very far in a white BMW with a registration plate that says FISHEE.'

'I guess not. Listen, Mr Tuggey – I run Denman's Original Fish Depot, at La Jolla Cove. Here – here's my card. Why don't you call by sometime, and have a drink on the house?'

'Thanks. I might just take you up on that.'

They shook hands. Bob returned to McDonald's, and Lloyd walked back to his car, holding the charm tightly in his fist, as if he were afraid it might jump out of his hand. He unlocked his car, but as he was about to climb into it, he noticed a red neon sign on the opposite side of Rosecrans announcing *Copie Shoppe: Xerox, Printing, & Fax.* He picked up the sheets of libretto from the passenger-seat, relocked his car, and crossed the road.

As Bob reappeared in the kitchen, Sally the manageress called out to him, 'Unca Tug? You just missed a phone call.'

'Oh, yeah, who was it? Not the President again, asking for advice on the Middle East? I wish he'd formulate his own policies, for God's sake, and leave me alone.'

'It was a girl. She sounded sexy, too.'

Bob looked up from the grill. 'A girl?'

'Sure. Real hoarse and provocative, know what I mean?'

'For me?'

'Well, not *specifically* for you. She wanted to know if anybody had handed in a gold charm. Apparently she lost it in the parking-lot.'

Bob put down his spatula in exasperation. 'Would you believe it? I just gave that charm to that guy out there. Well, he *was* out there. He's gone now.'

'What did you do that for?'

'He said that girl who burned herself was his fiancée. I was sure the charm must have been hers.'

'This girl sure didn't sound dead.'

'Well, the guy didn't recognize the charm, either, so I guess it couldn't have belonged to his fiancée, after all. Damn it.'

'Do you know who he is?' asked Sally.

'Oh, sure. He owns a fish restaurant at La Jolla. Guess I'll just have to call him and get it back.'

'I told the girl on the phone you had it,' said Sally. 'She said she'd call by later to collect it.'

'She described it?'

'Sure, kind of a lizard, in a ring, that's what she said.'

Bob nodded. He left the kitchen and went through to the corridor, and picked up the payphone. He punched out the number of Denman's Original Fish Depot, and waited while it rang.

Waldo answered. Bob explained what had happened, but Waldo told him that 'Monsieur Denman weel not veezeet ze restaurant *aujourd'hui*. Pairhaps tomorrow.'

'Just tell him the gold charm didn't belong to his fiancée, please, and maybe he could call me.'

'*Avec plaisir, monsieur.*'

Bot put down the phone, and went back to the Big Macs and the Fillet-o-Fishes and the Egg McMuffins. The afternoon passed quickly: his shift was due to end at seven-thirty. Tonight he was planning on bowling with his friend Stan Kostolowicz, another marooned penpusher from the Far Eastern embassies of the 1960s.

As it gradually grew dark, however, he failed to notice the large silver-grey Mercedes saloon with darkly-tinted windows which drew up outside the restaurant, and which remained parked there, even though none of its doors opened. Whoever was inside it had obviously decided to remain inside it, waiting.

Lloyd arrived outside Sylvia Cuddy's downtown apartment building a little more than ten minutes early, and Sylvia wasn't yet ready. He walked up the tile-flagged steps to the second floor, and Sylvia let him in.

'Excuse the chaos,' she said, kissing his cheek.

Like the living accommodation of many people he knew, even successful musicians and restaurateurs and interior designers, Sylvia's apartment was tiny. Real-estate prices in San Diego had risen stunningly, and even a cramped two-room apartment was beyond the reach of all but the most affluent.

Only one drawer had to be left open, or one newspaper dropped on the floor, and the whole place looked untidy.

Sylvia's 'chaos' amounted to nothing more than a coffee-cup left in the kitchen area, and an open file of drawings for the San Diego Opera's forthcoming production of *Mefistofele*.

'Have a seat,' she said. 'There's wine in the icebox. Or Perrier. Or freshly-squeezed pineapple. There's even some stuffed olives. Or some strawberry Jell-O.'

Lloyd poured himself a glassful of cold Cakebread chardonnay, and stepped out on to Sylvia's tiny redwood balcony. The balcony had been built up to chest-height to give her extra privacy, and to mask the view of water-towers and warehouses and tract housing rooftops. If you didn't peer over the edge, all you could see was Banker's Hill and the Coronado Bay, glittering gold in the distance.

'You've worked miracles with this place,' he told her,

turning around with his back to the parapet. 'I love this dark green wallpaper, and all these drapes.'

'I have to have drapes because I don't have room for closets,' she called back. 'I'm so tired of living in Lilliput, you know? It's so damned small here I can do swan-dives off the ironing-board, straight down the toilet.'

She stepped out onto the balcony beside him. She was short, only a little over five-three, with a wild tangle of backbrushed Titian hair, an owlish pair of Paloma Picasso spectacles, lips as plump as pink-silk cushions, and huge rounded breasts that were wrapped up like well-ripened canteloupes in a crimson-and-green floral blouse by André Laug.

'You know what Celia used to say about this blouse?' asked Sylvia. 'She said it was like somebody shouting in the jungle. Wasn't that just *typical*?'

'I went to see the place today,' said Lloyd. 'The place where she died.'

Sylvia didn't answer, but waited to hear what Lloyd would say next.

'It's a car-park, that's all,' he told her. 'A concrete car-park. What a goddamned awful place to die.'

'Any place is a goddamned awful place to die,' Sylvia told him, taking his hand and squeezing it. 'Come on, let's go find ourselves a real drink.'

They left the apartment and Lloyd drove them out to Harbor Island Drive, to Tom Ham's Lighthouse. Apart from being a bar and a restaurant, Tom Ham's was a genuine certified coastguard lighthouse, with a spectacular view of the harbour. It was dark now, except for a last diagonal streak of grainy orange light across the horizon. They sat at a window table, looking out over the dipping lights and the reflections of downtown San Diego. Sylvia ordered a Kahlua on the rocks, but Lloyd stuck to whisky. There were times when only whisky was any use.

'You said you thought there might be some connection between Celia and Marianna,' said Syliva.

'I don't know. I don't have any proof. It seems too much of a coincidence, that's all.'

'Coincidences do happen.'

'Well, sure ... but I've got a weird kind of feeling about it. That's one of the reasons I wanted to talk to this Otto character.'

'I'm afraid I haven't had any luck finding out about him. Don hasn't heard of him, but I'm sure that Joe North sometimes used to go along to see him, with Celia and Marianna. He's back at the theatre the day after tomorrow. I'll ask him then.'

'Thanks,' said Lloyd. Then, 'Do you happen to know what was the last opera that Wagner ever wrote?'

'That's a peculiar question.'

'Some pretty peculiar things have been happening.'

Sylvia frowned at him. 'Listen, you've had a dreadful shock. Are you sure you're okay?'

'I'm not too sure of anything, to tell you the truth. But tell me what was Wagner's last opera.'

'Well,' she said, 'the last opera that Wagner wrote was *Parsifal*, 1882. In 1883 he went to Venice and died of a heart attack.'

'He didn't write an opera in 1883?'

Sylvia took off her glasses. Her eyes were unfocused and a little bulbous, but they were richest shade of Belgian-chocolate-brown. 'Lloyd, I could talk about Wagner till the cows come home. However, the question is, is this relevant to anything at all?'

'I don't know. But inside Celia's piano, I found this manuscript.' He reached under the table and produced the plastic envelope. 'It's probably a fake, or a mistake. I'm not sure what. But it looks like part of a Wagner libretto, for an opera called *Junius*. It's dated 1883.'

'Let me see that,' asked Sylvia. She took the envelope, eased out one of the pages of manuscript, and peered at it closely. Lloyd watched her, feeling uneasy, as if he were the fall guy for some elaborate practical joke.

'What do you think?' he asked her, at last.

'This isn't a leg-pull?' she asked him, suddenly suspicious.

But she realized from the expression on his face that he

81

was serious, and why would he joke, at a time like this? She examined the pages carefully, turning them over one by one and laying them face down on the table.

'If this is genuine,' she said, 'then it's incredible. Do you have any idea where Celia might have found it?'

'I have no idea. She never mentioned it to me. It was sellotaped inside the piano.'

Sylvia said, 'Of course you won't be able to tell if it's genuine until you have the paper and the ink properly analyzed. But if it *is* genuine, you're going to be rich – especially if you can locate the rest of the opera, too.'

She peered at one of the pages closely. 'It certainly *looks* like Wagner's handwriting.'

'And if it is?'

'Come on, Lloyd, think about it! If that's an original score for an unknown opera written by Richard Wagner in the last year of his life, and you can show that you own it, then you're made for life. You can retire. I can think of at least four musical publishing companies who would pay you millions for it.'

Lloyd said, 'To tell you the truth, I wasn't so much interested in the money. I'm more interested in how Celia got hold of it, and why she hid it, and whether anybody else knows about it. Obviously she never talked about it to you ... but somebody broke into the house the night she died and I think this was what they were looking for. If it's worth millions, then that could have been a motive for somebody killing her.'

'You didn't tell me that somebody broke in! That's terrible! What did the police say?'

'They didn't say anything,' Lloyd admitted. 'I didn't tell them, either.'

'Any particular reason?' asked Sylvia.

'I don't know ... just a feeling, I guess.'

'But if you think she might have been killed ...'

'Oh, I don't think that. I mean, I guess I'm satisfied that she actually took her own life. But I want to know is, *why* – and whether anybody put her into a suicidal frame of mind.'

'Are you sure that's something you really want to find out?' Sylvia asked him. There was no doubting Sylvia's kindness or wisdom.

Lloyd nodded. 'I know what you're suggesting. There could have been another man involved. But, believe me, Sylvia, not knowing is worse than knowing.'

Their waitress came up and asked them if they wanted another cocktail.

'No, no,' said Sylvia. 'Two's my limit. Otherwise I start singing "Loike Old Times in Kilkenny, Begorra" and dancing on the tables.'

'We'll just have the bill,' said Lloyd. But as he did so, he caught sight of a girl on the far side of the bar, in the corner of one of the booths, and she looked so much like Celia that he shivered as if somebody had unexpectedly laid a cold hand on the small of his back. She was deep in the shadows, and she wore dark glasses, and a black scarf that covered her head like a turban. But there was sufficient light from the small crimson-glass lantern on the table in front of her to illuminate her face, and if she wasn't Celia then she was certainly Celia's *doppelgänger.* He couldn't take his eyes away from her, but her glasses were so dark that it was impossible to tell if she had noticed him.

Sylvia touched his hand. Then – when she failed to attract his attention – she turned around to see what he was staring at. 'Am I missing something?' she asked. 'I'm terrible like that. I was out with Don the other night and Robin Williams came into the restaurant and I didn't even see him.'

'That girl opposite ... in the corner booth.'

'Excuse me, I must put my specs on. Which girl?'

'That girl in the scarf and the dark glasses. There – right in the corner.'

But as he was trying to explain to Sylvia which girl he meant, a crowd of six or seven laughing businessmen came into the bar and stood between them. Lloyd leaned from right to left, desperate not to lose sight of the girl, but then the businessmen were joined by their wives, and for two or three minutes he couldn't see the booth at all.

'Lloyd – what on earth's the matter?' Sylvia asked him.

He grasped her hand. 'It sounds totally crazy, but I keep seeing Celia. Or girls who look like Celia. I saw one just after I left the morgue. I tried to follow her, but she disappeared in the crowds.'

'And now there's another girl over there who looks like Celia?'

'Exactly. It's uncanny. She's wearing dark glasses but she's so much like her.'

Sylvia gave Lloyd's hand a gentle squeeze. 'Lloyd – Lloyd, sweetheart.'

He looked at her quickly, then went back to searching for the girl in the booth.

'Lloyd, you're only torturing yourself. Celia's dead.'

'But the resemblance is totally uncanny.'

'Lloyd, she's *dead*. Dead people don't come back and sit opposite you in cocktail bars. You're just projecting your grief on to a girl who looks a little bit like Celia. It's like an after-image. I did it myself when my father died. I spent four thousand dollars on two shrinks, to sort myself out.'

At last, the crowd of businessmen moved away, still laughing noisily. '*There* ...' said Lloyd. But as the last man walked with infuriating slowness out of his sightline, he saw that the booth was empty, and that the girl was gone.

Sylvia looked at Lloyd with sorrow. 'Oh, Lloyd. I know how much you must be hurting.'

Lloyd stood up, and searched around the bar for any sign of the girl. The front door was slowly closing, as if somebody had just walked through it, and through the brown-tinted glass he thought he saw a slim dark figure, and the back of a woman's calf, but then there was nothing but darkness, and the reflection of a man lighting a cigarette.

He drove Sylvia back to her apartment, and helped her out of the car. A cool wind was blowing from the harbour, and Sylvia shivered.

'Don't bother to come up,' she told him. 'Get yourself safely home and take a couple of Nytol. You'll feel better when you get some sleep.'

Lloyd kissed her, and hugged her. 'Thanks, Sylvia. You're a genuine authenticated angel.'

'Listen ...' said Sylvia. 'Do you mind if I keep that score? Oliver Drexler's coming in for rehearsals tomorrow, I could show it to him. I know that he'd adore to see it.'

'For sure,' Lloyd told her, and reached into his car for the plastic envelope. 'Take good care of it, though. It could be evidence.'

'Oh, I'll take care of it, all right. I'll guard it with my life.'

She watched Lloyd U-turn across the street, then waved as he headed off northward, back to La Jolla. She let herself in through the heavy bleached-oak door of her apartment building, and climbed the tiled stairs.

As she climbed, she softly trilled *Pace, pace* from Verdi's *La Forza Del Destino*. She felt worried about Lloyd. It was obvious that he hadn't even begun to face up to the reality of Celia's suicide. It was understandable, of course. Suddenly to lose the love of his life in such a grisly and baffling way must have been enough to drive him half-crazy. By concentrating with such ferocity on finding out *why* she had killed herself, his mind was still protecting itself from the shock. His hallucinations of Celia were probably a symptom of the same self-protective mechanism.

Sylvia opened the door of her apartment and stepped inside. She wished there were something she could do to help Lloyd get over Celia. But Celia had been so pretty and so talented and so full of life that nobody could ever take her place. Sylvia missed her, too. Until today, she hadn't realized how badly. She had heard from Don that Exxon were going to put up the money for a major production of *The Marriage of Figaro*. She had actually started to say, 'Wait till Celia hears about this,' until it had struck her with almost physical pain that she would never see Celia again.

She went to the fridge and took out a bottle of white wine. She didn't usually drink as much as she had today, but she felt like something to help her sleep. She shucked off her shoes and walked out of the kitchen into the tiny living-room, carrying a glass of wine in one hand and the libretto in the other. She sat down in her favourite spoon-back armchair, and put up her feet on the coffee table.

Provided they were authentic, the pages of this libretto was one of the greatest musical finds of the century. Even if Lloyd couldn't find the rest of the opera, they were still worth a fortune. She didn't read German very well – particularly Wagner's spidery script – but she managed to work out some of the meaning.

Junius: *I confess that I listened*
To His sweet and tempting words
And that I gave myself willingly,
Body and soul.

And

Many hundred thousand goodnights,
Dearly beloved Veronica,
Innocent have I come into prison
Innocent have I been tortured
Innocent must I die.

She leafed through to the pages of music, and hummed a few bars to herself. The score was unusually monotonous for Wagner, although it had all of the Teutonic sinew of the *Valkyries* and *Rhinegold*. Sylvia slapped the arm of her chair with her hand to emphasize the timing. The music sounded almost like a barbarian war-chant, the kind of song that would have been sung by Goths and Visigoths on their way to battle.

She was still humming and slapping when she began to have the feeling that she was being watched. She used to feel it quite often, before she had built the high balustrade around her balcony, and it was a feeling that particularly disturbed her. She had imagined that somebody

86

in one of the tract houses was spying on her with binoculars. Her then-headshrinker had told her that she suffered
from a mild form of paranoia.

But this evening, the feeling was different. She didn't
feel that she was being watched from a long way off, but
from very near. Almost as if somebody were standing right
behind her, and breathing on her shoulder.

She stopped humming, stopped slapping, and glanced
quickly and furtively around. There was nobody else in
the room. But the building did seem unusually quiet.
There were no televisions mumbling in other apartments,
no music playing, no feet chip-chipping up the tiled steps
outside.

A jet took off from Lindbergh Field, its engines
thundering. The sliding-door out on to the balcony
rattled and vibrated. For a moment, as the airliner circled
out over the ocean, Sylvia's whole world was engulfed by
shattering noise. She looked toward the balcony, and
there, to her intense fright, a dark figure was standing,
with its back to her. A woman, in a black raincoat, her
head wound around in a black turban-like scarf.

Carefully, her heart still caught on the hook of her
fright, Sylvia set down her wineglass and the pages of
Wagner's libretto, swung her feet off the coffee-table, and
stood up. She looked around for something to protect
herself with, and decided that the swan's-head umbrella
beside her writing-desk would do. This was only a
woman, after all, and not an especially big or powerful-
looking woman; and by the way she was standing on the
balcony with her back to the living-room, it certainly
didn't appear to Sylvia that she had the intention of doing
anything violent or sudden.

All the same, the very presence of a stranger outside
her living-room, treating her balcony as if it were her
own, was more threatening than Sylvia could have
believed possible.

Sylvia gripped the umbrella in her left hand, took a
deep breath to steady herself, and then slid back the
balcony door.

'Hallo,' she said, her mouth dried out. 'Do you mind telling me what the hell you think you're doing on my balcony?'

For a long time, the dark woman said nothing, but continued to stare out over the sparkling lights of downtown San Diego and Coronado.

'This is a private apartment,' Sylvia insisted. 'If you don't leave immediately, I'm going to call the super, and the super will call a cop.'

At last, the woman turned around. She wore glasses with lenses so perfectly black that she looked as if she had no eyes, just two circular holes in her head. Her skin was very pale, with almost a greyish pallor, but very smooth.

'Hallo, Sylvia,' the woman replied, with the faintest of smiles. 'I believe that you've got something of mine.'

Sylvia recognized the voice at once. A thrill of fright ran down her arms, like ice-cold centipedes racing each other to reach her wrists. It was Celia. It had to be Celia. Yet Celia was dead, burned. There had even been photographs in the San Diego newspapers of Celia burning, although Sylvia hadn't been able to do more than glance at them quickly. She had glimpsed flames, a bowed black head, knees that protruded through the fire like kindling-sticks.

Sylvia opened and closed her mouth. Celia stayed where she was, her hands in her raincoat pockets, watching Sylvia with just the faintest touch of a smile on her lips, her eyes masked by those two black circles, black as the Bible-paper that the pirates in *Treasure Island* had cut out to make the black spot.

'*Fine* way to welcome your best friend,' she said, and her tone was quite vinegary. 'Now, you have something of mine. Something I need. I'd appreciate it a whole lot if I could have it back.'

'*You're dead*,' Sylvia hissed at her. '*I'm imagining this. You're dead.*'

Her feet and ankles felt as if they had grown cold clinging tentacles which had wound around the balcony and left her powerless to move. Celia stepped closer, and Sylvia's brain said *run*, but she couldn't even step back. *Run, she's dead! Run!*

'I followed you out to the lighthouse,' said Celia. She didn't take off her dark glasses, didn't smile. She was so much like Celia, yet there was something about her which was unnervingly unfamiliar. 'Then I followed you back here. Of course I've still got that key you gave me.'

She paused, and then she added, 'Lloyd gave you my music, didn't he?'

'You're dead,' gasped Sylvia, breathlessly. Her voice sounded as if she had somehow spoken into her own ear – intimate, secretive, but utterly hopeless. She had never felt so frightened in her entire life. She couldn't bring herself to move a single inch, couldn't even raise her swan's-head umbrella. Celia approached so close that Sylvia could have lifted her mouth and kissed Celia's smooth grey cheek, but still her muscles refused to work. She wondered in dumb lungless panic if she would ever be able to move again.

'I was waiting for you to go to bed,' said Celia. 'I was hoping so much that you wouldn't see me.'

Sylvia at last managed to take one stiff step away from her, then another. 'You're ... *dead*,' she repeated. She couldn't think of anything else to say.

Celia moved past her into the living-room – moved strangely and silently, her raincoat rustling. Sylvia caught a distinctive smell as she passed her by. A smell of heat, like a burned ironing-board cover.

She turned around and watched in fascination and horror as Celia bent over the Wagner libretto. With one black-gloved hand, Celia sorted quickly through the pages, obviously making sure that none of them were missing.

'It was very wrong of Lloyd to give you this,' she remarked, without looking up.

'I'm sorry. I was only borrowing it, out of interest,' Sylvia replied. Then, 'You're not dead, then? Are you all right? Were you really burned? Or wasn't it you at all?'

Celia gathered up the pages and stood up straight. 'Do I *look* dead? I'm more alive than ever.'

'I don't understand. You don't seem like yourself at all.'

Celia almost smiled. 'On the contrary, my dearest, I've blossomed at last.'

'You're going to tell Lloyd that you're okay? He's so upset he's almost crazy.'

'I can't,' Celia told her, dismissively. 'Not yet. But I will, as soon as I can. Believe me. I miss him as much as he misses me.'

Sylvia came back into the living-room and managed to sit unsteadily down on the arm of her sofa. 'Celia ... you must tell me! What's happened to you? Where have you been? If *you* weren't burned, then who was? Whose body was it that Lloyd had to go to identify? And if you weren't burned, why have you put everybody through so much *anguish*?'

Celia stared at her for a long time with those smoke-black glasses, saying nothing.

Sylvia said, 'We love you, Celia. We care about you. If something's wrong ...'

Celia hesitated a moment longer, and then she said, 'The truth is, Sylvia, that I was given the chance of a life-time, and I took it. There was no other way.'

'A chance? What chance?'

'Look,' said Celia, 'I'm very sorry for all the pain that I've caused you, and everybody else. But I had no choice. It had to be done secretly. It had to be done without anybody knowing in advance. And until it's truly finished, it has to remain secret.'

'But what's the secret?' Sylvia demanded.

'Life, Sylvia. That's the secret. Life.'

'I don't understand.'

Celia said, as if she were quoting, 'There is one sure way to everlasting life, and that is the baptism of fire.'

'Celia,' Sylvia persisted. She was still afraid, but she was becoming irritated, too. She had seen the distress that Lloyd had suffered, because of her apparent death. She had experienced that same distress herself. She didn't consider it at all funny that Celia should now reappear, without regret, without apology, and behaving in the oddest, most arrogant way imaginable.

On the other hand (and here's where she had to be careful) it was possible that Celia had gone through some kind of mental breakdown. She had always been a brilliant musician, effervescent but highly strung, and she could have been suffering a nervous crisis without anyone realizing that anything was wrong. Sometimes it happened that way. She remembered Giorgi Boutone disappearing, the night before he was due to play Truffaldino in Prokofiev's *Love For Three Oranges*. The musical director had found him by accident three days later, on a child's swing in Balboa Park, unshaven and filthy, singing *muh-nuh-muh-nuh* from the Muppet Show.

'Celia ...' said Sylvia. 'Maybe I should drive you back home. You owe it to Lloyd, if nobody else.'

Celia shook her head. 'It isn't time yet. We have to wait until the solstice.'

'The *solstice*? What's the solstice got to do with anything. How do you think he's going to feel?'

'How do I think he's going to feel about what?' Dead words, deadly spoken.

'About your being alive, of course!'

Celia said, almost with regret, 'I was hoping very much that you wouldn't tell him.'

'How could I *not* tell him?'

'Even if I begged you not to?'

'Celia, Lloyd's been through *hell*, thinking you killed yourself. I couldn't let him suffer a moment longer.'

Celia turned away. Sylvia said, 'Celia? Celia?' But Celia was plainly thinking very deeply about something, and didn't even appear to hear her.

'Celia, I *have* to tell Lloyd. I simply have to.'

Celia looked back at her. When she spoke, her voice was measured and quiet and chillingly matter-of-fact. 'You know something, Sylvia, fire has two properties. The ability to destroy, and the ability to recreate. Do you know why the Germans burned the bodies of all the Jews they slaughtered?'

Sylvia was perplexed. 'I don't know what you're talking about.'

'The guards at the concentration camps didn't know why they had to do it,' said Celia. 'Nor did the SS officers. But higher up it was policy. When Jews are exterminated, they must be burned.'

'Celia ...' Sylvia protested. 'What on earth does this have to do with ...'

'Everything!' Celia retorted, and her voice came out in a soft, threatening roar. 'If your body is burned, your soul will be damned. The Germans were determined to torture the Jews not only in this world, but the next, for ever and ever, for time everlasting.'

'Celia, you're sick,' said Sylvia. 'Why don't you let me call Lloyd, or maybe your doctor?'

'No!' roared Celia. 'Don't you understand what I'm telling you? Fire can condemn you to hell, but it can save you, too! If the proper rites are observed when your body is burned, and if the proper sacrifices are made at the next changing of the year, your soul won't be damned, but saved. Saved! And not for a month or a year, or ten years, or even one human lifetime. Your soul will be saved for ever!'

Sylvia was trembling. 'Are you trying to tell me you *did* burn yourself?'

Celia nodded, triumphantly.

'And are you trying to tell me that what I'm seeing here ... this is just your *soul*?'

'I'm a Salamander, Sylvia. A life everlasting, made of fire and smoke and human soul. A creature of perfect purity. Superior in mind, indestructible in body. The ultimate race that humankind was always meant to become.'

'A Salamander?'

'That's what we call them. That's what we are.'

'Who's *we*? Is Marianna one of these Salamanders too?'

Celia circled the room, until she was standing quite close. 'Marianna and many others. Scores of others.'

'So that bus ...?'

'That's right! Burned on purpose. Burned happily. The time has almost arrived!'

Sylvia glanced up at her nervously. 'Celia ... this is *very* hard for me to believe.'

'It was hard for me, too, when I first heard about it,' said Celia. 'In fact, I dismissed it. But then I met Otto and Helmwige and then I understood.'

'What are you going to do next?' Sylvia asked her. 'Where are you staying?'

'With Otto and Helmwige,' Celia replied.

'And you won't talk to Lloyd?'

'Not yet. Not until the solstice. He mustn't see me yet. I'm not ... well, I'm not stable. Physically, I mean. Not mentally.'

Sylvia said, 'Do you want a drink? I could use one myself.'

'A glass of water would be good.'

'Is that all? Just water?'

Sylvia stood up, and circled around Celia, and went to the corner table where she kept her drinks. She poured herself a Kahlua, and then said to Celia, 'Just going to the kitchen ... get your water for you. And ice, too.'

Celia was standing with her back to her, leafing through Wagner's libretto. She gave the smallest nod of acknowledgement.

'You know something ... I was saying to Lloyd, that libretto must be worth a fortune,' called Sylvia, opening up the refrigerator, and rattling the ice-tray. 'Darn it, this ice is all stuck! I'll have to put it under the hot water tap!'

Celia said, 'We were lucky to find it. In fact, we've found almost all of it now. All the pieces that matter.'

'You mean there's a whole opera?' Sylvia dropped the ice-tray noisily into the sink and turned on the cold water tap at full volume. Then she quickly stepped across to the other side of the kitchen and unhooked the telephone. Holding her breath, she punched out Lloyd's home number and prayed and prayed that he had managed to get back by now. *Please Lloyd, please don't decide to visit the restaurant, I don't know the restaurant's number. Please just be home.*

Celia said, 'Wagner wrote it in 1883. He still hadn't quite finished it when he died. He took it with him to Venice, and after his heart attack it disappeared. Not many people know about it. His widow Cosima mentioned it in one of her diaries, but not by name.'

'Oh, really?' said Sylvia. 'Damn this ice! I think there's something wrong with my thermostat or something.'

Lloyd's phone was ringing now. *Please be there, Lloyd. For God's sake, please be there.*

'In fact Otto was the first person to make any kind of serious search for it,' Celia went on. 'That was back in 1938, when Hitler was in power. Otto had Hitler's personal approval to look for *Junius*, and as much Nazi party finance as he needed. And of course, Mussolini was only too eager to help.'

Lloyd picked up the phone, and said, 'Lloyd Denman here.'

'Lloyd,' breathed Sylvia, with her hand cupped closely over the receiver. 'Lloyd – it's Sylvia.'

'I'm sorry, I can't hear you,' Lloyd replied. 'I just got in – the door's open. Can you hold on for a moment?'

'Lloyd, for God's sake, it's Sylvia!'

Celia was saying, 'Otto was given a team of five musical historians. They searched the whole of Venice … following every possible clue. It took them three years, until 1941. But they found it in the end. It had been hidden by the Roman Catholic priest who had taken Wagner's confession on his deathbed.'

'*Lloyd*!' begged Sylvia.

She could hear Lloyd closing the front door. She could hear his footsteps crossing the hallway. He picked up the receiver with a squeaking, jostling noise, and said, 'I'm sorry about that. I just couldn't …'

Sylvia slowly lowered her phone. She wanted to shout to Lloyd *CELIA'S HERE, CELIA'S ALIVE* but her lungs were empty and she couldn't breathe. Celia was standing in the kitchen doorway, staring at her with those black, black glasses. Without a word, she came over to Sylvia and lifted the phone out of her hand, and laid it down on the kitchen counter. Lloyd's tiny voice said, 'Hallo? Hallo? Is anybody there? Hallo?'

Celia asked, 'Is that Lloyd?'

Sylvia nodded dumbly. She didn't know why she was so frightened. Perhaps it was Celia's black glasses. Perhaps it was the thought that she might take them off.

'Celia, he has to know. You can't ...'

Celia raised one black-gloved finger to her lips. 'You promised me, Sylvia. You promised you wouldn't tell.'

'Celia, this is quite absurd. I don't know what nonsense this Otto has been cramming into your head, but I really think this has all gone much too far ...'

'Sylvia! You promised!'

On an impulse, Sylvia reached up and snatched off Celia's glasses. She was prepared for almost anything – bruises, burns, blindness. But when she saw Celia's eyes she screamed and screamed and screamed and couldn't stop. They were as black and empty as her dark glasses, holes in the grey featureless skin of her face. They gave her an expression of utter deadness, like a death-mask. She was a thing which walked but shouldn't walk.

Celia seized Sylvia's wrist and prized the glasses out of her fingers. 'Stop screaming!' she commanded her. 'Stop screaming!'

'Ah! Ah! Ah!' Sylvia gasped, shuddering with terror.

'Stop it!' Celia shouted at her. 'Stop it! Shut up!'

'Oh God you're not real, oh God you're not real!' Sylvia shrieked at her. 'I'm having a nightmare! Go away! Go away!'

Celia seized the lapels of Sylvia's dress and shook her so hard that one of her earrings flew off. 'Shut up, shut up, shut up! Shut up! You're hysterical!'

But Sylvia screamed and gibbered and dropped to her knees. Her brain felt as if it had fused, and she couldn't stop herself. Seeing Celia alive when she thought she was dead had been frightening enough. But seeing her dead when she was obviously alive was more than her mind could accept.

Celia hesitated, turned, then turned back again. She could hear footsteps outside the apartment, then the doorbell jangled. 'Ms Cuddy?' called a man's voice. 'Ms Cuddy, you okay in there?'

Celia lifted her right glove and unbuttoned it, tossing it aside. Then her left glove. Her hands were as pale and as smooth and as grey as her face. Deftly, she unbuttoned her raincoat, all the way down, and slid out of it. Underneath the raincoat she was completely nude, except for her tightly-wrapped black turban, her black high-heeled shoes, and a wide black leather belt, cinched tightly around her waist. The skin of her naked body was the same pearly-grey – a grey that gleamed in the shadows of Sylvia's kitchen like softly-polished aluminium, or the skin of a baby, three days dead.

She took hold of Sylvia's hands, both of them. 'Come on, Sylvia,' she coaxed her. 'Come on, Sylvia, up.'

Sylvia stared at her, wide-eyed. 'You're naked. You're dead. ... Go away.'

'Come on, Sylvia, up you get.'

'Ms Cuddy!' the man's voice repeated. 'This is Ramone the Super, Ms Cuddy? Is everything okay?'

'Everything's fine, thank you, Ramone!' Celia called, in a fair imitation of Sylvia's Bostonian accent.

Sylvia was standing with her knees slightly bent, as if she couldn't find the strength to stand up straight. 'What are you going to do to me?' she asked, in a voice as scattered as a burst-open bag of dolly-mixtures. 'What are you going to do to me? Please! I won't tell! I promise you, Celia! I promise you!'

Celia held Sylvia close, wrapping her arms around, pressing Sylvia's cheek close to her breast.

Slowly, almost sensually, she began to stroke Sylvia's hair.

'You feel hot,' Sylvia muttered. 'I thought dead people were supposed to be cold.'

'Ah, but I'm not dead,' Celia told her, still stroking her

hair, over and over. 'I'm very much alive. I'm so much alive that I shall never die.'

'Celia, you're so hot. Don't hold me so close. I can't bear it.'

Pale grey fingers stroked her hair, over and over. A first wisp of smoke, from the top of her scalp. A first smell of burning.

'Celia, please! You're hurting me! You feel so *hot*!'

But Celia's eyelids closed over those empty eye-sockets as if she simply didn't choose to hear, and she kept on stroking Sylvia's hair, her fingers running deeply and sensually into her curls. Another wisp of smoke, a small sharp crackle of burning ends.

'I shall never die, Sylvia, my darling, and nor shall Marianna, nor David, nor Leonard, nor Carmen, nor Julie, nor any of us. We're all pure now, every one of us. Salamanders! And we shall find more to purify, thousands more.'

Her fingers stroked and stroked. Sylvia tried to struggle free, but Celia held her even more tightly. Celia's arms were so hot now that Sylvia's silk blouse began to scorch, and the flowery fabric shrivel up. Smoke was pouring from Sylvia's hair, and filling the kitchen with an acrid, eye-watering stench. Suddenly, her hair burst into flame, and she shouted in pain. Celia instantly clamped her hand over Sylvia's mouth, and her fingers were so hot that Sylvia's lips sizzled and seared, like raw steak pressed against a red-hot skillet.

Sylvia twisted and writhed and thrashed, but she couldn't get free. Celia's body temperature had risen so high that Sylvia's blouse and skirt had scorched through and her first layer of skin had actually fused to Celia's, breast and hip and thigh, so that for all practical purposes the two women were actually welded together.

Sylvia breathed in superheated air: it burned the hairs in her nostrils and dropped into her lungs like blazing petrol. She had burned herself badly only once before in her life, six or seven years ago, when she had dropped a panful of scalding water on her foot, and she had thought that what she had suffered then was agony. But she understood now that what she had suffered then was simply pain, and that true agony was so intense that it was beyond physical description. It was a spiritual experience, so unbearable that it was beautiful, so devastating in its effect on her central nervous system that she felt as if she had discovered at last the full implication of what it was to be a human being.

In Celia's incandescent arms, she understood that God had created His children with the ability to be able to suffer to such a degree that death would seem like blessed relief. That was the horrible beauty of it.

She was incapable of screaming out loud. But inside her mind she was screaming and screaming until she couldn't even think any more.

Celia held her tighter, caressing her shoulders, caressing her back. Celia's hands left wrinkled, blistering tracks wherever they touched her. Blistering sheers of skin dropped from her back, until she looked as if she was wearing a ballet-skirt of curled-up crackling.

Sylvia lifted her puckering blistered face to Celia, and Celia opened her black empty eyes. Even though Sylvia couldn't speak, she communicated with every shrivelling nerve in her body: *Kill me, kill me, please. Don't make me suffer any more.*

Celia stared at her with terrible black blindness, and then closed her eyes again. It was at that instant that Sylvia exploded into flame. Her lungs swelled, and then burst apart, and blood and flesh geysered out of her mouth. Chunks of burning muscle flew from her shoulders, her legs collapsed like charred chair-legs; her intestines fell through her cracked-apart pelvis in a roar of fatty flame; her skull detonated.

The whole kitchen was strewn with burning ashes and lumps of shrivelled flesh.

Sylvia's remains blazed on the kitchen floor with ever-intensifying glare and heat. Celia stood watching, naked unmoved, even when the ceramic floor-tiles began to break, one by one, with a gritty popcorn crackle.

Smoke filled the entire apartment, although it was slowly beginning to drift out through the open balcony door. Celia paced slowly around, as if she were reluctant to leave, tense, anxious, almost *angry.* She kept returning to the kitchen to look at the last guttering flames. It was extraordinary how it took nothing more than heat to reduce a living, talking human being to a small heap of oily ashes, in which flames fitfully burned.

Celia wondered if she felt sad, or regretful. She wasn't sure. She felt sorry that Sylvia was gone, yet Sylvia had brought it on herself and Otto had always said that we must all accept the consequences for what we do, no matter how painful those consequences might happen to be. In a way, she felt that she had saved Sylvia from something far worse, although she knew that Sylvia's soul would suffer and suffer for all eternity.

She approached the antique mirror next to the front door, and stared at herself. She knew how much she had changed. She looked the same, but she wasn't the same at all. She was purified, utterly purified. She could never again be swayed by lies or deceit or broken promises. She would never again succumb to any kind of weakness. She was one of the chosen, one of the truly eternal.

Her empty eyes, which had horrified Sylvia so much, were the symbol of everything she had now become. *The eyes are the windows to the soul,* somebody had once said. She needed no windows. She was *all* spirit, *all* soul, made flesh by the smoke of her own sacrifice. She had no need of eyes.

She cupped her hands over her small bare breasts. Her skin was cool now, the burning had passed. She thought of Lloyd and her nipples stiffened between her fingers. She knew how much pain she had caused him. She had known from the very beginning that he would have to suffer. But when the time came, they would be back together again, whole, perfect, and their passion would last for ever.

'My dear, you will never die,' Otto had told her, with a thin smile, clasping both of her hands between both of his.

She reached down and twined between her fingers and thumb the fine curly hair that grew between her legs. She watched herself in the mirror. She had always been highly sexed. She hadn't realized how much she would miss Lloyd's lovemaking, even though they had been apart now for only three days. It would be wonderful, after the solstice, when she could take him back into her arms.

It was then that the phone rang. She hesitated for a moment or two, then she walked back into the smoke-filled kitchen and picked it up.

A voice said, 'Sylvia? Sylvia? Is that you?'

Lloyd, she thought, closing her eyes. She was almost tempted to answer, although she knew that she mustn't.

'Sylvia ... I had a call about five minutes ago. I thought it was maybe from you.'

She didn't answer, but she placed the receiver against her lips, and kissed it, slowly and lingeringly.

'Sylvia?' she heard him say.

She pressed the earpiece against her breasts, touching her nipples against the tiny holes from which his voice was emerging.

'Lloyd ...' she murmured.

'Sylvia ... can you hear me? Are you able to talk? Should I call you back? Can you hear me okay?'

Now she massaged the receiver against her stomach, and between her legs. She rubbed it slowly around and around against her vulva, until the plastic was slippery and shiny. Bending her knees slightly, she opened herself with the fingers of her left hand, and pushed the end of the receiver inside herself. Cream plastic, shiny pink flesh.

'Who's there?' asked Lloyd, right inside her.

'Your lover,' she replied, and then laughed. But all the time the tears were running out of her empty eyes.

She forced the receiver up even harder, gasping, churning it around. She hadn't felt so desperately frustrated for years. She pushed it and pushed it, sinking gradually on to her knees, and pressing her forehead against the ash-strewn kitchen floor. Then, in the silence of Sylvia's smoke-filled apartment, she heard the telephone click, and whine, as Lloyd rang off.

She drew the receiver out of herself, and clutched it in her left hand, and screamed at it in fury. Blue smoke began to pour from between her fingers, and the receiver started to soften and twist. She screamed and she screamed, a scream of fear and frustration and dark black anger, and the telephone burst into flame. Molten plastic dripped and crawled down her wrist, and dropped flaring on to the tiled floor.

At last, she threw it away, a smoldering knot of polystyrene on the end of a twisted telephone cord, and she knelt on the floor, shaking with emotion.

She had understood right from the very beginning that she would have to suffer. She had understood that she would be one of the first – different, and dangerous, and difficult for her friends and her lovers to understand.

But she hadn't been prepared for the strangeness of it, nor for the huge surges of anger that she would feel. She was immortal. She had inherited the whole world, for ever. But what had she lost? *What had she lost?*

She stood up, picked up her raincoat, and hung it over her shoulders. Then she carefully replaced her smoke-black glasses. She would have given anything to see Lloyd that evening, but she knew that she couldn't trust him to keep her secret, and most of all she couldn't trust herself.

She collected the Wagner libretto, let herself out, and closed the door behind her.

— NINE —

'That's me for tonight, folks!'

Bob Tuggey tossed his apron into the linen-basket, balled up his paper hat, and gratefully unhooked his old tan leather jacket from the peg. He reached into the pocket and took out a crumpled pack of Lucky Strike Lights, and tucked one into the corner of his mouth. He was just about to light it when Sally bustled past and said, 'Unh-hunh, Unca Tug. No smoking in the kitchen, corridor, washrooms, or staff recreation areas. Besides, the Surgeon General has determined that smoking cigarettes is bad for your self-image.'

'You're a goddamned Tartar,' he retorted. 'Besides, I don't have a self-image. I sold my self-image in Paris, about twenty years ago, for a plateful of calves' kidneys, a bottle of Rully and twenty *Disque Bleu.*'

'That was pretty cheap, for a self-image.'

Unca Tug put his arm around Sally's shoulders and gave her freckled cheek an affectionate smackeroo. 'In those days, my darling, we were more interested in peace and love and wondering what the hell we were fighting for.'

'I know, I know. "Come On Baby Light My Fire", all that stuff.'

'See you tomorrow, Tartar,' Bob grinned, and left the building. He took two or three steps into the car-park, and then paused to light his cigarette. He hoped Stan Kostolowicz wouldn't have any trouble getting out tonight. His daughter-in-law could be something of a pain in the ass. She didn't like Stan drinking, that was the trouble. When he drank, he always got up in the middle of the night and flushed the toilet and made himself Polish sausage sandwiches and drank milk out of the carton and messed up her perfect kitchen.

Bob reckoned that there was quite a lot to be said for living on your own. You could come in when you chose, go out when you chose. You could smoke in the john. You could eat Kettle Chips in bed and nobody complained about the crumbs. You could blow off whenever you pleased, and nobody wrinkled their nose up or started spraying lavender air-freshener around the place.

He tugged up his collar and began walking across the car-park. His pale-blue '69 Pontiac Grand Prix with the tattered vinyl roof was parked close to the exit. He had been meaning to repair the roof for nearly four years now. He still liked the car. It was old, but it had plenty of muscle and, as he was fond of pointing out to anybody who would listen, it had the longest hood in GM production history.

He didn't even glance at the Mercedes with the darkened windows. The soft crunch of car doors being closed behind him didn't register. Even when he heard footsteps close behind him he didn't turn around.

But when a woman's voice called, 'You're Bob Tuggey, yes?' Bob stopped, and slowly turned, one eye closed against the smoke of his dangling cigarette, and said, 'Who wants to know?'

Who wanted to know was an overpoweringly tall, heavily built woman in a short black sleeveless leather dress. Her eyes were the colour of green seedless grapes. Her white-blonde hair was scraped mercilessly back from her broad pale forehead, and braided into a rope-like Teutonic crown. Her nose was straight and short, her jaw could have cracked walnuts. She wore fine black fishnet pantyhose, and short black high-heeled boots. Altogether she looked like a dominatrix out of a masochist's favourite nightmare.

Not far away with his hands in his pockets stood a painfully thin man in a loose grey business suit and a wide-brimmed hat. He was taller than the woman, but where she was robust and well fleshed and stocky, he was sere and fragile, and looked as if one healthy smack on the back would crumble him up like ashes.

His face was long and oval, with a generously bulbous nose, but collapsed cheeks, criss-crossed with dry wrinkles, and eyes that swam around in his face as if he couldn't make up his mind what to look at or what to feel. His shoes were as bulbous as his nose: old-fashioned Oxfords, with toecaps, from a generation of shoemakers long gone.

'You're Bob Tuggey, yes?' the woman repeated, without answering Bob's question. She sounded as if she had an accent of some kind, Swedish or German, something like that. Bob could talk Viet Namese like a native, and French like a Belgian, but he couldn't speak any of those hurdy-gurdy Nordic languages.

The woman came closer. She was at least six-foot-two, and her breasts were gigantic. Yet she walked with the ease of total fitness. Close up, she smelled of leather and cigar-smoke and Chanel No. 5.

'You have something that belongs to us,' she told Bob.

Bob meticulously took the cigarette out of his mouth, and blew smoke sideways. 'I have something that belongs to you? How do you work that out? I don't even have anything that belongs to myself.'

The thin man in the grey business suit raised his hat, revealing a soft mat of white crewcut hair. 'Otto Mander, at your service, good sir. And this is Helmwige von Koettlitz. We have no desire to alarm you. But of course we must insist that you return our property.'

'What property?' Bob demanded. 'I don't have anything that belongs to you.'

'I think, a small charm. An amulet,' Otto told him.

Bob glanced at the woman called Helmwige. 'Are you the lady who called the restaurant today?'

She didn't smile. 'How do you think I knew your name?'

'Well ... I'm real sorry,' Bob told her, 'but I picked up that little charm thinking it belonged to the girl who was burned here a couple of days ago. Did you hear about that?'

'Yes,' said Otto, 'we heard about that. The question is, what did you do with the charm?'

'I'm real sorry. It was a genuine mistake. I gave it to that girl's fee-ants.'

'What?' Helmwige demanded, sternly.

'I told you, it was a genuine mistake. The guy didn't know whether it was hers or not. He'd never seen it before. But he took it anyway in case it was.'

'I see,' said Otto, as if he hadn't really been listening. A moth flickered past, caught in the floodlights that illuminated the car-park. Without appearing to look at it, he snatched it out of the air. Then he opened his hand, and inspected it.

'Pretty quick reflexes,' Bob smiled at him.

Otto stared at him as blankly as if he had said something in Czech. Then he pushed the still-fluttering moth between his lips, sucked it in, chewed it for a moment, and swallowed it.

Bob found this distinctly unsettling. 'Bit of a damned nuisance, right, moths?' he joked. 'Good thing they're full of protein.' He let out a short, abrupt laugh, then stepped away. 'Listen, I'm calling the guy tomorrow. I'll get your charm back for you, even if I have to drive up to La Jolla myself.'

'That's all right,' Otto told him, raising one hand. 'That won't be necessary. We'll drive up to see him ourselves.'

'Well, if you want to go to all of that trouble ...'

'Believe me, Bob,' Helmwige told him, in a deep, operatic voice, 'it will be no trouble.'

Bob waited for a moment. Neither Otto nor Helmwige appeared to have anything to say, so he shrugged and said, 'Good night, then. Unless there was anything else.'

'Wait!' said Otto. 'Before you leave ... may I make an impertinent demand on you?'

'I don't know,' Bob replied, cautiously. 'Depends what it is.'

'You will say nothing about us, to anybody.'

Bob drew slowly and suspiciously on his cigarette. 'Why should I? I don't care whose charm it is, so long as the real owner gets it back.'

'But, you will say nothing?'

105

'Listen, mister,' Bob told him. 'It's a free world. If I want to talk about it, I'll talk about it. If I don't, I won't.'

'Helmwige?' Otto suggested.

Helmwige smiled. 'There was no charm. That would be easy to accept, *nicht wahr*? that there *was* no charm?'

Something told Bob that this confrontation had just gone beyond the parameters of acceptable everyday wackiness. He sensed danger, the same way that he had sensed danger in Saigon. *Avoid the wacky like the plague*, William Trueheart had once told him. *They can go from hilarious to homicidal as quick as a blink.*

'Sure,' he nodded, taking his cigarette out of his mouth. 'Sure, that would be easy to accept.'

Otto approached him. The breeze blew from Otto's direction, and smelled like milky Dutch cigars and lavender and death. Otto licked his middle finger and picked a tiny spider from Bob's shirt-collar, and bit it between his teeth. 'Arachnid caviar,' he remarked. 'Their little black bodies … they make the same sharp *pop!* when you bite them.'

'Listen,' said Bob, uneasily. 'I don't know what the fuck this all about.'

'You don't have to,' Helmwige insisted. 'All you have to do is to say nothing. Is it so difficult to forget?'

'What's so damned significant about this charm that I have to forget it anyway? If I'm going to forget it, I'd sure as hell like to know what I'm supposed to be forgetting it *for.*'

'Bob …' replied Otto, with great middle - European courtesy. 'This affair is really nothing that should concern you. You are better off accepting that there are things which happen in this world which are not for the likes of you. Go about your business. Say nothing. You are an ant, that is all.'

Bob was already tired and irritable from a long shift cooking hamburgers. 'Wait up here,' he snapped. 'Who are you calling an ant?'

'You're so sensitive, about the lowly reality of your existence? You are an ant. That is not an opinion. That is a fact.'

'At least I'm not a fucking stick-insect.'

Helmwige came around and stood in front of him. She gave him a quick little shake of her head. 'You are not to speak to Herr Mander in that way.'

'Pardon me, lady, but I can speak to him any way I please. And if you think I'm going to keep my mouth shut about this lucky charm, or you, or this little charade we're playing out here, you've got another thing coming. Special delivery.'

He lifted the two fingers in which he was holding his cigarette, and gave Otto a disrespectful salute.

'Well, be seeing you,' said Otto, with a smile as thin as the edge of a sheet of paper.

'Not if I see you first,' Bob replied.

He stepped around Helmwige and carried on walking toward his car. *Jesus Christ,* he thought to himself, *wackos wasn't the word for those two. Those two came from the Planet Bananas.*

He was halfway to his car when he suddenly began to realize that the soles of his feet felt hot. Not just tired-and-sweaty-from-cooking-all-afternoon hot, but *really* hot, like walking barefoot across the beach on a midsummer day.

He half hopped, and walked more quickly. It had been warm today, for sure, but not warm enough to heat the car-park up to *this* kind of temperature. His feet almost felt as if they were *burning*.

He glanced behind him. Otto and Helmwige were still standing where he had left them, except that Otto was shading his eyes with his bony hands.

Suddenly Bob's feet hurt so much that he shouted out loud, and danced from one foot to the other. 'Jesus! I'm on fire!' he yelled. 'Jesus! What have you done to me?'

He dropped to the ground, and yanked at the laces of his worn-out Keds. Smoke was dribbling out of the lace-holes, and out of the ventilation holes at the sides. His feet were actually on fire!

Panting with effort and pain, he dragged off his sneakers and tossed them smoking across the car-park.

God almighty, that Helmwige woman must have given him a double hotfoot! Even his socks were scorched! But he was just about to stand up when both feet actually burst into flame, flaring and spitting like candle wax.

He screamed, and tried to beat at the flames with his hands. But then his hands caught alight, too, and started to blaze just as fiercely.

'*Help me!*' Bob screamed. '*I'm burning! Help me!*'

But neither Otto nor Helmwige moved a muscle. Otto remained with his hands shading his eyes, as if he were thinking very intently about something inconsequential, like his nephew's birthday present, or what he was going to have for lunch. Helmwige simply watched, with her arms folded under her breasts – not pitiless, but not particularly interested, as if she saw men burning every day.

Bob struggled to his knees, his hands melting in front of his eyes. At first, the pain in his blazing fingers and blazing toes had been excruciating, but then they became numb, and the pain encircled his wrists and his ankles instead. He didn't realize that the fire had burned away his nerve-endings, and that his hands and feet were approaching sixth-degree burns, which meant their complete destruction.

They're not going to help me, he thought, with an overwhelming dullness. *They're just going to stand there and watch me burn*.

He shuffled forward on his knees. The flames from his feet licked up his back, and abruptly his trousers and the back of his tan leather jacket caught fire. *My ass, for God's sake, my ass is on fire!*

He could see his Pontiac parked only twenty feet away. The dull handpainted fenders, the shredded vinyl roof. There was a fire-extinguisher under the passenger seat, if only he could ...

Blazing, he stumbled on his knees toward his car. A fiery penitent, a man lurching in flames toward his God. He suddenly thought that he had been doomed to die this way, ever since he had first seen that monk burning himself in Saigon. It was one of those bizarre twists of destiny in which he had become inextricably entangled, the moment he had stepped out of his car on the Cholon Road and tried to prevent that monk from doing what he believed he had to do.

Cars and buses whished past, this way and that, on Rosecrans Avenue, only thirty or forty feet away from him. What their occupants thought when they caught sight of a man burning in the car-park, he couldn't even guess, but none of them stopped.

'*Oh, look, Morton, there's somebody on fire.*'

'*That's all right, dear, it's nobody we know.*'

Bob's back was burning furiously now, and tongues of flame licked up between his legs. He staggered forward on his knees. It didn't seem to hurt any more, he couldn't think why. It was like kneeling in a very hot wind, that was all. It was almost funny.

He reached his car, and managed to heave himself up with his elbow beside the passenger door. *Extinguisher, extinguisher ... then I can put it out, and everything's going to be fine.* He grasped the doorhandle with his blackened hand. Thank God the locks are broken, I could never turn a key. He pulled, and the door opened, but with a crackling, agonizing wrench, his hand broke off, too, as if his fingers were sticks of charcoal.

He lifted the blazing stump of his wrist in pain and amazement. He understood then that he was dead, that he was beyond healing, beyond any kind of help. In a way, it came as a huge relief, because it took away the burdensome lifelong responsibility for having to take care of his body, for having to survive. No more worries about driving safely and drinking sensibly and giving up smoking.

Bob Tuggey tried to yell, a sort of a rebel yell, to show Otto and Helmwige that he didn't give a damn, that he was going out defiant. But he breathed in nothing but flame, he choked on a throatful of fire, and fell forward into the passenger seat of his Grand Prix without another sound. His body shuddered wildly as it burned, but the movements were probably caused by shrivellng muscles.

The vinyl seats caught alight almost at once. Fanned by

the warm ocean wind, the interior of the car was soon blazing furiously. All that anybody could have seen of Bob Tuggey were his legs, protruding from the open passenger door.

Now that a vehicle was burning, somebody called the fire department, and sirens began to honk and wail and warble in the distance. Just as the first fire-engine turned into the car-park, Bob's coveted Grand Prix exploded, sending up a huge rolling ball of dazzling white flame that was far brighter and far fiercer than nine gallons of petrol could have produced.

Burning chunks of car tumbled across the car-park. Even the engine-block rolled over and over, like a monstrous blazing die. Fragments of blazing fabric were caught in what felt like a sudden strong gust, and whirled around and around.

In the eye of this fiery storm stood Otto, slowly lowering his hands from his eyes, and Helmwige, who was looking the other way now, obviously bored.

'Are we going to La Jolla tonight?' Helmwige asked, nonchalantly.

'Oh ... the morning will do,' Otto replied. 'If Celia's *liebling* believes that the amulet is hers, he will keep it quite safe.'

'*Bist du müde, meine kleine Taube?*' Helmwige cooed, her pink lips shining in the light of Bob Tuggey's burning car. 'Are you tired, my little dove?'

Otto didn't answer, but remained where he was, staring at the glittering embers of steel and rubber and upholstery, his face intermittently lit crimson by the flashing lights of the fire-engines. A moth flickered past in the darkness, attracted by the brightness of the fire. Without hesitation, Otto snatched it out of the air, and pressed it with two fingers flat on his protruding tongue. Then he slowly sucked it against the roof of his mouth.

Helmwige sighed restlessly, and began to pace up and down. Unlike Otto, she found death completely uninteresting. How could anybody be interested in death, when they knew that they were going to live for ever?

— TEN —

After his shower, Lloyd wrapped himself in a thick white Turkish bathrobe, and sat down in the living-room with a large glass of Wild Turkey and all the San Diego newspapers for the past three days. He hadn't looked at them until now. He had known that some of them had carried photographs of Celia on fire, and he hadn't been able to face the idea of seeing her last seconds alive, when there was no possible way that he could turn back the clock and save her.

He was afraid, too, that he would see how much she had suffered.

However, his fear had at last been overcome by his curiosity about the charm that Bob Tuggey had found. He wanted to see if Celia had been wearing her bracelet when she set herself on fire; and if this particular charm were visible in the newspaper pictures.

He turned it over and over, frowning at it. It was discoloured by fire, so it must have been *near* her, at least. And its link was broken, as if it had accidentally been twisted and snapped off. But why had she been wearing it at all, on a bracelet that was supposed to symbolize all the important things that had happened in her life?

Maybe it *was* important, but Lloyd certainly didn't know why. A lizard, in a circle? What had happened recently that had anything remotely to do with lizards?

His CD was playing Bellini's *La Sonnambula*. He remembered Celia singing along with it once, waving a glass of champagne from side to side as she sang, so that champagne flew all over the carpet.

'Celia ...' he said, although he knew that she could never answer him now. God damn it, why hadn't she told him what was wrong? Why hadn't she even left him a letter?

He picked up the *San Diego Tribune*, and slowly unfolded it. *Girl's Fiery Death In Rosecrans Ave. Parking Lot. Horrorstruck McDonald's Diners Witness apparent Suicide.* He stared at the photographs with a feeling of growing numbness. The *Times* picture was quite blurred, but Lloyd could still recognize Celia's face through the flames. Her hands were resting in her lap, and it was difficult to make out any detail, but there was a thin white line around her right wrist that was almost certainly her charm bracelet. Unfortunately none of the charms was visible.

He examined the picture on the front of the *San Diego County Post.* This must have been taken a few seconds later, because Celia's head had almost vanished into the flames, but it did show more distinctly that she was wearing her bracelet. Reaching across for his magnifying glass, Lloyd scrutinized the photograph intently. He thought he could distinguish the gold treble-clef that he had given her, but there was no obvious sign of the lizard charm.

He went through all the photographs again and again, but none of them were clear enough for him to be able to tell whether she had been wearing that particular charm or not. Maybe somebody at her religious study group had given it to her, and that's why she had kept it a secret from him. He decided to visit Civic Theater tomorrow to see what he could find out about this mysterious Otto and his curious get-togethers.

On the front page of yesterday's *Tribune* there was a photograph of the burned-out bus in the Anza Borrego, too, but there was nothing in the report next to it that told him anything he didn't already know.

La sonnambula came to a finish and, dropping the newspapers on the table, Lloyd stood up to put on another disc. He hated the house being completely silent. He kept imagining that he could hear Celia in the kitchen, or in the bathroom, and at night he didn't dare to look into her dressing-table mirror, in case he should glimpse her sitting there, making up her eyes, alight.

He put on *La Traviata* and returned to the sofa. Standing up, he could see the newspaper photographs side by side; and it was then that something odd struck him. He frowned first at one newspaper and then at another. He took out his magnifying glass. It was crazy, but the evidence was indisputable. And it was far too much of a coincidence to have happened by chance.

In the background of the photograph of Celia stood twenty or thirty people, most of them children. But two tall figures stood out. A man in what appeared to be a business suit and a soft wide-brimmed hat, and a blonde-haired woman, who had her hand clamped over her mouth.

Then, in the photograph of the burned-out bus, the same two people appeared. They were standing quite a long way from the bus, next to a car that looked like a large Mercedes saloon. There were several other by-standers there. Three men who were probably truckers, and a woman holding a dog on a leash. But there was no question about those two. The man with the soft wide-brimmed hat and the woman with the bright blonde hair.

As far as Lloyd was concerned, that was indisputable proof that Celia's death had been connected with the bus burning – and indisputable proof that these two people knew what the connection was. Damn it, they probably even knew *why* Celia had committed suicide.

He picked up the telephone and dialled Sylvia's number. He had already rung her two or three times during the evening because of two peculiar calls – one from a woman who had *sounded* a little like Sylvia, but who had refused to do anything but whisper, and the other made to somebody at her apartment who had made only kissing noises. Each time he had called since then, however, he had heard the drone of an out-of-service signal. He knew that she must be all right – after all, he had seen her go into her apartment building – but he would have liked to have been able to tell her about these

113

extraordinary bystanders, whose fascination with death by burning seemed to go way beyond even the worst excesses of human prurience.

Again, Sylvia's number was out of service. He replaced the receiver, and punched out Sergeant Houk's number instead.

'Sergeant Houk?'

'Houk's out on a call right now. This is Detective Gable. What can I do for you?'

'Oh ... this is Lloyd Denman. From Denman's Original Fish Depot, remember? My fiancée was the one who...'

'Sure, Mr Denman. I remember you. Is there anything that I can do?'

'Will Sergeant Houk be very long?'

'Naw ... shouldn't think so. Thirty minutes tops. Do you want he should call you?'

'Please ... yes, I'd appreciate it.'

He put down the phone and sat back with his fingers laced behind his head. Sergeant Houk had been assigned to assist the State police in their investigation of the burned-bus fatalities, and so it was possible that he already had information which could help Lloyd find these two bystanders. Perhaps they'd been there when the bus was actually burning – in which case, the police would have taken their names and addresses.

He wondered what he ought to do if he found who they were.

He wondered what he ought to do if he found out that they were somehow responsible for Celia's death.

Should he report them to Sergeant Houk, or should he take the law into his own hands? At least if he took the law into his own hands, their punishment would be sure and certain and absolutely final.

He was still drinking and thinking when the telephone rang. He scooped it up and said, 'Denman.'

'Mr Denman? Sergeant Houk. I understand you called me.'

'That's right, Sergeant, I did.'

'You heard the news, then?'

'News? What news?'

'The news about your fiancée's friend, Ms Cuddy.'

'Sylvia? I was out with Sylvia earlier this evening. She's all right, I hope? I was trying to call her number, but it's out of service.'

'You didn't hear the news, then.'

'Well, don't you think you'd better tell me?' asked Lloyd.

There was a pause. It sounded as if Sergent Houk had put his hand over the receiver and was answering a question from somebody in his office, because he finished up by saying, 'Sure, and take it right down to the ME.'

Then he said, 'Sorry, Mr Denman, we're a little busy here this evening. I'm afraid that the news is bad. There was a serious fire at Ms Cuddy's apartment about two hours ago, and she was very regrettably unable to escape.'

Lloyd licked his lips. They felt as dry as insects' wing-cases. 'You're trying to tell me she's *dead*?'

'I'm sorry, Mr Denman. Really, truly, sorry.'

'God almighty. First Celia, then all of those people on the bus. Now Sylvia.'

'There's still no suggestion that there's any connection,' Sergeant Houk told him, with a noise like swallowing hot coffee. 'Since you were one of the last people to see Ms Cuddy alive, however, I'd like to come around and ask you some routine questions. You know how it is.'

'Sergeant ...' Lloyd began, and for a moment he was tempted to tell him about the bystanders. But something told him not to, to keep it to himself, at least for a while. He had the feeling that there was an extra double-knot in what had happened that logical detective work would never be able to unravel.

'Sure, Sergeant,' he finished. 'I'd be glad to help.' He took a breath, and then he asked, 'This fire at Sylvia's apartment ... does anyone know how it started?'

'Hard to tell. She was literally burnt to ashes. The fire department investigators were even talking about spontaneous combustion.'

'I thought spontaneous combustion was a myth?' said Lloyd. His voice shook.

'You haven't seen Ms Cuddy's apartment yet. All that got burned was her, and her telephone. Nothing else at all. We've got engineers from Pacific Bell working on it, too. Somebody came up with the theory that she might have been struck by a freak bolt of lightning down the telephone cable.'

Lloyd asked cautiously, 'Were there any witnesses?'

'None,' said Sergeant Houk. 'The super said he heard noises, laughing or screaming, but when they stopped, he thought she was having a bit of a private party, if you know what I mean. Nobody saw anybody enter the building, apart from Ms Cuddy, and nobody saw anybody leave the building, neither. And the door sure wasn't forced in any way, although the security chain was off.'

'Is there anything else I can do?' said Lloyd.

'Just sit tight, Mr Denman, that's all. Sit tight and stay in touch.'

'Very well, then,' Lloyd agreed, and put down the receiver.

Sylvia, burned to death! My God! He swallowed a mouthful of Wild Turkey and sat on the sofa, hunched up and shivering. This was like a forest fire, sweeping through his life, incinerating everybody he knew and loved. How could Sylvia have possibly burned to death? *Ashes*, Sergeant Houk had told him. *Nothing but ashes*.

After a while, he went back to the newspapers, spreading them out yet again, and reading every story with exaggerated care. Three eye-witnesses had been interviewed for the report on Celia's death. One was Bob Tuggey, whom Lloyd already knew. The others were a 25-year-old gas station attendant (who was unlikely to be dressed in a business suit and a trilby hat), a 32-year-old childminder called Maria Salazar (who was unlikely to be blonde), and a 66-year-old gardener with the improbable name of Dan Kan.

Lloyd turned to the report of the burned-out bus, to see if any of the names of the eyewitnesses matched those of Celia's burning. The story stated that:

... the only witness to the burning
of the bus was a 12-year-old Pechanga Indian
boy, nicknamed 'Tony Express', who has been
blind since birth. Tony told Highway Patrol
officers that he had heard a man's voice shouting
words that sounded like 'You knew us' in the vicinity
of the bus while it was ablaze.

Apart from a guess that the man was elderly,
however, he was unable to identify any marked
accent or linguistic peculiarity which might
have given detectives a pointer.

Lloyd looked back at the photograph of the man and the
woman watching Celia burn. The man's face was in
shadow, because of the wide brim of his hat, but his
stance and the stoop of his shoulders suggested to Lloyd
that he was about sixty, sixty-five, maybe even older.

But 'you knew us'? What did that mean? Maybe he had
torched the bus because the people in it could identify
him. 'You knew us'? 'You *knew* us'?

With that extraordinary power of which the human
mind is sometimes capable – the power to add two and
two together and come up with seven and a half – Lloyd
found his eyes drawn across the coffee-table, past the
spread-out newspapers, to the photocopies that he had
made of Wagner's libretto. The name was written in pencil,
almost as an afterthought. Junius, *Junius*. Pronounced,
in German, not with a 'J', but a 'Y'. As in, 'you-knew-us'.

He sat staring at the libretto, feeling chilled and
excited but not knowing what to do next, in case he
broke the spell. It fitted too damn well to be true, like a
crossword answer that seems to fit all of the spaces and
all of the known letters but turns out to be 'banished'
instead of 'boneyard'.

Could it really be possible that some elderly man had
been standing watching that bus burn, with thirteen
people inside it, shouting out, 'Junius!'? The same opera
that somebody had broken into his house to look for? The
same opera that ...

117

He closed his eyes in painful realization. *The same opera that Sylvia Cuddy had had in her possession when she was incinerated in her apartment.*

He poured himself another large whisky and paced up and down the living-room, his head churning with ideas. He could tell Sergeant Houk everything that he had guessed. But what did it really amount to? Would Sergeant Houk follow it up? And if he didn't follow it up, would he take active steps to prevent *Lloyd* from following it up? Lloyd knew how much police detectives disliked amateurs ... even certified PIs.

In any case, what did his discoveries really amount to? The coincidental appearance of the same bystanders in two news photographs ... the coincidental death-by-burning of three members of the San Diego Opera in as many days ... and the phonetic similarity between 'you knew us' and 'Junius'.

Not exactly what any hardnosed detective would call clues.

But Lloyd was so hurt and shocked by what had happened. Inside of him, such a rage had built up against whoever was responsible for Celia's burning, that he was prepared to pursue any fragments of evidence, no matter how circumstantial, no matter how coincidental – so long as he found out eventually who had done it, and why, and so long as he made them suffer as deeply and as savagely as he had, and Celia had, and Marianna had, and now Sylvia, too, whose death had agonized him so much that he could scarcely cry.

Tomorrow he would find this Otto character, if only to eliminate him from his investigation. Then he would drive out to the desert and find the Indian boy called Tony Express. He was determined to try anything and everything. He had far more time to spare than Sergeant Houk, and a far fiercer motivation for finding out what had happened.

He went into the kitchen, spooned out heaps of arabica coffee, and switched on the percolator. He wanted to stay sober from now on. No more self-pity, no more tears. Nothing but revenge.

The coffee had begun to *ploop-plip* noisily when the telephone rang.

'Mr Denman? Waldo. We've taken the last orders, I thought you would like to know that everything is very well.'

'Thanks, Waldo, I appreciate it.'

'The new-recipe bouillabaisse was not such a success. Louis thinks it has to have a different presentation somehow. It is too messy for somebody who is all dressed up for a special dinner. Too much shell, too many bones.'

'All right,' said Lloyd, not really listening. 'Tell him to work on it.'

'Oh ... one thing. A man called to tell you that the charm did not belong to Ms Williams. He said his name was ... wait a minute, please, I have it here. "Uncle Tug". You know this Uncle Tug?'

'Sure, I know him,' said Lloyd, with a frown.

'He said the charm did not belong to Ms Williams, and to call him.'

'Okay, then, I will. Thanks, Waldo. Anything else?'

'Everything's smooth, Mr Denman. Don't worry about nothing.'

Lloyd went through to the living-room and found the San Diego telephone directory. He leafed through it until he located the Rosecrans Avenue McDonald's, and punched out the number. It took a long time for anyone to answer, and when a girl's voice eventually said, 'McDonald's, how can I help you?' she sounded flustered and distinctly unhappy. Lloyd was sure he could hear sirens in the background.

'I'm trying to get in touch with one of your chefs,' said Lloyd. 'A guy who calls himself Unca Tug?'

The girl seemed to find it a struggle to reply. Lloyd heard more sirens, and somebody shouting.

'Hey, is everything all right?' he asked. 'It sounds like you've got yourselves some kind of panic down there.'

'It's Unca Tug,' the girl wept. 'His car caught fire.'

'*What?*' Lloyd demanded. 'His car caught fire? He's not

hurt, is he?' Understanding at once from the way the girl was sobbing that he *must* have been hurt, that he must have been worse than hurt, that he was dead.

The girl couldn't speak. Lloyd didn't know that it was Sally, Bob's manageress, but he could tell that she was somebody who had cared for Unca Tug very deeply.

A young man's voice came on the phone. 'I'm sorry, mister. Things are pretty crazy down here at the moment. A car blew up and one of our chefs got himself killed. I'm sorry. Maybe you could call back later.'

There was nothing that Lloyd could do except to hang up the phone and sit back on his sofa and wonder what the hell was going on. *Another* fire? *Another* death by burning? This was beginning to look like very much more than a series of coincidental accidents. This was beginning to look like somebody had opened up the oven-gates to hell, and was pitchforking people in there like Old Nick himself.

La Traviata came to its climactic ending, and suddenly there was silence. Lloyd felt very alone, and frightened, too. Frightened of his own imagination, frightened of fire, and frightened that people and things that were well beyond his comprehension might be walking the earth – even tonight, in ordinary familiar North San Diego County, while the insects sang and the breeze quietly blew from the ocean, and the moon rose from behind the mountains like a bleached shriek.

Joe North met him at the Science Museum in Balboa Park. It was one of those hot glaring afternoons when every tree and building seemed to have been drained of its colour; even the sky was white. Lloyd paid the museum entrance for both of them, and then they wandered into the main hall.

For a while, they stood side by side watching a small plump boy pedalling a fixed bicycle until he was red in the face, trying to generate enough electricity to light up the headlamps of a sawn-off Ford Fairlane.

'Nice going, kid,' said Joe, slapping the boy on the back.

'How'd you like a job lighting up Civic Theater?'

The boy stared at Joe as if he were mad. His black friend across the hall called, 'Look out, man. Gays!'

Joe stared at Lloyd and then inspected his own clothes. He was an assistant scenery designer at the San Diego Opera, and he looked it: thin and *nouveau*-hippie, dressed in off-white chinos and a red splattery shirt. His nose was noticeably pointed and he wore a natty little clipped moustache under his nostrils.

'Hey, do you think we look like gays?' he asked Lloyd.

Lloyd shrugged. 'Even if we were, I wouldn't go for that ugly kid.'

They climbed up to the mezzanine, and sat on either side of a vertical perspex screen, face to face. If Lloyd twisted the knobs on his side of the screen, he could gradually impose his own reflections on Joe North's features, until Joe North turned into him. On his side of the screen, Joe North could do the same.

'Tell me about Otto,' said Lloyd.

'Well, Otto . . .' Joe replied. 'What can I say? Very strange guy. Very charismatic, no doubt about it. One of those people you can't take your eyes off of.'

'What did he look like?' asked Lloyd.

'Sixtyish . . . no, probably older. Real dried-up looking, you know? Like you leave a bell pepper out in the sun.'

'But where did he come from? How come he got himself attached to the Opera?'

Joe cleared his throat with a high, hammering cough. 'I thought you would have known him already. Like Celia obviously knew him so well. It was Celia who introduced him to the opera company. She brought him around when we were rehearsing that Opera Gala Night, what was that, April last year? She said he was starting up kind of a born-again study group . . . couple of times a week.'

Lloyd twisted the knobs underneath his screen, and gradually his face melted into Joe North's face. The effect was unnerving, as if his whole personality had disappeared. Just like looking into a mirror, and seeing somebody else altogether.

Joe said, 'Otto gathered us all around him on the stage. He had this woman with him ... Jeez, you never saw such a woman. *The Valkyries* in the flesh. She didn't say too much, but she gave me the feeling that if you couldn't arm-wrestle her in three seconds flat, she'd treat you like dog-meat for the rest of your life.'

Lloyd sat back. 'What was her name? Did you ever find out?'

Joe shook his head. 'I heard it, you know? But it was like German, I couldn't remember it. Something like "Helmet", I don't know. Helmet, Earwig, I don't know.'

'What did Otto say?' asked Lloyd.

On the perspex screen, Joe's face began to recede, and Lloyd's face appeared in its place. Joe's voice came out of Lloyd's unmoving lips.

'He said that we'd all been suffering all of our lives from like a total misconception of what living was all about, you know? He said that we pretended to believe we had souls and that our souls were going to live for ever, but they weren't – not so long as we stayed in these rotting bodies.'

Joe hesitated, and then he said, vehemently, 'He really got through to us, man. Do you know that? He made us understand that right from the *very second* we were born, our bodies had already started to die. We're so incredibly vulnerable, you know? We can drown, we can fall off of a building. Some terrorist headcase can blow up our plane. Some asshole cabdriver can knock you down in the street. You know the woman who wrote *Gone With The Wind*, some cabdriver knocked her down in the street? Otto really made you feel, where's the logic in that? Where's the sense? What's the point of being born if all you're going to do at the end of it is die?

'A *germ* can kill you, for Christ's sake, that's what Otto said. Something you can't even see. You can be the kindest most philanthropic person in the whole entire universe, you can be a genius, you can be Einstein. But it only takes one germ, and all of that genius is wiped out forever. All of that kindness, all of that talent, *snap!* and it's gone.'

Lloyd stood up, walked across to the mezzanine railing, and looked out over the main hall of the science museum. Joe got up, too, and stood beside him.

Lloyd said, 'Some people say that if it wasn't for death, life wouldn't be worth living.'

Joe nodded. 'In the end, yes, that's what *I* said. Otto was too goddamned what's-it's-name. Fanatical, I guess. Totalitarian. I never liked nobody telling me what to do. Not even my mom. But for a while there, right at the very beginning … well, I guess he made me believe that I could live for ever. And a whole lot of the others went *on* believing it.'

'How many joined the group?' Lloyd asked him.

'From the Opera? I don't know. Maybe five, maybe six, maybe more. I went to the first couple of get-togethers myself, but like I said, Otto was too totalitarian for me. Those weren't discussion groups. Those were Otto-telling-you-how-it-was groups. He said that the pagans of northern Europe had discovered the secret of eternal life centuries before Christ, you know? But apparently the secret was lost when they were conquered by the Romans and interbred with other, inferior races.

'He was incredibly racist. I mean it was like listening to Adolf Hitler. But he always held out this promise that everybody in the group was going to live for ever, and a whole lot of the group really seemed to believe him.

'He said that a new master race was going to be born, a real master race, brilliant and pure and totally dominant. They would rule the whole world because they had no need for fear, or violence, any of that stuff. And the reason for that was, they were going to be immortal. They couldn't die.'

Joe took out a pack of banana-flavoured Hubba Bubba and unwrapped a piece. 'That was when I bowed out. I can make some pretty wild leaps of the old imagination, you know, especially when I've been freebasing, but no wrinkled old gent in a business suit can make me believe that I'm going to live for ever.'

Lloyd said, 'Did Otto explain to you *how* you were all going to live for ever?'

'Unh-hunh, not to me. I didn't stay around long enough to hear that bit. But there was a whole lot of mumbo-jumbo about secret hymns and special rituals and something they called "Salamanders".'

'Salamanders, what were they?'

'Search me. I never found out.'

'But Marianna stayed on, didn't she?' asked Lloyd. 'Didn't *she* ever talk about what they were doing?'

'Not a syllable, I'll tell you. All the people who carried on the study group kept totally silent about it. It was all some terrific secret. I used to ask Marianna about it, but all she said was "Wait and see ..." I said, "Wait and see what?" but all she said was "Wait and see ..."'

'Did it change her at all, going to Otto's group?'

Joe nodded. 'It changed everybody who went there. Not for the worse. I mean they didn't get depressed or unhappy or anything like that. Marianna was really light and bright, always singing, always happy.'

'But?' asked Lloyd.

Joe glanced at him quickly. 'Who said anything about "but"?'

'You did. I heard it in your voice.'

'Well, for sure. There was a "but". And the "but" was like Marianna never really *related* any more. You see that perspex screen back there? After she started going to that religious study group, I always felt like Marianna was talking through perspex. No contact.'

Lloyd said, 'Where did the group meet?'

Joe nodded. 'Otto rents this house on Passeo Delicias, out by Rancho Santa Fe. Well, I assume he rents it. Way back off the road, really secluded. Not one of your really expensive Rancho Santa Fe properties, though. It's pretty rundown. We used to meet in this kind of converted garage. The whole driveway was always jam-packed with Mercedes – four or five of them, one of them like Rommel's staff-car, something like that. Sometimes the

124

group met in different places, from what Marianna told me, but most of the time they met there.'

Lloyd slowly rubbed his forehead with his fingertips, around and around. Then he said, 'Do you have any idea what this Otto guy was really into? I mean, he was obviously peddling the idea of the life everlasting. All this talk about the body decaying with the soul trapped inside it. But what was he *into*? Did he charge for these meetings? Was it money he wanted? Or what?'

Joe slowly shook his head. 'Beats me. He never asked any of us for a penny.'

'And he was really offering immortality?'

'That's what he said. But I guess that message is nothing new. When you think about it, what does every TV ministry peddle? What does every spiritual healer promise you? Everlasting life, that's what it's all about.'

Joe looked at Lloyd with narrowed eyes, and lifted one finger. 'He made one promise, you know, that day he talked to us on the stage. He said, "any one of you who chooses to follow me, that one is going to live for ever and a day, I promise." And he didn't just say "I promise", like he was selling brushes or something. He said "*I promise*" like it was a cast-iron guarantee.'

'And Marianna believed him? Just like Celia must have done?'

'I guess. She kept on going to the meetings.'

Lloyd said, 'I'm just amazed that Celia never mentioned anything about it. Not one word.'

'Maybe she thought you wouldn't like the idea.'

'Too damn right. But you didn't like the idea, either, did you, and that didn't stop Marianna?'

'Come on, Lloyd, Marianna wasn't my wife-to-be. We were just good friends, who occasionally made it together. Blow hot, blow cold, you know the kind of deal. I wasn't in any kind of position to tell her anything.'

Lloyd said, 'It's the group, no doubt about it. It's Otto. They joined that group and Otto screwed their minds up. Like the Bhagwan, like the Moonies, like any one of those nutty religions. He promised them life everlasting and they believed him. How could anybody have acted so damned stupid?'

A museum orderly was eyeing them suspiciously. They must have looked and sounded like two quarrelling lovers. It was bad enough that a couple of ugly kids thought they were gay. Joe said, 'Come on, let's get out of here.'

They left the Science Museum and were walking across heat-dried grass of Balboa Park. Joe said, 'There was something else ... something that's been bugging me.'

They reached Lloyd's car. Lloyd unlocked it, but waited until Joe had told him what was on his mind before opening the door.

'I don't know whether it's relevant or not,' said Joe. 'But about two or three weeks before Otto appeared on the scene, we were spending the weekend together at the Dream Inn at Santa Cruz. Marianna had never seen the boardwalk before. Anyway, she was checking her breasts in the bathroom and she suddenly said that she could feel some kind of a lump.'

'It wasn't cancer, was it?'

'I never found out. I told her to go to the doctor, and she went to the doctor. But then she didn't say anything more about it. I kept asking her what she was going to do about it, and all she said was she'd been talking to Celia and Celia was going to sort it out.'

Lloyd wiped sweat from his forehead with the back of his hand. 'Celia was always talking about Marianna, but she certainly didn't mention anything about Marianna having a lump in her breast.'

'Well ... no particular reason why she should, I guess,' said Joe. ' "Girls' talk", if you know what I mean.'

'Come on, Joe. Celia and I talked about *everything*. And one of your best friends finding a lump on her breast isn't exactly unimportant, is it? Especially since *she* was supposed to be sorting it out. And in any case – how the hell *could* she sort it out?'

'Search me, pal,' Joe replied. 'But after Otto appeared on the scene she never mentioned it again, and when I asked her about it, she said, "it's fine, it's all fixed." '

He paused, and then he added, 'And with all due respect, Lloyd, Celia couldn't have told you *everything*, could she? There was a whole lot she was keeping to herself.'

Lloyd nodded, and opened the car door. 'You want a ride back to the theatre?'

'Joe shook his head. 'I want to walk for a while.'

'Okay,' Lloyd told him. 'I understand. I've been doing a lot of walking myself. Walking, and thinking.'

He drove away from the Science Museum and headed north. Joe watched him go, and then made his way slowly across the grass toward the shade of the trees.

Across the street, a woman was standing watching him. In spite of the heat, she wore a long white raincoat, and her head was tightly tied with a white silk scarf. Her eyes were concealed behind circular sunglasses with dead black lenses.

Joe glanced at her once, but her image was rippling in the heat from the concrete sidewalk, and he didn't recognize her. But after awhile, she began to follow him, keeping at least a hundred and fifty feet behind him, but never allowing him out of her sight.

— ELEVEN —

Lloyd reached the house on Paseo Delicias a few minutes after twelve. His mouth was dry, and he would have done anything for a glass of cold beer, but finding Otto was more important than quenching his thirst.

Joe had told him that the house was on the second-to-last curve before the road entered the town of Rancho Santa Fe itself. It hadn't been difficult to find. He had driven up the winding road through lemon groves and bursts of flowering bushes and located the house on a steep left-hand bend, behind a dusty-looking thicket of prickly pear. He had driven right past it, and then parked about three hundred feet further up the road, under the shade of some sadly-trailing eucalyptus trees.

He climbed out of the car and put on his sunglasses. It was very hot and quiet, up here in the hills. He had driven up here for lunch on days when the coast had been thick with fog, and it had always been clear. A lizard scuttered out of sight into the undergrowth. There was a strong aroma of evaporating eucalyptus in the air.

His shoes crunched on the dusty tarmac.

Now, how am I going to play this? What if I ring the bell at the front door, and he's actually there, and he answers it? What the hell am I going to say to him? Supposing he really did have something to do with Celia's death? And Marianna's, too? And Sylvia's? And poor Bob Tuggey's?

He reached the driveway. It sloped at a sharp angle in front of the house, with three large Mercedes-Benzes parked in it: an old-fashioned open-topped tourer, in a dull shade of German field grey; a large bulbous black 1950s' limousine; and a 1960s' 380SL sports car, in white. All three cars were grimy with dust and tree-pollen and spattered with fruit-coloured bird-droppings.

The house itself was equally neglected. It had once been a very elegant adobe, painted white, with a long front verandah and a curved Mexican-style porch. Now its single-storey roof was heaped with a thick toupee of dried-up creepers, the paint was flaking, and two of the steps leading up to the porch had rotted and collapsed.

Lloyd could see the garage that had been converted into a 'study centre'. It was a flat-roofed side-building built out of whitewashed cinder-blocks, with sun-bleached wooden doors. He found it difficult to imagine that Celia had willingly come to a place like this. She had always been so fastidious about everything. Her clothes, her hair, the slightest mark on the living-room rug.

What he found even harder to believe was that she could have fallen for Otto and his bullshit about master races and immortality. She had been nervy, yes, like a good many brilliant musicians. But she had never been gullible, nor superstitious, and she had certainly never been racist.

He stood in the entrance to the driveway for nearly five minutes, trying to make up his mind whether he ought to go in or not.

In the end, his mind was made up for him by a security patrol car cruising past. The driver slowed down on the bend and stared at him suspiciously through orange-lensed sunglasses. He gave the driver a nod and a smile, and tried to march into the driveway as if he belonged there. Behind the prickly pear, he heard the security car hesitate, and then drive on.

Lloyd climbed over the broken steps and approached the front door. It looked as if it hadn't been painted in twenty years. It had probably once been bottle-green, but now it was blistered and faded. The only fixture that looked new was a large brass doorknocker in the shape of a fat, snarling lizard, and even that was discoloured by the sun, and had never been cleaned.

He listened for a few moments, then he picked up the knocker and tapped it twice. It sounded flat, no echo at all, like striking a coffin with a walking-stick. He waited and waited but there was no reply, no sound at all. He knocked again, much louder this time. Again that curious flatness, as if the knocker could only be heard *outside* the house.

He stepped back a little way, and called out, 'Anybody home? Mr Otto? Anybody else?' The sweat was running down the back of his prune-coloured Bijan polo-shirt. He tried the knocker a third time, and shouted some more, but it was pretty damned obvious that there was nobody home or, if there *was* anybody home, they were quite determined not to come to the door.

He took off his sunglasses and peered in at one of the dusty windows. Now that it was early afternoon, the sun was sloping into the back of the house, and he could just make out the silhouette of a bulky rounded armchair, a side-table, and a 1930s-style sunray mirror gleaming on the wall. There was something about the decor of the room which disturbed him. It was obviously decorated in 1930s' style. But he couldn't believe that anybody would have gone to such trouble and expense to recreate a 1930s' room that looked so formidably dull.

It was almost as if the room had been left this way, untouched, for over fifty years.

Treading quietly on the boarded verandah, Lloyd crept along the next window. Another sitting-room, rather smaller, with a dark-oak desk facing the back wall. Again the furniture was all pure 1930s ... a bent plywood chair, a bent plywood table, and a plastic *Volksempfänger* radio, of the type cheaply produced by the German government in the 1930s to spread their propaganda message as widely as possible. On the wall above the desk was a large framed drawing of the same symbol that featured on the charm that Bob Tuggey had given him – a lizard with its head crooked to one side, and its tail bent the opposite way.

Lloyd rubbed the grimy glass with the side of his hand, but he couldn't distinguish very much more. The rooms were furnished very oppressively, but in an age when fifteen-year-old kids were roaming the streets of Watts with loaded Uzis, it was hardly a Federal offence to have oppressive rooms.

He walked around the end of the house, tugging aside a mass of creeper that had partially collapsed from the roof, bringing down two or three dozen shingles along with it. The only window he could reach was a small sash window next to the chimney-breast, and he could only just manage to peek into it if he stood up on tiptoe.

He saw a third room, much larger than the other two, and filled with sunlight. Against the left-hand wall stood a black Bechstein upright piano, its top covered in a dark red velour piano-drape. The top of the piano was clustered with black-and-white framed photographs, although Lloyd couldn't make out who they were. In this room, there were several large bulbous armchairs, covered in anchovy-brown cotton, with 'modern' patterns of red art-deco rectangles. Beside one of the chairs stood a tall chrome ashtray, on which a dead half-burned cigar butt was perched.

When Lloyd craned his neck around to have a look at the other side of the room, however, he felt a thrill of surprise and alarm. Kneeling on the carpet, with his head bowed, was a young blond man. Very muscular, deep-chested and narrow-hipped, and – from what Lloyd could see of him – very good-looking, if you went for slab-sided profiles and straight noses and deep-set eyes. A jock. More than a jock, a body-builder. The type that Celia would have half-mockingly called an ODYS – an over-developed young Siegfried.

Lloyd stared at the man in fascination, trying to keep as still as possible, so that he wouldn't attract his attention. The man was completely naked, and his wrists and ankles were manacled behind him with shiny steel bands, at least an inch and a half wide, and those manacles in turn were chained to a ring in the floor.

Lloyd had been concerned at first that the man would look up and see him, but the man kept his head unremittingly bowed, as if he were staring at the fireplace and

131

trying to make the hours pass by sheer force of will.

What the hell is this guy doing, chained up to the floor? Maybe he's been kidnapped. Maybe Otto's holding him hostage. Or maybe he has chained himself up. You get to hear of stranger perversions than that.

He was certainly in peak physical shape, so he couldn't spend all of his time chained up here. His hair was cropped as flat as a flight-deck, too, so he must have been to a hairdresser recently. His pubic hair was as blond as the hair on his head, and he had a huge heavy penis that hung halfway down his thighs, not circumcised, but with the foreskin rolled back to expose the glans.

Lloyd stood on tiptoe staring at him for as long as he could, until his calf muscles began to judder with the effort. Then he carefully left the window, and retraced his steps along the verandah. He considered knocking at the door again, and even raised the lizard in his hand, but he let it down again, with nothing but the faintest tap. What was the use, when the only occupant that he had seen was incapable of moving more than a couple of inches?

He left the driveway, and walked back to his car. He was strongly tempted now to call Sergeant Houk. After all, Otto must be committing some kind of offence, just by having that young man chained up. If he was guilty of *that*, then surely he could be guilty of almost anything. Didn't the Lindbergh law say that kidnappers were liable to be sent to the gas chamber? Or was that something he had read in that Joseph Wambaugh book about *The Onion Field*, and now half remembered?

He drove back home, playing *La Bohème* on his car stereo. He decided, on balance, not to get in touch with Sergeant Houk, not yet. First of all he wanted to talk to Otto in person, face-to-face, and ask him some searching questions about Celia. If he contacted Sergeant Houk he would never get the chance. He wanted to ask Otto how the hell a beautiful intelligent girl like Celia could have been bewitched by all the squalid claptrap of racial purity and dominant human species and immortality.

Then he wanted to ask him what had given him the

132

right to intrude on their love and their happiness – whether he was directly responsible for Celia's death or not.

And then he wanted to ask him what kind of a creature he really was.

He called Waldo on his carphone. It took Waldo a while to answer. It was the middle of lunch, and the Original Fish Depot was hectically busy. When he came to the phone, he sounded flustered but cheerful.

'It's going good, Mr Denman, believe me. Already this lunchtime fifteen lobsters and ten specials.'

'That's great. I'll look in later. Meanwhile I'm off to the desert.'

'You're going to the desert? Why for?'

'A little research, that's all. Any messages? Any calls?'

Waldo coughed. 'Two people called by to see you. They said you were expecting them.'

'I wasn't expecting anybody.'

'Well ... you didn't say that you would come to the restaurant today, so I guessed that you weren't.'

'Who were they? Did they leave their names?'

'An old man and a woman. Some kind of a woman, too. Too big for me.'

An old man, and a woman. Lloyd felt a cold pain of anxiety and suspicion that was almost like neuralgia. 'They didn't leave their names?' he asked.

'They said not to worry. They said they'd find you, whatever.'

Lloyd said. 'This old guy ... was he wearing a hat, and a suit?'

'That's right, hat and a suit. And the woman was wearing all black leather. Looked like a biker, you know? Or maybe a hooker. Biker or hooker, one of the two. Or maybe she was a restaurant critic.' Waldo thought that this was funny, and laughed until he coughed.

Lloyd laid down the phone. This was a new and distinctly disturbing development. He was looking for Otto, but at the same time it seemed as if Otto was looking for *him*. The only reason that Otto had been out when he called at the house on Paseo Delicias was because Otto had been calling at the Original Fish Depot.

So what did Otto want?

There was only one possibility. The charm with the lizard on it. The same lizard that Lloyd had seen on the wall of Otto's house. Unca Tug had called him to say that the charm hadn't belonged to Celia, and the only way that Unca Tug could have found *that* out is if somebody had come looking for it. Somebody had come looking for the lizard charm and Unca Tug had died by fire. Somebody had come looking for the Wagner libretto, too, and Sylvia had died by fire.

Lloyd was beginning to feel sure that all this burning was down to Otto, and that Otto was not simply some religious and racialist wacko, but gravely dangerous. A homicidal madman with a taste for random violence was frightening enough: but a homicidal madman with his own rationale for changing the world was even more terrifying.

He stopped at a gas station at Escondido, and a little tubby lady in a back-to-front baseball cap filled up his BMW.

'Nice car,' she commented.

'I like it,' said Lloyd.

'My old man, he wouldn't have a German car for all the world,' she remarked.

'Oh?'

She wiped a dab of grease from the end of her nose. 'He was in the 4th Armoured Division during the war. Liberated some of the concentration camps.'

Lloyd gave her his credit card. 'In that case, I guess he's got a reason.'

'Won't even drink Milwaukee-brewed beer, for fear that it's made by Germans.'

It was a long and pleasant, calming drive, out to the Anza Borrego Desert. The road wound up through trees and mountains, and the quiet communities of Ramona and Santa Ysabel. Lloyd stopped at Julian for a cheeseburger and a beer, and then drove onward, into the dusty scrubby outskirts of the desert itself.

On the car stereo, he played a tape that he had found of plangent rock'n'roll from the Woodstock days: Country Joe and the Fish, the Doors, Captain Beefheart and his Magic Band. It brought back memories of business college; furry sideburns and flared jeans; girlfriends with miniskirts and chains around their hips and long shining hair; his first car (a Beetle, with a Peace symbol painted on the door); his first joint (pukish); sitting crosslegged all night in a friend's poster-plastered apartment, drinking Thunderbird Red and talking about Meaning and Being Yourself, Man, and how they were all going to go to London and find out Where It Was At.

He had stopped looking for meaning a long time ago. Once he had started work, he hadn't had the time. As for being yourself, he had discovered how incredibly easy that was, once he had stopped trying to be like somebody else (Paul Newman, for example, in *Cool Hand Luke*, or George Peppard in *The Carpetbaggers*). He had never made it to London, but he guessed that since the Swinging Era had long since passed away, London probably wouldn't be much different from anyplace else, all Burger Kings and bumper-to-bumper traffic – no more Where It Was At than Indianapolis or Pittsburgh or San Francisco.

He thought of the first time he had seen Celia, at that charity dinner at the Rancho Bernardo Inn. She had stepped out of the doorway of El Bizcocho restaurant, and the sun had dropped into her hair like a sign from the angels above. *This is the girl for you, Lloyd, here she is, we'll even light her up for you, so there won't be any mistake.*

His throat tightened, and he sniffed. He missed her, by God how much he missed her. He found a tissue in the glove-box and loudly blew his nose.

He had been worried that it would be difficult to find the place where the bus had burned, but he came to the crest of a rise in the road, and there it was, about a couple

135

of hundred feet off to his left, a blackened skeleton, more like a charcoal sketch of a bus than a real bus.

Movingly, the skeleton had been decorated with scores of white ribbons, tied in fluttering bows – tributes from relatives and passing motorists to all the people who had died in it. A single car was parked beside it now, a red open-topped Camaro.

Lloyd turned off the blacktop and drove slowly across the scrub. He parked not far away from the Camaro and climbed out. White dust blew away from his tyres and the wind whistled softly past his car antenna. He walked toward the bus and stood staring at it, the saddest memorial to death by fire that he had ever seen.

As he stood there, a young woman came walking around the side of the wreck. She was dark-haired, tall, and she was wearing a short black dress. She came up to him, and said, 'Hallo, there. Are you a relative?'

Lloyd shook his head. 'Just a friend.'

'It was such a tragedy,' the young woman said. She was wearing wrap-around sunglasses, so that it was difficult for Lloyd to tell what she looked like. But she had high cheekbones and a strong jawline, that well-bred look that distinguishes many of the children of good-looking California parents. She was large-breasted but very narrow-waisted, and she had what a political friend of Lloyd's had once called congressional committee legs – in other words, they went on and on and you thought they were never going to come to an end.

She said, abstractedly, 'I didn't think I wanted to see it. But in the end I had to. It was like seeing Mike. I didn't think that I could bear it. But I did, and at least I won't have nightmares about it, trying to imagine what he looked like, and never knowing.'

'Mike?' asked Lloyd.

'My husband, Mike Kerwin. I'm Kathleen Kerwin.'

Lloyd shook hands. 'Lloyd Denman. I hope you'll accept my condolences. It must have been a terrible shock.'

She shrugged, to show her feeling of helplessness. 'I was working in my shop and two state troopers came in

136

and said that he was dead. I couldn't understand it. He wasn't even supposed to be here.'

'He wasn't?' asked Lloyd. 'I had a friend on this bus – well, a friend of my fiancée's ... well, a friend of my *late* fiancée's. She worked with the San Diego Opera Company. Nobody knew what the hell *she* was doing out here, either.'

Kathleen said, 'They kept saying things on TV, like it's a suspected Colombian drug massacre. Or it's a mass suicide pact. But Mike wasn't into drugs, he was a manager for San Diego Federal. And he was so happy ... we were going to start a family and everything.'

Lloyd said, 'Do you mind if we talk about this? I've been trying to do a little detective work on my own, trying to find out what happened. Maybe you can help me.'

'Well, certainly,' said Kathleen. 'Are you a private detective or something?'

'Not me. I run a fish restaurant.'

She almost managed to smile. 'Do you want to talk now, or later? It's very hot out here.'

'As a matter of fact, I came out here looking for an Indian kid,' said Lloyd. 'The newspapers said that he was the only witness to the burning. I was wondering if there was any chance that he could give me some kind of clue who did it.'

Kathleen looked around, as if she expected to see the Indian boy standing not far away. 'Didn't the police talk to him?'

'Oh, sure the police talked to him. But I'm not too sure that the police would have asked him the right questions. It seems to me that there's more going on here than meets the eye. I mean, this whole thing has some very weird aspects to it. Like your husband, for instance. You know he wasn't a crack dealer or a potential suicide. Neither was Marianna, the girl from the Opera, not a chance of it. So what were they both doing here, out in the desert, on a bus, getting themselves burned to death?'

Kathleen said, in a flat voice, 'The police told me that none of them tried to escape.'

'Well, that's right, they didn't. They just sat here and burned.'

They were silent for a moment. It was eerie out here, on the face of this baking-hot desert, with the wind sighing through the black-charred wreckage of the bus, and fluttering the white ribbons.

'I thought I'd drive up the road a way and see if I can track down that Indian kid,' said Lloyd. 'Why don't you come along, too? He can't live too far away, he's blind.'

Kathleen looked at Lloyd in surprise. 'But if he's blind . . .?'

'He didn't see anything, but he *heard* something. He may have heard more, if he could only remember it. Whatever, it's worth a try.'

'All right, then,' Kathleen agreed. 'But there's something I have to do. It won't take a minute.'

'Sure thing,' Lloyd told her.

While Lloyd waited, she went to her car, opened the trunk, and took out a wreath of white silk ribbons and white silk flowers. Across the centre was written the words *Michael Kerwin, My Beloved Husband, Now You'll Never Die*. She walked across to the bus, and tied it on to the front. Then she lowered her head for a moment in a silent farewell.

They drove less than a mile and a half further on before they reached a sharp left-hand turnoff. A sun-faded sign pointed north-westwards for GAS – FOOD – INDIAN R-T-FAX. Lloyd turned and Kathleen, in her Camaro, followed him.

They followed a range of low sprawling hills, occasionally dipping deep down into the shadows of an arroyo, and then rising up into the sunshine again. After about two more miles, they saw a 76 petrol station in the distance, with a small barn-like building standing next to it, and a ramshackle collection of trailers and pick-up trucks at the back, and a sign saying *Trailers 4 Rent*. Three windpumps circled overhead, and stray dogs roamed the perimeter.

As they came closer, they passed a large handpainted signboard which announced *Indian Jack's Genuine Pechanga Souvenirs. Beer—Hot Dogs—Blankets—Beads. Turkwise Jewelre. Video Rental.*

They pulled up outside the barnlike building, the double doors of which were opened wide, and hung around like a roadside shrine with feathered war-bonnets and saddles, and brightly coloured blankets and pipes-of-peace, rope and chaps and all kinds of Indian souvenir junk. A rusted Coca-Cola machine juddered noisily at the side of the doorway, and a little further away, at the end of a long chain, as if to prevent it from hopping off, stood an old-fashioned one-legged bubble-gum machine half-filled with sun-bleached gumballs.

A pre-teenage boy with dark glasses and black shoulder-length hair was sitting on a rocker in the doorway, smoking a cigarette and listening to Prince on a Sony Walkman. To him, the volume of 'When Doves Cry' must have been ear-achingly loud, because Lloyd could hear what the music was while he was still ten feet away.

'I'm looking for a kid called Tony Express,' said Lloyd.

The boy pulled a face, without taking off his earphones. Kathleen suggested, 'I don't think he heard you.'

Lloyd stepped forward, lifted up the boy's left earphone, and yelled into his ear, 'I'm looking for a kid called Tony Express.'

The boy lifted off his headset and resentfully rubbed his ear. 'Shit, man, I may be blind but I sure as hell ain't deaf.'

'I'm sorry,' Lloyd told him. 'You must be Tony Express.'

'What's it to you if I am?'

'I've been looking for you, that's what.'

'Well, now you've found me, man. What do you want?'

'A little help, that's all.'

'Sure thing. How about some really neat moccasins, all hand-made, or maybe a pipe-tamper made of genuine bone, or a cradleboard? These cradleboards look great, you know, you can fill them with arrangements of dried flowers, and hang them on your kitchen wall. I've sold a whole bunch of them to Cannell & Chaffin.'

'Cannell & Chaffin, the interior designers?' Lloyd looked at Kathleen in amazement. 'Can you believe this kid?' he asked her. 'A young upwardly mobile Pechanga.'

'You got to move with the mood, man,' Tony Express replied. 'How about a sundance doll?'

He groped to one side of his chair and lifted up a long stick decorated with skin and fur and squirrel-tails and beads. On the top of it, a small cross face had been painted.

'What's that for?' asked Kathleen.

'It grants you revenge, if you ask it nicely.'

'Who said anything about revenge?' said Lloyd.

Tony Express let out a high, cracking laugh. 'Nobody said nothing about revenge, man. You didn't have to. You didn't come here to buy nothing, did you, or else you'd've been asking me by now how much my blankets were, or did I take Visa, or coming out with stuff like "Look at that wonderful weather-dance shirt, darling, I could wear it to play golf."'

'You've got a pretty jaundiced view of the world, don't you?' Lloyd asked him, immediately regretting the use of the world 'view'.

'What's "jaundiced"?'

'Sour, cynical,' Lloyd told him.

Tony Express smiled. 'That's because I can't see it, man. I can't see its colours and I can't see its false bright faces. I can't even imagine what a colour *is*.'

'So what's all this about revenge?'

'That's what *you* should be telling *me*, man. You're the one who came here looking for it. You don't want to buy, so you must want to talk, and who comes all the way out here to Nothing Junction in a fancy foreign car, just to talk to some blind Indian kid about the weather, or how you can't get good help any more?

'Come on, man, get serious. You came here to talk about the only thing that's happened here in twenty years, man, that bus burning out, and all those people getting themselves killed.'

'I could be a cop,' Lloyd suggested.

'Unh-hunh,' said Tony Express. 'You're not a cop

because cops don't drive fancy foreign cars and they don't wear Geoffrey Beene aftershave, either. So you must be an insurance investigator or a relative of somebody who died. And since you didn't introduce yourself as soon as you arrived, "Listen, my name's Dick Head and I represent the Never-Pay Insurance Company Inc.", I guess you're a relative. And when somebody gets killed, what do relatives want more than anything else, especially in a Judeo-Christian society? They want revenge. Have a sun-dance doll, thirty-six bucks plus tax.'

Lloyd shook his head, and said to Kathleen, 'This guy's so sharp he's going to cut himself. How come you know "Judeo-Christian" but you don't know "jaundiced"?'

Tony Express tapped his nose with his finger. ' "Judeo-Christian" was on television, man. This brave always listens heap good, you understand? And when you listen – when you *really* listen – you can always tell exactly what's going down. Nobody can ever pull the wool over your eyes, man, because you ain't got no eyes to have the wool pulled over. I heard your car engine, man, and that's a six-cylinder import with overhead cams, and if you'd left it running a little longer I would have told you what it says on your bumper stickers. In fact I can tell you now, it says *Save The Whales*.'

'Actually it says *I Don't Brake For Smartass Blind Kids*,' Lloyd retorted.

Tony Express gave him a lopsided grin. 'All right, man, I'm sorry. I've been running off at the mouth again. I do it sometimes. Either I'm silent and moody and don't talk to nobody for weeks, or else I get this verbal dire-rear. I spend too much time alone, that's the problem. I guess I'm over-educated, too. I listen to the radio all day and the teevee for most of the night. What else is there to do? My teacher says I'm brilliant but wayward.'

'Are you really twelve years old?' Lloyd asked him.

Tony Express nodded. 'Twelve, going on thirteen.'

'In that case, you're too young to smoke. Does your father let you smoke?'

'My father's away on business. Avoiding the cops in

other words. My grandfer's taking care of me, John Dull Knife. He lives in that old Airstream trailer way in the back, by the fence.'

Lloyd said, 'Do you mind if I ask you a couple of questions about the day the bus burned?'

'No problem, what's it worth?'

'A sawbuck?'

'No problem.'

Kathleen had already perched herself on the hitching-rail at the front of the store. Lloyd dragged over a cracker-barrel and sat on that.

'It says in the paper you heard somebody talking while the bus was on fire.'

'That's right,' Tony Express agreed. 'He kept on saying "you knew us, you knew us".'

'Could it have been that he wasn't saying "you knew us", but "Junius"?'

Tony Express angled his head slightly. 'Say that again, man.'

'Junius. *Junius*, like somebody's name.'

'Again, man.'

Lloyd repeated it six or seven times. At last Tony Express lifted his small nail-bitten hand as an indication that he should stop.

'Well?' asked Lloyd.

'You're right,' said Tony Express. 'It was "Junius". I said "you knew us" because I never heard the name Junius before.'

'You're certain about that?' Lloyd asked him.

'Absolutely. I'd swear it on the Bible.'

'Now… this could be more difficult,' said Lloyd. 'Can you remember if he said anything else? Anything less distinct? Did he sing, maybe? Did he say anything in a foreign language?'

Tony Express thought about that, and then slowly shook his head. 'I don't think so, man. There was so much noise going on when that bus was burning. Crackling, popping. Like sticking your head in a bowl of Rice Krispies.'

142

Lloyd sat back in disappointment. 'So there was nothing at all?'

'Well ... one thing. But I couldn't be sure, man. I wouldn't swear to it.'

'Tell me anyway.'

'After the bus had been burning for quite a while, I thought I heard a sound like a trumpet or something. It was probably the bus, you know, the driver falling on to the horn, or maybe the alarm circuits melting. But that was all.'

'One thing more,' Lloyd asked him. 'If you heard the man's voice again, the one who said *Junius*, do you think you could identify it? Do you think you could pick it out and say, "yes, that's the guy."'

Tony Express didn't hesitate. 'Any time. Any time at all.'

'You seem very confident about that,' put in Kathleen.

'I've got a phonographic memory,' Tony Express told her. 'I can remember voices and sounds exactly. My teacher says it's uncanny. I don't know what's supposed to be so uncanny about it, especially since I can't see. I have this terrific nose for smells, too. You had garlic last night.'

'What?' said Lloyd.

'Just kidding around, man. But if you can find this dude, I can pick him out.'

'Good,' Lloyd told him. 'That's excellent. Here's your ten bucks, and here's another ten, in case it gets lonesome. Do you think I could call you, if I ever manage to find this guy, and ask you to identify his voice?'

'Sure thing. Do you think it was him who torched the bus?'

'I can't tell for certain, but it's beginning to look that way. Here ... here's my card. It's a restaurant in La Jolla. I won't be there most of the time, but if you ask for Waldo, he'll help you out.'

'Waldo, hunh?' asked Tony Express, with obvious scepticism. 'Like in Mr Magoo?'

'That's right, like in Mr Magoo.'

'You know what Mr Magoo's problem was, don't you, man?' asked Tony Express. 'He looked and he looked, and he *still* couldn't see.'

— TWELVE —

Joe North arrived back at his apartment above the Smiling Sashimi restaurant on West Washington Street shortly after seven o'clock. To reach his front door, he had to elbow his way through the chattering, unhelpful line of would-be diners who were already out in the street waiting for tables. The Smiling Sashimi was one of the cheapest and most popular Japanese restaurants around Hillcrest, although, after a month-long binge of eating there almost every evening after it had first opened, Joe hardly patronized it at all now.

Marianna had always made corny jokes about it. 'You're too tempura-mental,' she used to tease him.

He closed the street door behind him (red-painted, to match the restaurant) and climbed the narrow staircase to the second floor. The lights didn't work, and he had to feel his way up in darkness, carrying a heavy sack of marketing in the crook of his arm.

He wasn't surprised that the lights were out. Joe had sent the name of Mr Puls the landlord to the *Guinness Book of World Records* as the Meanest Bastard on God's Earth. Mr Puls believed that if it didn't specifically state in the rental agreement that the tenant had the right to see where he was going, then he had no legal obligation to supply lightbulbs.

'If you're shortsighted, do I have to buy you eyeglasses?' he always shouted.

Joe groped his way blindly along the landing until he found his front door. He had to set his shopping sack down on his feet while he struggled to find his key, and then to jab it into the lock.

He sniffed. He thought there was an odd *burnt* smell on the stairs. He was used to the smell of sukiyaki and chicken teriyaki, and once the whole kitchen downstairs had caught fire. From Joe's apartment, it had sounded like the sinking of the *Musashi* at Leyte Gulf, screaming and yelling and doors slamming, and afterwards the building had smelled like scorched bean-curd for weeks.

But this burnt smell was different. This smell was like overheated radiators, or saunas. A dry smell. Not oily, not smoky. He couldn't place it. It was like nothing he had ever smelled before.

He opened his front door and switched on the light. He kicked the door shut behind him. He had lived over the Smiling Sashimi ever since it had been the Siete Mares Mexican restaurant, and *he* had been deputy assistant scenery painter at Civic Theater. He kept telling himself that he ought to move somewhere classier, somewhere up the coast, but somehow there never seemed to be time. Or money. Even for one studio room, a shower, and a kitchen so small that you had to step into the hallway to open the oven door, he was paying what his mother was paying for a whole three-bedroomed house in Minnesota.

He backed into the kitchen and set his groceries down on the counter. A frozen lasagne, a large bag of cheese Nachos, a dozen Washington Red apples, some cinnamon-flavoured dental floss, a *TV Guide*, and a bottle of chianti. Now was that living, or was that a Loneliness Set in a brown paper sack?

He tore open the lasagne box and slid the lasagne into the microwave oven to defrost. He could still smell that strange overheated smell. Maybe the Nips had accidentally left one of their woks over a hot flame for too long. Maybe it was diesel oil wafting over from the naval station, or airplane fuel from the airport.

Rattling open his kitchen drawer, he scrabbled through shoals of ill-assorted cutlery until he found a waiter's friend. He opened up the bottle of chianti, and poured himself a large glass with his right hand while he adjusted the microwave with his left. He hummed the Humming Song from *Madame Butterfly.*

He was still humming it when he went through to the

studio room, and switched on the lamps in there.

He dropped his glass of wine on to the rug. He heard it fall, a dull ringing noise, but he didn't make any attempt to catch it, didn't look down.

Sitting on the end of his bed, quite upright, her hands held loosely in her lap, was Marianna. Against the jazzy red-and-yellow gaiety of the Mexican throwover that covered his bed, she looked monochromatic and severe. Her hair was tucked up into a black beret. She wore black sunglasses and a black belted raincoat and black stockings. Her face was as grey as clay.

'Jesus,' said Joe. 'I'm seeing things. Jesus, I'm seeing things.'

He turned around, and went directly back to the kitchen, and stared at the top half of his face in the mirror that was propped on top of his Smiling Sashimi calendar. The top half of his face stared back at him like a Venetian carnival mask. Blank, festive, and cruelly uncommunicative.

He told his eyes, 'I saw Marianna sitting on the bed.' His eyes stared back at him and didn't blink.

'Marianna's dead and I just went into the studio and there she was sitting on the end of the bed, wearing these shades and staring at me.'

He was trembling. He hadn't trembled as wildly as this since he had caught the Asian 'flu, his second year at the San Diego Opera, and almost died.

'She was there!' he yelled at the mirror, pounding his fist on the kitchen counter so hard that his box of dental floss jumped on to the floor. 'I walked into the studio and she was there!'

He covered his face with his hands. Marianna's death had shocked him, disoriented him badly. Even though he and Marianna hadn't always got along too well, he had always known that she was *there*, that he could call her, that he could surprise her, even if she told him to take a hike. It was only when she had completely disappeared from the world that he had been able to assess the size of his affection for her, the same way that you don't know how much you're going to miss a tooth until the dentist pulls it and you're left with this huge gaping Grand Canyon cavity in your mouth and you can't eat pizza for a month.

A soft voice said, 'You weren't dreaming, Joe.'

'See, now I'm hearing things,' Joe told himself, lowering his hands. 'It's the shock, right? I've been suppressing the shock. But now that I've talked to Lloyd about it, the dam's broken. I'm not shocked any more. Just seeing things, and hearing things.'

'Joe,' said the voice, amused.

He turned his neck stiffly sideways. Marianna was standing in the doorway, in that tilted black beret and those impenetrable black sunglasses, her hands thrust into her raincoat pockets.

'You're real,' he told her.

She smiled, and stepped into the kitchen. He smelled heat again, that dry metallic heat. 'Of course I'm real, Joe. I'm more real now than I was before.'

'Well – *hanh* – good! What's that supposed to mean? *More* real?'

'Didn't you ever love me?' asked Marianna. 'Don't you remember those times we went to Mexico? Dancing at Tijuana Tilly's? Eating ourselves sick on mixiote? Laughing, getting drunk? Remember that night at Popotla?'

'You died on that bus,' Joe told her.

She turned her head away. 'I was burned, Joe, but I didn't die.'

'Everybody died on that bus, Marianna. You included. I'm experiencing some kind of hallucination here, caused by delayed shock. You hear that, Joe? You're hallucinating.'

'No, Joe,' Marianna told him. 'I'm here, I'm here for real, and I'm here for ever.'

He stared at her. In spite of his natural scepticism, he was beginning to believe that *no*, she wasn't dead, and that *yes*, she was real. He slowly reached out his hand and touched her arm.

'I can feel you,' he said, but more to himself than to her.

147

'Yes, you can feel me. I'm real.'

'And for ever?'

'Yes.'

'So Otto was telling the truth all along?'

'Yes, Joe. Otto was telling us the truth all along.'

Joe covered his mouth with his hand, and leaned against the kitchen counter as if he couldn't think of anything to say.

'Did you tell Lloyd about Otto?' asked Marianna. He could still feel her heat. *Heat, heat, heat.* It was like standing next to an electric fire.

'I don't believe this,' Joe protested. 'You can't be real. It isn't possible.'

'Joe, it was easy, once I'd made that leap. Once I had that faith. I'm pure now, Joe, purified. Nothing but smoke and soul.'

Joe said, 'I'm going crazy. Listen – I'm going to leave now. Okay? I'm going to walk out of this apartment for a while and if you're real you'll still be here when I get back. But if you're not ... well, I don't know. I'm going to have to think about that. Kirsty McLaren said that her shrink was pretty good.'

'Joe,' said Marianna, 'I'm real.'

'Sure you are. Sure you're real. Just like Daffy Duck's real and Batman's real and Roadrunner's real. They must be real, you can see them on TV.'

'Joe ...' Marianna began, stepping forward.

Joe bunched up his fists and roared at her like an angry two-year-old. 'Damn it, Marianna! I'm scared! You scare me! You're dead, but here you are!'

'Joe, shush, it's okay. Everything's fine. I'm smoke and I'm soul and I'm absolutely fine.'

'I'm going to call Lloyd.'

'No, Joe, don't call Lloyd.'

'Jesus, Marianna, this is insane. I'm going to *have* to call Lloyd.'

'Did you tell Lloyd about Otto?'

'Of course I told Lloyd about Otto. What do you think?'

The smell of heat grew even stronger. Joe was so hot

that he was sweating, and the sweat stung his eyes. All the time he was backing away from Marianna but Marianna kept circling around and edging nearer, circling and edging, until Joe began to feel that he would never get away from her.

Marianna said, 'When you left the group, Joe, Otto made you promise that you would never tell. Don't you remember? You took an oath.'

'That wasn't any oath.'

'You laid your hand on the Book of the Salamander and you swore not to tell.'

Joe let out a half-broken laugh. 'Hey, come on. The Book of the Salamander isn't exactly the Holy Bible.'

'No, it isn't. It's greater than the Holy Bible. It doesn't just tell you that life has its miracles, it tells you what the miracles are and how they can be achieved.'

'It's bullshit.'

Marianna shook her head. 'Don't blaspheme, Joe. You've already broken your solemn oath. Don't blaspheme, too.'

'It may be blasphemy to you, but it's bullshit to me.'

He reached out for the telephone, but Marianna seized his wrist to stop him. There was a sharp sizzle of burned hair and seared skin, and Joe let out a bellow of pain. *'Aaaahhh! Christ! Aaaahhh!'* He wrenched his arm away and held it up. Marianna's fingers had burned five scarlet stripes around his wrist, and his skin was already bubbling up into a mass of blisters.

Shocked, he stalked stiffly into the kitchen, and turned the cold tap on full. He held his wrist under the running water until the agonizing burning was reduced to a thick, numb ache. Marianna came and stood beside him, watching him. Her grey face was impassive. There was no telling if she was pleased or sorry.

'You can get the fuck out of here,' Joe told her, his voice shaking.

'You have to keep your oath, Joe. You can't tell anyone. Otherwise we're all at risk.'

'Risk? What risk? Christ, how did you burn me like that?'

Marianna reached out for him again, but he backed away. 'Just keep off, okay? Just stay away.'

But Marianna continued to edge closer, and now she slowly twisted open the top button of her raincoat. Joe retreated to the opposite side of the kitchen, keeping his eyes on her all the time. He felt behind him for the counter, then for the drawer handle. As Marianna released the second button of her raincoat, and then the third, he tugged open the drawer and rooted around inside it for his carving-knife.

'Joe ... so long as you swear to keep your oath ... everything's going to be fine. But you have to swear.'

She unbuttoned the last button, and with a twist of her shoulders, the raincoat dropped on to the kitchen floor. Underneath, she was naked, her skin shining pearly-grey. Her small dark-nippled breasts were just the same as Joe remembered, her rounded stomach, her heavy thighs. But she had a dull subcutaneous glow that reminded him of nothing but death. As a boy, Joe had seen a drowned man dragged out of the Cahokia Canal in East St Louis, and his skin had glowed with the same dim putrescence.

Around her waist, Marianna wore a wide black belt that was buckled so tight that it made her flesh bulge out, top and bottom. The belt's clasp was in the shape of a lizard, inside a circle.

'Joe, don't you want to kiss me, Joe, the way we used to? Don't you want to hold me?'

'You just keep your fucking distance,' Joe warned her. His fingers closed around the blade of his sharpest vegetable-knife, and he felt it slice through flesh. He turned the knife around, and picked it up, and brandished it in front of Marianna's face. Blood was running down his fingers and dripping from his burned wrist.

'Don't you want to make love to me, Joe?' Marianna coaxed him, coming closer. She reached her hand down between her legs, and started rubbing herself sensually, and purring. 'Remember those nights in Tijuana, Joe? Not a wink of sleep. Make love to me, Joe, come on, make love to me.'

Joe stared in horrified fascination as she plunged her

hand deeper and deeper between her legs. She opened the lips of her vagina with one hand and slid the index finger of her other hand right inside, right up to the knuckle, and stirred it around and around. She closed her eyes, and threw back her head, and cooed, 'Come on, Joe, I need you so much ... come on, Joe, I love you.'

Joe hesitated for only a second. Then he dodged to the right, colliding with the edge of the icebox, and threw himself out of the kitchen door, into the hallway.

Marianna's reaction was instantaneous. She clawed for his shoulder as he hit the icebox, then jumped on to his back as he made his way to the front door. Immediately, Joe felt as if his back had been doused in blazing petrol. He screamed in pain, and staggered sideways under the weight. His shirt scorched, then burst into flames. He twisted and grunted, and tried to swing Marianna against the wall, but she was clinging on too tight, and her legs were burning into his sides, into his jeans, into his skin, into his flesh, and her arms were branding his shoulders like meat.

Reaching behind him, he stabbed at her frantically with his vegetable knife. But there didn't seem to be anything there to stab. In spite of her heat, in spite of her weight, she appeared to be completely insubstantial. Like smoke. Like someone's soul. Like nothing at all.

'*Marianna!*' he roared, with his clothes on fire and his hair shrivelling.

But Marianna shrieked, 'It's a game! It's a game! You have to guess who I am!'

'*Oh God!*' cried Joe, dropping to his knees. '*Oh God, Marianna, you're burning me!*'

'It's a game, Joe! Who am I? Who am I?' and she clapped her hands over his eyes, so that he wouldn't be able to see her.

Smoke poured out from between Marianna's fingers as she burned her way through Joe's upper cheeks and eyelids, and then fried his eyes. Through all of that pain, Joe felt his eyeballs burst, and heard the sharp sizzle of optic jelly. He was beyond screaming. The pain was too much. The horror of being blinded was more than his brain could accept. All his brain was interested in right now was survival.

He stabbed at her wildly, stabbed again. But she forced him down and rolled him over on to his back and forced him flat on to the floor.

All he could think of was pain. It flooded over him, as if he had been washed over by a tidal wave of concentrated hydrochloric acid. He shuddered and shuddered and windmilled wildly at her with his fists, but she pressed down on him more and more heavily, and there came a moment when he understood that it was futile, that he was going to die.

It was at that moment that he felt no pain at all. His brain had plainly decided that he didn't need any further warnings that his body was under attack. He had accepted death, pain was no longer necessary.

He lay still, not dead yet, but remarkably calm; as calm as the dead; as calm as anyone for whom there are no alternatives left.

He didn't even flinch when Marianna reached down and opened his jeans with fingers that scorched the denim.

'You broke your oath, Joe,' she sang. 'You broke your oath.'

With burning-hot hands she prized his penis out of his jeans, and stretched it upwards. The skin shrivelled and blistered. The spongy tissue crackled, and smoke poured out of the meatus. All around it, Joe's pubic hairs burned like scores of tiny fuses. Then Marianna was holding what looked like a flaring candle, the last fiery moments of Joe's manhood.

Sometime after that, Joe thought he heard someone singing. It was 'Bei Mir Bist Du Schön'. 'Please let me explain, *bei mir bist du schön*, means that you're grand ... again I'll explain ... it means you're the fairest in the land ...'

Marianna took off her dark glasses and stared down at him with empty eyes. Then she kissed him, and his mouth caught fire, and he died.

— THIRTEEN —

Kathleen lived in Escondido. On the night of her husband's death, her older sister Lucy had flown in from Tucson, Arizona, to stay with her. But Lloyd persuaded her to come back with him to La Jolla that evening, and to have dinner with him at the Original Fish Depot.

'You can't say that we don't have something in common,' Lloyd told her.

'But I don't have anything to wear.'

He smiled, shook his head. 'The Fish Depot isn't formal. Not unless you want it to be. And, besides, you look great as you are.'

Waldo was delighted to see Lloyd, and shook his hand up and down as if he were priming a reluctant pump. 'You want dinner, Mr Denman? Yes, of course! Look how busy we are! Full up to bursting! And every night this week!'

'Maybe I should stay away more often,' Lloyd suggested, as Waldo fussily piloted them over to the special guest table by the window, overlooking the Cove, and lit the candles.

'Mr Denman, we miss you,' Waldo told him. 'We work hard, we fill up the restaurant. But the restaurant is yours. Your dream, yes? Your inspiration. You know what my grandfather always used to say, when we walked on the beach? You can take everything away from a man. His family, his money, his clothes, his dignification. But you can never take away his ideas.' His voice dropped grimly. 'Not unless you are prepared to kill him.'

Lloyd clapped Waldo on the back. 'After Plato, this man is the world's greatest philosopher,' he told Kathleen. 'He's also the world's worst flatterer. Beware! That's how he gets whatever he wants.'

They sat facing each other over the dipping candle-light. Kathleen looked tired but very pretty. She had strong cheekbones, wide brown eyes. A mixture of determination and vulnerability that Lloyd found very appealing. The kind of woman who would cry when things went wrong; but who would wipe away the tears and promise herself that nothing would ever upset her so badly again.

Nil illegitimae carborundum. Don't let the bastards grind you down.

'When you've been married for so long, you forget what it's like, being alone,' Kathleen told him.

Lloyd nodded. 'Celia and I weren't officially married, but I guess you could say that we were married in the eyes of God. I never expected to spend my life with anyone else.'

'Tom misses him so much,' said Kathleen.

'Tom?'

'Our son. Our one and only.'

'I'm real sorry,' said Lloyd. 'Look – here's the starter.'

They began with coquilles St Jacques with a light mornay glaze. While they were eating, Louis came out from the kitchen and asked them how they liked it. He was a thin, diminutive Frenchman from Marseilles, by way of New Orleans, with a concave chest and a pale waxy face, and a limited grasp of English. But he could cook with verve and delicacy, and flavour his creations as precisely as a pianist hitting the right note; and he was a living denial of Paul Prudhomme's notion that any chef lighter than eighteen stone can't cook shit.

'Louis, this is brilliant,' said Lloyd.

Louis modestly shook his head. 'Not brilliant, *monsieur.* But just as it should be.'

After he had returned to the kitchen, Lloyd shook his head and smiled. 'Did you hear that? It is how it should be. That man is so uncompromising. I've seen him throw away lobsters because he didn't like the colour of their shells.'

Kathleen said, 'You surprise me, you know. You don't

seem like the kind of guy who would want to open a restaurant.'

Lloyd shrugged. 'I fell into it, I guess. I was tired of insurance, I wanted to be free. I thought of starting my own outboard motor company ... in fact, I was better qualified to start an outboard motor company than anything else. I can strip an Evinrude blindfold. But I thought to myself, where's the class, where's the image? Where's the fun?'

'But a restaurant must be such hard work.'

'Are you kidding? This isn't work. This is complete and utter self-imposed slavery, from morning till night. And still the customers complain.'

Their mutual bereavement sustained them through the *hors d'oeuvres*. But when they got into the crabbed halibut they began to realize that they had very much more in common than the sudden death of somebody that they had loved. They both liked theatre, they both liked music, they both liked water sports. They both liked Maria Callas and Robbie Robertson and Woody Allen.

'You've been marvellous,' Kathleen told him, as they left the Original Fish Depot and walked out into the warm night air. 'It's pretty hard to have fun after something like this, but I've had fun.'

'I guess the world keeps on turning, no matter what,' Lloyd told her. 'Now, how about a ride home? You could leave your car in the parking-lot here, and I could have one of the waiters bring it out to you tomorrow.'

'All the way to Escondido? Come on, Lloyd, you're tired. I could take a cab.'

'Well ... if it doesn't sound too forward, maybe you could come back to my place for a nightcap, and then make up your mind what you want to do.'

She took hold of his arm. 'That doesn't seem too forward at all. In fact it sounds very inviting.' He was breathing the smell of her perfume, Ombre Rose, and her hair was very fine-filamented and shiny in the streetlight. Somehow her plain black dress made her even more alluring. It was no good pretending: he liked her a lot.

155

They climbed into his BMW and Lloyd backed out of his parking-space.

'I just love your licence plate,' Kathleen told him.

'What, FISHEE? I don't know. The joke's kind of worn off.'

They drove down the long swooping curves of the road that would take them to North Torrey. It was slightly foggy, a late-night ocean fog, and the lights all around them were blurred and star-whiskered.

Kathleen said, 'Do you know what Mike always used to tell me?'

Lloyd glanced at her quickly. 'Go on. What did Mike always tell you?'

'Mike always used to tell me that when his grandfather died, he took off north, all the way to Eureka, even further. He said it was the greatest spiritual experience of his life. He stood on the seashore way up north, in winter, and he heard his grandfather speak to him clear as a bell. He said his grandfather told him that nobody dies until they're completely forgotten, until everybody that ever knew them dies, too.'

'I guess that's right,' Lloyd told her. 'I guess it makes it a little easier.'

'Well, maybe,' Kathleen replied. 'But I think I'd feel better if I thought that Mike had gone for good. Vanished, you know? Just like he never existed. My God, Lloyd, he was alive a week ago. He held me in his arms. Now there's nothing. Nothing! I find that pretty damned hard to accept.'

Lloyd said, 'Did Mike belong to any kind of religious study group?'

Kathleen stared at him. 'Mike? You're kidding! He wasn't into religion at all! What made you ask me something like that?'

'I don't know, just fishing,' Lloyd said guardedly. He didn't want to tell her too much about Otto, not yet.

'He used to go bowling a couple of nights a week,' Kathleen volunteered.

'Do you know where?'

She stared at him. 'No, I don't know where. He went with a gang from the office. You're making it sound like it's something really important.'

'It could be, yes.'

'Then what are you trying to say? Was he doing something wrong? Was he mixed up in something illegal or something? Come on, Lloyd, you can't just let it go.'

Lloyd turned toward North Torrey. His face was lit up by the passing streetlights – lit, then shadowed, then lit, then shadowed. 'It seems like Celia and Marianna were both attending regular religious study groups run by a character called Otto. Otto, apparently, was offering them everlasting life.'

Kathleen frowned at him. 'Everlasting life? Are you serious?'

'My feelings exactly,' Lloyd told her. 'But it seems like a whole lot of people believed it. Enough people to make up a coachload, anyway.'

'What are you trying to say?' Kathleen demanded. 'Mike was always so positive. He couldn't have been interested in everlasting life, or anything like that. He wasn't even superstitious. He didn't mind spilling salt or breaking mirrors from time to time, or black cats crossing his path.'

'He wasn't into drugs?'

Kathleen shook her head very firmly. 'He hated drugs. He didn't smoke and he didn't drink. He had a physique like Sylvester Stallone. He ran three miles every morning before breakfast and he voted Democrat.'

Lloyd turned into the drive of his house, and killed the BMW's engine. 'I'm sorry, Kathleen, I guess I shouldn't try to play detective. All I manage to do is upset people.'

Kathleen laid her hand on his arm. 'You've been great. Really. That's not just flattery. I was beginning to wonder if there was any kind of future after Mike, whether life was worth living. I admire what you're trying to do, you know that? Even if you find that Celia took her own life because of depression, or PMT, or who knows what … at least you're not giving in. You're looking for answers. You're fighting back. That makes life worth living, doesn't it? That alone.'

They got out of the car, and Lloyd ushered Kathleen toward the house.

Kathleen said, 'Do you smell burning? Do you smell smoke?'

Lloyd sniffed. The sourness of burning was unmistakable, and as they approached the house he saw a blueish curtain of smoke hanging over the back yard. *Dear God,* he thought, *they've burned my house down.* He unlocked the front door and, turning round to Kathleen, said, 'Stay back!'

'It's still alight!' called Kathleen, frantically pointing toward the bedroom windows at the back. Reflected flames danced in the window of the house next door. Lloyd hesitated for a moment. If he opened up the front door, he might feed the fire with a huge surge of oxygen. On the other hand, he had to get inside to put it out. No matter how fast the Fire Department made it to North Torrey, his precious house would be ashes before they could connect up their first hose.

'Call the Fire Department!' he yelled at Kathleen.

'What?'

'Call the Fire Department! Call them now! Use the car phone!'

Kathleen shouted at him, 'You're not going inside? You can't!'

'Just call the Fire Department, will you?'

He hesitated for only a second. Then he unlocked the front door, shouldered it open, and rolled head-over-heels across the hallway. He heard the fire bellow like a wild animal, and felt the side of his face scorched. Crouched by the foot of the stairs, his hands clasped protectively over his head, he waited until the flames had subsided, then he stood up and quickly looked around him.

The living-room had been ransacked. All the drawers were hanging open, and all of the display-cabinets had been smashed. The air was thick with smoke, and Lloyd coughed and spat to clear it out of his lungs. Then he ducked toward the kitchen.

In the kitchen, the story was the same. There was so

much cutlery on the floor that it looked as if a fisherman had emptied his baskets of sardines on to it. Every jar was broken open. Coffee, rice, cookies, salt. Even the burners had been prized out of the hob.

They were looking for their lizard charm, thought Lloyd. *They wanted it so much so that they lost sight of the fact that it doesn't mean anything to me. Not yet, anyway. But it will.*

He hop-jumped across the living-room. The bedroom door was wide open, and the bedroom itself was a mass of fire. He could see his bedside table burning, and the photograph of Celia twisting and curling up. He could see flames licking out from under his bed. It was so hot that he couldn't approach closer than six or seven feet, holding his hand up to protect his eyes. He didn't have a fire-extingusher in the house, but he guessed that a few bowlfuls of water might douse it down. He hurried back to the kitchen, flicked on the tap, and waited impatiently while the red plastic washbowl noisily filled up with water.

Then he hurried back again, balancing the bowl, slopping water, but as he approached the fiery entrance to the bedroom, he realized that what he was attempting was completely futile. The bed was alight, with huge flames roaring up to the ceiling, and fabric burning in a blackened blizzard. The heat was huge; it dried the moisture on his eyeballs as soon as he approached; and when he tossed the bowlful of water, it did nothing more than sizzle momentarily, and vanish into the smallest puff of steam. He might just as well have tried spitting.

He threw the plastic bowl aside, and hurried across to his desk, where he kept his accounts, and his diaries, and the photograph albums that his mother had given him. If he could save nothing else, he could save those.

He fumbled for his keys, slotted them into the keyhole, and it was only then that he realized that the desk wasn't locked. Somebody had been here before him. Somebody with a key. He opened the desk and saw that everything had been searched and shuffled aside: diaries, photographs,

159

files, papers, passports, cheque books.

Still, he didn't have time to worry about that. He stuffed the most important papers into two large envelopes, and hunched his way across the living-room with his arms full. The bedroom was burning so ferociously now that long tongues of fire were roaring out of it, and the bureau beside the door was already sprouting flames. It would be only a matter of minutes before the whole house was ablaze.

Lloyd had almost reached the hallway when he heard somebody calling him.

'Lloyd! Wait! Lloyd!'

At first he thought it was Kathleen, and he yelled out, 'Kathleen! I'm okay! I'm coming out!'

But then he suddenly realized that the voice was coming from his left. He stopped, disoriented, and dropped some of his photograph albums.

'Lloyd! Wait! Please, Lloyd, wait!'

He shielded his eyes against the heat. The living-room was filling up with smoke and he could scarcely breathe. He coughed, and coughed, and coughed again. At first, he couldn't see anything. But then he began to distinguish a shadowy figure in the bedroom doorway. He smeared his eyes with his fingers, trying to focus. The figure wavered in the flames, but didn't attempt to move; as if the flames meant nothing, as if the flames were no more than confetti, or flowers, or bright running water.

'Lloyd, wait.'

Lloyd thought: *it can't be.* But he knew with a terrible certainty that it was. You don't have to see somebody's face in close-up to know for certain who they are. A shape, a suggestion, that's all you need. And this figure standing in the flames was the same figure that he had seen running away from him on the *Star of India*, the same figure that he had seen sitting opposite him at Tom Ham's Lighthouse.

Celia, no question about it. *Celia, self-cremated but immortal.*

For a second, she emerged from the flames. They ran

up her grey naked body, ran up her face, and her hair stood on end in torrential fire. She stared at Lloyd with black, impenetrable eyes.

'Lloyd, I need that charm. If I don't have that charm, Lloyd, I'll die.'

He stared at her in horror. Flames licked at her breasts, but didn't consume them. Flames licked at her face. What fascinated and frightened Lloyd more than anything else was the way in which flames licked into her eye-sockets.

'I have to have that charm, Lloyd. Please, give it to me.'

Lloyd hesitated for one more second, mesmerized by Celia's appearance, but then he heard the whooping of fire sirens approaching the house, and the moment of hesitation was broken. He ducked out of the living-room, along the hallway, and out into the night.

Kathleen was waiting for him on the sidewalk, just as a shining firetruck came around the corner with its lights flashing and its horn bellowing.

'Lloyd, are you okay?' she asked him. She was trembling.

'Sure, yes, sure. I tried to put it out, but it had too much of a hold.'

'I moved your car back, just in case.'

'Thanks.'

A firefighter came stalking up to Lloyd, adjusting the straps of his helmet. 'This your property, sir?'

Lloyd nodded.

'Is there anybody in there?'

Lloyd thought of Celia, standing in the doorway, empty-eyed, alight.

'No, officer. There's nobody in there.'

'No domestic animals?'

'No, none.'

'How did the fire start?' the firefighter asked him. Already the first hose was connected to the hydrant across the street, and two more firefighters were approaching the house behind a wide high-pressure spray.

'I have no idea. We just came back from having dinner. It looked as if it started in the bedroom, but God knows how.'

'Chief!' called one of the firefighters. 'The back roof is coming down!'

'Okay,' the officer called back. Then, to Lloyd, 'I'll talk to you later, sir. Let's get this little bonfire under control first.'

Lloyd and Kathleen stood and watched as the firefighters axed their way into the back of the house and sprayed gallons of water into the kitchen. Lloyd felt shocked and detached. It was hard for him to believe that what he was witnessing was real. First of all he had lost Celia to fire, now his house. He felt like packing up and leaving everything behind him. Maybe travelling north to Eureka, the way that Kathleen's late husband had done.

Most of the neighbours had come out of their houses to watch the fire. Rog Kazowski from next door came across and asked Lloyd if he wanted to come in for a drink.

'It's okay, Rog, I think I'll just stand here and watch it burn.'

'I sure hope you got good insurance,' said Rog, the firelight dancing on his shiny bald head. 'If you have any problems, let me know.'

Lloyd looked around, and as he did so, he saw two unfamiliar figures standing amongst the main knot of neighbours. It was difficult to make them out clearly in the swivelling light from the fire and the flashing lights from the firetrucks, but the more intently he peered at them, the more convinced he became that he had found the man and woman he was hunting for. With a cold tingle of excitement and alarm, he recognized Otto and his tall German *fräulein*. Helmet, or Earwig, or whatever.

He couldn't be certain, but it looked very much as if they were watching him, too.

'Kathleen,' he suggested, 'I think it would be a good idea if we got away from here.'

'I'm sorry?'

'I'm not really too keen on watching my house burn to the ground, you know?'

Kathleen took hold of his hand. 'Well, of course, sure.

Do you want to come to my place?'

'That'd be great.'

He edged his way back through the onlookers, making sure that the fire chief didn't see them leaving. A police car had just arrived, too, and the last thing he wanted was to have to answer a lot of routine police-type questions. He glanced back across the street at Otto and his companion, and as he did so he saw a figure in dark glasses and a black turban skirting around the back of the crowd. *Celia*, no question about it. Or the grey-skinned empty-eye-socketed creature who had taken Celia's shape.

He gripped Kathleen's hand more tightly, and hurried her over to his car.

Kathleen said, 'Hold on! You're hurting me!'

'Quick, get in,' he told her. 'They've seen us.'

'Who's seen us? What are you talking about?'

Otto had detached himself from the main crowd and was walking toward them, straight and purposeful. The tall German woman followed him, although Celia remained where she was.

Kathleen said, 'I wish you'd tell me what's going on.'

'No time,' Lloyd told her, slamming the car door and starting the engine. As he did so, Otto abruptly stopped where he was, fifty or sixty feet away, and raised his hands to his forehead. He looked as if he were protecting his eyes from the glare. Lloyd released the parking-brake and swerved the BMW across the road in reverse.

'Lloyd!' Katheleen exclaimed.

Lloyd slammed the T-shift into 2, and the car skidded forward again. As they approached Otto, however, Lloyd felt the leather-covered steering-wheel heating up in the palms of his hands. Otto made no attempt to move aside as they slewed past him, and as they did so, the steering-wheel burst into flames.

'*Aaahhh!*' Lloyd yelled, trying to keep control of the swaying car with his fingertips. The leather steering-wheel cover was blazing furiously, and strips of fiery black hide kept dropping on to his unprotected thighs. His palms were branded, his fingers blistered, but in spite of the pain and the panic he managed to keep his hands dancing around the wheel, and to keep the car under some sort of control.

'Here!' said Kathleen, and dragged off her knitted shawl so that Lloyd could use it to smother the flames. He wound it around the top of the steering-wheel, and managed to damp down the worse of them.

They skidded on to the main highway next to the university entrance. Lloyd's teeth were clenched with pain, and his eyes were filled with tears.

'Under my seat,' he managed to tell her. 'Fire extinguisher.'

'For God's sake, can't you *stop*?'

Lloyd glanced in his rearview mirror. Already a large silver Mercedes sedan was swerving out of North Torrey, in obvious pursuit. It pulled right in front of a van, and Lloyd heard a horn blaring in indignation.

Kathleen unclipped the fire-extinguisher and blew five or six squirts of foam on to the last guttering flames on the steering-wheel.

'That's fine,' Lloyd told her, 'that's fine.'

'Why can't you stop?' Kathleen demanded, frantically. 'Who was that man? How on earth did our steering-wheel catch fire? Would you *please* mind telling me now what's going on?'

Lloyd checked his mirror again. 'You see that Mercedes? It's following us.'

Kathleen turned around in her seat. 'Are you sure? Why?'

'It's that man you saw in the road back there. As far as I can make out, that's Otto. The leader of that religious study group I was telling you about.'

'But what does he want?'

'This, I think,' said Lloyd, and reached into his coat pocket and took out the lizard charm. 'I don't know, it's some kind of symbol. He has the same symbol on the wall in his house.'

Kathleen turned the charm one way, and then the other. 'Why does he want it so badly?'

'I wish I knew. But it was found in the car park where Celia burned herself. If you look at the newspaper photographs, Otto was there, too, standing in the background. And Otto was *also* standing in the background in the newspaper photographs of that bus burning.

'What's more, anybody who has shown even the slightest interest in Otto and these burnings seems to have gotten themselves burned to death.'

Kathleen looked around again. 'They're gaining on us. Your poor hands. Are you going to be okay?'

Lloyd grimaced, and nodded. The sharp burning in his fingers had become a silently-roaring fire, and he was doing his best not to think about it. Pain? What pain? That pain doesn't belong to me.

Kathleen said, 'I don't understand it. How did your steering-wheel catch fire like that?'

'I don't understand it, either. But I think Otto did it. Maybe he can make things catch fire just by thinking about it. Did you ever see that movie about a little girl who could make things catch fire just by thinking about them? Maybe it's the same kind of thing. It's like using your mind as a magnifying-glass – concentrating all your energy on just one spot. The spot heats up, then *whoof!* it catches fire.'

The Mercedes was driving on full headlights, less than three car lengths behind, and Lloyd had to deflect his mirror so that he wouldn't be dazzled. 'There's something else,' he told Kathleen, as they negotiated the long lefthand downhill curve toward the ocean. 'I saw Celia in the house tonight.'

'You did what?'

'Believe me, Kathleen, I know it sounds crazy, but she was there. Or her ghost was there. Or some kind of apparition. She was standing in the bedroom and the bedroom was blazing and she wasn't even *touched*, wasn't even *singed*.'

'Lloyd ...' said Kathleen, gently. 'You don't think maybe that Celia's death has upset you more than you realize?'

Lloyd shook his head. 'It wasn't my imagination, Kathleen,

165

I swear to God. And if I'm really going screwy, how come this steering-wheel caught fire? It's all part of the same damn thing. Celia's death, the bus burning, Mike's death.'

'But I told you ... Mike didn't belong to any religious groups.'

'You mean that he didn't *tell* you that he did. But Celia didn't tell me, either. Celia, the love of my life, the girl who was going to share everything with me. She didn't even tell me that her best friend had cancer.'

'Her best friend had cancer?'

'That's right. Marianna, the one who was burned on the bus, along with Mike.'

They sped northward on the coast road. In the darkness, the Pacific foamed lonely and cold, and even the seagulls had found shelter for the night, the souls of the dead, the spirits of the lost.

'You know something,' said Kathleen. 'Mike went for a medical about three months ago, and when he got the results he was really quiet for a couple of weeks.'

'Did he tell you what was wrong?'

'Unh-hunh. He kept insisting that everything was fine. But I could tell that he was worried. In the end he said that he had problems at work, that was all. But he never did show me that medical.'

Lloyd quickly looked around. The Mercedes was still close behind, but it was keeping its distance. It seemed to be intent on following them, more than trying to overtake them. On the other hand, they were driving through Del Mar now, a well-lit, built-up stretch of the road, with rows of beach houses and bars and hotels and Chinese restaurants and bookstores, and if Otto tried anything too catastrophic, there would be scores of witnesses.

Kathleen said, 'Look ... there's a late-night drugstore. Let's get you something for your hands.'

Lloyd gave another quick glance behind. 'Okay ... they'll probably keep away from us here.'

He drew into the kerb beside Del Mar 24HR Drugs. It was a calculated risk, with Otto so close behind them, especially since Otto seemed to be capable of setting things on fire from such a long way off. If he could burn Lloyd's steering-wheel, there was no reason why he couldn't burn Lloyd, too. But Lloyd's hands were raging with pain, and both he and Kathleen needed a few moments to get their breath back.

They went into the drugstore just as the Mercedes drew up about sixty feet behind them, and remained at the kerb with its windows darkened and its motor running. Lloyd paused at the brightly lit drugstore door and gave the Mercedes a long, intent stare, but there was no way of telling what effect he was having on the Mercedes' occupants. The car was as blind-looking as Celia had been, if that burning figure in the bedroom door *had* truly been Celia.

He was beginning to realize that he no longer knew the difference between the living and the dead.

— FOURTEEN —

With a fatherly care that brought Lloyd closer to the brink of tears than the pain itself, the pharmacist at Del Mar 24HR Drugs covered his hands with antiseptic cream and then bandaged them up.

'You're pretty lucky, these are only very superficial,' he said, taking off his heavy tortoiseshell eyeglasses, and massaging the deep indentations in the side of his nose. 'Trouble is, it's always the superficial burns that give you the most pain. My mother always used to put on chicken fat. It healed the burns okay, but I used to have half the cats in the neighbourhood following me around for days. Take two Tylenol now, and another two before you go to bed tonight, and don't drive.'

They were about to go to the checkout desk when the drugstore door opened, and a thin elderly man in a wide hat and a grey business suit stepped in, followed by a tall girl with tight blonde braids and a floor-length black leather coat. The coat was unbuttoned, and underneath she was wearing what looked like a skintight black leather swimsuit. The two of them waited by the magazine rack, leafing through copies of *Sunset* and *Barbecue Recipes* until Lloyd and Kathleen began to make their way toward the door. Then the girl stepped forward to bar their way.

'Mr Denman,' the girl said, in a strong German accent. 'You have something that belongs to me.'

Lloyd hesitated, his heart beating fast.

'I don't see how that can be,' he replied. 'I don't even know you.'

The man slipped his magazine back into the rack, and stepped forward with a grin that looked like a pig's caul stretched across a wire coathanger. 'Allow me to introduce myself. Otto Mander, my dear sir. And this is Helmwige von Koettlitz.'

Helmet, or Earwig, something like that. Helmwige.

'Well, good to have met you,' said Lloyd. 'But if this is some kind of touch, then you're out of luck.'

Otto gave a dry, restricted cough. 'This is no touch, Mr Denman, as well you know. You have been looking for me as intently as I have been looking for you. Now, you have something that belongs to us, not to you, and I would appreciate your returning it without the necessity for any unpleasant confrontation.'

Lloyd said, 'Is Celia in the car?'

'I don't understand, Mr Denman. I was under the impression that your wife was dead.'

'The hell you say. I saw her tonight.'

Kathleen said, 'Lloyd ... I think I want to go.'

'All right,' Lloyd agreed. 'If this gentleman will agree to answer some questions.'

'Of course.' Otto nodded. His eyes roamed independently around the drugstore, as if he were constantly scanning the air, constantly searching for something. 'I am not a secretive man, Mr Denman, and I have done nothing of which I need to feel ashamed. I will answer any question that you care to put to me, as fully and as openly as I can. First, however, I want the charm.'

Lloyd shook his head. 'Questions first, charm later.'

'I must insist that you give me the charm, Mr Denman, and that you give it me now.'

'Even supposing I've got it, what's so darned important about it?'

Helmwige stepped forward and stood so close to Lloyd that her breast pressed against his arm and he could feel her breath on his cheek. 'Mr Denman, that charm is of no earthly use to you; yet it is critical to us.'

'You mean critical to Celia?'

'Your fiancée, regrettably, is dead. You identified her body yourself.'

Kathleen, anxious, begged, '*Please*, Lloyd, let's just leave.'

But Lloyd said, 'I saw her tonight. You can't convince me that I didn't. She's alive, in some way. She's been following me.'

Otto pursed his lips. 'An hallucination, my good sir. The living are living and the dead are very dead. There is no conceivable state of in-between.'

'That's not what you teach at your study groups.'

Otto's eyes momentarily concentrated on Lloyd's face as if he could have quite happily set fire to his forehead. But his eyes said one thing and his mouth said another. 'You are a gentleman, Mr Denman. A man of honour. You must understand that the charm does not belong to you. It is very important that we have it.'

'Is Celia alive?' Lloyd asked him.

Otto didn't answer, but continued to stare at him with that same incendiary stare. Helmwige said, 'You have the wrong ideas, Mr Denman. We are students and worshippers, not witchcraft workers.'

'I saw her with my own eyes, Miss von ...'

'Koettlitz,' said Helmwige. 'But of course this was impossible. Your fiancée, we are afraid, is quite gone.'

'She's alive,' Lloyd repeated.

Otto gave that stretched-caul grin. 'Perhaps you are then a fan of Goethe? *Und so lang daß du nicht hast dieses: Stirb und werde! Bist du nur ein trüber Gast auf der dunkeln Erde.*'

He kept on grinning, and said, 'It means "So long as you fail to understand the notion that death transforms you, you will only be a miserable guest on this gloomy planet."'

'I believe that Celia is still alive,' Lloyd repeated. 'I don't know how, I don't know why. Maybe I've totally flipped. But I believe that she's still alive, and I also believe that you know how, and why.'

'Well! Well! We are all entitled to our fantasies and our aberrations!' Otto replied. His laugh could have desiccated a coconut. 'But I insist on the charm.'

'Or what?' Lloyd challenged him.

Kathleen said, 'Lloyd, please let's go. I don't like any of this.'

'Or what?' Otto demanded. 'You want to know "or what?" Well, let me tell you this: if you refuse to give me the charm, if you *absolutely* refuse to give me the charm, then you must burn and burn until I can pick the charm from out of your ashes.'

Lloyd was shaking with pain and anger. He never would have counted himself as brave, but with his hands bandaged and his house burned down, with Celia dead or not dead, with Sylvia burned and Marianna burned and Kathleen's husband burned, he had passed that imaginary limit that his lawyer Dan Tabares called the GAS Line. After you've passed the GAS Line, whatever happens, you simply don't Give A Shit.

'Get out of my way, old man,' he told Otto.

'Hey! You don't speak to Mr Mander with such disrespect!' Helmwige interjected, jostling her shoulder forward.

Lloyd tried to be calm, but it was difficult. 'Get out of my way, all right?' he insisted. 'Because if you don't get out of my way, believe me, I'm not going to call the manager. I'm not going to call a cop. All I'm going to do is beat the living shit out of you, octogenarian or not, and then I'm going to do the same to Miss Cut-Price Leather Couch here.'

Otto lifted his chin in controlled fury. His neck rose out of his withered cream shirt-collar like a turtle. 'Mr Denman, you are not a wise man, my dear sir. All of your difficulties would be solved by simply returning the charm, please. In any event, it is not your property. You have no claim to it. I am sure the police will understand that.'

'Get out of my way,' Lloyd insisted.

There was a long moment in which none of them spoke: in which all of them were trying to outguess each other's reactions. Then, without warning, Lloyd shoved Helmwige back against the nail-varnish display, and there was a sudden brittle scattering of pink and red bottles. Then he jabbed his elbow deep into Otto's concave ribs. Otto gave a barking cough, and clutched himself tight.

171

Lloyd snatched Kathleen's hand and pushed open the drugstore door. They ran together across the pavement, colliding with a young skateboarder, tangling themselves with a couple in bermuda shorts and baseball caps, then climbed into Lloyd's BMW and skittered away from the curb with tyres howling and rubber 'Ss' snaking all across the street.

Otto threw open the drugstore door, and immediately pressed both hands to his forehead. Helmwige said, 'Otto! *Vorsicht! Er hat den Talisman!*' But Otto's fury was locked together jigsaw-tight, and nothing could have broken it, not then. A sharp arrow of fire chased across the blacktop after Lloyd's BMW, flaring against the car's rear bumper for an instant. But Lloyd was too quick, and the BMW had roared out of sight before the fire could take hold.

'Scheiß!' Otto cursed. He whirled around and walked stiffly back to his parked Mercedes, wrenching open the passenger door as if he wanted to tear it off its hinges. Helmwige walked around the car and opened the driver's door.

'What now?' she asked him.

'Go after them, of course!' Otto instructed her. 'Come on, quick, quick! Why do you stand there, staring at me like an idiot? Follow them!'

'They could have turned off anywhere,' Helmwige retorted.

Otto screeched at her. 'Do what I tell you! Follow them!'

The Mercedes bucked and heaved away from the curb. From the back seat, a grey-faced figure bent forward and said, 'If you catch him, you won't hurt him, will you?'

'What, you think I'm *verrückt*?' Otto snarled back. 'But where will you be, without your talisman? A Salamander, for ever! A living fire!'

Lloyd raced northward out of Del Mar, steering choppily and erratically with his gauze-bandaged fingertips. He skidded to a stop whenever they hit traffic signals, revved

172

impatiently, watching behind him, then ripped ahead as soon as the lights turned green.

Kathleen said, 'Lloyd! My God! Are they following us?'

Lloyd flicked his eyes to the rearview mirror. 'I can't see them yet.'

'Maybe they've given up.'

'No,' said Lloyd. 'They need that charm too badly.'

'But they're terrible! They're so threatening! Can't we call the police?'

'Sure we can call the police. But what do you think the police are going to do?'

'I don't know. But they set fire to your house, they set fire to your car! Look at your hands! Surely the police can charge them with *something*?'

Lloyd shook his head. 'Kathleen, I don't want to call the police. If I call the police, I'll never find out what's going on. They won't let me. Besides, what am I going to say to them? "My dead wife set fire to my house, then this cheesy old man set fire to my steering-wheel from fifty feet away"? You think they're going to believe me?'

'But they threatened us, they're chasing us.'

Lloyd said, 'Just tell me how we get to your house. They haven't caught up with us yet.'

'Lloyd, I'm frightened!'

'Me too. But calling the police isn't going to help. In fact, it'll probably make things worse.'

Kathleen was quiet for a moment. But then she said, 'Do you really think that Celia is still alive?'

'I'm beginning to believe that she is, yes.'

'I don't understand this at all,' said Kathleen.

Lloyd checked his rearview mirror again. 'I don't understand it, either. But Otto promised everybody who came to his group that they were going to live for ever. Somehow, it looks like he's managed it. With Celia, anyway. I saw her! She was different, but she was still Celia.'

'People can't die and then come alive again.'

Lloyd shook his head. 'I don't know. Maybe they can, in a different way. Burning seems to have something to do with it. Maybe you live for ever, if you burn.'

Kathleen said, tightly, distractedly. 'You can take a right here.'

They turned away from the ocean and started to drive up into the hills. But as they reached the first high crest beyond the interstate, Lloyd became aware that a single pair of headlights was following them, not too close, but close enough not to lose them.

'Look around,' he told Kathleen. 'Do you think that's them?'

She shaded her eyes. 'I can't be sure, but it *looks* like them.'

'Hold on tight, then. This is where we shake them off for good.'

Lloyd pressed the gas-pedal down to the floor, and the BMW surged forward at more than 90mph. It took them only a few seconds to reach the next intersection, and Lloyd immediately braked hard and swung off to the right, killing his headlights as he did so. Then he swung left, completely off the road, and the car jolted and bounced as he negotiated his way down a dusty slope, through a clump of birds-of-paradise and prickly pear. The BMW's suspension banged unnervingly as they drove over a series of rocky ruts, and the muffler grounded again and again. But then Lloyd wrestled the car around behind a high screen of bushes and brought it to a halt.

'There's no way they're going to find us now,' he told Kathleen. 'Let's give them ten minutes or so to get tired of looking for us, then we'll carry on to your place.'

Only a few seconds afterwards, they saw headlights flash past them on the main highway. Then a truck went past, and a procession of much slower cars. Lloyd let out a tight, anxious breath.

'I wonder what they want that charm *for*,' said Kathleen.

'I don't know. Maybe it's part of their religious ritual. Otto has the same design on the wall of his house, but much larger.'

'They're so *weird*, those people,' Kathleen shivered. 'I can hardly believe that Mike was mixed up with them.'

174

They waited in silence for five minutes longer. Then Lloyd said, 'I've been thinking about your husband's medical. Is there any way we could find out what the results were?'

'Why?'

'Just a guess. Marianna thought she might have had breast cancer, and if your husband had found out that he had something wrong with him – maybe that would have made them both a whole lot more receptive to the ideas of somebody like Otto. After all, he *was* promising everlasting life.'

'I suppose I could call Doctor Kranz.'

Lloyd checked his watch. His hands were still burning dully, but the Tylenol was deadening the worst of the pain. 'It's just a shot in the dark. But I've been trying to follow up every possible idea.'

'You don't think . . .' Kathleen began.

Lloyd glanced across at her. He knew what she was thinking, and what she was going to say. She had listened patiently to his stories about seeing Celia on the *Star of India* and at Tom Ham's Lighthouse, and about the break-ins, and the Wagner libretto inside the piano. But he wasn't surprised that he was stretching her credulity by insisting that Celia was somehow still alive.

All the same, he shook his head. 'No, I don't think I'm cracking up. I'm not superstitious, I don't even believe in star signs. I don't believe in the supernatural, either. But I saw Celia and she wasn't a mirage or an hallucination or a trick of the light. There's an explanation for all of this. I don't know what it is, but I'm sure as hell going to find out.'

He held up the charm. 'First of all I'm going to find out what *this* is all about. Then I'm going to take that Wagner libretto to somebody who knows something about music.'

'All right, then,' Kathleen agreed. 'And I'll phone Doctor Kranz, and ask about Mike's medical. But if none of this adds up to anything – well, I don't enjoy being chased around by people like this Otto of yours. It scares me.'

Lloyd raised one bandaged hand, and pledged, 'If we

can't come up with anything that makes any sense, then you're out of it. I promise.'

She leaned across the car and unexpectedly kissed his cheek. 'You were good, back there in the drugstore. Like *Lethal Weapon.*'

'Flattery will get you anywhere.'

'Well, home would be a good start.'

Lloyd cautiously steered the BMW out of the trees and back on to the road. There was no sign of the Mercedes anywhere. He turned right, and rejoined the winding road that would take them through Rancho Sante Fe and eventually out past Lake Hodges to Escondido. The night was exceptionally black, a strange liquid black, as if the world had been silently drowned by a seamless oil-spill.

Rancho Santa Fe was lit up, neat as toytown, its streets unnaturally deserted, as if all of its elderly residents had been taken away by friendly aliens. But once they had driven out into the hills, the blackness covered them yet again. Lake Hodges lay black between its black forested banks, betraying its presence only by an occasional secretive sparkle.

Kathleen tried to tune into KOGO on the radio to hear if there were any bulletins about Lloyd's house burning, but all they could pick up were six or seven country-rock stations and a long tedious interview about the Navy Hospital. She switched the radio off again.

Kathleen said, 'What are you going to do if Celia *is* still alive?'

'I've been trying not to think about it,' Lloyd replied. 'It gives me the shudders.'

'You still love her, though, don't you? The way that I still love Mike?'

Lloyd drove in silence for a short while. Then he said, 'I loved her the way she was. But the way I saw her tonight – well, she wasn't at all the same. She looked really strange. Her skin was kind of – I don't know – *greyish*, and she didn't seem to have any eyes. She was alive, for sure. At least she was walking and talking, and she recognized me. But she looked like she was dead.'

He cleared his throat. 'I keep trying not to think about the word "zombie". It sounds like some dumb teenage video with dead people shuffling through shopping malls.'

Kathleen didn't answer, but she gave a small shiver, as if somebody had stepped on her grave.

They turned toward Escondido. Kathleen's house was on the south-western outskirts, on a secluded road opposite the vineyards of the Altmann Brothers Winery. She touched Lloyd's shoulder as they approached it, and said, 'It's best to go dead slow. It's a real sharp turn into the drive.'

The BMW's headlights picked out the *San Diego Tribune* mailbox with the name M. KERWIN painted in silver reflective letters on it. The late M. Kerwin. Lloyd slowed the car down to a crawl, and steered carefully around the tightly curving driveway.

'Lucy and Tom are probably still over at Rancho Bernardo,' said Kathleen. 'They were visiting my parents this evening. Mom's been so good about everything.'

Lloyd saw bushes, flowers, a two-storey brick-and-wooden house. Then, to his horror, he saw a silver Mercedes sedan, parked facing him. Beside it stood the unmistakable and menacing figures of Otto and Helmwige. Somebody else, too, standing well back in the shadows behind them. Somebody with a black coat and a yellow scarf and blacked-out sunglasses.

'Oh God, it's them!' Kathleen breathed, her voice high-pitched with fright.

Lloyd slammed the BMW into reverse, and twisted around in his seat. The car's tyres shrieked in protest as it backed up the drive at full speed, swaying violently from side to side as Lloyd attempted to steer it straight. With a hideous thumping noise, they collided with a low retaining wall close to the entrance, and Lloyd had to shift back into 'Drive' and rev the car forward to unhook his bumper from the bricks.

In the glare of his halogen headlights, Lloyd saw Otto

step forward and lift his hands to his forehead. Otto's face was unnaturally white and his eyes were pinpricks of flashing yellow, as dead and as bright as a snake's eyes. Grunting with pain, Lloyd pushed the gearshift into reverse again, and began to steer his way backwards round the curve in the drive, scraping the wall all the way.

They almost reached the mailbox when the BMW's tyres exploded into flame, all four of them. Kathleen screamed. Lloyd shouted, 'Hold on! It's okay! We're almost there!' The car's rear bumper hit the mailbox and knocked it flat. Then Lloyd slewed the car around and they sped off into the darkness, their tyres blazing like Catherine-wheels, or the red-hot wheels of Union Pacific locomotives careening down the High Sierras on nothing but their brakes.

'How did they know where I lived?' Kathleen screamed, almost hysterical, as they roared along the highway with flames flickering all around them. 'How did they know where I *lived*?'

Lloyd was tempted to say, 'Maybe Mike's still alive, too. Maybe Mike told them', but he decided that Kathleen had been through enough horrors for one night. Besides, his most urgent concern now was to extinguish their tyres.

They flashed past an irrigation hydrant by the side of the road. Lloyd skidded the BMW to a halt, and backed up until they were parked right beside it. 'Out!' he told Kathleen. 'Careful! Don't stand too close! And keep an eye open for Otto!'

He climbed out of the car, and wrestled with the hydrant. He cried out, '*Shit, shit, shit!*' in agony as the knurled knob dug into his bandaged hands, but at last the faucet juddered and shook, and splattered blood-rusty water on to the ground. Lloyd found a discarded cardboard fruit-box only a few feet away, and filled it up to the top. The box gushed noisily from all its crevices, but it held enough for Lloyd to be able to heave water over the burning tyres, one by one, and to douse them in a sizzle of rubbery-smelling steam.

'Okay, let's get out of here!' he called. But as he tossed away the box and opened his door, he heard the rushing noise of a fast-approaching vehicle, and out of the darkness beside the Altmann winery sped the silver Mercedes with the blacked-out windows.

Kathleen ran back to the car, and Lloyd dropped into the driver's seat and twisted the key in the ignition. But before Kathleen could reach the passenger door, the Mercedes cut in front of them, and slid to a crunching, emphatic halt. The Mercedes' doors flew open at once; and Otto and Helmwige climbed out. Helmwige circled the BMW towards Kathleen, while Otto remained where he was, desiccated and thin, his hands clasped in front of him, his face darkly shadowed by the brim of his hat.

'No!' cried Kathleen, as Helmwige approached her. Lloyd came around the back of the car and stepped in between them, but Helmwige simply grinned at him.

'Now, with no more nonsense, you're going to give us the charm?' she demanded.

'Not a chance,' Lloyd told her, shakily. 'Now get the hell out of here and leave us alone. This time I'm going to call the cops.'

'Oh, yes? And what are you going to tell them, these cops?'

'I'm going to suggest that they search your little hideout on Paseo Delicias, for starters. Kidnapping and imprisonment are pretty serious offences, wouldn't you say?'

'Oh, you've been prying around our house, too?' asked Helmwige, still grinning. 'Well, I agree with you. Kidnapping and imprisonment are *very* serious offences. But there is no law against a man who *wants* to be chained up, now is there? That man would not be at all happy to be free. He is guilty, you see, that he has not lived up to his promise. He is only content when he is being punished.'

'You can tell that to the sheriff. I'm sure,' Lloyd challenged her.

'By all means. I will also tell him that you have an item

179

of valuable property which belongs to us, and that you refuse to return it.'

Lloyd help up the charm between his gauze-wrapped fingers. 'You show me who else you've got in that car, and tell me why you want this charm so badly, and then maybe I will.'

Otto called out dryly, 'What is he saying?'

Helmwige without relaxing her grin, turned back to him. 'He wants to see our passenger.'

'Then let him. Perhaps then he'll come to his senses.'

A large furry moth flickered into the beam of the Mercedes' headlights, and clung quivering for a moment to the dazzling lens. Otto reached out smoothly and cupped the mesmerized insect in his hand. Lloyd and Kathleen watched him in disgusted fascination as he licked it all over until its wings were stuck down with his saliva, then placed it into his mouth as if it were a piece of fruit. He sucked hard, and then swallowed.

'Celia!' called Helmwige. 'Why don't you come out, my dear?'

Although Lloyd had already guessed that it was Celia, he still felt an acid-sharp tingle of fear. He had seen her burned body in the police morgue downtown and he had seen her eyeless and terrible in their blazing bedroom. He didn't know how she could still be walking around, unless she had undergone some extraordinary kind of advanced operation, or unless she was a zombie, or a ghost, or a robot, or her own twin sister, or unless he had gone into shock when he had heard of her death, and this was nothing but a nightmare.

One slim ankle stepped out of the car. Then a long familiar leg. Then a slender girl in a black raincoat, with a scarf tied around her head like a turban, and impenetrable dark glasses. She stood close to the car, slowly buttoning first one black glove and then the other. Her face shone softly grey.

'Hallo, Lloyd,' she called, and it was Celia's voice, no question at all.

Lloyd was swept by such a surge of emotion, such a

turmoil of fear and longing and shock and disbelief, that he could hardly speak.

'Celia,' he said. 'Celia, what the hell is going on? Are you really alive?'

'I'm saved, Lloyd, that's what's happened.'

'Did you really burn yourself?'

But Otto interrupted. 'Mr Denman ... the less you know about this, the safer you will be. Please ... you have seen her. You know that she is saved. Give us the charm and the whole matter can be forgotten.'

Lloyd slowly and emphatically shook his head. 'That's where you're wrong, friend. This matter isn't going to be forgotten. No goddamned *way* is this matter going to be forgotten. You've been burning people to death, you've been terrorizing people, you've burned down my house, you've wrecked my car. Look at my hands, for God's sake! And now you bring Celia out, who's supposed to be dead, and tell me she's saved!'

'Mr Denman, she *is* saved, believe me.'

'I wouldn't believe you if you told me it gets dark at night. I want to know what the hell's going on.'

Celia said, 'Lloyd, my love, please. Don't argue now. Let them have the charm. Otherwise I can't survive.'

'I just want to know what this is all about,' Lloyd insisted.

Otto stepped nearer, brushing dust from the sleeves of his suit. 'Mr Denman, your fiancée is in a particular state at this moment which you might call *volatile*. When the year reaches its fullest point, at the summer solstice, we will be able to stabilize her condition and she will become whole. She will have attained a state of perfection that will make her nothing short of immortal. But, it is essential for her to have the talisman which she lost by accident on the day of her burning. Unless you wish her to remain in her present state, you will now return it.'

'Celia?' asked Lloyd, ignoring Otto as pointedly as he could.

'He's telling you the truth, Lloyd,' Celia replied. Her voice sounded like the softest of brushes on silver.

'But why?' Lloyd wanted to know. 'Why did you try to kill yourself like that? Weren't you happy? Was something wrong? Were you depressed? You didn't *have* to marry me, you know, if you didn't love me!'

'I loved you then and I love you now, and I will *always* love you,' Celia replied.

'So why did you burn yourself? What was it supposed to achieve?'

'Exactly what Otto told you. Perfection.'

'Don't you understand that as far as I was concerned, you *were* perfect? I wouldn't have changed you in any way for anything!'

Lloyd took a step toward her, and held out his hand. He couldn't stop his eyes from filling up with tears. 'Just tell me what's happened to you! Can't you do that? Tell me what's going on!'

Helmwige stepped between him and Celia, and said, firmly, 'No nearer, Mr Denman, or you will regret it. We will *all* regret it. Your interference has caused us enough trouble as it is.'

'But she's my fiancée, for Christ's sake!' Lloyd yelled at her. 'She's the woman I want to marry! *Wanted* to marry! Still want to, if you'll tell me what the hell's going on!'

Otto took off his hat, and wiped around the inside with his folded handkerchief. 'Enough of this lovemaking. We can't spare the time. Mr Denman, my lawyers will contact you regarding any damage that might have been done to your house and your car.'

'Your *lawyers*? Goddamn it, I'm going to the police! I'm going to have you locked up, you goddamned maniac!'

Otto ran his hand through his white felt-like hair, and looked away. 'Going to the police would be a grave mistake, Mr Denman. A wicked mistake. We would have to cut short our procedures, and delay Celia's transformation until the *next* solstice, in a year's time. Who knows what might happen to her in between now and then.'

'I don't understand this at all,' Lloyd told him.

Otto smiled, and replaced his hat. 'No, I don't suppose

you do. But then it isn't really necessary for you to understand it. In fact, you're probably not *capable* of understanding it. Like most men who place foreign cars and
designer clothes higher on their list of priorities than
spiritual strength and absolute achievement, you have an
intellect no higher than any of those cockroaches which
infest your restaurant.'

'Now, you damn well listen to me ...' Lloyd began,
angrily.

But Celia called, 'Please, Lloyd! Please! Just give Helmwige the charm.'

Lloyd hesitated, glancing from Celia to Otto and back
again. But then Helmwige suddenly seized his wrist, and
raised the fist in which he was holding the charm. Lloyd
gasped with effort, trying to push his arm down again.
But Helmwige was startlingly strong, and he couldn't
move a muscle.

At the same time, he began to feel Helmwige's fingers
growing gradually warmer and warmer. He frowned at
her in effort and disbelief. But it was only a matter of
seconds before her fingers were so hot that his skin
started to redden, and the edge of his gauze bandages
began to singe. The hairs on his wrist shrivelled, and
wisps of smoke rose from between his fingers.

'Lloyd, please!' Celia begged him.

But Kathleen slapped Helmwige's shoulder and
shouted, 'Let him go! You're all crazy! You're vicious and
you're crazy! Let him go!'

Otto gave her a fleeting, dismissive glance, 'Very
spirited, Mrs Kerwin. But it won't help at all.'

Lloyd kept his fist closed for as long as he could, but
the burning of Helmwige's fingers was more than he
could take. Gasping, sweating, shaking with pain, he
slowly opened his fingers and exposed the charm.
Without a word, Helmwige picked it fastidiously out of
his palm, and pressed it to her lips. Metal sizzled against
saliva.

'Thank you for your somewhat reluctant co-operation,
Mr Denman,' said Otto. He suddenly stooped forward, and

caught a hopping cicada by the leg. It struggled and danced, but he pushed it into his mouth until only its head was showing between his lips, its black beady eyes staring. Then he crunched it up between his teeth, and swallowed it. 'I like to give them one last look at the world they are leaving,' he remarked.

Shuddering with emotion and pain, his burned hand pressed against his chest, Lloyd could do nothing else but watch Celia climb back into the car, followed by Helmwige and Otto. Otto raised one gloved hand in dismissal, and then they drove off into the darkness. Their brake lights glared momentarily as they rejoined the main road, and then they were gone.

Kathleen came up to Lloyd with tears in her eyes, and put her arms around him. 'Oh God, are you all right? That must have hurt so much.'

'It's okay,' said Lloyd. 'I'll get over it. A college friend of mine lost both his legs in Viet Nam, and he got over it.'

'Was that really Celia?' Kathleen asked.

Lloyd nodded. 'It looked like her. It *sounded* like her. I don't know how it could be, though. I think I'm just about ready for the Yoyo Hotel.'

'But Lloyd,' Kathleen insisted, 'I saw her too, so she must be real. Just different, like that awful Otto said. God, he's disgusting! She's in a different state, that's what he said, didn't he? *Volatile.*'

Lloyd said, 'Let's see if we can get the car back to the house.'

'What are you going to do?' Kathleen asked him. 'Are you going to call the police?'

'Not yet ... not till I know what's going on. If there's a chance that Celia *could* be saved, then the last thing I want to do is blow it.'

Kathleen said nothing. There was nothing to be said. They had both been confronted with the evidence that the dead could really walk, that the grave and the crematorium might not be the end at all, but a new and mysterious beginning.

— FIFTEEN —

He was deeply asleep when the door chimes rang. He opened his eyes and for a long moment he couldn't think where he was, or what had happened to him, or even *who* he was.

He was lying on a chestnut-brown couch in a large rustic-style living-room. An empty red-wine bottle stood on the glass-topped table close by, with three wine-flecked glasses. On the brick-effect wall above the cabin-style fireplace hung a huge oil painting of Red Indians riding through a blizzard. It was entitled *Winter in the Sangre de Cristo Mountains*.

The doorbells chimed again. He sat up, and tried to rub his eyes, but found that his hands were thickly bound in clean bandages, like a boxer. He was wearing nothing but his boxer shorts. He looked around him, and saw his shirt neatly folded over the back of the chestnut-brown armchair opposite. It was only when he heard Kathleen calling from upstairs, 'Lloyd! Could you get the door please?' that he remembered exactly where he was.

He tugged on his pants and held them together with one hand because he couldn't fasten the button with his bandaged fingers. The dark wobbly shape of a man in a blue suit was visible through the hammered glass door. Using his hand like a big white lobster-claw, Lloyd opened the door on the chain and said, 'Who is it?'

The man turned around. It was Sergeant Houk. A little further away stood Detective Gable, with his hands in his pockets, whistling to himself. In the driveway, parked alongside Lloyd's burned and scraped BMW, stood Sergeant's Houk's Buick, and behind it, a blue-and-white squad car from the San Diego County Sheriff's Department, with a pale-faced young deputy sitting in it.

'Do you mind if we come in, or are we interrupting something?' asked Sergeant Houk.

Lloyd released the chain. 'Surprised you knew where to find me.'

'We *didn't* know where to find you, as a matter of fact. We put out a county-wide bulletin for your car last night, and that smart young deputy happened to notice it in Mrs Kerwin's driveway first thing this morning, and called us. There can't be too many white BMWs in Southern California with the licence FISHEE.'

As he stepped into the house, he looked back at Lloyd's car and commented, 'Pretty beat up, too. Hope you're not thinking of driving it on the highway in that condition.'

'I had a slight accident,' said Lloyd, trying to push the button of his pants through the buttonhole with the heel of his hand.

'You're not kidding. Was that how you hurt your hands?'

'That's right, burned them. It's not too serious. More blisters than anything else.'

Sergeant Houk walked into the living-room and looked around at the couch with its scrumpled-up cushions and its dragged-aside blanket, the empty bottle of wine, the three glasses. 'I didn't know that you and Mrs Kerwin were old acquaintances,' he remarked.

'We're not. We only met yesterday.'

'Impolite to ask you how?'

'Of course not. I went out to the Anza Borrego Desert to look at that burned-out bus, and Mrs Kerwin was there, tying on a wreath, in memory of her husband.'

Sergeant Houk nodded. 'Any particular reason you went out to look at that burned-out bus?'

'Celia was a member of the San Diego Opera, so was Marianna Gomes. I guess it struck me as something of a coincidence that both of them had burned to death within two days of each other.'

'So you went to look at the burned-out bus?'

'Yes, that's right.'

Sergeant Houk stood in the centre of the living-room

186

with his arms folded, making a show of thinking. 'Can I ask you what you thought you might find, if you went to look at the burned-out bus?'

'I don't know. Some kind of clue why Celia might have committed suicide.'

'Oh! And did you?' asked Sergeant Houk.

'Did I what?'

'Did you find any clues why Celia might have committed suicide?'

Lloyd gave a small, uncommunicative shake of his head. 'I guess I didn't.'

'But you did find Mrs Kerwin? Just by chance?'

'That's right. We got talking. In the end, I asked her to come back to La Jolla with me for dinner.'

'At your own restaurant, I presume?'

'That's right. We ate pretty early, as a matter of fact. But Mrs Kerwin seemed to be tired, so I suggested that she leave her car in the parking-lot and come back to my place for a nightcap.'

Sergeant Houk sniffed. 'With what intention?'

'I don't follow you.'

'What I'm trying to get at, Mr Denman, is what you had in mind when you invited Mrs Kerwin back to your house? Was it just for a drink, or did you have something more serious in mind?'

Lloyd stared at him indignantly. 'Are you sick in the head, or what? Both of us had just lost people we loved in the most horrible way you can think of. And you're trying to suggest that I asked Mrs Kerwin back to my house so that I could *seduce* her?'

Sergeant Houk was unfazed. 'I'm sorry, Mr Denman, I was simply trying to assess the degree of your intimacy with Mrs Kerwin. For all I know, you and Mrs Kerwin might have been acquaintances *before* these burning occurred.'

'And what's that supposed to mean?'

'I'm asking you.'

'You're not suggesting that *I* could have burned that bus?'

187

Sergeant Houk shrugged as if, well, it was *possible* sure, now that you came to mention it. 'You see the difficulty we have here is *why* Mr Kerwin was riding that bus at all. Or why *any* of the passengers were riding it. It was chartered by somebody calling himself Jim Ortal, and it was supposed to be a tour by the El Cajon Astronomical Society to visit Mount Palomar Observatory. Of course there is no El Cajon Astronomical Society and there is nobody with the name Ortal at the address that was given. The deposit on the bus and one day's rental plus full insurance was paid in advance in cash, so there's no bank account number and no credit card billing address.'

At that moment, Kathleen's older sister Lucy came downstairs in her black gingham robe, closely followed by a nine-year-old boy with dark hair and dark circles under his eyes. Lloyd had met Lucy and Tom late last night, when they had returned from visiting Lucy and Kathleen's parents in Rancho Bernardo. Kathleen had said nothing to Lucy about the unwelcome visit from Otto and Helmwige, and Lloyd had explained the devastated condition of his car by telling her that he had misjudged the turning into the drive, struck the garden wall, and that the car's fuel hose had fractured and started a fire. Lucy seemed to have believed him, and Tom had thought that any man who could cause such spectacular damage just by turning into somebody's drive was practically a superhero. And wreck a $65,000 BMW, too!

Lucy looked very much like Kathleen, only thinner and drier-skinned and more deeply suntanned, and she had acquired a slower Western drawl from all her years in Arizona. 'Kathleen'll be down in a minute,' she said. 'Have these gentlemen come about your accident?'

'That's right, ma'am,' grinned Sergeant Houk. 'Sorry to disturb you so early.'

'Don't concern yourself,' Lucy replied. 'Would you care for some coffee?'

'Black, please,' said Detective Gable.

'We won't. Thank you,' said Sergeant Houk. 'We're kind of pressed for time.'

'Lloyd?' asked Lucy.

'Yes, black please, Lucy,' Lloyd told her. Sergeant Houk was beginning to make him feel cornered, and he was glad of a momentary interruption. He didn't want to tell Sergeant Houk anything about Otto and Helmwige, not yet, not until he understood what Otto and Helmwige were actually into, and what was going to happen when Celia was 'transformed'. He could imagine far too vividly the police bursting into the house on Paseo Delicias and arresting everybody in sight, and condemning Celia for ever to that strange grey-faced state in which he had seen her last night.

Lloyd's whole night had been haunted by echoing, flaring nightmares. He had glimpsed Celia again and again, behind reflecting shop doors, on the opposite side of the street, on bridges, in the rain, masked by the windows of passing cars. He couldn't logically believe that she was still alive, in any shape, in any form. But he had seen her with his waking eyes and all he could do was to force himself to suspend his disbelief, to open his mind to any possibility, no matter how strange, no matter how grotesque.

It upset him that she was still in the hands of Otto and Helmwige, but in the end he supposed that there was no alternative for her. Even if they had originally been responsible for her burning herself (and by God he would kill them with his bare hands if he found out that they were), Otto and Helmwige had somehow raised her from the dead. He had to trust them to complete their ritual of 'transformation', whatever that was. If that was the only way in which Celia could be whole again, he couldn't interfere.

Sergeant Houk paced across to the fireplace and examined the oil-painting of Red Indians in the snow as closely as if it were a Van Dyck. 'Nice picture,' he remarked.

'Not exactly my taste,' Lloyd told him.

'Oh, yes. I've seen your restaurant. You're more into what d'you-call-'em, Depressionists.'

189

'Impressionists.'

'Whatever. They may impress you but they depress the hell out of me.'

Lloyd said tautly, 'If it sets your mind at rest, I never met Mrs Kerwin before yesterday, and the only reason I went out to the desert was because I wanted to take a look at the bus. Morbid interest, I guess.'

'Well, I'd say that hits the nail on the head,' Sergeant Houk replied. 'Morbid interest, Mr Denman, that's what you've got. But a very special variety of morbid interest.'

'I don't think I know what you're talking about.'

'You don't think you know what I'm talking about?' queried Sergeant Houk. He lifted one hand, and began to count items on his fingers. 'Your fiancée burns to death in the parking lot of McDonald's. You meet with Sylvia Cuddy of the San Diego Opera and then she burns to death in her apartment. You talk to Robert Tuggey, a short-order chef at McDonald's, and he dies in an unexplained fire in his automobile, in the same parking lot where your fiancée died. You visit the wreck of a burned-out bus, in which an acquaintance of yours from the San Diego Opera was killed. The same night, your house is seriously damaged by fire, and you and the widow of another victim of the burned-out bus are seen driving away from the scene of the fire with the interior of your car apparently in flames. This morning I arrive to find not only the interior of your car damaged by fire, but the tyres burned, too.'

Sergeant Houk had only a couple of fingers left to count on. 'Mr Denman,' he said, 'wouldn't you say that all of those incidents would lead a reasonable person to believe that you had a morbid interest in fire?'

Lloyd opened his mouth, then closed it again. Sergeant Houk had obviously spent all night trying to build a circumstantial case against him, but whatever he said, it would only make matters more difficult.

'You're not going to arrest me, are you?' he asked.

'No, sir, I'm not going to arrest you. I just wanted you to know how things look from our point of view.'

'I think I'd better speak to my lawyer,' said Lloyd.

'All right,' nodded Sergeant Houk. 'That's your privilege.'

Lloyd said, 'Let me tell you this, though. Whatever it looks like from your point of view, you're wrong. You're way off beam. I wasn't responsible for any of those deaths or any of those fires, and by the time this is over, you're going to find that out for yourself, and you're going to knock on my door the same way you did this morning, and you're going to have to say that you're sorry.'

'Be my pleasure,' grinned Sergeant Houk. 'Come on, detective, I think that's enough for now.'

'Yes, sir,' said Detective Gable, without taking his eyes off the tray of coffee that Lucy was carrying into the room.

'You're going so soon?' Lucy asked them.

'I think we have everything we need, thank you, ma'am,' said Sergeant Houk.

Lloyd showed them to the door, and opened it.

'Oh, by the way,' Sergeant Houk said, as if it had only just occurred to him. 'Did you by chance visit a house yesterday morning on Paseo Delicias, at Rancho Santa Fe? When we put out the APB on your car last night, an officer from White Shield Security called in to say that he'd seen a white BMW with the licence plate FISHEE out on Paseo Delicias yesterday morning. He'd also seen a man answering your description entering the property in a manner that made him look twice.'

Lloyd felt a tightness in his chest. The last thing he wanted was for Sergeant Houk to call at Otto's house. 'I'm sorry, I can't help you,' he replied.

'You mean you weren't there?'

'I mean the security officer must have been mistaken. I told you where I was yesterday, out in the Anza Borrego.'

'Well ... just asking,' Sergeant Houk smiled. 'Have you been back to your house yet?'

Lloyd shook his head. 'I was planning on calling my neighbour to find out how bad it was damaged.'

Sergeant Houk sniffed. 'It wasn't as serious as it might

have been, that's what the fire chief told me. Apparently the back roof collapsed, and the kitchen's burned out, but the main structure is still safe. You were lucky the fire-fighters got there so quick.'

He turned to leave, but then he hesitated and said, 'You'll stick around, won't you? And you'll let me know where I can get in touch?'

'Is that because I'm a suspect?' asked Lloyd.

'It's because I don't want to have to put out a county-wide APB every time I want to ask you a couple of questions, okay? Is that reasonable?'

Lloyd nodded, and closed the door. As an afterthought, he slid the security-chain into place.

Kathleen came down, wearing jeans and a plain white blouse. 'What was that all about?' she asked him.

'Just questions,' said Lloyd. 'He seems to have got it into his head that you and I might have planned to burn that bus so that we could collect your husband's in-surance and run off to Acapulco together.'

'You're not serious!'

Lloyd swallowed coffee. 'Almost. But that doesn't worry me. We didn't do it, and he can't produce any evidence that we did. What *does* worry me is that he knows where I went yesterday morning.'

'You mean to Otto's house?' Kathleen asked.

'That's right. And he's enough of a keen detective to try checking it out.'

'Oh, God. Otto will think that you tipped him off, won't he?'

Lloyd said, 'That possibility had occurred to me. And Otto isn't exactly your genial, forgiving type, is he? With any luck, he might allow me one last look at the world, like that cicada.'

'What can we do?' asked Kathleen.

Lloyd shrugged. 'Nothing. Have breakfast. Hope for the best.'

'*Piove sul bagnato*,' said Kathleen. 'It never rains but it pours.' When she caught Lloyd's quizzical look, she smiled gently and said, 'I used to have an Italian boyfriend once. Trouble is, I didn't fancy the idea of competing with a two-hundred-and-twenty-five-pound arm-wrestler for the rest of my life.'

'He was an arm-wrestler?'

'I'm talking about his mother.'

Sergeant Houk drew up underneath the overhanging eucalyptus trees on Paseo Delicias and switched off his engine. 'That's the house,' he told Detective Gable. 'Look at all those goddamned Mercedes. It looks like Hitler's garage.'

The deputy's car drew up behind them, and the deputy came up and leaned on the roof of Sergeant's Houk's Buick, next to the open window, and flipped his notebook. 'The sheriff just came through on the radio. The property is owned by Matt Orwell, the movie producer, and rented through Rand and Stewart, of Rancho Santa Fe. The present renter is the Salamander Corporation, registered in Butte, Montana. The rental documents were signed on behalf of the corporation by Mr J. Ortal.'

'Bingo!' breathed Sergeant Houk. 'And what's the betting that Mr J. Ortal turns out to be Mr L. Denman?'

'You seriously think that Denman burned that bus?' asked Detective Gable, taking off his sunglasses and hooking them into his shirt. 'He don't seem like the type to me.'

'*Type*, will you listen to him?' mocked Sergeant Houk. 'Did you ever see a single perpetrator who ever ran true to type? *Type* is for the movies. This guy Denman is a pyromaniac. You know? He loves to see things burn.'

'That still doesn't mean that he burned the bus,' Detective Gable insisted.

Sergeant Houk sighed. 'Let me suggest a scenario, right? Denman meets Mrs Kerwin at his restaurant one evening, very romantic, they flirt, etcetera, ectetera, they date, eventually they fall in love. Come on, he's a reasonable-looking guy and she's a pretty reasonable-looking woman, and one thing we know about Mr Michael Kerwin is that he was away most of the week on business.

193

Between the two of them Denman and Mrs Kerwin work out this plan to kill off *his* fiancée and *her* husband. Denman used to work in insurance, remember, he must know all the wrinkles. It's *Double Indemnity* all over again.'

'But why did they fry a whole busload of people, just to nail this one guy?' Detective Gable asked him, looking more like Jackie Gleason than ever. His hair was frizzy and wild, and there were clear beads of perspiration on his upper lip.

'It's been heard of before,' the young deputy remarked, trying to sound experienced and professional. 'You remember that case when a guy bombed an entire airplane, just to collect his mother's insurance? A hundred innocent passengers blown out of the sky, and for what? Just to get rid of one person. Hard case to solve, too: you've got scores of suspects, and as many motives as there are passengers.'

'Yes,' said Sergeant Houk, caustically, 'I saw that movie too.'

Detective Gable wiped his forehead with his sleeve. 'So what are we going to do? Are we going to go in there, or what?'

'Of course we're going to go in there,' Sergeant Houk told him, with exaggerated patience. 'You know what my motto is, "No Stone Unturned". Maybe Denman *didn't* do it. But maybe he did. Maybe he's Ortal and maybe he isn't. But we're not going to find out by sitting on our rear ends.'

He climbed out of the car, and combed his hair. Then he said, 'Let's go,' and they went.

They negotiated the interlocked maze of closely-parked Mercedes, and Sergeant Houk admired each one in turn. 'Beautiful, beautiful. Clean them up, and they'd be worth a fortune. You see that one, that tourer? One point five, easy.'

'Pretty small engine for a car that size,' Detective Gable remarked.

'Engine? Who's talking about engines? One point five million, at auction. They sold one at Christie's just like it.'

They climbed the broken steps to the verandah. 'Don't know how much Orwell charges for this dump, but it's got to be too much,' Sergeant Houk remarked. 'Have you seen the prices around here? Three quarters of a million for a three-bedroom home, and a view of what?'

They reached the door. The lizard doorknocker hung in front of them heavy and fat and black, more like a flaccid overripe fruit than a doorknocker cast out of brass. Sergeant Houk took a look along the verandah, at the broken boards, at the grimy windows. 'Place looks deserted to me. Deputy – why'nt you scout round the back – see what you can see? But be careful what you do. Don't touch anything, even if it looks like evidence. *Especially* if it looks like evidence. We don't have a warrant.'

He took hold of the knocker and clapped it forcefully against the door. It startled a brace of California quail on the roof-ridge, and sent them fluttering into the bright morning sky.

'Nobody here, Sergeant,' the deputy called back, as he reached the end of the verandah.

Detective Gable looked this way and that, as if he were trying to cross the street. 'You know something, Sergeant, this case is totally weird. This is the weirdest damned case I ever handled.'

Sergeant Houk shook his head. 'This case isn't weird. There's nothing weird about it at all. The perpetrator wants us to believe it's weird, that's all, to throw us off. A woman burns herself to death in a parking lot. A bus-load of people burn themselves to death in the desert. A woman gets burned in her apartment, a McDonald's chef gets burned in his car. It's not weird, Gable, it's just death, and death is death no matter how it happens. You wouldn't think it was weird if they were shot, or stabbed, or strangled.'

'Well, I know. But I still think it's weird.'

Sergeant Houk knocked again, but the front door remained adamantly closed. The deputy came back along the verandah, his boot-heels making a hollow rocking noise, his thumbs wedged into his belt.

'Okay, Matt Dillon. Go check the back,' Sergeant Houk instructed him.

'The name's Roger,' the deputy replied, somewhat put out.

'Okay, Roger, sorry Roger, go check the back, Roger.'

The deputy skirted the garage and timidly fought his way through the overgrown weeds, using his gun-barrel to push aside the thistles. Sergeant Houk watched him go with the expression of a man who had to learn patience the hard way.

'All right,' he said, at last. 'Let's give this doorknocker one last workout.' He banged it seven times, grotesquely loudly, and Detective Gable winced every time.

'If they don't answer that, they're either out, or dead,' said Sergeant Houk.

They waited and waited. 'Nobody in,' said Detective Gable. But as he did so, the front door suddenly unlatched itself and swung open, and there stood Helmwige, tightly swaddled in a bronze silk bathrobe, with a towel tied around her head.

'Yes?' she said, as if she hadn't heard Sergeant Houk beating at the door as if it were the Gates of Hell.

Caught off-balance, Sergeant Houk dropped his badge. As he bent down to retrieve it, he saw that Helmwige was wearing heavy silver anklets. 'I'm sorry to disturb you. We're investigating a series of homicides in the San Diego area. I was wondering if I could ask you some questions.'

Helmwige blinked at him with spiky wet eyelashes. 'What could I possibly know about homicides?'

Sergeant Houk coughed. 'I'm not suggesting that you know anything about them directly, ma'am. It's just that you may be able to assist the investigation by clearing up a couple of peripheral queries.'

Helmwige said nothing. Sergeant Houk wasn't at all sure that she had understood him.

'For instance,' he ventured, 'do you happen to be acquainted with a man called Lloyd Denman? He owns a fancy fish restaurant at La Jolla. Tall guy, thin, kind of aquiline nose.'

'Beaky,' added Detective Gable, when Helmwige still failed to respond.

Helmwige, without taking her eyes off them, called, 'Otto! *Kommen Sie nach hier, bitte!*'

After another lengthy pause, during which Helmwige stared back at Sergeant Houk and Detective Gable without volunteering a single word, Otto appeared from what was obviously the kitchen door at the back. He was wearing a white T-shirt and voluminous grey cotton shorts, which made him look even thinner and paler and more dried-out than ever. He was wiping his hands on a small threadbare towel, over and over and over.

Helmwige said, 'These gentlemen are detectives. They want to know if we have heard of anybody named – what was it, Detective?'

'Sergeant,' Sergeant Houk correct her. 'And the name of the man I was asking you about is Lloyd Denman.'

Otto inspected Sergeant Houk and Detective Gable with cold yellowish-grey eyes. He continued to rub his hands as if he were obsessive about having them completely dry. 'Why should you ask us this?' he wanted to know.

'Well, sir,' said Sergeant Houk. 'We're investigating a number of homicides … you may have heard about them, a whole lot of people in the San Diego area have been burned to death … and Mr Denman happens to be a suspect in this case.'

'A suspect?' asked Otto, and then nodded.

'Do you know him?' repeated Detective Gable.

Otto pursed his lips dismissively, and shook his head. '*Nein. Ich kenne ihn nicht.*'

Sergeant Houk opened his notebook. 'He was supposed to have visited these premises yesterday morning, round about eleven o'clock.'

'*Das ist ganz unmöglich,*' Otto replied.

'What'd he say?' Sergeant Houk asked Helmwige.

'He said, it is not possible.'

'He was seen entering these premises, sir.' Then, to Helmwige, 'Tell him that . Lloyd Denman was seen entering these premises.'

197

'Have you seen this man Denman?' Otto asked him, unexpectedly, in English.

'Sure I've seen him,' said Sergeant Houk guardedly. 'I saw him about a half-hour since. And if you can speak English, why the hell have we been ...'

He was interrupted by a splintering of glass from the back of the house, which sounded distinctly like a young deputy sheriff putting his boot-heel through a cucumber-frame. Otto's eyes instantly flared wide open, and he hissed at Sergeant Houk, 'You have sent somebody around to the back of the house?'

'Well, yes, I'm sorry, but we didn't think there was anybody here and we were just checking to make sure that ...'

'You have a warrant?'

'Not specifically as such, but ...'

'Who knows you are here? Which of your superiors? Which of your colleagues?'

'Sir – we weren't sent by anybody – this happens to be part of an ongoing investigation, that's all ... and if that deputy has damaged anything ...'

But Otto turned away from him, opened the kitchen door, and disappeared. Sergeant Houk said to Helmwige, 'Listen – I didn't intend to cause any problems here, but ...'

Without a word, her face grim, Helmwige slammed the door. Sergeant Houk and Detective Gable were left standing on the verandah.

'Didn't I tell you this case was weird?' said Detective Gable, hitching up his trousers.

'If I had a goddamned warrant I'd bust in there like fifteen tons of hot shit,' Sergeant Houk snarled. 'Goddamned Krauts. Just because we beat the shit out of them during the war, they seem to think we owe them some kind of apology.'

'Well, how can they expect that?' said Detective Gable. 'We weren't even *born* during the war.'

'Oh God give me strength,' Sergeant Houk retaliated.

At that moment, they heard an appalling high-pitched

scream. It sounded like a bird at first, or a coyote caught in a gin-trap. But it was quickly followed by another, more like a bellow of pain than a scream, and then a shout of '*Help me! Help me! Aaaahhh! Help me!*'

Sergeant Houk slapped Detective Gable on the shoulder and snapped, 'Round the back! Quick! You go that way, I'll go this!'

They both drew their guns. Detective Gable jumped heavily off the verandah and ran around the garage block, battling with the weeds as he went. Sergeant Houk sprinted along the verandah, round the other side of the house, and with a fierce kick broke the latch of the white-washed wooden gate at the side. He forced the gate wider, pushed himself through, and galloped up a flight of six or seven shallow brick steps to the back corner of the house. He caught his foot in a loosely-coiled garden hose; tripped, took three flying, loping, off-balance steps forward, and grazed his hand against the path.

The screaming went on, almost inhuman. As he came around the corner to the small back yard, Sergeant Houk saw the deputy engulfed in roaring flames, flapping at himself in a convulsive attempt to put them out. His arms jerked up and down like a clockwork toy, but all he was doing was fanning the flames even more. His eyes were squeezed shut. Both his ears were alight, shrivelling like radicchio leaves on a kitchen burner. Fire poured from the top of his head, sending up a column of black smoke that rose higher than the house.

Detective Gable appeared on the other side of the house, fighting aside the last of the weeds. He stopped and stared at the deputy in open-mouthed horror.

'Your coat, Gable, for Christ's sake!' yelled Sergeant Houk. 'Use your coat!'

He looked desperately around. How the hell do you extinguish a burning man? There was a swimming-pool in the yard, but it had obviously long been empty, and was peeling and cracked and silted up with dry eucalyptus leaves. The rest of the yard was mainly concrete, with a few sorry yuccas, a tangled flower border, and a glass vegetable frame hidden amongst the overgrown crabgrass.

The garden hose!

The deputy was still flapping, still dancing. Detective Gable had twisted himself out of his coat and was waving it at him like a matador, trying to get near enough the blazing deputy to smother the flames. Sergeant Houk ran back to the garden hose. The tap was stiff, but he hit it twice with the butt of his revolver, and it loosened.

Hurry, Christ, hurry, the man's on fire!

But all the time he knew that he was far too late, that it was no goddamned use, and that it would probably be kinder to let the deputy die. But he had been trained not to respond to thoughts like that. It was his duty to do what he could to save the deputy's life, human sympathy notwithstanding.

The hose was faded and inflexible from years of lying in the sun, and hideously knotted, but he managed to yank enough of it across the yard to reach the burning man. Water clattered on the dry ground all around him.

The deputy had fallen on to his side now, amongst the grass and the broken glass, and was shuddering and quaking in agony. Detective Gable was on his knees beside him, trying desperately to cover him up with his coat, but every time he moved the coat to suppress the flames that danced around his face, more flames would spring up around his thighs and his groin.

'Oh God!' whimpered Detective Gable, his own hands reddened and blistered. 'He's like one of those fucking candles you can't blow out!'

'Roger!' Sergeant Houk shouted. 'Roger, you hear me? It's okay! Get ready for a shock! This water's real cold!'

He couldn't tell whether the deputy had understood him or not. The boy's face was blackened like burned beef, his eyes had been poached into blindness, his hair was nothing but crisp black tufts. But somehow he was still alive, still hurting, still burning, still trembling in the very last moments of his life.

Sergeant Houk swung the hose around and drenched him.

200

Detective Gable heaved himself up, offering his own burned hands to the hosepipe jet, and saying, 'Here, Sergeant, for Christ's sake, just one splash.'

The second he said that, however, Sergeant Houk saw with horror that the hose hadn't extinguished the deputy at all. In fact, the flames were roaring up even more furiously, as if the water itself were flammable. He was about to say, '*Gable, no . . . !*' when the arc of water pouring out of the hose-nozzle burst into flame, and Detective Gable was drenched in fire.

Detective Gable screeched, and tried to wave away the fire with his arms, but his arms instantly caught alight. The hose almost immediately became too hot for Sergeant Houk to hold, and he dropped it. It snaked backwards and forwards under the wild pressure of the fluid, spraying Detective Gable again and again with liquid fire.

He fell to the ground, rolled over, thrashed, but he was burning even more fiercely than the deputy.

'Daddy!' he screamed. 'Daddy! For Christ's sake, Daddy!'

This time Sergeant Houk knew that the time for the rulebook had passed. He dodged the cascade of fire from the hose, and stepped up to Detective Gable quick and intent, his muscles tense as springs. He was holding his service revolver in both hands.

'God forgive me,' he said, and shot Detective Gable once in the head. Blood and brains sprayed outwards, and sizzled sharply in the heat.

Then Sergeant Houk turned around, his gun raised, and saw Otto standing at the kitchen window, his face white white white, his dry hands raised over his eyes as if he were staring at something very far in the distance. Helmwige stood a little further back in the shadows, but she wasn't even looking at the burning men in her back yard, she was admiring her fingernails.

Sergeant Houk pointed his gun stiffly at Otto and screamed, '*Freeze! Freeze, you bastard! You're under arrest!*'

But instantly he felt a wave of heat roar over him, as if a

201

huge furnace door had been opened right in front of his face. His hands blistered, his sleeve caught fire, his gun fired on its own, smashing the kitchen window. Instinctively, he threw the gun away, a split-second before the rest of its rounds exploded in the chamber, blasting fragments of shrapnel in all directions. One of them caught Sergeant Houk deep in his left-calf muscle.

You bastard! he thought. *You won't burn me!*

With his clothes alight, with his hair smoking, he ran back around the house, leaping over the hose, thundering along the verandah, vaulting the porch, and hurdling the long guano-spattered hood of Otto's Mercedes tourer.

He didn't notice the pain at first, but when his hair suddenly flared up, he felt a searing sensation on the top of his head that made him yell out. *He had to get away! He had to get away!*

His trousers were blazing, his shirt was almost completely burned off his back. Nylon was fused into skin, man-made fibre into man, until it was impossible even to separate them again. His shoes fell away from his feet in burning chunks, then the soles of his feet were torn off, with two sharp ripping noises, as his skin was fused to the blacktop.

He heard his breath coming in huge, Channel-swimmer's roars. He saw the road ahead of him, juggled in his vision like the view through a hand-held camera. He saw the eucalyptus trees swaying, although he couldn't hear them rustle. He saw his Buick, parked and ready for him, ready to take him away. He smelled fire, and smoke, and some indescribable odour that was *himself,* burning.

'*You ... Kraut ... bastard ... you ... won't ...*'

He reached his car, tugged open the driver's door with fingers that seemed to be dripping flesh.

Won't ... burn ... me ... you ...

His coat was gone, his shirt was gone. His torso was a mass of reddened flesh, on which small well-fed flames still licked. But he still had his car keys, embedded in his skin. With fingers that were tipped with nothing but bone, he prized the keys out of the blistered layers, pulling even more skin after them. He screamed in despair more than in pain.

'You won't burn me you bastard!' he shouted. He rammed the key into the Buick's ignition and the end of the key penetrated the palm of his hand, wedging itself right between his finger-bones. Still shouting, still blazing, he turned his hand so that the engine started, yanked the parking-brake, and skidded away from the side of the road in a blizzard of eucalyptus leaves and a cloud of dust. A Mexican gardener was raking the lawns of the house on the opposite side of Paseo Delicias. He turned around in horror as Sergeant Houk's Buick slewed past him, tyres shrieking like a chorus from *Tannhäuser*, with a man on fire in the driver's seat. The gardener dropped to his knees and crossed himself.

Swerving the Buick around the next bend, Sergeant Houk knew that it was over. His legs were still alight, his scalp was tightening and shrivelling like a bathing-cap. The pain was already so intense that he didn't know whether he could still feel it or not. It was like being *eaten*, rather than burned.

Ahead of him, up the winding hill of Paseo Delicias, he could see a huge blue-and-white truck toiling. *Genuine GM Auto Parts.*

Thank you, God, he thought to himself. *So you have forgiven me, after all.*

Behind the next embankment, he saw the top of the truck approaching. He pressed his foot as far down on the accelerator as he could, and wildly steered the Buick on to the lefthand side of the road.

He saw lemon trees passing, like trees in a dream. He saw rocks, bushes, fragments of sky, everything floating past him so gently and so normally, with the rocking motion of a carousel. He remembered the carousel at Disneyland, when he was a kid, floating up and down, up and down. But his tyres were still singing their merciless chorus, somewhere on the edge of his consciousness. *Fearful and loud thy rage is! Like a storm-wind you come!*

He opened his mouth to say something, but then his entire windshield was filled with the massive chrome radiator grille of the oncoming truck.

The Buick hit the truck at a closing speed of over seventy miles an hour. Its front end dived under the truck's front bumper, and the entire car vanished underneath the truck as if it had never existed. The truck driver didn't have the time to blow his horn.

Only a second afterward, however, the Buick's gas tank detonated with a sound like a huge and distant door slamming. The truck's body was blown apart in the middle, and a lethal hail of automobile parts was sprayed in all directions. A Caprice crankshaft was driven right through the back of the driver's cab, right through the back of his seat, and with a terrible and decisive crunch, right through his lower back. A spare Oldsmobile hub-cap sang through the air with the alien certainty of a flying-saucer, and sliced the head from the Mexican gardener who had witnessed Sergeant Houk's blazing ride down the hill. He stood headless with his sickle in his hand, as if, headless, he was unable to decide whether to fall over or not.

Then he dropped to the ground and began to irrigate the marigolds with a thick and glutinous stream of blood.

It was almost ten seconds before the last echoes of the explosion came back from the distant mountain, and the last fragments of shattered automobile parts came ringing down from the sky.

Otto turned away from the living-room window, and gave Helmwige a thin smile. 'It makes me impatient, you know, to show them who will be the masters next.'

'You should take more care,' Helmwige replied, in a voice which was meant to show him that she was deeply unimpressed.

'You heard what he said. Nobody knew that he was coming here, neither his superiors nor his colleagues. He came because our friend Herr Denman told him where to come. Herr Denman has an unpleasantly inquisitive turn of mind, you know, and the fact that we are keeping Celia here is obviously not enough to keep him from hounding us.'

'So what are you going to do?' asked Helmwige, flatly. 'You're not thinking of burning him, are you?'

'Of course not. Our future lies with men like Herr Denman. Good stock! Good fathers! Heaven knows that we are going to need all that we can get. But ... he is not behaving himself. I am going to be obliged to bring him here, and keep him out of harm's way until *der Umgestaltung*, the Transformation. Then he can burn. But not before. You remember what *der Führer* always said to me. "Otto," he always said to me, "the search for purity will take the lives of many martyrs. But we must seek purity first and last. *Die Reinheit zuerst, die Reinheit zuletzt. Die Reinheit it alles.*"'

Helmwige drew her silk bathrobe even more tightly around her, and stalked across to the far side of the living-room. The young naked man was still chained there, sitting cross-legged now, his face etched extremely sharp and pale against the southern California sunlight, every hard well-exercised muscle clearly defined. Helmwige stood over him for a long time, apparently admiring him, yet obviously despising him at the same time.

'The master race,' she said, shaking her head. 'What a pathetic specimen.'

Otto came and stood beside her, his hands in the pockets of his shorts. 'I suppose I have to agree. But then it was difficult for so many of those doctors to make such a leap of the mind. Mengele, what an idiot! And even the best of them, the very finest, Bloss and Hauer and von Harn, they could never understand that the master race was not just a question of genealogy, not just a question of breeding, but a question of the elements, too. The old, unquestioned power of the earth. That is what makes a master race.'

Helmwige ran her red-clawed hand through the young man's hair. 'Still, you know, I like him.'

'You like him!' Otto sneered. 'He is nothing more than a

failed experiment! A racial dead-end! My God, if *der Führer* hadn't made me promise, I would have destroyed him years ago, yes, and his father before him, and his father before him.'

'But you *did* promise,' Helmwige reminded him.

Otto walked across to the curved 1930s' cocktail cabinet, found a bottle of schnapps, and poured himself a drink. 'Yes, I did promise,' he agreed. 'And look at the result. A creature with perfect physique. Perfect body, perfect eyesight, perfect hearing. Pity his IQ is slightly below room-temperature.'

Helmwige continued to stroke the young man's blond, flat-cropped hair. He didn't lift his eyes to her once, didn't smile, didn't scowl, didn't acknowledge her at all, except when she began to run the very edges of her fingernails down the back of his neck, through those fine tiny almost-invisible hairs. Then his penis gradually swelled and uncurled, not fully erect, but visibly enlarged and thickened.

'Helmwige,' Otto admonished her, with a flatness in his voice which betrayed the fact that he was neither jealous nor interested. To him, the young man had less value than a laboratory chimpanzee. He was simply a nuisance, who had to be fed and exercised and accommodated. If Helmwige hadn't adored him so much, he probably would have set him alight years ago. That big fat prick would have burned like an altar candle.

Helmwige ran her fingernails all the way down the young man's knobbly spine. Then she traced the clearly developed lines of his deltoids, his teres minor and teres major, his latissimus dorsi. His chains clanked slightly as she stroked his shoulders, and his penis swelled even larger, until the foreskin gradually rolled back of its own accord, revealing the bare plum-like glans, with its high distinctive ridge, and its deeply cleft opening.

'You should have given him a name,' said Helmwige. 'How can anybody exist without a name?'

Otto sipped a little schnapps; ran a thin tongue-tip across thinner lips. 'He doesn't need a name.'

'How can he live, without a name?' Helmwige protested. They had been through this same argument more times than Otto could count.

'All he has to do is to *live*,' he retorted. 'A name is unnecessary. A dog may understand English, but you don't buy books, even for the cleverest dog.'

Helmwige stroked the young man's buttocks, and the sides of his thighs. Then she said to him, quite matter-of-factly, 'Turn over, you can be the cleverest dog.'

With a scraping and jangling of chains, the young man turned over until he was on all fours. He remained exquisitely handsome. His back beautifully curved, his thigh muscles taut. But he remained silent, too, and willing to obey.

'Now, look at him,' grinned Helmwige. 'Should I take him for a walk, on the end of a leash?'

'He will probably kill you one day,' Otto remarked, draining his schnapps and immediately pouring himself another.

'Oh, he won't kill me. He loves me. He adores me! I am the only one who treats him to what he likes!'

'That's what you think,' Otto told her. 'You humiliate him. Even a masochist has his pride, you know.' He patted his shorts, and said, 'Where are my cigarettes?'

'On the table,' Helmwige replied.

'Those are Marlboro. You know that I smoke only Ernte 23.'

Helmwige laughed, without humour. 'You smoke detectives, too, and all kinds of people!'

Otto snapped, 'Leave that boy alone! Go and find my cigarettes!'

'Oh, find your own cigarettes,' Helmwige replied. 'Just look at this.'

She spread apart the young man's buttock with her long red fingernails. Then, with the kind of taunting smile in her eyes that she knew Otto would find infuriating, she licked her index finger, and plunged it without hesitation into the knotted muscular rose of the young man's bottom. He flinched, uttered a low gasp, but accepted her

207

sharp-nailed finger without complaint.

'I suppose you were worse at Ohrdruf,' Otto commented.

'Everybody was worse at Ohrdruf. Guards, prisoners, everybody. The prisoners were as much to blame as we were. They brought it upon themselves. Have you ever experienced a race of people with such a death wish! How can a murderer be a murderer without a victim? In every murder, my dear Otto, the victim is an accomplice.'

Slowly, she withdrew her finger. Then she cupped the young man's testicles in her hand, and squeezed them, and massaged them, over and over, until they bulged between her fingers.

Otto looked away. 'You are appalling, my dear. You always were. I suppose your only redeeming feature is your complete disregard for human life, including your own.'

'Turn over,' Helmwige commanded the young man, and silently, he did so. Helmwige grasped the huge veined shaft of his penis in both hands, and rubbed it up and down, looking intently and questioningly into his eyes as she did so.

'How does *that* feel, then?' she asked him. 'Do you like it? Do you hate it? You don't really know, do you? What a vegetable!'

Now the head of his penis was gleaming and slick. Helmwige rubbed him harder and quicker. A faint flush of colour appeared on his perfect cheekbones; his stomach muscles tensed; and he closed his eyes. If possible, his penis appeared to grow even larger, and the opening gaped like a huge fish gasping for air.

'Now,' ordered Helmwige, with unexpected softness, and bent her head forward. Her mouth enclosed the head of his penis just as he shuddered, and ejaculated. She waited with her braided head bent forward in his lap for almost half a minute, and before she finally sat up, she pulled back the foreskin as far as it would go, and gave his shining skin one last definitive lick.

She stood up, and approached Otto with shining lips.

The young man remained where he was, his head still bowed, his penis shrinking.

'Don't you know what a tribute I pay you, Otto?' Helmwige teased him. Otto flinched and turned away, his thin fingers tightening on his schnapps glass.

'Otto – you are always the true master. Look what I have done for you! Mengele produced his so-called master race, and I have simply swallowed it!'

Otto refused to look at her. A few moments passed, the road outside was chaotic with sirens. Helmwige said, 'What is death, Otto? Where does it begin, where does it end? Supposing your mother had swallowed your father's sperm, on the night when you were due to be conceived? She would have killed you! You would have died, and been digested, and floated out to the Baltic, the tiniest atom in a whole universe of atoms.'

'Helmwige,' said Otto at last, still averting his face. 'If you touch that young man again, I will burn him to death in front of you. And that is my warning.'

Helmwige smiled. 'Why should I worry, Otto? You can frighten many, many people, but you can't frighten me. In any case, why should I care, when you plan to burn the whole world.'

— SIXTEEN —

Lloyd was pouring himself another cup of Kathleen's espresso when he saw the Mercedes pull up outside. After a moment, Otto climbed out, closely followed by Helmwige, but by nobody else. They came up to the front door, and rang the bell. Tom said, 'It's okay, I'll get it!'

Lloyd called, 'No! Leave it! Don't answer it!'

Kathleen was halfway down the stairs. 'What's the matter?' she asked. 'What's wrong?'

Lloyd strode quickly to the stairs and took her arm. 'It's them again. Otto and that woman.'

'They've come back? What do you think they want?'

'I don't know, but it might be better if you kept Lucy and Tom well out of the way.'

The doorbell rang again. They could see Otto's distorted shape through the window. Otto had already begun to inspire in Lloyd a kind of nagging dread, like waking up in the night with the fear that he might have cancer. Kathleen said, 'All right, just to be safe. Tom ... Auntie Lucy's upstairs, why don't you take her another cup of coffee?'

When Tom had carefully carried the cup upstairs, Lloyd went to the door and opened it. Otto was standing on the step in his old-fashioned grey suit and his wide-brimmed hat, smiling coldly in the sunshine, while Helmwige stood a short distance away, dressed in a black Spandex mini-skirt and a leather jacket which looked as if it had once belonged to Judge Dredd.

'What do you want now?' Lloyd asked Otto, tautly.

Otto peered into the house as if he were inspecting it for dry-rot. 'You don't mind if we come in?'

'Yes, I very much do mind if you come in. What do you want?'

Otto's roaming eyes settled on a crane fly that was trembling on the side of the doorway in the warm morning breeze. 'You gave me your word, Mr Denman, that you would tell nobody about us.'

'I've kept it.'

'Oh? Then perhaps you can explain a visit we received this morning from three police officers, inquiring if we knew you. A very unpleasant visit, I might add. A visit that ended in a most regrettable tragedy.'

'Tragedy?' queried Lloyd. He was aware that his left eyelid was involuntarily fluttering. He was exhausted, he was stressed, and most of all he was terrified of what Otto might take into his head to do to them.

'There was a fire, and an automobile accident,' Otto explained, his eyes still fixed on the crane fly. 'As I said, most regrettable. But we all know that police work has its risks.'

'A fire? You burned Sergeant Houk?'

'Was that his name? You shouldn't have told him where to find us, you know. That was a great mistake.'

'I didn't tell him anything.'

Otto's eyes sloped toward Lloyd, and he gave him a thin lazy grin. 'Oh, come now, Mr Denman. Do you take me for a *Dummkopf?*'

'Christ, you're insane,' Lloyd breathed at him.

'On the contrary,' Otto replied. 'In all the world, I am probably the only man who is in a state of complete mental balance.'

'What do you want?' Lloyd repeated.

'I want *you*, Mr Denman, and I want Mrs Kerwin.'

'I don't understand.' Lloyd hated him so much at that moment he could have seized him by the neck and throttled him. But as if she could sense the sudden surge in Lloyd's hostility, Helmwige stepped forward and stood close to Otto's shoulder, with an expression of threatening disinterest. Lloyd had seen the same expression on the faces of security guards at rock concerts. They'll break your back or they won't break your back, it's up to you. But they'll do it if necessary.

'Mr Denman,' Otto explained, 'the summer solstice is next Wednesday. Then our Transformation Ceremony will be complete. I will no longer have to worry if inquisitive people disrupt our preparations. But until that time, I must ask that you and Mrs Kerwin stay as my guests, in order not to spread undue alarm about us, amongst people who may not be friendly.'

'You expect *anybody* to be friendly to you, the way you're acting?' Lloyd demanded.

'I expect only to be left undisturbed,' Otto replied.

'Well, if you think we're going to stay with you, you're crazy.'

Otto couldn't resist the crane fly. His hand passed over it, and cupped it, and discreetly he pressed it into his mouth. Lloyd grimaced in disgust.

'You shouldn't rush to judgement, Mr Denman,' Otto told him. 'There are other ways of life, apart from *nouvelle cuisine* and the pursuit of custom homes with real brick fireplaces.'

'Don't you mock me, Herr Mander,' Lloyd cautioned him. 'Now get the hell out of here, and don't come back.'

Otto raised his hand. 'I've come to get you, Mr Denman, one way or another. If you don't agree to stay with me until the solstice, you and Mrs Kerwin, then believe me, you will burn, too.'

Lloyd said, 'You're bluffing. Now take a powder, before I do something I might be sorry for.'

Otto stared at him. Almost immediately, Lloyd felt a sharp pain in the middle of his forehead, and heard the snap of burning skin. He shouted out, and lifted his hand to his forehead. Otto had burned a small circular mark on him.

'You see that is "O" for Otto,' Otto smiled. 'You are branded now, Mr Denman, like a dumb animal. You belong to me.'

Lloyd took a cautious step back. His forehead felt as if it were still on fire. 'You want us to stay with you? At your house in Rancho Santa Fe?'

'Until next Wednesday, for the sake of my peace of

mind. You wouldn't want to disturb my peace of mind, would you, Mr Denman?'

'I guess I wouldn't,' Lloyd replied. Helmwige laughed.

At that moment Kathleen appeared. Otto bowed, and clicked his heels together. '*Guten Morgen, gnädige Frau.*'

'Lloyd?' asked Kathleen. 'What's going on? What's the matter with your forehead?'

They were driven to Rancho Santa Fe with the sounds of *Die Walküre* on the Mercedes stereo. Inside the car, it was like a black leather icebox, so cold that Kathleen shivered. Helmwige drove, Otto sat neatly in the passenger-seat with his knees together and smoked a cigarette with an amber holder. The music was too loud for sensible conversation.

Kathleen's sister Lucy had been confused and worried by her sudden request to take Tom for a week, and she had obviously been suspicious of Otto and Helmwige. But Kathleen had explained that Otto was a grief counsellor with the psychiatry faculty at UCSD, and that she needed to spend a few days with him to help her get over Mike.

'He's a good friend, too,' she had assured Lucy, as Helmwige had lifted their bags into the trunk.

'You never mentioned him before,' Lucy had replied, 'and he sure doesn't *look* like any kind of counsellor. Let alone anybody that *you'd* like.'

'It takes all kinds,' Kathleen had told her, and kissed her cheek. 'I'll be back Thursday morning. Take care of Tom for me.'

'You know I will.'

They reached the house on Paseo Delicias and turned into the sloping drive, parking close to the Mercedes 380SL. Helmwige opened the door and they dutifully climbed out.

'Helmwige will bring in your bags,' Otto told them. 'Follow me ... I will show you where you can stay.'

'Where's Celia?' asked Lloyd, looking around. 'Is she here someplace?'

Otto turned to him, his face as crumpled as white

213

tissue. 'I will explain everything to you in due course, Mr Denman. And in due course, I will show you your bride-to-be.'

'You're sick,' Lloyd told him.

'History will be the judge of that, not you,' smiled Otto.

'How about that friend of yours?' asked Lloyd. 'The guy in the chains?'

'What about him?'

'Is he still here? I'm not sure that he's exactly the kind of sight that Mrs Kerwin ought to be exposed to.'

'He's nothing. He's not even a person.'

'What do you mean, "he's not even a person"? What the hell is he, then – two orders of eggroll to go?'

Otto stopped on the verandah and fixed Lloyd with a look that could have set fire to a lake. 'Don't joke with me, Mr Denman. Don't think that you have that privilege. You have voluntarily and unwisely involved yourself in a matter which is no concern of yours, and now you are paying the price for your inquisitiveness. I could have burned you many times. Be thankful that I didn't, but watch what you say. I can always change my mind.'

Lloyd said nothing. He could sense that he had pushed Otto way too far, and just because Otto didn't have a gun, that didn't mean that he wasn't capable of killing him with all the effectiveness of a gun, and a hundred times more painfully. He allowed Otto to lead him into the house, and Kathleen followed a little way behind.

Otto showed them into the living-room. Lloyd noticed that the chain-rings were still in the floor, although the young man was gone. Inside, the living-room looked even more like a period piece from the 1930s than it had from the outside. The wallpaper was dull brown, the furniture was mostly laminated plywood and chrome. On the walls were dozens of sepia photographs of Germany before World War Two. Pretty girls in fur stoles, smiling young men, balconies and snowy mountaintops.

An old-fashioned gramophone stood in one corner, with a stack of 78 records beside it. The top record was *Die Wacht Am Rhein*.

Lloyd looked up at the huge drawing of the lizard on the wall. 'Our friend the crosslegged gecko,' he remarked.

Otto stared at him coldly. 'That, my friend, is a salamander. The symbol of our Transformation.'

Kathleen came in, and looked around. She gave Lloyd a meaningful glance, but both of them guessed that they would be safer if they remained quiet.

Helmwige showed them upstairs to their rooms. Both rooms were small, with sloping dormer ceilings, and in Lloyd's room the bed was no more than a mattress on the floor. He had a restricted view over the treetops, downhill toward the Fairbanks Ranch, but immediately he saw there was no prospect of escaping out of the window. Below the sill, there was a short slope of oak-shingled roof, and then a sheer drop down to the yard. He peered out and saw the young man who had been chained up in the living-room, digging in the yard with a shovel. The young man wore baggy shorts and a singlet, and the back of his singlet was dark with sweat. Lloyd wondered what he was doing gardening on such a blistering hot afternoon. At least he wasn't naked. But when Lloyd looked again, he saw that the young man was still restricted by a long chain around his right ankle. *Very* bizarre.

'You are free to do anything except leave,' Helmwige told them. 'You will be well taken care of. Otto is many things, but he is always a man of his word.'

'Glad to hear it,' said Lloyd. 'What time's lunch?'

Helmwige said, 'He will tell you everything this evening. I know Otto. He talks about secrecy but he is so impatient to show the world what he has achieved. Your Celia is part of that achievement, Mr Denman. He won't be able to resist the temptation to boast.'

'He burns people and then he boasts?'

Helmwige smiled, almost friendly. 'You still don't get it, do you, Mr Denman? It is right in front of your eyes. You should try perhaps to see things for what they are, instead of what you would like them to be.'

She went back downstairs, and left them alone. Kathleen came up to Lloyd and held him close, without saying

215

a word. Lloyd circled his arms around her and said, 'Don't worry ... really, don't worry. Everything's going to be fine. So long as we play it cool and easy, and don't lose our nerve.'

'But what are they *doing*?' asked Kathleen. 'Are they spies, or what? And if it's all such a big secret that we have to stay here, why does Otto want to boast about it so much?'

'And what is it that's right in front of my eyes, that I don't see?'

Kathleen shook her head. 'It's all so strange. I feel like I'm going to wake up any minute and Mike will be lying in bed next to me and none of this will ever have happened.'

Lunch didn't materialize, but by six o'clock they began to smell the strong aroma of cabbage throughout the house. Shortly after seven, the young man knocked at their doors, and asked them to come downstairs to eat. He was wearing the same shorts and singlet that he had been wearing in the yard, and he smelled of sweat.

Kathleen said to him, 'You like gardening, huh? I just love it!'

The young man looked at her without expression.

'We saw you in the yard,' Kathleen told him, trying to sound bright. 'You were digging, yes? We saw you digging.'

Still the young man said nothing.

'Looks like the lights are on, but there's nobody home,' Lloyd remarked.

'You do *comprenez anglais*?' Kathleen asked the young man. 'I mean, you asked us to come eat. Or was that just something that Otto taught you?'

'Come on, Kathleen, forget it,' said Lloyd. 'Let's just go eat.'

The young man led them downstairs, and showed them through to a small dining-room furnished in dark oak. Otto was already sitting at the head of the table, Helmwige on his left. Around the walls hung lurid amateurish paintings of Bavaria, purple mountains and black pine-trees and lime-green lakes, although pride of place was given to a framed photograph of a stern, rectangular-faced man with acne-scarred cheeks and long bushy side-whiskers.

'Wagner,' said Lloyd, immediately. He had seen so many pictures of Wagner in Celia's treatises.

Otto nodded. 'Yes, Wagner, to whom we owe so much.'

'Isn't ... *he* ... eating with us?' asked Kathleen, nodding toward the young man.

'No, no,' said Otto, quite surprised. 'He doesn't eat with us.'

Helmwige lifted the lid from a huge blue-and-white china casserole dish. A strong aroma of pickled cabbage and ham filled the room. 'Choucroute,' Helmwige announced. 'I make it myself. Pickled cabbage with pork belly and liver dumplings.'

She heaped three plates high, and handed them to Kathleen, to Lloyd, and to herself. Otto ate nothing but a little dry bread, which he broke into tiny pieces. *Too many bugs in between meals*, thought Lloyd, but decided against saying it out loud. Helmwige's food was fatty and unappetising enough without thinking about Otto eating insects.

Kathleen lifted up a huge slice of white vibrant pork fat on the end of her fork. 'I'm sorry,' she said. 'I can't eat this. I'm on the F-Plan diet.'

Plainly irritated, Helmwige took the fork and shook the fat on to her own plate. She cut it up and ate it with gusto, juice running down her chin. 'I've seen people kill each other for such food,' she said.

Lloyd put down his fork. 'I guess that must have been before the days of *nouvelle cuisine*,' he remarked. Actually, if he had been able to eat the kind of heavyweight food that sustains Alsatian farmworkers, he probably would have found Helmwige's cooking very good. He tried a little of the cabbage and it was strong and savoury and delicious.

Lloyd and Kathleen picked at their food in silence for a

few minutes, while Helmwige noisily devoured fat and sausage and potatoes and pickled cabbage. Occasionally Otto fastidiously ate another small piece of bread, or sipped a glass of Alsace riesling, but most of the time he sat at the head of the table as if he were waiting for something, but didn't know what. He cracked his knuckles one by one, and sighed.

Kathleen said, 'Who is that young man?'

Otto turned to stare at her. 'Are you speaking to me?'

'Yes. I wanted to know who that young man is. The one who called us down to supper.'

'He isn't anybody,' Otto replied.

'What do you mean? Everybody's *somebody*.'

'Not him. He belongs to a genealogical line which should never have existed. He is ... what do you call it? ... a freak, a mistake.'

'He looks all right to me,' said Kathleen.

'Of course!' Otto smiled. 'Physically he is flawless. But inside his mind ... well, who knows what goes on inside his mind. When you ask him where he lives, he says that he lives inside of a black sack. You can't take him out at night, because he keeps throwing stones at the moon, trying to hit it.'

'Well, that's terrible,' said Kathleen. 'He's so good-looking.'

'A master race is not made up of looks alone,' Otto told her.

It was then that Lloyd raised his eyes from his half-finished meal and saw the symbol of the salamander inside the circle, and understood at last what it was that had been right in front of his eyes, and which he had failed to see. *Master race.* The salamander's head was crooked, its feet were crooked. If he half closed his eyes, he found that he was looking at nothing less than a swastika.

'Let me explain what we are doing,' said Otto. 'It won't do any harm, since you will be staying here until the Transformation is over.'

Helmwige, with her mouth full, rolled her eyes up at

Otto's predictability. She gestured with her fork at Kathleen's plate and said, 'Mmm-hm, mm-hmm!' – encouraging her to eat up.

Otto said, 'In 1936, as soon as he was appointed Chancellor, Hitler commissioned doctors from many different scientific disciplines to explore the possibility of creating a master race, based on the natural supremacy of the Aryan. Immediately these doctors set to work in their laboratories and their hospitals, trying to breed perfect little babies.'

He sat back in his seat, and interlaced his fingers. '*Der Führer* also asked me to contribute to this programme. I was very young in those days, a philosophy student in Basel, but already I had shown my interest in the National Socialist ideals, and come to the attention of Josef Goebbels. It was Goebbels who recommended me to Hitler.

'I pursued other ideas, quite different from breeding babies. I was a thinker, not a farmer! Besides, I thought breeding was too slow, too uncontrollable! *Der Führer* wanted to change the racial characteristics of the world in a decade, not wait for the unpredictable results of several centuries!

'How many generations does it take to produce children who are blond and beautiful and possess the required size of brainpan? And what guarantee would you ever have that these perfect creatures would grow up capable as well as beautiful?

'No ...' he said, smiling as he sipped his wine. 'I was searching for a master race that was guaranteed not only to be beautiful and mentally brilliant, but also to be ready within a matter of years, perhaps months, perhaps even weeks! That meant selecting people who had already shown themselves to have these desirable characteristics. Not breeding babies, you see, but transforming adults.'

He scraped back his chair, and stood up. 'I spent years and years at Salzburg University, looking for a way. I searched right back in history and legend, right back to the days of the Vikings, looking for any kind of clue. At last I began to come across references to a Transformation ceremony in Northern Jutland, in which the bravest and most intelligent people in several communities were burned alive *in order that they might never die.*

'If the proper ritual was observed, the fire did not destroy them, but transfigured them, immortalized them. In other words, the Danes were burning alive their best people to preserve them for ever, and to make them the founding members of a pure and immortal race. They had tried to preserve people before, by pressing them into their peat-bogs, but without success. The answer was fire!'

Kathleen looked across the table at Lloyd, but the expression on her face was one of apprehension, not disbelief. They had both seen enough of Otto's abilities to know that at least some of what he was saying must be true.

'In Salzburg I also came across previously unpublished diaries by Paracelsus, the sixteenth-century alchemist, who had proved to his own satisfaction that there is a direct physical and mystic connection between life and fire. Both life and fire fed on other lives, but if they were *combined* they created first a life that was fire, and then, at the moment of complete Transformation, a fire that was life.

'This was my breakthrough! I searched libraries in Leipzig and Dresden and London, too, and time and time again I came across references to the life-giving properties of fire. I discovered that when a living human being is burned, there is a Norse ritual which ensures that the soul and the fire combine, to form a half-being which I call a Salamander, after the legendary lizard which hides itself in the hottest recesses of blacksmiths' forges.

'Salamanders are highly volatile. They can be as cool as flesh or as hot as fire, according to their temperament. They are susceptible to spontaneous combustion, so they have to keep themselves masked from the air. Hence the scarves, and the coats, and the gloves. Too much oxygen, and they can burn like phosphorus. Like Walpurgis night!'

220

He paused, and cleared his throat. His snake-yellow eyes seemed to be focused not just on something else but on *somewhere* else. Another time, another place, when fires had burned at night, and black-and-red banners had flapped, and voices had roared like the sea.

Helmwige finished eating, and began noisily to clear away this dishes. Otto said, 'The Transformation Ceremony must take place at the summer solstice, when the forces of the earth are at their strongest. I am not talking about magic here, or mysticism! These forces are gravitational and magnetic and psychokinetic – *measurable* forces, which have controlled the balance of the planet Earth for millions of years.

'The ancient music must be played, and the ancient words must be sung. Then the Salamanders will become flesh. Not just flesh, but immortal flesh! And flesh that still has the power of fire!'

Lloyd nodded toward Helmwige. 'Is she ...?'

Otto nodded. 'Immortal, and blessed with the power of fire. You felt her fingers on your wrist. But she is no use to me, as a propagator of the master race. She was a camp doctor of Ohrdruf during the war, and she caught some filthy Semitic disease which left her barren. It would have killed her, if she hadn't agreed to be burned.'

Lloyd swallowed, in an effort to control the revulsion that Otto aroused in him. 'So when somebody's burned, with all the appropriate chants, they cheat whatever illness they have, and live for ever?'

Otto smiled. '*Ach so*, Mr Denman. You learn quickly. Because – until it has unequivocally been shown to be true – who could you convince to burn themselves alive but those who know that they are terminally ill?'

'Like Marianna, with her breast cancer?' asked Lloyd.

Otto nodded. 'And your husband, Mrs Kerwin. He was suffering from a brain tumour which would have killed him within six or seven months.'

'So *that* was why he was so depressed after his medical,' said Kathleen, shocked.

'Dr Kranz referred him directly to me,' said Otto. 'In

221

South California, there is a whole network of doctors of German background who refer their terminal patients directly to me. Because, what choice do these people have? To die a mundane death, having achieved nothing at all? Or to become immortal, and to change the whole course of human history? That is why they agree to burn themselves alive. That is why they agree to become Salamanders.'

'But Celia wasn't sick,' Lloyd protested. 'She never even caught a cold.'

Otto laughed. 'They always say, don't they, that the husband is the last to find out! Or, in your case, the husband-to-be. Your beloved Celia was very sick, Mr Denman. The only thing was that she was desperate that you didn't find out. You would have insisted that she go for treatment. She would never have had the opportunity to do what she did. Where could she have found petrol and matches, in a clinic? Or at home, under your watchful eye?'

'What was wrong with her?' asked Lloyd, his mouth as dry as a torn-open kapok mattress.

Otto turned away for a moment, as if he hadn't heard, but then he turned back and said, 'Multiple sclerosis. Gradual wasting, gradual loss of muscular control, inevitable early death.'

'I don't believe you. You killed her!'

'Do you want to see Dr Warburg's records? I have them all in my files. You're not a doctor of course, but perhaps you noticed that when you stroked the soles of her feet, her great toe bent upwards, and her toes spread apart? That's the Babinski sign. In normal people, when you stroke the soles of their feet, the toes bend downwards.'

Otto couldn't have said anything more telling. Lloyd could clearly remember stroking her feet one night when they were making love, and noticing the way her toes spread out. 'How do you *do* that?' he had asked her. 'I can't do that!'

She had smiled and kissed him, and said, 'I hope you never find out.'

222

Lloyd was shaken. 'She had multiple sclerosis? And that was for sure?'

'That was for sure,' Otto replied. 'She could never have given you the children you wanted, she could never have been anything else but an invalid wife. Your married life together would have been a tragedy.'

'So she burned herself? She turned herself into one of these – what do you call them – Salamanders?'

'That is correct. That is what she is now. But when we hold our Transformation Ceremony at the summer solstice, she will become flesh, or flesh of a kind. Fire transformed into life. You will have her back, Mr Denman, never fear – and with the threat of illness erased for ever!'

Lloyd said, 'All of those people on the bus? Were they sick, too?'

'Every one of them. Some had years to live, some no more than weeks. But they had all decided that the way of the Salamander was the way for them, and they were prepared to suffer the pain of burning in the hope of the life everlasting.

'They had faith, Mr Denman. They were like Shadrach, Meshach and Abed-nego, who defied King Nebuchad-nezzar and stepped into the burning fiery furnace. In fact, there is historical evidence that the Babylonians in the sixth century before Christ had a ritual which was very similar to the Salamander ritual.'

Lloyd asked tautly, 'Why did Celia burn herself alone, when everybody else was burned together on the bus?'

'Celia was impulsive, Mr Denman. You know how impulsive she was. We were driving her back downtown after our last meeting when she suddenly said, "Now, let's do it now."

'I argued with her. I asked her if she was sure. But she insisted. She wanted to do it immediately.'

'And you let her,' Lloyd said, his voice as dull as a '53 nickel.

Otto's hand was spread flat on the table. His fingernails were ridged and chalky. 'I had no choice, Mr Denman. It takes so much for a person to build up the confidence to set fire to themselves. How do you express it? They have to be "on a high". At that moment, driving along Rose-crans Avenue, Celia reached that peak. She had to burn herself then and there, or else she may never have done it. We stopped at the petrol station and bought a jerrycan and five gallons of petrol, and the rest you know.'

Lloyd didn't know what to say. Celia had summoned up the courage to burn, Celia had summoned up the courage to change her life, Celia had summoned up the courage to become immortal. But she hadn't confided in him, her husband-to-be. Hadn't said a word. He didn't know who had failed whom. Maybe he had failed Celia, because he hadn't recognized that she was sick. Maybe Celia had failed him, because she hadn't trusted him to help her.

He could have nursed her, he could have taken care of her. But maybe she hadn't wanted nursing. Maybe she hadn't wanted him to take care of her. Maybe she had wanted what she had always wanted. Independence, freedom, and the pursuit of happiness, no matter what.

Helmwige came into the room, bearing a huge cut-glass bowl filled with aggressively pink trifle.

'Wait, wait,' Otto told her. 'We can have that later. Let me show Mr Denman the Salamanders who are awaiting the solstice with the same impatience that he is.'

'Your pride will be the death of you one day,' Helmwige replied.

'And your insolence will see you burn!' Otto rapped back.

Helmwige bared her teeth at him. 'Remember which one of us is immortal, Otto. I shan't be laying any flowers on your grave.'

Otto pushed his chair back and stood up. 'Come with me,' he told Lloyd and Kathleen, and led the way out of the dining-room. They hesitated for a moment, glancing at Helmwige, but Helmwige was already spooning a vast triangular cliff of bright pink trifle on to her plate, and she didn't seem to be interested in what they were doing at all.

They walked through the kitchen and out to the back of the house. The sun had just set, and the sky was the colour of pasqueflowers, high and clear. Kathleen suddenly reached out for Lloyd's hand. Slim fingers, soft warm skin. Lloyd felt something that he hadn't felt for years, not even with Celia. A sense of being responsible. A sense that a woman was depending on him to make things work out right. In high school, he had once dated a thin grey-eyed girl called Jane who had made him feel like that. Jane had probably married a real-estate agent or one of those used-car salesmen who scream at you on television.

Otto unlocked the back door of the garage, pushed it open, and switched on the overhead light. 'Go ahead! Look! *Hier schläft die Zukunft!*'

Lloyd peered inside. The huge garage had been built with whitewashed cinder block walls, and a low white-washed ceiling. In the far corner stood a solid and well-used workbench, with rows of drillbits and wrenches, a professional vice, and a car battery-charger. But there were no cars here, not one. Every available inch of floor-space was taken up by grey-faced bodies, lying down, dead or sleeping. Every one of them wore impenetrably dark sunglasses, and every one of them had a heavy grey blanket drawn up to the neck. It looked like a morgue for dead sun-worshippers, rather than a sanctum for people who were desperate enough to want to live for ever.

There was a heated smell in the air, like a communal sauna, or singeing wool, and the temperature was way up above normal. Lloyd noticed a small thermostat on the wall which was registering into the red.

'Salamanders,' Otto announced. 'Smoke and soul, combined. Eighty of them, so far.'

Kathleen, in a voice as pale and as transparent as a glass of water, said, 'Oh, God, Lloyd. That's him. That's Michael. That one there, close to the wall. That's Michael, I swear it. Oh, God.'

She started forward, but Otto held her arm and restrained her. 'Believe me, Mrs Kerwin, you will be doing

225

yourself no favours if you wake him up. At the moment, he is not the man you knew. Only when he has undergone the Transformation will you recognize him again, and then you can keep him for ever.'

'Can't I even *talk* to him? Let him know that I'm here?'

Otto gave her the tiniest dismissive shake of his head. 'He is too volatile. He could be quite calm, when he sees you. But on the other hand, he could explode. He might feel resentful. He might feel angry. You never know. But the point is that he could burn you. He could burn everybody around him, too. I can't risk a fire in this garage, not with all of the Salamanders here. Well, it doesn't bear thinking about, does it, Mr Denman? There's Celia, too, can you see her? There, by the door.'

Kathleen twisted her arm free of his fingers. 'I want to look at him, that's all. He's my husband.'

'Very well,' Otto agreed. 'But if you disturb him, and wake him, then do not blame me for what happens. I have worked too many years for this to allow some hysterical *hausfrau* to destroy it.'

Kathleen stepped carefully between the grey-blanketed bodies until she reached the far side of the garage. She stood over the wrapped-up body of a white-faced man, her hand clasped over her mouth, her eyes glistening with tears.

'She has no need to cry,' Otto told Lloyd. 'Michael will live for ever, long after she has gone. It is *he* who should be crying for *her*.'

Lloyd couldn't keep his eyes off Celia. She looked so grey. She looked so waxy. She looked so dead.

'When they're transformed ...' he asked Otto. 'What kind of life are they going to be able to lead?'

'Very different, in some way. Very ordinary, in others.'

'What does that mean?'

'It means, Mr Denman, that what you are looking at here is the beginning of the master race. These people, and many like them, will recreate that ideal world which we tried to establish during the war, but failed. They are all people of pure blood, of great talent, and of high intelligence.

226

'When they are transformed, they will able to do anything they please, because simply by touch they will be able to generate enormous natural power. If they are angered, they will be able to burn anything they please, and anyone they please. They will be invulnerable.'

'So Celia could set fire to me, if I annoyed her?'

Otto laughed. 'She could burn you to a cinder, my friend! But we don't want her to do that. We want you to be married, and to have children together.'

'She'll be able to have children?'

'Oh, yes,' Otto nodded. 'She certainly will. In fact, we encourage it. The future belongs to the young ones, yes? The special children ... half-human, half-fire.'

Kathleen came back across the garage. Her face was very pale.

'You, too, Mrs Kerwin,' smiled Otto. 'All the children you wish!'

— SEVENTEEN —

'By the end of nineteen forty-three I was quite sure that I had found what I was looking for,' Otto told them, as they sat in the living-room with Asbach brandy and cigars. The air was thick with blue flat-smelling smoke. The room was growing cold. With theatrical inappropriateness, Otto was trying to play the genial host, sitting in his huge 1930s' armchair with his leg swinging, smoking and drinking relentlessly and telling them all about the heyday of the National Socialist party. 'What times we had in Berlin! *Unter den Linden*, at night, in nineteen thirty-six! We shall never see times like that again!'

Kathleen was exhausted, and sat with her head bowed, saying nothing. Lloyd was tired, too, but he wanted to hear Otto out. He sipped his brandy to keep himself awake, and he glanced from time to time at Helmwige, who was so bored with what Otto was saying that she was finishing the crossword in the *San Diego Tribune*, sniffing and talking to herself.

Otto said, 'I had heard of an ancient ritual chant which could change a burning human into a Salamander, but although I searched through thousands of books, I could not find it! At Ohrdruf concentration camp, with Helmwige's assistance, I tried seven hundred different Norse and Hebrew prayers, burning a Jew each time in order to test the prayer's effectiveness, sometimes sixty or seventy Jews a day! Years went by, thousands were burned, but still to no avail. Not one of them survived, not one of them became a Salamander!

'However in March, nineteen forty-three, an old rabbi came to my office and asked me why I was burning these people. I explained that I was looking for the secret chant which could give a man immortality by fire. He begged me to stop burning people. He said that he would try to find out for me what the chant was, if only I would stop burning people. Well, what kind of an offer was that? I was a German officer and the experiment had been personally ordered by the Führer, and I said no.

'Eventually, however, this same rabbi returned to me. He said that the word had been sent throughout the camps, and that there was a young Jewish music professor at Flossenburg who could tell me everything that I wanted to know.'

He offered Lloyd more brandy, but Lloyd held his hand over his glass. He found it disturbing enough having to share a room with Otto, without having to accept his hospitality, too.

Otto said, 'The young professor had made a special study of Wagner and the origins of Wagner's music. He had heard that Wagner was supposed to have been interested in basing an opera on the Norse fire-burial chants, but he wasn't convinced that Wagner had ever written it. Apparently, the chants had been lost in the eighth century, during the Viking Migration period. The Book of Salamander, the runic book in which all the chants were contained, was sent by sea from Tollund to England, but it was sunk in a winter storm. However, the wreck must have been washed up on the northern coast of Germany, and the book salvaged. It reappeared in Bavaria, in the seventeenth century.

'By a very circuitous route, and after many dubious transactions, it had come into the possession of the Bürgermeister of Bamberg, Johann Junius. Junius had long been fascinated by alchemy and by the secrets of eternal life. He translated the Norse runes, and began experimenting by setting fire to live cats and dogs. The story goes that eventually he succeeded in creating an unkillable cat.

'However, Junius was spied on by his neighbours. He was arrested and taken before the courts, and accused of witchery. He was tortured with thumb screws and leg vices and the strappado, and in the end, of course, he confessed. Anything to escape further pain! He was burned at the stake, and apparently he shrieked and sang while the flames devoured him. Perhaps the good witch-finders of Bamberg managed to kill, perhaps they didn't. But the story has it that Junius was seen many weeks afterward in various towns in Bavaria, looking pale and strange.'

Lloyd said nothing. He found it almost impossible to speak to a man who had calmly confessed that he had burned thousands of innocent people for the sake of a mystical theory, no matter how earth-shattering that mystical theory might be. It hadn't been worth a single one of those lives. Not one. But who remembered those lives today?

Otto said, 'The Book of Salamander and all of Junius' notes were locked up in the *Rathaus* in Bamberg for two hundred years. But somebody found them, we don't know who. It could have been a plague doctor called Gunther Hammer, or an astrologer known only as Stange. Whoever it was, he must have been a fanatical devotee of Richard Wagner, because in November, 1882, he sent it immediately to Wagner with a long unsigned letter pleading that Wagner use it to achieve immortality.

'Richard Wagner had begun to fall ill in the last year of his life. Bad heart, you understand. In the letter, Hammer or Stange wrote to him, "Play these melodies, O Master, and you will live for ever." Wagner was deeply impressed by the Norse chants. They were so *barbarisch*, so powerful! But he completely misunderstood his well-wisher's intentions. He thought that he was being exhorted to turn the chants into an opera, so that he would achieve everlasting *fame*. It simply didn't occur to him that he could actually live for ever.

'At Flossenburg concentration camp, the young Jewish music professor told me that in his view the existence of the opera *Junius* was only a myth, and that it was quite probable that Wagner had never written it. But now I had a scent to follow! With five historians to assist me, I discovered from the private diaries of Wagner's friends that he had been working on a new opera in the last year of his life which he jokingly referred to as his *Wikings-gesangbuch*. He took it with him to Venice and he was still working on it when he died.

'Unfortunately, when Wagner died, neither the opera nor the Book of Salamander was found amongst his possessions. For a long time, I thought that I had reached a dead-end, and that the young music professor was right about the opera being nothing but a story. But in a moment of inspiration, I discovered the name of the doctor and of the priest who had attended Wagner on his deathbed. The priest was Father Xavier Montini, a Jesuit, and a famous scholar on the subject of pagan ritual.

'Now I used my logic, Mr Denman! My powers of deduction; and also my lifelong suspicion of Jesuits! I deduced that when Father Xavier Montini saw what Wagner had been working on, he became alarmed, and smuggled the Book of Salamander and the unfinished opera out of Wagner's house, and hid them. After all, isn't immortality supposed to be the exclusive territory of God Almighty? His unique selling point? The priest didn't want that challenged by some pre-Christian mumbo-jumbo from Jutland!

'Mussolini's military staff gave us all the co-operation we needed to comb Venice looking for the opera and the book. In the end, after three months, we found them, bricked into the cellar wall of a house that had belonged to one of Father Xavier Montini's friends. We were sad to discover that the cellar had flooded four or five times since the book had been concealed there, and that most of the original runes in the Book of Salamander had been obscured by damp. But the opera had been carefully wrapped in oilskin, and was almost as fresh and as bright as the day that Wagner had laid down his pen.

'We had in our hands the means to create the master race of which Hitler had always dreamed, a race of pure-blooded immortals who would rule the world with force and wisdom.'

'So what stopped you?' asked Lloyd.

Otto's eyes followed a blowfly as it droned across the

room, and the tip of his tongue ran across his lips. 'Wagner had taken many liberties with the original chants. He hadn't understood their importance, you see, and he had made many changes, for the sake of his opera. It was necessary for musical experts to work through the opera, note by note, in comparison, with Wagner's diaries, and with what we had managed to salvage from the Book of Salamander, in order to recreate the original ritual music.

'Otherwise, our dream would have been *totgeboren*, you understand? Born dead.'

He stood up. He swayed a little, as if the Asbach brandy had made him drunk. He seemed taller than before, a giant ash-grey stick-insect. Thin and tall and long-legged. Lloyd watched him with apprehension. He walked over to the window where the blowfly was furiously bizzling against the glass.

'Our work was still not complete when the Russians entered Berlin. I was in the *Führerbunker* with Hitler and those who remained. Goebbels, Bormann, and the rest. On Hitler's instructions, I was still working with Helmwige on the opera. We burned alive two young volunteers from the Hitler Youth, without success. They simply died in terrible pain. Then on the night of April 29, with the Russians only hours away from us, Helmwige volunteered to be burned. Hitler's chauffeur Erich Hempka went to fetch two hundred litres of petrol, and two SS men dug a sandy pit in the Chancellery garden.'

He paused for a second, then scooped the blowfly into his hand. He held it up, and Lloyd could hear it furiously buzzing.

'We chanted the ritual chant, and then we drenched Helmwige with petrol and she set fire to herself with a lighted rag. She said nothing. Didn't scream, didn't protest. At last the fire-chants had worked. Her smoke and her soul arose, and although her body remained, her spiritual essence became a Salamander, a creature of fire and spirit. It was amazing to watch. Hitler witnessed it for himself, and he was in tears.

'Helmwige and I escaped from the *Führerbunker* along with Martin Bormann, and we were helped by SS officers to obtain International Red Cross passports, and to make our way to America. We arrived in New Orleans in time for the summer solstice, and we were able to complete the ritual in a room at the Pontchartrain Hotel. Helmwige then became what she is today. A living example of the master race.'

Otto held his fist close to his ear, so that he could hear the blowfly's desperate struggles. He smiled in anticipation of the tiny treat that he was going to give himself.

'What about Hitler?' asked Lloyd. 'If he saw what happened to Helmwige ... didn't he want to try it for himself?'

Otto gave a non-committal shrug. 'The *Führer* was, of course, deeply impressed with what I had achieved. I was immediately put in charge of all genetic and racial experiments, including those of Mengele and von Harn. Not that it counted for much, of course. By that time, the Russians had already reached Potsdamer Platz, and the Reich was obviously at an end.

'Hitler told me to leave Berlin with Helmwige and with a young Aryan boy whom Mengele had bred ... the father of the young man who acts as our servant now.'

'But Hitler didn't take to the idea of setting fire to himself?' Lloyd persisted.

Otto turned and stared at him narrowly, although the curved shadow from the mock-parchment lampshade made it difficult for Lloyd to see his face.

Otto said nothing for a while. Then he looked away. 'What happened to the *Führer* will always remain a secret,' he said.

'Did you turn him into a Salamander?'

Otto shook his head. '*Ich weiß nicht.* If the *Führer* went through the ritual, he did after I left the *Führerbunker.* Helmwige and I and the boy escaped from Berlin in the early hours of April 30th. Later that same day, Hitler's body was burned, yes, that is a matter of historical record. But the historical record does not say whether he was alive when he was burned, or whether he was already dead. He was supposed to have shot himself in the mouth, but when they carried his body out of his room, his head was covered with a blanket, so that none of the eye-witnesses could tell for certain.'

'But if he *did* go through the ritual ...?'

Otto shrugged. 'If he *did* go through the ritual, then the probability is that he is still alive. But where ... who knows?

He opened his hand, and lifted out the blowfly by one leg. He picked off its wings with the concentration of a man picking the stalk off a raisin. Then he popped it quickly on to his tongue, and held it in his mouth for a moment, so that he could feel it vibrating against his cheeks. He sucked, and swallowed. 'Helmwige,' he said, 'switch on the television.' The conversation appeared to have ended.

They watched *21 Jump Street* for a while. Then Otto switched over to the eight o'clock news. Lloyd looked at Kathleen but there was nothing that either of them could do. Otto watched a long item about crack dealing in San Diego schools, frowning and muttering to himself. Then the news turned to the accidental death of San Diego Detective Sergeant Houk, and the disappearance of Detective Gable and Deputy Bredero.

'Sergeant Houk and Detective Gable were assisting State police in their investigation of the death by burning of thirteen men and women in the Anza Borrego State Park ... While Sergeant Houk's death appears to have been an automobile accident, state and metropolitan police are still unable to account for the complete disappearance of Detective Gable and Deputy Bredero ... Deputy Bredero's patrol car was found abandoned at the Five Flags shopping centre close to Highway I-5, with no fingerprints on it apart from his own ...'

'You're very thorough,' Lloyd remarked.

'I had a scientific training,' said Otto. 'Besides, what we are doing here is too important to allow any margin for mistakes.'

'You don't think the police are going to track you down?'

Otto used his thumbnail to pick something black from between his teeth. 'You are talking to someone who escaped from Berlin on the very last day of Hitler's Reich,' he said. 'You are talking to a man who discovered an opera which had been hidden for sixty years, and who was able to revive a mystic ritual which had been lost for eleven centuries. Now ... I have work to do, letters to write. I would appreciate it if you and Mrs Kerwin would retire to your rooms. And, please, make no attempts to leave the house. Our young man had been instructed to use physical force if necessary, to keep you here, and you have seen for yourself what I can do.'

'But you're not one of these Salamander people, are you?' asked Kathleen. 'How come you can set things on fire?'

Otto closed his eyes. He remained silent for such a long time that they thought that he wasn't going to answer. But then he opened his eyes again, and said, 'I have told you quite enough. Some secrets must remain secrets. On your dying day you will remember that you once knew me, and you will shudder in awe.'

Lloyd retorted, 'I'll shudder with something, but it damned well won't be awe.'

Otto flicked him a look as sharp as a whipcrack. 'Don't tempt me, Mr Denman. It's growing cold, and I'm sure we'd all appreciate a fire.'

The young man escorted them wordlessly up to their rooms, opened their doors for them, and then locked them in. Lloyd sat down on his mattress, eased off his shoes, and then lay back, feeling exhausted and grimy and shocked, as if he had just survived a minor but unpleasant automobile accident. His hands were sore, and he thought that it was probably time his bandages were changed, but at the moment there was nothing he could do about it. He watched the nodding fang-like shadows of yucca fronds on the sloping ceiling. There was still so

235

much that he couldn't accept, even though he had heard Otto's cruel and lascivious confessions with his own ears, and seen with his own eyes how remorseless Otto could be.

All those grey-skinned people on the garage floor – how could they really be composed of nothing more than smoke and spirit? How could a ritual change transform an agonizing death into a fiery rebirth? How could anyone live for ever?

He thought of Celia lying there; and wondered what she was thinking, if she was thinking anything at all. Out on the road at Escondido, she had said that she still loved him. But could *he* still love *her*? How could you love somebody who had died and come back to life – somebody who wasn't really flesh any more? Most difficult of all, how could he accept her back into his life when she had so readily embraced a creature like Otto – a man who had burned alive thousands of innocent people for the sake of one insane ideal?

Beneath everything that Otto was doing, Lloyd could feel the terrifying legacy of the Third Reich moving like a black silently thunderous glacier. Hitler had reawakened something in the human mind that would take more than guns and bombs and forty-five years of economic reconstruction to destroy. When he had claimed that his Reich would last for a thousand years, he had been right. And if Otto was able to transform all of those Salamanders sleeping on his garage floor, it would be even more than a thousand-year Reich. It would be a Reich that dominated mankind for ever.

Lloyd had read plenty of books and articles about the war. But until now he had never felt the real fear of war, the fear of living under somebody else's will. It was more disturbing than he had ever imagined possible, and he suddenly began to understand why people were prepared to risk their lives for political freedom. Without political freedom, life was simply not worth living.

He fell asleep, and almost immediately he dreamed of Celia again. He dreamed that he was wading across a glossy-green meadow, through varnished grass and huge wide-awake daisies, under a sky the colour of tarnished bronze. Celia was standing naked on a distant levee, beside a gnarled and whiskery plane tree. Her hair was alight, and a plume of orange fire was rising from her head. He tried to shout out, but his voice sounded as tiny and ineffective as the blowfly buzzing in Otto's fist. He tried to run, but the grass was too deep.

The key turned in his door. He opened his eyes. For a moment he could hear nothing but the insects in the yard outside, and the soft chattering of his wristwatch. He thought for a moment that he must have dreamed the sound of the key, but then he heard a floorboard creak.

'Who's there?' he demanded, his heart racing – knowing all the time that he couldn't do anything to defend himself, no matter who it was. The nameless young man was obviously powerful enough to break his neck. Helmwige could fry him alive just by touching him. And Otto could turn him into a human incendiary bomb simply by *looking* at him.

The door slowly opened. He lay still, although every tendon in his body was pulled tight. A single second passed as slowly as the world turning on its axis. Then the young man appeared, and stood beside the open door, watching him.

'What do you want?' Lloyd asked him, at last.

'I came to see if you were asleep.' The young man's voice was soft, and curiously distorted, like the voice of somebody deaf, somebody who has learned to speak only by watching the movement of other people's lips.

'I *was* asleep, until you came in.'

'I'm sorry. I wanted to ask you something.'

Lloyd propped himself up on one elbow. The young man's apologetic tone was in direct contrast to Otto's dry-voiced hectoring. 'Does Otto know that you're here?' he asked him.

The young man glanced quickly behind him, as if the mere mention of Otto's name could somehow invoke Otto's presence. 'No. Otto is working. He ...' making a scribbling gesture with his hand '... writes, you know? Always writing.'

'What did you want to ask?'

The young man closed the door behind him, and knelt down next to Lloyd's mattress. Although he was so muscular, he had the gentlest of airs about him. A boy, rather than a man. Uncertain, anxious, unexpectedly shy.

'They have always hated me, Otto and Helmwige. They have always told me that I am nothing but an animal. They hated Mengele, you see, because up until the very end, Mengele was always the *Führer*'s favourite. They talk about it over and over, as if it happened only yesterday.'

Lloyd said nothing, but waited for the young man to carry on.

'I have no name. I have nothing,' the young man told him. 'I asked Otto what was my name, and he said, you're not even a person, you deserve no name. Do I give names to cabbages, or eggs, or chairs? That's what he said.'

Lloyd said, 'Otto isn't exactly the most sympathetic person I've ever met.'

'I have to do everything for them, everything. I have to clean, I have to do everything. Helmwige expects me to have love with her, any time that she wants to. They told me that to work for them was my punishment, because so many people had died so that I could live. I was made by Josef Mengele, and this is my punishment for having been made.'

'Nobody's to blame for their own existence,' said Lloyd.

'I am to blame for myself.'

'Bullshit, you were born because somebody else wanted you born, for whatever reason. It doesn't matter what the reason was, you had no hand in it. It's not your fault.'

The young man raised his head so that the light from the corridor fell across his face, and shone in his eyes. Eyes like crystal-clear marbles, young and hopeful and innocent. 'I wanted to ask you if you would like to leave this place, and take me with you.'

Lloyd sat up. 'You're going to help us to escape?'

'Only if you wish to.'

'Only if we wish to? Are you kidding? You think we're here because we felt like an early vacation? We're here because Otto threatened to burn us alive.'

The young man nodded. 'He has done that many times, to many people. He does not say so, but burning people is Otto's pleasure.'

'But you're going to help us get away?'

The young man nodded. 'Very early in the morning, when Otto sleeps his deepest. I will come to your room and guide you away. We can take Otto's own car, that will prevent him from following, for a while. None of the other cars is working.'

'What about Celia?' asked Lloyd. 'He won't do anything to her, will he? He won't harm her in any way?'

The young man shook his head. 'Your Celia is most important to him. Celia is the only one who can understand the music. He will never harm Celia.'

'You're sure about that?'

The young man nodded. 'I heard him talking to Helmwige. He said that Celia was his Godsend ... his saviour. When they escaped from Germany, you see, they lost many of their notes, and Celia was the first person they had found who was able to play the music for them.'

'Okay, then ... it's a go,' Lloyd told him. 'Wake me up whenever you're ready, and I'll be right behind you.'

The young man checked his wristwatch. 'Three o'clock ... that will be the best time.'

Lloyd said, 'You're sure I can trust you?'

The young man lowered his head again.

'Supposing I give you a name?' Lloyd asked him. 'Can I trust you then?'

'A name?' the young man asked him, incredulously.

'Sure, a name. Your very own name.'

'How can you give me a name?' the young man asked. 'You're not my father.'

'For Christ's sake, I don't have to be your father to give you a name. What do you want me to call you?'

The young man shrugged. 'I don't know any names.'

'All right, then ... we'll call you Franklin, after Franklin Roosevelt. How about that? Franklin Free, because you're going to be free.'

The young man pressed his hand to his chest. 'And that can be me? That name? Franklin Free?'

Lloyd nodded. 'That can be you.'

Never in his life had Lloyd seen anybody lifted so quickly from his own lack of self-importance as Franklin Free. He quivered with new strength, like a butterfly emerging from a chrysalis; he breathed more deeply, and knelt up straight. 'That can be me? Franklin Free?'

'That *is* you. You're a human being, every human being has a name, and your name is Franklin Free.'

Franklin stood up. He didn't seem to know which way to turn. Softly, he repeated the incantation, 'My name is Franklin Free, and that can be me. My name is Franklin Franklin Free and that can be me.'

Lloyd checked his watch. 'Listen, Franklin ... it's way after eleven. Let me try to grab some more zees. If you're planning on breaking out of here at three o'clock in the morning, we all need to be fresh and alert and ready for anything.'

'*Franklin,*' Franklin repeated, in awe.

He reached out and grasped Lloyd's hand, and squeezed it with the trembling restraint of someone who would dearly love to have hugged him, but knew that he couldn't.

'Franklin,' he said. 'That's good.'

'Glad you like it,' Lloyd told him. He felt genuinely touched, more touched than Franklin could have understood.

Just then, they heard Helmwige calling from downstairs. 'Bath! Come on! I want my bath!'

The newly-named Franklin gave Lloyd's hand one last squeeze, and then said, 'I have to go. Helmwige wants me.'

'I'll see you at three,' Lloyd replied.

Franklin said, 'If it doesn't work out ... if we don't get away ...'

'We *will* get away,' Lloyd assured him. 'Don't even think about it.'

'But if we don't, if he burns us . . .'

'He's not going to burn us, all right?'

'But if he *does* . . . I just want you to know that what you've given me . . . well, it's worth more than anything that Otto and Helmwige have ever given me. It's worth the world.'

'Draw my bath!' Helmwige screamed.

Franklin went to the door. 'Three o'clock,' he promised. He held up the doorkey. 'And just to show you that I mean what I say . . . I won't lock the door.'

He hesitated, bit his lip. 'If I do that . . . you won't escape without me?'

'I trust you,' said Lloyd. 'Don't you think that you can trust me?'

'I don't know,' Franklin replied, suddenly hesitant. He obviously wasn't used to making up his own mind about anything.

'Do you have any *choice*, but to trust me?' Lloyd suggested.

Franklin thought about it, and then he said, 'No, I guess I don't.' He tried to give Lloyd a brave smile, and then he left the room and closed the door behind him. Lloyd waited to hear the key turning in the lock, but it didn't. Franklin had kept his word. One way or another, they were going to be free.

He heard water running like muffled thunder out of the hot-water tank. Then footsteps on the stairs, and creaking boards on the landing, and Helmwige talking as if she were slightly drunk. He lay on his mattress without moving. He had tried to sound confident about escaping, but he wasn't at all sure that Franklin was bright enough to be able to get them out of the house, or that Otto and Helmwige would be sleeping deeply enough to allow them to go. If they could just get out of range of Otto's fire-raising, they would be safe. But he wasn't at all sure how far away that actually was. For all he knew, Otto only had to think hard enough, and he could ignite a fire in the next county, or the next state, or anywhere he liked in the world. His talent for fire-raising was the one secret that Otto had refused to discuss.

Still, Lloyd recalled that when Otto had set fire to his steering-wheel, he had taken two or three steps forward, as if to bring himself closer. And when he had chased them out of the 24-hour drugstore in Del Mar, his arrow of fire had been able to pursue them only for thirty or forty feet.

If they could just get clear of the house, he guessed that they would probably be safe. Then all they had to do was to find somewhere safe to hide and to wait for the solstice – wait for Otto and Helmwige to perform the ceremony of Transformation – and then rescue Celia and Mike Kerwin, too.

Nothing to worry about. Nothing that the Lone Ranger couldn't have handled, or maybe Dirty Harry. Lloyd would have loved Otto to make his day.

After a few minutes, he eased himself up off the mattress and went to the door. He turned the handle, and found that Franklin had been telling the truth. He had left it unlocked. Lloyd opened it two or three inches, and listened. At the far end of the landing, the bathroom door was ajar, and he could hear splashing and murmuring, and then Helmwige saying, 'Gently, gently, *du bist* so plump.'

He hesitated for a short while, and then he opened the door wider, and crept out into the corridor. It sounded as if Otto was still downstairs, writing. The whirling sounds of *The Ride of the Valkyries* came from the record-player in the living-room, played at top volume, and Lloyd heard the clinking of Otto's brandy-bottle as he poured himself another drink.

Holding his breath, he tiptoed along the corridor until he reached the half-open bathroom door. Cautiously, he put his eye to the crack in the door. The whole room was foggy with rose-smelling steam, and from where he was standing he could see only the edge of a large white enameled bathtub, a bottle of Vidal Sassoon shampoo, and a glistening pink curve which he took to be Helmwige's shoulder. Helmwige was sitting with her back to him, so he took the risk of leaning across the doorway and peering right into the room.

Franklin was kneeling beside the bathtub wearing nothing but white Fruit-of-the-Loom shorts. He was facing the door and he saw Lloyd at once. He frowned, and mouthed the word. '*Wha* ... ?' but Lloyd gave him a quick wave to reassure him that everything was fine, and that he wasn't trying to escape just yet.

There was nothing that Franklin could do, in any case. Helmwige was watching him too intently. He was massaging her shoulders with soap, while she ran her hands up and down his muscular forearms, and kept saying, '*Mmmmmmm*, that's better ... gently, gently.'

Lloyd watched as Franklin rubbed more soap on his hands, and then began to lather Helmwige's enormous breasts. Her wet skin squeaked as he grasped her breasts tightly, and rolled her nipples between finger and thumb. She continued to murmur, and to splash, and to run her hands up and down his arms.

'Harder, you can do that harder. Pinch me! I like to be pinched! Ohhh ...'

Franklin rinsed her breasts with a huge natural sponge. Then he scooped his arm into the bath, so that his hand was right underneath her bottom, and he raised her hips right out of the water. She had heavy thighs, and a rounded stomach, but she was still in voluptuous shape for a woman who must have been immortalized when she was well into her forties.

'You must make sure that I am *completely* clean,' she told Franklin.

'Yes,' said Franklin. His voice was flat. He glanced at Lloyd but Lloyd remained where he was, not moving. Downstairs the *Valkyries* continued to thrash and to tumble, although it sounded as if this part of the record had suffered from years of being played almost every evening.

Helmwige reached down with both hands into her dark blonde pubic hair, and opened her vulva as wide as she could, so that Franklin could soap his finger and slip it inside. '*Ohhh, höchst erfreulich,*' she murmured.

Franklin slid his finger in and out of her, and she threw back her head and moaned and warbled like a dove. Then he slid in a second finger, and a third. Helmwige gasped and splashed, and pulled herself even wider open. At last, panting, his muscular chest glistening with perspiration, Franklin worked his entire soapy hand up into her, right up to the wrist.

Helmwige made an extraordinary growling deep-breathing noise that reminded Lloyd of a sea-lioness. She gripped Franklin's wrist fiercely in both hands. Then she suddenly shuddered, and shook, and screamed out loud. The bathwater churned as wildly as if it were full of piranha fish. Fascinated and horrified by what he had seen, but strangely aroused, too, Lloyd turned quickly away. He tiptoed back along the corridor until he reached the door of Kathleen's room. Franklin had left the key in the lock, so all he had to do was quickly to turn it, open the door, and slip inside.

Kathleen was awake and sitting up in bed. When he came in, she switched on the bedside lamp, a cheap clip-on with a broken plastic shade. 'Lloyd? What's happening? How did you get out? Somebody's screaming!'

'Don't worry about that – that's Helmwige, having a little bathtime fun. Listen – that boy came into my room a few minutes ago. It seems like he's had it up to here with Otto and Helmwige, and he wants us all to make a break for it.'

'You mean escape? Do you think you can trust him?'

'I don't see any reason not to. He's not exactly Albert Einstein, but he seems willing enough. And he doesn't have any *reason* to double-cross us, does he?'

'But what if Otto catches us? He'll burn us alive!'

'I wouldn't be too sure that he's not planning on doing that anyway. He's determined to start where Hitler left off, and, believe me, he's not going to let anybody stand in his way.'

Kathleen brushed back her hair with her hand. 'He'll never manage it, though, will he? The police are bound to track him down sooner or later.'

Lloyd shrugged. 'I'm not so sure. He's got people who can burn you as soon as look at you – people who can live for ever. How are you going to stand up against people like that? And how many other people are going to be tempted to join him, once they realize that they really could be immortal? Besides, you've got Otto himself to contend with. You heard what he did to Sergeant Houk. He could do that to anybody who tries to stop him. One glance and you're humanburger.'

He heard water emptying out of the bathtub, and the sound of voices. 'Listen – I'd better get back to my room. The plan is that we sneak out of the house at three o'clock in the morning, when Otto and Helmwige are really out of it. Franklin is going to wake us up, if we're asleep.'

'Franklin? I thought he didn't have a name.'

'I christened him. He was as pleased as a dog with two tails.'

'Lloyd … do you really believe that we're going to be able to get away? I mean, safely? If anything should happen to me … well, I don't know what Thomas would do.'

'Do you want to stay?' Lloyd asked her.

Kathleen shook her head. 'I guess it's just that I never felt frightened before. Not like this.'

'Franklin told me that Otto wouldn't harm Celia at all, if I escaped. I guess he wouldn't harm your husband, either.'

Kathleen said, 'That man lying out in the garage, Lloyd – that isn't Mike Kerwin. Leastways, it's not the Mike Kerwin I married. The Mike Kerwin I married was burned to death on that bus in the desert.'

Lloyd saw the tears glisten in her eyes. He couldn't help admiring her bravery and her realism. He hadn't yet accepted that he had lost Celia for ever. Somehow, with a Disneylike optimism, he had kept on believing that the Celia he had hoped to marry was still there; that she would reappear just as she was before and say, 'Fooled you!'

But he knew now that he was going to have face the truth. Celia had been burned, Celia was gone. The creature that had taken her place was a creature of fire and sorcery, a creature that he would never be able to accept back into his life. He could understand why Celia had chosen youthful immortality over a gradually worsening disability and an early death. But the more he learned about Otto and his Salamanders, the more difficult he found it to come to terms with the fact that Celia had embraced his idea of a master race. The Celia that Lloyd had loved would never have accepted a single minute of life that had been bought at the price of thousands of innocent people being deliberately incinerated.

He had lost Celia now, lost her for good. The world had had enough of camps, enough of gas-chambers, enough of ovens.

Kathleen must have sensed what he was feeling, because she put her arms around him and laid her head against his chest. Tears slid down his cheeks and dropped into her hair like warm pearls.

'Ssh, it's over,' she said.

Lloyd wiped his eyes with the heels of his hands. 'Thanks,' he said. 'I guess I've been the victim of my own bravado.'

She kissed his cheek. 'I'll see you at three.'

LLoyd went to the door, listened, then opened it. He returned to his room, quietly closed the door behind him, and lay back down on his mattress.

He hadn't expected to be able to sleep, so he had recited the lyrics of all the rock songs that he could think of, then all the poems that he could remember (*By the shore of Gitche Gume ... by the shining Big Sea Water ...*); then the address section of his Filofax, with the full telephone numbers and zip codes of all of his friends; then the Padres' batting averages for the past three seasons.

He was only aware that it was three o'clock when he felt Franklin shaking his shoulder and whispering, 'Mr Denman? Mr Denman? Wake up, Mr Denman, it's time to go.'

He stared into the darkness. 'Is it three o'clock already?' he asked, his mouth thick and woolly. He sat up, and rubbed his eyes. 'Jesus, I dreamed I was having dinner at Mr A's.'

'Come on,' breathed Franklin. 'as quietly as you can. Otto is so deeply asleep that he's practically dead, but Helmwige is very jumpy.'

Lloyd cleared his throat. 'I'm not surprised, the way she was playing in the tub tonight.'

'She will do anything and everything,' said Franklin. 'What does she care, she's going to live for ever? She's a morphine addict, Hermann Goering got her on to morphine during the war. But she takes every kind of drug you can imagine. She has sex with anybody she feels like it. She doesn't have to care about AIDS. She will perform any kind of sex act you can imagine, and some that you can't. I've seen her have sex with two dogs, while Otto watched her and ate flies.'

'Let's go,' said Lloyd. He didn't particularly want to hear any more. He stood up, and caught his head on the sharply sloping ceiling. He swore more foully than he had sworn for years, not so much because it hurt but because he was tense and tired and frightened. In some ways, Helmwige frightened him more than Otto. At least Otto was mortal, at least Otto could be killed. But how could you fight against somebody who had no regard for their own life whatsoever?

Franklin opened the door, and crept out into the corridor, with Lloyd following closely behind. They crossed to Kathleen's room, and Franklin quietly turned the key. Kathleen must have heard them whispering, because she was waiting for them right behind the door.

'Are they asleep?' she breathed. Lloyd nodded, and took hold of her hand.

Quickly and silently they tiptoed along the corridor, past the half-open bathroom, and then past Helmwige's bedroom, which was wide open. By the light of a flickering black-and-white television movie, they could see Helmwige sprawled naked on her frilled four-poster bed, her legs wide apart, her mouth open. She was breathing coarsely and irregularly, as if she were having a nightmare. The movie was *The Thin Man*, with William Powell and Myrna Loy.

'I read you were shot five times in the tabloid.'

'It's not true. He didn't come near my tabloid.'

With infinite care, they went downstairs. Franklin was so heavy that the treads squeaked whenever he put his weight on them, and Lloyd winced. But at last they reached the darkened hallway, and the house remained silent.

Franklin beckoned Lloyd and Kathleen to come closer. 'All we have to do now is get out of the front door, head for the car, get into it, and go.' He held up the car keys. 'I lifted these from Helmwige's purse this afternoon.'

'What about the other cars?' asked Lloyd.

'Only the coupé works, and I let down the tyres.'

'Where does Otto sleep?' Lloyd whispered. 'Will he hear us leave?'

'Oh, he'll hear us leave all right. He works in the living-room every night till one or two o'clock, playing his records and drinking brandy. Then he goes to sleep on the couch, fully dressed. He doesn't even bother to wash.'

'Thanks a lot,' Lloyd replied. 'He's already won the Lloyd Denman Award for the Man Most Likely to Make You Barf On Sight.'

'Okay, let's go,' Franklin told them. 'But let's make it real quick.'

He released the security chain, and then silently slid back the bolts. He opened the latch, and the front door swung open with the faintest of creaks. Outside, the night was as black as only a Southern California night can be. They could barely distinguish the faint gleam on the roof of Otto's Mercedes sedan.

'Okay, go!' whispered Franklin. Together, they ran across the porch, into the drive, and quarter-backed their way between the parked Mercedes. Kathleen caught her knee against the rear bumper of the 380SL, and hissed, 'Shit!' but they reached the sedan, wrenched open the doors, and threw themselves into the leather-upholstered seats. Franklin pushed the key into the ignition, roared the car into life, and switched on the headlights.

'Oh, God, no!' said Kathleen, in panic.

The headlights had instantly illuminated the thin uncompromising figure of Otto, standing in front of them in a short-sleeved shirt and grey slacks, his arms folded, his withered mouth puckered with anger.

'Run the bastard down!' Lloyd shouted at Franklin. But Franklin sat in the driver's seat staring at Otto in complete paralysis. Franklin had been bred by Otto and raised by Otto. Franklin's will had been subjugated by Otto from the moment he was born.

Otto walked up to the side of the car and held out his hand. 'The keys, please,' he demanded.

— EIGHTEEN —

'Franklin, *go!*' yelled Lloyd, and yanked the Mercedes' gearshift into drive.

Franklin stared at him as if he didn't recognize him. 'I ... what ...?'

'Go, Franklin, go for Christ's sake!'

Otto snapped, 'Don't you dare!'

But at that critical instant, Lloyd had one call on Franklin's loyalty that Otto couldn't match. He had given Franklin a name.

'Go, Franklin, go!' he shouted at him, almost screaming.

Franklin slammed his foot on to the Mercedes' gas pedal, and the huge sedan swerved and snaked, its rear tyres blasting out pebbles and dust. Otto made a desperate bid to snatch the keys out of the ignition, but he couldn't quite reach them. However, he seized hold of the steering-wheel and wouldn't release his grip, and as the Mercedes roared out of the driveway, and bucked on to the road, he was still clutching it, running at first, then allowing himself to be dragged.

His white face glared into the window of the moving car like a nightmare. They had reached over twenty miles an hour on the curve toward Rancho Santa Fe, and they were still accelerating. '*Du bist ein Verräter!*' he shrieked at Franklin. '*Wo ist deine Dankbarkeit?*'

Franklin whimpered in terror, but Lloyd continued to shout at him, 'Keep going! Keep going! He can't hurt you now!'

'*Verräter!*' cried Otto. '*Schon bist du Tot!*'

Franklin frantically twisted the steering-wheel from side to side, trying to dislodge Otto's grip, and the car rolled and dipped from one side of the road to the other, its tyres giving out a chorus of continuous howls. But

Otto hung on, his shoes dragging and scrabbling on the tarmac, showers of sparks flying from his heels.

They slewed into the brightly lit streets of Rancho Santa Fe, with Otto still holding on.

'*Stop the car, you traitor!*' he panted at Franklin. '*Stop the car or I'll kill you now!*'

But Kathleen, from the back seat, shouted out, 'Lloyd! Here!' and passed over one of the car's cigarette-lighters. The spiral tip was glowing red-hot.

Without hesitation, Lloyd pressed the cigarette-lighter on to the back of Otto's hand. There was a sizzle of puckering skin, and Otto let out a deep, outraged roar. Just as they skidded past the entrance to the inn at Rancho Santa Fe, he released his hold on the steering-wheel, and Lloyd twisted around in his seat to see him flying and tumbling across the triangular green, arms and legs, over and over, a malevolent cartwheel, the long-legged scissorman from *Struwwelpeter.*

'We did it!' Franklin whooped. 'We did it! We did it! Hot dog, hot dog!'

Lloyd kept his eyes on Otto as they sped around the next curve and headed toward the coast. A second before the green disappeared from view, Lloyd saw him climbing on to his feet. With a sense of dread and disappointment, he realized that Otto obviously hadn't been badly hurt. Kathleen had seen him, too, because she turned to Lloyd and her expression was grim.

'He's not going to forgive us for that,' she said.

'Hot dog!' Franklin kept repeating, with that odd deaf-school pronunciation. It came out more like 'Hudduh, hudduh!'

'You did good, Franklin,' Lloyd praised him.

'The question is, where do we go now?' Kathleen wanted to know. 'We may have got away, but Otto's going to come after us, for sure.'

Lloyd said, 'I just want to lie low till Wednesday, till they've completed their Transformation. Then at least we'll have a chance of getting Celia and your husband back. I know they'll have changed. I know we may not even be able to love them any more. Maybe they won't be able to love *us* any more. But we have to give them that one chance. They can't stay as Salamanders. You heard what Otto said, they're really volatile. They're as much of a danger to themselves as they are to other people.'

'Maybe we should drive up the coast, and find ourselves a quiet hotel,' Kathleen suggested.

'Well, that sounds romantic, but I've got a better idea. Let's drive out to that Indian place in the Anza Borrego. They had trailers to rent out there, and that's just about the last place that Otto would think of looking for us. Then as soon as the Transformation's over, we can take that young Indian boy to the police.'

'What for?'

'He's our only witness that Otto was chanting when the bus was burning, that's what for. What other witnesses do we have?'

Kathleen shrugged. 'I guess you're right.'

Franklin said, 'I can't believe it. We did it, we got away!'

'It's all thanks to you, buddy,' Lloyd told him.

'I never saw Otto so angry,' Franklin grinned.

'Oh good, that makes me feel a whole lot better. As if he isn't frightening enough when he *isn't* angry.'

Kathleen said, 'We could call the police now, you know. They'd find the Salamanders, at least.'

Lloyd shook his head. 'There'd be a massacre, no doubt about it. And you'd blow any chance of seeing Mike again.'

Kathleen stared at her own reflection in the black-tinted window. 'I'm not too sure that I want to.'

'Well,' said Lloyd. He suddenly realized he was still holding the cigarette-lighter, and he handed it back to Kathleen with a wry grin. 'It's a damned hard life, so long as you don't weaken.'

'Weaken?' she said, and he could see in the window that she was crying. 'No, I'm not going to weaken. I'm just a little tired.'

'Were things okay between you and Mike?' Lloyd asked her.

She wiped her eyes with her fingers, 'Not particularly, even before he went for his medical.'

'Now you feel guilty because you don't care for him as much as you think you should?'

She nodded. 'The trouble is, how can I explain that to Tom? He worshipped Mike, really worshipped him. Half the time I don't know whether I'm really feeling grief-stricken, or whether I'm acting it for Tom's sake. That makes me feel so bad.'

Lloyd said, 'I guess that everybody feels the same way, when they lose somebody close. I remember when my grandfather died. I was really upset, but at the same time I had this peculiar sense of relief that I didn't have to worry about him any more. I was almost happy for him. We all get born, we all have to die. I guess there really isn't any reason why we shouldn't be happy at both events.'

Franklin said, 'Helmwige will never die.'

'That's a creepy thought, isn't it?' said Lloyd. 'That woman's still going to be forty-something when we're dead and gone.'

Kathleen asked, 'Will she really never die? Never, ever? Can't anybody kill her? What happens if she's involved in an auto accident, or somebody shoots her, or something like that?'

They were driving down toward Solana Beach, under the interstate. Lloyd said, 'Take a left here, on to the freeway. I want to take a flying look at my house, before we head out for the desert, and maybe check with Waldo, if I can.'

Franklin swerved on to the entry ramp with squealing tyres. Lloyd glanced behind them. 'It's okay, you can slow down now. I don't want to get pulled over by the cops for a traffic violation, not now.'

'Sorry,' said Franklin, although it sounded more like 'howwy'. But as they joined the almost-deserted I-5, he said, 'They can be killed by Him.'

'Who?' asked Lloyd. 'Who can be killed by whom?'

'The ones who live for ever. Helmwige, any of them.

They can be killed by Him.'

'Him? Who's He, when He's at home? Did Otto say?'

Franklin shook his head. 'But I heard him talking to Helmwige one night. That was when Celia first came. He said, "She doesn't know about Him, does she? Even you can be killed by Him, and so can all of our master race." '

Lloyd gave Kathleen a quick, excited look. 'Did Otto come out with any clues about who He might be?'

'No,' said Franklin. 'But the reason I remember what he said was because he kept talking about it, over and over, like he was really worried about it.'

Lloyd sat back. Otto had half suggested that Hitler might have been Transformed, burned and immortalized. Maybe 'He' was Hitler. Maybe *Der Führer* still held absolute sway over all of his followers, just as he had during World War Two.

'Are you thinking what I'm thinking?' he asked Kathleen.

'I don't know. What are you thinking?'

He explained, but he could see that she found it difficult to believe. 'I'm sure Hitler's dead,' she said. 'Didn't they identify his dental records?'

'It doesn't matter if they did. His original body's dead, for certain. Just like Celia was dead and Mike was dead. But what happened to the smoke and the soul that rose right out of that body? It's hard to believe that Hitler could have seen Helmwige turn into a Salamander, without wanting to try to do the same thing for himself.'

'It doesn't bear thinking about,' said Kathleen.

'No, it doesn't. But it could be true.'

It was still two hours before dawn when Franklin drove the Mercedes quietly through North Torrey, so that Lloyd could inspect his house. Lloyd climbed out of the car and walked up the sloping driveway, then circled the house to the back. The kitchen doors and windows had been boarded up, and plastic sheeting had been draped over the kitchen roof. There was a strong noxious reek of smoke, and when he peered in through one of the side

254

windows, Lloyd could tell that, apart from rebuilding the kitchen, he was going to have to redecorate almost the entire house. Still, having once been an insurance salesman, he had made sure that his fire policy was comprehensive and up-to-date. For the money he was going to get, he could afford almost to tear down this house and build another one, from scratch. In a way, he found that a very tempting thought. This house reminded him so strongly of Celia, and the life they had been planning to live together. They had even thought of filling in the grave-like conversation-pit, in case baby fell into it.

Lloyd rattled the front door to make sure it was locked. The house seemed to be reasonably secure, and around here the neighbours were too nosey to make burglary much of a practical proposition. Jesus, the Kazowskis even noticed when he put out the trash in new pyjamas. 'Noticed your new pyjamas, Lloyd. The Ascot shop?'

Lloyd left the house and walked back to the car. Kathleen said, 'Is there any place we can get some coffee and something to eat? I think I'm just about to pass out. I keep tasting Helmwige's sauerkraut.'

'Sure, we can go to the restaurant,' said Lloyd. 'I can ask Waldo to meet us there.'

The sky was beginning to lighten as they drove toward La Jolla. Lloyd was feeling tired, but strangely changed. Stronger, somehow, as if he had at last accepted the burning of his house and the burning of the woman he loved, and was preparing to face what a new day was going to bring him. He looked around at Kathleen and she managed to summon a smile.

Waldo was delighted to see him, but horrified by his appearance.

'You look like you won first prize in a Mickey Rourke look-alike contest,' he said, bringing over a large white jug of espresso coffee and a stack of steaming baguettes. 'Why don't I call Louis, and have him come over and cook you a proper breakfast?'

'We don't have time for that,' Lloyd told him. 'Listen –

we have to keep our heads down for a few days. We won't be too far away, but I'm not going to tell you where we're going to go, in case you get asked by somebody who won't take no for an answer.'

'Mr Denman, my lips are sealed,' Waldo assured him.

'How's business?' Lloyd asked him. He looked around at the restaurant, at the neatly laid tables, the neatly folded napkins and the shining wine-glasses, and for some reason he didn't find it enchanting any more. Instead, it looked prissy and claustrophobic, the kind of place where people were more concerned about *foie gras chaud poêlé aux blancs de poireaux* than they were about life, and the struggle that most of the world went through daily, simply to stay free.

Waldo offered Franklin some more baguettes. 'Business is fine. Do you want to see the books? Maybe levelling out a little, but nothing to worry about. People will always demand good fish, cooked good. Do you know what I read yesterday? The reason human beings got such big brains, they always ate fish. People who don't eat fish, they're going backward, like evolution in reverse. You don't eat fish, you're going to wind up like Barney Rubble.'

Kathleen gave a tired smile. 'You've got yourself a wonderful *maitre d'* here, Lloyd. I never knew any restaurauteur who worried about Darwin as well as Paul Bocuse.'

'Where'd you read that stuff, Waldo?' Lloyd demanded.

'It's true,' Waldo insisted. 'Same with birds. They used to be land creatures, but then they started eating shellfish that didn't contain hardly no calcium. Their bones got lighter and lighter, and in the end they literally blew away into the air.'

'This is true?' asked Franklin, fascinated. Waldo glanced at Lloyd, alarmed by Franklin's loudness. 'Hithith *hroo?*' Franklin had demanded, as far as Waldo could tell.

They talked for almost an hour. Outside, the sun had risen, and La Jolla cove shone golden and pale in the early-morning fog. Lloyd went to the men's room for a wash and a shave, while Kathleen called Lucy and asked after Tom, and Franklin unashamedly devoured more baguettes.

'Your friend has an appetite,' smiled Waldo, taking hold of Lloyd's hand.

Lloyd smiled, and nodded.

'Listen,' said Waldo, 'I don't know what you've got yourself into here. Maybe you want me to call the cops about it?'

'Not yet,' Lloyd told him. 'I have to get my revenge first.'

'Revenge?' sniffed Waldo. 'I don't know. I used to think about revenge. I used to think about going back to Europe, and looking for the people who killed my family. I could have been like those Nazi-hunters, you know? I could have brought them all to trial. But what's it worth, in the end, this wonderful revenge? It doesn't achieve nothing. It doesn't make you feel any better. It ends up making you worse than the people you're trying to punish.'

'Maybe,' said Lloyd, and gave Waldo's hand a last affectionate squeeze. This little fat guy, who took so much pride in his work, and had so much to give to the world that the world probably didn't have room for it all. 'Sometimes you have to think of the future, as well as the past.'

They left La Jolla a few minutes before nine o'clock, and headed eastward, with the sun in front of them. This time, Lloyd did the driving, wearing Otto's tiny green-lensed sunglasses, which he had discovered in the Mercedes' glove compartment. Kathleen said, 'God, you look like Himmler.' Franklin had made himself comfortable in the back seat, and by the time they started climbing toward Santa Ysabel, he was already snoring.

'You want me to talk to you?' asked Kathleen, suppressing a yawn.

'Not if you want to sleep.'

'I'll just close my eyes for a moment, okay?'

And that's how it was that Lloyd sped across the scrubby outskirts of the Anza Borrego State Park in a

257

stolen Mercedes sedan with Kathleen lolling in the front seat, her forehead knocking softly against the passenger window with every bump in the road, and Franklin stretched out on the back seat, snoring in two distinct keys. Lloyd wryly wished that Celia were with them: she could have identified the exact key in which Franklin was snoring, and maybe sung along to it, too.

Celia had been brilliant, bright, and always funny. Lloyd tuned the Mercedes radio to KFSD on 94.1, and caught Bruch's *Kol Nidrei*, played by Vladimir Ashkenazy. It was uncanny: the *Kol Nidrei* had always been one of Celia's favourites, and Lloyd felt almost as if Celia were trying to get in touch with him.

Ahead of him, the desert burned bright, a land of hills and mirrors. Behind him, the dust blew high. But Lloyd felt neither lonely nor sad, nor particularly grief-stricken, not now. He had a job to do which nobody else in the world could do, and for which (in all probability) nobody would thank him. He hummed along with Bruch, and watched the miles ticking steadily upward on the Mercedes' clock.

By early lunchtime, they drove past the place where the bus had burned. The wreck had been towed away now, and there was no reminder of what had happened except for a cross that somebody had fashioned out of two charred aluminium roof-supports, a cross that was hung with dried-out wreaths and withered flowers. Kathleen was still asleep as they drove by, and Lloyd didn't wake her. Some places are worth remembering, other places are best forgotten.

But Kathleen woke as they drew up outside Tony Express's store, and stared at Lloyd for a moment as if she couldn't think who he was.

'You know, I was having the weirdest dream? I dreamed I was swimming off Baja with Mike. The ocean kept rocking me up and down. I guess it must have been the car.' But then she frowned, and said, 'Mike looked so *strange*, in this dream. He looked like he didn't have any eyes.'

'Come on,' said Lloyd, and opened the car door. 'Let's go see what accommodation we can find for ourselves.'

He found Tony Express sitting inside the shadowy darkness of the store, threading beads. Considering he was blind, Tony Express was working with extraordinary speed, his fingers sorting out beads of different colour and texture, and swiftly impaling them on his threading-needle, almost as if he were an insect-collector. *Or an eater of flies*, thought Lloyd, obliquely, and it was a thought which seemed to take a long time to go away, like a train disappearing across the flattest of horizons.

'Tony? How're you doing?' he asked.

The blind Indian boy kept on picking out beads, picking out beads. 'Doing fine, thanks. Doing what Red Indians are best at. Walla-walla-walla, heap good necklace, all that stuff.'

'Looks good to me,' said Lloyd.

'Ho-ho.' Tony Express retaliated. 'A heap of shit would look good to you, if I painted it red, white and blue.'

'Do you remember me?' Lloyd asked him. Because – God almighty – if he couldn't remember Lloyd's voice – then how could he clearly remember the voice of the man who had called out *'Junius! Junius!'* to a busload of burning disciples?

'Sure I know you, man,' said Tony Express. 'What you come back here for? I told you everything, there's nothing else.' *I'll tell you everything I can, there's little to relate.*

'I was wondering if we could maybe hang out here for a while.'

'You're wearing Hugo Boss aftershave and you want to hang out *here*?'

'I'm looking for a little peace, that's all. A few days' break from the hurly-burly of yuppiedom.'

'You're not hiding from the law?'

'Of course not.'

Tony Express suddenly lifted his head. 'Who's the big guy, man? He wasn't with you before.'

Lloyd was taken aback, and turned around to Franklin

259

and shrugged. Maybe Tony Express was only kidding that he was blind.

But Tony Express immediately said, 'It's a knack, man. I can only do it in the afternoons, when the sun's shining into the store. I can feel him blot out the warmth.'

'I'm sorry,' said Franklin, stepping out of the sunshine.

'Don't worry about it, man,' said Tony Express. He deftly knotted the necklace he was stringing, and closed the lid on the cigar-box full of beads. 'There's an empty trailer next to ours. It belongs to an Indian called Zuni Tone. He's no damn Zuni and he sure doesn't have no tone, but there you go. You can rent it for twenty a week.'

He led them around the back of the store, where instantly two brindled mongrels launched themselves furiously from their makeshift packing-case kennel, their eyes bulging, until they were brought to a throttling halt by the chains around their throats. 'Don't mind them,' said Tony Express. 'They only eat lawmen and truancy officers. They've got the Good Housekeeping Seal of Approval.'

Kathleen held Lloyd's arm as they skirted around the growling, slavering dogs. 'That's one guarantee that I wouldn't like to put to the test,' she told Tony Express.

Tony Express opened the high wire gate to the compound, waited patiently while they filed in, and led them between the trailers with the nonchalance of somebody who knows exactly where he wants to go. He dodged potholes, washing-lines, upturned Coca-Cola crates. He acknowledged old men sitting on dilapidated armchairs under tattered awnings, he called to women and children, and even said, 'Hi, Geronimo!' to a cat that was sleeping in the middle of a worn-down tyre.

'It's hard for me to believe that this boy is blind,' Franklin remarked.

'In his way, he can see more than we can,' Lloyd replied. 'He's a damned sight more intelligent, too.'

Tony Express didn't say anything, didn't turn around, but he lifted one finger in the air to show Lloyd that he had heard.

At last they reached a large, sagging, green-painted trailer with overgrown window-boxes and a Charley Noble stovepipe sticking out of the black-tarred roof. Tony Express opened the front door for them and let them take a look inside.

The trailer was gloomy and fiercely hot, but almost the first thing they bumped into was a huge Westinghouse air-conditioner which looked as if it had previously been used to cool the Superbowl. The rest of the interior was surprisingly clean and tidy. There was a table, set with a vase of dried flowers, a dresser with willow-pattern plates arranged along it, an old-fashioned but scrupulously neat kitchenette, and a tiny bathroom with a mahogany-veneered Civil War washstand and a bean-shaped re-enamelled bath.

Lloyd went to one of the bookshelves and picked out a paperback at random. 'The poems of Sterling Brown?' he queried.

Tony Express laughed and quoted.

> *O Ma Rainey*
> *Li'l and low,*
> *Sing us 'bout de hard luck*
> *Roun' our do';*
> *Sing us 'bout de lonesome road*
> *We mus' go*

He added, with a smile, 'Zuni Tone is heavily into the emancipation of oppressed people, man.'

'Yes, well, I think we are too,' Lloyd replied.

Tony Express circled around and around in the middle of the floor, as if he were looking at everything. Maybe he was picking up vibrations, maybe he was picking up smells, or noises, all of those nuances which sighted people are usually too insensitive to notice.

'You like it, man? What do you think?'

'It's better than I could have expected. Cleaner, for sure.'

Tony Express stopped circling. 'You think that Indians are dirty or something?'

Lloyd felt uncomfortable. 'No, no. Of course not. What I meant was ...'

Tony Express flapped his hand at him as if to tell him to forget it. 'The twenty up front, man. In folding. Our credit-machine's broke.'

Lloyd produced a twenty, and pressed it into Tony Express's hand. 'It's yours,' said Tony Express. 'Power extra, depending on what you use. There should be clean linen in the closet, Zuni Tone's very particular. Like he always sweeps up the rug after he's been clipping his toenails.'

'Glad to know it,' said Lloyd.

Tony Express was about to leave the mobile home when they heard a car horn honking, out by the front of the store. 'Wait up,' he said, and swung himself down the steps, and jogged off between the mobile homes. Lloyd went through to the kitchenette and tested the gas and the water. The gas was working and after a brief, asthmatic pause, the water came coughing out of the tap.

Kathleen sat down on the bed. 'You know, you always picture these trailer-parks as being so slummy. But look how neat everything is. I guess it's the discipline of living in such a small space.'

They were still talking when Franklin lifted the net curtain and peered out. 'The boy's coming back,' he said. 'He's got two policemen with him.'

'Oh, what?' Lloyd demanded. He lifted the other side of the curtain and saw that Franklin was right. Tony Express was weaving his way back between the trailers closely followed by a fat ruddy-complexioned highway patrolman, and a thinner, darker officer in designer sunglasses and a sharply pressed shirt.

'What are we going to do?' Kathleen asked, as Lloyd let the curtain fall back.

'Nothing we can do,' Lloyd told her. 'Tough it out, is all.'

They stood waiting in silence while Tony Express and the two highway patrolmen approached the trailer. The door opened, and the entire trailer groaned and dipped to one side as Sergeant Jim Griglak climbed aboard, closely followed by Ric Munoz. Jim Griglak shuffled his way toward the living-area, holding his wide-brimmed hat pressed against his chest, as if he were paying a respectful visit to some friends of the family. Ric Munoz was relentlessly chewing Orbit, and he left his sunglasses on.

'Sergeant Jim Griglak, Highway Patrol,' said Jim Griglak, although Lloyd could read that for himself. 'We've been asked to stop a Mercedes-Benz sedan answering the description of the vehicle parked by the roadway back there, and detain the occupants. Are you the occupants?'

Lloyd shook his head. 'Don't know what you're talking about, Sergeant. I never owned a Mercedes-Benz in my life. Beverly Hills Skodas. I'm a BMW man, myself.'

Jim Griglak breathed patiently. 'We're not talking ownership, here, sir. We're talking grand theft auto.'

'Still don't know what you're talking about. If I don't *like* Mercedes-Benzes, why should I steal one?'

Ric Munoz put in, 'Sometimes any vee-hickle is better than no vee-hickle.'

Jim Griglak looked around the three of them. 'Do you want to tell me your names, and what you're doing here?'

Lloyd said, 'We're an ethnic study group from UC San Diego. I'm Professor Holden Caulfield, these are my assistants. We're putting together a social profile of small disaffected Indian communities, such as this trailer park.'

Jim Griglak closed his eyes for a moment as if summoning huge internal reserves of patience. At last he said, 'I'm arresting all three of you on suspicion of grand theft auto. I've read *The Catcher in the Rye*, too, Professor Caulfield. Pity you couldn't have thought of some much more convincing alias, like Bruce Wayne.'

He sniffed, and recited their rights. Then he said, 'Let's go. You're going to make me late for my lunch.'

Ric Munoz added, 'Sergeant Griglak get seriously pissed if he's late for his lunch.'

There was nothing they could do. Led by Tony Express, they filed out of the trailer and back through the gate toward the store, where the dogs snarled and yapped and hurled themselves wildly against their chains.

263

'Thanks a lot, pal,' Lloyd told Tony Express, as they walked around the side of the store. 'Remind me to do *you* a favour some day.'

'I couldn't help it, man,' Tony Express replied. 'They'd already seen the car, they knew you had to be around someplace.'

Lloyd said, 'That guy we're trying to catch ... the one who said "*Junius! Junius!*" when the bus was burning ... I want you to know that he's just about the most disgusting slime on two legs. So if we *do* manage to get this sorted, and we *do* manage to catch him, I hope you're going to be ready to come forward and identify his voice.'

'What if I don't?'

'Then he and his friends are going to do to today's Americans what yesterday's Americans did to the Indians. *Capiche?* He and his friends think they're some kind of master race, do you understand what I mean? They think the world belongs to them, and they're the people to rule it. You ever heard of Adolf Hitler?'

'Sure I heard of Adolf Hitler. I told you I was over-educated for a kid of my age.'

'Well, what this Junius guy is trying to do is carry on where Adolf Hitler left off.'

'Here? In California?'

'Why not? It's one of the richest and most influential places in the world. What California does today, the rest of the world is going to be doing tomorrow.'

'Give your mouth a rest, will you?' Jim Griglak called out. 'You elected to remain silent, so frigging well *remain* silent.'

Tony Express looked pale and his breathing was oddly shallow. 'I couldn't help it, man. They'd already seen the car.'

They reached the road. It was grillingly hot, and heat rose from the blacktop like the shallows of a wind-ruffled lake. Jim Griglak opened the rear door of his Highway Patrol car and indicated with a curt nod of his head that Franklin should climb in. Franklin hesitated, and looked dubious.

'Come on, bonehead, we're going for the scenic tour,' Jim Griglak rasped.

They climbed into the back of the patrol car and Jim Griglak locked the doors. Then they U-turned and headed back toward the main highway, while Tony Express stood forlornly by the side of the road listening to them go.

Ric Munoz picked up the intercom and reported back to headquarters that they were bringing in three suspects for the theft of Otto Mander's Mercedes. Jim Griglak sang to himself under his breath as he drove, and occasionally made comments about the passing scenery, or if there was life after retirement, or baseball. He went with tedious detail into an explanation of the Boudreau Shift, which is when a manager counters a slugger who always pulls to the right by shifting all of his fielders to the right of second.

Lloyd and Kathleen and Franklin said nothing. Franklin was bemused: Lloyd and Kathleen were both physically and emotionally exhausted. The jiggling of the car began to send them to sleep.

'*I have often walked ... down this tooty-wooty before ...*' sang Jim Griglak. '*And the pavements tooty-wooty frooty-woot before ...* Hey, did I ever tell you that story about Yogi Berra, when they gave him a cheque that said, "Pay to Bearer"?'

'I'm not sure,' Ric replied, manfully. He was beginning to look forward to Jim Griglak's retirement.

Jim Griglak chuckled. 'He said, "Hey, they spelled my name wrong!"'

They had travelled nearly six miles across the dazzling desert landscape before Jim Griglak suddenly began to slow down. The change in speed woke Lloyd almost immediately, and he sat up abruptly and said, 'What is it? What's happening?'

But Jim Griglak didn't answer. Instead he drove slower and slower, peering ahead of him as if he couldn't believe what he was seeing.

Kathleen grasped Lloyd's arm and said, 'Lloyd, look!'

Lloyd shifted his position and frowned ahead into the

265

sunlight. What he saw gave him a feeling of delight and terror, both at once, as if he had woken up one morning and found that he could fly.

'*This can't be so,*' whispered Jim Griglak.

'It's so all right,' said Ric Munoz, echoing the moment that they had found that burned bus, and all of its charred and grisly occupants.

Standing beside the road not a hundred feet ahead of them were two figures. One was an elderly Indian, in jeans and red plaid shirt. The other was the skinny, wind-tattered figure of Tony Express. In his hand he was holding the long stick decorated with strips of skin and fur, squirrel-tails and beads, the sundance doll that he had shown them back at the store, the first time they had met him.

The sun lanced off the lenses of his sunglasses. He wasn't afraid. He was simply waiting. Jim Griglak slowed the patrol car to a whining crawl, and at last to a halt, still thirty feet shy of the skinny Pechanga blind boy with the ragged stick.

He applied the parking-brake with a heave of his foot, and then switched off the engine. It was hot and bright and suddenly silent.

'What's wrong?' Lloyd asked him, at last.

Jim Griglak shifted himself around in the driver's seat and stared at Lloyd balefully. 'You're looking at a young blind Indian kid who has just managed to overtake a car travelling at fifty-five miles an hour, on foot, across a desert landscape heated well in excess of one hundred and ten degrees fahrenheit. And you're asking me what's wrong?'

'Maybe he has a brother,' Kathleen suggested, without much hope. 'Maybe he telephoned him, and arranged for him to meet up with us here – you know, pretending to be him.'

Jim Griglak slowly and flatly shook his head. 'That is the same kid. That is the exact same kid who stood outside his dad's store less than fifteen minutes ago and watched us drive away.'

Ric Munoz gave an unbalanced laugh. 'Come on, Sergeant, what are we saying here? We know there's only one kid. Anyway – who's the old guy with him? You're making a mistake, you must be. All ethnic minorities look the same.'

'You're an ethnic minority,' Jim Griglak reminded him.

'Oh, sure, but some of us transcend our origins, right?'

'You think a frigging Toyota Turbo and a frigging pair of designer sunglasses changes what you are? That's the same frigging kid, Munoz, on my mother's grave.'

Jim Griglak turned back to Lloyd and Kathleen and Franklin and said, 'Stay put, you got it. Watch my lips. S-t-a-y p-u-t.'

He heaved himself out of the car. Ric Munoz hesitated for a moment, then unclipped the pump-gun from its rack in front of the dashboard, and followed him, keeping the gun held high. Lloyd watched them walk slowly toward the two Indians, the old Indian in the baggy jeans and the young blind Indian in the headband, and for a moment he found himself unable to speak. It was like watching history.

Kathleen whispered, 'Is that really him? It looks like him!'

'It can't be him,' Lloyd told her. 'How could anybody run six miles in less than ten minutes, and arrive here well ahead of us? He may be precocious, and he may be just a little crazy, but he's human.'

'So you think that's his double?'

'It makes a damned sight more sense than it being him!'

'But supposing . . .'

'Supposing what?'

'I don't know,' Kathleen replied, flustered. 'It just seems to me that if Otto is capable of burning people and bringing them back to life again, maybe there's more to this world than we usually allow ourselves to see.'

— NINETEEN —

Jim Griglak approached the old man and the young boy with all the caution that a working lifetime in the Highway Patrol had taught him. Watch the eyes. Watch for the slightest flicker of movement. Watch the hands, too. Apart from good old straightforward honest-to-God handguns, there are plenty of other weapons that can kill and maim. Knives, small-calibre guns that spring out of the sleeve, and all of that ninja crap like stars and chains.

The boy was standing with his head held slightly higher than a sighted person would have held it, his lips drawn back across his teeth, but with great poise and certainty. The furs and tails that decorated his sundance doll swung around and around in the hot afternoon wind. Jim Griglak saw the tiny malevolent face on top of it and decided that he didn't care for it *at all*.

In contrast, the old man appeared to be quite benign, just one of those old coots that you might see at a charity lunch for senior citizens. His face had that distinctive leathery look that only Indians have, his eyes were blood-shot and filmed-over, but he was smiling to himself as if everything was just the way he liked it.

Jim Griglak stopped, and sniffed, and wiped his nose with the back of his hand. 'How'd you get here?' he asked, bluntly.

'How'd *you* get here?' the boy replied, with a blind smile.

'Listen,' said Jim. 'Don't you start jerking me around. I want to know how you got here.'

The old man said, 'Same way that you did, sir. By air, by fire, by wind, and by water.'

'What's your name?' Jim Griglak asked him.

'John Dull Knife. What's yours?'

'Mind your own goddamned business.'

'Interesting,' John Dull Knife nodded. 'Don't like it much, though. Your parents atheists?'

'Listen,' said Jim Griglak. 'I don't know how the hell you managed to get here so quick, less'n you've got yourselves a Ferrari Testarossa hidden behind that dune. But I do know one thing. You're going to get yourselves back where you came from, both of you, and stay well out of stuff that's not your frigging concern.'

John Dull Knife said, 'My parents always taught me to speak to everybody, even my enemy, with respect. Respect is power, my friend. Contempt is weakness. The greatest power in the universe is the appreciation of one human being for the strengths of another. Only the weak seek out weakness.'

'How'd you get here so quick?' Ric Munoz asked him. 'Come on, let's hear it. You know some secret shortcut, or what?'

John Dull Knife turned to the boy and smiled. 'We were not quick, my friend. It is you who were slow. Look at the time. Look at the position of the sun. How did it take you six hours to travel no more than six miles?'

Jim Griglak lifted his head and looked around. John Dull Knife was right. All of the shadows had mysteriously swivelled from one side of the compass to the other. High up above them, the sky was already beginning to show signs of darkening. He checked his wristwatch and it was almost five. They had been driving at the legal limit all the way from Tony Express's store, and yet they couldn't have chalked up more than one mile an hour. At that speed, John Dull Knife and Tony Express could have strolled past them with their hands in their pockets.

'Ric,' said Jim Griglak, between tightened teeth, 'what time do you have, please?'

'Almost five, Sergeant.'

'That's what I have, too. And look around you. It's definitely five o'clock, no mistake about it. But you know and I know that it takes less than seven minutes to travel six miles at fifty-five, and you know me. I always hit fifty-five right on the nose. So what the hell's going on, I'd like to know?'

The blind Indian boy shook the sundance doll. 'We don't have your firepower, man. We never want to, and we never will. But this land is ours, and always will be. So if we want you to go slow, then all we have to do is to ask the land to carry you slow. You don't even understand "travelling", do you? Why "travelling" is so important? When you travel, it's not just you moving over the ground, it's the ground moving underneath you. Time and distance, they're elastic, don't you understand that? After all that Einstein taught you? It's not fantasy, it's not magic, it's *true*.'

'How old are you?' Jim Griglak asked him.

'Thirteen come February.'

'Jesus,' said Jim Griglak. 'When I was thirteen, my parents thought I was a genius because I could recite *Casey At The Bat*.'

Ric Munoz took the gum distastefully from his mouth, gum that he must have been chewing for over six hours. '*Thought* the goddamned flavour'd gone out of it.'

'Listen,' Jim Griglak told Tony Express and John Dull Knife. 'I don't know what the hell kind of a stunt you've pulled here, but it amounts to interference with officers of the law in the execution of their duty. I don't have room for you in my vehicle right now, but I'm warning you that you face possible arrest, and that as soon as I've delivered these three suspects to San Diego, I'm coming back for you.'

'That could take you many hours,' smiled John Dull Knife.

'I don't care how frigging long it takes,' Jim Griglak retorted. 'I don't care if it takes me past my frigging retirement. You've been frigging around with me, injun, and nobody frigs around with me and gets away with it, never.'

'*Never* is a white man's idea,' John Dull Knife answered him. 'My people only say "ever".'

'Well get this,' Jim Griglak snapped back, 'nobody never

frigs around with me, ever. Understandee?'

He jerked his head to Ric Munoz and said, 'Come on, Munoz. I'm getting hungry.'

He turned around, but to his astonishment, their patrol car had disappeared. As far as the eye could see, there was nothing but empty road.

He turned furiously back to Tony Express and John Dull Knife, but they had disappeared, too, and the road was just as empty ahead as it was behind. He turned and stared at Ric Munoz but all Ric Munoz could do was stare back at him.

'Where'd they go?' he demanded. 'Did you see them go?'

Ric Munoz shook his head. 'I didn't see nothing.'

Jim Griglak stood in the middle of the Anza Borrego desert, and for the first time in his career he let out a long bellow of frustration and rage.

To Lloyd and Kathleen and Franklin, who had been sitting in the back of the hot patrol car waiting, it had seemed that Tony Express and John Dull Knife had simply walked around the two Highway Patrol officers, leaving them standing by the side of the road.

John Dull Knife leaned into the open driver's window with a smile. 'Do you think you can drive this vehicle back to the trailer park?' he asked Lloyd. 'Then you can collect your own car and be on your way.'

Lloyd frowned at Jim Griglak and Ric Munoz. 'What about those two? They're not exactly going to stand and wave while we take off in their patrol car, are they?'

John Dull Knife continued to smile, unconcerned. 'For the next hour, those two will be living at a different pace from the rest of us. By the time they regain their normal perception, we will have long been gone.'

'How do you *do* that?' asked Kathleen, amazed.

'You must have heard of the Yaqi, and their ability to change perception. What I have done to our friends from the Highway Patrol is a very similar procedure, not at all unusual or difficult to achieve.'

271

Lloyd gave Jim Griglak and Ric Munoz a long uncertain stare, and then opened the patrol car door and stepped out. The two officers remained where they were, not even turning their heads around. 'That's incredible,' Lloyd told John Dull Knife. 'That's the weirdest thing I ever saw.'

'How do you think Crazy Horse managed to outflank General Custer at the Little Bighorn?' asked John Dull Knife. 'So many eyewitnesses said that first the Sioux were there, and then they were not there. But of course they were there. It was simply that Custer couldn't see them.'

Lloyd climbed into the driver's seat. 'Do you want a ride?' he asked John Dull Knife, 'or will you get back the same way you came?'

'I'll have a ride, thank you,' John Dull Knife told him. 'We may have appeared to you to have arrived here quickly, but we still had to walk six miles in hot sun.'

Tony Express sat next to Lloyd, and John Dull Knife climbed stiffly in beside him. 'Hey man, can we switch on the siren?' asked Tony Express, as Lloyd started the engine and turned the patrol car around.

'Don't talk like a child,' John Dull Knife told him.

Kathleen leaned over from the back seat. 'What are we going to do now?' she asked Lloyd. 'Once those two patrolmen wake up, they're going to come directly to the trailer-park looking for us, aren't they?'

'My laywer has a small beach house at Del Mar,' Lloyd told her. 'I'll see if we can use it for a few days. I don't think Celia would think of looking for me there.'

John Dull Knife said, 'You should take Tony with you. He has told me of your struggle. He knows the magic, and he knows how to use the sundance doll.'

'Why don't you come along?' Lloyd asked him.

John Dull Knife shook his head. 'I am too old, my friend. My days of adventure are long gone.'

'Tony?' asked Lloyd. He was more than a little dubious of taking responsibility for a twelve-year-old blind boy, particularly when they were being pursued by somebody as dangerous as Otto Mander.

'Sure, man, I'll come,' Tony agreed. 'Franklin can be my bodyguard, hey, Franklin?'

Franklin grinned and nodded, although he was still plainly bemused by what had been happening to them. 'I'll be your eyes, too. You can do all the thinking. I can do all the looking.'

'Hm,' said Tony, as if he wasn't completely convinced by this arrangement.

They drove back to Tony's store, where Otto's Mercedes was still parked. John Dull Knife shook them by the hand, and wished them well. 'If I had been many years younger, I would have gladly come with you,' he said, 'but all I can say to you is what Chief Speckled Snake said to his Creek warriors when the white people began to invade their territory.'

'What was that?' asked Kathleen.

'You would not understand the Creek, but the words exactly mean, "go out there and kick the crap out of them".'

Lloyd used the store telephone to call his lawyer, Dan Tabares. But the phone rang and rang and nobody picked it up. He hesitated for a moment, and then he called Waldo at the restaurant.

'Waldo, it's me.'

'You're okay, Mr Denman?'

'I'm fine. But I have to change my plans a little. I'm thinking of using Dan Tabares' beach house at Del Mar for a few days. The only trouble is, he's not at home right now. I wonder if you could call him in about an hour and ask him to leave the beach house keys under the step, same place as he did when Celia and me – well, the same place as he did before.'

'Okay, Mr Denman, sure thing.'

After Lloyd had hung up, Kathleen used the phone to call her sister and talk to Tom. Lloyd stood outside the store in the long shadows of the setting sun and watched her. There was no mistaking the light in Kathleen's eyes when she eventually got through. Lloyd looked away, and thought about Celia, and about the children that *they* would never have.

Tony Express came up, carrying an Adidas sports bag crammed with jeans and T-shirts and greyish-looking undershorts, which John Dull Knife had packed for him. A spare pair of sneakers were knotted around his neck, and he was swinging the shaggy, stringy-looking sundance doll. His eyes were invisible behind his dark glasses.

'We ready to roll, man?' he wanted to know.

Lloyd nodded. 'I guess so. But you listen. If this looks like it's going to get at all dangerous, then you're right back here on the next available bus.'

'I can take care of myself, man,' Tony Express pouted. ''Sides, I got my bodyguard now, don't I?'

Franklin grinned at him, and said, 'You bet,' and Lloyd rolled his eyes up, wondering what the hell he had got himself into.

— TWENTY —

Waldo waited until he had closed the door behind Angie, the last waitress to leave, and seen her safely across the sidewalk to her boyfriend's Corvette. Then he turned the key in the door, shot the bolts, and turned around the American Express placard that said *CLOSED*. He walked back across the darkened restaurant, between the tables set with fresh napkins and softly gleaming cutlery, and opened the sliding door that led out on to the balcony.

All around him, the lights of La Jolla glittered in the warm night wind, and the sea fussed and phosphoresced on the rocks of the cove. He had rescued a third of a bottle of Barossa Valley Cabernet Sauvignon from a party of elderly ladies who had got too giggly to finish it all, and he poured himself a glass and leaned on the wooden rail and took a deep breath of ocean air.

Although he wouldn't have presumed to usurp Lloyd's authority, he was beginning to enjoy the responsibility and the rewards of running the Original Fish Depot on his own. He had managed to keep the place busy and lively, and he had allowed Louis a free hand to try dozens of new fish dishes, including a spectacularly successful brill with oysters.

He had also become much more cheerful and sociable, and as his confidence had increased, his French accent had become less and less exaggerated – until, as Louis had remarked, he was practically speaking English.

He sipped the sauvignon and rolled it around his tongue. It wasn't quite cold enough but that didn't matter. He was enjoying the night too much.

He had been out on the deck for only a few minutes when he became aware that the seagulls were crying. He had never heard them cry in the dark before. He sensed a disturbance in the wind, an anxiety in the seething of the surf. He stood up straight and listened, and he was sure that he could hear somebody calling his name.

Waldo, don't run too far, don't run too fast! Grandpa is coming, Waldo. Grandpa is coming!

'Grandpa?' he said, out loud. Then he shook his head, and smiled at his own stupidity. He must be really tired to imagine that he had heard his grandpa. 'Finish your wine and lock up for the night ... and get yourself some sleep,' he told himself, trying to sound the way his grandpa used to sound.

He turned, and shouted out loud in shock. Standing in the shadows at the end of the deck was a black figure with a pale face and dark glasses. A figure that stood and watched him and said nothing at all.

'Who are you?' Waldo cried out, his throat tight. 'This is private property. A private restaurant. Nobody is allowed here.'

The figure stepped forward, into the dim light that shone through the restaurant from the half-open kitchen door.

'Not even the owner's fiancée?' she said, with a grey-lipped smile.

Waldo shuddered, and made an odd noise through his nose that sounded like *hnyuh!* The figure stepped closer still, so that Waldo could see himself reflected in her glasses, and the air was strong with the aroma of heated metal.

'I'm looking for Lloyd,' she said, very quietly.

Waldo breathed with terrified heaviness, and he could feel his heart racing and plunging like a surfer trying to paddle out beyond the incoming waves.

'I am having a nightmare about you,' he told her. 'I am asleep, and you have come out of my dream. You must go away.'

'Waldo,' Celia insisted, 'I'm looking for Lloyd. I have to find him, before it's too late.'

She came a fraction closer, and Waldo screamed and lifted his arm to protect himself. 'You must go away! You

276

are absolutely dead!' He stumbled back against one of the chairs and had to snatch at the wooden rail to stop himself from falling. 'Go away! Go away!'

'How can I be dead, Waldo, when I'm right here in front of your eyes?'

Waldo had retreated right to the end of the balcony, and his back was pressed against the rail. He glanced quickly behind him, and it was a long drop down to the concrete footpath below. 'Oh God help me, oh God help me!' he muttered.

Celia pushed aside the chair that Waldo had toppled over and came after him. The smell of heated metal seemed even more pungent, and Waldo coughed.

'What do you want?' he asked her. 'What do you want? You're a dead person, what do you want?'

'Waldo, I'm not dead. This is me. This is Celia.'

'But you're hot! I can feel it! You're hot!'

'Waldo, my earthly body burned but my soul survived. You mustn't be frightened of my *soul*! It's still *me*, it's still the same Celia!'

'Don't touch me!' shouted Waldo.

'I'm not going to touch you.'

'Then what do you want?'

Celia took off her dark glasses. In the shadows of the balcony, her eyes appeared to Waldo to be extraordinarily dark. More like pits than eyes. More like holes. He felt that he could see right inside the blackness of her head.

'Waldo – I have to know where Lloyd is, that's all.'

'He's not at home?' Waldo quaked.

'Don't take me for a fool, Waldo. We both know that the house burned down.'

'Well, I don't know,' said Waldo. 'He doesn't tell me nothing.'

'You're running the restaurant. You're in charge of his pride and joy. You must know where he is.'

'Ms Williams – I swear – I don't have no idea.'

Celia unbuttoned her glove, and rolled it up. She tucked it into her raincoat pocket. Then, without warning, she snatched hold of Waldo's hand, and squeezed it tightly. Waldo shouted out, 'Hey!' and shook his arm violently, to break free of her. But Celia clung on, and her fingers weren't only tenacious but burning hot.

'Hey, you're hot, you're hot, you're burning my hand!' Waldo shouted out. 'Get off me, go away!'

'Where's Lloyd, Waldo? I have to know!'

'I don't know where he is. I swear it! He went away and he didn't tell me where he was going! He did it on purpose, in case somebody should find out. I didn't know it was *you*!'

'Waldo – I don't believe a word of it. Lloyd is one of those careful, careful men who never leaves anything to chance. He doesn't leave his restaurant to chance, he doesn't leave his house to chance, he doesn't leave his *life* to chance. But here's some unpredictability, Waldo. Here's a bit of improvisation. If you don't tell me where he is, I'm going to set fire to you.'

Gasping, Waldo tried to pull his hand away from Celia's, but suddenly her fingers flared so hot that she burned through skin and muscle and tendons, and fused their hands together. Waldo shrieked in pain, and dropped to his knees on to the balcony, but still he was unable to pull himself free. *God, if I pull myself free, I'll pull my whole hand off!*

'Don't! Don't! Don't!' he cried, but then Celia tugged open her raincoat with her free hand, and revealed herself naked and grey-skinned, and smelling of molten zinc. A curl of metallic smoke rose out of her coat-tails.

'Tell me where he is, Waldo,' Celia insisted. 'I have to know!'

'I don't know, I don't know. I swear to God I don't know!'

But then Celia tugged off her left-hand glove with her teeth, and placed her bare hand on top of Waldo's balding head. There was a furious sizzling noise, and his scalp puckered up red and blistered. Smoke poured out from between Celia's fingers, and Waldo opened his mouth wide and let out a white scream of agony and fear.

Celia abruptly stopped that. With her fingers burned

278

deep into the flesh on top of his head, so that Waldo couldn't have wrenched himself away without being scalped, she pressed his face flat against her bare stomach. His scream was muffled for two or three seconds. Then smoke billowed up between Celia's breasts, the smoke of Waldo's face burning; and she breathed it in with lubricious satisfaction.

'Haven't you wanted to do that to me ever since you first saw me?' she taunted him. Then she rubbed his face up and down her stomach, and between her thighs, and he shuddered and shook in overwhelming agony. It was like having his face rubbed against an electric hotplate. With each rub, more strips of burned skin were dragged from his face. He felt the flesh seared from the side of his nose. His cheeks almost seemed to *melt*, like wax. But Celia kept on rubbing his face against her until his nose-bone was being clicked up and down against her like a skeletal trigger.

He could scarcely speak. His face was raw and blistered, and nobody would have recognized him now, nor would again. His eyes bulged from reddened sockets, his nose was nothing more than a twist of fried gristle, with two huge gaping nostrils, and his lips had swollen to three times their normal size. He was trembling in shock, but still Celia wouldn't let him go.

'Listen to me, Waldo! I have to know where he is!'

She began to pull his face toward her again, but Waldo lifted a hand to stop her. His fingers crackled against the ferocious heat of her thighs, but he was too far gone to scream any more.

'Be-beach-house. Dan Tabares' beach-house. Up at Del Mar.'

'Thank you, Waldo,' said Celia. 'Why didn't you tell me that in the first place? You could have saved yourself such pain!'

Waldo tried to climb to his feet, but he was shuddering too much. Celia stood watching him, her coat flapping softly against her naked body, her skin subtly fuming like a metal baking-sheet. 'You know what your trouble is,

Waldo?' Celia asked him, although he probably failed to hear her. 'You were always too loyal! A man like Lloyd needs people to question him. He needs people to needle him, people to upset him. You shouldn't give a man like Lloyd too much of an easy life. He'll take advantage of you, and forget to pay you for it, too.'

Dumbly, with the head-dipping motion of a wounded hippopotamus, Waldo shuffled on his knees toward her. She stepped back once, then twice, then stepped back again.

'I'll *kill* you,' Waldo blubbered, through grotesquely inflated lips. 'I swear to God that I'll *kill* you!'

He threw aside one of the chairs, then tipped over the table.

'Whatever you are, I'm going to *kill* you!'

He tried to pick himself up, stumbled, and fell heavily on top of her. She jarred backwards on the balcony, and where her hand clawed against the planking, she burned black bitter-smelling fingerprints into the wood. '*Kill* you!' Waldo repeated, and lifted both fists high above his head, ready to smash them down on to her face, the way that he had once seen his father kill a berserk dog.

But Celia clung on to him, arms and thighs, and said wildly, 'Come on, Waldo! Maybe you and I were always meant to make love together! A special kind of love, yes? Really hot!'

She pressed his blistered face against her bare breasts, and then she ignited him, like a bonfire. He shrieked and twisted and clawed for anything to help him get away. His shoes drummed against the planking of the balcony. 'Help me! Somebody help me!' But the flames consumed him as fiercely as if he had been moulded out of paraffin wax.

The pain became so intolerable that he managed to drag himself somehow up on to his knees again, and then on to his feet. He was blazing from head to foot. His shoes crackled and spat as the polish burned.

He stood by the rail with the ocean wind fanning his flames until they roared. The pain, at first excruciating, seemed to burn out and fade, and soon he felt that it was possible to stand here ablaze and not to die. The seagulls were crying. It was dark but the seagulls were crying. He was sure he would hear his grandpa as they walked along the seashore. *Don't worry, young Waldo. Never fear. Now you can fly, too.*

He climbed burning on to the wooden rail around the balcony, and balanced for a moment with flames flying out behind him like a monstrous cloak. He opened his mouth to call to his grandpa and fire burst out from between his teeth. He felt as if he were alight both inside and out.

You can fly, Waldo. You can fly.

So, he flew. Over and over in the darkness, forty blazing feet, until he landed with a thunder of flame and a smack of steam into a bubbling hot tub on the balcony below. The tub was occupied by a hairy-chested orthodontist and a redheaded girl who wasn't his wife, and Waldo's fiery arrival in his hot tub marked the moment when his marriage, his affair, his practice and his sanity instantaneously and simultaneously vanished.

On the balcony above them, Celia listened to them screaming and gibbering in horror. Then she buttoned her gloves, walked through the restaurant, and let herself out. A Merecedes 380SL was waiting by the kerb, its engine running, its hood dull with bird-droppings and grime. Otto was sitting behind the wheel, his mouth pursed, his cheeks puffed out oddly.

'Del Mar,' said Celia. 'They're hiding in his lawyer's beach-house. I'll direct you.'

Otto nodded, without saying a word.

'Are you all right?' Celia asked him.

Otto nodded again, and then opened his mouth. His tongue was crowded with twenty or thirty glistening green-and-black blowflies, all alive, all struggling, but stuck to his tongue with saliva. Otto closed his mouth again, then sucked, then crunched, then swallowed.

Celia said very little on the way to Del Mar, except 'Right here ...' or 'Slow ...' or 'Watch this intersection ...' She was beginning to feel that perhaps her burning had changed her more than she had realized ... more than Otto had promised her. She knew that she had liked Waldo – loved him, almost. Yet she had felt no remorse when she had burned his face. She had felt no regret when he had plunged blazing off the balcony. In fact, she had felt something disturbing and dangerous – a pleasure in witnessing the · agonized death throes of another human being that was almost sexual.

She slipped her hand into her raincoat, and cupped herself between her legs. Moisture and fire. Death and delight. She could hardly wait to find Lloyd again. She could hardly wait to hold him. She trembled at the thought of what they would be doing on the night of the solstice, when the year turned, and the fires burned, and the master race would be reborn.

Otto glanced at her out of the corner of his eye. '*Was machst du*, Celia?' he asked her.

'I'm thinking, that's all.'

'Did you burn Slonimsky?'

She whispered, 'Yes.'

Otto wiped stray fly-wings from his lips with the back of his withered hand. 'So for all Jews,' he remarked. 'They escaped once, we won't fail a second time.'

Lloyd managed to adjust the antenna of the clapped-out Zenith television so that they could watch the late-night news. For most of the bulletin, the Chinese anchor-woman's face was livid blue, with a thin wavering green moustache, but intelligible sound was all that they needed.

'Highway Patrol officers were forced to walk five and a half miles across the Anza Borrego State Park this evening when their patrol car was borrowed by two men and a woman whom they had arrested on suspicion of grand theft auto. The barefaced suspects commandeered the Highway Patrol vehicle when the officers temporarily vacated it to interview two hitch-hikers, and used it to return to the Mercedes sedan which they were originally suspected of having stolen ...'

'Hitch-hikers!' exclaimed Tony Express, scornfully. 'Even the cops can't tell the truth these days!'

'What did you expect them to say?' asked Lloyd. ' " We stopped to talk to these two Pechanga Indians, one twelve and one seventy, because they overtook us on foot when we were travelling at fifty-five miles an hour in a car"? Give the poor guys a break.'

They had made themselves as comfortable as they could in Dan Tabares' beach-house. It was one of a row of twenty or thirty shabby oceanfront properties, reached by a derelict back street behind restaurants and stores and automobile body shops. Most of the beach-houses were owned by inland hotels who liked to boast that they had somewhere for guests to enjoy the ocean, or by down-town San Diego businessmen like Dan Tabares who brought noisy gangs of middle-aged men out for a weekend of fishing and Miller-drinking and leering at the local nubility.

The large damp-smelling living-room was furnished with white-painted cane sofas, which were scattered with bamboo-patterned foam cushions, and it was appallingly lit from above, so that they all looked much more tired than they really were. The kitchen was decorated in brown and orange, and boasted a filthy microwave, an electric can-opener encrusted with age-blackened tomato-sauce, and an old Betty Furness-style refrigerator containing two bottles of flat soda-water and something khaki and effervescent that, in another life, had probably been a quarter of a pound of liverwurst.

After they had arrived, Lloyd and Kathleen had driven to the nearest late-night market for bread, bacon, fresh vegetables, peaches, doughnuts, Cheerios, coffee, 7-Up, chocolate bars, Smirnoff vodka, Wild Turkey whisky, and all the other essentials of a civilized existence.

There was nothing in the beach-house that didn't look as if it hadn't been rejected from Dan Tabares' main house, right down to the Goodyear ashtray and the tattered real-estate poster for Rancho Jamul Estates, *Your place ... in the country (actual view)*. Two of the bedrooms were smallish and mean, with folding beds. The main bedroom had been painted in garish purple, with a tasteless reproduction oil-painting above the bed of a girl in a wide-brimmed hat standing on the seashore with her skirt billowing up, so that her bare bottom was revealed.

Kathleen went out on to the boardwalk in front of the beach-house. From there, half-a-dozen wooden steps led down to the sand. She stood for a while listening to the sound of the surf. Once he had listened to the rest of the news, Lloyd came to join her.

'Hope those highway patrolmen didn't get into too much trouble,' he said.

'I don't care if they did,' Kathleen replied. The wind blew her hair across her face. 'The fat one was obnoxious and the young one was just plain stupid.'

'Freshen your drink?' Lloyd asked her.

She shook her head. 'I'm going inside in a moment. The ocean always scares me at night-time. It sounds like hungry bears.'

'Maybe you should get some sleep,' Lloyd suggested. 'I've straightened the bed for you.'

'So where were you thinking of sleeping?'

'I'll take one of the couches.'

She shook her head. 'Those couches are disgusting. They stink of beer. I'm sure that you and I can manage to sleep together without doing anything immoral.'

Lloyd smiled, and swallowed whisky. 'Depends what you mean by immoral.'

'Just try me.'

They stood outside a while longer, finishing their drinks, and then they went back inside. Tony Express had showered and washed his teeth, and was already in bed, his dark glasses folded neatly on his bedside table. His milkwhite eyes stared at the ceiling, his hands were clasped across his chest.

Lloyd sat on the side of his bed. 'Do you ever pray before you go to sleep?' he asked him.

'Unh-hunh,' said Tony Express. 'Praying's for the birds, man.'

'You'd be surprised how often it helps, even if you don't believe in it.'

'Well, I'm desperate, man, but I'm not *that* desperate.'

'Didn't your grandfather ever read to you?'

'John Dull Knife? He can't read, man. But he knows some pretty good stories about the old days, before the paleface honky long-knives stole our land, took all our women and turned our sacred lodges into Safeways.'

Lloyd smiled. 'And what does he say to you, before he turns out the light?'

'He always says, "I don't know why the hell I'm doing this, you can't see it anyway."'

Lloyd reached out and took hold of Tony Express' hand. 'You're something special, you know that?'

'Yeah, man, I know it.'

Switching off the cheap bedside lamp, Lloyd left Tony Express and went to see Franklin, who was lying on his bed fully dressed, looking tense.

'Everything all right?' Lloyd wanted to know.

'I guess so. I feel funny, that's all. Edgy. I'm not used to being free.'

'You'll get used to it quick enough. You sure don't want to go back to Otto and Helmwige, do you?'

'I don't know. I still don't feel right.'

'What do you want me to do, chain you to the bed?'

Franklin glanced up at him, and then said hoarsely, 'No. No more of that. That was when I didn't have a name, and they made me feel like everything bad that happened in the world was my father's fault, because my father had been bred by Josef Mengele, and because it was all my father's fault, it was *my* fault, too.'

He paused for a moment, and then he said, 'It's still hard for me to think that it isn't.'

'What made you change your mind about it? What made you decide to run away?'

'It was something I heard you say to Otto, when you first came to the house. He told you that I wasn't even a person, and I heard you say, so angrily, "what the hell is he, then, two orders of eggroll to go?"'

Lloyd couldn't help laughing, but Franklin was quite serious. There were tears in his eyes. 'That was the first time that anybody had said that I was a person, and was angry with Otto because he tried to say that I wasn't.'

Lloyd said, 'All right, eggroll. Time to get some sleep.'

'You know something?' said Franklin. 'I never knew my father, although Helmwige showed me some pictures they took in New Orleans when they came to America after the war. I never knew my mother either. Otto had to choose somebody. I don't know who, or how.'

'Your father wasn't around when you were young?'

Franklin shook his head. 'Nor my mother. I never even saw a picture of my mother.'

There was nothing that Lloyd could say. He was already aware that Otto was completely cold-blooded, and that he would do anything to anyone in order to achieve the birth of his master race, but somehow the way in which he had arranged for Franklin's conception and upbringing – not because *he* had wanted to, but because the *Führer* had decreed it – was beyond the edge of any kind of human cruelty that Lloyd could think of. It was almost unbearable for him to think of Franklin's childhood years – nameless, unloved, beaten and sexually abused. The fact that he had somehow managed to survive with his sanity intact was a miracle which was deserving of anybody's prayers, even Tony Express's.

Franklin said, 'You know what I used to pretend? You won't laugh, will you?'

'Of course not. Tell me.'

'I used to pretend that the mom and dad in *Flicka* were my real parents. Whenever they came on to the TV, I used to turn down the sound and talk to them.'

Lloyd laid his hand on Franklin's shoulder. 'A whole lot of kids do the same kind of thing, Franklin. A whole lot of adults, too.' He was suddenly taken back to his own childhood, lying on his stomach on the worn-out brown rug in front of the black-and-white television watching Duncan Renaldo cantering across the screen. *Adios, amigos, see you soon!*

286

He closed Franklin's door and returned to the living-room. Some old late-night movie was playing, and he switched it off. Kathleen was already in the bedroom: the door was ajar and the light was on. There was a smell of Badedas shower-gel, too. He went to the bedroom door and knocked.

'You want a nightcap?' he asked her.

'Sure. You can come on in, if you want to.'

Hesitantly, he edged open the door, and then stepped inside. The bedcovers were folded back, the pillows plumped up. Kathleen was standing in front of the bath-room basin, washing her pantyhose. She was wearing a man's striped shirt that she had found in Dan Tabares' closet.

Lloyd said, 'This reminds me of an old Clark Gable movie. You're sure you don't mind if we sleep together?'

She hung up her pantyhose on a wire coathanger and came into the bedroom. 'That's very gentlemanly of you. But aren't you being a little arrogant?'

'What do you mean?'

'Aren't you being a little arrogant in assuming that I might even *think* of doing anything but sleeping?'

Lloyd sat down on the end of the bed and prised off his shoes. 'I'm sorry. I didn't mean it to come out that way. I guess I'm just exhausted.'

He went through to the tiny bathroom and stepped into the pink-tiled shower-stall. He turned on the shower and stood for a long time letting the water gush straight into his face. He hoped to God that he had the strength to carry this thing through, and that he would understand how to deal with Otto and Helmwige when the time came.

Even more than that, he hoped that he would under-stand how to deal with Celia.

He dried himself and dressed in voluminous white shorts and a T-shirt which said *Mothers And Fathers Italian Association*. By the time he came back into the bedroom with his mouth tasting of Crest, Kathleen was already in bed, reading an ancient copy of *Reader's*

Digest. He climbed in beside her. She felt warm; and he was surprised how good it was to lie next to a woman again.

'Anything good?' he asked her, nodding toward the magazine.

She shook her head. 'The usual. How the pilot of a crashed plane crawled nine miles with his leg torn off.'

He rested his head on the pillow and looked at her closely. 'Are you a tough lady or is that just the impression you're trying to give me?'

She closed the *Digest* and dropped it on to the floor. 'I lived for twelve years with a man I wasn't sure I loved, and then I lost him. I've cried about it, for sure, although I'm not sure why. Maybe I've been crying for me, rather than him. All those years that could have been better, and weren't. Maybe it took Mike's death to wake me up.'

Lloyd said, 'You've got Tom.'

Kathleen nodded. 'Yes, you're right, and I wouldn't give up Tom for anything. But if I'd never met Mike, Tom would never have been born. I would have had some other child, by somebody else.'

'I don't know whether you can think like that,' Lloyd replied.

'Well, maybe not,' she said, her finger tracing invisible patterns on the quilt. 'But everybody's entitled to some "might-have-beens", don't you think so?'

'I guess.'

Lloyd tugged the light-pull, and the bedroom was swallowed in darkness. Kathleen leaned over him and kissed his cheek and said, 'Sleep well.' He was very conscious of the weight and warmth of her breast inside the shirt she was wearing, but he didn't want to think about getting involved with her. Not now, not with this crisis on his hands. And besides, he wasn't even sure how much he liked her. She seemed to have a cool, well-suppressed side to her, a willingness to suffer in silence but to resent her suffering afterwards. Lloyd preferred people to say what they meant, right up front. He didn't have any talent for duplicity.

288

'Good night,' he told her, and turned over.

He lay awake for a long time, listening to Kathleen breathing next to him and the nearby churning of the surf. He kept thinking of that rhyme that Tony Express had repeated,

> *O Ma Rainey*
> *Li'l and low,*
> *Sing us 'bout de hard luck*
> *Roun' our do';*
> *Sing us 'bout de lonesome road*
> *We mus' go.*

He slept. He dreamed that Celia was standing watching him, with fire pouring from her eyes and mouth. He dreamed that Celia was sliding closer. He dreamed that she was bending over him. He dreamed that she was kissing his cheek.

He opened his eyes and found that she was.

'Lloyd?' she whispered.

He lay absolutely still, sweat-soaked, stiff with terror.

'Lloyd, it's me, Celia.'

Still he found himself unable to move, unable to speak. His mind was clamped tight like a vice that wouldn't unlock, his teeth were immovably clenched.

'You have to come back with us, Lloyd. This is much too important. It's only two days now to the solstice … things mustn't go wrong.'

Kathleen murmured and shifted in her sleep. Celia glanced at her behind her impenetrable dark glasses, and said, 'Unfaithful so soon?'

Lloyd lifted himself up on one elbow, and whispered back at her, 'Back off, all right? Stand away from me. Let's talk about this next door.'

He climbed out of bed as carefully as he could, and then quietly opened the bedroom door and went through to the living-room, with Celia following close behind him. He could smell that hot metallic smell, and it frightened him. He closed the bedroom door so that Kathleen wouldn't be disturbed.

'*Guten Abend,*' said a dry voice, as he switched on the overhead light. Otto was sitting in one of the bamboo armchairs, with his legs crossed, his face shadowed by his hat. '*Ihr T-shirt ist sehr amüsant.*'

'How did you find us?' Lloyd asked him. 'Why the hell can't you leave us alone?'

'Some fellow called Slonimsky told us where you were,' Otto remarked, picking with his fingernails at the fraying raffia which held his chair together. 'He was *most* co-operative.'

'Waldo? *Waldo* told you where we were? I can't believe that!'

Otto shrugged. 'It took a little persuasion. But – as I say – he was most co-operative.'

'Jesus Christ, if you've hurt Waldo – I'll see you in hell!'

'My dear Mr Denman, you will probably see me in hell in any event.'

'Celia,' asked Lloyd. 'Is Waldo okay?'

Celia nodded. 'Waldo's fine, darling. Just fine.'

'Are they all here?' Otto wanted to know. 'Mrs Kerwin? Mengele's creature?'

'A boy, too.'

Otto frowned. The overhead light made the criss-cross wrinkles on his cheeks look like soft beige quilting. 'What boy is this, Mr Denman?'

'He's kind of an orphan. I promised to take care of him.'

'What a strange man you are, Mr Denman. Running away, stealing my car, threatening my life's work. And at the same time taking the trouble to care for some human mongrel. Well, I suppose it can't be helped. He'll have to come too.'

'You're taking us back to Rancho Santa Fe?'

'I have no choice, Mr Denman. The day after tomorrow we are holding the grand Transformation at Civic Theater. You cannot be allowed to jeopardize my greatest moment – the moment for which I have prepared for so many years.'

Lloyd said, 'What time do you have?'

'Three minutes after three,' Otto replied. 'Why do you ask?'

'It's just that – okay, we'll come back to Rancho Santa Fe. We don't really have any alternative, do we? It's either that or having ourselves burned alive.'

'You're beginning to grasp the situation rather well,' Otto smiled.

'Just let these people have a few hours' sleep,' pleaded Lloyd. 'They've been under all kinds of stress. Why don't you have a drink? I'll make some coffee if you like. We'll leave promptly at eight o'clock, how's that? But don't get them up now, especially the kid.'

Otto thought about that, and then said, 'Very well. I have no particular objection. I could use a little sleep myself. Perhaps you and your bride-to-be can use the time to become re-acquainted. After all, the future will soon be yours, *nicht wahr*?'

He reached down and unlaced his large black welted shoes. Then he propped both of his stockinged feet on to the coffee table. His socks were made of thin grey wool, covered with pills. They looked as if he had been hand-washing them in hotel basins since the war. He interlaced his fingers, and closed his eyes.

Lloyd looked at Celia, in her black turban and her dark glasses and her black raincoat. 'Is that it?' he asked her. 'He's asleep?'

'He'll sleep till seven now,' she told him. 'He goes to sleep almost instantly, and he sleeps very deeply. No dreams. He says it's something to do with what happened to him during the war.'

'Let's go through to the kitchen,' Lloyd suggested. Celia walked in front of him, but he made sure that he kept his distance. He couldn't bear the strange greyness of her skin.

'Do you want a drink?' he asked her. '*Can* you drink?'

She took a glass from the drainer beside the sink and poured herself a glass of water. She swallowed a mouthful, and left her mouth open, watching him with what looked like a mocking expression. He heard the water boil sharply, inside her stomach. Steam rose out of her mouth and nose.

Lloyd's hand was shaking as he splashed out a large glassful of whisky. 'I wish you'd told me what you were going to do,' he told her. 'Maybe I could have coped with it better. Maybe I could have understood it.'

'I'm sorry, Lloyd,' she said. 'I truly am. But I was never the kind of woman who could give up without a fight. And when Otto promised me that I would live for ever ... never sick, never growing old ... well, I'd already begun to feel the effects of multiple sclerosis. I'd seen what happened to Jacqueline Du Pré. I didn't want the same thing to happen to me.'

'And you think this is better, being a Salamander? You think this is really *you*?'

'It's my soul, Lloyd. It's my spirit. I'm still Celia. I still love you. Inside of me, I'm just the same as I always was.'

Lloyd vigorously shook his head. 'The Celia that I knew wasn't interested in immortality or master races or shrivelled old Germans who eat bugs.'

'Lloyd – it's not like that! You should have heard Otto, the first time he talked to me! I was terrified of what was happening to me, and he gave me such hope! All of a sudden, I had a future; and not just one future, but a thousand futures, and a thousand futures that I could share with you!'

Lloyd swallowed whisky. 'Celia – *I'm* not going to live for ever. I don't even *want* to live for ever. I want to get married and run a successful restaurant and have a couple of kids and grow old gracefully ... that's what I want to do. I don't want to burn myself alive so that I turn into some kind of Nazi nightmare.'

'You don't have to live for ever, if you don't want to,' said Celia. 'But you can still have a child. On the night of the Transformation, when all the songs are sung and all the rituals have been recited, I'll be flesh again, like Helmwige. There's no reason why you and I can't live together just the way we always planned it.'

Lloyd let out a sarcastic grunt. 'Oh, yes, for sure ... with me growing steadily older and you staying young. With you capable of burning the living shit out of me every time I make you angry. I can see it now!'

'Lloyd, darling ... it wouldn't have to be like that at all.'

'So what *would* it be like? And apart from anything else, what would our children be like? Half-immortal and half-mortal? And if so, which half?'

'Ah ... that's the whole point,' said Celia. 'The true master race will eventually be made up of the children of people like me – people who have burned and Transformed – and their human lovers. Those children will have all the properties of immortality and humanity, combined. Don't you see, that's why Otto didn't want to let you go before the solstice ... he wants us to have a child ... *I* want us to have a child ... one of the first of the new everlasting order. Ancient magic, modern flesh. The combination will be irresistible, Lloyd.'

'Well, heil Hitler,' Lloyd told her.

'Lloyd – you don't understand. A child of ours could be almost holy! A beautiful magical creature who could rule the whole world!'

'Like the Hitler Youth were beautiful magical creatures who were going to rule the whole world? What the hell did Otto do to you, Celia?'

'He showed me the future!' Celia retorted. 'He showed me this rotten, diseased, crime-ridden, fear-ridden world for what it is, and he showed me the future!'

'Oh, did he?' Lloyd countered. 'Well, there's one thing he predicted wrong, and that was that you and I would ever have a child. Because if you think I'm going to touch you ever again, you're very mistaken, my lady. I wouldn't touch you again if you were the last woman left on the whole goddamned planet!'

Celia was quiet for a moment. She lowered her head, as if she were thinking, but she had no eyes to give her away.

'I was hoping I could persuade you,' she said, at last, with a catch in her throat that made her sound much more like the Celia he had known before.

Lloyd said, 'It's nothing personal, believe me. It's just that I don't happen to believe in master races. And I don't believe that people should live for ever, either. What value can your life possibly have, if you're never at risk of losing it?'

'Maybe, when the Transformation's done, you'll think differently.'

'I doubt it.'

'You'll come, though, won't you?'

'Do I have any choice?'

'We're holding it at Civic Theater. One thousand and one specially invited guests. Music by the San Diego Opera Company.'

Lloyd frowned at her. 'You have a thousand guests and music by the opera company? How the hell did you arrange that? The opera company's convinced that you're dead and gone.'

'It wasn't difficult,' said Celia. 'About six months ago, I asked Don Abrams, the production supervisor, to let me mount an evening of Wagernian-style opera – operas written by other composers as a tribute to Wagner. I played him some of the music from *Junius*, and of course he agreed. It's magnificent, one of Wagner's most dramatic operas ever – his masterpiece! And even more persuasive, I was even able to fix up a Gramma Fisher Foundation grant to fund it.

'But of course the opera company is still completely unaware that they're going to be singing an actual lost opera by Wagner himself. The only people who *will* be aware of it will be Otto and Helmwige and all of us Salamanders, who will come on stage at the climax of the opera, when the company sings the Transformation chant.

'At the climactic note of that chant, we will all be transformed into flesh; and the master race will at last be born. Think of it!'

'And what will your thousand and one invited guests do then? Stand up and sing the Horst Wessel song?'

'Lloyd, my darling,' Celia pleaded. 'This isn't Nazi Germany in the 1930s. This is California, today. Otto knows that. He's not trying to recreate the Third Reich, nothing like that. He just wants to see the world put into the hands of people who have the strength and the ability to run it as it should be run. He wants to see an end to suffering and cruelty and drug-addiction and poverty.'

Lloyd poured himself another drink. 'God almighty. If only Wagner had known what he was doing.'

'But Wagner did know.'

Lloyd dragged over a barstool, and sat down. 'Otto was sure that he *didn't*.'

Celia shook her head. 'He didn't know at first. But he found out. When he was in Venice, he played the Fire Ritual from *Junius* to a young music student called Guido Castelnuovo who was helping him to write the libretto. Two days later Castelnuovo set fire to his own clothes and killed himself. Wagner assumed that Castelnuovo was dead, and of course he was very upset. But about a week later, the student reappeared at dawn in St Mark's Square, when Wagner was out walking. He was a Salamander, just like me. He begged Wagner to play the Transformation music for him, in order to turn him into immortal flesh.'

'And did Wagner oblige?'

Celia said, 'Of course – and it worked. But Wagner was so horrified by what had happened that he sought out a famous Jesuit priest called Father Xavier Montini, who was an expert on pagan rituals, and told him all about it. Father Montini told Wagner that the only way in which he could put Guido Castelnuovo to rest was to write a Hymn of Atonement.

'This hymn had to include Wagner's own prayer for forgiveness, as well as the famous runic chant which the Pope had sent to St Augustine in Britain in 597 AD. St Augustine had needed it to destroy the immortal followers of a bloodthirsty pagan called Ethelfrid.

'So that's what Wagner did – he wrote a Hymn of Atonement. Then he invited Guido Castelnuovo to his apartments in Venice, and played it to him. Nobody will ever know what happened that night, but at the end of it, one room was found fiercely burned, and Wagner was found dead of a heart-attack.'

'How do you know all this?' Lloyd asked Celia, searchingly.

Celia gave a thin, grey-lipped smile. 'It was all in Father Montini's diaries and notebooks, in the Boston University library, of all places. They were sent there with a whole heap of other nineteenth-century Jesuit literature in 1924.'

'Nineteen twenty-four? So when Otto was searching for *Junius* during the war, he could never have found them?'

'Of course not.'

Lloyd narrowed his eyes. 'So Otto doesn't *know* about this Hymn of Atonement?'

'Oh, he knows about it, all right,' said Celia, 'but he doesn't realize I have it. It was all there, where Father Montini had hidden it, mixed in with all the rest of the opera. But Otto's musical advisers never got around to interpreting it. All they were interested in were the Fire Ritual and the Transformation Ritual. What did they care for a hymn?'

Celia glanced quickly toward the living-room door, but they both knew that Otto would still be deeply asleep, dreaming of nothing at all.

'Why didn't you tell him about it?' asked Lloyd, and for one instant he thought he sensed a flash of the old Celia – the Celia he had once loved. Headstrong, clever and determined.

'I didn't tell him because I knew what he would do. He would take it as a threat to the master race, and he would burn it. But I worship Wagner. To me, you know, it would be absolutely inexcusable to burn the only copy of a Wagner hymn, written in the master's own hand. That would be like burning the Mona Lisa.'

'So you hid it at home in your piano?' said Lloyd. 'And that's what you came looking for, the night you set fire to yourself?'

Celia said, 'No ... originally I came looking for my salamander talisman. I'd lost it, I didn't know where. Otto insisted that I had to have it for the Transformation ceremony. I thought I might have dropped the talisman inside the piano when I was hiding the manuscript there.'

Lloyd was silent for a long time.

'What's wrong?' asked Celia.

'For Christ's sake, tell me what's *right*.'

'The world is going to be a better place to live in, Lloyd. Believe me.'

'Did you burn Sylvia?' he asked her.

Celia looked away. 'No, I didn't burn Sylvia.'

'Sylvia had the hymn. You wanted it back. Who else could have burned her?'

'I went to get it and she gave it to me. I don't know what happened to her afterwards!'

But Lloyd wouldn't let her get away with that. 'You burned her, Celia,' he repeated. 'You personally cremated her. Maybe Otto was responsible for the others, but if Otto still doesn't know that you have the Hymn, then Sylvia's burning must have been down to you.'

Celia was oddly flustered. She spoke in a quick, side-ways manner, like Joan Crawford denying that she had ever punished her children. 'Lloyd, I swear – things haven't been easy. Burning yourself, it isn't easy. Coming out of your body as nothing but smoke and soul, do you have any idea what that's *like*? I felt as if I were walking into a blast-furnace. Pain, panic, terrible self-doubt. Thinking to myself, Why did I do it? Why?'

'Celia,' said Lloyd, 'when this Transformation ceremony is over, and just as soon as Otto will let me, I'm walking. I don't want to hear any more about your master race, I don't want to hear any more about your immortality. As far as I'm concerned, we were finished the moment you struck that match and set fire to yourself. In fact, we were finished the first day you went to Otto for help, and not to me. Talk about trust – Jesus! Talk about truthfulness!'

'Could you have cured me of multiple sclerosis?'

'Of course I damn well couldn't.'

Celia removed her dark glasses and revealed eye-sockets as black as memories, as black as the insides of cameras. 'You could join me, you know. It would be wonderful if you could join me.'

'I've told you, Celia. I don't want to live for ever. I'm not that goddamned proud. I'm not that goddamned *important*. You know, to the general scheme of things.'

'Many hundreds of people will.'

'Not your invited audience, I hope?'

'Otto chose them personally, you know. It took him years. Each one had to be checked and cross-filed. It took so long that some of them had died before we could send out the invitations.'

'So who's coming?'

Celia made a face. 'The faithful, I guess. The old Germans, the new young rich. The right-wing intellectuals. The scientists. Half of UC San Diego. Some from the Scripps Institute. Anybody intelligent and good-looking and progressive.'

'And white?'

'Otto doesn't insist on that. He says we have to adapt to changing times. We have Japanese, Hispanics, Italians.'

'No blacks?'

'Not as far as I know.'

'No Jews?'

'Lloyd!' smiled Celia, in disbelief. 'We won't have enough room for *everybody*!'

Lloyd finished his drink, and set down his glass on the drainer with exaggerated care. 'I think that's what they said the last time they tried to create a master race.'

They were still talking when the kitchen door opened and Franklin appeared, tucking his shirt-tails into his jeans, and blinking in the light. 'What's going on?' he asked. 'I heard voices.'

Celia stepped out from behind the refrigerator with a smile on her face. 'Hallo, you've woken up? That's a good boy. We're all going back to Rancho Santa Fe in just a while.'

'His name's Franklin,' said Lloyd.

Celia frowned at him. 'What?'

'His name's Franklin. That's what we've named him. Franklin Free.'

'Well … not free just yet, I'm afraid,' Celia told him. 'Not until Otto decides it.'

Franklin's face fell. 'Lloyd, I don't want to go back. Please don't make me go back, Lloyd.'

Lloyd said, 'Listen, Franklin, it's all right. Everything's going to work out fine. Why don't you go get your little doll? You understand me? Go get your little doll, and then we can all think about leaving.'

Franklin didn't appear to understand at first, but then he left the kitchen and went back toward the bedrooms, closing the door behind him.

'Poor mutt,' Celia remarked. 'I guess he *means* well.'

'Yes, I guess he does,' Lloyd agreed, trying not to sound too sharp.

They waited for a minute or two, and then they heard footsteps coming back toward the kitchen. They stopped right outside the door, and for a long moment there was silence. Celia stepped back in uncertainty. 'Why doesn't he just come in?' she asked.

'I think he wants to make a dramatic entrance,' said Lloyd.

He did. With one massive kick, he flattened the door to the floor, ripping out the hinges and splintering the door-frame. He stepped into the kitchen with one buccaneering stride; and what was even more dramatic was that he was carrying Tony Express on his back, white of eye and grinning with sleep, brandishing the 'little doll' – the shaggy, dead-decorated sundance doll, with its tiny cross face and its tattered fur hangings.

Celia immediately seized the lapel of her raincoat and tore it open, buttons bouncing and rattling across the kitchen floor. She faced Franklin and Tony Express completely nude, her grayish skin already beginning to darken and rise in temperature. Smoke rose flatly from her shoulders.

'For God's sake, be careful!' Lloyd shouted. 'Don't let her touch you!'

The kitchen was filled with the nostril-burning smell of intense metallic heat. Celia stalked up toward Franklin and Tony Express, trailing one hand along the kitchen counter, and where she trailed it, she left a deeply-burned furrow, and the acrid smoke of plastic laminate and chipboard.

'Tony! Franklin!' Lloyd shouted at them. 'Forget it! She'll cremate you alive!'

Celia whipped her head around and stared at him, grinning. She plucked off her dark glasses and he saw her for what she really was: a creature of smoke and fire. Both open eye-sockets flared with orange flame, like blow-torches, and her grin seethed with sparks.

— TWENTY-ONE —

But Tony Express, out of all of them, was unafraid. Tony Express couldn't see Celia, although he could hear her, and feel her heat, and smell the smoke of melting Formica. He sat piggy-back on Franklin's broad shoulders, lifted his sundance doll, and shook it violently.

'*Weksa-dek!*' he shrilled. '*Weksa-dek!*' He shook the sundance doll until it rattled and rattled, bones and beads.

'Don't you *dare* ...' Celia began, but then she was suddenly silent. She stayed where she was, not moving, not advancing, although flames still funnelled out of her eyes, and rainbows of coppery heat crawled across the skin of her back.

Tony Express shook his doll yet again, and began to build up a strange rhythm with it, shouting out, '*Weksit-patesk! Weksit-patesk! Na! Na! Weksit-patesk!*'

At last Celia stood completely still, and even from three or four feet away, Lloyd could feel that she was cooling. Tony Express slid down from Franklin's back and approached her, and laid his hand on her bare breast.

'See, she's cold now. Easy.'

'What the hell did you do? Some kind of Pechanga magic?'

'Algonquin, as a matter of fact. Their stuff is older, much more in tune with the Norse magic, know what I mean? Like the Norse people lived in America years before Christ. You know "*weksa-dek*" is Algonquin for "it's getting hotter" – and the Norse for "it's getting hotter" is "*vaeckser hedt*". You know, like, "it's waxing hot". Everybody in the world speaks the same language, except the Japs, and who wants to go around saying "kamikaze Toyota sushi" all the time, man?'

Lloyd walked around Celia slowly, touched her shoulder. She was quite cool, and she didn't seem to react at all.

'Did you hypnotize her, too?'

Tony Express groped for Franklin's hand. 'I did the same to her as I did to those cops. Lowered her vital what's-their-names, so that she's living at about a hundredth of the normal speed. As far as she's concerned, we're moving around this kitchen so fast now that she can't even see us.'

'What about Otto?' asked Lloyd.

'Who's Otto?'

'Otto's the Junius man. The one who burned the bus. He's sitting in the next room asleep. Least, I *hope* he's asleep.'

'Is he hot, like this one?'

'No;' said Lloyd. 'He's mortal. But he can start fires, just by thinking about them. He's pretty damned dangerous. Look what he did to my hands.'

'He can set light to things just by *thinking* about them?'

'That's right.'

'Then maybe we can make him think about something else, man, apart from us.'

'I'm not too sure what you mean.'

Tony Express squeezed Franklin's hand and said, 'Go see if Otto's still asleep, would you, Franklin?'

Franklin looked anxiously across at Lloyd, as if to say, *what's going to happen if Otto's awake, and he orders me to stay where I am, and I can't disobey him?* But Lloyd nodded and said, 'Go ahead, Franklin, you'll be okay. You're Franklin, right?'

'Sure, I'm Franklin.'

He circled around Celia, glancing at her from time to time as he did so, obviously afraid that she was going to spring back to life, and set fire to him. As a matter of fact, Lloyd could actually see Celia moving, as gradually as the hour-hand on a clock, but her movement was so long-

302

drawn-out that it would have taken her the rest of the day to cross the kitchen floor.

Franklin pushed the door open a little way so that he could see into the living-room. 'He's there,' he reported back hoarsely. 'He's still asleep.'

'Men with no mothers sleep like the dead,' Tony Express remarked. When Lloyd raised an eyebrow in response, he said, 'Old Pechanga saying, man. Don't ask *me* what it means.'

Lloyd said, 'We're going to have to get out of here, now that Otto's found us. They're holding the Transformation ceremony at Civic Theater tomorrow evening. It sounds like Otto's got a whole lot of arranging to do, so it should be pretty easy to stay out of his way. First of all I need to get back to Escondido.'

'Escondido?' asked Tony Express. 'Why d'you have to get back to Escondido?'

Lloyd looked at Celia. Her metabolic rate may have been reduced to that of a turtle, but he still preferred not to say anything about Wagner's Hymn of Atonement right in front of her. 'I'll tell you later,' he answered. 'Meanwhile, let's get our stuff together and get the hell out of here.'

He took hold of Franklin's arm and indicated to him in dumbshow that he should go pack up his clothes, and Tony Express's clothes, too. Then he stepped quietly into the living-room and crossed the rug on tiptoe, right past the sleeping Otto.

Otto's eyes were deeply sunken, his mouth was slightly open, and he was breathing so quietly that he might just as well have been dead. Only the slighest tic in the muscle of his left hand indicated that he was still alive. Lloyd passed within six inches of him, grimacing with the effort of keeping so quiet.

He went into the bedroom. In spite of all the noise they had been making in the kitchen, Kathleen was still asleep. She must have been totally exhausted by everything that had happened to her. Lloyd sat on the bed beside her and shook her shoulder.

'Kathleen? Kathleen? Wake up, we have to get out of here.'

She stirred, then tangled her fingers into her hair, and turned over.

'Kathleen, come on, we have to go.'

At last she sat up. 'What time is it?' she asked, blurrily.

'Nearly dawn. Otto's found us, he's here, we have to leave.'

'*He's here?*'

'He's asleep, but I don't know for how long.'

Kathleen climbed out of bed, and while Lloyd kept an eye on the door, she dressed. 'I didn't hear a thing,' she admitted. 'I must have been completely out of it. I was dreaming about Mike again.'

'Quick as you can,' Lloyd urged her.

As soon as she was ready, they crept out of the bedroom and back across the living-room. Otto remained where he was, silently breathing. It was only when they had reached the kitchen door that he opened his eyes and said in that husk-dry voice of his, 'You're not leaving, Mr Denman?'

Lloyd gritted his teeth. *Shit*, he thought. *Nearly made it, and now the bastard's woken up*. He pushed Kathleen ahead of him into the kitchen and indicated wildly that she should call Tony Express.

He heard Kathleen say '*Ah!*' as she encountered Celia in the kitchen, but then there was silence.

Lloyd turned back to Otto, chafing his hands together, and said, 'We were getting ourselves packed and ready to go back to Rancho Santa Fe, that's all.'

'And are you ready now?'

'Yes, well, pretty much.'

Otto gave himself an almost imperceptible stretch, and Lloyd heard the cracking of vertebrae. Then Otto stood up, and replaced his hat, and stood looking at Lloyd with an expression that Lloyd found impossible to interpret. It was partly amusement, partly cruelty, partly the tiredness of the post-war years. After the fall of Berlin, the rest of the twentieth century, for Otto at least, had been one long anticlimax. Only tomorrow's Transformation could possibly redeem it. Only the re-establishment of the master race.

He said, distractedly, 'We'd better think of leaving, then. Do you have any food here? You'd better take that, too.'

Lloyd said, 'Celia told me what you plan to do tomorrow ... all about the Transformation.'

'Oh, yes? And what was your reaction to *that*, Mr Denman?'

'I, uh – well, you know how I felt at first. But I think I begin to see the logic of it now. You know, the master race, all of that. I didn't think too much of it to begin with. I guess I thought you were trying to bring back Nazi Germany. But Celia explained that you weren't.' He hesitated, and shrugged. 'And, uh – she told me that we could still have a child. Still live together, just like we planned. It sounds ... well, it sounds attractive. Magical, almost.'

Otto listened to this fastidiously. Then he said, 'You're trying to tell me, then, that you have changed your mind? That you will be helpful, rather than obstructive?'

'I guess that's the size of it, yes.' He looked quickly over his shoulder. *Where the hell are you, Tony? We have to get out of here!*

Otto tugged his fingers so that his knuckles popped. 'It will be the greatest occasion in modern history. The very creation of a new race of demi-gods! Men and women at whose feet you will be glad to fall.'

'Oh, sure thing,' said Lloyd, and at that moment the kitchen door opened and Tony Express stepped in, a slight mis-step to the left, holding up his sundance doll, and shaking it.

'*Na! Na!*' Tony Express screamed out.

'This is the boy?' asked Otto, calmly.

'Er, yes,' said Lloyd. 'He's kind of ... ebullient, I'd guess you'd call it.'

'He's blind.'

'Yes, he's blind. He's also an Indian. His parents called him Child-Who-Looked-At-The-Sun. He's okay. Very well meaning.'

Tony Express came slowly forward on the softest of soles. He held the sundance doll up to Otto's face and shook it very, very gently, so that it sounded flat and threatening like a rattlesnake under a rock.

'You're the one, man,' he declared.

'I'm *which* one?' Otto asked Lloyd. He seemed to be unable to address himself to Tony Express directly, as if his blindness made him deaf and mentally defective, too. 'What is he talking about?'

'You were the one who torched the bus, man, out in the Anza Borrego.'

'How does he think he knows such a thing?' asked Otto, with a smile. 'He has no eyes.'

'I can recognize voices, man,' Tony Express told him. 'And I can recognize yours. "*Junius*!" That's what you said! "*Junius*!"'

'Well ... I hope you think this will do you some good,' Otto replied.

'Good testimony, in a court of law, man,' Tony Express suggested.

'I don't think so,' said Otto. He was growing irritable now. 'Let's get out of this place, now we've all had our sleep, and get back to Paseo Delicias.'

Tony Express shook his sundance doll. 'No, Otto,' he said, and his voice sounded peculiarly sweet and high, almost feminine. '*We're* going, but *you're* staying.'

'Enough of this nonsense!' Otto snapped at him. 'You will all get into the sedan, now, and drive to Rancho Santa Fe. Celia and I will follow in the sports car.'

'Otto ... not a second time,' Tony Express told him, in that clear girlish voice. He shook his sundance doll once, twice, three times.

Right in front of Otto, the air began to curdle and eddy, as if it were water. Then gradually a figure began to take shape, dim and shadowy at first, but gradually clearer. Lloyd stared at it and a thrill of fright scuttled right up the back of his neck. It was a young girl, no more than fifteen or sixteen, with long shining blonde hair. She was standing between Otto and Tony Express with her head

306

bowed. She wore a dark pinafore dress with a white smock over it, and short white socks, and black lace-up boots.

'Don't leave me again, Otto,' Tony Express repeated, and this time it sounded as if he were talking in stereo, two voices overlapping.

Otto stared at the apparition of the little girl in fascination and shock. He took off his hat and leaned forward, so that he could see her better.

'Gretchen?' he trembled. 'Is that really Gretchen?'

'Don't leave me again, Otto,' the girl pleaded, although she still wouldn't lift her head so that Otto could see her face. 'You hurt me so much the last time ... But the worst hurt was when you left me.'

Otto stroked her hair, over and over, and even though it was almost invisible, it built up static electricity, and rose softly crackling into the palm of his hand. 'Gretchen, I had to leave you ... how could I have taken you with me, when you were dead?'

'I hated that ditch,' Gretchen whined. 'It was so cold, and wet, and dark, and I was all tied up with wire. Why did you leave me, Otto?'

Tony Express took one step back, then another, and then nudged Lloyd's elbow. Lloyd was so enthralled by the apparition that Tony Express had conjured up that he was reluctant to leave, but Tony Express hissed at him, '*Go! Go! This won't last much longer!*'

'Oh, Otto, why did you hurt me so much?' Gretchen kept on whining.

'Little one ... you were so beautiful,' Otto told her, his voice cracking with dryness. 'I had to have you, I had to take everything that you had to offer. Even in that ditch when you were dead, white skin smeared with black mud – even in that ditch you were beautiful. I knelt in that ditch and I didn't care about my clothes and I took you one last time.'

'I honoured you, Otto,' Gretchen replied, as Lloyd and Tony Express slipped out into the kitchen and softly closed the door behind them. 'I respected you, and worshipped you. To me you were more like a knight from the days of old than a real man.'

Otto bent forward and kissed her hand. 'You were always so sweet, my little Gretchen. You could not have died better.'

'Creep,' said Gretchen.

Otto thought he had misheard her. He lifted his head and said, 'What? What did you say?'

'I said creep rat fink A-hole, that's what I said.'

Gretchen lifted her one stiffened middle-finger at him, and then raised her face so that he could see it. Her silky blonde hair fell back and there was the blind black grinning expression of Tony Express.

Otto stood very still and rigid. *So! Die Zauberei!* He had never realized that America was a land of sorcerers, too! And what kind of magic was this – that the girl on whom he had inflicted the cruellest acts of his entire life could be materialized in front of his eyes – could *speak* to him, accuse him directly of everything that he had done? He had left Gretchen in that ditch near Wuppertal in the winter of 1943, and nobody else had known about it except him.

'Got you worried, man?' Gretchen asked him, in Tony Express's voice.

Otto snarled, his thin lips dragging themselves back across his teeth. He lifted both hands to his head, and stared at this mocking apparition of Gretchen in rising fury. 'Nobody does this to me! *Nobody*! Ever!'

There was a deafening burst of incandescent flame, and the apparition exploded in front of Otto's eyes. But instantly he screamed, and slammed the heels of his hands against his temples, and dropped to the rug in agony. The sundance doll had drawn the ghost of Gretchen out of his own memory, and all that he had succeeded in burning was his own memory-cells. In fact, he had cauterized his recollection of her altogether, so that he would never be able to remember her again.

He lay on the floor, folded up like a storm-broken umbrella, shaking. *Gott in Himmel*, what had happened to him? He knew that it was something huge and dramatic, but he couldn't think for a moment what it was. Somebody had laughed at him. Somebody had mocked him.

'Celia!' he called out. He climbed on to his knees. 'Celia, *wo bist du*, Celia?'

He called again and again, but there was no reply. Eventually he managed to drag himself on to his feet and shuffle toward the kitchen, holding on to the furniture for support. He felt as if he had been hit in the head with the back end of an axe, and the light of dawn straining through the venetian blinds in the kitchen made his eyes water.

Celia was standing only a quarter-inch further from the spot where Tony Express had first suspended her metabolism. Otto walked up to her, and stared directly into her face, and said, 'Celia, *was ist los?* What have they done to you? Why don't you move? Why don't you speak?'

But Celia remained practically motionless, her empty eye-sockets wide in surprise, one arm lifted, a cold grey statue of a woman in a shabby oceanside kitchen.

Die Zauberei, Otto repeated to himself, in disgust. Indian tricks, hocus-pocus, men who were there and then they weren't there, shamans who turned themselves into eagles, tricks, mirrors. Sand which poured upwards, clouds which refused to rain. He had heard about it but he had never taken it seriously. He didn't take it seriously now. The day of the Transformation was almost here, and *then* the magicians of every culture would see who ruled the realms of the dead, as well as the realms of the living.

He was still standing in the middle of the kitchen with angrily clenched fists when he heard the tyres of his Mercedes sedan squealing on the road outside. He ripped apart the slats of the venetian blind in time to see Lloyd wildly U-turning, and driving back toward the main Pacific highway. He also saw that they had let down the tyres of his 380SL.

Angrily, he scooped handfuls of dead blowflies and moths from the window-sill, and crammed them into his mouth, swallowing most of them without chewing. He coughed on one large mouthful, and as he did so, Celia suddenly phased out of her slowed-down metabolic state and turned to stare at him.

Tony Express and his sundance doll must have driven away too far to influence her any longer.

'Otto?' she asked, bewildered. 'Otto – what's wrong?'

Otto spat out flies so that they clung quivering with trails of saliva to his chin. Then he slapped Celia so hard across the face that he bruised his ring-finger, and shouted out, '*Scheisse! Scheisse!*'

'Otto . . .' Celia quavered, picking up her fallen raincoat, and wrapping it around her.

'The first thing we do after the Transformation is that we hunt down every Indian in every reservation and we finish with them! *Versteh*'? We finish them!'

TWENTY-TWO

'Here,' said Lloyd, with relief, lifting the envelope out of the door-pocket of his BMW. 'Wagner's Hymn of Atonement, courtesy the Rosecrans Avenue Copie Shoppe.'

Kathleen took the pages and leafed through them carefully. 'Do you really believe this can stop them?'

'Celia seemed to think so. And remember what Franklin overheard Otto saying to Helmwige ... "They can only be destroyed by Him ..." I think Franklin probably misheard. Otto wasn't talking about *Him*, he meant the *Hymn*.'

'Well, I suppose if they can be *created* by a ritual chant, they can be destroyed by one,' said Kathleen, although she sounded dubious.

'Of course the problem is having this properly scored and played,' said Lloyd, as they walked back to the house. 'Not only that, but having it played at exactly the right moment, after the Transformation.'

'You must know some of the musicians at the opera,' Kathleen suggested.

'For sure ... but I don't know how many of them are members of Otto's jolly little study group ... or which of them might give us away without realizing it.' He checked his watch, and looked around Kathleen's house. 'We won't be able to stay here too long, either ... not without Otto or the cops catching up with us. We're not exactly the least conspicuous quartet of people I've ever seen. I mean we don't have that ability of melting into a crowd, do we?'

Kathleen opened the front door to her house, and let them in. 'Lucy!' she called. 'Tom! We're back!'

There was no reply. Kathleen ran upstairs and checked the bedrooms, and then came down again. 'They're not here. They must have gone over to my parents.' She picked up the phone and punched out the number. Lloyd asked her, 'You want some coffee?'

'I'd kill for some coffee.'

'Franklin? Tony? How about some orange juice?'

'I'd sell my grandpa for a root-beer,' said Tony Express. 'You don't realize how much you miss it till you don't have it.'

Lloyd was scooping espresso into the coffee-machine when Kathleen came into the kitchen looking anxious. 'I've called my parents' house and there's no reply.'

'Hey, I shouldn't let it worry you,' Lloyd told her. 'They probably went to the market, or out to the zoo.'

'Weird day for the zoo.'

Lloyd touched her shoulder. 'We're living in weird times.'

All the same, he started to feel a small sharp anxiety of his own when he called the Original Fish Depot and there was no reply from Waldo. It was a little too early, maybe, but when he called Waldo's home number, Waldo wasn't there, either. Oh, well: maybe he was on his way to La Jolla, stuck in the rush-hour traffic on I-5, or maybe he was down at the embarcadero, buying snapper.

They risked staying at Kathleen's house long enough to have a good breakfast of eggs and corned beef hash, although Tony Express wasn't too keen on corned beef hash because he said it reminded him of adobe.

Kathleen kept trying to call her parents, but still nobody answered.

'You don't think that anything's happened to them?' she asked.

'What could have happened? Your parents are old enough to go out without telling you, aren't they?'

But Kathleen remained worried and there was nothing he could do about it. And *he* remained worried because Waldo still didn't pick up the phone at the Original Fish Depot. He prayed that Celia and Otto hadn't taken their questioning too far.

'We'll take the BMW,' Lloyd decided. 'But I'll switch

plates with your Camaro, Kathleen. FISHEE's a little too conspicuous. Franklin – do you want to do that for me?'

'There's a whole set of wrenches in the garage,' said Kathleen. 'Mike always kept his tools so tidy. Totally tidy guy, on the whole.'

Although it was only twenty to eleven, Lloyd poured himself a medicinal whisky. Then he went back to the phone and tried the restaurant again. This time, the phone was instantly picked up.

'Waldo?' he asked.

'Who is this?' a flat voice demanded.

'I'm trying to get in touch with Waldo Slonimsky.'

'You a friend of his?'

Lloyd frowned. 'Well, kind of. What's going on?'

'I'm sorry, sir. The only way that anybody can get in touch with Waldo Slonimsky is through a medium. He was killed last night, burned in a fire.'

Lloyd opened his mouth and then closed it again. So Celia had been lying when she had told him that she hadn't hurt Waldo. And she had probably been lying when she had sworn that she hadn't burned Sylvia Cuddy.

But Waldo, goddamnit. He couldn't bear the thought of losing Waldo. Waldo had been so much more than a friend, he had been the last surviving member of a family who had sent him desperately and optimistically to America in the hope that he would carry on their name, long after *they* had all been burned and forgotten.

His eyes filled with tears. He couldn't speak any more, and he put down the phone. He was going to kill Otto now. He was going to kill Helmwige. His feeling of revenge, already strong because of what Otto had done to Celia, now surged up inside him like a huge black tidal wave.

In the den, with his feet up on the magazine-table while he listened to *The Real Ghostbusters* on television, Tony Express suddenly lifted his head. He had heard something, the softest of rattles. It was the sundance doll, which he had left propped up in the hall. The sundance doll, which was especially sensitive to men's revenge –

ask what revenge you want, and it will give it to you.

Now why should the doll suddenly rattle? thought Tony Express. It only rattled if somebody came close to it who was so hungry for revenge that they could scarcely wait.

He stood up and groped his way to the den doorway. He heard footsteps.

'Who's that?' he asked.

'It's me, Lloyd,' a choked-up voice replied.

Without hesitation, Tony Express said, 'Waldo's dead.'

'How'd you know that?'

'The doll can feel your revenge, man. And from the way you've been talking, there's only one person you care about enough to want to kill for.'

He paused, and then he added, 'I'm really sorry, man. I know he meant a lot to you.'

'Well, yeah,' said Lloyd, scarcely able to catch his breath.

But hardly had Lloyd told Kathleen what had happened, when Franklin came in from the garage, and Tony Express could tell from his quick, harsh breathing that he was seriously upset.

'Lloyd,' he said, 'can I talk to you?'

'If it's about the registration plates, Franklin, don't bother. I've just this minute heard that Waldo died last night.'

Franklin was confused. 'Oh, no, that's terrible. Was it Otto, do you think?'

'Otto or Celia, one of the two. I don't know. Who cares. They're both as mad and as dangerous as each other.'

'Lloyd –' Franklin began. He glanced with uncertainty at Kathleen.

'What is it? Come on, can't it wait until later?'

Franklin dumbly shook his head. 'You'd better come see for yourself.'

They went outside to the garage. Franklin had closed the automatic doors, but as they approached, he said, 'You're sure you're ready for this?'

'Just open up, for Christ's sake,' said Lloyd.

He didn't know what he had expected, but he certainly hadn't expected a corpse. A black charred figure was sitting upright in the middle of the concrete floor. The figure was so comprehensively burned that it was impossible to tell whether it was a man or a woman, or even if it was an adult or a child. It was sickening, but what made it slightly less shocking was that it had no identity. It could have been an artist's wooden figure, which somebody had perversely decided to char all over with a cigarette-lighter.

Lloyd approached the body slowly, and then stood quite still in front of it.

'Who do you think it is?' Franklin asked him. 'Look at this garage – there's black smoke all over everything.'

Lloyd circled around the burned body and ran his finger across the roof of Kathleen's Camaro. Its elk-grain padded vinyl was sticky with black powdery ashes and human grease.

At that moment, Kathleen appeared around the corner. Lloyd had asked Tony Express to keep her away, but there wasn't much that a twelve-year-old blind boy could do to control a determined middle-aged mother who was worried about her only son.

'Kathleen …' Lloyd began, and tried to step in front of her.

'Oh my God,' she said, her face as white as wax. 'It isn't …?'

Lloyd took hold of her arms, but she quickly twisted herself free. 'Who is it?' she said, in a breathless scream. 'Lloyd, who is it?'

It was then that the draught through the garage toppled the figure's precarious sitting position, and it fell to the floor with a soft crunching sound. One charred arm broke free, revealing a thin discoloured gold ring, set with diamonds.

Soundlessly, Kathleen pressed her hand to her face. She stood shaking for a moment, and then she almost collapsed, and between them Lloyd and Franklin had to help her back to the house.

'Lucy, oh my God, Lucy,' she said, over and over again in a high-pitched hysterical voice. 'Oh my God, Lucy.'

In the hallway, the sundance doll rattled ominously as she passed it by.

Lloyd gave Kathleen a dose of the valium which her doctor had prescribed for her after Mike had died, and put her to bed. She came downstairs three or four times, trembling and quivering, but in the end Franklin went upstairs with her, and sat beside her, and talked to her and stroked her forehead until she relaxed.

Lloyd poured himself another drink, and another root-beer for Tony Express. Then he stood and stared out of the window for a long time, while Tony Express sat beside him, humming to himself.

'It must have been Helmwige,' said Lloyd, at last.

'Sure,' Tony Express agreed. 'Celia and Otto went that-away to look for us, Helmwige came thisaway.'

'God, that poor woman,' said Lloyd. 'None of this was anything to do with her. Nor was it anything to do with Waldo. God knows what's happened to Tom.'

'As a matter of record, man, it wasn't actually nothing to do with *me*, either,' said Tony Express. 'Not wishing to sound ungrateful or nothing.'

'I'm sorry,' said Lloyd. 'I seem to have got all of these innocent people caught up in my own crusade.'

'Don't worry about it, man,' Tony Express told him. 'My horoscope said that I was going to do something useful this month, for a change.'

'John Dull Knife tells horoscopes?'

'No, man, the *San Diego Tribune.*'

Lloyd thought for a while, and then he said, 'I don't know what the hell we're going to do. You were pretty damn good at holding off Otto and Celia this morning, but could you do the same at the opera tomorrow night? I mean, what's the extent of your strength?'

'Let's put it this way,' said Tony Express, 'I can't fight any Little Bighorn for you. The sundance doll can help you take personal revenge on somebody you hate real bad

... like the way it slowed Celia down because she was threatening Franklin, and the way it used a spirit out of Otto's own mind – a spirit that really hated Otto – just to hold him off for a while.

'But I don't think I've got the power to *kill* anybody with a sundance doll. And I sure couldn't hold off a thousand people, maybe not even ten. The old Indian sorcery's gone, man. It came out of the ground and it came out of the sky and it came out of the water. Now the ground's all built on and the sky's all chopped up into pieces by airplanes and you sure wouldn't want to drink the water.'

Lloyd picked up the Wagner libretto. 'So what you're saying is ... this is our only hope?'

'Wagner raised these Salamanders up, man. Only Wagner can send 'em back again.'

'So how am I going to get it played? The only person I know who could have done it is dead.'

'Who was she, when she was at home?'

'Sylvia Cuddy. She worked for the opera company with Celia. She was almost as much of an expert on Wagner as Celia was. In fact in some ways she was better.'

'You were telling me about her. You reckon that it was Celia who burned her?'

Lloyd nodded. 'I could sure use her now.'

'Well, man,' sniffed Tony Express. 'Maybe you can.'

'What are you talking about?'

'If Sylvia Cuddy is suffering in hell because Celia burned her, then she's going to be feeling pretty damned vengeful, right? And revenge is what we're tapping into here. Anybody who gets unjustly sent to hell can get themselves released by taking revenge on whoever it was who unjustly sent them there. Come on, man, *everybody* knows that. What do you think ghosts are? Why do you think they moan and they groan? They're spirits who think they shouldn't be suffering in hell, searching for the bastards who put them there.'

Lloyd said gently, 'Am I beginning to understand you correctly? Because if I am ... God help me!'

'Pass me the doll, man,' said Tony Express, lifting himself off the sofa and sitting crosslegged on the rug. 'I'm going to show you something now you won't forget.'

Lloyd reluctantly picked up the sundance doll and gave it to Tony Express. It felt almost *alive* in his hand, throbbing, swollen and pliable, like a man's erection felt through a woman's fox-fur coat.

'Sylvia Cuddy you say?' asked Tony Express.

'That's right,' Lloyd agreed.

'Okay, then ... what I want you to do is to think hard about Sylvia Cuddy. Try to remember what she looked like ... where she lived. Her belongings. The sound of her voice. Imagine a real small Sylvia Cuddy standing inside of your head. Do you think you can do that?'

'I can sure as hell *try.*'

He closed his eyes. Tony Express said, 'Come on, man, keep your eyes open. How'm I going to be able to see her, if you don't keep your eyes open?'

'How did you know I had my eyes closed?'

'It's a characteristic of white people. They can't think and look at the same time. It confuses them.'

'All right, I'll do my best.'

They sat facing each other on the rug, while the morning sunlight fell like a golden fog between them. Tony Express hummed very softly to himself, occasionally articulating words which Lloyd couldn't quite understand, but which sounded as if they meant something. '*Nequet ... mmmmm ... nadtow-wompu ... mmmmm .. wejoo-suk ...*'

At the same time, he gently rattled his sundance doll, and the malevolent little face on top of it hopped and bobbed in front of Lloyd's eyes like a taunting puppet-show.

'*Wejoo-suk ... mmm ... wejoo-suk ... mmm ...*'.

Lloyd did his best to think of Sylvia. He thought of her backbrushed hair and her red lips and her huge designer eyeglasses. Then he thought of her neck, with the first sign of middle-aged wrinkles, and a heavy gold necklace

He thought of her hands, of her jungle-patterned blouse. He thought of her tiny apartment, and he could almost hear her voice saying, 'I'm so tired of living in Lilliput. It's so damned small here I can do swan-dives off the ironing-board, straight down the toilet.'

'Think of her,' Tony Express was urging him. 'Think of her clearly, man, think of her hard.'

'I can see her,' said Lloyd, and he could. She was standing inside his head like a tiny holographic image. She was standing inside his head and she was sharp, she was clear and she was *real*.

Tony Express said, 'Look at me.' Or perhaps Lloyd only imagined that he said it. But all the same, he turned to him and stared at him directly, with the tiny image of Sylvia still bright and sharp behind his eyes.

Tony Express took off his dark glasses. Lloyd saw his sightless milky white eyes. But in that instant, he felt as if something bright had been sucked right out of his own eyes, a brilliant image that had left him dazzled.

Although he was dazzled, however, he was able to see that Tony Express's eyes were dully glowing like 40-watt bulbs. Then Tony turned his head, and stared toward the far corner of the living-room.

Lloyd had already seen today the materialization of the girl called Gretchen, whom Otto had tortured and killed. Gretchen had been the faintest picture from a long-dead past. But he still shuddered when the sunlit air in the far corner of the room began to flow and coagulate, and gradually the shimmering outline of a woman began to form. Not just any woman, either. As the image grew more distinct and more colourful, he could see that it was unmistakably Sylvia Cuddy.

She took on no more substance than a translucent image in the air. An over-exposed transparency, its colours so thin – ivories and roses and pale jade greens – that Lloyd could barely see what they were. But it was Sylvia, all the same, and she moved, and turned her head, and her eyes looked at Lloyd with a sadness that made him feel impossibly guilty. After all, if he hadn't been rash enough to lend her the *Junius* libretto, she might still be alive.

'Sylvia?' he called her.

'Lloyd, what's ...' her voice strengthened and faded, as if they were hearing something on the very edge of a shortwave radio frequency.

Lloyd stood up and approached her. 'Sylvia, I'm sorry. I'm so sorry for what happened.'

'... n't your fault, she ...'

'Sylvia ... are you suffering at all? Sylvia, listen to me! Are you suffering at all?'

'... always the day ... every day ...'

'What day, Sylvia?' He was so close to her now, yet she was so transparent that he felt he could have stirred her image around like sheets of coloured gelatine dissolving in warm water.

'... day my father died ... every day ... so much grief ...'

Tony Express was standing close beside Lloyd's elbow. 'In hell, you suffer the worst thing that ever happened to you when you were alive, over and over, every day. Didn't you know that? That's what hell is. You white people don't know nothing.'

Lloyd hesitated, and then he said, 'Sylvia ... that libretto I gave you to look at ... the Wagner libretto ... could you score that for me? Could you sing it for me, so that I know what it's supposed to sound like?'

'... n't understa ...'

'Score it for me, teach me how to sing it! It's desperately important! It's a hymn, written by Wagner, to destroy all of the fire people ... to make atonement for all of the Salamanders!'

At last, Sylvia began to nod, as if she had grasped what it was that he wanted her to do. Lloyd went over to Kathleen's upright piano, opened the lid, and set the manuscript pages on the music-stand. Then he turned back to the glassy, flowing image of Sylvia, standing in the sunlight, and there were tears in his eyes.

'Try, Sylvia, please.'

For the next two hours, they were treated to an eerie

but enchanting scene. Sylvia's image sat at the piano, carefully scoring Wagner's music with a pencil that almost seemed to jiggle in mid-air by itself. Every now and then, she would play a short phrase from the hymn on the piano, and the room would resonate as if the notes were being played on every frequency in the known universe.

At last, Sylvia announced that she had finished, that she was ready: that her scoring and arrangement of Wagner's Hymn of Atonement was as close to Wagner's original as she could manage.

Tony Express elbowed Lloyd's ribs. 'Tape-recorder,' he reminded him.

'Oh, sure,' said Lloyd; and switched Kathleen's Sony to record.

The Hymn was strong and primitive, a pagan hymn rather than a Christian hymn. But it had a soft wild beauty that stirred a feeling in Lloyd that he hadn't felt for years.

> *Forgive the beacons we have lit,*
> *Forgive our wraith; our ire*
> *Forgive the souls that dared to burn*
> *Within th'immortal fire.*

Sylvia sang the words high and clear: so high and clear that Franklin suddenly appeared in the doorway, and stood staring at the piano mesmerized.

The Hymn died away. Sylvia turned to Lloyd and raised both hands to her lips. Her eyes were filled with affection and regret. But at least she had a chance now to live an afterlife that was free of suffering and agonizing grief.

'... 'bye, Lloyd ... remember, I ...'

She was gone. The pages of the libretto were ruffled by a sudden breeze, and blew one by one on to the floor. Lloyd knelt down and collected them up.

'Who was playing the piano?' asked Franklin, stupefied.

'Didn't you see anybody?' Lloyd replied.

Franklin came closer, and peered around the piano. He lifted the drapes and looked behind them, too. Then he stared at Lloyd in complete bewilderment.

'Were you playing that piano?'

'No,' said Lloyd. 'Didn't you see her – the woman in the floral blouse?'

Very slowly, Franklin shook his head. 'I didn't see anybody. There was nobody here.'

Lloyd looked across at Tony Express, but Tony Express was still sitting crosslegged on the floor, his head thrown back a little like Stevie Wonder, rocking on his haunches and humming to himself. Lloyd had read about the doors of perception, and the extraordinary levels of different reality into which Indian shamans had always been capable of removing themselves, but this was the first time he had experienced it so intensely and so emotionally for himself. He wondered who was experiencing whom, and if Tony Express should ever regain his sight, whether the rest of the world would instantly become blind.

— TWENTY-THREE —

'I have to come with you,' Kathleen insisted. 'If they've got Tom, then I simply have to.'

'You realize how dangerous it could be,' said Lloyd, although he had known all along that he wouldn't be able to persuade her to stay at home.

'It's no less dangerous here,' Kathleen argued. 'Look what they did to Lucy.'

'All right,' Lloyd agreed. There was no arguing with that. They had decided yesterday not to try running on anywhere else, because they had all been tired and Kathleen had still been suffering from shock. But they had taken it in turns to keep watch all night, in case Otto or Helmwige or any of the Salamanders came after them.

It had been difficult for Lloyd to persuade Kathleen not to call the police. After all, Lucy had been killed and Tom was missing, and there was no guarantee that their Hymn would have any effect on the Salamanders at all. Lloyd only had Celia's word for it – that, and a half-heard conversation which Franklin had reported. It was quite possible that Celia had been lying, the way she had lied about almost everything else, and that Franklin had simply misunderstood what Otto had been talking about.

Nevertheless, they were carrying two duplicate cassettes with Wagner's Hymn on them – in case one of them should get lost or caught – and their plan was simply to play it over the Civic Theater loudspeaker system at the end of the opera.

'Simple, man,' remarked Tony Express. 'All we have to do is gatecrash an invitation-only opera, hide, stop ourselves from being burned alive, mess with the Salamanders' hi-fi, duck their subsequent wrath, rescue Kathleen's kid, call the cops, make the cops believe that we're not totally out to lunch, and bingo.'

'You make it sound so easy,' Lloyd remarked.

By calling the Civic Theater enquiries, they had discovered that tonight's opera evening started at nine o'clock, and finished at midnight. 'But, I'm sorry, sir, it's strictly by invitation only, and there are no more seats available.'

They spent the day resting and pacing about and nervously watching television. Lloyd would have done anything for a drink, but he resisted it. He sat in the kitchen watching Kathleen make sandwiches for everybody, and drank Perrier with a wedge of lime and salt round the rim, a teetotaller's tequila.

Kathleen seemed to have lost a lot of her defensiveness since they had discovered her sister burned in the garage. She was still practical, still disinclined to show her feelings, but as he watched her against the afternoon light he could see her femininity shining through. Those graceful movements, those soft and appealing expressions.

He could see, too, that she wasn't the woman for him. He might have acquired a restaurant and a BMW and house with a peek, but he was still his parents' son.

At the moment, however, it didn't matter whether they would ever stay together or not. What bonded them together was their hatred of Otto and Helmwige and the master race, and their need for revenge. They both needed revenge so much that it physically hurt them, like the need for crack.

'Do you think Tom's safe?' Kathleen asked him, as she cut the last of the sandwiches.

Lloyd nodded. 'Almost certain of it. Otto can't catch us, but I reckon he's going to keep Tom as his insurance policy, in case we start making trouble.'

'What happens when we *do* make trouble?'

'Then I'll do everything I can to make sure that Tom gets out of there safely.'

Kathleen was silent for a moment, as if she were making her mind up about something. Then she said, 'Okay, thank you. I guess that's the most that anybody could promise.'

324

They drove south towards San Diego on I-5, so nervous that they could scarcely speak to each other. Lloyd switched on the radio for a moment, but it was Chris Rea singing 'The Road To Hell', and so he switched it off again. He would have done anything for a drink, a cigarette, an excuse to take the next turnoff and head back to La Jolla. But it was too late now. He had far more lives to think about than his own. Even Celia's. Perhaps Celia's more than any of the others, because he had failed her.

And what would happen, when Otto's master race emerged, and began to impose its will on a nation whose moral certainties were already foundering? *God*, thought Lloyd, *I've been afraid before, but never like this. I've never been afraid that I'm going to wake up tomorrow, and America's going to have changed for ever.*

They passed the Seaworld turnoff, and the glittering lights of downtown San Diego began to rise up in front of them. Tony Express crossed himself.

'I didn't know you were a Catholic,' Kathleen remarked.

'I'm not,' he said. 'But, you know man, you might as well give yourself all the protection you can.'

It was a hot, windless night. There was no smell of ocean, only burned petrol and stale air-conditioning and cigarette smoke. The sky reflected the lights of the city so that it was almost purple. Lloyd took the Civic Centre turnoff, and then bore left until he reached the Civic Theatre garage entrance at 2nd and A.

It was 8:35. Already the theater garage was busy with lines of glistening Cadillacs and Mercedes and Porsches, and crowds of people in evening dress were taking the elevators down to the street. There was a smell of imported cigarettes and pot and Giorgio perfume.

'All right?' asked Lloyd, as they parked. 'Anybody want to back out?'

'Come on, Lloyd,' said Franklin, laying his hand on Lloyd's shoulder. 'Let's just go. Don't let's think about backing out.'

They climbed out of the car. They had raided Mike Kerwin's closets to make themselves look as presentable as possible. Lloyd was a little taller than Mike, so the trousers of his dinner suit flapped around his ankles, but the dress-shirt fitted quite well. Franklin had managed to wedge himself into a blue Yves St Laurent blazer and a pair of slacks that made his muscular legs look as if they had been sprayed with dull grey paint, while Tony Express had found a black jacket of Kathleen's that fitted him. He had gelled his hair and combed it like Robert de Niro's.

Kathleen wore a black velvet evening-gown, low-cut, with a large diamond pin on her left breast. She was tired, and her cheeks were colourless, but then she was just beginning to feel the full effects of Tom's disappearance, and of her sister's ugly cremation in the garage. All the same, Lloyd thought she looked exceptionally alluring, and he was proud to have her on his arm.

As they walked across the parking level, Lloyd noticed two black minibuses with mirror windows parked close together in the far corner. *Balboa Hi-Way Bus Rental* was lettered on the side panels of each of them. And what was the betting they, too, had been rented by Mr Ortal? Mr Imm-Ortal, big joke, Otto.

They took the elevator down to street-level and then turned left to the Civic Theater entrance. It was bright and crowded, although there were uniformed security guards at every door checking invitations, and the sidewalk was roped off to prevent anybody from straying into the theatre entrance by accident.

'How on earth are we going to get in?' Kathleen asked, behind her black-gloved hand, as they approached the doors. A man behind her was laughing loudly and saying, 'She came for rhinoplasty and went away with new lips, new ears, new breasts, and twelve thousand dollars' worth of liposuction.'

'Well, Kurt, you're a good salesman, I'll admit that,' his companion was saying. 'You probably couldn't remodel an outhouse, but you sure can sell.'

They both laughed loudly. Then Tony Express and Lloyd reached the door, closely followed by Franklin and

Kathleen. The security guard was a big-bellied black man with a glossy peaked cap pulled down low over his eyes.

'Check your invitations, please?' he asked, suspiciously.

Tony Express lifted his sundance doll and shook it twice. '*Na, na'lwiwi!*' he said, sharply.

The security guard frowned at him, and said, 'What you doin' that fo'?' so he shook it again.

'*Na! Na! Na'lwiwi!*'

Lloyd was sure that the security guard was going to turn them away, but then an extraordinary thing happened. The air in front of the security guard's face seemed to *bend*, like a distorting mirror at a funfair, and no matter how much he turned his head from side to side, he appeared to be unable to see past it.

In the end he turned to the two cosmetic surgeons right behind them and said, 'Okay, gentlemen. How about *your* invitations?'

'But you didn't check ...' one of the surgeons began, pointing at Lloyd and Franklin and Kathleen and Tony Express.

The security guard looked back at them, but the air was still flexing, and it was obvious to Lloyd that he simply couldn't see them. Tony Express had somehow summoned his powers of light and air to distort the man's vision.

'Come on, man,' Tony Express urged him. 'That's nothing but a trick and it don't last more'n a minute.' Together, they shove-shuffled their way through the crowded lobby and up the stairs, and through the open doors into the main auditorium.

The Civic Theater could take nearly twice as many people as Otto had invited, and so there were plenty of spare seats. Lloyd and Kathleen found themselves stalls seats close to the left-hand exit, while Franklin and Tony Express went to sit on the opposite side. The stage curtains were still closed, but already some sections of the orchestra were beginning to tune up. Their persistent off-key scraping and whining did nothing for Lloyd's already-tightened nerves.

He looked around him at the gradually filling theatre. If

327

he hadn't known that each of them had been personally selected by Otto for their racial characteristics, their politics, and their intelligence, it would have taken him a long time to realize that there were no blacks here, nobody who was obviously Jewish, no Slavs. There were several light-skinned Hispanics, and some Orientals, but none of them looked anything but wealthy and well-domesticated Southern Californians.

Under the sparkling chandeliers sat a thousand and one of Southern California's finest and most successful – doctors, lawyers, dentists, accountants, politicians. Although they didn't yet know it, they were the master-race-to-be.

'Where do you think Tom is?' asked Kathleen, looking anxiously around.

'If Otto's got him, he'll be here,' Lloyd reassured her. 'He's Otto's hostage, remember, in case we try to mess things up for him.' In spite of his confident tone, however, he wasn't at all sure that Otto would have brought Tom here – nor even that Tom was still alive.

'Oh God protect him,' Kathleen whispered.

Franklin gave Lloyd the thumbs-up from the far side of the theatre. They had planned to sit through the first part of the opera, until the second interval, and then for Franklin and Tony Express to make their way backstage to see if they could find Tom and locate the theatre's audio equipment. As the opera drew to its climax, towards midnight, Lloyd and Kathleen would join them. They would play the Hymn, if they could, and with luck, make their getaway.

It wasn't much of a plan, and they would probably have to decide what to do as they went along, but then Lloyd's vice-president at San Diego Marine Trust had always said, 'When you haven't got a fucking clue, extemporize.'

It was that advice that had led Lloyd to quit the insurance business and open the Original Fish Depot. He hoped it would hold out tonight, on the night of the summer solstice, on the night of Otto's sorcerous Transformation.

Kathleen took hold of his hand and squeezed it. 'Come on, Lloyd,' she whispered. 'We've got God on our side.'

Lloyd gave her a tightly drawn smile, and tried to look as if he believed it.

As nine o'clock drew near, the doors of the auditorium were closed, and Lloyd noticed that a security guard stood by each. Maybe the invited audience thought they had been posted there to keep out gatecrashers, but Lloyd was pretty damned sure that they were intended to keep the invited audience from getting out.

Gradually the lights were dimmed, and the hubbub of conversation died down. There was a breathless moment when a thousand and one people sat in complete silence, and then the curtains parted and Otto stepped out, in white tie and tailcoat, prissily tugging at his shirt-cuffs. There was a smattering of applause across the stalls, although it was obvious that nobody in the audience knew who Otto was.

He lifted his hand for quiet, and then he said, 'Good evening, ladies and gentlemen. You have all received from me a personal invitation to this gala evening of Wagnerian opera. You were selected because each of you has attended several classical concerts in the past five years, and because most of you are very successful at what you do.

'I am hoping that tonight we will form amongst ourselves an exclusive and special society of those who are devoted to the works of Richard Wagner and the fundamental principles which inspired his music. But more of that later.

'What I have to tell you is that what you are about to witness is not what you *thought* you were going to witness ... not a collection of works by various composers, paying tribute to Richard Wagner. What you are going to witness is a complete and previously unknown opera by Richard Wagner, his last.'

A low roaring of excitement and surprise went through the audience. Even the orchestra turned to each other in amazement. Celia must have given them scores which appeared to be several unconnected pieces, but which in fact made up the entire opera, cunningly disassembled.

Willard Bright, the conductor, stood up and said something to Otto which Lloyd couldn't hear. But Otto simply smiled and said, 'You have rehearsed it, *ja*? You know how to play it? You will be magnificent!'

The conductor consulted with his orchestra for a moment, but none of them appeared to have any objections. In fact most of them looked eager to start playing.

'Here then,' said Otto, 'is Richard Wagner's lost masterpiece *Junius*. It tells the story of a Bavarian bürgermeister who made a pact with the powers of darkness in return for immortality ... how he was misunderstood by his fellow citizens and sacrificed ... but how he triumphed over death, and how glory and brilliance came out of that darkness, and forged an empire the like of which had never been seen before, but which will rise again!'

Immediately, the orchestra broke into a thunderous overture, wilder and more powerful than any Wagner that Lloyd had heard before. The music was primitive, sweeping, unbridled, like a hurricane blowing through the theatre. Already overwhelmed by Otto's compliments, and by the fact that they were going to hear the premier performance of a long-lost opera, the audience sat enthralled.

For most of the overture, the auditorium was plunged into complete darkness, but then the curtains were drawn back, and the kettle-drums set up a rolling, reverberating, primitive rhythm, and a hundred-strong chorus, all dressed in black and carrying lighted torches, sang a deep, dirgelike repetitive chant.

> *Who has been trading with His Satanic Majesty?*
> *Who has been offering his very soul for sale?*
> *Who has turned his back on the Lord His God?*

In spite of his fear, in spite of his hatred of Otto, Lloyd found the opera hugely moving and disturbing. It had all the elements of a Nazi rally ... darkness, torches, flags, symbols ... and chants of triumph that swelled like the ocean at night.

Turning around, he could see that the rest of the audience were transfixed by it, too. It had drummed up their deepest terrors, it had stirred up all of their suppressed prejudices. It had given their hatreds a musical voice.

At the end of the first act, the orchestra finished with a deafening finale of horns and drums, through which the chorus chanted 'Glory! Purity! Power and strength!' over and over and over again, until Lloyd could hear some of the audience chanting it with them.

'Glory! Purity! Power! Strength!'

God, thought Lloyd. How easy it was to start it all over again.

By the close of the first act, the audience was in a frenzy of excitement. They rose from their seats and gave the opera company a standing ovation that roared on and on and seemed to rise rather than diminish. The second act started with a long, quiet passage set in the twilit mountains of Bavaria. The scenery was dimly blue and luminous, and the voice of the leading soprano, Eloïs Steiger, seemed to slide through it with a coldness that Lloyd could feel in his bones.

> *I have seen with my own eyes*
> *Dead men walking in the streets*
> *Dead men tapping at the children's windows*
> *Not speaking, not calling*
> *But waiting for me at every corner*

Gradually the aria became another chant, a low throbbing chant that put Lloyd in mind of a galley-drum, or the beat to which a Viking longboat might have been rowed. He had the unsettling feeling that this was the prelude to the Fire Ritual, the magical chant which prepared a would-be Salamander for the flames.

He was right. The mountains of Bavaria moved away to

reveal a barbarians' encampment, and in the centre of the encampment a monstrous bonfire blazed. The effect had been achieved with flickering lights and shreds of flying tissue-paper, but the stage technicians had achieved the right degree of lurid, mesmerizing light. The chorus appeared, and began a chant which underlay everything sung by Eloïs Steiger, and by Robert Kupka, the baritone who was playing the sorcerous bürgermeister Johann Junius.

Lloyd looked along the chorus. They wore grey monk-like habits, and their faces were partially concealed in shadow. But he was sure that he recognized Celia, fourth from the left, and he nudged Kathleen and whispered, 'Can you see Mike there? Somewhere in the chorus.'

Kathleen picked up the opera-glasses from the seat in front of her, and carefully scrutinized the stage. 'There ...' she said at last. 'I think that's him ... the tall one just behind the fire.'

They both watched the remainder of the second act in dread and curiosity. Lloyd checked his watch and there were only forty minutes remaining until midnight. Forty minutes to complete the last act of Wagner's opera, and the first act of the master race.

As the fire scene came to a drumming, low-key ending, Lloyd leaned across and signalled to Franklin that it was time for him to go. Franklin nodded, and as the audience rose for the last interval, he and Tony Express disappeared into the crowds.

Although the audience were allowed through to the Civic Theater bars for champagne cocktails, Lloyd noticed that all the street exits were closed and guarded. He and Kathleen stood in a corner saying nothing to each other, but listening to the chatter all around them.

'... says something you could never say in print without somebody branding you a bigot ...'

'... it's loud, for sure, and very Germanic. But what music! Do you realize what a privilege it is, to hear that music for the very first time ...'

'... makes me feel strange – like I've heard it before, but I can't think where ...'

'... music's been dominated by blacks and Jews for so long, people have forgotten what real pure classical music sounds like ...'

Lloyd took Kathleen's hand and together they walked back to the auditorium and sat down.

'Did you *hear* them?' said Kathleen. 'It's happening already.'

'I know,' Lloyd agreed. 'The Third Reich, all over again. And *here*, in Southern California.'

'I'm afraid,' Kathleen told him.

He leaned across and kissed her. 'Do you want to know something?' he told her. 'Me too.'

There was feverish excitement as the audience returned to the theatre for the final act. Somehow a rumour had circulated that the last aria was magnificent beyond belief, that tonight was going to be legendary in world opera for decades to come. 'The night that *Junius* was performed in public for the first time ... The night that Eloïs Steiger reached a fortissimo A-natural above high C that had the audience screaming in denial that such a sound could exist.'

Lloyd recognized the rumour for what it was: propaganda. A way of stirring up more excitement in an audience that was already tired and excited and ready for almost anything.

The curtains drew back, revealing a megalithic Aryan city, under a threatening sky. Lightning flickered and thunder crashed. Horns bayed in unison. Then the chorus marched diagonally right and left across the stage, wearing breastplates and heavy helmets, and carrying spears.

'We march toward the future ...
We will make war on decadence and sloth
Like a black wind we will storm through the world'

The music grew louder and louder, the chorus shrilled and roared. Lloyd peered at his watch and saw that there were only a few minutes to go before midnight, the critical moment of Transformation. The chorus were gathering in a semicircle, holding hands, and chanting '*Storm! Storm! Storm! Storm!*'

Eloïs Steiger moved centre-stage, wearing a huge black cape and a black horned helmet. Several of the audience stood up in awe, and nobody attempted to make them sit down again. Drums rolled, thunder shook the auditorium.

'*Now is the moment of our Transformation!*' she sang, in a voice as powerful as a gale. '*Now is the moment when men become gods!*'

'*Storm! Storm! Storm! Storm!*' chanted the chorus, raising their joined hands with every chant.

Women were shrieking in the audience. Some of the men were stamping their feet in time to the chant of the chorus, others stood with their mouths open in disbelief as Elöıs Steiger reached the final measures of the opera. The orchestra swept them all along like survivors clinging to a life-raft.

'*Now is the moment of our triumph! Now is the moment when all will fall before us!*'

Eloïs hung for a moment on the penultimate E-flat. The orchestra was suddenly silent, the audience hushed. Lightning danced in the painted sky, and there was a suppressed buzzing of electrical contacts, but that was all. Kathleen clutched Lloyd's hand, although neither of them were really sure what they were expecting.

It was then that they heard a sound that didn't sound like a human voice at all. It sounded like some uninvented, unimaginable instrument. A shiver of dread ran through the audience that they would only hear this once in their lives, and this was the moment.

The sound broadened and widened and swelled and rose. Eloïs Steiger flung wide her arms and threw back her head, and in that rippling black cloak she uttered an A-natural that filled the theatre like an atomic explosion, dazzling and deafening, wider and wider and louder and louder until Lloyd felt that the whole auditorium would collapse on top of them.

But there was more to come. At the instant the note died – in that stunned hiatus before an audience usually roars its approval – the chorus threw back their cloaks and revealed themselves naked, gleaming with the grey metallic skin of Salamanders. They raised their joined hands, and shouted together, '*Glory! Purity! Power!*'

The entire theatre shook. Pieces of plaster dropped from the ceiling, and a battery of spotlights fell on to the stage and smashed. Somebody screamed, 'Earthquake!' and a moan of terror went through the audience. But then they immediately saw that it wasn't an earthquake. It was the power that was rippling through the chorus, a sullen crimson light that throbbed from one to the other, through their arms, through their hands, until all of them were glowing the colour of red-hot coals.

The audience stood and stared at them in bewilderment, but Lloyd and Kathleen knew what was happening. Their volatile bodies of smoke and spirit were being transformed by the most ancient of pagan powers into something which resembled human flesh – the flesh of the gods. These were going to be the parents of the master race.

Gradually, the light died and the smoke drifted away. The audience were left in stupefied silence. Some of the women were sobbing. They didn't understand that the enormous emotions stirred up by the opera hadn't been for their benefit, but for the benefit of Otto's Salamanders. They were left aroused, excited, but completely disoriented, unable to understand what they had witnessed.

'Now,' Lloyd muttered. 'Now, Franklin – the Hymn, for God's sake! The Hymn!'

But no Hymn came. Instead, the curtains slowly and silently descended, and Otto reappeared on the stage, his hands raised in a call for calm.

'Sit, please, sit,' he said, and the audience gradually sat. He waited until they were completely quiet, and then he

335

said, 'You will not know what it is that you have seen, not yet. It was a Transformation, of fire into flesh, of insubstantial souls into immortal beings who can walk this earth as gods.

'You too can be gods like they are. In fact, that is why I chose you. All of you here can take part in the ritual of fire, and become leaders of men such as the world has never known.'

Nobody spoke. Nobody challenged him. Nobody knew what to say.

'You are not aware of it,' Otto continued, 'but the ritual chant in the first act prepared all of you for what is going to happen now. You will survive it – as the men and women of my chorus survived it – to be transformed, when the time is right, into glorious creatures such as they.'

Otto raised both his hands to his temples. There was a low murmur of bewilderment, but so far nobody had dared to speak up.

'My God,' Lloyd whispered to Kathleen. 'We have to get out of here! Do you see what he's going to do?'

'What? What is it?' asked Kathleen, still bemused by the climax of the opera.

'Salamanders!' Lloyd hissed at her. 'He's chosen this audience to be Salamanders! This is his master race! He's going to burn the whole goddamned theatre!'

At the instant he spoke, there was a shrill scream of surprise from the back row of the stalls. Lloyd turned, and saw that a man's head had caught alight, and was furiously burning. The woman next to him was trying to flap at the flames with her fur stole, but then she burst into flame, too. One by one, with alarming speed, like a lighted taper running along a row of candles, the whole row of people were ignited, and then the next row, and then the next.

'*Out!*' Lloyd yelled at Kathleen, and pushed her along to the end of the row to the exit. A security guard was standing in the way, but he looked as shocked by the fires as they were, and Lloyd shouldered him to one side and kicked open the exit before he had time to stop them. He twisted around, and shouted, 'Hey!' but then the front rows detonated into flame, and he was caught in a roaring fireball of superheated air which took off his face as if it were a plastic Hallowe'en mask.

Lloyd and Kathleen ran along the corridor, until they reached a door marked *Offices: Private*. The door was locked, but Lloyd gave it three violent kicks, and it fell flat into the drab carpet-tiled office beyond. On the opposite side of the office was a door which obviously led backstage.

'Come on,' Lloyd urged Kathleen. 'We have to play that hymn!'

They ran along another long corridor, up a flight of stairs, and then they pushed open a swing door and found themselves in the gloom at the back of the stage, among flats and props and cardboard trees and gold-painted thrones and coils of rope. There was nobody around, so they stepped cautiously behind the scenery, looking for the hi-fi console.

'Listen,' said Kathleen, holding his hand. 'You can hear the fire alarms.'

Lloyd paused, and listened. 'Sure. But no screaming. Have you noticed that? Nobody's screaming. They're not even fighting to get out.'

They could smell smoke and heat and the unmistakable barbecue stench of charred human flesh, but apart from the distant alarms the quiet was uncanny. They crept forward behind the Bavarian mountains, and suddenly found themselves front stage, only partially concealed by what were supposed to be alder-trees.

On the stage, the chorus now stood in a circle, still naked, but no longer greyish-skinned, the way they had been before. They had eyes, too, like Helmwige's; pale and glistening and unnaturally calm, the eyes of people who will never have to fear for their lives. Otto stood outside the circle, still facing the auditorium.

The theatre was the most grisly sight that Lloyd had ever seen. Through a dense veil of human smoke, he could see that all thousand and one guests had burned, and that they were lolling in their seats, still smoking. Raw grins stretched over burned teeth. Jewels had melted into charred necks. Everywhere Lloyd looked, bodies sat stiff and blackened. Here and there, a toupee still burned with a guttering flame, or a patent purse flared.

Lloyd had never understood how a Salamander was formed, but now he saw it for himself, over and over again. It was silent, and it was quite uncanny. He had seen many supernatural occurrences over the past week, but nothing as strange as this.

A thick-set man lay slumped in his seat in the front row. The smoke rose from his burned body, and seemed to twist and thicken above his head. As it drifted higher and higher toward the ceiling, it gradually took on a human shape, and reached a point where it started to sink again, until it had reached the floor. The ritual chant had mixed smoke with the rising soul, so that the soul couldn't leave the earth's gravity, so that it was denied its place in heaven.

At the back of the smoky auditorium, more and more Salamanders fell soft as quilts from the air, and gathered together in silence, mute witnesses to their own burned bodies.

Otto turned back to his chorus in triumph, his yellow eyes wide.

'It has begun!' he cried. 'It has begun! Now for the greatest transformation of all!'

The chorus parted to allow him into the centre of their circle. Otto stood there for a moment, admiring them. 'You, my immortals! My master race! Parents of the gods!'

Then he walked around the circle, touching each of them on the arm by turn. 'You have an army now, an army of Salamanders ... and those who do well for you can be Transformed like you at the next solstice. You need fear no resistance ... you cannot be killed, you cannot die. You are the greatest of all living creatures.'

He continued walking around and around. 'All of you have mortal partners with whom you can breed one child

... those children will be the foundation of our future, the demi-gods.'

He stopped when he reached Celia and Mike Kerwin, and laid his hand on their shoulders. 'You, unfortunately, have a partner who let suspicion overcome love ... Mike, so did you. But for you, I have two special partners. Partners with whom it is more than an honour to breed.'

He looked around once more, and took a long, dry breath. 'Now ...' he said, 'the talismen, please.'

The chorus held up their salamander charms, fourteen of them in all. Otto took Celia's and placed it on his tongue, and Celia stepped back out of the circle. The other thirteen held theirs up, and began to chant.

'What's happening now?' asked Kathleen. She had her handkerchief pressed to her mouth to stop herself from choking. 'What's he *doing*?'

As the chanting grew louder and more strident, Otto appeared, oddly, to grow taller. Lloyd wiped the smoke from his eyes and looked again. But it was true. Otto was growing taller and taller, until he was nearly eight feet tall, thin and attenuated and insect-like. He was grinning down at the stage, his yellow eyes bright, triumphant, fierce.

Suddenly, the top of his scalp parted, and his skin peeled away from his skull like a rubber glove. Underneath Lloyd saw black glistening bone, and yellow slanting eyes that were as dead and as calculating as any gargoyle's.

Now the skin split down Otto's back, and a forest of shining black spines rose up. 'I have done what I was summoned to do,' he said, in a croaking rasp that was scarcely human. 'I have recreated the master race. Now I can return.'

Kathleen gripped Lloyd's arm. 'Lloyd ... he's not even a ... *Lloyd!* He's some sort of a ...! Oh my God! *What is it, Lloyd? What is it?*'

Lloyd stepped back. 'Whatever it is, we have to play that hymn ... Once this is over, all of those people are going to go their different ways, and then we'll *never* stop them!'

They backed away from the stage, and around the back of the scenery again. On the far side of the stage was a short flight of steps and a door marked *Grams: Silence*. A small lighted window overlooked the stage itself.

'That's it,' said Lloyd. 'Follow me, but for God's sake keep a look out behind you.'

They climbed the steps as quietly as they could. The treads creaked, but the chanting of the chorus was so loud now that nobody could have heard them. In the centre of the circle, the reptilian monstrosity into which Otto was slowly being transformed was swaying and clicking and uttering harsh breathing noises. Lloyd glanced at it quickly and then decided not to look at it again. Black claws were tearing their way out of the skin of Otto's fingers.

He cautiously turned the knob of the sound room, and opened the door. Inside he could smell heated electrical equipment. He took the cassette out of his pocket, and stepped inside, nodding to Kathleen to follow him.

'All I have to do is find the tape-player,' he said, inspecting the rows of switches and lights on the console. 'Why the hell don't they have a Walkman, like everybody else?'

He found the tape-player, and was trying to slot in the tape when the door burst open again. In blundered Franklin, holding hands with Tony Express. Right behind them came Helmwige, looking darkly angry, with Tom. She was dressed in a skintight black leather leotard, cut impossibly high at the thigh, and black thigh-length boots. She was tugging Tom after her on a steel neck-collar. His neck was raw and his eyes were blotchy from crying.

'Tom!' said Kathleen. 'You bitch, let him go!'

'Let him go? I'm going to flay him alive and eat him for my breakfast if you don't shut up! You! Denman! Take out that tape and give it to me!'

Lloyd looked around at Franklin and Tony Express

340

Franklin said, 'We tried, Lloyd. We tried real hard. But she said she was going to kill him if we didn't give her the tape.'

'Tony?' asked Lloyd carefully, meaning 'what about your sundance doll?'

'You can't use a revenge totem against somebody who's technically dead already,' Tony Express explained carefully, as if he were demonstrating a vacuum-cleaner. He swung the sundance doll from side to side, and nothing happened.

Helmwige said, 'The tape, Denman, or else I burn the boy to a cinder, right in front of your eyes, like I burned his aunt.'

'Lloyd ...' said Kathleen, anxiously.

'Guess I don't have any choice,' said Lloyd. He glanced out of the window of the grams room, and he could see something black and gleaming swaying in the centre of the stage. Otto, sloughing his human appearance, and returning to what he really was. The chant of the chorus was muffled in here, but Lloyd could hear that it was reaching a high pitch of hysteria.

He held out the cassette to Helmwige, just two or three inches out of her reach. 'What *is* that thing?' he asked her. '*That* ...' nodding toward Otto.

Helmwige smiled. 'Otto? He used to be a student in Salzburg, before the war. But you see, he discovered a way to make himself not just a scholar but a genius. He made a trade with something dark, I don't know what. He allowed that thing to live inside his body until he had made his mark in history. Now, he has made his mark, and the thing is leaving, back to where it came from.'

Lloyd shuddered. Then, without warning, he swung his right arm and punched Helmwige straight in the face. Helmwige staggered back, lost her balance, and hit her side against the hi-fi console. But immediately she was back again, and she slapped Lloyd open-handed across the head so hard that he was thrown against the opposite wall.

'Fool!' she spat at him. He tried to get up, but she

kicked him in the ribs, and then in the stomach.

At that moment, however, Franklin grabbed hold of her, and gripped her in a bear-hug. At the same time, he yanked Tom's chain out of her hand, and threw it aside.

'Lloyd!' he yelled. 'Put on the Hymn! Kathleen! Tom! Tony! *Go!*'

'You cretin!' spat Helmwige. 'You know what I can do to you!'

'Lloyd!' Franklin bellowed. 'The tape!'

Dazed, coughing, bleeding, Lloyd climbed to his feet. He picked up the cassette and jabbed it into the tape-player.

Kathleen hesitated at the door, but Franklin shouted, 'Go! Go! Go!'

'Mengele's *Dümmling!*' Helmwige screeched. But Franklin kept her tight in his bear-hug, her arms by her sides, her face scarlet with fury and exertion.

Quickly, she began to increase her body heat. Franklin gasped, but he took a huge breath and continued to hold her. Lloyd pressed the *Start* button on the tape-player, and after a second or two, he heard the crackling rush of the lead-in.

Helmwige was now burning hotter and hotter. Her leather costume began to smoulder and stretch, but she kept on increasing her temperature. Sweat streamed down Franklin's face, and he gritted his teeth. But still he clung on to Helmwige, even when smoke began to rise from his scorched shirt, and the skin on his chest and his thighs began to blister.

'*Aaaaahhhh!!!*' screamed Franklin, as Helmwige's body began to burn into his nerve-endings.

'You fool! You pitiful fool!' Helmwige hissed at him. 'You're nothing! You're nobody! You never were!'

The first notes of Wagner's Hymn of Atonement suddenly broke out of the theatre's public-address system. Down on the stage, the spindly black creature swayed and turned, and threw back its head. The chanting chorus obviously didn't hear the Hymn at first, but then one or two of them began to look around, and frown.

342

'You're nothing!' Helmwige raged. 'You're a nameless nothing!'

'Oh, God!' Franklin cried out. 'Oh God, help me! I'm Franklin! I'm Franklin Free! I'm Franklin Free!'

Steady and calm and strong, the piano-playing of the dead Sylvia Cuddy filled the auditorium of the Civic Theater. For one heart-stopping moment, Lloyd thought that the Hymn wasn't going to work, and that they were all going to die. But Helmwige suddenly incandesced, as bright as magnesium flaring, and both she and Franklin screamed at each other in mutual agony.

There was an ear-shattering explosion inside the grams room, and Helmwige collapsed into grey bones and silvery ash. Franklin dropped to the floor, trembling violently at first, then still.

Lloyd wrenched open the grams room door and stood on the top step. One by one, the chorus were incandescing, blazing bright as flares, and leaving nothing on the stage but drifts of ash. Lloyd glimpsed Celia for a moment, her hands pressed against her ears, but then he lost sight of her behind Mike Kerwin, who flared up as brightly as a fallen comet.

In the centre of the stage, the black glistening creature had dropped to the boards, and lay quivering malevolently. Its yellow eyes glared at Lloyd with such cold hatred that he had to turn away.

'*You have assured my return,*' the creature croaked at him. '*Until I can capture the soul of a mortal who can change the course of human history, I shall always return.*'

Lloyd turned around and faced it and there were tears running down his cheeks. There was nothing he could say to evil like this.

With a hideous clattering sound, the creature slid between the cracks of two single floorboards, spines and claws and tail, and vanished from sight. Lloyd went to the side of the stage and retched, but all he could bring up was warm saliva.

He looked toward the auditorium. The burned bodies

of a thousand of Southern California's most successful suburbanites sat charred beyond recognition. Of the Salamanders, there was no sign at all. They were always volatile, that's what Otto had said, when Otto was Otto, and not some black thing out of hell. He walked up the aisle and saw the deep scorch marks on the carpet where each of them had stood.

He had almost reached the exit when the first firefighter came hacking and splintering his way through the locked doors with his axe. The firefighter took one look at the autidorium, one look at Lloyd, and said, 'Jesus.'

In a suite at the El Cajon Hotel, downtown, a fiftyish man in a tan-coloured shirt sat in front of his television set, round-shouldered, silent. Across the room sat a dark-haired woman, watching him anxiously.

'So he failed,' said the man, at last.

'We don't yet know why, or how,' the woman replied.

The man stood up and went to the window. He drew back the grimy net curtains and stared down into the street. 'It doesn't matter why. It doesn't matter how. They always fail. They always betray me. "You can father a child," he said. "I have just the woman for you. And just the man for Eva."'

'What are you going to do now?' the woman asked him.

'Do?' he said. 'I shall start again, *natürlich*. I have all the time in the world.'

Lloyd was playing cards with John Dull Knife in Zuni Tone's trailer when the telephone rang.

'Heads you answer it, tails we let it ring,' he suggested.

Without even looking at it, John Dull Knife flicked a quarter with his thumbnail. He slapped it on to the back of his withered, liver-spotted hand, and it was tails.

'I should have learned not to gamble with you,' Lloyd complained, and struggled up off the couchette to pick up the phone.

'You shouldn't gamble with anybody,' replied John Dull Knife. 'You gamble like a woman.'

'Screw you, too,' Lloyd told him, just as a girl's voice said, 'Hello?'

'Oh, hi, yes, I'm, sorry.'

'Is that Mr Denman? I rang your fish restaurant but they told me you sold up and moved away.'

'Well, that's right. I'm out in the desert at the moment, taking a sabbatical. It's what's called getting your head together. How can I help you?'

'You probably don't remember me, but my name's Lawreign. Law like in *LA Law*? I work at the souvenir counter in the *Star of India* ...'

'Hey, I remember you. You're the pretty one.'

'Thanks! But actually I called you because you asked me to watch out for a woman in a white raincoat and a yellow headscarf and dark glasses.'

'Well, that's right, sure, but ...'

'She came in, day before yesterday.'

A soft feeling of dread crept down Lloyd's back, like a cold-furred cat. 'Say again.'

'She came in, day before yesterday and bought a piece of scrimshaw. Quite an expensive piece, too. She said she was going to send it to somebody as a gift, so we wrapped it and everything.'

'How did she pay? With a credit card? Cheque? Did she give her name?'

'No, she paid in cash. But it was a beautiful piece. It was engraved with dolphins and mermaids, and the words said I'll Love You For All Eternity.'

'Those exact words?'

'That's right.'

'Lawreign, I owe you one,' said Lloyd, and before she could say any more, he hung up. He stood for a long time with his hand thoughtfully covering his mouth, and then he said to John Dull Knife, 'Did you check the mailbox lately?'

John Dull Knife looked up at him with rheumy eyes. 'Sorry, keep forgetting. Ever since Tony went to live with that Kathleen woman of yours ... well, he always used to do it.'

'Won't be a minute,' said Lloyd. He left the trailer, climbed down the steps, and walked across the trailer park. Although it was well past seven o'clock, the evening was still dry and hot, and there was a smell of mesquite in the air.

He walked slowly at first, but as he neared the mailbox he began to hurry. He hadn't even opened the wire fence before he could see that the flag was down.

NIGHT PLAGUE

Top U.S. Fiddler Flies In

Master U.S. violinist Stanley Eisner, 44, arrived in London today to join the Kensington Chamber Orchestra for eleven months. Eisner, the star of the San Francisco Baroque Ensemble, will give master classes to especially talented young musicians, and also play first violin in a series of new recordings of Bach suites and inventions. His place in San Francisco is being taken by John Bright, the Kensington orchestra's 41-year-old first violin.

—*Evening Standard*, November 25, 1989

I was that man—in a dream
And each world's night in vain
I patient wait on sleep to unveil
Those vivid hills again.

—Walter de la Mare

ONE
Knitted Hood

HE HAD NEVER FELT RATTLED IN LONDON BEFORE. IN NEW York, yes; and once in Haiti, in Port-au-Prince, When his car had been stopped and searched by the *Tontons Macoute* Ray-Bans and machine guns. Never in good old down-at-heel London.

But when he came down the steps of his apartment building at eight o'clock that frostbit morning, whistling the rondo from Mozart's *Posthorn Serenade*, the man in the gray knitted hood was already waiting for him on the opposite corner, just as he had been waiting on the opposite corner yesterday morning, and the morning before that, and the morning before that.

And Stanley, who had always considered London to be chummy and noisy and as safe as a city can be (as safe as Stockholm, anyway, or Bonn), stopped short, chin lifted, abruptly cautious, as if somebody had fingertip-slapped him, not too hard, but hard enough to irritate him, to shake his confidence. *Three straight mornings, and here he is again.* Stanley tasted salt and pewter in his mouth and that was the taste of authentic fear.

A radio played "*. . . great music for a great city . . .*" from somewhere not too far away.

Stanley in slo-mo closed the black-painted garden gate behind him, *squeak, clang.* Alert, frowning, breathing too deeply, he glanced around the streets of flat-fronted early Victorian terraces, yellow-ocher brick and freshly painted stucco. There was nobody else around, only the man in the gray knitted hood, and him, and a brindled cat with a live candy-pink fledgling in its mouth slinking low-bellied and guilty over the camber of the street. Less than fifty yards away the King's Road grumbled and thundered with the morning rush hour, but Langton Street was an abandoned world of its own.

"Traffic update . . . with the Flying Eye . . ."

All along the curb, bumper-to-bumper, the parked cars stood empty, unwashed Citroëns with dog-smeared windows and brand-new Rovers with dented fenders and overflowing ashtrays. In Fulham it was *infra dig* to treat your car with any reverence. The sky was low and cold and corroded-looking, as if it were soon going to snow.

Stanley stood still with his violin case in his hand and stared at the man in the knitted hood, willing him to turn around, but the man in the knitted hood didn't move or give any indication at all that he was aware that Stanley was staring at him. Underneath the knitted hood, the man wore a long gray gaberdine raincoat and oddly box-shaped shoes, like surgical boots or medieval clogs. He stood awkwardly, too, tilted to one side, as if he had been twisted by a spine injury.

Every day since his first appearance on Tuesday morning, the man in the knitted hood waited on the opposite corner of Langton Street until Stanley had started walking toward the King's Road; then he had promptly started off after him. He had remained twenty or thirty yards away, and whenever Stanley had slowed or stopped, he had slowed or stopped, too—not immediately, and not so obviously that Stanley could have been quite certain that he was being purposely or even *purposefully* followed.

While Stanley had waited for his bus, the man in the knitted hood had stayed well away from the bus stop, mooching this way and that, restless as a character in a Popeye cartoon, always keeping his head bowed and his face averted. When the bus had arrived, he had disappeared into the jostle of people. But somehow he had always managed to reappear on top of the bus, sitting six or seven rows behind Stanley, his face turned toward the window. By the time Stanley had reached his stop, however, and stood up, the man in the knitted hood had already vanished.

Now Knitted Hood was back for the fourth morning in succession, standing on the opposite corner by the postbox, slightly hunched, hands in pockets, not moving. The wind was as sharp as a lino-cutting knife. Stanley licked his lips in apprehension, then wiped them with his handkerchief so that they wouldn't get chapped. He wasn't sure what to do. The man obviously didn't intend to attack him, he always stayed so far away. He couldn't be panhandling, either, not unless he had the most abstruse technique of any beggar ever . . . frightening his intended benefactors just by *being* there, just by silently lurking, until they approached him with money to leave them alone.

Irrationally (and this was *seriously* irrational), Stanley had even entertained the remote possibility that Knitted Hood could have been a private investigator, acting for Eve, his wife. But Eve was back with her mother and father in Napa, California, in their neat expensive house with the mushroom-colored shag-pile carpets, and Stanley couldn't really imagine Eve doing anything so quirky as hiring a private investigator from six thousand miles away—nor anything so expensive, either. For sure, Eve and he had wrangled for months over alimony for Leon, and Eve had accused him of arranging his exchange job in England to evade his paternal responsibilities and to conceal his true income (which was slightly true); but he couldn't imagine what good it would do her to send a clubfooted cripple in a gray knitted hood to follow him on to the bus every morning.

"Today's weather . . . cold and raw, with eight octaves of cloud and a strong north-east wind . . . temperatures in town down to—"

A more sensible proposition was that Knitted Hood was probably nothing more alarming than a down-and-out—one of those filthy but harmless fruit-loops who shuffle through London in their thousands. One of those aggrieved derelicts who live in abandoned cardboard boxes; or one of those gentlemanly eccentrics who play spoons in the street, or sit under bird-splattered statues of colonial heroes drinking Tennent's extra-strong lager and railing at the city as it thunderously ignores them on every side. It was even possible that Knitted Hood wasn't following Stanley at all, but just happened to catch the same bus—although if *that* were the case, why did he wait every morning until Stanley had started walking toward the King's Road before he himself set off, at almost exactly the same distance?

Stanley waited for two or three minutes, trying to make up his mind if he ought to cross the street and ask Knitted Hood what he wanted. He wasn't usually afraid to confront strangers. In New York, he had lived in the Village for eight and a half years, and he had been mugged twice; the second time unsuccessfully, because he had faced right up to the geeks and fought back. Three blacks with Mike Tyson necks, and eyes like rivets. They had hit him in the face with an adjustable wrench and broken his cheekbone, and then they had kicked him in the mouth. He had scarcely felt it. He had been high on vodkatinis and self-righteousness at the time, not to mention a recent viewing of Woody Allen's *September* and *Death Wish III*, but this morning he didn't feel so high.

There was something else, too. Something in Knitted Hood's appearance which invoked a feeling of disquiet that he had never experienced before. It was a quality which he could only think of as *medieval*. It reminded him of monks and lazars and some of those crippled creatures with gray-bandaged stumps in Breughel paintings.

Something *diseased*.

He hesitated for nearly half a minute; then tugged back his woollen glove and checked his watch: 8:17. His bus would be coming any minute, although the traffic looked thick this morning. It was the second day of the January sales.

"Hey!" he called across the street.

Knitted Hood remained where he was and gave no indication that he might have heard.

"Hey!" shouted Stanley, louder but higher.

Still Knitted Hood didn't respond. Stanley was tempted to forget all about him and go; but it had taken quite a surge of adrenaline just to shout, and it seemed incredibly wimpish and defeatist just to walk off and leave Knitted Hood where he was—especially if Knitted Hood started following him again.

He stepped off the curb and started to cross the road. A single van passed him, a bright yellow British Telecom van, and for a moment he had to wait. But then the van was gone and there was nobody but him and Knitted Hood.

"I say, hey, excuse me!" he called, trying to sound English.

Knitted Hood remained motionless and silent.

"Excuse me!" he repeated, taking two or three steps nearer. "Excuse me, sir, but I have the distinct impression that you've been following me!"

He waited. Knitted Hood gave no indication that he might have heard. The wind curled up the tails of his gray gaberdine coat, exposing soiled striped trousers tied at the cuff with knotted parcel twine. *No private eye he*, thought Stanley. *Even the sleaziest shamus doesn't tie his pants up with string.*

Stanley circled around Knitted Hood, trying to see his face. But as he did so, Knitted Hood somehow managed to edge himself around so that he was still facing diagonally away from him.

For a whole minute there was silent impasse between them— a shortish American musician with thinning brown hair and a velvet-collared Harrod's overcoat; a tall lumpish English scarecrow in a gray knitted hood. Neither of them moved, neither of them spoke. Eventually, Stanley coughed into his hand and looked away, like a teacher trying to be patient, and then looked back again.

"Listen, friend, unless I get some kind of answer out of you, I'm going to miss my bus, okay? And if I miss my bus I'm going to get measurably mad. Okay?"

Still no response. Above their heads, a jet scratched invisibly through the clouds on its descent toward Heathrow, and even if Knitted Hood had said anything, Stanley wouldn't have been able to hear what it was. The street remained peculiarly empty. They could have been thousands of miles from anywhere, instead of fifty yards away from one of the busiest roads in London.

"All right," said Stanley, "if that's the way you want it, forget it. But let me tell you this. If you're standing here tomorrow morning, I'm going to call the police. Do you hear me? I see you here one more time, that's it.''

Knitted Hood turned his back. Stanley had been about to walk away, but when Knitted Hood did that, he felt madder than he had for a long time, and he stopped and turned back. He felt madder than he had with Eve, in a way. At least he had understood what Eve was up to. Eve had been chiseling money and obstructing his visitation rights. Plain and simple, Eve had been chiseling money and obstructing his visitation rights. Plain and simple, Eve had wanted revenge. But what did Knitted Hood want? If it was money, he had a goddamned weird way of asking for it. But what else could he possibly want, except for money?

Conversation? Company? Who could tell? Maybe Knitted Hood had heard that Stanley was a well-known international violinist. Maybe he was some kind of brilliant but horribly disfigured musician who desperately wanted private lessons, but didn't dare go to the Kensington Chamber Orchestra to ask for them. You know, like *The Phantom of the Opera*, something like that.

"Listen, friend," said Stanley, taking three or four paces closer. "If there's something you want, why don't you tell me what it is? I may not be able to help you, but I can listen. You know what they say. If you can share a problem, it's only half a problem."

He tried to skip between Knitted Hood and the postbox, so that he could see Knitted Hood's face. But the figure managed to swivel around at the last possible instant, so that all he glimpsed was the glossy-white tip of a nose.

"Listen!" Stanley repeated. "This is totally crazy! You've been following me practically every morning for the past week, now you won't even show me your face! For Christ's sake, if you want something, come down off the fucking ceiling and tell me what it is. If you don't, then stop showing up here, do you mind? Stop following me! Goddammit, there's a law against following people!" He wasn't at all sure that there *was* a law against it, but it sounded authoritative.

Knitted Hood remained silent, with his back turned. Stanley checked his watch. He had a choice now—either to manhandle

Knitted Hood, to turn him around by force, or to forget the whole thing and go catch his bus.

He didn't relish touching that greasy gaberdine raincoat, and if he was honest, he didn't much relish seeing what Knitted Hood really looked like. But there was some kind of principle involved here. Stanley was willing to admit that it could be the kind of principle that only an American would be concerned about. Maybe English people followed other English people for no reason at all and nobody got upset about it. In less than three months, he had already begun to perceive that English people had a radically different concept about civil liberties. They were secretive and deflective; and they seemed to think that the sharing of information was almost as unhygienic as sharing the same toothbrush.

Stanley suddenly thought: *This is absurd. Walk away from it. This guy isn't going to tell me anything. He probably has nothing to tell. He's just a public nuisance, like traffic wardens or flag-day collectors or black plastic bags of trash in the street.*

He turned away. But, as he did so, Knitted Hood uttered an extraordinary sound, halfway between a whistle and a cough.

A slide whistle, *hooo-eee, oop* with a barking end to it.

Stanley said, "Oh, you've decided to explain yourself, have you?" and turned back.

His scalp prickled with shock. He found himself confronted by a face as white and as glossy as celluloid, a face that could have been a mask, neither man nor woman, but frighteningly beautiful. A saint's face; an angel's face.

Because it was so seraphic, it was ten times more terrifying than it would have been if it had been ugly. How could such a misshapen creature have been blessed with such ravishing looks?

Stanley stepped back, and he was deeply scared. The face was empty-eyed—black-eyed, anyway. Night–black-eyed. Expressionless, sweet, glistening, a Mardi Gras martyr.

"What do you want?" Stanley demanded, his throat choked up with a hair-ball of fear.

Knitted Hood said nothing, but took one awkward step towards him. *Chip-shuffle.*

Stanley heard soft, harsh breathing. Breath against celluloid.

"What do you want?" he repeated. He felt pee in his trousers. He was ready to run.

Knitted Hood's perfect white forehead began to crinkle. His black eyes became distorted and small, and spread themselves further and further apart. The chin warped and dropped.

Stanley had the terrible feeling that he was witnessing somebody die; watching somebody's whole physical integrity collapse, right in front of his eyes. How could that happen? How could somebody simply fall apart, one piece from another?

There was a split second in which he could have run; could have escaped. But then—without warning—Knitted Hood snatched at his sleeve, swung him around, and half jumped, half collapsed on top of him.

"*Jesus!*" Stanley cried out. Knitted Hood's weight was enormous, like a five-hundred-pound sack of beets, and instantly Stanley's knees gave way. He fell into the gutter, twisting off one of his shoes, his brown tweed trousers torn. "*Get off me! Jesus Christ, get off me!*"

But Knitted Hood seized the back of his neck with a hand like a claw and forced his face right down to the pavement. Stanley felt one of his front teeth break. His lower lip dragged against concrete, his forehead scraped. His wrists were pulled right up behind him in a full nelson, so fiercely and quickly that he heard cartilage crack. A pain as fierce as white-hot iron was poured into the crucibles of his shoulder sockets and brimmed over into his arm muscles. He tried to shout out but his lungs were empty and he couldn't snatch enough breath. *Dear God, don't let him dislocate my arms.*

Knitted Hood was not only oppressively heavy. His body was lumpy and awkward and wrapped up in all kinds of rags and scarves and metal-buckled belts and pieces of blanket. He stank of grease and sweat and some nostril-burning synthetic-violet odor, like air freshener for toilet bowls. Facedown on the pavement, Stanley gasped, "Get off, will you? For God's sake, you're breaking my arms, get off!"

Without a word, Knitted Hood grasped Stanley's hair and banged his head against the concrete, almost knocking him out. Stanley tasted blood and sicked-up coffee and floods of saliva. He could hardly believe what was happening to him. All he knew was that he wanted it to stop.

He heard traffic, radio music, people talking. Surely some-body could see what was happening to him.

But then he felt a relentless claw-nailed hand pulling at his coat and then his trousers. There was some fierce and prurient fumbling between his legs. The buckle was torn from his Gucci belt; then he felt corduroy tearing, cotton shorts tearing.

"God! Get off me! What are you doing?" he shrieked out, his voice as high as a woman's.

They crouched struggling on the pavement under Knitted Hood's raincoat, one on top of the other, like some grotesque gray camel. Stanley tried to crawl forward, pushing against the curb with his knees. He couldn't cry out any more. He was too frightened even to speak. He was too desperate to get away.

But then Knitted Hood's filthy clawed hand closed around his bare genitals; not crushing them, but squeezing them just tightly enough for Stanley to gasp, and to stay where he was, shivering, his vision intermittently blocked out by the wind-blown tails of Knitted Hood's raincoat.

Knitted Hood's thumbnail found the opening of Stanley's penis and started gently and almost lovingly to scratch at it. Stanley's stomach tightened, his eyes filled with tears. *Oh, dear God, this can't be happening.* His testicles shrank; his whole soul shrank. *Riboyne Shel Olam, protect me.*

"Oh, God!" he managed to choke out. "I'm rich, look, I'll give you money!"

But all he heard from the creature pressing down on top of him was course, irregular breathing. And at the same time, that terrible scratching continued, until Stanley was sure that he must be bleeding.

"Can you speak?" he gasped. "Listen—can you understand what I'm saying?" He scarcely recognized his own voice.

Knitted Hood grunted and whooped in two different tones, almost like two people speaking at once. But he pressed his weight even harder on Stanley's back, and probed his fingernail even deeper into Stanley's penis; and then he mounted Stanley with all the unthinking forcefulness of one animal mounting another; the same way a bull heaves itself up on a cow. Stanley felt his buttocks clawed apart, skin ripped. Then something rubbery and greasy and uncompromisingly hard pushed up against him. Something as big as a baseball bat, pungent and obscenely hot, forcing itself into his anus.

It hurt him so much that he wept, bitterly wept, in a way that he hadn't wept since he was a child. He bit his lip with his broken tooth, and blood ran down the side of his mouth. But the pain wouldn't stop; and he couldn't stop it. It drove into his bottom and he felt that his back was cracking apart. It pushed and it pushed until he was screaming out loud (or silently, he couldn't tell). He felt the cold, heavy, regular swing of Knitted Hood's scrotum against his thigh. He heard breathing that sounded like leather bellows. Then he felt his bowels flooded with hotness and wetness, deep up inside him; and Knitted Hood immediately slithering out of him; and he vomited coffee and half-chewed crackers all over his hands.

His cheek was resting against a surface that was hard and flat and deadeningly cold. He wondered if he had been sleeping. He didn't like falling asleep during the day. There was always that feeling when you woke up that the world had irrevocably changed while you weren't looking; that muffle-footed scene-shifters had been rearranging your life.

He saw black patent high-heeled shoes, with bows on the front, very close to his eyes. Then he heard a girl coughing and a worried voice say, " 'Ere, you ain't dead?"

He tried to shake his head. "No," he whispered. "I'm not dead."

"Well, you stay there. I'll call a namblunce."

"I just want to get up."

"What?"

"I just want to get up, get on to my feet."

There was a silence. Then the girl's voice said, "I wouldn't do that if I were you, mate. You wait there. I'll call a namblunce."

He felt that he was being jostled. He saw lighted windows going by. Faces that danced in front of his eyes like clouds of midges. He was surrounded by whiteness and coolness and the sliding whisper of sheets; and a strong smell of antiseptic. A warm voice with a foreign accent reverberated deep inside his brain, reassuring him that he was being taken care of, that he was in hospital, and that everything was going to be fine.

You're going to be fine, Mr. Eisner! Can you hear me? You're going to be fine! Fine. Fiyyynnee. Yiiiiine.

He felt the vinegary prick of a needle. He wanted to say, *I hate needles. I never have needles.* But then his consciousness fled backwards into empty darkness, and there was nobody to hear him.

He was back out on the street again. The clouds moved past the rooftops at a strange hurried speed. A cat slunk past him, carrying something in its mouth. He knew that it was something terrible but he didn't want to look.

He heard a whistle, high and hollow, with a whoop at the end of it. He turned in alarm, and on the other side of the street he saw Knitted Hood, waiting for him, taunting him.

Hooo-eeeee, oop.

Knitted Hood slowly began to turn his head. Stanley stared wide-eyed, expecting to see that white exquisite face. But then Knitted Hood's head turned around and around, rotating slowly at first, then faster, while his shoulders remained hunched in the same position. Stanley realized that the gray hood covered his head completely, without any hole for his face. It was more like a hangman's hood than a balaclava.

Heart beating, mouth dry, Stanley started to cross the street. Not walking, but sliding. He was less than halfway across, however, when he knew for a certain fact that he didn't have the nerve to continue. Knitted Hood would turn around and jump on top of him.

Stanley tried to stop himself, to turn around, to dig his heels into the road surface. But the gray tarmac rumpled up like a thick soft carpet, and he continued to slide towards Knitted Hood, quicker and quicker, and he couldn't scream; couldn't even speak.

Knitted Hood whirled around, faceless. As he whirled, he grew impossibly taller, up and up and up, until he blotted out the sky. He paused and swayed, his coattails softly thundering in the morning wind. *No*, thought Stanley. *No.* But then Knitted Hood collapsed on top of him like the sky falling in.

Stanley screamed. But he knew that nobody could hear him. The screaming was only inside his head.

He convulsed, rigid, his teeth clenched, still unable to scream, still unable to do anything but tighten his muscles until he felt as if they were going to burst out of his skin. Then he opened his eyes. He saw shifting, dancing whiteness, blurry figures.

"Pulse rate's up," said a young woman's voice.

"Otherwise stable?" asked a young man's voice, further away.

There was some shuffling, and somebody coughed. Then the young man's voice said, "Has Gordon Rutherford been in?"

"Dr. Patel told him to wait till later."

"What about the filth?"

"Oh, *they're* here. Detective Sergeant Brian Morris, waiting in reception."

"You've told him to wait?"

"Of course. But he didn't seem to mind much. He's brought a book."

Stanley slowly opened his eyes. His body felt as if it had been bruised all over, muscle and bone. Even the palms of his hands felt sensitive and sore. But it was the pain in his back that he couldn't bear. A bitter, cracking pain right in the lumbar region that made him feel like bursting into tears.

A broad young gingery-bearded face loomed in front of him, so close that it looked more like a freckled landscape than a face. Stanley breathed in the smell of cigarettes, masked with Trebor extra-strong mints. "Ah! We're awake, then!" The young doctor grinned at him.

Stanley nodded.

"Do you know where you are?" the young doctor demanded.

Stanley shook his head.

"St. Stephen's," the young doctor replied. "You've been— well, attacked, sort of."

"St. Stephen's where?" Stanley whispered.

The young doctor stared at him with eyes like blue glass marbles. Sea-blue sailors, they used to call marbles that looked like that.

"I've only been in London since November," Stanley explained, almost apologetically, as if it were his fault that he didn't know where St. Stephen's was.

"Fulham Road," the young doctor told him. "Just opposite the gas fire shop," as if that should make it any clearer.

Stanley cleared this throat. "What time is it?" he asked.

"Quarter to two. You've been sedated for most of the morning."

"I have a pain in my back."

"Only to be expected, I'm afraid, after what you've been through."

Stanley swallowed. He was silent for a long time. The young doctor watched him and smiled; but there was no genuine humor in his smile; and no genuine sympathy, either.

"Is there any . . . damage?" Stanley asked him.

"You mean physical trauma?"

"Sure. Physical trauma."

The young doctor looked at him steadily. "Grazing, bruising. Broken incisor. External lacerations of the buttocks. Some internal laceration of the lower rectum. Dr. Patel gave you seven internal stitches. Nothing too serious, though. Some bruising, of course. But give it a little time."

"How long will I have to stay here?"

"Depends. You're pretty fit, on the whole. A week, ten days. Not much longer."

"I have two major recording sessions scheduled for Monday and Tuesday."

"Not a hope, I'm afraid. You won't be able to walk for at least three days; and you won't find sitting down very comfortable, either."

Without warning, Stanley found that his eyes filled up with tears. He wiped them away with the edge of his sheet, and then the young doctor offered him some tissues.

"I'm sorry," he said. "I don't know what the hell came over me."

There was a long silence. The young doctor continued to stare at him. "We'll be carrying out some tests," he said at last.

"What kind of tests?" Stanley asked him.

"Oh, the usual. Blood pressure, heart rate, liver function. Sexually-communicable diseases."

Stanley tightened his mouth with pain. "Sexually-communicable diseases?"

"Gonorrhea, that kind of thing."

"I don't have gonorrhea. I don't have any sexually-communicable diseases. For God's sake. I've been in London less than three months. I haven't done any sexual communicating."

"You did this morning," the young doctor told him, in a tone of almost threatening blandness. "Or, at least, somebody sexually communicated with you."

"Goddammit, he—" Stanley began; but then his body winced, and his brain winced, too. He felt the dark greasy flapping of Knitted Hood's raincoat, like the wing of some huge diseased bird. He heard the thick whistling of Knitted Hood's breath.

The young doctor stood up straight and sniffed. "You'll be tested for HIV, too."

"You means AIDS?"

"That's right, Mr. Eisner. AIDS. I'm sorry, but given the nature of what happened to you. Exchange of bodily fluids, and all that."

Stanley couldn't do anything but nod and tremble. When he had been hit in the face in New York, the pain had been very much worse. But this, in a different way, was almost unbearable. This was the most terrible thing that had ever happened to him. He felt as if his entire soul had been invaded; as if everything that made him a human being had been forfeited, his emotional buttons pulled off, the sword of his virility broken. His cottage in Los Angeles had been burgled two or three years ago, and the thieves had torn down the drapes and urinated on the bed. He had felt then that his privacy and his personal dignity had been threatened. But this was something else altogether. Right out in the street, for everybody to see, this had been the brutal denial that he had any freedom of choice, that his body was his own, and that he was anything more than a receptacle for another man's hideous urges.

"Listen," said the young doctor, suddenly more sympathetic, "just at the moment you probably feel as if it's the end of the world. You're still in shock. Also—well, it wasn't a very pleasant experience, was it, to say the least? A chap called

Gordon Rutherford is coming to see you. He's very understanding about this kind of thing.''

"Did they catch the guy who did it?'' asked Stanley.

"I don't think so. The police are here, too, but you don't have to talk to them yet. Does them good to keep them waiting. Reminds them where they stand in the hierarchy. A shade below bus conductors and about two points above estate agents.''

"What about the people I work for?'' said Stanley. "I should put in a call to the orchestra.''

"Don't worry,'' said the young woman's voice from the door. "The bursar telephoned your orchestra as soon as you were brought in. Somebody's coming to see you later on.''

Stanley raised the head a little and saw a blond-haired woman in red designer spectacles and a white doctor's coat, standing by the door. "Thanks,'' he told her.

"You should get some rest now,'' the blond woman told him. "Drink as much as you possibly can. I'm afraid you won't be able to touch solids for at least a week.''

Stanley lay back on his pillow. He felt bruised and exhausted. The gingery-bearded young doctor told him, "Don't worry, Mr. Eisner. People do get over these things. You just have to give yourself a little time.''

Later that afternoon, he propped himself up on his pillows and watched *Neighbours* and *The Young Doctors* and drank half a bottle of orange barley water. The day began to darken around four o'clock, and he looked across the air shaft at the lighted windows on the other side of the hospital. He was beginning to feel oddly detached and unreal, but the gingery-bearded young doctor had told him that it was only natural, after shock and concussion.

There was something else, though: a feeling inside him that he couldn't quite put his finger on. A kind of prickling in his blood, as if his arteries were filled with thistles. And no matter how much he drank, he always seemed to be thirsty.

At half past five, there was a knock at his door, and a tall, thin young man with brown wavy hair appeared. "Mr. Eisner?'' he asked in a breathy, excited voice.

"That's right.''

"I'm Gordon Rutherford. I'm sorry I've taken so long. I had to collect my cat."

He came into the room and dragged a blue plastic chair up to the side of the bed. He was very intense-looking, with a large bony nose constructed of complicated angles of bone and cartilage, and bright pink bow-shaped lips. He wore a large shapeless jacket of hairy green tweed, and he was so thin that he had punctured an extra hole in his leather belt, so that it would fit around his waist.

"Poor Roger," he said, opening his cheap W.H. Smith briefcase and taking out a clipboard. "He was so resentful he wouldn't even *speak* to me afterwards."

"I'm sorry," said Stanley. "Who's Roger?"

"My cat. I had him neutered this morning. Well, he was causing such a disturbance. All that yowling and screaming in the middle of the night. The neighbors used to throw stones at him. He couldn't leave the lady cats alone for a minute."

Stanley said, "Are you a cop? A social worker? What?"

"Didn't they tell you? I'm from the Rape Crisis Center," Gordon explained.

Stanley frowned. "You deal with men as well as women?"

Gordon looked surprised that Stanley had even found it necessary to ask.

"Oh, yes. It doesn't matter what sex you are. If you've been raped, you're going to suffer the same problems. Sometimes *worse* problem if you're a man. Your average heterosexual male is completely psychologically unprepared for the experience of being sexually penetrated. Physiologically, too, of course."

Stanley started to speak, then found that he couldn't. His throat was constricted with self-pity. "I didn't—" he began.

Gordon reached out and squeezed his hand. "The first thing you're going to have to come to terms with is that it wasn't your fault; not in any way at all."

"He was just standing there," Stanley gasped. "I asked him what the hell he was doing—and then he fell right down on top of me."

He couldn't stop himself; he started to tremble again, and tears ran down his cheeks as freely as they had the day that his mother died. "He was so goddamned *heavy*, so goddamned *strong*. I struggled as much as I could, but he hit my face on the sidewalk and damn near knocked me cold. Then he just did it, and there wasn't a thing I could do to stop him."

Gordon listened and then nodded. "Do you really believe that?" he asked.

"Do I really believe what?"

"Do you really believe that there wasn't a thing you could have done to stop him? Do you really believe that you did everything within your power to prevent him from raping you?"

Stanley wiped his eyes with a wad of screwed-up tissue. "I don't know. I keep thinking I should have kicked him, or reached in back of me and tried to gouge his eyes. I keep thinking how stupid I was to try to challenge him at all. I mean you should have seen this guy. He had some kind of woollen hood on, and he was all hunched up like Quasimodo. *No*body would have challenged him; nobody streetwise, anyway, like I keep trying to make out I am."

He took a shallow, shuddering breath. "I must have been crazy. Or else I was asking for it."

Gordon pursed his lips. "What you're feeling is very common among rape victims. It doesn't matter what sex they are; or even what the circumstances were. I've talked to women who were held down by four men and raped by a fifth, and they *still* believe in the back of their minds that it was partly their own fault."

Stanley said, "I could kill him, you know? I could physically kill him with my bare hands. I never felt that way about anybody, ever before."

"That's not unusual, either. You feel guilty about what happened to you; and your subconscious mind is suggesting to you that one way to get rid of your guilt is to punish the person who made you feel that way."

Gordon paused, and then he added, "Sometimes, Mr. Eisner, rape victims feel so guilty that they try to punish the only person they can lay their hands on, which is themselves. I think you're probably intelligent enough for me to be able to tell you that, and for you to understand the symptoms, if and when you start to feel them. In other words, Mr. Eisner, when the initial shock has worn off, you're going to start feeling depressed; and your estimation of yourself is going to take a steep nosedive.

"At that time, you're going to feel self-destructive."

"You mean I'm going to feel like killing myself?"

Gordon nodded. "It happened to me, too."

"But you survived?"

"I'm a survivor."

"Did they ever catch the guy who did it to you?"

"Guys plural, actually. I was hanging around Piccadilly, trying to make myself enough money to cover my rent. I was picked up by four Turkish gentlemen in a Mercedes. They took me back to some woman's flat in Shepherd's Bush and did things to me that you wouldn't even want to have *nightmares* about."

He patted Stanley's hand and smiled. "And, no, they never caught them. They never even tried. Diplomatic immunity, all that sort of thing. And who was I? Nothing but a spotty young rent boy, from Leeds. All I got from the police was, 'Piss off, you horrible little pooftah, before we break the other arm.' "

Stanley said, "They broke your arm?"

"They almost broke my soul, believe me. And I was gay to start with."

"I'm sorry."

"*You're* sorry? How do you think I felt? Actually, you know jolly well how I felt. Or you will, anyway, when you talk to the police. As far as most coppers are concerned, Mr. Eisner, male rape is one of those offenses which give rise to nothing but innuendo and ribald humor. They'll accuse you of being gay, too. I hope you're ready for that. They'll suggest that you egged this character on, whether he looked like Quasimodo or not. You're a musician, too, that doesn't help. Anything to do with the arts is limp-wristed, as far as your average British woodentop is concerned. *And* you're American; *and* you're Jewish."

"What I am doesn't alter the facts," Stanley insisted, trying to keep his reasoning straight, trying not to cry. "All I did was *talk* to the guy, for God's sake—ask him what he was doing there. Then he jumped on me. No warning, no come-on, nothing."

Gordon shrugged. "All the same, the police will certainly try to suggest otherwise. It makes life easier for them if you're guilty, too. It fits in with their pig-Freemason-racist view of the universe. Sod justice, my dear—*every*body's guilty, victims and perpetrators alike. In fact, as far as the police are concerned, the victims are usually more guilty than the perpetrators. Serves them right for getting in the way, do you know what I mean? Apart from that, if you're just as guilty as the guy who attacked you, the police won't feel that they're under so much of an obligation to find him."

"I always heard your British policemen were wonderful," said Stanley dryly.

"Oh, good gracious, that was in the days of Jayne Mansfield," Gordon replied. "But don't misunderstand me. I'm not a professional cynic. I'm a firm believer in flowers and balloons and lambs gamboling in the sunshine, not to mention the fortitude of the human spirit. I'm simply saying that you should gird your loins for the kind of questions that Detective Sergeant Brian Morris, God bless him, will be putting to you. Detective Sergeant Brian Morris is Anglican, white, thirty-three, and straight. He lives in Wandsworth with his wife, his Alsatian dog, his budgerigars, and two-point-four children. Detective Sergeant Brian Morris is also overworked, overpaid, nauseated by gays and druggies and football hooligans and people who park their cars on double yellow lines, and is very interested in getting an easy result."

Stanley swallowed. His mouth was feeling dry again. Without being asked, Gordon reached over and poured him another glass of orange barley water, which Stanley drank in two long drafts, without breathing.

"Let me tell you this," said Stanley. "If the police aren't interested in finding this character, then I will, and I'll kill him personally."

Gordon slowly and mechanically shook his head from side to side. "Believe me, Stanley—you don't mind if I call you Stanley?—taking the law into your own hands would be the very worst thing you could do. That would prove to the police beyond a shadow of a doubt that you and Quasimodo were nothing but a couple of quarreling ginger-beers; and you'd probably be banged up forever, amen."

"So what do you suggest I do?"

"I suggest you answer every question factually; and unemotionally; and as fully as you can. Try to imagine that what happened, happened to somebody else, not you, and you're simply a witness. Whatever Detective Sergeant Morris suggests to you, don't lose your temper. Don't theorize, don't speculate, stick to the facts."

Gordon hesitated, and then he added, "One more thing."

"What's that?"

"Whatever you do, don't allow yourself to burst into tears."

Dr. Patel came to visit Stanley before Detective Sergeant Morris was allowed in. He was slender and dark-eyed and sad-looking, like a disillusioned Indian ascetic, and his touch was infinitely gentle. Two young Chinese nurses manhandled Stanley on to his stomach, so that his face was pressed against the pillow, and waited with their arms folded and their eyes bright while Dr. Patel examined Stanley's stitches.

"You have been quite lucky," Dr. Patel remarked.

"If this is lucky, what's unlucky?" Stanley wanted to know.

Dr. Patel covered him up and signaled to the nurses to turn him back over.

"You were forcibly penetrated by an object that was nine or ten inches in length, with a diameter of two and a half inches," he replied in his soft, melancholy voice. "Unlucky would have been a perforated bowel, Mr. Eisner. Unlucky would have been dead."

Detective Sergeant Brian Morris was short and bull-shouldered, with a mustache that was clipped too small for his face and a complexion the color of Sainsbury's unsmoked bacon. His eyebrows were so fair they were almost invisible, and this gave him the appearance of being astonished at everything he came across, but not much.

He had a bent-back copy of *Little Gloria Happy at Last* in the pocket of his pale blue windcheater, which struck Stanley as incongruous enough to be threatening. Right now, however, Stanley found almost everything threatening. He had never realized how vulnerable he actually was; how easily hurt; how quickly his dignity could be stripped away from him.

The room was very poorly lit. Detective Sergeant Morris didn't help matters by sitting in the far corner, in a black shadow the shape of a teacher's mortarboard, next to a faded

color print of *The Wye at Symonds Yat*. He kept his head lowered over his notebook, so that all that Stanley could see of
him was the meticulously accurate parting in his hair. He was
the kind of man who used shoe trees, and resharpened his old
razor blades, and bashed at his hair before he left for work
with two hog's-bristle brushes.

"Dr. Patel was cooperative enough to retain a semen sample and to pass it on to us for pathological examination," he
remarked in a flat accent which sounded to Stanley like cockney; but which Gordon Rutherford could have told him was
South London, not a stone's frow from Streatham Bus Gar-
ridge.

Stanley didn't know what to say. The thought that his attacker had discharged semen into his body made the assault
seem even more disgusting. There had been no passion in it,
no reproductive purpose. Just brutal penetration and the ejaculation of fluid, for his attacker's own filthy and mindless satisfaction.

"Obviously, once your assailant is apprehended, the semen
sample can be used for the purpose of genetic identification,
and very useful, too," Detective Sergeant Morris continued.
"But what we urgently require from you, Mr. Eesner, is some
sort of physical description so that we can circulate our forces
on the ground."

"Eisner," Stanley corrected him. "It's not Eesner, it's Eisner."

Detective Sergeant Morris looked up with a carefully-
prepared expression of policemanly surprise. "Well, sir, you
say 'eether' and I say 'either.' You say 'neether' and I say
'neither.' "

"He wore a gray knitted hood," said Stanley.

"Ah," said Detective Sergeant Morris.

Stanley watched him for a while. Then, "Aren't you going
to write that down?"

"Not much point, is there, Mr. Eesner? Gray knitted hood,
probably would've taken it off by now. Disposed of it."

"Well, sure, but somebody may know who he is. I mean, if
he was in the *habit* of wearing a gray knitted hood—"

Detective Sergeant Morris reached into the pocket of his
windbreaker, where three pens and two pencils were neatly

fastened by nerd clips, and produced a ballpen. On the top line of his notebook, he wrote (softly mouthing the words as he did so) *"gray . . . knitted . . . hood."*

"He was tall," said Stanley. "Six one, six two. And heavy. I never felt anyone so heavy."

"Heavy," wrote Detective Sergeant Morris. Then he looked up. "See his face, sir?"

"Yes, I saw his face. It didn't fit his general appearance at all. It was very white, almost like a mask. Have you ever seen a Mardi Gras mask, or a saint's day mask?"

"No, Mr. Eesner, can't say that I have."

"Well, I can probably find a picture for you. But it was like that. White, and glossy, and very beautiful. I mean exquisitely beautiful."

Detective Sergeant Morris gave Stanley an odd small-eyed stare. "Not sure what you mean, sir."

"He wore a gray knitted hood, right? A really disgusting gray knitted hood. And a greasy old raincoat, and boots like—I don't know—coal miner's boots. He looked like a hobo, a tramp. But when he turned around and looked at me, his face was incredible."

"You mean beautiful, sir?"

"That's right. He had the most beautiful face that I've ever seen in my life."

Detective Sergeant Morris wrote this down, slowly and laboriously, with lots of loops in his writing. It was the writing of a small boy who is trying hard to impress his teacher.

"What time did you leave your flat, Mr. Eesner?" he asked at last.

"Eight-ten, dead on the nose."

"And when did you first see your assailant?"

"Immediately. He was waiting for me across the street."

Detective Sergeant Morris clenched his tongue tip between his teeth, writing and murmuring, *"He was . . . waiting . . . for me . . ."*

Stanley said, "This was the fourth straight day. He's been waiting for me every day since Tuesday. He's been following me, all the way to the King's Road and on to the bus."

"Had you *asked* him to wait for you?"

"What do you mean? Of course not, I didn't even know the guy!"

"Then why was he waiting for you?"

"How should I know? You should ask him! I tried to find out, and look what the hell happened to me!"

Detective Sergeant Morris carefully wrote this down. Then he said, "If you didn't know this gentleman, sir, and he didn't know you, it seems very odd that he should be waiting for you every morning. Had you met him at all before, in any context whatsoever?"

"I told you, I didn't know him from Adam. I never met him before anywhere, ever."

"What you mean is, you hadn't seen him before he started waiting for you across the street—which was, ah, Tuesday?"

"That's correct."

"And to quote your own words, Mr. Eesner, he had the most beautiful face that you had ever seen in your life?" In the expressionless way that Detective Sergeant Morris intoned them, Stanley's words sounded absurd, like a line out of Monty Python. He could almost have added, "nudge, nudge, wink, wink."

Stanley tried to keep a tight rein on his irritation. *Answer every question factually and unemotionally*, Gordon Rutherford had warned him. "That's right," he agreed.

Detective Sergeant Morris remained silent for a moment, still writing. Then he said, "Who approached whom, sir?"

"I'm sorry?"

"What I'm trying to establish, sir, did you approach him or did he approach you?"

Stanley winced and frowned. "What the hell difference does that make? He attacked me!"

"I realize that, sir, but if we're thinking about prosecution, in the courts, we're going to have to come up in front of a judge, and twelve good men and true. And that judge, and those twelve good men and true, they're going to be asking themselves, was this beautiful young chap in the gray knitted hood approached by you; and, if he *was* approached by you, was it possible that he was justified in assuming that you were actively seeking the kind of sexual pleasures which he then proceeded to provide?"

Detective Sergeant Morris leafed back through his notebook and added, "In simple words, sir, were you essentially, as it were, asking for it?"

Stanley lifted himself up on his elbows, trembling with shock and anger. "He attacked me! What the hell are you trying to say here? He attacked me! He smashed my face against the sidewalk, he broke my tooth!"

Detective Sergeant Morris was undeterred. "There are some who like it a bit rough, sir."

"Rough? What are you, some kind of retard? He practically killed me! He hit my head against the sidewalk and then he sodomized me, can't you understand that? He raped me, against my will!"

Slowly, with more loops, Detective Sergeant Morris wrote, *"raped me . . . against my . . ."* When he finished, he added in that leaden tone, "And, believe me, Mr. Eesner, insults won't help us at all."

Stanley was juddering with tension. His heart banged dryly against his ribs, too much adrenaline, too much stress.

Detective Sergeant Morris said, "How was the rape actually effected, Mr. Eesner?"

"What?" asked Stanley.

Detective Sergeant Morris was obviously trying not to smirk. "Can you tell me how the rape was actually effected? I mean, without putting too fine a point on it, sir, there are practical difficulties. Quarts into pint pots, if you follow me."

"I don't understand, he raped me," Stanley replied.

"Yes, sir," Detective Sergeant Morris repeated patiently. "But what the judge and the jury will want to know is, how? Perhaps you remember *Last Tango in Paris*, sir? In that case the practical difficulties were overcome with butter."

"Butter?" Stanley repeated. *"Butter?"* and then, fatally, began to cry.

He had one more visitor that day—Frederick Orme, the director of the Kensington Chamber Orchestra, who arrived with a bunch of daffodils from the flower stall outside the hospital, and a copy of Jeffrey Archer's *Twist in the Tale*. Frederick Orme was tall and airy and vague, and sat back on his chair showing seven inches of white leg, his russet eyebrows rising up his forehead like flames.

"The evening papers seem to have been discreet about it," he remarked. "They say simply that you were mugged, rather than go into the grisly details of—well, what actually happened to you."

Stanley had the disturbing suspicion that Frederick Orme felt the same way as Detective Sergeant Morris—that even if he hadn't actually *encouraged* it, any man who had been anally raped must at least have accepted his attack submissively. ("Catch me letting anybody near *my* rear end!")

Frederick Orme reached over and picked one of Stanley's grapes. "The doctor told me that you were quite lucky."

"He seems to think so," said Stanley. "At least I'm still alive."

"But I gather you won't be playing with us for quite a while. Six weeks' convalescence at least, that's what the doctor suggested."

Stanley nodded.

"That's really quite a nuisance, you know," Frederick Orme told him, eating one grape and picking himself another. "We have Nils Planck coming over from Düsseldorf next week to finish recording the Adagio and Fugue in C Minor; and then we were hoping to arrange a concert at the Royal Festival Hall."

"I apologize for being attacked," Stanley told him flatly.

"My dear boy, it wasn't your fault. We all sympathize dreadfully. But it does make life rather difficult. I would have thought an American would be rather more, what do you call it? Roadworthy?"

"Streetwise," Stanley corrected him. His painkillers were beginning to wear off, and the aching in his back was almost intolerable. He watched Frederick Orme eat another grape, and then he said, "I'll ask Dr. Patel if I can come out sooner. I could play from a wheelchair, I guess."

Frederick Orme nodded. "Helpful if you could." He stood up quite abruptly and tugged down his brown tweed waistcoat. "Everybody sends their best, anyway. Fanny Lawrence said she'd pop in to see you tomorrow. And if there's anything you need . . ."

"A little rest, as a matter of fact," Stanley told him.

"Of course, dear boy. I must be off, in any case. Wonderful grapes. Are you allowed Guinness?"

He slept badly that night. Again and again, he woke up with a start, convinced that there was somebody in the room with him. But he was alone, and the room remained overheated and silent, except for the muffled grinding of London's traffic and the occasional whistling of a night porter.

He felt feverish and hot; and not completely real; and his blood prickled as it coursed around his body as if it were filled with fine hairlike fibers.

He tried to think of some soothing musical score, to calm himself down. *Eine Kleine Nachtmusik*, maybe. It usually worked: he had never gone past the andante without falling asleep. But all he could picture tonight was a stave without notes or notations, ribboning out of one side of his mind like an empty five-lane highway, and ribboning away out of the other. He felt as if he were musically illiterate: as if he had forgotten every crotchet that he had every played.

There was something wrong with him. It wasn't just shock. It wasn't just concussion and bruising and violently-torn tissues. There was something inside him; something was hiding inside his body that wasn't him, and wasn't his; something was hiding inside his mind.

You're sick, he told himself, dry-lipped, in the half-darkness of his hospital room. *You're badly, seriously sick.*

For the first time since he had left New York in November, he felt like talking to his father. He checked the time. He would be sleeping by now; but he promised himself that he would phone him during the day. He would have liked to be able to talk to Eve, too; and he would have called her right now, if he could. Two A.M. in London, six P.M. the previous day in Napa. She would probably just be starting supper. He wished now that they hadn't argued so bitterly over money. It had probably been the only way they knew how to punish each other. Ever since they had known each other, way back at Berkeley in the days of Leon Russell songs and flared jeans, he and Eve had always been able to discuss their problems and their anxieties together, even if they hadn't really loved each other enough to stay married. Stanley's old college pal Pete Chominski had always said that he and Eve should have stayed friends; and never tried to pretend that they could be man and wife.

He missed Leon, too; serious-faced Leon, who had been named for Leon Russell; he missed him more than he could ever have imagined.

He lay back on his pillow with his eyes open. At the same time, he had the extraordinary feeling that at some time in the past few minutes he had fallen asleep—that he had passed from waking to dreaming without even noticing the transition. He wouldn't have believed that his mind could have arranged for him to pass so seamlessly from one state to another. Not even a blink; and London's traffic still thundering outside, exactly as it had been before.

Now, however, somebody was standing in the shadows, in the darkest corner of the room. A tall hunched figure, with its face concealed. A figure that must be a dream because the door hadn't opened and closed, and he heard no footsteps; no rustling of clothing.

A figure that must be a dream, because he felt no sense of terror, only a helpless curiosity.

"Who are you?" he whispered.

The figure said nothing, and remained buried in darkness.

"Who are you?" Stanley repeated. "What do you want?"

After a long pause, the figure slowly raised its head, and Stanley saw the cold beautiful face of the man in the knitted hood. Pristine, angelic, glistening.

"I am the pestilence that was promised."

"You're what? What are you talking about?"

"Don't you remember? If you were unwilling to obey, you were promised that the plague on you would be increased by seven times, according to your sins."

"You're crazy."

"Am I? Who could be crazier than you, who disobeyed? Don't you remember what you were told—that when you gathered together in your cities, pestilence would be sent among you, so that you should be delivered into the hands of your enemies."

"I'm dreaming," said Stanley.

The figure uttered a strange, soft, mocking sound; not so much like a laugh, more like a sack being slowly dragged across an unswept cement floor. *"Who dreams? Who's awake? Am I dreaming you, or are you dreaming me?"*

Stanley said, "You attacked me, you bastard. You could have killed me."

"Ha! We are cutting a swathe through the world. You can hardly complain if you were chosen to be the first."

"I don't understand a word of this," said Stanley. "Dream or no dream, I'm going to call for the doctor." He heaved himself up on to one elbow.

"It will serve no purpose," Knitted Hood told him. *"We are dreams, you and I, both of us. We are wraiths of each other's imagination, nothing more."*

Stanley hesitated for a moment, then stripped off the surgical tape which held his dextrose drip in place, tugged out the tube, and swung his legs off the side of the bed. "All right, then, pal, if this is all a dream, and it's just me and you, then let's see what you're made of."

Again Knitted Hood uttered that gritty whispering noise. Then—while Stanley eased himself carefully and painfully off the edge of his bed—he moved to the window and drew aside the curtain with his gray-bandaged hand.

"You doubt the truth of what I say?" he asked Stanley, his eyes black, his face seraphic but utterly expressionless, *"Look out of the window, tell me what you see."*

Stanley approached the window at a slow, geriatric hobble. Blood slid from his wrist where he had pulled out his drip. Now that he was closer to Knitted Hood, he could smell that same sourish odor that he had smelled yesterday morning, when he was attacked; that same strong scent of lavender. His stomach knotted up, and the roof of his mouth felt as if it were coated with grease.

"Look," Knitted Hood insisted.

Stanley looked out of the hospital window and saw that the sky was beginning to lighten. The landscape was a hard, chilly gray, a winter's morning as cold as a witch's teat. But there was no traffic to be seen, no buildings, no streets and buses and backyards. All he could see were boggy, deserted fields, and disconsolate trees, and a small collection of huts and sheds and pigpens.

Fulham seemed to have vanished. In its place was nothing but marshy farmland and winding tracks of glistening black mud, as far as Stanley could see.

"I don't understand," he said hoarsely.

"Perhaps it's a dream," Knitted Hood suggested. *"Then again, perhaps it's a memory."* He was silent for a moment, and then he added, *"Then again, perhaps it's real."*

As Stanley watched, a woman in a bonnet and a shawl emerged from behind the huts, pushing a handcart. She was too far away for him to be able to see her clearly, but she didn't look older than twenty-one or twenty-two. She had greasy blond hair tied up in a scarf, and a blue-gray dress with a plain square neck and skirts that were heavy with mud. The handcart appeared to be heaped up with old rags.

"Is this a dream?" Stanley demanded.

Knitted Hood said nothing, but turned away from the window and stood in the shadows, so that Stanley could barely see him.

"Is this a dream?" Stanley repeated. "Am I asleep, or what?"

"Who can say what it is?" Knitted Hood replied. *"It could be your past, it could be your future. Ha! It could be nothing more frightening than something you ate."*

Stanley turned back to the window. The girl had managed to wrestle the handcart onto the muddy track, and for a moment she paused, looking in his direction. Although she was pale and her cheek was marked with mud, she was almost beautiful, in a starved kind of way, and strangely familiar.

Stanley raised his hand, compelled for some reason to wave to her. He felt that he wanted to call our her name, although he didn't know what her name was. Could she see him? Was he really here? Could she see the hospital even? How could a large red-brick Victorian hospital be standing in the middle of a boggy country farm?

We shall cut a swathe through the world, Knitted Hood had assured him; and now Stanley was beginning to feel frightened and chilled. He turned around quickly, terrified that Knitted

Hood had suddenly come up close behind him; but Knitted
Hood had folded himself so darkly in the shadows that Stanley
wasn't sure that he was there at all.

He looked back at the girl with the handcart. She was
struggling to push it over a rutted part of the path, close to
the farmyard gate. One of the wheels became deeply en-
mired; and no matter how hard she pushed it, and jostled it
backwards and forwards, the handcart refused to move any
further.

The girl looked around, as if she needed help, but didn't
know whom to call, as if there wasn't anybody she *could* call.
She glanced towards the hospital, and Stanley pressed his
hand against the window; but he couldn't decide whether she
had seen him or not. *Who's dreaming whom? Maybe this farm
girl is dreaming about me. Maybe Knitted Hood is dreaming
about both of us. Maybe we're all dreams. Maybe we're all
dead.*

The girl tried rocking the cart yet again, but the wheels sank
even more inextricably into the mud. She was almost knee-
deep in black ooze, and her dress trailed heavy and bedraggled
in the puddles.

Each time she pushed, the rags on the handcart slipped
further and further to one side, and suddenly Stanley saw
something pale appearing from underneath them. Two more
pushes, and he realized with horrible fascination that he was
looking at a human arm. It lolled lifelessly from one side to
another as the girl struggled to push the handcart out of the
mud.

*How can this conceivably be a dream? This is far too real
to be a dream. All right, London has disappeared, I don't know
how, and I'm out in the country someplace. But this girl is
pushing a dead body on a handcart and I can see it as clear
as if I'm awake.*

He had to find his way outside. The girl desperately needed
his help. Yet somehow he couldn't bring himself to leave the
window. Supposing she vanished, and London came back?
How could he possibly help her then?

The girl appeared to lose her temper, and she shook the
handcart violently from side to side. As she did so, the rags
dropped away, and a heap of greenish-white naked bodies slith-

ered off the edge of it, like fish being emptied out of a basket, and into the mud.

Stanley stood at the window, panting with shock. *Oh, God. Oh, God.* A dead child, no more than two years old, had fallen facedown into a puddle. Close beside him, with her eyes wide open, lay a dead girl with dark bushy hair, her sticklike arms crossed over her chest, her ribs emaciated like a Belsen victim. She could have been anything from ten to fourteen years old. A little further away, curiously crouched up, lay a dead woman in her early thirties, gray-faced, wearing a gray linen cap. She had such an appalling expression of despair on her face that Stanley could almost have believed that she was still alive. A dead newly-born baby had been strapped tightly to her back with strips of torn bandage; a tiny purple doll with terrible black eyes; as if she were expected to carry it with her into death in a way that she had never been able to carry it in life. A punishment or a consolation? Stanley couldn't even begin to guess.

"Your plague shall be increased seven times, and we shall cut a swathe through the world."

Behind him, the door of his room suddenly opened. Stanley turned around, still trembling, still gasping. He found himself face-to-face with one of his Chinese nurses.

"What are you *doing*, Mr. Eisner?" she demanded in astonishment. "You are under very strict orders to stay in bed till Dr. Patel says you can get up! And what have you done to your drip?"

Stanley swayed. The nurse caught him with matter-of-fact efficiency as he began to faint, and helped him back on to the bed.

"I saw something—" he began, but the nurse sharply, "Ssh! No more talking!"

Briskly, she reconnected his drip. Then she made sure that he was settled in bed and firmly tucked up. "You rest, Mr. Eisner! Don't you dare to move! In a minute we'll be bringing you some breakfast. I must call Dr. Patel, too, to make sure you haven't pulled any of your stitches."

Stanley lay on his side, tucked up as tightly as a small child, his face turned away from the window, while the morning gradually grew brighter. Outside, quite distinctly, he could hear the churning of early-morning traffic, the juddering of taxis, the sniffing and bellowing of buses. He thought once that he could hear a girl's voice crying out, plaintive and high, but with his cheek against the starched hospital sheet he had to admit to himself that it was probably nothing more than a dream.

TWO

Nylon Stocking

HE SAT BY THE WINDOW OF HIS FLAT FOR OVER AN HOUR, watching Langton Street grow darker and darker. A mug of espresso coffee grew cold on the table beside him. He made no attempt to switch on the lights, or to change the record which circled silently and endlessly on the hi-fi on the opposite side of the room.

He was watching the corner where Knitted Hood had waited, on that hideous morning four and a half weeks ago. The pavement was deserted now; Langton Street remained empty.

At half past six he pushed back his chair and stood up. *It's no use thinking about it, Stanley. It happened, and all the thinking in the world isn't going to make it un-happen.* He picked up the coffee cup and took it through to the kitchen, and switched on the lights.

This was his first night back in his own flat since leaving hospital. The *Sun* newspaper had printed a front-page story, "Attack on Top U.S. Violinist 'Was Rape,'" complete with a photograph of Stanley shaking hands with Sir Georg Solti in Chicago; and for the sake of Stanley's "emotional convalescence" and the orchestra's "general equilibrium," Frederick

Orme had decided it would be "generally preferred" if he didn't immediately return to the orchestra. The second bassoon, Nigel Bromhead-Jones, had given Stanley the use of his late mother's bungalow in Oxshott, in the Surrey commuter belt, and Stanley had spent over three weeks reading and going for walks and watching television.

In all that time he had spoken to hardly anybody, except the woman in the local post office, who believed that her migraines were caused by the depletion in the ozone layer, and the landlord of the Feathers, who was gruff and belligerent and thought that anybody who couldn't trace their English ancestry back at least three generations should be forcibly repatriated at their own expense, regardless of the fact that this would have emptied the cities of Bradford and Wolverhampton overnight.

Only one of Stanley's fellow musicians from the orchestra had come down from London to see him—Fanny Lawrence, a pale bespectacled girl with wild pre-Raphaelite hair and hems that dangled with fraying cotton threads. She worshiped Stanley. She had told him so several times. "You're my god, you know," she had announced when they were sitting in the pub eating chicken-in-the-basket. Stanley had taken her to the station afterwards and kissed her cold, plump cheek.

The days had passed gray and detailed and tedious, like the spokes of a bicycle wheel ticking around and around. Walking along the puddly roads, Stanley had almost forgotten who he was, or why he was here. He had found himself increasingly afflicted by a huge inertia. Some afternoons he had sat for two or three hours at a time, listening to his heart beat, feeling that strange thistly prickling in his veins, thinking of nothing at all.

He could have stayed in Oxshott forever, gradually absorbed by English suburbia until he became a mirage, a reflective disturbance in the air, and nothing more.

Yesterday, however, he had caught sight of himself in a fisheye security mirror in the local supermarket. He had stopped, stepped back towards the mirror, and stared at himself more closely. A tired Buster Keaton-looking man with a wire basket full of cheese and kitchen towels and shredded wheat. A voice inside him had asked urgently, *What the hell's happening to you, Stanley? Are you sick or something? Are you dying? You look like you're dying!*

Very carefully, he had walked back around the supermarket and replaced all his shopping on the shelves. Then he had walked back along the narrow pavement to the bungalow, turned off the gas and the power, and telephoned for a taxi to take him to London.

In the back of the taxi, staring at the passing suburbs, hairdressers, garages, mile after mile of 1930s semidetached houses, gray skies, pylons, he had admitted to himself that Knitted Hood's assault had taken something away from him that he might never be able to recapture. It had taken away his spirit, his joy in being alive; and that man he had seen in the Oxshott supermarket mirror had only just been managing to cling on to his identity by his fingernails. It had been more like peering through the spyhole of a padded cell and seeing a lunatic peering back at him.

Tonight he walked around his flat, tugging the brown velour drapes and switching on the lamps. He resisted the temptation to take one last look out into the street.

On the television screen, in a thick Northumbrian accent that Stanley could scarcely understand, the BBC weatherman was explaining that tomorrow would be bitterly cold. Somehow the BBC seemed to have convinced itself that weathermen with thick regional accents would be more believable, like shepherds or crofters.

Red sky at night, shepherd's delight. Red sky in the morning, shepherd's warning. Red sky in the afternoon, shepherd's house is on fire.

Stanley's flat was spacious and quite comfortable, in a stuffy London way. He had a large living room, with beige-papered walls and brown furnishings, and a beige tiled fireplace with a six-bar electric fire. Above the fireplace hung a huge reproduction of *Prince Baltasar Carlos with a Dwarf*, by Velázquez, bought from Boots the Chemists. Stanley found the portrait unsettling and strange. It showed two small creatures in elaborately-embroidered dresses—one of them pale and royal, and painted in an odd perspective, as if he were floating in the air, the other one stunted.

Stanley carried his cold coffee through to the kitchen, trying to hum Handel but sounding flat. The kitchen was modern, fitted in brown oak, with a large Zanussi refrigerator and a window that overlooked some dark small yard between the houses; a yard which intrigued Stanley because he had heard children playing there, but couldn't see how anybody could gain access to it.

Stanley tipped away his coffee and went to the refrigerator and took out a half-empty bottle of Pouilly-Fumé. Dr. Patel had advised him against drinking alcohol while he was still on medication, but the way he felt tonight, what the hell. He shook two capsules into the palm of his hand, clapped his hand against his mouth, and washed the capsules down with cold wine.

He went back into the living room and sat down in front of the television. Channel 4 news was reporting on the day's debates in the House of Commons. The Conservative MP Mr. Robert Adley had called the Labour MP Mr. John Prescott "a freak." The Speaker of the House had decided that this remark was "not un-Parliamentary but certainly inelegant."

The longer he stayed in England, the quainter and more claustrophobic Stanley found it. It was like living in a novel by Charles Dickens, *Our Suffocating Friend.*

The news turned to the subject of the Channel Tunnel. Protestors in woolly hats were claiming that it would "cut a swathe of devastation through the sublime county of Kent."

A swathe, thought Stanley. *We shall cut a swathe through the world.*

He could still feel that prickling in his blood. He had told Dr. Patel about it while he was in hospital, but Dr. Patel had assured him there was nothing wrong. His blood samples had been sent back twice for re-analysis—once to the Hospital for Tropical Diseases—but now Dr. Patel was fairly sure that he hadn't caught anything nasty from his encounter with Knitted Hood. "You are a physically well man, Mr. Eisner. If you are feeling anything in your body, then it is your mind that it is creating that feeling."

Stanley leaned his head back in his armchair and closed his eyes. He had never felt so tired in his life, although he couldn't understand why. He had been resting for almost a month, after all. He hadn't even practiced his violin. It lay on the chair beside the window, its case closed. He had taken it down to Oxshott with him, but he had only taken it out once. He had played two quick, scraping, discordant notes, and then immediately put it back again. He didn't seem to have any music in him any more.

The clipped monotonous voice of the Channel 4 newscaster went on and on; humorless and English and peculiarly unintelligible. *And today clams were still being mabel that fortitude was passing wild recessions.* Stanley began to breathe more deeply and more regularly. His hand slid from the arm of his chair.

He wasn't quite asleep, but he could feel his consciousness slowly sinking, like a saucepan gradually filling up with water. He thought about the landlord of the Feathers. *Never in calming positions, but always in falling necessities.* He thought about the woman in the Oxshott post office. *Even today, when almost all tankards have interested trees.*

He slept. He thought he was asleep. But then he opened his eyes and the television news was still on, and the living room seemed exactly the same as before. He felt cold, however, uncomfortably cold. He sat up shivering and trembling; and as he did so he was conscious of that sharp prickling sensation in his veins.

He eased himself out of his chair and knelt down in front of the fireplace to switch on the electric fire. Why did he suddenly feel so cold? He felt as if all the skin had been stripped off him and his raw flesh had been exposed to the wind. He switched on all six bars of the electric fire and hunched down close to it while the bars gradually reddened.

As the fire warmed up, he held his hands close to it. *Why do I feel so terrible? Why do I feel so goddamned shivery and weak?* He was beginning to wonder if his experience might not have brought out something worse, like chronic delayed shock, or even ME—myalgic encephalomyelitis. He had never felt so sensitive before.

He coughed. He coughed again; and this time his cough was thicker. His stomach felt queasy, as if he had been swallowing phlegm. He coughed again and again, thicker and thicker; and between each bout of coughing he found he had to fight for breath.

Oh, God, I feel so lousy. What the hell's the matter with me? He coughed for almost a minute, pressing his handkerchief over his mouth. Then suddenly he felt something slippery in the back of his throat; and he retched loudly, a terrible ripping retch that made his stomach contract, and almost made him vomit. A large slimy gray lump, the size and shape of an oyster, slithered out of his mouth and into his handkerchief.

He stared at it, sweating and panting, his stomach still convulsing, his mouth flooded with foul-tasting saliva.

What is it? A lump of mucus? A lump of coughed-up lung? Perhaps he had cancer and Dr. Patel hadn't wanted to tell him. He felt weak with exhaustion and fear, and his head swam. He could smell the burned-dust smell of the electric fire, and it almost choked him.

Cautiously, he squeezed the gray lump in his handkerchief. At first, nothing happened, so he squeezed it again. It felt exactly like an oyster, or a soft cyst. He opened up his handkerchief again so that he could examine it more closely. He was still swallowing with nausea. He prodded it with his fingertip, and then took hold of one of its slippery tubules and tried to tug it apart.

Instantly, it tightened and convulsed, as if it were alive. Stanley cried out, *"Ah!"* and flung it away from him in disgust and fright, and it landed on the top bar of the electric fire. A sharp sizzling noise; a smell so repulsive that Stanley clamped his hand over his nose and mouth; and then the lump dropped into the fireplace, twitching furiously, rolling and unrolling, as if it were suffering hideous agony.

Stanley picked up the wine bottle and tried to crush the thing; but it felt just like a human tongue, and he couldn't stand the feeling of it, wriggling between the bottle and the tiled hearth, as if it were determined to stay alive, no matter what pain it had to endure, no matter how hard Stanley tried to kill it.

He grasped the arm of his chair and heaved himself upright. He retched again and almost vomited. *God Almighty, what was happening to him?*

He turned, half expecting to see what he saw.

There—in the shadow of the curtains—close beside the chair where his violin case lay, stood Knitted Hood. White-faced, silent, shining, as beautiful as sin.

Stanley stood shivering, saying nothing. This was a dream

now, he knew it. It had to be a dream. The only terrifying part about it was that he didn't know how to wake up.

"It could be your past," Knitted Hood whispered. *"It could be your future. It could be nothing more frightening than something you ate."*

"Leave me alone." Stanley swallowed, wiping his mouth with his hand.

"We have something in common now, you and me," Knitted Hood told him. *"What was mine has now passed to you; and what is now yours will pass to the rest of the world; one to another; and together we shall cut a swathe through all mankind."*

"Wake up!" Stanley shouted to himself.

"Perhaps you're awake already," whispered Knitted Hood, and his voice was chillingly benign.

Stanley swung his arm and slapped himself hard across the face. "Wake up! Wake up, you stupid *putz*! Wake up!"

He shut his eyes tightly and slapped himself again and again.

"Wake—*up*!—wake—*up*!—wake—*UP*!—wake—*UP*!"

He was suddenly aware that something was different; that the atmosphere in the living room had subtly altered. Slowly, his cheeks stinging, he opened his eyes.

The Channel 4 newscaster was saying, ". . . and that's all for this evening . . . and a very good evening to you."

Stanley looked around the room, sniffing and trembling. Behind the curtains there was nothing but shadow; and in the hearth there was nothing but broken glass, and a steadily-widening pool of white wine, in which the scarlet bars of the electric fire were reflected.

"God protect me," he said out loud.

He went through to the kitchen to find a mopping-up cloth. On the scribble board next to the telephone he had written Gordon Rutherford's number. He stared at it for a while, undecided, then he picked up the telephone and mechanically punched it out.

The phone rang for almost a minute. Then a cautious voice answered, "Ye-e-es?"

"Gordon?" said Stanley with a catch in his throat.

"Ye-e-es?" Quite archly, this time.

"Gordon, it's Stanley Eisner. Listen, Gordon, I have to see you."

"Are you all *right*, Stanley? You sound positively—I don't know—discombobulated."

"Can I see you? Please? It's very important," Stanley paused. Then he said, "To be frank with you, Gordon, I don't have anyone else."

The next morning the weather was brighter and warmer, almost like spring. For all of his burr, the BBC shepherd had been dramatically wrong. Stanley took the bus to St. Stephen's to keep a last appointment with Dr. Patel. It was little more than a formality. Dr. Patel had already told him that his internal injuries had healed well, and that he had suffered no brain damage from hitting his head on the pavement.

"But somehow you don't seem convinced that you *are* well," Dr. Patel remarked as he shuffled Stanley's notes and closed the folder.

Stanley tried to sound calm. "I keep having dreams that I'm sick . . . that I'm coughing lumps of terrible stuff. I look out of the window and all I can see is people lying dead."

Dr. Patel looked melancholy and steepled his long, slender fingers. "Your mind is simply trying to find a way of dealing with what has happened to you, Mr. Eisner. Let me put it this way: your subconscious is seeking an explanation for something which is still inexplicable. Why did this fellow attack me? He hasn't yet been caught; he didn't explain himself in any way. So your mind is trying to construct an explanation—based on your religious upbringing, perhaps, and also on your quite-natural fear of contagious disease."

Dr. Patel took out a blindingly clean handkerchief and wiped his sad, watery eyes. "There is some element in your blood sample which has caused us some mystification, but as you already know, you are HIV-negative, and as far as we can say, you have no trace of any communicable infection of which modern pathology is aware."

Stanley swallowed tightly. "Thank you."

"I could recommend a psychiatrist, if you feel you have the need," Dr. Patel suggested.

Stanley shrugged. "I need something, but I don't know what. Revenge, maybe. I don't know. I didn't do anything, you know? Some goddamned revolting creature knocked me down on the sidewalk and raped me. I fought back. I mean, I really fought back. But he was so goddamned strong. And what did he weigh? Three hundred fifty, four hundred pounds. A gorilla."

"Yes, a gorilla," Dr. Patel replied, as if he had been thinking about something else altogether. Then he stood up and extended his hand. "Your body is healed, Mr. Eisner. You are free from infection. Any other difficulties you are experiencing are unfortunately outside my field of expertise. But do speak to my secretary if you wish to know the name of a psychiatrist. Whatever happens, I wish you all the best."

He hesitated and smiled faintly, and then he added, "You may be interested to know that I am quite a fan of yours, you know. I have all of your quintets on CD."

Gordon sat on the concrete embankment swinging his scuffed suede shoes. Beside him, he had almost ritualistically laid out his Carlsberg Special Brew and his packet of Silk Cut cigarettes and his Zippo-style lighter with a picture of Cliff Richard on it. Only a few yards away, trains echoed and rattled across a light-green-painted latticework bridge, on their way to Richmond, south of the Thames; and the narrow riverside path outside the Bull's Head pub was crowded with drinking and laughing weekenders; but Gordon lifted his beaklike nose to the unseasonably warm sunshine as if he were sitting alone, out in the countryside.

"Do you know something?" he remarked. "You could get quite a respectable tan if you sat here long enough."

"Sure, but who wants to sit here for a year?" Stanley replied. He was leaning on the railings, looking out at the broad wind-ruffled surface of the Thames. The tide had turned about a half hour ago, and already a small dinghy moored by the steps was beginning to bob and spin in the rising current. Ducks paddled around, snatching at cheese-and-onion potato chips that a ginger-headed Duchess of York look-alike was tossing into the water.

"You're not beginning to feel homesick, are you?" Gordon asked him, basking, his eyes closed.

"Not yet. I guess I'm just disoriented, that's all. A stranger in a strange land."

"Any news when you might be invited to play again?"

Stanley shook his head. "In the opinion of the great and omnipotent Frederick Orme, it would be wiser for me to make completely certain of my recovery before I rejoin the orchestra."

"Did he say that before or after that report in the *Sun* that you'd been you-know-whatted?" Gordon wasn't usually shy of the word "rape" but the embankment outside the pub was very crowded and he didn't particularly want anyone to overhear. Stanley had suffered enough.

"After, of course," Stanley replied. "What do you think?"

"I think that the sooner you get back to normal, the better."

Stanley sipped his Guinness and shrugged. "I don't know. Frederick has some kind of a point. The way I'm feeling at the moment, I couldn't play anything worth shit."

"Have you *tried* playing? Or practicing, even? Even shit's better than nothing."

Stanley kept his eyes on the squabbling ducks. "I haven't even opened my violin case since I was attacked. Well, once, but I put it straight back again."

"Any particular reason?" asked Gordon. "I thought that music was therapeutic. They play Andy Williams records to people in comas. It's practically infallible. Nine out of ten times the patients wake up, shouting 'No more, no more! I'll wake up, please, but no more!' "

Stanley smiled. He liked the way Gordon refused to allow him to take himself too seriously. "I don't know. All the music seems to have drained out of me. I used to be able to think in staves, night and day. I used to be able to write music in my head. Now my whole brain seems to be filled up with guys in gray knitted hoods, and peculiar nightmares, and how crappy I feel."

"I still think that getting back to the orchestra would do you good. You know, get you cranked up again."

"That all depends on Frederick. My contract says that I'm obliged to play whenever the musical director asks me to play; but it doesn't give me any kind of guarantee that he *will* ask me to play. If he wants to pay me for sitting on my hands, there's nothing I can do about it.''

"Have you spoken to him about it?''

"Not lately.''

"Perhaps you should. Perhaps you *need* to play.''

"I don't know. I'll think about it.''

"You're not embarrassed, are you? You know, by what's happened to you?''

"I don't know,'' said Stanley. "I suppose that's part of it. Embarrassed; maybe a little humiliated, too.''

"What on earth do you have to be humiliated about?'' Gordon asked him.

Stanley sipped his Guinness. It was strange stuff, black and earthy and gloomy, more like molasses than beer, but he was growing to like it. It had a bitterness that seemed appropriate. "Frederick seems to believe that what happened to me was entirely my own fault, that I actually left home that morning with the *intention* of getting myself assaulted.''

Gordon, his eyes still closed, slowly nodded. "Tell me the old, old story,'' he said.

"What do you mean?''

"I mean, my dear Stanley, that you've come up against the English perception of sex. Sex, in England, is bracketed with road accidents: it's always considered to be somebody's *fault*, and more often than not it's the fault of the victim. The raped rather than the raper, the buggered rather than the bugger.''

Stanley said, "I didn't think that this was going to be so hard to deal with.''

"I told you it wouldn't be easy.''

Stanley swilled the last of his Guinness around in his glass, and drained it. Watching him, Gordon suggested, "You could always go back home to New York.''

"Not yet,'' said Stanley. "I need to face up to what's happened to me. I need to understand it. If I go back to the States, I might forget about it superficially, you know, but it's always going to be there, right in the back of my head, and I'm always going to be thinking *why*? Why did it happen to me? Why did I cross that street? Why did that guy attack me? Why couldn't I stop him? Why *didn't* I stop him?''

He paused, and then he looked around and added, "Besides,

I feel that I haven't finished up here yet. There's something I have to do. Something I'm kind of caught up in."

"Such as?" asked Gordon.

"I don't know. It's just a feeling."

"Do you want another drink?" Gordon asked him.

"Sure, I'll pay for it."

"No, no. Have this one on Desert Orchid," said Gordon. When Stanley looked blank, he smiled, "It's a horse. It won."

He climbed to his feet and smacked the dust from the seat of his jeans.

Stanley said, "Do *you* think that it was my fault? Maybe just *partly* my fault? I mean, was there something inside of me, something subconscious, that actually encouraged that guy to jump on me?"

"Let me tell you something," Gordon replied. "I deal with six or seven rape victims every single month. Some of them are men—remand prisoners, or army cadets, or young male prostitutes. Most of them are women, from all kinds of backgrounds. You couldn't meet a more varied collection of people anywhere. But they all have to come to terms with the same feeling of self-doubt, and they all have to come to terms with the change in the way that people treat them after it's happened.

"Nine times out of ten, a rape victim will find that her friends and colleagues treat her radically differently from the way they did before she was assaulted. Her women friends will find excuses not to be quite so close any more, almost as if she's caught some terrible disease. And the men in her life will ostracize her, too, because she didn't play the game. A chap's entitled to a bit of fun, after all, and if she got knocked about a bit, well, sorry and all that, but that's sex for you. No need to whine about it."

Stanley said very softly, "How do they cope with it? These other victims you deal with? How the hell do they come to terms with it?"

Gordon took his empty glass. "The way that you're having to come to terms with it: by learning to ignore the monstrous prejudices of the world at large . . . at least for as long as it takes you to convince yourself in your heart that what happened to you was a violent and totally unpreventable act for which you weren't at all to blame.

"Coming to terms with it, my dear Stanley, starts here, inside your own head. Treat yourself first; worry about the rest of the world later. Now, do you want some crisps?"

"Crisps, sure. Worcester sauce flavor, if they have them."

"Yuck. You're becoming too bloody Anglicized for your own good. Apart from the fact that it's pronounced *Wooster*, not *Whirr-sess-ter*."

" 'Wooster,' got you."

Stanley watched the river traffic passing as he waited for Gordon to come back with their drinks; and listened to the ferocious rapid-fire sniping of weekend conversation.

"Dennis stripped the dado, and then we rag-rolled the walls in apricot," a young woman in a horsey headscarf was explaining.

"Well, I don't know, I've gone orf rag-rolling," another woman replied, her Butler & Wilson costume earrings swinging in the February sunlight. "It looks so desperately Habitat."

Behind Stanley, a meaty-shouldered young man in a houndstooth jacket was booming with satisfaction, "—beautiful job on it, tweaked the carbs, stiffened the rear suspension, goes like an absolute bomb."

A sight-seeing boat puttered slowly past, and everybody on deck waved at the shore, although nobody outside the Bull's Head waved back, or even looked at them. Stanley found himself wondering why they had waved. To show that they were having fun, even if they weren't? To try to reassure themselves that they were real? They wouldn't have waved if they had been simply walking past. In fact, they would have turned their faces away.

He wished he would stop having thoughts like that. But there was something about England that brought it on. Something not quite right, as if everybody were in a play.

He was still watching the sight-seeing boat when he glimpsed somebody standing on the opposite bank of the river, over a quarter of a mile away. The trees were dark on the opposite bank, tall and melancholy poplars, their leaves glittering oc-

casionally in the wind. The kind of trees that reminded Stanley
of cemeteries, or municipal buildings.

He wasn't sure what it was that first attracted him to look at
the figure. Maybe it was the way that it was just standing there,
close to some broken-down railings and a boat shed, not moving. It was too far away for him to be able to see it clearly, but
when he narrowed his eyes, he managed to distinguish that it
was wearing a gray coat and some kind of gray hat.

A terrible cold feeling poured down him. He couldn't tell
for sure, but supposing it was Knitted Hood? It *looked* like
Knitted Hood, the way it was standing there, not moving. Its
face was white—white as a distant handkerchief—but Stanley
couldn't distinguish any more than that.

Should he call the police, even if he wasn't one hundred
percent sure that it *was* Knitted Hood? Jesus—supposing Knitted Hood was watching him? Supposing Knitted Hood was out
to get him again?

He looked urgently around for Gordon, but the pub was
crowded to the doors, and Gordon was probably still waiting
to be served.

It was then that he saw a pigskin binocular case that somebody had left on one of the outdoor tables. He pushed his way
over to it and picked it up. "Pardon me!" he called out, holding them over his head. "Who do these belong to?"

The young man in the houndstooth jacket replied, "Me, as
a matter of fact, and you can jolly well put them down. They're
Zeiss."

"Would you mind if I borrowed them for just a couple of
minutes?"

"Actually, I make it a rule not to lend anything, old man.
Even my girlfriends."

His friends hooted with laughter.

"Listen, how about drinks all round?" Stanley suggested.
He glanced quickly back across the river. The figure was still
there, unmoving.

"Come on, Alex, that's a fair deal," one of the young men
called out.

"Yes, come on, Alex, what about the special relationship?"

"Well, all right," said Alex. "But for God's sake don't drop
them."

Stanley took out the binoculars and elbowed his way back to the railings. His place had already been taken by a tall girl with straight blond hair and a cigarette, and she was very reluctant to give him any room.

"Would you mind?" he asked her.

She looked at him down her nose and moved at least an eighth of an inch.

Stanley lifted the binoculars and focused them on the opposite bank of the river. He found the boat shed, the broken-down railings. He inched the binoculars a little to the left, where the figure had been standing, but the figure had vanished. Immediately, he swung the binoculars to the right, but there was no sign of the figure in that direction, either. He lowered the binoculars and peered across the river with his hand shielding his eyes against the sunlight.

He was still trying to see where the figure had disappeared to when Gordon came back with their drinks.

"What are you doing, birdwatching?" he asked.

Stanley was almost about to tell him, when it suddenly occurred to him that he had probably been mistaken, and that the likelihood of the figure across the river being Knitted Hood was not only remote but ridiculous. It had probably been nothing more sinister than some old man taking his dog for a walk. If he told Gordon what he thought he had seen, Gordon would either call the police, with all the humiliation and embarrassment *that* would cause, or else he would begin to think that Stanley was becoming obsessive.

"I was watching the boats, is all," Stanley explained sheepishly. "That young fellow was kind enough to lend them to me."

"At a price!" called out one of Alex's friends loudly. "At a price!"

"That's right, mine's a large Bells and American," put in a leggy dark-haired girl with a profile like a thoroughbred horse.

"Holsten Pils for me," Alex declared.

Gordon asked Stanley, "What *have* you got yourself into, my dear? The Chiswick Mafia?"

"Give me a minute, I promised to buy them a round," Stanley told him.

Inside the Bull's Head it was smoky and noisy and jam-packed with drinkers. Stanley managed to force his way up to the oak-beamed bar, where he had to stand for nearly five minutes pressed between an old rheumy-eyed man with a hand-rolled cigarette smoldering between his lips and a potbellied young Australian with a bellowing laugh.

At last he was able to catch the attention of the young black man serving behind the bar; but while he was waiting for the drinks to be poured out, he felt somebody tapping him on the shoulder. He turned around and found himself face-to-face with a petite girl of eighteen or nineteen, her blond-streaked hair pulled up into a ribbon on top of her head so that she looked like a firework. Her blue eyes were heavily made up with glittery purple eye shadow, and her lips were almost white. She wore a black leather jacket and the shortest black miniskirt that Stanley had ever seen, exposing three inches of bare thigh, black nylon stocking tops, and black garters. In Napa she would have caused a serious public disturbance.

"Wotcha!" she shouted above the noise of laughter and conversation.

"Hi." Stanley smiled.

She looked him right in the eyes, smiling mischievously. "You don't know 'oo I am, do you?" she demanded.

"Have we met?" he asked her.

"Once," she told him. "That day you was attacked. I was the one what called a namblunce."

"Oh," said Stanley, nodding furiously. "In that case I owe you one."

"Are you all right now?" the girl wanted to know. "I read about it in the paper."

"I think the entire universe read about it in the paper," Stanley replied. "But, sure, I'm fine now, thanks. I'm still waiting to have my tooth fixed. You know, capped. Apart from that, though, I guess I'm pretty much fully recovered."

"That was really awful," the girl told him. She was watching his eyes with a sort of innocent relentlessness, to see how he was going to react.

"Yeah, it was—really awful," Stanley agreed. He couldn't stop himself from flinching, turning away.

"Did they ever catch the bloke?"

Stanley shook his head. "Doubt if they ever will. I don't

know whether you saw it, but he was wearing some kind of mask. Not to mention that hood.''

'' 'E was so bloody 'orrible, don't you think? Ugh. All dirty and greasy. Know what I mean? Are you all right now, then?''

"I'm fine, believe me. Can I buy you a drink?''

"I'm supposed to be with my boyfriend.''

"Will your boyfriend mind if I buy you a drink?''

"Not so long as you buy 'im one, too.''

Stanley asked for a pint of Fosters for the boyfriend and a gin-and-orange for the girl. The whole round cost him nearly twenty-two pounds. While he was rummaging through his coat pocket for change, the girl said, "My name's Angie, by the way. Angie Dunning.''

Stanley shook her hand. "Pleased to know you. Do you live around here?''

"Just across the road, 'erbert Gardens. Got a flat there— well, there's five of us sharing. Lived 'ere for ages, ever since I come to London. The only reason I was in Fulham that day you was attacked was that I was coming 'ome from a party.''

"Well, listen,'' said Stanley, "maybe there's something I can give you . . . you know, something to say thank you. A record, maybe. What kind of music do you like?''

"Oh, I dunno. Roachford, Bros, Kylie Minogue.''

Stanley smiled. "Not quite what I'm into, I'm afraid.''

"What do you play, then? Classical? Like James Last and stuff?''

"Something like that.''

A tall young man with cropped fair hair and scarlet-erupting cheeks came pushing his way over from the adjacent bar.

'' 'Oo's this, then?'' he asked Angie.

"Stanley Eisner,'' said Stanley, holding out his hand.

'' 'E's the violinist bloke what got attacked and I was the witness,'' Angie explained.

"Oh, yeah?'' demanded the young man belligerently.

"This is Paul,'' said Angie, as if that explained everything.

"I, uh, bought you a drink, Paul,'' said Stanley.

"Oh, yeah?'' said Paul.

Stanley went back outside and rejoined Gordon, who was checking his watch and looking tetchy.

"Your Whirrsesster crisps are getting stale," said Gordon rather tartly.

"I'm sorry," Stanley told him. "I just met the girl who called the ambulance when I was attacked. I wanted to say thank you."

Gordon looked at his watch again. "I'm going to have to leave you in a minute. My brother and his family are coming up from Maidenhead."

"Listen," said Stanley, "I haven't thanked you yet for everything you've been doing for me. I want you to know that I appreciate it. I don't know how I would have kept my sanity if it hadn't been for you."

Gordon pursed his lips, then smiled and nodded. "I'm not sure that sanity is worth keeping, but you're quite welcome."

Stanley opened up his bag of crisps and leaned back against the railings. The river was so high now that waves were beginning to slop over the embankment, and the ducks could swim right up beside their feet. "Do you know much about dreams?" he asked Gordon.

"In what way?" said Gordon. "You mean Freud, symbolism, that kind of thing? Carrot equals penis, grotto equals vagina?"

"I'm not sure," Stanley told him. "I had a dream when I was still in hospital, about the guy in the knitted hood, and it wasn't like a dream at all. It was like it was really happening. I mean, I wasn't at all aware that I'd fallen asleep. Then I had another dream last night. It was just the same . . . I went straight into the dream without any real sensation of going to sleep. I was sick, I puked up this lump like a clam or an oyster, and it was alive. And Knitted Hood was there, too."

Gordon swallowed beer and said nothing.

"Do you think I'm going crazy?" Stanley asked him.

"Maybe," said Gordon. "Sometimes I think that being crazy is the only thing that keeps me sane."

"I mean seriously."

"Did you mention these dreams to Dr. Patel?"

"He thinks my subconscious is trying to come to terms with my being raped. He said I should go see a shrink if it got too bad."

"I used to dream about my Aunt Millie's knickers once,"

said Gordon. "I think that was what finally decided me to go gay."

"I thought I saw him just now," said Stanley.

"Who?" Gordon asked him, squinting against the sunlight.

"Knitted Hood. I thought I saw him across the river."

Gordon frowned across the Thames, towards the tall dark trees. Then he looked back at Stanley. "Is that what you were doing with those binoculars?"

Stanley said, "I didn't want to tell you directly. I didn't want you to do anything—I don't know, *official*, like calling the cops. It could have been a hallucination. It could have been somebody else altogether—somebody who looked like Knitted Hood, but wasn't. It's a good half mile off."

"I wouldn't have called the police, you know," Gordon replied. "Not unless you'd wanted me to. As far as I'm concerned, the most important thing is for you to get your head back together again. Catching this Knitted Hood character comes a pretty long way behind that."

He finished his beer. "I'd better go now, Bryan and Margie will kill me. But if there's anything you want, you can always call the center, anytime you like. You've got a long way to go, you know. Inside your head, you haven't even started to accept what's happened to you. So, take it easy, *comprende*?"

He gave Stanley a ride in his unwashed Austin Montego as far as Kew Bridge. On the back seat were stacks of old Sunday newspapers and a stuffed otter that had seen better days. Around his feet as he drove were tides of crumpled red Topic wrappers. "I never get time to eat lunch. A Topic's a meal in itself, don't you think?"

Stanley had intended to catch a bus or a taxi back home; but after Gordon dropped him off, he realized that he was only three or four minutes' walk from the Royal Botanic Gardens. He crossed the river, half deafened by passing buses and trucks, and then walked along Kew Green, bordered on both sides by elegant eighteenth-century town houses. As he passed St. Ann's Church, bells began to toll, slowly, funereally, and a breeze scurried across the bright green grass like frightened cats. Stanley wished he had brought his Burberry. The sun was glaring, but out in the wind the day was still chilly.

He entered the gates of Kew Gardens and walked alone along

the wide, open pathway. On either side, trees nodded in the wind, nondescript to Stanley, who knew nothing about trees, but each with a label announcing that it was rare or special. The trees were still leafless, most of them, but already budding, and in the middle distance Stanley could see crowds of daffodils, almost too yellow to be real. He walked for almost five minutes, hearing nothing but the wind, and his own breathing, and the crunch of his shoes, and seeing scarcely anybody at all, just a few raincoated figures moving on other diagonal paths between the trees, their faces blurred in the shadows.

He passed a bench where a very old man sat in a plaid scarf and a barathea coat and a beautifully-brushed homburg. The very old man was patiently eating an ice-cream cone with two chocolate flake bars stuck in it like rabbit's ears. He passed another bench where a worried-looking black woman sat, endlessly rocking a baby buggy. A small coffee-colored half-caste boy with curly blond hair sat in the buggy, fast asleep.

A swathe through the world, thought Stanley.

At last he emerged beside a wide slate-black lake, where swans circled. Overlooking the lake was a vast Victorian glasshouse, two or three stories high. Its windows were steamed up, but through the misted glass panes, Stanley could make out the shapes of huge tropical palms and creepers, and iron catwalks that allowed visitors to view them from high above.

It was like something out of a dream; or *The Lost World*, by Arthur Conan Doyle, a vision of pterodactyls in Victorian London. Although he couldn't put his finger on the reason why, Stanley began to feel stressed and disturbed, and his mouth felt dry.

He looked around. A toddler was lying on the ground, kicking his legs, refusing to walk any further. His mother called, "Stay there, then! See if I care!" The wind was blowing even more penetratingly, and although he felt unsettled, there was no doubt that the Palm House looked warm. Stanley circled around to the end of it, opened the white-painted door, and stepped inside. Immediately he started to cough. It wasn't just warm inside, it was tropical, and the humidity was overwhelming. Stanley had to stay by the door for a moment, taking deep breaths to acclimatize himself.

With every breath, he took in the dank smell of equatorial vegetation. An old woman in yellow-tinted spectacles was standing not far away, watching him oddly, almost as if she recognized him. He tried to smile at her, and gasped, ''Good morning.''

After a while, however, the woman abruptly disappeared, and he caught his breath. He waited for a moment or two, and then he ventured further inside, making his way through huge feathery palms and twisted trunks. He saw two or three other visitors, at the far end of the glasshouse, but apart from them he appeared to be alone. He wiped his forehead with the back of his hand. The humidity was so high that perspiration was beginning to trickle down his back.

He walked to the very center of the Palm House, craning his neck so that he could see the tallest trees. He had almost decided that he was warm enough now—*too* warm, in fact—when he glimpsed somebody high on one of the iron catwalks above him, half hidden by the dark silhouetted leaves.

He shivered. There was something about the way the figure was standing—leaning, not moving—that reminded him too much of Knitted Hood. He cautiously circled the pathway around the palms, glancing upwards from time to time to make sure that the figure hadn't vanished. But it remained where it was, motionless. Who went to visit a Palm House and just *stood* there?

Stanley came around the iron pillars, keeping well back among the palm fronds so that the figure wouldn't be able to see him. He parted the fronds with his fingers and peered up at the catwalk. The figure had somehow contrived to keep its back to him, but there was no doubt about it. That soiled gray raincoat, that gray knitted hood; that hunched and peculiarly distorted posture.

Stanley looked around. No bobbies in sight. Never were, when you really needed one. So what was he going to do? Climb up to the catwalk and challenge Knitted Hood to a face-to-face fistfight? Run for the nearest telephone booth and risk Knitted Hood escaping?

He bit his lip. He was still feeling a whole lot less than one hundred percent physically, and he had already experienced enough of Knitted Hood's strength and weight to know that he wouldn't stand a chance, not without a baseball bat or a .44 Magnum. He was a classical violinist, for God's sake. His fingers were strong, he played a mean game of squash, but his pectorals could hardly be described as Ramboesque. Quite apart from sheer physical strength, he would need something else to deal with Knitted Hood, and that was will. Right now he wasn't sure how much of that particular commodity he possessed.

Supposing he went for the cops? There didn't seem to be much future in that, either. Knitted Hood had obviously been following him, and would see him straightaway, and guess what he was doing. He would have to be a retard to be still waiting here when Stanley returned with the boys in blue.

No, thought Stanley. *What I'm going to do is, I'm going to turn the tables on you, my friend. I'm going to follow you.*

He shuffled back into the palm fronds, just far enough to make it more difficult for Knitted Hood to see where he was; but not too far to restrict his own reasonably clear view of both ends of the Palm House. There was no chance now that Knitted Hood would be able to leave the building without Stanley spotting him.

Then Stanley waited, quietly perspiring, his hands clasped in front of him like a saint, or a tailor's dummy, trying to remain calm, trying to remain still.

Several people passed him by and stared at him curiously. Two young girls said, "Excuse me, are you Tarzan?" and burst into fits of hysterical giggles. All Stanley could do was smile, and hope that Knitted Hood hadn't heard them. He glanced surreptitiously sideways now and again. Each time he looked, the grayish figure was still standing there, hunched over the white-painted railings of the catwalk.

Waiting for Knitted Hood was both tedious and frightening. Although it seemed highly probable, he didn't know for sure that Knitted Hood had been following him. There was still the possibility that Knitted Hood didn't even realize that Stanley was around; and that his appearance here was nothing but a hideous coincidence. Maybe he was waiting for somebody else. Maybe he was watching somebody else. Maybe he had come here to look at the palms, and to warm himself up, just like Stanley had done.

Almost twenty minutes went past. Outside the misted-up windows, the sun abruptly swirled itself behind the clouds, like a temperamental opera singer flouncing off the stage, and without warning the afternoon turned photographic and hard. Inside the Palm House, it was suddenly so gloomy that Stanley could scarcely see from one end to the other.

He looked up at the catwalk. Knitted Hood had turned into a fretted shadow; but as far as Stanley could make out, he was still there, still motionless, still waiting. Stanley tugged his handkerchief out of his pocket and wiped the perspiration from his face. His shirt was clinging to his back, and his handmade Alan McAfee shoes felt as if they were totally sodden.

Another five minutes went by. Then Stanley heard the door of the Palm House open, and close again. A woman in a long black silky-finished coat came rustling through the palms. Stanley couldn't distinguish her face very well in the shadows, but her hair gleamed thin and fine and very long, so blond that it was almost silver. Her shoes tip-tapped softly on the wet flagged pathways between the plants.

She came directly to the center of the Palm House, around the pillars, and suddenly stopped, only four or five feet away from Stanley's hiding place, although she didn't look at him. She appeared to be young middle-aged, late thirties or early forties, with the kind of high-cheekboned Zsa Zsa Gabor looks that had been popular in Hollywood in the 1960s. Stanley caught the scent of Giorgio perfume, Beverly Hills' best.

The woman hesitated, and looked around, and then up at the towering palms.

"You're interested in palms, Mr. Eisner?" the woman asked him, still without looking at him. She emphasized the word "interested."

Stanley stared at her. "You know me?" he asked her, keeping his voice to a hoarse whisper.

She turned and smiled. Her eyes were the palest amber, the color of agates.

"Of course I know you. Why are you so surprised? You are a musician of international standing. There is a photograph of you in the *Encyclopedia of Music.*"

Stanley shrugged. "I don't know. I'm sorry. To me that seems like some kind of exceptional talent, you know? To be able to walk right into a tropical greenhouse in London and recognize a musician from San Francisco without even taking a breath. I mean, I'm a classical violinist, not a pop star."

"You have other qualities, Mr. Eisner."

Stanley quickly glanced up at the catwalk to see if Knitted Hood was still there. The Palm House was so shadowy now that it was impossible to tell for sure. But he hadn't heard Knitted Hood's cloglike feet on the iron staircases that led down from the catwalks, and he hadn't heard either of the doors opening, so it was pretty safe to assume that Knitted Hood was still here.

"Listen," he said softly, making a patting gesture in the air with his hand. "I'm very flattered that you recognized me, ma'am. But I'm a little preoccupied right now. I'm sort of waiting for someone."

The woman made no attempt to move on. "Palms are worth studying, you know," she told him. "We get raffia from palms, we get oil from palms, we get sago from palms. They are all so different, yet so alike. Look at this huge tree here, *Lodoicea*, the coco-de-mer. It has a nut which weighs several kilograms. Yet it belongs to the same family as this long thin rattan, of the genus *Calamus*, which can grow to a length of one hundred and fifty meters, occasionally more."

"That's very interesting, ma'am, very nice," Stanley told her. "The only trouble is—I really have to wait for this person—and if I miss them—"

"He has already left," the woman replied.

Stanley coughed. "I beg—I beg your pardon? What?"

"The person for whom you are waiting. He has already left."

Stanley gingerly parted the palm fronds with his hand. Then he stepped out and peered directly up at the catwalk. The woman was right: Knitted Hood was no longer there.

"Son of a bitch," Stanley muttered under his breath.

The woman watched him calmly and without comment as he hurried across to the spiral staircase and clanged noisily up to the place where Knitted Hood had been standing. It was unnervingly high up here, overlooking the tops of the palms, like an aerial view of the jungle. Sparrows twittered all around him, rushing from one perch to another in noisy flocks. He looked from one end of the Palm House to the other, but there was no sign of Knitted Hood anywhere. No movement, no shadow. Only the darkly-steaming palm leaves, and the trailing creepers, and the first flicker of lightning in the far distance, toward the southwest.

"Did you see him go?" Stanley demanded, his voice echoing.

The woman shook her head. "He decided to leave, that's all; and so he left."

"I don't understand."

"There is much that you don't understand; but you will."

"What, are you a friend of his or something?"

"Of course not. But come down here, and I will tell you."

Stanley took one last look around the upper galleries of the Palm House; then slowly he descended the iron stairs. The woman was waiting for him when he came down.

"I think you owe me some kind of an explanation," he told her. His voice was trembling.

The woman smiled; and Stanley saw then that there was more to her personality than her appearance had led him to think. She may have looked like Zsa Zsa Gabor, but she knew who he was; and she knew her botany; and she knew where Knitted Hood had gone, too; and even the fact that Stanley had been looking for him.

"Mr. Eisner," the woman told him, "I owe you nothing at all. On the contrary, it is *you* who owe something to me; or, at least, you owe something to those whom I represent."

She held out her hand. Her fingernails were very long and painted Hawaiian pink. She wore five or six diamond rings on one hand alone; peculiarly ostentatious for a woman whose words were so subtle and oblique. Stanley noticed one thing: the skin on the back of her hands was very taut and smooth, suggesting that she was much younger than she had first appeared. Eve had sat in front of the dressing-table mirror every evening, pinching the skin on the back of her hands. The time it took for the pinch of skin to return to normal was an infallible giveaway to a person's genuine age. "You can tighten your face, you can lift up your boobs, but you can never change your hands." That was Eve's theory, anyway; and whenever Stanley was introduced to women these days, he found himself discreetly checking the backs of their hands.

Stanley said, "I don't even know who you are. How can I owe you anything?"

"Come for a walk," the woman suggested. "I will show you where you can find the person you have been looking for; and I will also tell you why I have come to meet you."

"Now, wait up a goddamn minute, will you?" Stanley objected. "I don't even know who you are. I mean, for all I know, you could be this guy's friend—accomplice, or whatever."

"If you come with me, I will try my best to explain everything," the woman told him. Stanley found it impossible to place her accent. It certainly wasn't British; and it wasn't French; but it was flatter and more precise than any American regional variations that he had ever heard; an unidentifiable mixture of gentrified Charleston and privately-educated Swiss. Posh, but somehow lacking in poshness because it boasted no recognized background.

Stanley wiped his forehead with the back of his hand. "Okay," he agreed at last. There didn't seem to be anything else that he could do.

They left the Palm House and walked around the lake. Behind them, the sky was as black as Bibles, and there were spatters of rain in the wind. The swans had left the water and were strutting inelegantly across the pathway. The woman's coat flapped and rustled as she walked. She said, "You don't have to hurry, he's not going very far."

"Do you know who he is?" Stanley asked her.

"I know *what* he is."

"All right, then, what is he?"

"He's what we call a Carrier. There are ten or eleven of them at least, perhaps more."

"A Carrier? You mean like a truck driver?"

"No, Mr. Eisner. Not like a truck driver. He carries a virus, of sorts. A kind of disease."

Stanley swallowed. "A disease? He has a *disease*? Is it catching?"

"That depends."

Stanley stopped, and the woman stopped, too, just outside the garden turnstiles. "Listen," he said, "don't think I'm being deliberately offensive here, but do you mind telling me who the hell you are? You didn't come here by accident, did you? How come you know so much about this Knitted Hood guy, this Carrier? How come you know so much about *me*?"

"You've been having dreams, haven't you?" the woman asked him. The wind blew her fine blond hair across her face.

Stanley gave her an almost imperceptible nod, which he tried to turn into a shake of denial, but too late.

"Dreams of sickness? Dreams of plague?"

"Yes," Stanley told her. He felt disturbed, panicky. Dr. Patel had told him he was clear of any infection, but he hadn't been feeling particularly well, and the dreams had unsettled him even during the day. He didn't even have to close his eyes to recall the way those corpses had come sliding off the push-cart, like a load of dead fish. The mother's face, agonized. The smudged black eyes of the baby.

The woman said, "You feel anxious, am I correct? Your blood feels as if it's full of tiny prickly particles? You feel giddy and disoriented, as if you're jet-lagged?"

"What is it?" Stanley insisted, "Does it get worse? How serious is it?"

The woman glanced toward the turnstiles. "We'd better be moving on, we don't want to miss him."

"You know what happened to me, don't you?" said Stanley, breathless, keeping close beside her. "You know why I'm following this son of a bitch?"

"Yes, I know," the woman replied. "I knew about it almost as soon as it happened. That was how you contracted your infection."

"But what the hell is it? Is it some kind of blood disease, what?"

"It's a form of immune deficiency."

Stanley's lips felt numb, as if his mouth had been anesthetized. "You mean I have AIDS?"

"You have an infection. It has parallels with AIDS in some respects. It's passed on by sexual intercourse, particularly by anal intercourse, but also by biting and by sharing of hypodermic needles.''

"It's similar to AIDS but it's not AIDS, is that it?''

"That's right.''

"Is it as serious as AIDS?''

They had left the gardens now and were waiting by the curb to cross the main road outside. Buses and trucks bellowed past them, blowing up showers of fine grit.

The woman said, "I would be deceiving you, Mr. Eisner, if I pretended that it wasn't.''

"Does it have a name?''

"In the seventeenth century they called it the Bard's Disease, because Shakespeare was supposed to have died of it. It has also been called the Haitian Pox. There is no question at all that Mozart was infected.''

"I never heard of it. Believe me, I never even heard of it.''

"It's been lying dormant for a long time, Mr. Eisner. There haven't been any major outbreaks recorded since the late 1600s. One or two isolated cases, yes; some of them well recorded; but nothing widespread.''

Stanley swallowed again. He felt as if he were suddenly going mad. "Is it, uh . . . ? This—what—Bard's Disease? Is it terminal? I mean, is there any chance of recovery? Any kind of treatment?''

"That will depend on you; and those who are chosen to help you.''

"I don't understand.''

"You will, Mr. Eisner, if you trust me.''

"Trust you? I don't even *know* you!''

The woman, unexpectedly, smiled at him. "You're *sure* you don't know me?''

"Why should I know you? Are you a doctor? A reporter? This doesn't make any kind of sense to me at all!''

"Please, Mr. Eisner, don't get angry. I'm here to help you, if I can; as well as to ask for *your* help, in return.''

"Help? You want *my* help? You're telling me I've contracted some fatal disease that Shakespeare died of, I mean what kind of crap is that? *Shakespeare?* And then you want me to help you?''

A tour coach had parked across the street, *"Glückliche*

Fahrt, Düsseldorf,'' and as they disembarked, a group of German teenagers turned to stare at them as if they were a local tourist attraction: Stanley's sudden anger, the woman's dated beauty.

"Mr. Eisner—" the woman cautioned him. "Please, don't get upset."

"Don't get upset? What are you trying to do to me here?"

"Mr. Eisner, the Carrier didn't attack you at random. He knew who you were. He was waiting for you."

"He purposely wanted to infect a violinist, is that it?"

"Aaron, you're much, much more than just a violinist."

Stanley stared at her. "What did you call me?"

"Aaron. It's your name, isn't it?"

"Sure, yes, but how did *you* know?" Stanley retorted. "The only living people who know that my name is Aaron are my mother and my sister. That's it, nobody else."

"Please, Mr. Eisner, I'm sorry," the woman soothed him. "You were named Aaron, but everybody called you Stanley when you were little because you had such a squeaky voice and your hair stuck up like Stan Laurel's, and you just—well, you just *looked* like Stan Laurel."

"How the *hell* did you know that?" Stanley raged at her.

"Will you stop being angry and let me explain?"

"I don't think I want to stop being angry."

"Mr. Eisner—Stanley . . . listen, let's just carry on walking. Walk, listen. Don't be angry. The truth is, you've become involved in something that you can't really deal with, not on your own, and not as yourself."

"Not as myself? What's that supposed to mean?"

The woman took his arm; the gesture was sisterly and peculiarly comforting. They were walking up a side street now, between dull big Victorian houses and rows of blistered plane trees.

"My name is Madeleine Springer," the woman explained.

"You're not British, are you?" Stanley asked her.

"Not exactly. But not exactly American, either. But that really doesn't matter so much. What matters is who *you* are; and who your ancestors were."

"Why should that matter?"

Madeleine Springer smiled at him. "To most people, Stanley, it isn't important who their ancestors were. Miners, weavers, farmers, what does it matter? Their skills and their failings died when they died, and they were never remembered. But some ancestors had a special duty and accepted special obligations—not only on their own behalf but on behalf of all of their descendants, forever."

Stanley had a sudden urge to escape, to pull himself free from Madeleine Springer's arm and walk briskly away. In most respects, however, she appeared to be sane; and more than anything else it was this penetrating sanity that kept him from leaving. He found the obscurity of her conversation infuriating. He was a man who was used to saying what he had to say, in the simplest words he could think of. Her patronizing attitude annoyed him, too. Yet she was calm and beautiful, and she had already convinced him that what she had to tell him was important: life-and-death important.

He just wished that she would come out with it direct. His mind was in enough of a turmoil, holding on to his sense of reality, holding on to his musical talent, trying to deal with Eve and Leon and all the physical and emotional consequences of Knitted Hood's attack; and there would be even more for him to cope with if Madeleine Springer was telling the truth and Knitted Hood had infected him with some AIDS-like disease.

He said sharply, "You're talking about *my* ancestors, or what?"

"Of course."

"My ancestors had some special duty, and they passed that duty on to me?"

"Yes, in a word."

Stanley stopped beside a low brick garden wall and a privet hedge clogged with discarded ice-lolly wrappers. "Listen, Ms. Springer, I don't even know who my ancestors were. My family goes back as far as Hamburg, Germany, in 1880 something. We were emigrants. That's all I know."

"Your ancestors, Stanley, go back much further; to 1620 at least; and to London. Thirteen generations ago, Jacob Eisner was a ragpicker in Whitechapel."

Stanley lifted both hands in mock surrender. "Ms. Springer,

this is really very entertaining, but I think that you've mistaken me for somebody else. I'm a Jewish American, my grandfather came from Hamburg, my family have no connection with Britain whatsoever. I'm here on a professional exchange scheme, that's all. A British musician went to San Francisco, I came here."

"How did I find you?" Madeleine Springer challenged him. "How did I know your name was Aaron?"

"I don't know, Ms. Springer; and I don't really think that I care. Maybe you read the *Sun* newspaper and have a perverted interest in men who have been assaulted by other men. I don't know. But I think I'm going to leave now, and go back to my apartment, and pour myself a very large drink."

Madeleine Springer suddenly switched her gaze to look over Stanley's shoulder. "There he is," she said, her voice quiet but very clear.

Stanley immediately turned around. On the opposite corner of the street stood a large brindled-brick house, with broken guttering and a sadly-neglected garden. But Stanley had turned just a split second too late to see anyone entering it. All he saw was the weather-faded front door slamming shut, its knocker barking once. The lights switched on, then lights switched off.

"That was him?" Stanley demanded.

"Tall, with a gray raincoat and a gray woollen balaclava?" Madeleine Springer asked him.

"That's it, kind of a hood."

"Yes, that was him. He was the one who attacked you, wasn't he?"

"Does he *live* there?" said Stanley.

Madeleine smiled faintly at the brindled-brick house. A sign on the half-collapsed front gate announced that somebody had once named it "Tennyson." "Nobody *lives* there, Mr. Eisner. Not in the sense that you think of anybody living there."

"What is it—a what-do-you-call-it—a squat? I mean, if that's his permanent address—if he comes back every night—"

Madeleine said, "It's no use calling the police, Mr. Eisner. The police couldn't find him, not in there, and neither could you. I can't stop him. The police can't stop him. *You* can't stop him, not as you are. You could search that house until doomsday; and he simply wouldn't be there."

"You told me he just went in through the door."

"That's right, he did. And you were waiting for him in the Palm House."

Stanley thrust his hands into his pockets. "Ms. Springer, I think I've had it up to here with this game. I don't know who you are, or why you're here, but enough is enough."

Almost immediately a black taxi came around the corner with its For Hire light on. Stanley raised his arm and gave the cabbie his special Broadway-after-the-theater whistle; the one that was guaranteed to stop a Doberman pinscher in its tracks. The taxi pulled into the curb, and Stanley opened the door.

At the last moment, however, he relented a little. He turned to Madeleine Springer, opened his wallet, and took out one of his cards. "Look, listen—if you want to call me sometime . . . provided you want to tell me something that makes some kind of sense . . . ."

Madeleine Springer smiled and shook her head. "Don't worry, Aaron, I know where to find you."

He frowned at her. "You're not upset, are you?"

"Of course not," she replied.

"You knew that I was going to lose my temper, didn't you?"

"I would have lost my temper, too, if I had been you."

"Then what happens next?" he asked her.

"What happens next is that you go home, and you think about what I have told you. Then, when you are ready, we will talk some more."

"You know that I don't want to believe you."

"Of course you don't."

Without saying anything further, Stanley climbed into the taxi and slammed the door. "Langton Street," he told the driver.

They drove away. Stanley turned and looked out of the taxi's rear window. Madeleine Springer remained where she was on the sidewalk, not smiling, her hair lifted by the wind. For a flicker of a moment, Stanley thought, *Yes, you're right, I do know you. I've met you before.* But then the feeling vanished, and the cabbie was saying, "Langton Street, that's just past the World's End, innit, mate?" and all that Stanley could do was sit back in his seat and think about Knitted Hood, the Carrier; and the real or imagined infection known as the Bard's Disease.

THREE
Violin Song

BACK AT STANLEY'S APARTMENT, A LETTER WAS WAITING FOR him, hand-delivered. He didn't open it immediately, but tossed it on to the table in the dining area and left it there while he drew the curtains and switched on the fire. In the left-hand corner, the envelope carried an embossed treble clef and the name "Kensington Chamber Orchestra." Whatever Frederick Orme had to say, Stanley didn't want to know what it was; not yet.

He went to the kitchen, chipped three or four ice cubes out of the freezer with a dinner knife, and poured himself a jumbo-sized glass of Wodka Wyborowa. Then he went back into the living room and put on a CD of Handel's *Messiah*.

He had the strangest feeling that ever since Knitted Hood had attacked him, he had lost control of his own destiny—that it didn't matter where he went or what he did, he was playing out a part in a carefully-arranged plan. Why had he gone to Kew Gardens, for instance, when he could have gone anywhere, from Richmond Park to Hampstead Heath?

Or perhaps Knitted Hood would have been waiting for him

on Hampstead Heath, too, with Madeleine Springer not far behind.

He sat down in his armchair and took a large mouthful of vodka. Tomorrow he would go back to Kew, he decided, and take a look at the house in which Knitted Hood was supposed to live—or *not* live, however Madeleine Springer's words could be interpreted.

Hallelujah! sang the Handel chorus, *Hallelujah! Hallelujah!*

Stanley drank more vodka and loosened his necktie. He felt slightly feverish, and although he had been trying to persuade himself all afternoon that the prickling sensation in his blood was less uncomfortable than it had been before, it was still noticeable, and if it was anything at all, it was slightly worse.

Hallelujah! screamed the chorus. *Hallelujah!*

Although he couldn't understand why, he found the singing irritating. What the hell did they think they were doing, screeching out their adoration like that, to some completely illusory God? They sounded worse than orangutans screeching in the trees, and just as mindless.

Hallelujah! Hallelujah! Halle-loo-oo-jah!

Stanley stood up again. He went to the sideboard and unscrewed the top of the vodka bottle and poured himself another large drink. He was confused and irritated, and the bottle rattled against the side of the glass. He had always adored the *Messiah* in the past. Why did it grate on him so much now? Yet the longer it went on, the more it annoyed him, almost as if the chorus were insulting him personally by praising the Lord.

He crossed the room and opened the curtains a little way, so that he could see outside. Maybe Knitted Hood was prowling around again. Maybe that was what was causing his blood to prickle and his nerves to scrape like a badly-tuned violin. But outside in the sodium-orange street, there was nobody. Only parked cars, and a cat that fled across the intersection like a drop of mercury pouring across an orange carpet.

I am the pestilence that was promised, Knitted Hood had warned him.

He stood staring at the empty street for minute after minute, his teeth clenched together, while the chorus sang *Hallelujah* and his hand gripped the curtain so tightly that he heard the metal curtain hooks tearing one by one out of the fabric binding.

King of kings! Hallelujah! Hallelujah!

He couldn't stand it. It was worse than listening to a thousand knives scraped across a thousand plates. It wasn't just cacophonous, either. It was insulting; and it was *painful*. It made his blood feel like barbed wire, racing viciously furiously through his arteries, snagging and tearing at his veins, all the way down his legs and his arms, around his shoulders, into his neck, ripping at the membranes of his brain, catching and snagging at his heart muscles.

He tried to control himself. He squeezed his eyes tight shut and bit the flesh inside his mouth until blood-streaked saliva began to creep down his chin. He uttered an extraordinary noise: halfway between a groan and a deep hum. Then everything burst.

He stormed across the room, heaved up the hi-fi, and smashed it down on the table. The CD gave a single warped shriek and stopped. Stanley tore out all of the hi-fi's wire, lifted it over his head, and threw it across the room, so that it hit the doorjamb with a deafening crash and tumbled over and over into the kitchen.

He stood in the middle of the room, panting and shivering. *I am the pestilence that was promised!* He felt as if he had been running hard for six or seven blocks, his mouth parched, his breathing harsh, his heart pounding. Very slowly, rubbing his upper arms like a man trying to reassure himself that he was still real, he sank to his knees, and remained on his knees.

What's happening to me? I used to adore Handel. The Messiah *used to bring tears to my eyes. Now it sounds lewd and discordant, an outpouring of smutty absurdity, set to music. King of kings, what kind of shit was that?*

After a long time, he grasped the arm of the sofa and levered himself up into a standing position again. He turned and went back to the window. He had tugged the curtain so violently that half of it was hanging down and could no longer be drawn all the way across. He tried, feeling irritated and petulant, but all he succeeded in doing was tearing more of it down.

Langton Street remained orange-lit and deserted. "What's happening to you?" Stanley asked himself, out loud this time, as if he were somebody else. *Am I really sick, or is this nothing more than delayed shock? Dr. Patel explained that people in shock can suffer strange changes in personality. They can become strangers to themselves, as well as to other people.*

He swallowed the rest of his vodka and retched loudly, bringing some of it back up into his mouth, awash with half-digested shepherd's pie, from the lunch he had eaten at the Bull's Head. Strangely, it tasted good. Sour and thick, a soup of alcohol and potato and grainy fragments of ground lamb, which Gordon had called "mince." He swallowed it back slowly, relishing it. *That's better. Who cares what doctors think? Dr. Patel can go screw himself. Madeleine Springer can go screw herself. The whole screwing world can go screw itself.*

He went back to the sideboard to refill his glass, his tongue still probing fragments of sour mince from the side of his mouth. As he unscrewed the cap of the Wyborowa bottle, he looked down and saw the letter from Frederick Orme. He turned it this way and that as he poured out more vodka; then he ripped the envelope open with his teeth and shook the letter out one-handed.

Dear Stanley: We have arranged a magnificent charity concert at the Albert Hall on March 8, comprising all of Mozart's six string quintets. The concert will benefit the National Society for the Prevention of Cruelty to Children, and we are hoping that at least one member of the Royal Family will agree to attend. This concert would be a most auspicious and fitting occasion for your return to the orchestra, and I am hoping—"

Slowly, Stanley crumpled up the letter and tossed it across the living room. Who the hell did Frederick Orme think he was? When Stanley had been hurt and degraded, Frederick Orme had given him nothing. Nothing but a bunch of five forced daffodils and a cretinous book of short stories. But it was different now. Now that his rape had been forgotten by the daily press, Frederick Orme wanted him back. *A most auspicious and fitting occasion*, bullshit.

He took a large mouthful of vodka, swilling it around his mouth before he swallowed it. The whole world was crowded with liars and idiots and sycophants. There was no future in it, everybody knew that. We were all wallowing in our own shit and our own self-righteousness. How could anybody sing "Hallelujah!" when we were up to our necks in our own sewage, and even the air we took into our lungs to praise this so-called Lord of Creation was unfit for human consumption?

The world was a joke. A ridiculous maniacal joke. And if Knitted Hood had infected him, and he passed on that same infection to somebody else; and if that somebody else passed on the same infection to two somebody elses; and those two somebody elses passed it on to eight somebody elses; and so on; forever; until the whole damned world was infected and damned; then what of it?

He went angrily back to the window, tore down the curtain completely, and swirled it across the room like a heavy brown cloak.

When he turned back to the window, however, he stopped absolutely still. A cold prickling feeling brushed down the back of his neck. His hyperventilated breathing abruptly quietened; so much so that his lungs felt starved of oxygen, and he started to pant.

Langton Street was still orange-lit and lined with parked cars. But down the center of the street, very slowly, with all the determination of great disgust and inconsolable grief, a girl was pushing a handcart heaped high with lolling bodies. The corpses were so silvery-white that they were almost fluorescent, like the skin of decaying mackerel. Their eyes were dark with the anger of dying. A tousle-bearded man, his head hanging so that it shook from side to side with every jolt of the pushcart, a silent but endlessly-repeated denial of his own extinction. A young girl, not more than fourteen years old, her arms crossed over her chest like sticks, her hair wild and dark and matted with grease. A woman, her face contorted in desperation, one leg twisted beneath her in a posture that would have been impossible for anyone living. Babies—who knew how many babies?—their fat white limbs heaped together like a plateful of slippery cod's roes.

The girl who was pushing the handcart was dressed in a long brown skirt, so heavy with damp and dirt that it dragged along the road surface. Her face was half shadowed by a brown linen headscarf, but she was startlingly beautiful, in a tragic hollow-cheeked way; the kind of girl you could sit and watch and wonder about for hours. Her expression was extraordinary. In the whole of his life, Stanley had never seen anybody look like that before. Exhausted but uplifted. Nauseated but strong. She pushed her grisly load with such terrible calmness that Stanley felt ashamed of himself for having insulted God and for having believed that the world He had created was such a cruel joke.

He remained where he was; quite still; trembling; with tears running down his cheeks. Already, he could faintly distinguish the grinding of the pushcart's wheels; and he had never heard anything so terrible. Grind, grind, grind. Metal rims on tarmacadam. And the lifeless jiggling of all of those bodies, as if they were jostling and pushing each other in rage and humiliation, because they were dead.

Stanley was still staring out of the window when his doorbell rang. His mouth flooded with saliva. He turned around. He wasn't expecting anybody. He thought for one terrifying moment that it was the girl with the pushcart—that she had somehow managed to enter his house and climb the stairs with her ghastly burden of bodies. He turned back to the window. She had gone; and the grinding of her pushcart's wheels had died away.

The doorbell rang again, longer this time. Stanley said, "Coming." Then, when it rang again, "I'm coming, for God's sake!"

He opened the door. The landing was so dark that at first he couldn't see who it was. A shadowy figure with a pale face. He didn't speak, couldn't speak. His whole being felt clenched up like a fist. Then she leaned forward a little and asked him, "Is it awkward? I only come to see you on the off chance, like."

"It's you," he said in a watery voice.

She peered into his apartment. "Can I come in? I was supposed to be going to a party with Glenys but she's got ever such a stinker."

"A stinker?" Stanley asked her in disbelief.

"You know, a cold. So I thought to meself, why not see 'ow poor old wossname's getting on? Stanley."

"Come in," Stanley invited her. He had been so sure that she was the girl with the pushcart that he still hadn't stopped shivering. But when she stepped into the hallway, she was so clearly Angie Dunning that he felt immediately calmer, almost himself again. He closed the door and asked her, "How about a drink?"

"I'll 'ave a glass of wine if you've got one. If not, cup of tea'll do."

"I've got some Pouilly-Fumé."

"Pooey Foomay? Not sure I like the sound of *that*."

"It's dry white wine, French."

"All right, then."

She was obviously dressed for a party. She took off her black ankle-length coat and threw it over the arm of the sofa. Underneath she was wearing a short tight dress of red ribbed wool, and red panty hose, and red shoes with heels like Lucrezia Borgia's daggers. Her wrists jangled with cheap chunky chromium-plated bracelets.

Stanley went into the kitchen. The smashed hi-fi lay on its side in the middle of the floor. He heaved it aside with his foot and opened the icebox. Angie stood in the doorway and said, "What 'appened to your record player? You drop it?"

Stanley took out the chilled bottle of wine and filled a large Boda goblet with it. "I threw it," he told her. He might just as well tell her the truth.

"What, didn't it work or nothing?"

"It worked fine. I didn't like the record it was playing, that's all."

Angie took her wine and gave him an exaggeratedly taken-aback look. "Bit drastic, wasn't it?" she asked him.

He guided her back into the living room again. "I've been having what you might call moods."

"What, since that bloke attacked you?"

Stanley nodded. He poured himself another vodka and sat down next to the fire. Angie perched herself on the edge of the sofa, hitching her dress up dangerously high. "Paul has moods," she remarked.

"Your boyfriend?"

"I've been going out with 'im ever since I left school. I think he thinks we're going to get married or something."

"And are you?"

"Not likely. A stupid wally like 'im? Anyway, I want to 'ave a bit of fun before I get married. I met one of my best friends from school just before Christmas, and she 'ad two kids already, and a pushchair, and she looked like she'd been pulled through an 'edge backwards. And she used to be ever so fashionable.''

"You don't have to get married at all, you know," Stanley told her. "It's not obligatory."

"Are you married?"

"I was. I'm divorced now."

"Got any kids?"

"One son."

Angie crossed and uncrossed her slippery red-sheathed legs and laughed. "Is that your way of telling me that you're old enough to be my father?"

"Maybe. But that doesn't mean that I don't wish I was twenty years younger."

" 'Ow old would you be if you was twenty years younger?"

Stanley swallowed vodka. Angie really amused him. "Twenty-four."

"Still too old," she told him.

Stanley laughed. "God almighty." And then thought, *God Almighty, am I really that old? This girl makes me feel like I'm ready to be laid out.*

She stood up, pranced over to the window, and looked out. "What 'appened to the curtain?" she wanted to know. "Did you 'ave another mood? Didn't like the way it was drawn or something?"

Stanley gave her a sloping smile. "Something like that."

He watched her over the rim of his vodka glass as she continued to poke around the living room, picking up ornaments, picking up his gray fedora hat. In hatless London, Stanley hadn't yet had the nerve to wear his fedora, but Angie put it on top of her own blond firework of a hairstyle, and he had to admit that she looked good in it. In fact, he had to admit that she looked good, period. He found his yes straying around the curves of her hips; at the way her dress clung to the tops of her thighs. Her legs were so slender that there was an inverted triangle of clear space in between her thighs, wide enough to accommodate a man's hand, without it touching the sides. That had always turned him on, and it turned him on now.

"I always fancied a titfer," she said. She stood in front of

the mirror, pouting her lips and tilting his hat this way and
that. When she raised her arms, Stanley could see how large
her breasts were—large and high and almost impossibly firm.
Eve's were small and droopy and slanted, with olive-dark nipples. He had never liked Eve's breasts. In fact, he had mentioned it to her, in a letter about Leon's support money. *P.S.
Even your tits were dull.* He wished now that he hadn't written
it, but he supposed that a certain amount of craziness was
always permissible during divorce, on both sides. Eve had
probably thought that his ass was dull, too, although she had
never said so.

Angie had turned around and was giving him a questioning
look. "You look like you're thinking about something," she
told him.

"I am. I'm wondering whether my ex-wife thought my ass
was boring."

Angie turned back to the mirror. "You've gone bonkers, if
you ask me."

"Yes, maybe I have." He was watching the way the hem of
her dress lifted a fraction of an inch over the rounded cheeks
of her bottom, whenever she raised her arms. He had never
felt this way before. Girls had aroused him, for sure. Girls on
the beach, girls who asked for his autograph, and when he was
twenty-seven he had fallen so furiously for a lady cellist from
the Limoges Baroque Ensemble (bobbed chestnut hair that
swung when she played, classic nose, lips like pink satin cushions) that he had followed her home and played his violin for
her outside her front door. After ten minutes her scruffy husband had come out with a Gitanes between his lips and told
him to **** off, you *catiche*.

But the way that Angie was stimulating him was different.
He felt lustful, even violent. He could imagine himself seizing
hold of her, forcing her facedown over the sofa, and pulling
up her dress. He could imagine twisting her arms behind her
back and hurting her. He could imagine forcing her thighs
apart and pushing his fist inside her. Damp curls, slippery
knuckles, gasps of pain.

"Do you know what the time is?" she asked him.

His eyes refocused. He glanced at the clock above the fireplace. It had stopped. He looked down at his wristwatch. That

had stopped, too. He held it up to his ear and shook it. "I guess it's a little after eight."

"Do you fancy going for a drink?" Angie asked him.

"I don't know. I think I've drunk too much already."

" 'Ave you 'ad any tea yet?"

Stanley had learned enough about the English working class to know that "tea" meant a full-cooked early-evening meal, sausages and chips or fish fingers and chips or steakburger and chips.

"I haven't eaten since lunchtime," he told Angie. He kept shaking his watch, but it remained obstinately silent. A Jaeger-le-Coultre, too. It had stopped at the same time as the clock, 7:01.

He looked up. "What do you say we go get something to eat?" he suggested. "Do you like Thai?"

"Never 'ad it. But I'll eat anything. Paul calls me gannet-face."

They left Stanley's apartment and walked to the Busabong Restaurant in Fulham Road, only five minutes away. The night was clear but piercingly cold. Angie unselfconsciously held Stanley's hand as they crossed Limerston Street, as if she were his daughter, or even his girlfriend. He could feel that her nails were bitten down, and for some reason that made her all the more appealing. It was something to do with girlish innocence, he supposed. The child-woman.

In the restaurant, among the usual ethnic-restaurant paraphernalia of mock palm roofs and copper pots and tapestries, they sat on cushions on the floor in the *khan toke* style and ate the sour prawn soup called *tom yam kung* and the chili beef called *nua pad prik* and the chicken in peanut and coconut sauce called *kai penang*. Two Thai waiters changed into satin boxing shorts and gave a demonstration of kick boxing, perilously close to where they were sitting.

Angie liked the boxing (she clapped and cheered out loud) but she wasn't sure about the food. "It's ever so 'ot, some of it," she said. "Not '*ot* 'ot, like, but peppery 'ot. And I don't like this green stuff," which was fresh coriander. "Tastes like the inside of old ladies' 'andbags."

It was well past eleven by the time they left. They stood on the pavement outside the restaurant in the freezing wind, and Stanley said, "How about a nightcap?"

"No, thanks, Stanley," Angie told him with considerable kindness. She reached up and pecked him on the cheek. "I've got to get up early tomorrer. Thanks for the nosh, though."

"That's all right," Stanley replied. "Maybe you can cook me some tea sometime. Egg and chips?"

He whistled for a taxi; too loud the first time, because the cabbie gave him two fingers and drove past without stopping.

"Tell you what, Stanley," said Angie as he opened the door of a second taxi for her. "You come round next week and we'll 'ave bangers and mash."

Bangers and mash. That sounded exciting; like fireworks. Angie herself was a firework. He stood on the pavement waving to her as the taxi took her back to Chiswick. Pronounced *Chizzick*, thought Stanley. For the first time since he had arrived in London, he began to feel like a native, or at least an honorary native.

Perhaps he was growing acclimatized. Perhaps, on the other hand, London had worked its baleful influence on him, like an old gray grandmother who takes in orphaned children from all over the world, but then refuses to let them go.

He was sitting up in bed at two-twenty A.M. reading *Our Mutual Friend* when he thought he heard the street door open and close. He lowered his book, took off his reading glasses, and listened. Nothing. Only that low, endless muttering of traffic.

He was too tired to sleep; too tired and too distressed. He had tried switching off his bedside lamp and closing his eyes, but every time he did so, his blood seemed to prickle furiously, so that he felt as if he could scratch his flesh to ribbons, and all he could think about was Madeleine Springer in her rustling black coat, and Knitted Hood, perching up on the catwalk of Kew Gardens' Palm House like some hideous worm-ridden bird of prey.

He kept picturing that house of brindled brick, with its shabby and derelict front garden. He kept hearing the grinding of metal-bound wheels.

Once tonight he had climbed out of bed and walked through to the kitchen, just to stare at the smashed-up hi-fi lying on the floor. Had he really thrown it himself? Had he really torn down the drapes? Maybe Angie was right. Maybe he was going bonkers.

Or maybe Madeleine Springer was right, and he was infected.

He picked up his book again. *"So deeply engaged had the living-dead man been, in thus communing with himself, that he had regarded neither the wind nor the way, and had resisted the former as instinctively as he had pursued the latter."*

He heard footsteps, somewhere in the house. The creaking of early-Victorian floorboards. By American standards, this house was old when *Our Mutual Friend* was written. Charles Dickens himself might well have passed it, glanced up at Stanley's window, and never known that a hundred years in the future Stanley would be sitting up in bed with his book on his knees, listening for footsteps, listening for doors that opened and closed.

He heard the front door of his apartment open. The chain slide in its socket. The chain swing free.

How could the chain swing free?

He closed the book and laid it on the right-hand nightstand, next to his alarm clock and his empty vodka glass and his leather-framed photograph of Leon. Eve had always said that Leon looked just like him, "poor boy." The bedroom, like the living room, was decorated in dull expensive browns. Brown hessian walls, brown curtains, and a beige shag-pile carpet that was so matted that it looked like the coat of an Old English sheepdog. Dull brown lithographs all around.

He heard somebody walking along the hallway.

"Who's there?" he called out.

There was no reply.

"Who's there? Is anyone there?"

Still there was no reply.

He looked around, half panicking, for some kind of weapon. On the other side of the bed, on the left-hand nightstand, was a heavy ashtray of brown and white onyx. He leaned across the bed, straining his chest muscles as he did so, and hefted it up in his hand.

"All right!" he shouted, feeling bolder now. "Who's there?"

His bedroom door, which had been two or three inches ajar,

was pushed open a little wider. Stanley knelt up in the center of the bed and eased the ashtray back in his hand like a baseball pitcher. He used to be terrific at baseball, in high school. Anybody who walked into the room right now was going to get the hardest-hitting surprise of their whole goddamned life. Solid ashtray, with the mustard on it.

A face peeked around the door. It was Angie, firework hairstyle and spiky black eyelashes and everything.

Stanley, surprised, relieved, lowered the ashtray and sat back. "Angie? What the hell are you doing here? I thought the goddamn door was locked."

"It was." She grinned. Then she came prancing right into the middle of the room, and she was wearing nothing but her shiny red panty hose and her skyscraper-heeled shoes.

Stanley stared at her. His mouth changed shape, ready to say something, ready to protest, ready to ask her what the hell she thought she was doing, but words didn't seem like enough. All he could do was to watch her in fascinated perplexity as she came right up to the end of the bed and bowed to him.

Her skin was pale and soft; so pale that it gleamed. Her breasts had looked large beneath her tight red woollen dress; but bare they looked even larger, with wide magnolia-pink areolas, and the faintest tracery of bluish veins, and a way of counter-swinging against the way that she moved that reminded Stanley of the French cellist's counter-swinging hair.

Her panty hose had the hard shine of scarlet nail varnish, giving the curves of her thighs and her bottom a gleaming emphasis that Stanley found startlingly erotic. Her pubic hair was trapped beneath the nylon in a fine fan-shape.

She betrayed no trace of shyness whatsoever. On the contrary, she seemed to be deliberately displaying herself. She giggled and swung her hips, and her breasts swung, too.

"Angie?" asked Stanley in disbelief.

"I thought you'd like me to play for you." Angie smiled. "You know, the gypsy violinist. Sorry I couldn't find a rose to grip between me choppers. All the shops was shut."

Like a conjuring trick, Angie produced from behind her back Stanley's Vuillaume violin. " 'Ere we are! What would you like me to play? 'Ow about ''Oo's Taking You 'Ome Tonight, 'Oo's the Lucky Gel?' "

Stanley lifted a cautioning hand. "Angie . . . come on now,
no playing around. That violin is worth more than fifteen thousand dollars. It was custom-made, okay? And that's a Tourte
bow, worth more than the goddamned violin."

"Oh, come on, Stanl-ee, don't be a spoilsport!" Angie
teased him. She lifted the violin and nestled it under her chin.

"Angie, please—that violin is so damned delicate!"

Stanley hop-vaulted across the bed in his pale blue Saks pajamas. But Angie stepped back, so that he couldn't reach her,
and immediately began to play. Not "Who's Taking You Home
Tonight?" or any other cockney ballad, but the *Allegro molto
appassionato* from Mendelssohn's violin concerto in E minor;
and played as exquisitely as Stanley had ever heard it, even
better than Anne-Sophie Mutter had played it with Herbert von
Karajan.

He stood up and watched Angie playing, transfixed. She kept
smiling and winking at him as she played, as if she had been
playing like this for years, as if it were all a huge joke. He
took another step towards her, but she took another step back.
He couldn't try to snatch the violin away from her; it was far
too fragile for that. His insurance company would go apeshit
if they found out that he had let anybody else breathe in the
same room as his violin, let alone *play* it.

Yet her playing was incredible. She made the strings weep
with emotion. He had heard the allegro a thousand times; he
had rehearsed and played it himself. But he had never heard
anything like this. It soared; it shrilled. It filled him with grief
and it filled him with delight. He fell to his knees in front of
her, staring at her. She brought the allegro up to its climax and
smiled down at him tartly. Why hadn't she told him before that
she could play like this? Why had she spent the whole of their
evening together talking about Paul and his secondhand Ford
Granada, and her friend what had the cold, and why she
wouldn't never go to an 'oliday camp for her 'olidays, never
again. "Bloody knocking-shops, those 'oliday camps, that's all
they are."

And yet she could play like this, without hesitation, without
rehearsal, on an unfamiliar, untuned violin!

He reached up and grasped her hips. The nylon of her panty
hose felt harsh and glossy and cheap. He dug his fingertips in

between her soft skin and the elasticized waistband, and rolled the waistband down, over her hips, down her thighs, until her legs were completely bared. He could feel the warmth radiating from her skin against his face. He disentangled her feet from the rolled-down nylon. She kept playing, her elbow vigorously sawing, her breasts swaying, her entire body tense with passion.

Stanley cupped her right buttock in his upraised hand, drew her towards him. He kissed her soft, flat stomach. He slid the tip of his tongue through her pubic hair and into the liquid warmth of her vulva. She shuddered; she smiled; but she continued to play.

He licked her, persistently and quickly. All of a sudden she stopped playing and lowered the violin. The silence fell around them like a cloak.

He closed his eyes. Her liquids coursed down his chin. Her thighs were tensed. One bitten finger tapped and scratched at the strings of his Vuillaume, off-key, irritating, but peculiarly arousing, too.

And we are cutting a swathe . . . tra la la, tra la la . . . through the world . . . tra la la, tra la la . . .

She opened wider and wider like a soft, sweet-tasting oyster. The muscles in her thighs were so taut that they trembled. Then she whispered something that sounded like *"Oh, deus,"* and dropped quaking to her knees, her cheek against the carpet, her arms outstretched, panting, her pale white bottom lifted.

Now Stanley rose to his feet, stripped back his pajama top, pulled open the fly of his pajama pants. Brandishing his raging crimson-headed penis, he forced himself violently into her, so harshly that she cried out. But all that Stanley could hear was the thundering of blood against his eardrums, like tropical rain cascading against a tarpaulin, and somewhere beyond this thundering, the Mendelssohn violin concerto scraping its elegant and painful way across his consciousness.

He clawed the firm white cheeks of her bottom as far apart as he could. He was confronted by a flower as small and as reticent as a hothouse pink. He pressed his fingertip against it, as if to protect it, while all the time he slogged himself in and out of her, his thick slippery shaft between her swollen slippery lips, setting up a rhythm that was insistent and crude and yet cheerful, too, like a crowd clapping loose-wristed at a Mardi Gras carnival.

She said nothing, but kept her cheek pressed against the carpet and her bottom dutifully uplifted. The bird-dog position, his college pal Meanie Collins had called that. He slogged in and out, gasping.

And, yea, we are cutting . . .

. . . a swathe through the world . . .

At the final instant, he took himself out, and his sperm surged all over her. It stuck to everything in hot strings and globules. He fell to the carpet beside her, gasping, pleased, exhausted. He hadn't had sex like that for years. Crude and brutal and completely demanding. No foreplay, no whispered promises. Just shoving and panting and gasping, and a climax like an automobile accident.

Her face was turned away from him. All he could see was the disorganized firework of her hair. He reached across the carpet and stroked it, and twisted it around his fingers.

"You're brilliant," he whispered. "Do you know that? You're brilliant. I never met anyone like you."

Angie said nothing, but her rib cage rose and fell as she slowly got her breath back.

"Are you going to play for me?" asked Stanley. "Why didn't you tell me you could play like that? You're amazing."

Still Angie said nothing, but continued to pant.

Stanley lifted himself up on one elbow. "Listen, what do you say we take a shower together, then have a drink? Or help ourselves to a drink first and take a shower afterwards?"

No response, only the rising and falling of those thin ribs.

Stanley said, "You know something . . . what you've done for me tonight—I haven't felt this way for years. You can play music like an angel, you make love like a devil."

He reached across and cupped her heavy bare breast in his hand. Her nipple tightened and crinkled. But she continued to pant, almost like an animal now; a dog left dehydrated in a sun-baked station wagon. Stanley began to have the smallest inclination that something was wrong; that he might have hurt her somehow; maybe not physically but emotionally. He had been rough, after all. He had dragged down her panty hose and forced himself into her. Maybe she wasn't used to that kind of treatment. Maybe she had hated it, even, but hadn't had the courage to tell him or the strength to resist him. *Oh, hell.* She spoke in a brash cockney accent, for sure—or what Stanley assumed was a brash cockney accent—and her behavior had seemed fairground-brazen, but she had played violin with stunning virtuosity. The kind of virtuosity that made tears spring into your eyes; the way that tears had sprung into Stanley's father's eyes, on his deathbed, when Stanley played him Al Jolson favorites, "Mammy" and "Wonder Bar." He could have read her all wrong. Maybe her nudity had been meant to be artistic, rather than erotic.

"Angie, listen to me, are you okay?"

She stirred. She growled, "I'm all right." Her voice sounded off-key, as if she were talking into a chloroformed handkerchief.

"Angie?"

"I'm all right, you bastard, how many more times?" she roared at him, and twisted her head around; and he wasn't looking at a young snub-nosed punk from Herbert Gardens, Chiswick, but the glacial celluloid face of Knitted Hood, with its perfect nose and its perfect cheeks and its perfect bow-shaped mouth, and its eyes as black as railroad tunnels rushing toward him.

Oh, God, I'm—

Oh, God, I'm—aaahhh!!

Intense shriveling terror wriggled through every nerve in his body. He rolled over, his arms flailing. His head struck the side of the bureau. He clambered to his feet, gasping, thrashing around for balance.

It took a moment or two before he realized that he was quite alone; that his bedroom was empty; that all he could hear was traffic and the sound of pop music from a room upstairs. Rick Astley, "Hold Me in Your Arms." A song so banal that Stanley couldn't distinguish it from rattling plumbing.

Angie was gone; his violin was gone. He looked down at himself. He was naked, with something wet and sticky drying on his thighs. *Oh, God. I've been dreaming. That was all a dream. I must be so goddamned frustrated—*

He bent over, feeling old, and picked up his pajamas. He tried to drag his pajama pants on to his right foot, but stepped

on the fabric and almost toppled over. In the end he had to sit
on the end of the bed and dress himself. He could smell the
pungent briny aroma of semen. He felt ashamed and shocked
and frightened all at once. It was almost impossible to believe
that his ferocious lovemaking with Angie had been nothing
more than a fleeting erotic dream. How could a dream talk like
that, play music like that? How could a dream *feel* like that,
so fleshy and substantial?

Quaking, he stood up, steadied himself, and walked across
the bedroom to the half-open door. He waited and listened.
"Angie?" he called out. His voice cracked, and he had to
cough to clear it. "Angie?"

There was no reply. Only the tinny *thump-thumpity-thump*
of Rick Astley. He was tempted to call Angie again, but then
he decided against it. If there was somebody else in his apartment, he didn't want to advertise where he was. It might be a
burglar. It might be Knitted Hood.

He eased open the bedroom door and went along the corridor to the living room. The brown furnishings were harshly lit
by sodium light. As far as he could see, there was nobody
there. He hesitated a moment longer; then made his way around
the back of the sofa to the chair where his violin case lay. He
stood staring at it for a while; then he flicked open the catches
and eased back the lid.

At first he couldn't understand what he was looking at. His
violin seemed to have turned pale, a ghost of itself. Yet it was
alive, too. It moved and shifted, as if he were looking at it
through rippling hot air, or underwater. He frowned and leaned
forward. It was only then that he understood that it was a
powdery outline of a violin, a dust-covered shell, almost completely devoured by writhing woodworm.

He let the lid drop. Dusty varnish puffed silently out of it
like talcum powder. *"Gevalt!"* he whispered. His sanity felt
like a balancing rock in a Road Runner cartoon. Was this a
dream, too? Or had dreams and waking become so inextricably
tangled up together that he would never know whether he was
awake or asleep? It would have been different back home. He
could have gone to the drugstore on the corner of Lexington
and Fifty-ninth and asked Mo behind the lunch counter if he
was real; and Mo would have told him yes or no. Mo could

tell kosher franks from nonkosher franks, just by the way they squeaked. He could tell a *gontser macher* from a *lump*. But here in London, who could Stanley rely on? Mr. Rasool, in the mini-market? Fanny Lawrence, from the orchestra? Frederick Orme? Maybe he should try phoning Eve, and asking her if she was dreaming or awake?

His throat was parched and his breath stank of stale alcohol. He felt as if he were even sweating alcohol. He went through to the kitchen and poured himself a pint of water in a glass tankard that he had liberated from the World's End pub, and drank it straight down, so that it poured out of the sides of his mouth. He closed his eyes. He didn't feel as if *this* were a dream. It was too mundane; too believable. Yet he had walked straight out of the living room where he had seen his violin riddled by grubs, and into here, without any perception of having woken up.

Perhaps an inability to distinguish between sleeping and waking was a characteristic of Bard's Disease. Perhaps, in the end, Shakespeare had been unable to decide which was real, his life or his plays. And Mozart? Hadn't Madeleine Springer said that Mozart died of the same infection? How could anybody bear to live their lives not knowing for sure if they were asleep or awake? How could you continue to write music if you knew that you might open your eyes at any moment, and it would all be gone, as if it had never existed?

He opened his telephone book, the small maroon moroccobound volume that Leon had given him for his last birthday, with his own name and address entered in it already, Leon Eisner, Atlas Peak Road, Napa, California. *Just in case you forget, when you go away.* Dear God, children could say the most innocent words, and yet they resounded down the days. *Just in case you forget, when you go away.* As if he ever could.

He punched out Gordon Rutherford's number in Putney. The phone rang and rang and rang, and Stanley was about to put it down when a tired, effeminate voice said, "Y-e-es?"

"Gordon?"

A tight sniff. "Who wants him?"

"Stanley, Stanley Eisner."

"He's asleep. He's had a difficult night."

Stanley cleared his throat. "I'd really appreciate it if you woke him up."

"I'm really—I'm *terribly* sorry. But Gordon's had such a grotty time of it."

"Please," Stanley begged him. "It's really critical. I wouldn't ask you to wake him if it weren't."

A very long, unsociable pause. Then the voice said, "Who shall I say wants to talk to him?"

"Stanley Eisner. I'm a violinist, with the Kensington Chamber Orchestra. Well, temporarily anyhow."

"A violinist, *hmmmmmmm*? I think you've got the wrong man. Gordon isn't interested in anything classical. His favorite record is 'Relax.' You know, *relax, don't do it, when you want to commmee*."

Stanley took a deep breath. "Listen, my friend, I'm sorry, but I think you have the wrong idea about this."

"Oh, yes? Don't you know what time it is?"

"I'm sorry, no. Around midnight, I guess."

"It's just gone *two*, my old china!"

Stanley glanced at the digital clock on his New World oven. For some reason, he couldn't focus on it; it didn't seem to make any sense. "I'm sorry. But do you think I could speak to Gordon . . . just for a couple of minutes? I wouldn't ask if it wasn't really urgent."

Long pause. Undecided breathing. Then the receiver was put down, sharply, on a table or a shelf. Voices in the background. Somebody arguing? Then the sound of footsteps, and a sleep-clogged voice saying, "Stanley? What's the matter? It's the middle of the night."

"Gordon, I need you to meet me."

Another long pause; a sniff. "What's the matter, Stanley? Tell me."

Stanley unexpectedly found himself very close to breaking down. "Gordon, I need you to meet me, that's all."

"You don't mean now?"

"How about an hour?"

"Stanley, I had a really long day at Shepherd's Bush Green police station, then I had a meeting in Hammersmith. I didn't get to bed until one. I'm exhausted. I'm naked."

"Go on, tell the world," said the fussy, effeminate voice in the background.

Stanley asked Gordon, unbalanced and unsteady, "Gordon, do I sound *real?*"

"*Real?* What do you mean by *real?*"

"Are you awake?"

"Of course I'm awake! I wouldn't be talking to you if I wasn't awake!"

"Does it sound like *I'm* awake?"

Guardedly, Gordon asked him, "Stanley . . . what's the matter? I want you to tell me."

Stanley covered his eyes with his hand. "I don't know what's happening, Gordon . . . I keep seeing things and feeling things and talking to people, and I don't know whether I'm sleeping or awake or what. I feel like I'm going out of my head."

"Do you want me to come around to your place?" asked Gordon.

"Oh, God!" said the voice in the background. "To the batpoles, we haven't a moment to lose!"

Stanley said, "I'll meet you at Kew. Do you know that café called the Original Maids of Honor?"

"You want to meet me at the Original Maids of Honor at three o'clock in the morning?"

Stanley said, dry-mouthed, "Yes."

"I hope you'll be there, that's all."

"Oh, yes, I'll be there. Because if I'm not, you can forget that I ever existed."

"Stanley—"

"If I'm not there, Gordon, it will be because this phone call is a dream, and you're a dream, and I never really asked you to meet me anywhere."

"All right then, three o'clock," Gordon assured him.

He went back to the living room and opened his violin case. His polished Vuillaume violin nestled in its purple velour bed, uneaten by worms, shining, unplayed, intact. He looked at it for a very long time, then he lifted it out and plucked each of the strings in turn, and tightened them, just to make sure that they were in tune. Then he lifted his bow and played a short improvised melody in the style known as *ondeggiando*, or undulating.

He lowered the violin, his face composed and serious, and then returned it to its case and snapped down the catches. He was beginning to believe that the woodworms he had seen had not wriggled out of his own imagination, or out of his dreams, but that they were real, in an inexplicable way; that they existed outside of his own shock; outside of his own dreams, outside of his own hallucinations. Perhaps they had been left for him to find as a clue. Perhaps they had been intended to frighten him. Perhaps they were simply *there*, as blind and uncomplaining as any mass of creatures, humans included. Perhaps that was the point.

Even great music was bound to decay in the end; because the men who could play it were bound to decay; and their instruments would corrode and collapse into dust.

He went back to the bedroom and dressed in fawn corduroy pants and a white Scottish sweater. He knew that it would probably be impossible to find a taxi on the streets at this time of night, so he called the Carib Cab Company. A strong West Indian accent told him that the cab would be "wit' you in a quahtah of an owah, man; and it's dobble fayuh aftah mid-*night*."

He poured himself a vodka. For courage, for luck. If he was dreaming, he might just as well be drunk. If you got drunk in a dream, did you wake up with a hangover? He stood by the window waiting for the minicab to arrive. There was no traffic, no passersby. The view was so static that it could have been an orange-tinted photograph.

Only five minutes had passed when his doorbell rang. It startled him, and he stood rigid for a moment wondering whether he ought to answer it or not. If it was the cabdriver, he had arrived here incredibly quickly. He leaned close to the window and peered down into the street. No sign of a car. The doorbell rang again, then again, then again.

Knitted Hood, he thought, his stomach shrinking. But then he heard hammering on the door and a voice calling, "Stanley! Stanley! It's me!"

He put down his glass and went to open the door. It was Angie. She hurried past him into the hallway, directly into the living room, and went straight to the chair where his violin case was lying. She started to wrestle with the catches.

"What?" Stanley demanded. "What?"

She turned to stare at him and her eyes were wide and glistening and smeared with black mascara. "I 'ad a dream," she said. "I was round my friend's place but I thought I was 'ere. But it wasn't like a normal dream. I really couldn't work out whether I was really 'ere or whether I wasn't."

Stanley glanced sideways at the violin case. "You had a very clear . . . very realistic dream that you were here?"

Angie shrugged. She suddenly realized how ridiculous it sounded.

"Okay," said Stanley, trying to stay calm. "What were you doing in the dream?"

She laughed, although her laugh was more hysterical than humorous. "It's stupid, really. I was playing your violin. I mean not just scraping it or nothing, but playing it brilliant. I woke up and I couldn't work out whether it was real or not. I just 'ad to come round and find out whether I could. You know . . . play it," she concluded rather lamely.

Stanley felt as if the wing of death had brushed across him. "Do you know what time it is?" he asked her, his mouth dry.

She nodded. She remained straight-backed, wide-eyed, small fists clenched. Defiant, fearful; but no more fearful than Stanley.

Stanley said, "It's two o'clock in the morning. And you came back here just to find out if you could play the violin?"

"It wasn't just that," she admitted. "I mean it wasn't just the violin."

Stanley said nothing. He waited for Angie to find her own words. She lowered her head, then lifted it again and said, "I had a dream about you and me. We was . . . well, you know. We was 'aving it away."

"You dreamed that you and I had sex together," said Stanley.

Angie nodded.

"God," said Stanley, turning away from her.

"Stanley?" she asked him. "You never 'ad the same dream?"

"Yes. I had the same dream."

"You never!"

"It's true, Angie. You came into my bedroom wearing nothing but your red panty hose and you played my violin. You played Mendelssohn. You played Mendelssohn better than I ever heard anybody play Mendelssohn before, ever, in the whole of my life. Then we made love."

Angie approached Stanley slowly and touched his sleeve. "Oh, Stanley."

Stanley let out a quaking breath. "Angie, I don't know what's happening to me. I don't know whether I'm dreaming or awake."

"You're awake, of course, silly. Do you want me to pinch you?"

"But when you came into my room . . . when you started playing my violin like that . . . I wasn't even aware that I'd fallen asleep. I was even getting all ticked off and mad at you, because I didn't want you to touch it."

"I know," said Angie.

Stanley pressed his hands against his face, as if he were breathing into an oxygen mask. "It's impossible," he said. "Two people can't have exactly the same dream."

Angie continued to hold his sleeve, as if she didn't want to let him go. "I read in the *Readers' Digest* once that identical twins can 'ave the same sort of dream."

"The same *sort* of dream, for sure. And they're identical twins. But you and me, we're total strangers, and our dream was *exactly* the same."

Angie hesitated for a moment, and then she said, "Well, we're not *total* strangers, are we? I mean, not any more."

Stanley stared at her. "You don't think I—? Come on, that was only a dream, right, whatever we did?"

"Just because it was a dream, that's not to say that I didn't enjoy it."

"Angie—I'm forty-four years old."

"I know. Old enough to be my dad. But don't tell me *you* didn't enjoy it, either."

Stanley swallowed, shrugged, looked around. "I don't know. I'm not sure that *enjoy* is quite the right word."

"Well, you didn't actually 'ate it, did you? It was better than a poke in the eye with a dirty stick?"

"Yes," Stanley admitted, and couldn't help smiling. "But I don't know . . . I've gotten myself involved in something weird. Something I don't fully understand. I don't want you to get involved in it, too."

Too late, a voice inside him whispered. *You've dreamed your dream about her; and she's involved already. You've passed your infection on. And why should you worry, anyway? Why not use her while you have the chance? She's young, she has a beautiful body. She's impressed by what you are and the way you look. Have her, have a good time. There won't be many more good times left for anyone now.*

"I don't mind being involved," said Angie. "I've always liked fortune-telling, that kind of thing. And 'orror stories, you know. Dennis Wheatley and that. Paul's always saying I'm weird. I don't think you're going to make me any weirder."

Angie's going to dream of Paul; and Paul's going to dream of all the other girls he goes out with. Two times two makes four, four times four makes sixteen, sixteen times sixteen makes two hundred fifty-six. An unstoppable equation of unstoppable infection.

Stanley said, "Maybe you ought to try the violin."

"Beg your pardon?"

"Maybe you ought to try the violin . . . see if you can really play it."

"Well, that's what I come 'ere for. But now that I'm 'ere . . ."

"Go on, give it a try. Just so long as you don't drop it."

Stanley lifted the Vuillaume out of its case and handed it to her. He demonstrated how she should hold it, how to adjust the chin rest; then he gave her the bow. As he stood beside her, showing her how to draw the bow across the strings, she turned and looked at him in such intense close-up that he could feel the breath from her nostrils on his cheek.

"What's that after-shave you've got on?" she asked him.

He stared back at her. Their eyes were so near that they could hardly focus. "Grey Flannel," he told her.

"Did your ex-wife buy it for you?"

He shook his head. "I bought it myself. At Harrod's."

"It's nice. It's like lavender."

Stanley said, "Would you like to try playing now?"

She looked away. He could see the soft curve of her cheek. The fine curly hair at the back of her neck tickled his ear. "I was wet," she whispered.

"What?"

"After that dream, I was wet. It was just like we'd actually done it."

Stanley took a shallow breath. "You mean . . ."

She turned back. "Spunk, that's what I mean. We 'ad it away in a dream only we really did it."

He stepped away from her, lifting both hands defensively. "Angie . . . I told you this was weird. I think it would be a whole lot better if you and I just kind of parted company, you know? Just forgot about it. Forgot about each other."

"But what if I don't *want* to forget about it?"

"Angie, this is for your own good. Ever since that guy attacked me—well, I'm not normal any more. I have some kind of illness. I don't think that you and I should see each other again."

"Supposing we dream about each other again, what then?"

"Dreams are dreams, Angie. That's all. They're just shadow theater. Figments of stressful imaginations."

"I was full of spunk, Stanley," retorted Angie. "It was real and I liked it."

"It wasn't mine," Stanley told her. "There is no possible way in the world that it could have been mine. Maybe you were tired and Paul made love to you and you forgot."

"Paul wasn't there. It was you."

"Angie, for God's sake! It was a dream! If it wasn't a dream, I'm going out of my mind!"

"Oh, yeah?" Angie demanded, and lifted the violin, and without hesitation played a dazzling flourish from Mendelssohn's violin concerto. "I suppose *that's* a dream, too?"

Stanley stared at her. Angie stared back. Slowly, she lowered the violin, her face white, her lips quivering. First she looked at the bow; then she looked at the violin.

"I can't play the violin," she whispered.

"What?"

"I can't play the violin. I never, ever, in my whole life, even *touched* a violin."

Stanley stepped forward and gently took the instrument away

from her and replaced it in its case. He kissed her forehead, and she pressed herself close to his chest.

"Something really weird is going down here," Stanley told her. "I want you to keep well away from it."

"I want to stay with you," Angie appealed. "Please, Stanley. We made love in that dream together. I played the violin and I can't even play the violin. I have to stay. I have a right to."

"A *right*?"

"I'm not leaving, Stanley. Can I call you Stan?"

Stanley heard a car door slam outside; then a few moments later the street doorbell rang. "Okay," he told her. "But don't say I didn't warn you."

FOUR
Empty House

WEST LONDON WAS DESERTED AS STANLEY AND ANGIE WERE driven at high speed over the Hammersmith flyover toward Chiswick and Kew. The flyover passed within feet of a block of Victorian flats, and Stanley could see a man and a woman furiously talking to each other through an uncurtained window. The digital clock on the RCA building reminded them that it was 3:02, and that the temperature was two degrees Celsius. The orange glare from the streetlights was reflected on the low, slowly-moving clouds.

Stanley felt exhausted; but much more real. He was reasonably sure now that he wasn't dreaming. Perhaps tiredness alone had restored his sense or wakefulness and sleep. He held Angie's hand on the back seat of the car and watched the rooftops of Hammersmith revolve around them. Off to the left, the Thames gleamed like a steel door key.

They had been collected at Stanley's door by a tall spidery Rasta in a huge woollen tom. His silver Granada had stood by the curb, throbbing with reggae music like a cartoon car from *Roger Rabbit*. Stanley had asked him to turn the music down a little as they drove to Kew. "I like it, okay, but I'm a little tired."

The driver had turned his radio off completely. "There is no comprom-eyes with the real music, man. There is no way that you can listen to it kwai-hut."

"You're right," Stanley had agreed. "You can't listen to Mozart quiet, either."

They were driven across the river, through Kew Green, and past the dark brick walls of the Royal Botanic Gardens. "Left, left here," said Stanley. "Just by the Original Maids of Honor."

The Rasta dropped them off next to the old-fashioned tea-rooms, and Stanley gave him ten pounds for the double fare and a five-pound tip. The Rasta called him back and dropped three pound coins into his hand. "That was too much, man."

"Excuse me?" Stanley couldn't believe what he was hearing.

"Five-pon' tip on a ten-pon' fare is too much, man. I wouldn't give it to *you*; I don' expect you to give it to *me*."

"I think I just witnessed a miracle," Stanley told Angie as he returned to the Original Maids of Honor.

Angie clung to his arm and pressed her head against his shoulder. "Bloody taters out 'ere," she told him.

Stanley was taken aback. "Bloody taters? I never heard that one before."

"Taters, you know, cold. Potaters in the mold, cold."

"Oscar Wilde was right," Stanley remarked.

"I don't like jazz much," said Angie.

"Jazz? What the hell does jazz have to do with it?"

"Oscar Wilde. 'E played piano, didn't 'e?"

"I think you're thinking about Oscar Peterson. Oscar Wilde was a poet and a dramatist. The reason I mentioned him was that he said Britain and America were separated by a common language."

"Oh."

They waited, Angie clinging close. Stanley said, "You probably want to know what we're doing here."

"Well, waiting for your mate, aren't we?"

"Sure, but we're here for a reason. That guy who attacked

me . . . the guy in the knitted hood. He lives just around the corner.''

Angie stared up at him. "So what you going to do?'' she asked him. "You're not going to do 'im over or nothing, are you? You and your mate?''

"I don't know. I don't think it's going to be as simple as that.''

Angie twisted her head around. "Well, 'ow d'you know 'e lives 'ere? 'Ow d'you find that out, then?''

"It's a long story, but I met this woman in Kew Gardens, in the Palm House . . . and *she* showed me.''

"Oh,'' said Angie, apparently satisfied. Stanley was amazed at the way in which some topics aroused intense curiosity in her, while she would accept others without blinking an eye— particularly anything concerned with authority or grown-ups. He supposed it was something to do with the British education system. "This woman'' had sounded authoritative—as author- itative as Mrs. Thatcher—and therefore Angie had accepted the truth of what she had said without question.

After ten minutes of shuffling around in the cold, Gordon's Austin appeared from the direction of Kew Green and drew in beside the curb. Gordon leaned over the passenger seat and wound down the window. "I hope this is bloody well worth it,'' he said. He was wearing a maroon sweater, with a collar folded over it that looked suspiciously like the collar of a pair of pajamas.

"Take the first left, then park,'' Stanley told him.

Gordon parked his car in Kew Gardens Road and switched off the lights. "Jeremy was furious,'' he said as he locked the door.

"Oh, yes. You told me about him. Jeremy the Jealous.''

Angie nudged Stanley and raised her eyebrows. "He's not a gay, is 'e?''

Stanley pressed his finger to his lips, but Gordon said loudly, "Gay as the day is long, *ma petite*.''

"I don't reckon gays,'' Angie retorted in a challenging voice.

"Oh, no?'' Gordon replied. "I don't suppose many gays would reckon you much, either, darling.''

"For God's sake,'' said Stanley. "Do you know what happened to Angie and me tonight? We both experienced the identical dream.''

"Oh, yes?'' said Gordon. In the lamplight he looked haggard and scruffy. ''And for that you got me out of bed?''

''Gordon, we both dreamed the identical dream. Just like we'd lived it. Don't you understand how *extraordinary* that is? What are the chances of that happening?''

Gordon raked his fingers through his hair, trying to comb it straight. ''All right, that's very unusual. But it's hardly a crisis, is it? And why the hell did I have to drive all the way *here* to discuss it?''

Stanley told him how he had encountered Knitted Hood in the Palm House; and how Madeleine Springer had brought him here. He explained about the Carriers, and Bard's Disease, and what had happened to him after he had returned to Langton Street.

Gordon took out his Silk Cut cigarettes and lit one, blowing smoke across the street. His eyes remained foxy and uncommunicative. He waited until Stanley finished, and then he said, without any preamble, ''You should take Dr. Patel's advice. Go and see a psychiatrist.''

''Gordon—I don't need a psychiatrist! If I need a psychiatrist, then Angie needs a psychiatrist, too, and she's not crazy! Goddammit, Gordon, I'm telling you the truth!''

Gordon pursed his lips. ''Did this Madeleine Springer leave you a number where you could contact her?''

''Unh-hunh.''

''Do you think you might have imagined her?''

''What do you mean?''

''Well, Stanley, my dear fellow, you don't know whether you're asleep or awake. Isn't it possible that after I left you on Kew Bridge, you took a taxi back home and went to sleep, and simply *dreamed* that all of this happened? Isn't it possible that you dreamed you saw Knitted Hood in the Palm House? That there *is* no Madeleine Springer?''

Stanley was defensive. ''I guess it's possible. But that's not what happened.''

''Stanley,'' Gordon persisted, ''are you actually awake now? There is a chance, you know, that you're suffering from some incredibly convincing form of somnambulism. Do you understand what I'm suggesting? Your mind won't accept the world the way it is, not while you're awake, so most of the time you're technically sleepwalking.''

"What, are you crazy?" Stanley shouted. "Sleepwalking, what is this? Are *you* awake?"

"What?"

"Are *you* awake?"

"Well, I don't know," Gordon replied. "I may appear to *you* to be awake. On the other hand, you might be dreaming that I'm telling you that I'm awake. For all you know, I might be home in bed with Jeremy, absolutely fasters.''

Without any hesitation, Stanley slapped Gordon across the face; so hard that Gordon staggered two or three steps back across the narrow grass verge, and trod in some dog's muck.

"Jesus!" he exclaimed, holding the cheek. "What the hell did you do that for?"

"Are you awake now?" Stanley shouted at him. "Or am I just dreaming that you're awake?"

"I'm awake, for Christ's sake, I'm awake! Look at the state of my bloody slipper!"

"Oo-ah, 'e's got 'is Marks & Spencer's slippers on." Angie giggled.

"Jesus," said Gordon, scraping his slipper against the pavement.

Stanley clasped Angie's arm. "I'm going to take a look at Knitted Hood's house," he told Gordon. "You don't have to come if you don't want to. I just thought you were the kind of guy who was prepared to go out on a limb."

Gordon stopped wiping his slipper and stared at Stanley resentfully. "Who the hell helped you to recover after you were raped? Felix the Cat?"

"No," Stanley replied emotionally. "*You* did; and you'll never in your whole life understand how much you helped me. But what happened to me was something different than anything you've ever had to handle before—totally different. It was a rape, sure, on the surface of it. But it wasn't just a physical rape. It was like my whole soul was raped. Knitted Hood didn't just take away my physical dignity. He didn't simply traumatize my conscious mind. He took something else, too. My dreams

. . . the way I feel about the world . . . he raped everything I believed about right and wrong.''

"Stanley," said Gordon, like a parent talking to a small child, "I don't think I understand a single word you're saying."

"You want it straight?" Stanley retorted. "He's *infected* me."

Gordon made a conspicuous effort to hold his ground; not to back away. "Not with AIDS?"

"For God's sake. Of course not with AIDS." Stanley jabbed a finger at his right temple. "He's infected me right inside my mind. Inside of my head."

"Inside your *head*?"

"I keep thinking things that I don't want to think. I can't work out if I'm dreaming or awake."

"So what are we doing in Kew?" Gordon demanded. "If you believe that you've been infected, in your head or anywhere else, you'd be better off back at St. Stephen's, instead of here, in the middle of the night, slapping people and making them step in dog's dirt."

"Because the *answer* is here," Stanley insisted.

"What answer? The answer to what?"

"The answer to who these guys are, these Carriers, and what they're carrying, and why I was attacked, and what the hell is happening to me."

"Stanley," said Gordon very soberly, "I don't think anything is happening to you, except stress and delayed shock. People think you can get over shock in days, or weeks, but you can't. I think you need to talk to somebody who can help you."

"You're damn right! And that's why we're here! You see that house? That's where the guy with the knitted hood lives. We're going to go directly to the front door and we're going to confront him. Him and his fellow Carriers, if they're at home, too."

Gordon looked dubious. "Do you think that's a good idea?"

"What else can I do? Wait until I've gone completely crazy?"

"I don't know. You could call dear old Detective Sergeant Morris."

"Are you serious? He didn't believe a word of what I said

when he interviewed me in hospital. You don't think he's going to believe me now?"

"I'm not too sure that *I* believe you now."

"It's true, Gordon. All of it. It's disgusting and it's weird, but it's true."

"So you want to beard Knitted Hood in his den, so to speak? And what do you think *that* will achieve?"

"At least I might find out what he's done to me."

Gordon glanced at Angie. "And what do *you* think about all of this?"

Angie shrugged, "We 'ad the same dream, didn't we? Both at the same time. Something must 'ave 'appened."

"God, I wish I was back in bed," said Gordon.

That may not have been a statement of unqualified enthusiasm for knocking at Knitted Hood's door; but Stanley took it at the very least as reluctant cooperation. He took hold of Angie's hand, and together they crossed Kew Gardens Road to Knitted Hood's house and went right up to the dilapidated front gate. They looked around. The night was bone-cold; the distant traffic echoed like a roaming herd of mournful buffalo. They waited while Gordon caught up with them. Stanley squeezed Angie's fingers. They had both experienced the same dream. Perhaps, in some peculiar sideways dimension, they had actually made love for real. She had pressed her face against the carpet, in the dream; in a gesture of complete submission. She had whispered words that he still failed to understand. He and Angie had nothing in common, only fate. But maybe fate was more than enough. Maybe the greatest of historical events were assembled from coincidence, accidents, two people meeting by chance.

He wondered how much of a chance it was that he had been attacked by Knitted Hood.

Gordon stopped in the middle of the deserted street to chafe his slipper against the tarmac. "Is this it? *Tennyson?* 'Do we indeed desire the dead should still be near us at our side? Is there no baseness we would hide? No inner vileness that we dread?' "

"What's that?" asked Stanley.

"Tennyson," said Gordon. "Alfred Lord, 1809, 1892."

Tennyson was typical of the large suburban dwellings that

had been built in southwest London in the years before the Great War, in the years before zeppelins and Passchendaele Ridge and "Pack Up Your Troubles in Your Old Kit Bag." The house was unfashionably but handsomely constructed of hard red brick, with tile-patterned pathways and stained-glass decoration in the downstairs windows. Around Kew and Barnes, most of the larger family houses had been subdivided into flats and were occupied now by lonely building-society clerks and promiscuous British Airways stewardesses and fat Australian girls who had found nothing in Brisbane, no husband, no love, and wouldn't find anything here, either.

Angie said, "What you going to do, knock once and ask for Mr. 'Ood?"

"Why not?" asked Stanley. "You know what they say: the best way to deal with your fears is to face them head-on."

" 'Oo said that?" Angie wanted to know.

"I don't know. My mother, I think." Stanley forced open the gate. The front garden was small and clotted with rubbish and stank sourly of dereliction and bad drains and cat's pee. The bottom of the gate scraped against the tiled pathway with a sharp squeaking sound. Something black and alive fled into the grass: a rat probably, London was still alive with rats.

"But s'posin' 'e answers?" Angie wanted to know.

"If he answers, I'll know for sure that meeting Madeleine Springer wasn't a dream, and that I'm not dreaming now, I've got Gordon here as a witness."

Gordon said, "Madeleine Springer? That name rings a bell. Was she your mysterious lady?"

Stanley nodded.

"Well," said Gordon, "even if Knitted Hood *does* answer, that's no absolute guarantee that you're not dreaming, is it? I mean—the way I feel—I'm probably at home, even as I speak, and fast asleep in bed."

Stanley gripped Gordon's fingers and almost crushed them. "You're here, right? You're awake. I need you."

"Ow! Shit! All right," Gordon protested, blowing on his hand.

Stanley stood halfway up Tennyson's path and looked up to the second floor. Unlike every other house in the street—even those houses which remained unlit—Tennyson appeared to be empty. More than empty—derelict. A house in which unhappy lives had been lived out; lives that were gone now; ways that were parted. Stanley had often wondered whether houses could be witnesses to the pain of the people who lived in them. He thought of his own house, the house that he had shared with Eve and Leon on Dolores, in San Francisco. If somebody moved into that house in a hundred years' time, would they still pick up the echoes of all of those rows that he and Eve had been through, all of those screaming matches?

Was it still there, somehow, the moment when he and Eve had faced each other across the living room, their faces like masks, and known without even vocalizing it that this was the moment, this was the end? *Thus far, and no further. And we shall cut a swathe through the world.*

Gordon said, a shade petulantly, "Are you going to knock, dear, or not? Because if not, my beddeth calleth."

"You aint 'alf gay," Angie scolded him.

"Listen to it," Gordon complained. "She's more like Samantha Fox than Samantha Fox."

"For God's sake," Stanley said, shushing them. He approached the front porch. It was generously deep, and plunged in shadow. Seven or eight empty milk bottles were arranged in a soldierly line along one side of it, half filled with green murky rainwater. What Stanley couldn't have known was that they were all of a style of tall thin milk bottle that had been changed more than twenty years ago.

He reached out for the front door. The paint felt weather-dulled and dry, and cracked in places into razor-sharp blisters. He couldn't see very much, but he ran his hands over leaded windows, scarred putty, a corroded brass letter box. Then gradually he raised both hands up the center of the door and felt something bronze and heavy and gnarled. Something metallic, something which had always possessed its own cold-hearted independence, as some metallic things do, even if they have been made by men. Horseshoes, and hammers, and hooks.

"Gordon," he whispered. "Pass me your lighter."

"My what?" asked Gordon in a stridently normal voice.

"Your lighter, you idiot! And keep it down!"

Gordon passed over his Zippo. "Who are you calling an idiot? I came down here, didn't I?"

"*A shanim donk in pupik,*" Stanley retorted.

"I don't even know what that *means*," Gordon hissed back furiously. "I'm not the United Nations, for Christ's sake!"

"It means, much appreciated thanks in your belly button. In other words, thanks for nothing." He flicked the Zippo's metal-grated wheel with the ball of his thumb, and the wick immediately flared up, smoky and orange and pungent.

"This thing stinks," Stanley told him.

Gordon nodded, as if Stanley had paid him a compliment. "I fill it with eighty-five percent petrol, five percent methylated spirits, five percent olive oil, and five percent Brylcreem body splash. Works a treat, doesn't it?"

Stanley held the flickering cigarette lighter up to the door. When its guttering flames eventually illuminated the knocker, however, he involuntarily took two steps back.

"God Almighty," he breathed.

The door knocker was the head of a woman, with a blindfold wrapped tightly around her eyes. Her mouth was stretched wide open, and three fat tongues protruded from it. A coronet of spikes encircled her hair—spikes which, on closer examination, turned out to be twisted nails.

Something else became apparent as Stanley scrutinized the door knocker more closely. Her three tongues were not tongues but toads, warty and swollen, forcing their way out from between her lips, as if they were determined to choke her.

For some reason that he couldn't understand, Stanley felt a splintering sensation of alarm—but of excitement, too, as if after years of searching he had come face-to-face with something whose existence he had suspected ever since he was a boy.

It seemed absurd, but he felt for an instant that this horrifying woman's face was the key to his whole existence—as if he had been born under its influence, as if he had been schooled for the sole purpose of finding it, as if he had been bar mitzvahed in order to acquire the ethical and moral courage to face up to it.

The woman's face was terrible because she was being tortured. But what made it doubly terrible was the look of triumph which the artist had somehow managed to convey; as if she were proud of her debasement.

"Dear me," said Gordon, leaning forward to look at the door knocker more closely. "I'm surprised nobody's nicked it before now." He stepped back again and looked around the front of the house. "I mean the whole place looks completely empty, doesn't it?"

"I definitely saw him come here," said Stanley. "Maybe he's let things slide."

"Understatement of the year," Gordon replied. He rubbed the heel of his hand against the stained-glass windows in the front door. "Look at the state of these windows."

Stanley lifted the cigarette lighter higher. The stained glass was grimy, and some of the panes were chipped and cracked. But as he strained his eyes against the swiveling flame, he gradually made out the pictures which had been formed out of triangles and curves of colored glass. Unlike most Edwardian houses, which displayed stylized arts-and-crafts flowers or Elizabethan galleons under full sail, these windows showed a ghastly parade of human death. Heaps of naked white bodies were being carted through narrow streets, in the shadow of tilted buildings. Skeletons walked with skeletal dogs at their heels, elegant and terrible, with scythes over their shoulders and hourglasses in their bony hands. Fat men were lashed to posts, their bellies slashed open with huge double-headed axes, so that their bowels gushed over the feet of their executioners. Women were paraded around high in the air, impaled on tall poles, holding their arms out wide so that they wouldn't lose their balance and have even more horrifying damage inflicted on their insides.

The lower quarter of the windows was taken up by the depiction of an open mass grave, into which hundreds of bodies had already been tipped, like shoals of herring.

Just as the expression on the face of the door knocker suggested a kind of masochistic triumph, this stained-glass charivari of agony and death was made all the more grisly because of the glee on the faces of both torturers and tortured; as if pain were something to be celebrated; as if death were a huge delight.

"Jesus," Gordon whispered.

Angie came and looked at the windows, too, openmouthed, standing very close to Stanley and exuding warm wafts of Lou-lou perfume. "Bloody 'ell," she said at last. "It's 'orrible. 'Oo on earf would want a bloody 'orrible winder like that?"

"I'm having a nightmare," said Stanley, with no confidence whatsoever. "I'm still asleep and I'm having a nightmare. *No-*body has stained-glass windows like that, not in London."

"You ain't asleep, Stan, love," Angie told him, taking hold of his hand. "I promise you. I can see it, too."

Stanley kept the cigarette lighter lifted. Normally, he was repelled by pornography, and particularly by sadistic pornography. A friend in the San Francisco orchestra had once shown him a Dutch magazine with pictures of women tied up and tortured. The brightly-colored images had remained in his mind for weeks afterwards, lurid and inexplicable. What kind of woman would want to pose for a magazine like that? What kind of person would want to take pictures of her? Who could possibly derive any erotic pleasure from looking at them?

Yet tonight he found himself fascinated by the parade of torture and mutilation that flickered in the light of Gordon's Zippo. Repelled, and yet aroused. Almost as if— He extinguished that thought like extinguishing a candle flame with wet fingers.

Almost as if you'd relish such torture yourself?

"Are you going to knock, then?" asked Gordon. "I don't really feel like standing here for the rest of the night."

"What do you think?" asked Stanley dubiously.

"I think you should do what you came to do, especially since you've dragged Angie and me along, too. To be quite honest with you, I shouldn't think there's anybody at home, Knitted Hood or not, and if there is, he certainly isn't Mr. Tasteful Home of the Year, is he?"

"These windows . . ." whispered Stanley, running his fin-gertips across the grimy images. He held the lighter flame re-ally close, so that he could distinguish the colors of the glass. They were drab ambers and sickly grays and diseased-looking greens.

"Certainly not things of beauty and a joy forever, are they?" Gordon remarked.

"Are you going to knock, then?" asked Angie. Even she was growing impatient.

Stanley reached out gingerly for the huge, frightening door knocker. As he did so, however, Gordon said, "There's a bell here."

Stanley pressed the brass button. They heard the faint trilling of the bell somewhere in the back of the house, where (in hinter times) the servants would have heard it.

"Bet you five quid there's nobody in," said Gordon with a confident sniff.

"You ain't 'alf pessimistic," Angie told him.

"That's me," Gordon retorted. "The gay pessimist."

But it appeared as if Gordon was right: the arcane door remained closed, and they heard no noises or footsteps inside the house. Stanley, with some reluctance, hefted up the door knocker and gave it a timid bang, but again there was no response.

"Well . . . I'm sorry, it looks like I've dragged you out of bed for nothing," Stanley admitted.

"Oh, come on, give it one more shot," said Gordon, and gave the knocker three tremendous slams against the door. A dog started barking across the road, and in the house opposite, a bedroom light was switched on, and then a curtain was drawn back.

"You didn't have to wake the whole damned neighborhood," Stanley hissed. "You were right, okay? There's nobody home."

As he said that, however, the front door squeaked very quietly on its hinges and opened a little way, no more than two or three inches. Stanley and Gordon collided with each other as they both stepped hastily away from it, expecting to see Knitted Hood confronting them, or worse.

Angie said, "You're not *scared*, are you?"

Stanley kept his eyes on the slightly-open door. It was completely dark inside, and as far as he could make out there was nobody there, although he thought he could detect the faintest pattering noise, and he thought that he could smell cold and damp. Rotten carpets, dry rot, disused store cupboards with unnamable fungus growing in them.

"Hello?" he called, his voice strangulated. "Hello?"

Gordon gave the door a cautious push. It swung open even wider, revealing a shadowy hallway, with stairs rising on the right-hand side. At the very end of the hallway, another door stood ajar; and through that door they could dimly make out another stained-glass window, a very pallid and yellowy stained-glass window, on which was depicted yet again the face of the blindfolded woman. This time, however, she wore no coronet of twisted nails, and her mouth was tightly closed.

"Hello?" Gordon ventured. "Is there anybody home?"

"Coo-ee!" called Angie.

Gordon turned to stare at her. " 'Coo-ee'? That's no way to call on a diseased maniac rapist, for God's sake."

Angie flushed and looked embarrassed, until she realized that Gordon was ribbing her. In fact, Gordon had woken up sufficiently to have regained his waspish sense of mischief; and even if they weren't going to have a real adventure, at least they could have some laughs.

"I vote we go inside and take a look," he suggested. "I mean, just look at the state of this place, nobody lives here. Then if you see your lady again, your Madeleine Stringer or whatever her name is, you can tell her that she's talking through the back of her head."

"Actually, she said that he *didn't* live here," said Stanley thoughtfully, remembering Madeleine Springer's words.

Gordon planted his hands on his lips. "She said he *didn't* live here? Then what on earth are we doing here at all? I thought you said that—"

"No, no," Stanley interrupted him. "She didn't mean in the sense that he didn't live here . . . more like he didn't *live* here."

"I fail to see the distinction," said Gordon.

"To tell you the truth, I didn't totally understand myself what she meant. But the more I think about it, the more it seems like she was trying to say that he's here, but he's not alive—I mean not in the sense that you're alive and I'm alive."

Gordon gave an exasperated little sigh. "Oh, *very* clear."

"You mean 'e's dead?" asked Angie.

"I don't know. Maybe he's neither."

"Are we going inside or not?" Gordon wanted to know.

Stanley turned back towards the shadowy doorway. He could

still hear that faint pattering noise . . . still smell that terminal sourness. It was like the sourness of death, corpses washed in vinegar.

—*swathe through the*—, somebody whispered.

He stepped into the hallway without another word. If he had spoken, he may not have had the courage to go in. He had always thought that people in horror movies who deliberately go to investigate strange noises in the night (*always* in the dark, *always* alone) were acting completely at odds with human nature. With *his* nature, anyway. He didn't mind facing up to real-life threats, he wasn't scared of bullies or blowhards, but when it came to noises in the night he was an advocate of the famous bury-your-head-under-the-blankets-and-wait-until-it-goes-away technique.

Gordon hesitated for a moment, then followed him inside, holding out his hand for Angie. Angie hesitated, too, looking dubiously at Gordon's hand.

"Homosexuality isn't *catching*, you know," Gordon told her.

They stood together in the darkness. Inside the hallway, the smell of decay was almost overwhelming; partly sweet, partly fishy, partly acidic.

"Smells like a mortuary," Gordon remarked.

Angie said, "Ssh! Can you 'ear anything?"

Again, that light pattering sound; steady and insistent. Gordon looked at Stanley, and Stanley looked at Gordon. "Sounds like dripping water," said Stanley at length. "Maybe a pipe's burst. That could account for the smell, too."

"Only one way to find out," said Gordon. He flicked his cigarette lighter and held it up in front of him. Its dripping flame made shadows come alive on the walls, leaping and froghopping all around them. The walls were papered in a pattern of huge faded roses. So much of the color had soaked out of them that they looked more like decaying cabbages. There were no pictures on the walls, although grimy rectangular outlines marked the places where pictures had once hung. At the far side of the hallway was suspended an old barometer, its veneered case corrugated by years of damp. Its face was thick with dust; its needle was stuck at *Rain*.

Gordon ventured further along the hallway, and Stanley followed him. Angie came close behind, clinging on to Stanley's

sleeve. Ahead of them, the stained-glass window of the blindfolded woman gleamed and stirred in the light of Gordon's
Zippo, almost as if it had suddenly awakened. Now that they
were closer to it, Stanley could see that the background to the
woman's head was made up of dozens of hooded figures, facing
left and right, their outlines interlocking like one of the illusory
drawings of M. C. Escher.

"What do you make of that window?" Stanley asked Gordon. But he was interrupted by Angie exclaiming, "Urggh!"
and suddenly lifting up her left foot. "This carpet's bloody
soaking!"

In her strappy little shoes, she had noticed the sodden carpet
first. Gordon lowered the lighter, and Stanley could see that
the crimson-patterned Axminster was swollen with water, and
that every time he put his foot down, he squeezed out a large
wet footprint.

"Burst pipe, no doubt about it," said Gordon.

They had reached what Stanley presumed to the the door to
the main downstairs living room. They paused; and now they
could hear the water much more clearly. Gordon placed his
hand against the door and said, "Soaked through, absolutely
soaked through."

That pattering sound, thought Stanley. *That doesn't sound
like a burst pipe. That sounds like—*

"Can we go now?" Angie fretted. "I'm going to ruin me
shoes."

"Let's just take a shufti in here," said Gordon, and turned
the door handle. But the door wouldn't budge. He turned the
green key and announced, "It's not locked. The frame must
have swollen in the wet. How about putting our shoulders to
it?"

Angie held the cigarette lighter while Stanley and Gordon
thumped their shoulders against the door panels. "Come on,"
she jeered. "You two couldn't fight your way out of a paper
bag."

Gordon gave the door a petulant kick.

"We have to do it together," Stanley told him. "It's no good
us bouncing backwards and forwards alternately. It's like music, okay? Timing!"

"All right, then," Gordon agreed. "One, two, three, Geronimo!"

Together they walloped their shoulders against the door; and this time they jarred it inwards a quarter of an inch, wet wood protesting against wet wood. "Again!" shouted Stanley, and this time they almost managed to open it. "One more!"

The door hurtled open and juddered a quarter of the way back again. Angie let out a sarcastic "Hoo-ray!" but she swallowed it almost as soon as she said it. Inside the living room, it was gloomy and cold, and a persistent wind blew. The walls snaked with running water, the carpeted floor was awash. In the middle of the room a three-piece suite of heavy brown 1930s design stood miserably dripping. The tiled hearth overflowed; on the sideboard water trickled out of the brimming fruit bowl, in which three or four swollen apples still bobbed, blotchy and brown, like human kidneys in a specimen jar.

Inside the living room, there were no burst pipes. *Inside the living room, it was raining.*

Stanley held out his hand. It was rain, there was no mistaking it. He stared up at the ceiling but there was nothing to be seen there except water-stained plaster. The rain was falling out of the ceiling as if the ceiling simply weren't there; as if it were open sky. Yet he could see the ceiling clearly. He could see its damp-blurred acanthus-leaf moldings and the ugly brown glass lampshade that was suspended from the center of it.

He took one step into the room, then another. The wind was the same as the rain—it blew keenly through the room as if the walls simply didn't exist. Yet the walls *did* exist; he could see that they existed, he could feel them, and even though the rain was falling from nowhere at all, it was making the walls wet.

Stanley touched the sofa. It was upholstered with soggy brocade. He lifted an antimacassar from one of its cushions and held it up for a moment. It dripped, he dropped it. It was real, he could *feel* it was real. But this whole room was very much more than it appeared. It wasn't just a dowdy wet living room in southwest London; it was somewhere else, too. In defiance of all the laws of matter, in defiance of any kind of logic or sense, this room was two places at the same time.

Stanley turned back to Gordon, who was standing in the doorway, with an odd expression on his face, as if somebody had just tried to explain the theory of relativity to him and failed.

"Am I dreaming?" Stanley asked.

Gordon stared at him. "It's *raining*. How can it be raining?"

"Am I asleep or am I awake?" Stanley demanded.

Gordon stepped into the room, too, and lifted his face to the ceiling, and to the falling rain. "You're awake, Stanley. And I'm awake, too. What about you, Angie? Come on in!"

"No fear," said Angie. "It's bad enough getting me shoes wet wivout getting me hair wet, too."

Stanley walked around the room in a slow, measured circle. The rain plastered his hair against his forehead and darkened the shoulders of his coat. It was extraordinary. It felt exactly the same as if they were standing outside, and yet here they were, in somebody's living room. He drew back the brown brocade curtains, heavy with water, and through the murky, misted-up window he could see the orange sodium lights of Kew Gardens Road.

"Maybe this is what Madeleine Springer meant by not living here," Stanley suggested. "Maybe this is two places at once . . . two different places kind of overlapping each other. So you could be here and not here, both at the same time."

"It's rain," Gordon repeated. "That's what I can't get over. It's actual rain."

He went to the wall beside the fireplace and laid his hands flat against the wallpaper. "I can feel the wind on my hands, but I can feel the wall, too. It's incredible. It's the most incredible thing I've ever seen."

Angie, who was still patiently holding up Gordon's cigarette lighter, asked, "Can we go now? I'm ever so cold."

"Do you see this, Angie? It's rain," Stanley explained.

There was a look in Angie's eyes which told Stanley that she didn't want to talk about it; that it was all too frightening for her. She didn't even want to marvel at it. She just wanted to leave, as quickly as she could.

"Okay," he told her, "let's go. Maybe you'd all like to come back to my place for breakfast."

"Don't you think we ought to take a look upstairs?" said Gordon.

"Upstairs?"

Gordon nodded toward the ceiling. "I'd be interested to know if it's raining upstairs, that's all. I mean—is the rain coming through the ceiling from the room above, or is it in this room only?"

Stanley turned his face toward the wind. It was pungent, the wind. It smelled of river. "I don't know," he told Gordon. "I really don't know. I'm not so sure that I care any more."

"You came here to face down this Knitted Hood character, didn't you? You came here to find out what he was all about?"

"I don't know, I'm confused. How the hell can it be *raining* in here?"

"My dearest Stanley, I haven't a clue. But let's try to find out, shall we?"

Stanley felt an unexpected surge of hatred for Gordon. He couldn't think why he had invited him to come here to Kew in the first place. It was raining, the wind was blowing, what more did Gordon want? Sometimes things happened because they happened, and you didn't question them. Why did Gordon want to interfere?

Gordon came out of the living room and shook his wet hair like a dog. He came up close to Stanley so that Stanley could smell the wet leather of his jacket and the strong undertone of Cerruti after-shave. "I'm converted," he announced. "Just like Saul, on the road to Damascus, I done seen the light. You, my dear, have got yourself involved with something really"—he searched for the word—*"outré."*

"I just want to know whether I'm asleep or awake," Stanley replied stiffly. His whole being felt as if it were rigid with panic, like a jammed-up ten-lever dead-lock.

Gordon looked at him for quite a long time. "You really don't know?"

Stanley shook his head.

"He's done something serious to you, hasn't he?" Gordon asked. "Even if he hasn't actually infected you . . . he's had an effect on your mind. He's altered your whole perception of things."

"What the hell is it to you?" roared Stanley. "What the hell difference—!"

"Hey now, shush, come on now," said Gordon. "You're under a strain, right? You're still trying to make sense of what happened to you. That's why you came here today. But let me tell you this . . . you're awake and I'm awake, okay? You can see that rain and feel that wind, but so can I. It's all *real*, my love. So if we're going to find out what your problem is, we're going to have to understand what's happening in this house. Yes?''

Angie said, ''Can we go now? My plates are freezing.''

Stanley was instantly enraged, almost as if he were drunk. ''Will you shut up?'' he screamed at her. And then, angrily, at Gordon, ''I'm sorry! All right? I'm very, very, very sorry! I'm sorry I dragged you out of bed, I'm sorry I brought you here, I'm sorry I came here myself! You were right the first time! It's a burst pipe! It's nothing! It's a waste of time! So we're going, all right? *Vamos!* Forget it!''

Gordon folded his arms and leaned obstinately back against the door frame. ''I'm still going upstairs, Stanley. You don't witness the greatest miracle since the loaves and the fishes, and turn your back on it and go back home for Gold Blend coffee and a bowl of Rice Krispies.''

''Gordon, this is *my* life and *my* problem,'' Stanley replied, trying his best to be patient, his voice wet-sand-slushy with badly-contained rage.

''Exactly,'' Gordon replied. ''And that's why I'm going to go on helping you, whether you want me to help you or not.''

''God preserve me,'' said Stanley.

''He will.'' Gordon smiled. ''And so will I.''

Gordon took the hot flickering lighter from Angie and squelched back along the wet-carpeted hallway to the foot of the stairs. He mounted one stair, then another, then another, while Stanley stayed where he was, with his back against the faded rose wallpaper, watching him, and Angie shivered like a young child lost at Coney Island. After a sixth or seventh stair, Gordon leaned over the banister rail, the lighter flame held close to his face, so that it looked like an illuminated clown's mask suspended in the air, and asked, ''Coming, are we? Or are we scared?''

''Do we 'ave to?'' Angie asked Stanley.

''I'll go,'' Stanley told her. ''You wait outside. We won't be long.''

''I'm not waiting outside by myself.''

"Well, in that case, come on upstairs with us. I doubt if there's anything up there."

They walked to the foot of the stairs, and Stanley went up first, turning to Angie and saying, "It's okay. There's nothing to be frightened of. It's just some kind of weird natural phenomenon. You know, like St. Elmo's Fire, or mirages in the desert."

"All right," Angie agreed, although she didn't sound very happy about it.

Gordon climbed on ahead, taking three and four stairs at a time. He turned a bend in the stairs, and for a moment all they could see of him was his huge hunchbacked shadow. "Sounds like it's raining upstairs, too!" he called back.

"Bloody 'ell," Angie muttered. "Right 'ow's-your-father this is."

"Come on," Stanley encouraged her. Gordon's insouciance had given him new courage. "It's only rain, after all."

They joined Gordon on the upstairs landing. There were five doors off it, four bedrooms, probably, and a bathroom. On the walls hung dozens of dark and diminutive paintings and prints, so small that they were almost miniatures, of the same blind-folded woman whose likeness appeared on the door knocker, and in the stained-glass window at the end of the hallway. Stanley peered closely at the pictures and discovered that each of them varied slightly. In one, the woman had a coronet of what looked like fishhooks piercing the skin of her forehead. In another, her mouth was crammed full to choking with a green herb that looked like parsley or coriander. In a third, the head of a dead martlet protruded from her lips.

"What the hell do you think these pictures are all about?" he asked Gordon.

Gordon, leaning over his shoulder, slowly shook his head. "I haven't the faintest idea. Perhaps they're all symbolic. They remind me of tarot cards a bit. Rather *medieval*, if you know what I mean."

When Stanley examined the paintings even more closely, he could see that their backgrounds varied, too. In some, there were gloomy forested landscapes or the battlements of broken-down Teutonic castles. In others, there were deserted beaches, or overgrown gardens, or long empty corridors with harlequin-patterned tiles. All that every one of the paintings seemed to carry in common was the blindfolded girl and a small hooded figure in the distance—a figure that was always looking away or hurrying off in the opposite direction.

Stanley stopped in front of a painting in which the blind-folded girl was depicted in front of a landscape of boggy, deserted fields, and a ramshackle collection of huts and lean-tos and pigpens. In this picture, thick whitish fluid was pouring from the sides of her mouth, and Stanley could only guess what it was supposed to be.

"I recognize that landscape," he whispered to Gordon.

"You *recognize* it?"

"I saw it when I was in hospital . . . in a dream or some kind of hallucination. It's the same landscape, I swear it."

Angie shivered. "D'you mind if we 'urry up, please?"

They all looked around the landing and listened. The same sound of rain pattering on to wet carpets was just as apparent up here as it had been downstairs in the hallway. "Let's try some of these doors," Stanley suggested. "This room looks like it's directly on top of the living room, right?"

They opened it up but it was nothing more than a linen cupboard, still filled with neat stacks of pillowcases and towels and yellowing sheets. Gordon said, "I get the feeling that whoever lived here left in rather a hurry, don't you? I mean, who's going to leave all their best linen behind?"

"P'raps they died," said Angie.

"Yes, well, perhaps they did," Gordon agreed. "But I'm beginning to think that Stanley could be right, and that Knitted Hood *does* live here. Or *not* live here, whichever way you want to put it."

"You're actually beginning to sound like you believe me," said Stanley.

"Well, yes," Gordon admitted with a complicated little smile. "It's not every day you see it raining inside somebody's living room, is it? And—listen—if you're right about that landscape—if it's really the identical landscape you saw when you were in hospital—then there must be some connection between whoever lives here and what happened to you when you were attacked."

"You should've been a lawyer," Stanley complimented him.

"I nearly was," said Gordon. "Unfortunately, you know . . . I was always a little bit too flamboyant." He turned to Angie. "Too much of a raging gay, in other words, my little buttercup."

"Are we going or what?" Angie wanted to know. Her teeth were chattering, and she was obviously far too frightened to be riled by Gordon's bantering. Stanley thought that it was remarkable that Gordon was able to remain so lighthearted. He might be effeminate and over-sensitive, but now that he had decided that he was going to find out what was happening in this extraordinary house, he seemed to be nerveless, completely lacking in fear.

He remembered his father telling him about a transvestite sergeant in the Japanese-American 442nd, in Italy during the war, who had taken a German dugout by galloping towards them in an electric-blue ball gown, screeching a soprano battle cry, and firing his machine gun from the hip. The Germans had been too stunned by his appearance to fire back.

"There are brave *timtums* and coward *timtums* just like normal people," his father had told him, and anybody else who was prepared to listen to his war memoirs. But Stanley knew that he would have been mortally grieved if Stanley had turned out to be homosexual. He was almost pleased that his father hadn't lived to witness the breakup of his marriage to Eve.

"All right, what do we next?" asked Gordon.

"Let's try this one," Stanley suggested, taking hold of the handle of the door to the left of the linen closet. The handle was duller and more corroded than any of the others. The wood felt damp.

The door was easier to open than the living room door downstairs, although Gordon had to give it a sharp kick to free it from its frame. Inside, it was raining hard; but it was much lighter than the living room, because the streetlamp directly opposite Tennyson was able to shine into the window. The floor was covered with linoleum, scattered with sodden rugs. The only furniture appeared to be an iron-framed bed, heaped with blankets, and a small battered bureau, which somebody had once painted medicine-pink and covered with My Little Pony stickers.

Gordon and Stanley walked into the room and looked around.

Stanley raised his collar against the persistent rain. It seemed to fall right out of the ceiling and right through the floor, into the living room below. If anything, it was even heavier up here; and the wind was certainly keener.

"Maybe it's some kind of microclimate," Stanley volunteered. "Some kind of electrical disturbance."

"Maybe it's raining in somebody's bedroom," Gordon replied. "No more, no less. One of those things you have to accept."

He walked across the window and looked out. Then he crossed to the fireplace. It was small and arched; a typical Edwardian bedroom fireplace, in olive-green tiles, with stylized lilies curving around it.

"These fireplaces are worth a bit, these days," said Gordon, "Everybody ripped them out when they put in central heating, so they're getting quite rare. Burglars don't take stereos and televisions any more, they dismantle your Victorian staircases and tear out your period fireplaces. Sign of the times, hmh? I used to hate these fireplaces when I was a kid. They remind me of my grannie; and toast-and-dripping, because that's all she could afford to feed me."

They were just about to leave when they heard a high, shuddering sigh. Stanley stared at Gordon in alarm, his wet neck tingling. "What was that?" he whispered. "Did you hear that?"

"Yes, I don't know," said Gordon. "It sounded like it came from the bed."

Angie, from the landing, pleaded, "Can't we go now? Please? This is 'orrible."

"Just a minute," Stanley begged her. He circled around the end of the bed and frowned at the filthy ragged blankets that were heaped up on it.

"Is anybody there?" he asked, as sharply as he dared.

"It looks like nothing but a heap of bedding to me," Gordon remarked.

Stanley leaned closer. "You want to lift some of it up and find out?"

"No. Do you?"

"No. Me neither."

They waited, and listened, while the rain continued to patter against the carpet, and water continued to drip down the walls. For no logical reason, Stanley began to feel an immense sense of fear; a sense of fear unequaled to anything he had ever experienced. It was even worse than that light-airplane tour of the Napa Valley wine country that Eve had given him three years ago for a birthday present. He hated to fly at the best of times: but the Cessna's engine had cut out just as they were climbing toward Lake Berryessa, and the mountains had relentlessly swollen larger and larger like a panful of milk boiling over, and he had bent his head forward and squeezed his eyes tight shut and prayed that dying wouldn't hurt too much.

Now he felt a sensation that was deeper and more gut-wrenching than anything he had ever known; as if his actual *soul* were being swayed from side to side; as if the world he walked on wasn't safe.

We shall cut a swathe, the voice whispered in his ear. *It could be your past, it could be your future.*

In his dream, the girl's handcart had been heaped up with old rags. Just like these rags that were heaped on the bed. Filthy, soft, and swaying.

They're bodies, he thought, and froze rigid.

"Stan?" queried Gordon. "Stanley?"

They're bodies, he repeated, although he wasn't sure that he had spoken out loud.

"Stanley, what's the matter?"

On the bed. They're bodies.

He swiveled his head around slowly and looked toward Angie standing in the doorway. For a split shuddering second he could have believed that Angie was blindfolded; but then she opened her eyes and she was staring at him in terror. Her mouth opened and closed, and the words reached him through the rain, like somebody talking on a radio through thick electric static. *Stanley I'm scared Stanley I want to go now please Stanley please.*

He turned back to Gordon, and Gordon was reaching his hand out towards the heap of rags and so much fear collided in his mind that he couldn't even find the air in his lungs to shout out *Don't!*

All he could think of was the girl pushing the handcart up that muddy road, and the bodies nodding as she pushed them, nod, nod, nod, in the obscene helplessness of death, almost as if they were taunting him because they were nothing but meat now and their movements were controlled not by muscle and not by consciousness, but by inertia and by gravity.

"Don't," he said; and this time he heard his own voice, clear and quiet.

Gordon had already lifted one of the blankets. "They're blankets," he said, although the look on his face made it clear that he understood what Stanley had been thinking. "Stanley? They're blankets."

He stripped them off the bed, one by one. They were rancid, and heavily stained, and clotted with rainwater, but they were only blankets, after all.

Stanley wiped rain from his forehead with the back of his hand. "I'm sorry. I didn't realize."

"What else did you see in that dream?" Gordon asked him.

Stanley lowered his head. He felt unexpectedly emotional. "Dead people," he said. "Like the plague, you know? When they came around to collect dead bodies on handcarts. Or like the Holocaust maybe, Belsen or Auschwitz. I've seen it two or three times since then. A girl, a young woman, pushing a handcart heaped up with bodies."

Gordon smeared rain from his face with his hand. Stanley had never seen him look so serious. At least he was convinced that Stanley wasn't traumatized or mad. How could he not be convinced, in a house full of blindfolded faces, a house where it rained indoors?

"I think before we go any further we'd better find somebody who understands this kind of thing," Gordon said. "I'm a counselor, not an exorcist."

"Maybe a priest might know," Stanley suggested.

"I don't know. Either a priest or a meteorologist."

Gordon dropped the blanket he was holding, and they turned to leave.

"Are we going?" asked Angie in shivering relief.

They had almost reached the door when they heard a scratching, tumbling noise in the fireplace. Stanley hesitated, and frowned at it. "Did you hear that?"

"Sounded like a starling, falling down the chimney. They do that sometimes."

They stood in the chilly, persistent rain, listening. Another scratch; and then a quick, furtive dragging sound, and a sharp *pitter-patter* that sounded like a dog's claws on parquet flooring.

"There's definitely something there," said Stanley.

"If it isn't a bird, then it's probably a rat," Gordon told him. "I wouldn't go too close. They're infected with just about every disgusting disease you can think of, and a few more you wouldn't even *want* to think of."

But Stanley shielded his eyes against the rain and peered intently at the small arched Edwardian fireplace, and he could see brownish soot showering softly down inside it, into the narrow rusted grate, and hear scratching and scuffling and *whispering*, he was sure of it, somebody was *whispering*.

"Hello?" he called unsteadily.

Gordon said, "For goodness' sake, Stanley, there can't be anybody stuck in the chimney. It simply isn't big enough. You're saying hello to a rat."

"Gordon, I can hear whispering."

Gordon listened. "It's the rain, that's all."

"Can we please go now?" Angie called, even more plaintively than before. "It's absolutely brass monkeys in 'ere."

Gordon ignored her and knelt down in front of the fireplace. He listened again, and this time he nodded. "I'm sorry, Stanley, you're right. I *can* hear somebody whispering. Maybe it's somebody in the house next door; or somebody's radio."

"Can you hear what they're saying?" asked Stanley.

Gordon shook his head. "Sounds like they're laughing, or *growling*, I don't know. It's very odd."

Stanley said, "It's almost three-thirty. Maybe we'd better leave. It doesn't look like we're going to find Knitted Hood."

"Just a minute," said Gordon, angling his head so that he could see up the chimney. "There's something here. An opening."

Cautiously, he reached his hand into the fireplace and felt up inside the canopy. "There's an opening here, definitely. I can feel the draft coming through. It feels as if somebody's knocked the bricks out of the back of the flue."

He withdrew his hand and looked up the chimney again.

"Damn soot keeps dropping in my eyes. I'm going to look like Al Jolson after this."

He stared up into the darkness for almost a minute. Stanley, with his hand resting on the rain-spotted tiles of the mantel, began to feel impatient. Outside on the landing, Angie was pacing nervously and irritably backwards and forwards, and letting out louder and louder sighs of annoyance.

Stanley was about to suggest that they call it a night when—without any warning at all—Gordon jerked away from the fireplace and fell back against the bed, knocking his shoulder against the iron upright.

"What?" Stanley demanded. "What?"

Gordon looked up at him in astonishment. "There's a boy in there."

"A what? What are you talking about?"

"There's a boy up the chimney! I saw his face."

"For God's sake, Gordon. How can there be a boy up the chimney?"

"How the hell should I know? I was trying to make out where that opening was, and all of a sudden I saw this white round face, with black eyes, and this sort of bristly hair, and it was staring right back at me."

Stanley swallowed dryly. He dropped down on to one knee himself, and slightly lowered his head, and looked up inside the chimney canopy.

"I don't see anything."

"I saw him, I swear it."

Stanley waited for a moment and then called, "Hey! Up in the chimney! Anybody there?"

A flurry of scratching; another soft shower of soot; but no reply.

Gordon came closer. "Hello? Hello, can you hear me? Are you stuck up there?"

Still nothing; so Gordon said, "We're friends, we can help you! If you're stuck, we can call the fire brigade. Are you stuck up there, or did you just climb up there?"

A short, harsh noise, but still no reply.

Stanley called, "Why don't you tell us your name? Did you come here alone, or did you have friends with you? You won't get into any trouble, I promise. But if you're stuck, we sure can't leave you up there, can we?''

Angie came into the room, her collar turned up against the rain. She hunkered down close behind Stanley and laid her hand on his shoulder.

" 'Oo you talking to?'' she wanted to know.

"Gordon says he saw a boy up the chimney.''

"You what?''

"Gordon says that when he looked up the chimney, he saw a boy's face. White, with bristly hair.''

"P'raps it's a reflection. But if it's got bristly 'air, p'raps it's an old sweep's brush, aye?''

"There's a boy there,'' Gordon insisted. "I saw his face quite clearly.''

" 'E ain't answering back, though, is 'e?''

"Maybe he's in shock,'' said Stanley. "Maybe his chest is wedged so tightly in the chimney that he can't draw enough breath to speak.''

"He doesn't *sound* as if he's tightly wedged. He sounds as though he's almost—I don't know—running around up there.''

"Maybe the opening goes through from the chimney into another room, and he's just poking his head out.''

Gordon shuffled himself right up against the fireplace. "Boy!'' he called. "Hey, you up there! Boy! We're going to call the fire brigade, do you understand me? We're going to call the fire brigade and get you out!''

There was a moment's pause, and then Gordon suddenly said, "There! He's looking at me! I can see his face! Hey, you up there! Can you nod or blink? How about one blink for yes, two for no?''

"Let me take a look,'' said Stanley, and crouched down beside Gordon's left shoulder.

He couldn't see anything at first, the inside of the chimney was so dark compared with the dim orange light in the bedroom. But then gradually he distinguished a pale round face, with dark and rather protuberant eyes, and short bristling hair. The face was looking at him from just above the breast of the flue. Looking at him, without any expression at all, so that Stanley couldn't even be certain that the boy could see him.

Maybe it just appeared that he was looking at him. Maybe he was blind.

Maybe—and this was the most chilling thought of all—*maybe he was dead. Maybe he was wedged tight upside down in this chimney, within four feet of the open fireplace, and that's where he had suffocated, or starved. A lonely, agonizing, long-drawn-out death. He had heard of Victorian boy chimney sweeps dying that way. Maybe it had happened by accident to this boy, too.*

Yet, if he were dead, who had been doing all that scratching and shuffling?

Rats, maybe, gnawing his flesh? Or crows. Crows picked at dead flesh, too.

Stanley glanced back at Gordon. "Do you think he's still alive?"

"I don't know," Gordon replied. "He could be comatose, from lack of oxygen."

"I think we ought to call a namblunce," said Angie. "And the fire brigade. *And* the Old Bill."

"Yes, you're right, we ought to," Gordon agreed. "Perhaps I should try to reach him . . . I should be able to feel if he's breathing or not, or if he's still warm."

"Well, for God's sake be careful," Stanley cautioned him.

Gordon sat in the tiled hearth tailor-fashion with his legs crossed, and tugged up the sleeve of his coat. Then he rested his cheek against the curved iron canopy over the hearth and reached as far up the chimney as he could.

"Can you reach him?" asked Stanley.

"Unh-hunh, not quite yet. He's just—"

He shuffled himself a little closer to the hearth and grimaced as he reached even further up the flue.

"You should be able to feel 'is breaf on yer fingers," said Angie. "That's if 'e's breaving."

"I can't feel anything." Gordon winced. "Not so far, anyway."

"Oh, God, he's dead," said Stanley. Although another voice said, *Serve him right, the stupid dumb bastard kid. Serve him right if he suffered and choked. I hope he panicked. I hope he cried. I hope he understood what death was going to be, before he died.*

He saw Angie looking at him suspiciously; her face rain-streaked, her mascara smudged, her hair bedraggled, not bright, but child-pretty, and sharp as a knife; far too knowing and erotic for a girl of nineteen. He suddenly realized how insanely he was smiling and tried to reassure her by smiling more naturally. It didn't seem to work. He seemed to have lost control of his face. All he could think about was the way (in his dream) that she had played his Vuillaume violin, her bitten fingernails skip-dancing up and down the fingerboard. All he could think about was the curves of her naked bottom and his own ejaculation. It was like watching a pornographic video set to the most exquisite sound track.

"I can feel him," said Gordon. "I can feel his forehead. He feels *cold* . . . I can't feel any breathing."

"That's it, he's dead," Stanley heard himself saying.

Gordon said, "Hold on, wait . . . I thought his eyelashes flickered. Perhaps he's—

"*Aaaahhhhhh!*" Gordon screamed, his voice so high-pitched and penetrating that Stanley's brain didn't register at first that his ears had heard anything at all—only that the air in the room had been somehow condensed into an expression of concentrated pain.

"*Aaaah, my hand! Oh, Christ, my hand!*"

Stanley threw himself down on his knees beside him and gripped the shoulder of his coat. "Gordon? *Gordon?*"

Gordon stared at him wildly, his face emptied of color. He blurted out something, but it sounded like a foreign language, the dialect of unremitting agony.

"What?" Stanley demanded. "What's happened? For God's sake, Gordon, what's happened?"

"My ha—" Gordon began. But his survival instinct must have decided that rescuing himself from further pain was far more important than talking, because he twisted his head away, his teeth gritted, the tendons in his neck as tight as violin strings, and wrenched his arm downwards, out of the chimney, in a shower of soot and a bursting splatter of rusty-colored blood.

But something else flopped heavily out of the chimney, into the hearth, and thrashed furiously from side to side on the end of Gordon's bloodied arm. Angie screamed and tripped backwards against the wall. Stanley grabbed the end of the bed and pulled himself on to his feet—terrified, incredulous, his mind exploding like a fission bomb.

This cannot be! This simply cannot be! And yet it must be, because I'm here now, watching it, and it's jerking and tussling around in front of me.

Clinging ferociously to Gordon's hand was a boy's head; a white-faced, bristly-haired boy's head, with protuberant eyes and a snubbish nose. His teeth were sunk deeply into the meaty flesh just above Gordon's thumb, and already Gordon's thumb was waggling dangerously sideways as if the boy's teeth were an eighth of an inch away from ripping it off altogether. Gordon's hand was smothered in blood; and the boy's face looked as if it had been toothbrush-sprayed in carmine red.

But it wasn't the blood or the savagery of the boy's attack that caused Stanley to stumble away so quickly. It was the boy himself. He had the head of a boy, but the short brutish body of a dog. He looked like a pit bull with a human head. Four paws, a deep-barreled chest, brindled fur, and a tail. And although his face was handsome, in a bulgy-eyed Donald Sutherland kind of way, his teeth were curved and bloody, and he snapped and snarled with all the ferocity of a dog.

Gordon heaved himself sideways, hitting the boy-dog loudly and wetly against the floor. He was screaming all the time, out of rage, out of pain, but mostly out of absolute terror. Angie screamed, too, and the rain lashed down from the ceiling, and for a moment Stanley didn't know whether he was in London or in hell.

What brought him back to stark reality was the sight of the boy-dog's teeth tearing the rumpled skin from the back of Gordon's hand, and then—with a sharp crackling sound—the raw scarlet flesh of the lumbrical muscles, the palmar muscles, and even the interosseous muscles between the fingerbones. It was like watching a bloody glove being wrenched off; because then the arteries fountained, the deep palmar arch and the princeps pollicis, which feeds the thumb.

Angie shrieked, "Stan-*leeee!*"

Stanley didn't really know what to do. But he dragged one of the sodden blankets from the bed, swung it around like Dracula's cloak, and hurled it over the boy-dog's back. It landed with a thick, felty slap. The boy-dog snarled and whiplashed,

but Stanley took hold of its body and tried to heft it away from
Gordon's hand. He could scarcely hold it. It was solid bunched-
up muscle from head to toe, writhing and fighting and wriggling. He couldn't believe how much it *weighed*. Its claws
lashed his knuckles, then his wrists. He gripped it as tightly
as he could; but then the blanket slipped away from its head
and it twisted around and snarled at him and *God Almighty! It
was the face of a boy!* and his fingers locked and he let it drop
to the floor.

It retreated across the bedroom floor, growling softly, with
the bloody rags that it had torn from Gordon's hand dripping
from its mouth. Rusty-red splashes, instantly diluted with rainwater.

Stanley gave Gordon one quick sickened sideways glance.
Gordon was lying on his side, too shocked to whimper, his
right hand reduced to red-stripped bones, his left thumb pressed
on to his wrist to stop the blond pumping straight out of his
ulnar artery all over the floor. He looked as if he had borrowed
his eyes from Peter Falk: black, glassy, not quite focusing.

Angie said, in an off-key voice, "It's not real, is it?"

"I don't know," Stanley replied, picking up the wet-heavy
blanket and holding it up in front of the pit-bull boy like a
cautious matador. "Maybe we're dreaming, maybe we're not.
Do you think you could make it to the door? Call an ambulance?"

"God, I'll try," Angie told him.

"Gordon?" asked Stanley. "Gordon, are you okay?"

Gordon stared back at him, desperate to speak, but shuddering too violently to say anything coherent.

The boy-dog gagged down the rest of the flesh that he had
torn from Gordon's hand with two sickening twists of his neck.
As he chewed it, he watched Stanley with bulbous, suspicious
eyes. Stanley lifted the blanket and shook it, trying to be
threatening. The boy-dog took two or three paces back, his
claws clicking on the floor, but he didn't look frightened. He
was obviously more interested in finishing his meal than in
attacking Stanley's blanket.

Shakily, Stanley challenged him. "What are you? Hunh? Are
you a boy, or a dog, or what?"

The boy-dog watched him and continually licked his lips and said nothing.

"Am I dreaming about you?" Stanley asked him. "Are you a dream? Come on, let's have some honesty here. Dogs with boy's heads? No such creature! *A nechtiger tog!*"

The boy-dog swallowed, and snarled a blood-bubbly snarl.

"Angie?" asked Stanley without turning around. "Did you call that ambulance yet?"

"Stanley," Angie called him. Not loudly; a shade above a stage whisper. The rain still sifted down between them.

Stanley flicked his eyes sideways once; twice. And then he saw what was worrying her. Two more boy-dogs were standing in the doorway, blocking Angie's escape, one white and one greasy-brown, with human heads, their tails slapping noisily against their haunches. A boy who looked almost angelic, with bright blue eyes; and a darker boy, with freckles and a mad serious look, as if he could happily tear out Angie's throat.

"Stanley . . ." moaned Angie. "Stanley . . ."

Stanley backed away from the fireplace, still holding up the blanket, with the intention of circling around Angie and protecting her from the two boy-dogs in the doorway. But as soon as he took one step back, the boy-dog by the hearth took two or three steps towards Gordon.

"Stanley, for Christ's sake," Gordon croaked, his hand all bones and blood. "Stanley, he's going to kill me."

The boy-dog snarled and barked, although it sounded more like a sharp high-pitched human shout than a dog barking. The other two boy-dogs growled, too, and came into the rain-drenched room with their teeth bared and their eyes bulging. Strings of saliva swung from their chins, and the boy-dog with the bright blue eyes began to foam around the mouth. Their claws *chip-chip-chipped* at the linoleum flooring.

Angie retreated until she and Stanley were standing back-to-back. She reached behind her and clung on to Stanley's rain-soaked coat. "Stanley, I'm so bloody scared. Is it a dream, Stanley? Can't you wake me up?"

"Just take it easy," Stanley told her. He could feel her shivering. "So long as we don't make any sudden moves . . . upset them, or anything."

"Upset them? Bloody 'ell, Stanley, they want to kill us, that's all!"

Stanley was numb with cold and soaking wet and his arms were already aching from holding up the heavy wet blanket for so long. The boy-dogs edged closer still, never taking their eyes off them. It occurred to Stanley in a detached way that Angie was right, and the boy-dogs were quite determined to tear them to pieces, and that there was no hope at all of any of them leaving Tennyson alive.

FIVE
Braided Whip

THE TWO BOY-DOGS STRETCHED BACK THEIR LIPS AND BARED their teeth, and started to advance on them with quick little steps, their tails stiffened and their ears flat back against the sides of their heads. Angie gasped and gripped Stanley even more tightly. On the floor, weak from shock and loss of blood, Gordon abruptly dropped back and lay helplessly panting, while the first boy-dog ventured close enough to sniff at his shoe.

Stanley was sure now that the boy-dogs couldn't be reasoned with. They might have human heads, but they were totally animalistic and blindly ferocious. All the same, it was difficult to look down at the freckled face of the boy who was sniffing at Gordon's ankle and not believe that he was capable of human speech; or at least of human thought. All the time that he was stalking Gordon, his eyes remained fixed on Stanley, as if he were daring Stanley to stop him.

Go on, then, stop me. Try to stop me. You don't dare, do you, Stanley? You just don't dare.

Stanley leaned his head back towards Angie. Out of the corner of his mouth, he murmured, "It's no use staying here. We won't stand a chance. We're going to have to try to rush our way out. If we wrap this blanket around ourselves, it should stop them from biting at our legs.''

"What about Gordon?" asked Angie, her teeth chattering.

"I don't know. Gordon?"

Gordon opened his eyes, but his face was gray, and he didn't seem to have heard.

"Gordon, it's Stanley! Gordon? Can you hear me?"

The boy-dogs hesitated and listened. *Supposing they can't speak, but can understand what we're saying?*

"Gordon, we have to get out of here!"

Gordon coughed and slowly lolled his head from side to side. "Can't be done, dear. Can't even feel my feet."

"Gordon, if you stay here they're going to tear you apart."

Gordon half smiled, and coughed again. The rain was falling directly into his face. "Jeremy always said I looked like a dog's dinner."

"Gordon!" Angie screamed. *"Gordon, you've got to!"*

Her scream instantly triggered off one of the boy-dogs, who leapt at her, caught his teeth in her sleeve, and swung from her arm snarling and scrabbling his legs. Stanley twisted around and grabbed hold of the boy-dog in his blanket and tore it off Angie. For a second, he thought that he had managed to get a grip on its throat, but it lashed so wildly from side to side that he had to drop it back on to the floor.

Angie was gasping, and shaking, and sobbing. "Oh, Stanley, I've wet meself. Oh God, Stanley, what are we going to do?"

The boy-dogs didn't hesitate. Now that their blood was roused, they came snapping back at Stanley's and Angie's ankles. The fair-haired creature ripped at Stanley's trouser leg and snagged the skin of his calf. He felt blood stream down his leg. Swearing, he kicked the boy-dog away, but it rolled over and came snarling back at him, its blue eyes swollen with fury.

Angie screamed again. The other boy-dog had jumped on her shoulders and was trying to bite at the back of her neck. Stanley kicked the fair-haired boy-dog away a second time and punched the boy-dog on Angie's shoulders in the side of the head. It yipped and clawed at him, but he punched it again, straight between the eyes, and it dropped backwards on to the floor with a thump.

Gordon cried out: a terrible whining cry of pain and despair. The first boy-dog was tearing at his thigh, ripping a long scarlet string of flesh and skin away from him. Stanley could actually *hear* it: like calico being ripped apart.

"Gordon!" Stanley shouted, but the fair-haired boy-dog jumped up at his face and raked his cheek with three hard claws.

At that moment, however, over the snapping and the snarling of the boy-dogs, and the ceaseless trickling of the rain, they heard another sound. A sharp, explosive crack, and then another, and then another. At first Stanley thought that somebody had started shooting; but then he turned towards the door and saw Madeleine Springer standing there, in black leather thigh-length boots and an impossible outfit like a black leather corselette, with a long black leather cape thrown around her shoulders. Her hair was still blond but dramatically upswept. Her face was alight with commanding righteousness. In her left hand she was holding a bullwhip, a heavy braided black leather whip with a long silver-knobbed handle, the kind used by South African stockbreeders.

She cracked her whip at the fair-haired boy-dog, caught it around his forepaw, and sent him swinging against the wall. He tumbled over, snarled; but Madeleine Springer whipped him again, lashing his cheek open. Then again, splitting the tight wiry fur across his back. Then again, across his shoulder. Bleeding, limping, uttering a low curlike whining, the boy-dog limped toward her, with foam crackling thickly out of his mouth. Madeleine Springer whipped him once more, *kkkrakkkkk*! and then again *kkkrakkkk*! and his blue eyes burst. He rolled over on to his back, his legs thrashing, blinded, shrieking, twisting his spine from side to side.

Madeleine Springer lashed his exposed belly. The tip of her whip cut through the skin like squid being sliced. Intestines bulged from every slice; then bile; then blood. The boy-dog lay quivering on his back, one paw scratching at thin air; then died.

The other two boy-dogs backed cautiously away. But Madeleine Springer wasn't going to allow them to escape. She whipped one, then the other, so that they gradually retreated towards the hearth, whining and cringing. Angie clung to Stanley clockspring-tight; in hysteria and fear and elation. "Who is she? Who is she? What's she *doing*?" she screamed; but she didn't really want to know. She was too frightened and excited by the sight of Madeleine Springer's whip lashing and cutting at the boy-dogs, laying open fur and flesh and cheeks and muscle.

Madeleine Springer cornered the boy-dog who had torn at Gordon's hand, and snapped her whip three times around his neck. Then, with a stormlike shake of her wrist, she heaved him clear of the floor and flung him violently against the side of the cast-iron hearth. They heard his bones smash inside his body like a china jug smashing inside a sack.

Stanley tried to stop forward to help Gordon, who had passed out. The arteries in his mutilated wrist were jetting blood in Jackson Pollock squiggles all over the floor, and his trouser leg was darkly strained, too. But Madeleine Springer said, "Wait!" and lashed the last of the boy-dogs until it lay trembling in the hearth in the throes of imminent death.

Only then did she kneel down beside Gordon and lift his spurting wrist.

"Shall I go and get that amblunce now?" asked Angie in a quaking voice.

Madeleine Springer glanced up at her. "No. Stay. I should have known this was going to happen."

"But he's bleeding to death!" Stanley protested. "We *have* to call an ambulance!"

Without saying a word, Madeleine Springer touched Gordon's bloodied hand with the tips of her fingers. *"Ashapola, help me,"* she whispered, and closed her eyes. Stanley frowned at Angie and then back at Gordon's hand. Almost immediately, in front of his eyes, the bleeding dribbled and stopped, and the torn skin folded in on itself, like the petals of a flower closing up at twilight. In less than a minute, Gordon was left with a stump of a wrist that was still crimson-sore, but which was almost completely healed.

"Is he okay?" Stanley asked Madeleine Springer in astonishment.

"He'll survive. But we must get him at once to a place of safety."

She felt around on the floor and picked up the bones and tendons of Gordon's dismembered hand, as deftly as if she were scooping up tiles in mah-jongg. She carried a large black silk purse around her waist, and she dropped the bones into it and tugged the drawstring tight.

"It can't possibly be put back together, can it?" asked Stanley with a pit-of-the-stomach feeling of disgust.

Madeleine Springer shook her head. "There is a saying that the man without a hand can never say farewell. Besides, we should leave no evidence that we were here."

Already the rain was streaking and diluting the blood that Gordon had pumped all over the floor, and it was swirling away through the cracks in the floorboards. Presumably, in the room below, it would rain blood for a while.

Between them, Stanley and Madeleine Springer heaved Gordon on to his feet. He was still semiconscious, and his feet dragged on the floor. For somebody so slim, Stanley wouldn't have believed how heavy he was.

"Where are we going?" he asked Madeleine Springer, wiping the rain from his face with the sleeve of Gordon's coat.

"I have a car outside," she told him. "I'll take you to my place. You'll be safe there. Safer than Langton Street, anyway."

It took them three or four awkward, jostling minutes to half carry, half shoulder Gordon down to the hallway and out into the street. It was still dark. The sun wouldn't rise for another three and a half hours, and in any case it was probably going to be a gloomy, overcast day. A friend of Stanley's had once described winter Sundays in London as the nearest simulation to the end of the world that anybody could imagine. (That was before he spent a winter Sunday in Wolverhampton, in the north of England.)

Angie opened the front door for them, and they helped Gordon along the path and out of the front gate. The cold wind was beginning to revive him, and he kept letting out grunts and moans, like a man experiencing a nightmare.

Madeleine Springer's car was parked across the street, half-

way around the corner, hidden from anybody who might have
been watching out of the house. It was a large gray British car
from the mid-1960s; Stanley couldn't remember having seen
one like it before. He and Angie supported Gordon while Madeleine Springer unlocked the door. Then, between them, they
gently lifted Gordon on to the back seat.

"I'll sit with 'im," Angie volunteered.

"Thought you were down on gays," said Stanley, although
he wasn't seriously mocking her.

"I can change me mind, can't I?"

Stanley climbed into the front passenger seat beside Madeleine Springer. The interior smelled of leather and old carpets
and engine oil. The engine started with an irregular blaring
noise, and when she pulled away from the curb, Stanley heard
a nasty nasal whine in the transmission. It sounded more like
a truck than a car.

"How long have you had this?" he asked her.

She glanced at him. "Ever since it was new. It's a Humber
Super Snipe. They used to be plutocratic, once upon a time."

"Where are you taking us?"

"Richmond. It isn't very far away. We have rooms there."

"Those . . . dog-creatures," Stanley began.

"You want to know what they were?"

"Did they really have human heads, or did they just look
that way?"

Madeleine Springer turned left at Kew Road and headed
south. The wide road that ran beside the black brick wall of
the Royal Botanic Gardens was completely deserted; not even
a police car.

"They weren't human in the sense that you might understand
them to be human. It depends how much humiliation you're
prepared to suffer in order to stay alive."

"Are there many more of them?"

"It's impossible to say for sure. This latest outbreak of the
Night Plague has only been with us for two or three years.
Historically, though, it looks like the worst by far."

"The Night Plague?"

"Bard's Disease, Mozart's Syndrome, call it what you like."

Stanley was silent for a moment. Then he said, "I think I'm
going to need to know a whole lot more about this."

"I intend to tell you," Madeleine Springer promised him. She drove oddly, a little too fast for Stanley's liking, with mechanical, exaggerated movements, as if she had only recently learned. He supposed that it couldn't be easy driving in high-heeled black leather thigh boots. He caught himself looking at the smooth whiteness of her bare thigh, in between the top of her boot and the black satin frills around the legs of her corselette. *I wonder what it would like to plunge my hand now between those warm white thighs, while she's driving and unable to stop me.*

"How have you been feeling?" Madeleine Springer asked him, as if she had read his thought as clearly as the motto in a Christmas cracker. They had reached the traffic lights at Lower Mortlake Road. The large roundabout, usually teeming with cars and buses, was silent and deserted. Stanley could easily have believed that they were the only people left alive.

"I've—uh . . . I've been experiencing a little confusion from time to time."

"What kind of confusion?"

" 'E don't know whether 'e's kipping or whether 'e's awake," Angie put in, trying to be helpful.

"Not only that," said Stanley. "But this mixed-up feeling that I can only call *moral* confusion."

"Oh, yes? And how does that manifest itself?"

"In all kinds of different ways. I keep having waves of anger and disgust against God, and music, and other people. Even people I like. Even people I *love.*"

The lights changed to green and Madeleine Springer changed gear. "You have waves of violence, too, right? And sexual lust?"

He looked at her acutely. She smiled, although she didn't look back at him. "I know how strong your urge was to thrust your hands in between my legs, Mr. Eisner. 'She's driving, she won't be able to stop me.' And it's warm there, and smells of leather and woman and some perfume that you can't even identify."

"I reckon Gordon's coming around," called Angie, who obviously hadn't heard what Madeleine Springer was saying.

Stanley stared at Madeleine Springer hard. "How do you know all that? Are you a mind reader, or what?"

"I'm a very good psychic, that's all," she replied. "You saw what I did to Gordon's wrist, back at the house. That was nothing more than faith healing, as it's usually called; although it was very much more effective faith healing than most psychics are capable of."

"You're not kidding," Stanley told her.

Madeleine Springer said, "There are natural powers in the universe of really devastating magnitude. I know how to call on them; and to direct them; and there's nothing more mystical to it than that. These days, nobody would think of gasping in astonishment when they switch on an electric light bulb; yet what I do is no more remarkable than that, and in some ways a great deal simpler. The natural powers have certainly been around a whole lot longer."

They were turning toward Richmond Hill when two police officers stepped out into the road and lifted their hands. "Damn it," said Madeleine, and slowed the Humber down to a whinnying walking pace, and then to a stop. One of the police officers approached Stanley's window and rapped on it gently with his knuckles. Stanley wound it down.

"Morning," the policeman greeted him. His breath steamed in the cold, and his nose was pinched red, and he looked what Angie would have called "right cheesed off." His companion had steel-rimmed shatterproof spectacles and kept sniffing and wiping his nose with his glove.

"Can I help you, Officer?" Stanley asked him.

The policeman peered inside the car. Then he said, "Just interested to know where you're going at a quarter to four in the morning."

Stanley turned to Madeleine, his lips already forming the shape *W* to ask "Where are we going, Ms. Springer?" when he saw that she wasn't there. There was no steering wheel, no brake or accelerator pedals, no gearshift. All of those controls had mysteriously moved across the car and materialized in front of him, as if he were driving.

He twisted quickly around. The back seat was empty, too. He was sitting in the car alone.

It had been a dream. Tennyson, the boy-dogs, everything. It had all been a dream. But what was he doing in this strange car, in the middle of the night?

"American, aren't we?" the police officer asked him.

"Well, *I* am," Stanley replied.

Unamused, the police officer inspected the tax disc on the windshield. "This your vehicle, is it?" The policeman with the eyeglasses was walking slowly around the other side of the Humber, inspecting the tires and the lights.

"Well, ah . . ." Stanley began, but then out of the corner of his eye he saw the shimmering transparent whiteness of Madeleine Springer's upper thigh, almost completely invisible, like the reflection of a thigh glimpsed in a dark window. He spread his fingers across the steering wheel in front of him, too, and realized with an involuntary shiver that it had no actual substance, it was the *illusion* of a steering wheel and nothing more. He just hoped that the police officer hadn't seen his hands pass right through it.

If Madeleine Springer had gone to all the trouble of rendering herself invisible—and Angie and Gordon, too—then she must very badly want to conceal the fact of her presence here tonight—perhaps her very existence.

"Yes, it's . . . my car," he concluded.

"Do you mind telling me what the license number is?"

"Sure, it's—" *NLT 683*, said Madeleine Springer's voice, right inside of his head, as clearly as if she had spoken out loud in his ear.

"That's right, sir." The policeman produced a black leather pad and began to write. "You've got a faulty offside indicator light, sir. Flashing too slowly. Can you make sure you get it seen to?"

"Oh, sure, yes, I'm sorry. I didn't realize."

The policeman tore off the ticket he had been writing. "And if you'd care to produce your driving license and MoT certificate and insurance documents within the next seven days, sir, at the police station of your choice?"

"Yes," said Stanley. He was aware of a huge charge of static inside the car, like passing his hand in front of a television screen, and his hair prickled on the back of his neck.

The police officers returned to their car, swinging their arms and clapping their hands together to warm themselves up. The Humber's engine started up again, and the elderly car began to pull away. As he passed the police car, Stanley pretended that he was holding the steering wheel, even though he could feel no substance whatsoever, only the soft crackling of psychically-focused electricity.

It was only when they had reached the top of Richmond Hill that Madeleine Springer gradually reappeared, grainily at first, like the picture on a poorly-tuned television; then completely.

"Blimey, that was totally weird, that was!" Angie blurted out. She held her hand in front of her face to make sure that she was still there. " 'Ow d'you do that?"

"It's a little bit of conjuring with refractive light, that's all," Madeleine Springer told her. Stanley turned around in his seat, and for Angie's benefit pulled a face that showed how impressed he was.

"Can you imagine being able to do that all the time?" he asked her. "You could sit right next to people and listen to what they're saying about you, and they wouldn't even know."

"I'm afraid it takes too much natural energy for anybody to sustain invisibility for very long," said Madeleine Springer. They passed an old-fashioned pub called the Lass of Richmond Hill where Stanley was disappointed to notice that they were offering New Orleans-style barbecue. When he first arrived in England, he had expected it to be crowded with fish-and-chips shops and eel-and-pie stalls and Dickensian chophouses. Instead it had exactly the same fast-food franchises as downtown Napa, all Burger King and McDonald's and Kentucky Fried Chicken.

They had reached the very crest of Richmond Hill, high above a wide curve of the Thames. The terraced gardens that led steeply down to the river were buried this morning in a deep foggy shadow, but the river itself shone dully through the trees as it flowed between Petersham Meadows on its eastern bank and Marble Hill Gardens on its west. A haunted, melancholy view, one of the most romantic in southern England. To think that Henry Tudor had seen the same view; that Elizabeth I had passed this way in her carriage. Sometimes London's sense of history made Stanley feel elated; sometimes it made him feel oppressed.

The suspension of Madeleine Springer's twenty-five-year-old car clonked noisily as she turned it into a narrow private slip road. She parked, switched off the engine, and announced, "We're here. I'll help you carry Gordon inside."

They climbed out of the car. They were parked beside a stately terrace of cream-painted four-story houses, which had now been divided into apartments. Madeleine Springer led them through the front door and into the hallway. It smelled of new Axminster carpets and stifling central heating. An arrangement of dried flowers stood on a small table in front of a mirror, and Madeleine Springer went across while they waited for the elevator to arrive, and refurbished her lipstick.

Gordon had recovered sufficiently to be able to walk, although Stanley insisted that he lean on his shoulder. "Quite a place," he whispered in a gray voice.

"It's wonderful in the summer," said Madeleine Springer. "The view over the Terrace Gardens is absolutely beautiful." She looked at Gordon in the mirror and smiled. "You're just the way I imagined you would be," she told him.

They rose in the quietly-humming elevator to the top floor; and then Madeleine Springer ushered them along the corridor to her apartment. She opened the door, and they stepped inside, and at last Stanley felt that they were safe.

Madeleine Springer had furnished her apartment ascetically, to say the least. Their footsteps echoed on a bare oak-parquet floor, absolutely immaculate, so highly polished that they looked as if they were walking across the surface of a lake. The walls were painted the faintest shade of yellow. The only furniture in the living area was three Chippendale armchairs with faded pink satin seats, a yucca plant in a basketwork planter, and a curious hybrid sofa, part French Provincial, part Chinese, with an elaborately-carved back. There were no paintings on the walls, no drapes, no net curtains. The night filled the windows, black and uncompromising.

They helped Gordon to sit on to the sofa. He was still deathly pale, but he was almost cheerful. Madeleine Springer went through to another room and returned with a white gauzy scarf, which she wound around the stump of his left hand, and then ripped, so that she could tie it in a bow.

"You saved my life," said Gordon as he watched her.

"You would have survived in any case," Madeleine Springer told him. "It was always your destiny to survive; for the time being, at least; just as it was always your destiny to lose your left hand.''

"I don't understand," Gordon told her.

"Of course you don't, not yet. But what I am trying to tell you is that you would have lost your hand somehow, sometime soon; and that nothing you could have done would have prevented it.''

"I don't believe in fate," said Gordon.

"Not believing in it doesn't stop it happening.''

"I could use a drink," said Stanley.

"There's vodka in the kitchen," said Madeleine Springer. "You'll find some glasses there, too.''

"Can I use the toilet?" asked Angie.

Stanley switched on the fluorescent lights in the kitchen. They flickered, jolted, and then stayed on. It was an expensive, modern kitchen, a real cook's kitchen, with white cupboards and a polished brass rail around the counters. But Stanley swung open one wall cupboard after another and found them all empty. The entire kitchen was innocent of food, or any suggestion that anybody ever intended to prepare any food here.

"Looks like you're fresh out of vodka," he called to Madeleine Springer. "In fact, it looks like you're fresh out of everything.''

He opened one of the drawers and found a cutlery tray containing two very ancient and corroded knives, with hair twined around their handles, and a corroded iron talisman on a leather thong. It was a Celtic cross, with a blindfold of rotten linen tied tightly around it.

Stanley picked the talisman out of the drawer and held it up. It swung from side to side, and spun around and around. As it turned around, he saw that there was a face on the obverse side. He caught it in the palm of his hand and examined it more closely. There was no question about it. It was the same face that he had seen again and again at the house called Tennyson.

The blindfold woman, with the coronet of twisted nails.

Stanley was suddenly aware that Madeleine Springer was standing in the doorway watching him, with a faint smile on her face.

"Can't you find the vodka?" she asked him. She crossed

the kitchen and slid out a tall narrow drinks drawer. She took out a full bottle of Finnish vodka and unscrewed the cap.

Stanley turned to her while she knocked ice out of the ice tray, still holding up the talisman. "What is this?" he asked her. "I saw it everywhere back in that house at Kew. The door knocker, the stained-glass window. Then dozens of paintings and etchings, all around the upstairs landing. Now I open a drawer looking for vodka, and here it is again."

Madeleine Springer handed him his drink. It was clear and cold and aromatic, in a tastefully-designed Boda glass.

"I would prefer to begin at the beginning," she said. "But I can tell you who the face is supposed to represent. The name by which she is most commonly known is Isabel Gowdie."

"That doesn't strike any chords at all."

"There's no reason why it should."

"But when I first saw her, on the door knocker, I had the feeling that she was kind of familiar."

"It's possible that you've seen her picture before. You could even have met her. She's lived as many lives under as many different names as—"

Stanley swallowed vodka. "As a cat?" he suggested.

"I'm sorry?"

"Cats have nine lives, don't they?"

"Oh, I see what you mean," said Madeleine Springer. "But no, Isabel Gowdie has lived far more lives than any cat. Every one of those paintings and prints of her on the first-floor landing at Tennyson showed a different Isabel Gowdie, in a different life."

"What about the rain? And the boy-dogs?"

"They were both manifestations of Isabel Gowdie's influence."

Stanley said, "I think you'd better begin at the beginning."

Madeleine Springer nodded. "All three of you are more than ready."

Stanley clinked the ice in his drink. "Before we start, I think I'd better thank you for saving us back there. I don't know how you knew we were there; or how you managed to show up just when we really needed you. But you did, and I'm grateful."

"Well . . . I shouldn't really have been there," Madeleine

Springer told him. "But there are times when even fate requires a little assistance."

She led him back to the living room, where Angie and Gordon were sitting together on the strange French-Oriental sofa. She dragged over one of the Chippendale chairs for Stanley, but remained standing herself. As she talked, she paced slowly backwards and forwards, and her long black leather cape hissed softly on the polished oak floor.

"There are dire warnings in the Old Testament time and time again about the punishment that God has in store for those who disobey Him. The punishment is plague. *'The Lord will smite you with consumption and with fever and with inflammation. The Lord will smite you with madness and blindness and bewilderment of the heart. The Lord will smite you with the boils of Egypt and with tumors and with the scab and with the itch, from which you cannot be healed.'* "

"Charming," said Gordon weakly. But considering his hand had been violently torn from his arm less than an hour ago, his composure was extraordinary. It was Gordon's recovery more than anything else that convinced Stanley that he ought to listen to what Madeleine Springer had to say. The disappearing trick in the car was one thing. But he had seen Gordon bleeding to death in front of his eyes; and now he was ridiculously well.

Madeleine Springer smiled. "Whether God really *does* punish anybody who disobeys him by striking them down with the plague . . . well, that's a matter for theological argument. Paracelsus believed that syphilis was a punishment invented by God for those who were guilty of 'general licentiousness,' and there are plenty of people today who are quite willing to believe that AIDS is God's punishment for homosexuality.

"They ignore the simple truth that an illness is an illness, however it happens to be transmitted; and not a metaphor for divine judgment."

"All the same," Stanley interrupted, "Knitted Hood gave me a very direct warning. He said, 'I am the pestilence that was promised, if you disobeyed.' "

"Did he specifically mention God?"

"I don't really remember too clearly. I don't think so."

"He wouldn't have. The Carriers loathe to utter the name of

God, in any of its forms. If he did he was lying and trying to confuse you. The Night Plague isn't a divine punishment any more than AIDS is. The Night Plague is what you might call an infection of the soul. It's the moral virus which Satan himself uses to spread his influence through human society."

Angie glanced worriedly at Stanley. Madeleine Springer may have rescued them from Tennyson, but already she was beginning to sound as if she wasn't teeing off with a full set of clubs.

Stanley said, "Can we wait up a minute? On the one hand, you're telling us that plagues aren't a punishment handed out by God. But on the other hand, you're telling us that they're a punishment handed out by Satan."

"I don't even *believe* in Satan," put in Angie. "I mean, not with 'orns and a tail and a toasting fork."

Madeleine Springer continued to smile. "Out of all the epidemic diseases, only the Night Plague is spread by Satan. And he certainly doesn't spread it as a punishment. He spreads it as a way of turning the hearts of men and women away from the principles that have always denied him dominion over the world. Trust, faith, self-control, truthfulness, and loving other people as you love yourself.

"It's a particularly vicious joke that he uses the sexual act, the act of love, as a means of spreading his disease."

"So you reckon 'e's real?" asked Angie.

"With horns and a tail and a toasting fork? Not quite. But the entity which people call Satan *does* exist; and although I call him 'hc,' as if he were nothing more than a black-hearted man, he is much more understandable as an 'it.' A huge intense concentration of horror."

"Where does 'e live, then?" Angie wanted to know. " 'Ave you ever seen 'im? Or it, or whatever?"

Madeleine Springer was completely undisturbed by Angie's skepticism. She swirled her soft whispering cloak around her, and her heels tapped on the hardwood floor. "He occupies the furthest recesses of human awareness; that unlit lake of shared consciousness that Jung described as the collective mind. There are times when you can sense his actual presence in the back of your head. Something very cold, something very dark, sliding past you like a giant stingray sliding over an underwater shoal, but *inside* your mind, inside your own imagination."

''Can he be summoned into the physical world?'' asked
Stanley. ''I mean, all that stuff about Black Sabbats, raising
the devil . . . is there any substance in that?''

Madeleine Springer nodded. ''He can be called; and of
course a few people *do* call him. The Sumerians were aware
of the feeling of evil in the backs of their minds, and there are
several recorded instances of Sumerian priests raising out of a
particular well in the desert some terrible black creature that
fed on masses of children and goats. The Egyptians raised him,
too, believing that they could use him to overcome the mystic
power of the Israelites; and that was how the biblical plague
was first spread through Egypt.

''In a sense, the outbreak in Egypt *was* a punishment for
disobeying God; although more accurately it was the pathological consequence of trying to enlist the power of evil against
the principles of good.''

''So how is this Night Plague communicated?'' asked Stanley. ''What does it actually do?''

''You've probably heard how witches are supposed to cop-
ulate with Satan during the Black Sabbat,'' said Madeleine
Springer. ''That's not just an incidental part of the Sabbat, it's
the entire point and purpose of the Sabbat.

''Satan infects the witches with his virus by violent intercourse which tears the internal tissues of the witch's body and
opens a wound through which her blood can be infected.

''The witch retains the Night Plague virus in her body for
the rest of her life. She has intercourse herself with seven men.
Each of them is chosen because he is terminally ill with some
ordinary physical disease, such as leprosy or cancer or AIDS.
In return for becoming Carriers, the witch grants them extended life. Their task is to pass on the Night Plague virus to
as many innocent people as they possibly can, especially people who are imaginative and creative and who have a strong
influence on society. That was why Shakespeare was infected.
He was visited by an apparition who looked to him like a Dark
Lady. That was why Mozart found a horrific gray stranger
knocking at his door. Something happened to Mozart that night,
nobody quite knows what, but his health and his music never
recovered from it.''

"I think I'll 'ave a drink now, if you don't mind," said Angie.

"Gin-and-orange, isn't it?" asked Madeleine Springer. "You'll find everything you want in the kitchen."

Angie said, " 'Ow . . . ?" but Stanley lifted his finger to his lips to shush her.

Madeleine Springer went on: "Once the Night Plague virus has entered the bloodstream of an innocent person, it enters the brain and invades the hypothalamus. Here, it gradually alters; and it begins to exert an insidious effect on the sufferer's mind. It begins to change his morality. It causes him to have spasms of petty hatred, and spitefulness, and irrational violence. It loosens his perception of reality, so that he never quite knows whether he's dreaming or awake. It creates grotesque symptoms of physical sickness, such as vomiting worms or molluscs or great choking balls of animal hair, or urinating streams of blood. All of these symptoms serve to heighten the sufferer's sense of degradation and self-disgust."

Stanley said nothing. He knew exactly what Madeleine Springer was talking about. Even now, he could feel himself growing impatient with her and feeling an irrational urge to slap her and twist her hair.

She turned to look at him. She must have been able to sense what he was thinking. She kept her eyes on him steadily as she spoke.

"Gradually, the symptoms of Night Plague become increasingly severe. The sufferer becomes depressed and irascible, and there will be a noticeable coarsening of his personality. He will start using foul language, drinking more, making crude remarks. Usually, he becomes much more sexually active, sometimes frantically so, even though he will find it more and more difficult to achieve a physical climax. He will often become sadistic, too.

"By this stage, the Night Plague has transmuted itself into an infection of the spirit; a disease of the unconscious mind. And it is spread from one person to another through dreams—dreams of sexual intercourse or rape. It is remarkably similar in its pathology to recent strains of syphilis . . . except that it infects the soul rather than the body."

Stanley swallowed vodka. "This is all very well, Ms.

Springer . . . but what's the *point* of it? Assuming that Satan does exist . . . assuming that this Night Plague is exactly what you say it is . . . why does Satan want to spread it in the first place?''

Madeleine Springer replied softly and sadly. ''Because a soul infected by the Night Plague is a soul which cannot be admitted to heaven, that is why. The Night Plague can be passed on from one soul to another even after death. So any soul who is infected must be denied entry to the Kingdom of Light. Satan has already contaminated the temporal world; we cannot allow him to contaminate the hereafter, too.

''The Night Plague is Satan's way of garnering souls, Mr. Eisner. And this time, he seems determined that he shall infect not just the Caribbean and a third of Europe, as he did in the days when Columbus and his crew brought it back from Haiti; nor most of England, as he did in the days of the Black Death. This time, he seems determined to infect the whole global population; to make *all* of us his, forever.''

Gordon was beginning to shudder, although Stanley wasn't sure if he was shuddering from the shock of losing his hand or in dread of what Madeleine Springer was telling them. Because—to his own surprise—he *did* have a feeling of dread. He had seen enough of Knitted Hood and the horrors of the house called Tennyson to believe that Madeleine Springer was telling them the truth, or at least the truth as far as she understood it.

He had also felt the symptoms of the Night Plague for himself; and he was fighting against them now.

''Is there any cure?'' he asked Madeleine Springer.

''There is only one antidote,'' she told him. ''You must find the witch who originally infected the Carrier who infected you. In your case, it was Isabel Gowdie, the blindfolded woman whose likeness appears all over Tennyson. You must find her and have relations with her, to pass back the virus in the same way that it was transmitted. As soon as you have done that, *while* you are doing that, you must kill her, so that she cannot pass it back again.''

''Relations?'' Stanley demanded. ''What kind of relations? You mean *sex*?''

Madeleine Springer nodded. ''It's the only way.''

''But supposing she doesn't want to have sex? Supposing *I*

don't want to have sex? Supposing I can't even find her to have sex with?''

"You will have to find her. You will have to have sex with her; or your immortal soul will be forfeit forever."

"You're not putting me on?"

"I wish in the name of Ashapola that I were."

"Well, do you have any idea where this Isabel Gowdie is?"

"None at all. She was eventually captured and imprisoned by Night Warriors, but it is a strict rule that Night Warriors never reveal to anybody where a witch or a demon has been imprisoned. In that way, nobody can ever be tempted to release them. And, believe me, the temptation can be great. Satan and his agents can offer you almost anything that you have ever desired."

"Don't you even have an inkling of where she might be?"

"No. The last known official record was that Isabel Gowdie was sentenced to be burned at the stake on May 13, 1662, after she confessed to the Scottish court that she was a special domestic servant of the Devil, and that she had conjured up storms all round England's coastline by slapping a rock with a wet rag, and that those storms had drowned scores of fishermen."

"Then she's dead?" asked Stanley."

Madeleine Springer shook her head. "Somehow she managed to escape. Whatever was burned at the stake, it wasn't her. In fact, one eyewitness said that it looked more like the ashes of a Great Dane.

"She *must* be alive, and even if she hasn't broken free from her imprisonment, she must at least have broken free from the bonds which the Night Warriors used to seal her mind. Her Carriers are roaming abroad and spreading her infection, and they cannot do that unless she is conscious and capable of giving them strength and mobility. Without her, they are nothing, literally, but corpses. She is dreaming, too. Powerful, vivid dreams of the way things were when she was locked away. That is why the house called Tennyson is full of her pictures, and why it rains there, just as it rained in the same spot in 1666, when Isabel Gowdie was still free. Her influence is very strong; she was said to have placed one hand on her head and one hand on her foot, and renounced everything in between her two hands to Satan.

"Satan dearly favors her. That is why he awarded her such powers. Your hallucinations of plague-ridden landscapes are the result of *her* influence in your infection. Her psychic DNA is inside you now, inside your mind. When Isabel Gowdie sleeps, her dreams are just as real to you as they are to her."

There was a long silence. Angie came back with her gin-and-orange and sat close to Stanley, resting one hand on his knee.

Madeleine Springer said, "You haven't yet asked me what *I* have to do with all of this."

"I had the feeling you were going to tell us, anyway," Stanley replied.

"In actual fact," said Madeleine Springer, "what *you* have to do with it is much more important than what *I* have to do with it."

"I don't follow you."

"You don't think that you were infected at random, do you?"

"What are you saying? That Knitted Hood picked me out specially?"

"Of course he did, because you're the direct descendant of a Night Warrior. Not just any Night Warrior, either—one of the Night Warriors whom Isabel Gowdie killed before she was finally captured."

"Now you've really lost me," Stanley complained.

Madeleine Springer walked across to him and touched his shoulder with her fingertips. Stanley felt a tingling sensation, as if he had touched a live electric wire. But it was something more than electricity: it had a resonance, too, like thunderous silent music.

"You feel that?" she asked him. "You're the direct descendant of Jacob Eisner, the ragpicker from Whitechapel. Jacob was a Night Warrior, and that means that *you* are a Night Warrior, too. That was why you were followed and assaulted by Knitted Hood. He wanted to make sure that Isabel Gowdie's infection got to you before *you* got to Isabel Gowdie."

"I came to London to play the violin. I didn't come here to look for some witch."

"In time, I would have called on you and required you to do it."

"*Required* me?"

"You're a Night Warrior, Mr. Eisner. You have no choice."

"I don't understand any of this," Stanley told her, trying to be patient. "Do you mind explaining exactly what you mean by a Night Warrior?" The feeling that she was playing a gigantic hoax on them began to resurface; and apart from that his head had started to throb with a vicious migraine. He hadn't had a migraine in ten or eleven years, but there was no mistaking it.

Madeleine Springer said, "There was a time when the earth was infested with demons and devils, like vermin. In those days, the Night Warriors were both necessary and numerous. They were a holy army, if you like, who were charged with the task of hunting down evil creatures in the landscape of the human unconscious . . . in dreams, where demons and devils had previously been able to conceal themselves and remain unscathed and undetected.

"In human dreams, you see, demons could escape being exorcised. The priests simply couldn't reach them. Dreams were a sanctuary for some of the most horrific of all the medieval creatures. People who didn't believe in demons in waking life were quite prepared to believe in the demons they encountered in dreams; and demons thrive on those who believe in them, just as they are weakened by those who don't.

"But, over the centuries, the Night Warriors entered the dreams of thousands of people, and tracked the demons down, and destroyed them; and those whom they didn't destroy they imprisoned forever with sanctified locks and holy seals. They imprisoned witches, too, and all of those agents and familiars of Satan that they could find.

"The Great Fire of London in 1666 was started not by a careless baker, but by one of the greatest dream battles of all history. Five Night Warriors entered the dream of a ratcatcher who lived close to Pudding Lane. They laid an ambush for thirteen of Satan's most favored witches, who had agreed to meet there. *'When shall we thirteen meet again?'* They were laying their plans to spread the Black Death even more widely.

"The witches were caught by surprise, and most of them were destroyed within the first few minutes. But one of them— who was probably Isabel Gowdie—caused the ratcatcher's brain to explode and catch fire. She escaped from the dream, but all five Night Warriors were killed, and the ratcatcher's house caught alight. As you know, most of London was burned to the ground.''

Madeleine Springer's eyes remained fastened on Stanley. They were the strangest eyes that he had ever seen. Faint kaleidoscopic colors seemed to flicker through them, and in some extraordinary way they seemed to be focused *inwards* rather than *outwards*, as if all that she needed to see, she could see inside her own mind.

''Jacob Eisner was one of the Night Warriors who died that night,'' she explained. ''The other Night Warriors were *your* great-grandmother many times removed, Miss Dunning, and *your* great-grandfather many times removed, Mr. Rutherford, and one other, the ancestor of an American professor called Henry Watkins. So you can see now that destiny truly brought you all together.''

''That's only four Night Warriors,'' Stanley interrupted. ''You said there were five.''

''That's right. Jacob Eisner's older son Joshua was a trainee Night Warrior. He died, too.''

''Well, that's too bad,'' said Stanley. ''But what does it have to do with us? We're not Night Warriors.''

Madeleine Springer unfastened her cloak and let it slide to the floor. ''The oaths that were taken by your ancestors bind you, too. They always have. You are beholden to fight this plague, just as much as your ancestors would have been.''

''This is a joke,'' Stanley retorted irritably.

''No joke,'' Madeleine Springer replied. ''And what's more, it's your only hope of finding Isabel Gowdie and ridding yourself of the Night Plague.''

''Listen, who the hell *are* you?'' Stanley barked at her. ''You've been sounding off for ten minutes now, all this ridiculous baloney about Night Warriors and witches and plagues and God knows what.''

Madeleine Springer smiled calmly. ''Not *God* knows what, Mr. Eisner; Ashapola knows what.''

''Ashapola? What are you talking about? What's Ashapola?''

''Ashapola, if you like, is the god of all gods. When anybody on this planet speaks of their god, no matter how they happen to imagine Him, they are referring to Ashapola. It is Ashapola who created the world. He is what the Freemasons call the Great Architect of the Universe. It is Ashapola who takes care of you. If you are threatened by the forces of darkness, it is Ashapola who dispatches *me* and those like me to warn you, and to marshal your forces. He cannot directly intervene in the destiny of the world. If He were to do that, then the world as you know it would cease to exist; because a human society that is not required to face the consequences of its own actions is a paradox.

"But there is nothing paradoxical about a Creator caring for his creation, and sending somebody like me to warn you of overwhelming danger."

"You mean you're an angel?" said Angie.

Madeleine Springer glanced at her. "You're a bright girl. I *am* an angel, if an angel is a messenger sent by a divine being. But I am less of a messenger than a message. The body in which you see me is a borrowed memory. You remember the little holographic image of Princess Leia which R2-D2 carried in *Star Wars*? I am much more like that, a picture, an illusion."

As she looked at Stanley, he thought he could see her face and her body subtly altering. Her wide, feline face began to narrow, as if he were seeing negatives of two different faces, one on top of the other. Her voice, which had been quite gentle and mellifluous as she had told them about the Night Plague, began to sound choppier and gruffer. Stanley could almost have sworn that she was changing into a thin-faced young man, right in front of his eyes.

"And you expect us to believe all of this cock-and-bull story?" he demanded, clearing his throat.

"I expect nothing, except that you will do your sworn duty."

"I don't have to do squat, and neither do my friends here."

Madeleine Springer came forward and stood very close to him. The remarkable thing about her was that she didn't have any smell, none whatsoever. No perfume, no leather, no skin smell, nothing. Without asking him, she reached out her hand and laid it on top of his head.

"Hey, what—!"

She smiled. "You have a sick headache," she said. "Quite

often, when the Night Plague takes hold of you, you start to suffer from all the illnesses you've ever had, all over again. Colds, chickenpox, measles, flu. It's raging immune deficiency, with a vengeance.''

She paused. Then she nodded and said, "It's gone now, yes?'' and it was true, his migraine had vanished, just like the tiny glowing spot in the center of a switched-off television tube.

"How did you do that?'' he asked warily. Madeleine Springer was looking more like a man than ever. Her blond hair seemed to be shorter; her jaw was much sharper, and he could see fraying gingery hairs under her arms. *Am I awake, or am I asleep? Is this really happening or not?*

"You're awake,'' Madeleine Springer told him. "And, as I've told you, I'm a message more than a messenger; and a message can take many different shapes and forms.''

Stanley slowly rubbed his forehead with his fingertips. He turned to look at Angie, who sat close beside him, still trembling a little, peaky and distressed; and at Gordon, who had closed his eyes now, and appeared to be asleep, his mouth open, his scarf-wrapped stump lying in his lap. If he were awake, and all this were real, if he were actually *here*, in this apartment, then he knew that he had no alternatives.

"Tell me about the Night Warriors,'' he asked Madeleine Springer.

"Your ancestor Jacob Eisner was one of the most powerful and respected of the Night Warriors,'' Madeleine Springer told Stanley. "His name was Mol Besa, and he was what in the seventeenth century they used to call a Mathematick Grenadier. These days, we call them Equation Warriors. He was able to make the mathematical calculations that would change energy into matter, matter into heat, heat into speed, speed into time—and apply them to his immediate surroundings. For instance, he could work out that if a horde of horse-demons were riding towards him at twenty miles an hour, the kinetic heat that they were producing as they rode was sufficient to raise a wall of bricks in front of them which would stop them dead. He couldn't create bricks out of nothing. Einstein and Newton still apply, even in dreams. But he could convert their own energy into something which would stop them. Mol Besa was the master of what you might call mental judo . . . using your enemy's own strength to bring him down.

"Here," said Madeleine Springer, and beckoned Stanley to follow her across the room. "Stand quite still—here, that's right—and *relax*. I know it's difficult. I know you're fighting the Night Plague. But you can do it, if you try. You can beat the plague and you can beat Isabel Gowdie and you can beat Satan, too, because he's out there, Stanley, he's out there now, tonight, while everybody's dreaming, and he's determined that this time, *this time*, he's going to have us all."

She laid her hand on his shoulder, and he felt that same prickling electricity. "It's the end of the world, Stanley, if we don't beat him now. You can forget about ozone layers and cutting down the rain forests. He'll take our morals, he'll take our families, he'll take everything, including our immortal souls. This is *it*, this is Armageddon. This is the pestilence that we were promised."

Stanley looked towards Angie; but Angie was too tired to do anything but shrug. Gordon was fast asleep now, his head resting on the cushion of the sofa.

"Watch the window," said Madeleine Springer.

Stanley faced the window. He could see himself reflected sharply against the night, and Madeleine Springer, too. They seemed to be standing outside in the darkness, three stories up, like Peter Pan beseeching admission to the nursery window, or Victorian levitationists.

As he watched, a gleaming outline began to form itself around Stanley's head and shoulders: the outline of a spherical helmet, like an old-fashioned diver's helmet, but made of thick glass instead of brass, and surrounded by a cage of metal circlets, which appeared to be constantly contra-rotating.

His shoulders were armored with upswept fins, which reminded him of the air inlets of a Ferrari Testarossa. On his chest he carried a huge bank of instruments and switches and computers, including a holographic astrolabe and the most complicated mathematical calculator that he had ever seen in his life. The visual displays winked at him in sapphire blue and infrared.

Around his waist he wore a heavy-duty telephone-linesman's-type belt, from which swung a huge pistol-grip instrument, the size of an Uzi submachine gun, and a whole variety of cylindrical nickel-plated containers that looked like cartridges.

"This is incredible," said Stanley, staring at his reflection in the window, and then looking down at himself to make sure that it wasn't just a trick of the light. "But it's almost—I don't know, transparent. I can't see it too well."

"That's because you're still awake," Madeleine Springer explained. "I'm creating an illusion of your armor for you out of my own memory, to show you what it looks like. When you're asleep, and dreaming, this will all take on its own reality."

"But I don't know how to *use* all of this stuff."

"You will, once you start dreaming. You have inherited Jacob Eisner's mathematical skills, as well as his duties. Those circlets around your helmet will enable you to pinpoint your psycho-geographical location within the sleeper's imagined landscape. And you'll be able to use those calculators and computers to convert latent energy into heat, heat into matter, matter into time, time into water, whatever you wish.

"Once you've made your calculations, all you have to do is insert one of those empty equation cartridges into the side of the computer and load the program into it. Then you slide the equation cartridge into the gun—like this—and you fire it. Your program arrives where you've fired it; and pure math is instantaneously detonated into pure action."

"I hate to disillusion you, but I flunked math," Stanley admitted. "I couldn't even remember my times tables. I'm not sure I could even recite them *now*."

"This is something different," said Madeleine Springer. "This is mathematics with a mission."

She stepped away from him, and gradually his suit of armor crackled and faded. Stanley felt depleted somehow—as if the armor had given him courage, and strength, and a new sense of purpose. He hadn't felt that kind of determination since he had first played with a professional orchestra. In those days (God Almighty, in those days, twenty years ago) it had seemed like the whole world was his.

Maybe, some day soon, he could claim it back.

"What about me?" asked Angie, who had been watching Stanley's transformation wide-eyed.

Madeleine Springer walked over to the sofa, took Angie's

hand, and led her back to the center of the room. "Your ancestor was called Elisabeth Pardoe, and she was the wife of a
fisherman in Dover. Not a very faithful wife, I'm sorry to say,
but not many fisherwives were. Not many of the prettier fisherwives, anyway. I think you can excuse her. She was married
on her twelfth birthday to a man nearly twenty years older than
she was; and the fishing fleet was usually away for days, or
weeks if the weather was rough. She was very alluring, too;
as you are."

Angie blushed. Madeleine Springer was now so manlike, her
voice so deep, that it wasn't difficult to believe from what she
was saying that she found Angie attractive.

"But what sort of a what's-its-name was she? What sort of
a Night Warrior?"

Madeleine Springer stood behind Angie and took hold of her
shoulders in both hands, directing her attention towards the
black reflecting window.

"She was Effis; and so are you. Effis the light-skater. One
of the very fastest of the Night Warriors, even faster than Xaxxa
the slide-boxer. You can skate on light, wherever that light may
happen to be. It may be the sun, dancing on the surface of the
sea; it may be shining through a window. It may be a klieg
light, pointing at the sky, or the flickering of pilgrim's candles.
You need only the merest pinpoint, and you are away, fast as
a flash."

"What if it's totally dark?" asked Stanley. "What happens
then?"

Madeleine Springer turned to him and she was undeniably a
young man now. A rather handsome young man, with a self-
indulgent languor about him, but no less likable. His costume
had altered, too. It was more of a leather jerkin than a basque;
and although his thighs were still bare and he still wore thigh
boots, he had developed smooth powerful muscles, and his
boots were more like eighteenth-century riding boots, with
turned-over tops.

Madeleine Springer said, "It's rarely dark in people's
dreams—even in their nightmares—with the exception of some
psychotic claustrophobics, who dream of being imprisoned in
cellars or having their faces pushed into pillows. Effis can always find some light to skate on. She can dance on the flame

of a single match. Besides, she almost always stays close to
Kasyx the charge-keeper. He can usually give her sufficient
light.''

"Kasyx? Is that who Gordon's going to be?"

"No . . . you will have to wait to meet Kasyx. But first of
all, let me show you what you will look like, Miss Dunning,
when you enter the world of dreams.''

Springer kept his hands on Angie's shoulders and closed his
eyes for a moment. Gradually, in a sprinkling of tiny electrical
pinpoints, her appearance shifted and flowed, and Stanley saw
her not as Angie Dunning any more, the almost-punk from
Herbert Gardens, London, but as Effis the light-skater, one of
the swiftest and deadliest of the Night Warriors.

She wore a helmet that was constructed out of a lacework of
fine silver wire, elaborately pierced and decorated, and twinkling with hundreds of minuscule white lights. The sides of
the helmet were scalloped, like a clamshell, but the facepiece
was shaped like a mask of Angie's face, a second skin of lights
and flowers and pierced silverwork.

"This headpiece may *look* frail," Springer remarked, "but
it is made of a combination of metals which was discovered by
the Ecuadorian Indians thousands of years ago when they were
trying to sinter platinum and gold. It feels like the softest lace,
but it can withstand higher temperatures than platinum, over
three thousand degrees; and it can also deflect a blow from any
kind of battle-ax that you can imagine.''

"What about battle-axes that we *can't* imagine?" asked
Stanley.

Springer nodded and smiled at his perspicacity. "Battle-axes
that you *can't* imagine have to be deflected by trial.''

"No error?"

"If you make an error with an unimaginable battle-ax, you
don't usually get a second chance.''

Angie looked fantastically otherworldly in her mask-helmet;
a butterfly-woman; a creature out of a carnival; but startlingly
pretty. Her eyes were very wide and glistening and lambent,
and Stanley saw an expression in them that he hadn't seen
before. A greater alertness, a sharper intelligence, a *questioning* look. It was a look he had seen in the eyes of well-educated
children who attended his master classes in violin. They were

not necessarily prodigies. In fact, some of them were quite slow when it came to math and history and spelling. But they possessed a burning keenness to question; and to question again; and to find out. They consumed new knowledge like a brush fire burns oxygen, and still they raged for more.

Angie Dunning had never had that fire; but Effis did; and Stanley found it remarkable how much more self-possessed it made her, how much more magnetic. She still talked in her common South London accent, but she held her head straight, and every movement seemed to have more grace.

So much did Effis's body armor remind Stanley of the glitteringly ostentatious show costume of a star figure skater that he didn't realize at first that it *was* armor. It was a sheer leotard, halter-necked but cut so high on the thighs that her legs looked endless. Patterns of white light played and danced ceaselessly across the fabric, unfolding flower patterns, silently-exploding stars, diamonds, and ruffles. The halter neck was very high, and fastened tightly at her throat with a brilliantly-jeweled choker, four rows of dazzling diamonds, pressed into a thick band of solid platinum.

While it seemed so thin, and clung to her skin so tightly, the body stocking lifted and separated Effis's breasts so that they looked even fuller and rounder and shaped her waist. She appeared to be taller, trimmer.

"What do you think?" Springer asked her. "The finest suit of dreamlight armor ever made."

Effis stared at herself in the window and said, "This ain't supposed to be *armor*, is it? It don't feel like armor."

Springer laid his hand appreciatively on her back. The dancing patterns of light sparkled along his fingers and around his fingertips. A few small sparks even showered from his lips as he spoke.

"This suit will protect you from every lightweight weapon that has ever been encountered by the Night Warriors in ten centuries of human dreams. The fabric's rather like the surface of a CD record . . . it's programmed to alter its structure to deal with anything that happens to be fired at it. Darts, arrows, death-stars, stones, you name it; and a few things for which there *are* no names. For instance, what do you call a lance that's fashioned out of solid darkness, and nothing else?"

"You said it protects against lightweight weapons," Stanley put in. "What about heavyweight weapons?"

Springer shook his gradually-darkening hair. "Effis will be far too fast to have to worry about anything heavier. Once she's started skating on a strong light-source, she can pick up the momentum of the light itself, and travel faster than you and I or anybody else can even *think*."

"Right now, I don't know *what* to think," said Stanley.

Effis did a twirl in the window and then lifted both arms. She wore full-length gloves, as fine and as lacy as her helmet. But along the outside edge of each glove, all the way from the tips of her little fingers to her elbows, was a thin folded fan of shining silver metal.

"What are these for?" she wanted to know.

"Those are your razor-fans, your principal weapons," Springer told her. "You approach your target as fast as you can. You hold your arm straight out in front of you, hand flat. Then you flex the muscles in your arm and the razor-fan opens up."

Effis hesitated, but Springer lifted her right arm for her and showed her. "Now, *flex*."

Instantly, silently, the fan opened up into a series of five metal fins. The fin on the side of her hand was only two or three inches wide, but the fin on her wrist was a little wider, and the one halfway along her forearm a little wider still, until the fin at her elbow was over a foot wide.

Effis turned her arm this way and that, and reflections from the shining fins skipped and shivered around the room. "I don't see 'ow it works."

"Crouch down like a skater," Springer instructed her. "Imagine you're traveling at two hundred feet per second. That's not too fast, you can skate much faster than that. Hold both arms rigidly out in front of you, keeping your hands locked together, like a diver. There's a whole row of demons in front of you, all right? You flex your muscles, your razor-fans open up. You shout your battle cry, *Ashapola!* and you skate right through those demons on your ray of light, and you slice off everything that gets in your way."

Effis relaxed her arm muscles, and the razor-fan slowly

closed. She looked uncertain. "I'm not too sure I like the sound of that."

Springer shrugged. "Effis the light-skater is one of the most feared of all the Night Warriors, believe me."

"That still don't mean I like the sound of cutting people to bits."

"Those who inspire the greatest fear in Ashapola's enemies have the greatest duty to perform," said Springer.

"But—"

"Before you say 'but,' take a look at your skates. They've changed a great deal from the days when Elisabeth Pardoe was Effis. In her day they were ash wood, with sharpened iron blades, and hand-ground lenses to take in the light. But so much of the Night Warriors' equipment has changed and developed. We would have been overwhelmed and routed centuries ago if we had allowed ourselves to remain complacent. Modern dreams require modern weaponry."

Effis looked down. Little by little, a pair of skating boots materialized around her ankles. They were gleaming silver metal, streamlined and wedge-shaped, with clusters of six or seven large white lenses around the ankles. The boots appeared to have no skates: Effis was standing flat on the floor.

"This is the greatest advance," said Springer, hunkering down beside Effis. "In the seventeenth century, the light was taken in through the lenses, focused, and directed along the cutting edge of the blade, so that it acted as a lubricant between the skate and the ground surface. With these skates, the light is taken in through the lenses, intensified over ten thousand times, and guided by fiber optics through to the sole of the boot, where it forms an actual skate blade made of pure light."

"But there's nothing there," Effis protested.

"There will be, when you're all charged up, believe me."

At last they approached Gordon, who had just woken up from a restless doze on the sofa. Springer knelt down beside him and gently laid his hand on his scarf-wrapped wrist. Gordon's face was colorless, and his eyes were widely dilated. When he spoke, his voice was slurred, as if he were recovering from anesthetic.

Stanley wondered if Springer had somehow "put him un-

der" to ease the shock and the pain of what had happened to
him. No matter how miraculous Springer's healing might have
been, the loss of a hand must still have been hideously trau-
matic.

"Gordon . . ." said Springer in a gentle voice. "How are
you feeling?"

"Terrible," Gordon replied. "I feel as if a gerbil's been
sleeping in my mouth. Do you think I could have a drink of
water?"

"Of course. Stanley, would you mind? It's going to take you
a week or two to get over the shock."

"What were those things . . . those dog-things?"

"Guard dogs, if you like. Witches create them for their own
amusement; and also to serve them and protect them. You've
read fairy stories about witches stealing children . . . Rapun-
zel, Hansel and Gretel . . . they're based on truth. Witches
used to steal babies and children and meld them supernaturally
with the bodies of dogs, or cats, or goats. The children were
always promised that—one day—they would be changed back
into human shape, but in return they had to serve and obey
their mistress without question. Those boy-dogs who attacked
you at Tennyson were guarding the entrance to their mistress's
memories . . . that rainy landscape, that barbaric world of pain
and disease."

Stanley brought Gordon a glass of water, which Gordon
drank thirstily and unsteadily, spilling some of it down the
front of his coat.

"The boy-dogs were told to kill all intruders, whatever the
cost," said Springer. "You were lucky to escape with your
lives."

"I left my hand behind," said Gordon.

Springer slowly stood up and looked at Gordon with a mixture of compassion and acceptance. Stanley saw in his eyes the
steadiness of somebody who knows that events must turn out
as events must turn out; but somebody who can regret it, all
the same. There are greater conflicts in the universe than the
squabbles of men. There are far more monstrous planets turning than the planet earth; and far more agonizing losses than
the loss of Gordon's hand.

All the same, the distance between the earth and Jupiter, at conjunction, was only 928 million kilometers; and the distance between Gordon and his lost hand was infinite.

Springer said, "Since you were born, Gordon, you were fated to lose that hand. You probably don't know it, but your great-great-grandfather lost the same hand, when he was called to the service of the Night Warriors. And three generations before that, *his* great-great-grandfather also lost his left hand."

"But *why*?" asked Gordon in a hoarse voice.

"It was a sacrifice, of a sort. A way of improving your ability to fight for Ashapola. Just as Amazon women removed one breast to make it easier for them to use a bow and arrow, your hand was given in the cause of the greatest battle of all."

"How the hell does losing my hand help me to fight better?" Gordon demanded.

"Let me show you. Are you strong enough to stand?"

Gordon nodded. "I think so. If I fall flat on my face, then you'll know that I'm not."

Springer helped him up and guided him over to the middle of the room. Gordon walked unsteadily and swayed a little as he stood facing the window, but Springer stood close beside him and held his arm.

"You are Keldak the fistfighter. Watch the window . . . this is your armor."

Gordon said sarcastically. "*Fist*fighter? With only one fist?" but Springer said, "Wait, and watch."

Slowly, the outline of a heavy squarish helmet appeared around Gordon's head . . . a helmet of softly-gleaming green metal, with the narrowest slit of a tinted visor. Attached to the left side of the helmet was a square illuminated grid, and less than an inch away from this grid, hovering in the air, was a holographic image of a globe, about four inches in diameter. Whichever way Keldak turned his head, the globe remained hovering at the same distance from the left side of his helmet, like an obedient planet.

"You use the globe to aim your weapon," Springer told him. "When the time comes for you to go into combat, it will swing around in front of your eyes, and you will be able to create a model of your adversary within it. Once your adversary has been targeted, and his image has been locked into the globe, he can never escape, even if it eludes you at that particular moment, and you don't come across it again until months or even years later."

Below his helmet, Keldak's chest and stomach were protected by green metallic body armor. A shaped triangular codpiece of the same green metal protected his genitals, and was fastened tightly between his buttocks with a thin leather strap. He wore green metallic boots with illuminated studs all the way down the sides, but otherwise he was naked.

"So where's my weapon?" he asked. He raised his bare right fist. "This isn't going to be very much use against demons. Come on, Springer, I couldn't punch my way out of a wet paper bag."

Springer smiled and said, "Hold up your left wrist."

Keldak did as he was told. Springer took hold of it and carefully unwrapped the scarf, baring the swollen skin of his stump. Although it was still reddened, it was miraculous how well it had healed. With conventional medicine, Keldak would probably have still been undergoing surgery.

Springer said, "The power that I am going to give you now is only a tiny proportion of the power that Kasyx the chargekeeper will give you. But it will be sufficient for a demonstration."

He closed his eyes for a moment, still gripping Keldak's left wrist. Keldak glanced uncertainly at Stanley, but all that Stanley could do was to shrug. He couldn't guess what was going to happen any more than Keldak could.

Angie whispered, "It's *unbelievable*, innit?"

So gradually that Stanley couldn't be sure at first that he was not simply imagining it, a pale luminous hand-shape appeared on the end of Keldak's left wrist. Springer kept his eyes tightly closed, and with each passing second the luminous hand grew brighter and brighter, until it shone almost as brightly as a halogen lamp.

Keldak turned his wrist this way and that, staring at the dazzling hand in amazement. It threw vast distorted shadows of all of them around the room. "I can *feel* it," he said. "I can actually *feel* it. I can wiggle my fingers."

"It's one hundred percent pure power," said Springer, opening his eyes. "When Kasyx has charged you up, it will be absolutely blinding. On the left side of your chest armor, you will find a gauntlet. Normally, your fist will remain covered; but when you are ready to fight, you will pull off the gauntlet, target your fist, and release it.''

Keldak frowned. "*Release* it?"

"Do you want to try it?" asked Springer. "Why not target that vase?"

On the opposite side of the room, on the floor, stood a tall black glass vase, containing a stylized arrangement of silvery dried honesty.

"Are you sure?" asked Keldak.

"Go ahead, everything's replaceable."

Keldak hesitated for a moment, then raised his right hand and slid a small switch on the left of his breastplate. Immediately, silently, unerringly, the holographic globe quarter-circled around from the side of his helmet and floated right in front of his narrow visor.

"How did I know how to do that?" he asked in bewilderment.

"The skills of the Night Warriors are passed mystically from generation to generation," said Springer. "With a little practice, you will become as adept as your forefathers. Now—target the vase."

Keldak pressed a series of small illuminated buttons on his breastplate, and a three-dimensional picture of the vase began to build up inside the sphere. It took no more than three or four seconds. Once it was done, Keldak pressed another button, and the glove returned to its "parked" position on the left side of his helmet.

"Raise your arm," Springer instructed him. Keldak did as he was told, looking quickly at Stanley and Angie for reassurance.

"All right, fire."

"Fire?"

"Go ahead. Don't you know how to do it?"

"I—" Keldak began, but without warning, his shining left fist shot from the end of his arm with a startling *sshhhhhheeeeeee-krakkkkkk!* and punched the vase from over ten feet away. The vase exploded in a fine spray of glittering black glass, and the sprigs of honesty were tossed across the floor.

Springer laughed. Keldak looked down at his stump. Another hand had already appeared, more pale and ghostly this time.

"That's amazing," he said. "That's absolutely amazing."

"Of course, your combat fist will be infinitely more powerful," Springer explained. "And each new fist will normally be just as powerful as the one before it. That's until you run short of charge. Then you'll have to go back to Kasyx for more."

Keldak's armor and helmet faded, leaving Gordon standing tiredly in the middle of the room. "Come on," Springer urged him, "sit down. You've had enough for one night."

Gordon returned to the sofa. Stanley drained his vodka glass and went to the kitchen to help himself to a refill. Springer followed him and stood in the doorway watching him as he poured himself what British India-hands would have called a *burra-peg*, three fingers and a splash more.

"Well?" asked Springer. Somehow, he was beginning to change again, to become younger and more feminine. His hair seemed silkier and longer than it had just a moment ago, when he was showing Keldak his armor.

"Well, what?" asked Stanley. "Do you want me to say that I'm impressed? All right, I'm impressed. I can't say that I'm delighted, but I'm impressed."

"I hope you don't expect me to pretend that being a Night Warrior isn't anything but a burdensome and dangerous responsibility," said Springer in a tone that almost turned his words into a question. "But your forefathers made promises which bind you today; and which bind your children; and which will bind your children's children."

"The sins of the fathers visited on the sons," said Stanley caustically into his vodka glass.

Springer said, "You do understand, don't you, that for you personally, finding and destroying Isabel Gowdie isn't just a matter of controlling this epidemic of Night Plague? It's your only hope of saving your soul, Stanley."

"I'm not sure how much I *want* my soul to be saved."

"Well, you'll feel that way a lot of the time . . . that's one of the symptoms. You'll feel depressed and hopeless. You may even feel suicidal."

Stanley said nothing, but swallowed more vodka and shivered.

Springer came up to him. He was much smaller now, and his blond hair was almost touching his shoulders. He had become a young girl of eighteen or nineteen, very slim, almost breastless, with dreamy heavy-lidded eyes and a delicate mouth.

"I've seen the Carriers come and go," Springer told him. "I've even managed to follow them, two or three times. They've been searching for more Night Warriors to infect. But I still have no idea where Isabel Gowdie might be; not even a clue. You'll have to go into her dreams to find her."

"What are our chances if we do?"

"Better than your chances if you don't."

"So when do we start looking for her?" asked Stanley.

"Just as soon as Kasyx the charge-keeper and the fifth Night Warrior arrive."

"The fifth Night Warrior?"

"Zasta the knife-juggler. His forefather was killed, too, when Isabel Gowdie ignited the ratcatcher's brain. He has to have his revenge."

Stanley said, "How soon are they coming?"

"Within two or three days, no longer."

"And how are we supposed to know when they arrive?"

"You'll know. I promise you. You'll know for sure."

Stanley looked at Springer; pretty and youthful and gentle as a young animal; and for no reason that he could truly comprehend, the most appalling feeling of dread came over him.

SIX

Rotten Rags

THE TELEPHONE WAS RINGING WHEN STANLEY AND ANGIE ARrived back at Stanley's flat at half past seven that morning. They had driven Gordon home first and then borrowed Gordon's car to get back to Langton Street. Stanley had been obliged to let Angie do the driving, even though she hadn't yet passed her test. He had never driven a car with a manual gearbox before—especially not a shuddering, rusty, rubbish-littered junker like Gordon's Montego.

The morning was gloomy and fogbound, and even though it wasn't raining, the deserted streets of Fulham and Chelsea were shining with wet. It was so bitterly cold that Stanley had kept his hands thrust deep in his pockets.

He first heard the phone as he slotted the key into the downstairs door. "What are you going to do?" he asked Angie. "Drive straight back to Herbert Gardens or stay for some breakfast?"

"Ain't you going to answer the phone?" Angie wanted to know.

"It's a wrong number, more than likely. I get dozens of them. 'Is Stephanie in?' mostly. I think this flat used to be rented by the most industrious call girl in Fulham. Don't worry, if it's all that important, they'll call back later.''

Angie looked at her wristwatch. ''All right, I'll 'ave a cup of coffee. Don't s'pose Brenda and Sharon are awake yet, anyway. They usually 'ave a lie-in, Saturdays.''

They went upstairs, and Stanley opened the door to his flat. The phone continued to ring, but he didn't answer it straightaway. He drew back the curtains and switched on the lights first, and stripped off his coat. Only then did he pick up the receiver and tuck it under his chin.

''Miss Thomson doesn't live here any more, I'm sorry to say,'' he answered. Then he paused and listened, and the expression on his face slowly melted from tired-flippant to tired-serious, ''Eve? Eve, what's wrong?''

He placed his hand over the receiver and said to Angie, ''It's my ex. She's calling from San Francisco.''

Angie had dropped on to the big brown sofa and was sitting with her knees tucked up. There were violet smudges of exhaustion under her eyes. She didn't say anything, but untied the ribbon around her firework-style hair and shook it loose like a poodle.

Eve said, ''What time is it? I tried to call you earlier, but there was no reply.''

''It's seven thirty-five in the morning.''

''Did I wake you?''

''I've been out. That's why you couldn't get me before.''

''You've been out all night?''

''Eve, we're not married any more. I can do what I like.''

''Stanley, my father's had a coronary. He's very, very sick.''

''I'm sorry to hear that, Eve. Where is he?''

''He's still in Napa right now, but Dr. Fishman is talking about transferring him to the Polk Clinic in San Francisco when he's strong enough.''

''Well, I'm sorry to hear that, Eve. Is he conscious?''

''He can understand what we say to him, but he can't speak just yet.''

''Well, tell him how sorry I am—and if there's anything that I can do . . .''

''As a matter of fact, Stanley, that's why I'm calling. There *is* something that you can do.''

Stanley looked across at Angie and rolled his eyes up to show her that Eve was going on again, the way she always went on. Angie grinned at him.

"Stanley . . . I'd like you to take care of Leon for a while."

"You'd like me to what?"

"Stanley, it isn't much to ask. Leon's so upset about his grandfather . . . and he misses you so bad. I just think it would do him so much good if he could join you in London for a month. It would get him away from all of this trauma. And it would reestablish your relationship, too. Don't you think that's important? Father and son?"

"That's not what your lawyer told my lawyer, the last time they spoke on the subject of visitation rights. Your lawyer told my lawyer that you would rather have Leon spend weekends with the Wolfman than spend any time with me."

"I was upset, Stanley. Now I'm not upset. Well, not as upset as I was then."

"You mean this time you need me."

"All right, Stanley, I need you. Leon needs you. Maybe you need Leon, too, even if you don't need me."

"Eve, it's very early in the morning, I haven't slept all night, and this is getting too complicated. What exactly are you proposing to do?"

"I want to put Leon on the six twenty-five Pan Am Clipper tomorrow night. I want you to meet him at London airport. If you can have him in London for three weeks minimum, that'll be wonderful. If you can have him longer . . . well, that would be even more wonderful."

Stanley was silent for a very long time. He didn't intend to play with the Kensington Chamber Orchestra for at least another month. That was if he ever played anything with anyone, ever again. The thought of opening up his violin case made him feel cold with anxiety. It might be teeming with worms. His violin might have collapsed into soft, silent dust. There might be something worse in there . . . something infinitely vile.

Angie came over and stood beside him and looked directly into his eyes.

"What is it?" she asked him.

"My ex wants my son to come stay with me, here in London."

"Why not? I'll 'elp you. It might be a laugh."

Eve said, "Stanley? Stanley? Are you still there?"

"Yes, Eve, I'm still here."

"Well? Will you have him? He's your own flesh and blood, after all."

Stanley nodded wearily. "All right, Eve, pack his bag and send him over. What did you say? The six twenty-five Clipper from San Francisco?"

"PA 126 . . . For goodness' sake, make sure you're there waiting for him. And call me when he arrives. Don't wait to get home, call me from the airport."

"You've got it."

"Stanley—"

"Yes, Eve?"

"Nothing. I know this is short notice, Stanley, and I really do appreciate your having him, especially after everything that's happened."

"You made it happen, sugar, not me."

"Stanley, I—"

"It's too late, Eve. It's all too late. Just give my best to your old man, would you? And tell your old lady I take it all back, what I said about her black-bottom pie. And tell Leon I love him."

He put down the phone. For some odd reason, he suddenly thought of what Springer had said to him about the other two Night Warriors. *You'll know when they arrive.*

Angie said, "You don't look particularly chuffed about 'im coming."

"I don't know. I don't know what to think. Everything's so weird. That house last night . . . all that stuff about Night Warriors. I feel like I'm losing my marbles."

"Oh, cheer up," Angie insisted. She was standing very close to him, and when he tried to move away she caught hold of his shirt sleeve.

"I was going to perk some coffee," he told her.

She still didn't let go of his sleeve. "I don't think you're losing your marbles, you know," she told him. "It's true, all of it."

"You're very sure, all of a sudden."

"I've caught it, too, that's why," she said in a challenging voice.

"You've caught what?"

"That disease that Springer was talking about—that Night Plague. I've caught it, too, caught it from you. I know what it feels like because I can feel it inside of meself. I feel like shouting out loud, I feel like 'itting you, 'ard as I can. I feel like scratching your eyes out. I can't stand the sight of you. But I want to go to bed with you, too. I want to go to bed with you and do it and do it and do it in every single way you can think of and never stop."

Stanley slowly lifted her hand away from his sleeve. *Why not? She's a beautiful girl. And if she's really desperate for it, why not? Don't you remember what you said to Eve. "Eve, we're not married any more. I can do what I like." Prove it— prove you can do what you like. Take her to bed and do it.*

"You're overtired, that's all," he heard himself saying.

"Stanley, I'm not. I've caught it."

"How could you have caught it?"

"We 'ad it away, didn't we? We 'ad a dream that we 'ad it away. That's when I caught it."

Stanley laid his hands on her shoulders, almost fatherly. "Angie . . . you're overtired, that's all there is to it. I know what Springer said about passing on the Night Plague in dreams . . . but it's far more likely that you're exhausted, and that you're still suffering from shock. Let's face up to it, what happened last night was pretty damned extraordinary."

Angie stared at him for a long, tense second, her body taut, her back straight, her lower lip quivering.

"Stan," she said, "I've caught it."

He lowered his head, trying to be patient, "Listen, sweetheart—"

"I've caught it, you stupid bastard! I've caught it!"

She tore open the two top buttons of her clinging red woollen dress, then she wrenched the wool apart, exposing her scarlet nylon bra, filled to overflowing with her brimming white breasts. She wrenched the wool again, and again, and tore the dress completely off, so that she was standing in front of him in her scarlet bra and her scarlet panty hose and her high-heeled scarlet shoes, and that was all.

Stanley said, "Angie, this just isn't the time or the *(why not? why not? look at those breasts, look at the way those panty hose are tucked tight right between her legs)* impossible, not you and me, especially if Springer's right and we're *(you could lose your whole hand in those breasts, like plunging your fingers into soft bread dough)* can't do it, can't even *think* about doing it."

Angie paused. Her eyes seemed to be unfocused, as if she were high, or hypnotized. In exaggeratedly slow motion, she reached behind her and unfastened the clasp of her bra. Her breasts swung bare, with tiny tight sugar-pink nipples.

"Angie—" Stanley began; but the look in her eyes was enough to convince him to stay back. Her pupils were so widely dilated that he felt that if he looked into them with a flashlight, he would be able to see right down inside of her body, all the way down to the soles of her feet.

She kicked off her shoes, and then she tugged down her panty hose, stepping out of them and tossing them aside. Completely naked, she stood in front of him again. He hadn't realized how short she was, without her high heels. Her nipples were on the same level as his waist.

Look at her, look at that body, smell that perfume, smell that sex. She wants you so much that she has tears in her eyes.

"I want it," she mouthed.

He said nothing, couldn't think of anything to say.

"I want it," she repeated.

He turned away, toward the window. Outside, in the foggy air, he could see woodsmoke lying almost horizontal a few feet above the ground, motionless, unstirred by any wind; and a muddy rutted field, and a half-collapsed building that looked like a pig farm or an abattoir. He could see people walking through the fog huddled in gray blankets and tattered shawls; people who walked as if they had nowhere to go to, and no hope whatever.

I want it, said Angie inside of his mind.

Then—without any further warning—she took one step forward and raked her rough-bitten nails all the way down his left cheek, tearing the skin three layers deep.

The sting of nails was instant and excruciating. It hurt so much that for a split second he thought that she had thrown acid at him. But his reaction was so fast that he had slapped her across the face before he had even decided whether he was going to retaliate or not. She slapped him back, almost as quickly. He slapped her again.

"You bastard!" she screeched at him. Her face had turned into a contorted mask, terrifying in its hate and its intensity. *"You bastard!"*

He seized hold of her wrist and twisted her around, jamming her hand up between her shoulder blades in a hammerlock. She screamed and kicked and tried to struggle her way free *bastard bastard bastard bastard* but he managed to snatch her other wrist and catch both hands behind her back, gripping both of her wrists in his left hand.

He forced her forward in an awkward four-legged dance. She spat at him over her shoulder and swore at him filthily, a monotonous litany of blasphemy and hatred and dirt.

She staggered, and he pushed her against the door, which slammed shut. He pressed his weight against her, keeping her hands high up between her shoulder blades, and forcing them higher whenever she kicked back at him. *God you bastard you bastard I'm going to kill you for this you bastard.*

He grunted, pushed her harder. Her bare breasts were squashed against the panels of the door. With his free hand he tugged loose his belt buckle, wrenched at his buttons, tore open his zipper. His hardened penis rose from his shorts like a thick sculpture in dark red marble, the gleaming heart-shaped head, the corded shaft.

If she's crying out for it, the whore, she can have it. She can have it hard and she can have it till she screams at me to stop. And then she can have it some more. He opened her up with his fingers, stretched her lips apart. She shrieked and tried to break free, but he stretched her even wider. He was grunting, he could hear himself grunting. He sounded more like a beast than a human, a savage crouching primitive creature with a rearing erection.

He pushed himself into her, right up as far as he could go, forcing her even harder against the door. He pushed her again and again, and she wrestled and swore at him, but he kept on pushing even when she screamed, and his whole mind was filled up with shattering blackness, like the black glass vase that Keldak had shattered with his explosive fist of light.

He could feel his climax tightening between his legs. *Bastard*, she was screaming at him, *bastard bastard bastard thousand times bastard!*

He said, "Oh, God" but at that instant she roared at him, roared at him *Nooo!* and twisted herself around so violently that she broke his grip on her wrists. She dropped to her knees in front of him, seized his buttocks with fingers that dug into his flesh like claws, and pulled him forward into her open mouth, deeper than he could have believed possible, as deep as he could go. He gripped her hair, wound it around his fingers. He felt her teeth catching at his skin *God she's going to bite it off* then climaxed in terror and pain and incomprehensible ecstasy *ngugh nnngghh nghh* quaking and crying out as if all the doors of hell had slammed at once.

She said something, he couldn't understand what. She swallowed and swallowed again.

Then it was over and they lay side by side on the carpet staring at each other and saying nothing, their fingertips touching, that was all, and Stanley was sure and certain that Springer had been telling them the truth. They were in danger of losing not only their morals but their mortal souls, and there was only one way for them to save themselves.

They slept for most of the morning. Stanley woke at ten after eleven and lay staring at the ceiling for a while. He felt tired and nauseous, and his mouth was filled with sickly-tasting saliva. Without waking Angie, he eased himself out of bed and tippytoed through to the bathroom.

He switched on the fluorescent light over the bathroom mirror. He stared at himself. His face appeared to be gray and bloated, like a man who has been found drowned in the Thames. His left cheek was scored with four scab-encrusted parallel lines where Angie had scratched it. There were reddened bite marks on his neck, too, and on his shoulders.

"Stanley," he told himself. "You look like you fought a monkey in a trash can and lost."

His stomach gurgled, and his mouth was filled with bile. He

spat it out and reached for the water glass, but as he did so he
suddenly coughed. He could feel something twisted and rubbery caught in his throat, and his stomach rebelled against it
so violently that he let out a huge cackling retch and bent
double over the washbasin.

His throat contracted again and again, and slowly, out of his
stretched-open mouth, he forced out a tangled mass of brown
squid's legs, glistening and suckered and still curling and un-
curling as if they were alive, all stuck together with a wet gray
mass that looked like hair and soap scum that had been cleared
out of a blocked bathroom drain.

The thing completely choked him, so that he couldn't cry
out. He retched and retched again, shuddering with pain and
disgust, his eyes crowded with tears. Just when he thought it
was going to suffocate him, it gave a last convulsive wriggle
and dropped into the washbasin, where it lay writhing and
twisting and unrolling, as if it, too, were suffering agonizing
pain.

Stanley bent his head over the bath and turned on the cold
faucet as far as it would go, and splashed handful after handful
of water into his mouth. His stomach was still growling and
protesting, and he couldn't stop himself from convulsing in
horror.

At last, however, he sniffed, and stood up, and dragged a
bath towel from the rail and momentarily buried his face in it.
When he looked back at the washbasin, the tentacles were still
wriggling, and he had to cover his mouth with his hand to
prevent himself from puking yet again.

He heard Angie calling from the bedroom, "Stan? Stanley,
are you all right?"

"I'm okay," he choked back. "I'm okay. Just don't come in
here."

"Stan, what's the matter?"

"I'm fine . . . I've been sick, that's all. Just don't come in
here."

The thing in the washbasin was trying slowly and painfully
to slide up the sides of the slippery white ceramic. Stanley
swallowed and shuddered. It was alive, damn it, it was really
alive. It almost made him heave just to think that it must have
been growing inside of his stomach. He picked up the lavatory

brush and tried to poke it back down into the basin, but immediately its tentacles twisted themselves around the bristles and it started to climb out of the basin, dripping gray juice.

Stanley smacked the brush smartly against the side of the basin but the thing refused to release its grip. Whatever it was, it was tenacious and resilient and it was determined to get out of the basin. He smacked the brush again and again, but still the thing clung on.

"Stan-*lee*! What are you doing?" Angie demanded.

"Don't come in here, that's all!"

He dropped the lavatory brush, wrenched open the bathroom door, and hurried across the hallway to the living room. A half bottle of Wyborowa stood on the mantelpiece over the fire, beneath the strange painting of *Prince Baltasar Carlos with a Dwarf*. He picked up the bottle, and then crossed to the bureau in the corner and took a box of Swan matches out of the drawer.

By the time he returned to the bathroom, the tentacled thing had succeeded in struggling painfully up the head of the lavatory brush, and was beginning to entwine its suckers around the handle.

His hands shaking, Stanley emptied the vodka bottle all over it. The instant the spirit touched it, the thing suddenly writhed and wriggled, and Stanley breathed, "Shit!" and jumped smartly back, knocking his knee against the side of the bath. But he steadied himself for long enough to fumble a match out of the box and strike it. The match flared, but then its head dropped off on to the floor and sizzled out. Stanley scrabbled desperately in the box for another one. Already the dripping thing was halfway out of the washbasin, trying to overbalance itself on to the floor.

Stanley struck the match one—twice—then tossed it while it was still blazing into the middle of the creature's tentacles. There was a soft crackling *whoomph* and the thing was engulfed in a halo of blue flame.

Stanley kept his back pressed against the cold tiles on the opposite wall of the bathroom as the thing lashed and twisted and shuddered in agony. The lavatory brush caught alight, too, and the bathroom began to fill with thick looping curls of acrid smoke, and black feathers of burned plastic.

Gradually, the thing in the washbasin puckered and shriveled, its glistening tentacles drying out and curling up, its gray slime reduced to a fibrous ash. The flames guttered and burned out. Stanley cautiously approached the washbasin, picked up the handle of the half-burned brush, and prodded the thing to make sure that it was dead.

To his fascinated disgust, the brown mushroom-wrinkled skin in the middle of the thing peeled open, and he saw a single dead eye looking up at him. He prodded the creature, hesitated, then lifted it up with the brush and dropped it into the lavatory. He flushed it, and immediately it was swirled away.

He was still staring into the lavatory when the bathroom door opened and Angie came in, wrapped in a sheet.

"Gordon Bennett," she said. "What the 'ell's been going on in 'ere?"

Stanley ushered her out of the bathroom and back into the bedroom, closing the door behind him. He went quickly across to the window and tugged open the drapes. Outside, the landscape was the same as it had been last night. Dreary, rain-swept marshes, squalid buildings, and a girl pushing a handcart laden with joggling corpses.

"Can you see that?" he asked Angie, taking her by the arm.

She nodded, her face pale. "What is it? What does it mean?"

"I'm not sure. But don't you remember what Springer said—that it was raining inside Tennyson because Isabel Gowdie was dreaming it was raining, the way that it used to rain there, before the house was built? Well, the same thing must be happening here. If you ask me, this is Isabel Gowdie's memory of what this part of London looked like, before the Night Warriors finally got to her and locked her up.

"She can make her own dream world exist at the same time as our world. She can make all these fields and these buildings look as if they're really there. Maybe they *are* really there. Her dreams are so damned strong that they have as much reality as the real thing."

"But how can it be a dream if I'm not asleep?" asked Angie.

"It's a dream but it's not *your* dream . . . that's why you can't work out whether you're asleep or awake. It doesn't matter whether you're asleep or awake because you're not dreaming it yourself. That's why you and I were able to have an identical dream about making love. It wasn't *our* dream at all. It was hers. It was Isabel Gowdie's.''

"But how can we be in somebody else's dream?" asked Angie.

"I don't know. That's what Knitted Hood asked me. *Who's dreaming whom?* Maybe there's no real answer to that. Maybe—in a way—we're all dreaming each other. You know, Jung's idea about everybody sharing the same unconscious mind. When you come to think about it, it would account for a whole lot of things, wouldn't it? Psychic experiences, mind reading, premonitions.''

It was plain that Angie didn't really follow what Stanley was trying to say, but she must have thought it *sounded* convincing, because she nodded as if she did.

Stanley said, ''Maybe witches weren't really witches at all . . . not flying around on broomsticks or anything . . . but women who happened to understand the power of the human mind and can use it to their own advantage.''

"Trouble is, 'ow can we get ourselves cured?" asked Angie. "I mean—Stan, I like you ever so much. But we can't go on doing what we did this morning. I mean, I just don't *love* you. I mean, not *that* much.''

In his mind's eye, Stanley experienced a flickering Instamatic picture of Angie's eyes, wide open, as he climaxed, his fingers entangled in her hair. He said, "If Springer was telling us the truth, we have to find Isabel Gowdie, wherever she is, and kill her.''

"But we can't do it until the rest of the what's-their-names get 'ere, can we? The rest of the Night Warriors?''

"I don't know," Stanley told her. "For you and me, it's urgent. Maybe we should try making a start today.''

"What, actually go outside? Just as we are? Without any armor or nothing?''

Stanley went right up to the window and stared out at the gloomy, rain-glistening fields. The gray Thames clay looked like the clay of a freshly-dug communal grave. "I don't know . . . why not? The sooner we find her, the sooner we can get ourselves cured.''

Angie stood with her sheet wound around her like a Roman toga. "I don't think we ought to," she said dubiously. "I don't think Springer would like it, would 'e, or *she*, or whatever 'e is? It's a bit like jumping the gun, ain't it?''

"Let's get dressed," Stanley suggested. "Then . . . if the fields are still there when we go outside, let's go looking for Isabel Gowdie. How about that?''

"What about all those dead people out there?''

"They're dead. What can they do?''

"Well, nothing. But what did they die of?''

"Bubonic plague, I expect, but don't let it worry you. These days, we have a cure for bubonic plague.''

"Oh, thanks a lot.''

They dressed. Angie was more modest this morning and turned her back on him. He couldn't help noticing the red bruises and the scratch marks on her shoulders and her bottom, however. It seemed extraordinary to think that he had practically raped her this morning. Now they were talking to each other in their actual, uninfected roles, as two affectionate acquaintances with nothing at all in common.

Stanley glanced toward the window; partly to make sure that Isabel Gowdie's dreadful dream landscape was still there; partly because he had felt something quiver in his consciousness, like a spider suddenly quivering on its web.

—swathe through the—

A few feet away from the broken-down fence of the pig farm stood Knitted Hood, motionless, the shoulders of his raincoat dark with rain. Had Langton Street been there, instead of this nightmare hallucination of the seventeenth century, he would have been standing exactly where he had stood on the morning that he attacked Stanley and infected him with the Night Plague, on the opposite corner, beside the postbox. Stanley shivered. He felt one reality overlapping with another; dream upon dream; until he couldn't be sure if he was really seeing Isabel Gowdie's dream, or if he was dreaming that he was, or if Knitted Hood was dreaming that he was.

He saw Langton Street as it was today. He saw it run backwards through a thousand changes, three hundred years skipping and dancing in front of his eyes like a speeded-up movie in reverse. Passersby blurred this way and that along the sidewalks, their lives no more than an evanescent flicker of light. Vehicles whirled around the street in a furious phantom carousel—bicycles, horse-drawn carriages, pushcarts, hansom cabs, horses. Trees flared up and shrank away again. Clouds raced threateningly overhead. Houses tumbled apart, cottages collapsed.

And then there was nothing outside his window but the rain and the mud and the silent, patient figure of Knitted Hood; more like a diseased hawk than a man; his perfect face nothing but a white smudge in the shadow of his hood.

Angie said, "Are you sure you want to do this, Stan?"

Stanley tugged on a thick maroon polo-neck sweater. "Couldn't be surer," he replied, although the only certainty he felt was a panic so rigid that he could almost feel it in his chest. "Let's go, hunh? There's a raincoat in the hall closet you can borrow."

They went downstairs. The house was gloomy and deserted. The only sound was the rustling of Angie's raincoat as she shrugged it on, and the noise of their feet on the thinly-carpeted stairs.

In the hall, before Stanley opened the door, Angie caught hold of his hand. "I 'ope you realize this is mad," she said.

Stanley gave her a humorless nod.

"I mean walking off into some old witch's dream. It's totally bonkers. I mean what 'appens if she wakes up, and we're right in the middle of a brick wall or something?"

"I don't know."

Angie looked away, hesitant. Then she said, "I'm scared."

"We have to do it, Angie. We don't have any choice."

"Supposing—" Angie began, but she couldn't find the words. Stanley lifted the collar of her raincoat and fastened up the top button for her, in a distinctively fatherly way. He kissed her on the forehead.

"You and me, we've both fallen foul of some kind of fight between the probably-good guys and the very, very super-mega-evil guys. The problem is, we *have* to get involved; otherwise this thing in our heads is going to make us wilder and weirder and if we don't end up killing each other we'll probably end up killing somebody else. *And* spreading this Night Plague around to God knows how many unsuspecting people, every time we dream."

Angie said, "You're just as scared as what I am, ain't you?"

"Yes," Stanley admitted. "I'm just as scared as what you are."

"One more thing," said Angie. "What was you burning in the bathroom?"

"You don't want to know."

"It must 'ave been something 'orrible. It *smelled* 'orrible."

"Listen—believe me—you really don't want to know."

"Was it something to do with you being ill?"

Stanley said, "Yes, it was. But just remember I've had this infection longer than you, and if we find Isabel Gowdie . . . well, we'll put an end to this plague before the same thing happens to you."

Angie said nothing, but it was clear from the expression on her face that Stanley had decided her. They had to go hunt for the witch, and they had to find her soon. What they had done this morning, the brutality of their sex together, was disturbing enough, but already Stanley had begun to have jagged splinters of fantasy about forcing Angie into even more sadistic and ferocious acts, and to encourage her to inflict pain on *him*, too. Chains, and locks, and straps, and blood.

His fantasies weren't only about Angie, either. He continually glimpsed zoetropic images of greeting Leon at Heathrow Airport, shaking hands with him, and squeezing him so tightly that he crushed all the bones in his fingers. *Welcome to London, you little asswipe,* and then laughing a huge Vincent Price laugh while Leon screamed. He thought about catching the cat that caught all the mice and fledglings around Langton Street and shutting its head in a car door. *Crunch.* And how would the car's owner react when he came back to his vehicle and found a cat's body standing with the patience of rigor mortis beside his fender?

We shall cut a swathe, said Stanley inside his head. *We are the pestilence that was promised.*

He opened the front door. The fields were still there. Rain pattered on the churned-up clay, creating thousands and thousands of greasy gray puddles, wherever they looked. There was a strange smell in the air: wet and pungent, with a hint of sharpness in it. It was the smell of air that had never known the pollution of automobiles or factories, but which was cider-tangy with horse manure and pigs' urine and sweet-laden with charcoal-burning and death.

Nobody could have prepared Stanley for the overwhelming smell of death.

"Cor, it don't 'alf stink," Angie complained. "Is this what it was really like, back in 'istory?"

Stanley took a cautious step into the mud. He sank up to his ankle, but after two or three inches, the clay seemed reasonably firm. He looked around, at the run-down cottages, at the scrubby trees and gorse bushes; at the neutral gray English sky which conceded nothing and promised nothing. *Plague that was.*

"What year do you think this is?" asked Stanley. His voice seemed oddly flat, as if he were speaking in a closed room.

"Search me," Angie replied, taking hold of his hand to steady herself. "This mud's going to ruin me shoes."

"I'll buy you another pair, okay?"

"Not like these. I got them from Footloose."

Stanley narrowed his eyes against the rain. He could see the pig farm only twenty or thirty yards away, its thatched roof dripping, its slatted walls black with wet-rot. Knitted Hood seemed to have disappeared, although he could easily have concealed himself behind the piggery, or a nearby copse of leprous-looking silver birches, or even beyond the horizon. Because the fields sloped so dramatically towards the Thames, the horizon was only a hundred yards away, and who could guess what lay beyond it?

We are the plague that was.

They trudged through the mud to the pig farm and looked around it. It was deserted, except for a starved and half-bald black cat that stared at them hysterically out of the darkness, a witch's familiar without a witch.

" 'Ere, pussy, pussy, pussy," Angie coaxed it.

"I wouldn't encourage it if I were you," Stanley told her. "Most domestic animals in the seventeenth century must have had some kind of disease."

"Still—wish I'd brought a tin of Whiskas with me," said Angie.

They walked eastwards, trudging and stumbling through the ruts and the puddles. The rain continued to drum down on them, cold and casual and unrelenting. *Promised promised promised*. Stanley was surprised how hilly London was. It was so built up that he had always thought of it as reasonably flat, especially in comparison with his home city of San Francisco. But in spite of lying in the muddy basin of the Thames, the terrain undulated at least as much as New York's. They plodded up a long, low incline, and when they reached the top of it they were able to see the river off to their right, dull as unpolished pewter in the morning light. A few barges and triangular-sailed boats hung suspended in the haze. Off to their left, a line of gray forbidding hills overlooked London from the north, hills that would one day be Highgate and Hampstead and Harrow-on-the-Hill. Ravens wheeled slowly through the rain, silent and tattered and menacing.

Directly ahead of them, through a pall of rain and pungent woodsmoke, they could see the cluttered rooftops of the City of London. It was nothing like Stanley had expected. No steeples, no spires, no grandiose guild buildings, no palaces. Instead, it was a squalid huddle of narrow streets and low, dilapidated buildings, surrounded by woods and fields and a sprawling makeshift community of sheds and shanties.

He remembered from high school history that the Great Fire of London had raged for over four days, but he had never been taught that it had devastated thirteen thousand houses, St. Paul's Cathedral, ninety parish churches, the Guildhall, jails, markets, fifty-two halls, countless other public buildings, and that it had made nearly a quarter of a million people homeless.

It was the wretched dwellings of those homeless people that he was looking at now. *For, yea, we shall cut a swathe through the world*. And outside London, the Great Plague had still not subsided.

They were close enough now to be able to hear the dolorous tolling of a single bell, and the squalling of a hungry child, and dogs barking. There was another sound in the background, too, a low persistent moaning, like the wind blowing under a door, or hundreds of monks humming a dirge, or mourners at a Spanish funeral.

"Do you think it's safe?" asked Angie. Her hair was dripping wet now, and there was a smudge of mud on her cheek.

"I don't know. It's only a dream."

"It's not *our* dream, though, is it?"

"It's a dream, all the same."

"The rain's wet. The mud's muddy. It can't be that much of a dream."

Stanley wiped his face with his hand. "I guess that's a risk we're just going to have to take. We *have* to find Isabel Gowdie. We don't have any damn choice."

"Do you think you're going to find 'er 'ere?"

"Maybe. The idea is to look for my ancestors, the Eisner family. If anybody can tell me, they can."

"But if this is Isabel Gowdie's dream, she's not going to let you find 'er, is she?"

"I'm not too sure about that. I have a feeling she might. I think that's why Knitted Hood turned up at Kew Gardens . . . he was encouraging me to follow him. It was only because Madeleine Springer intervened that I didn't."

" 'E's 'ere now," said Angie, taking hold of Stanley's arm.

Stanley peered over to the far left, in the direction that Angie had indicated. She was right. Knitted Hood was standing gray and tall beside a half-collapsed lean-to. A damp fire was burning close by, and every now and then he disappeared from view behind the smoke; but there was no doubt that he was watching them, and waiting for them.

"It begins to make sense now," said Stanley. "Isabel Gowdie wants me for some reason . . . and the only way to make sure that I absolutely *had* to come was to send Knitted Hood to give me the Night Plague."

"Why do you think she wants you so much?" asked Angie. It was miserably cold, here on the outskirts of the city, and she was shivering.

"I don't know. I guess we're just going to have to find her and ask her ourselves."

Knitted Hood vanished in the smoke. Stanley looked up at the sky and frowned. "It looks like it's beginning to get dark. We'd better get our asses in gear."

They plodded along a narrow track of poisonous black mud, churned up by cartwheels and horses and stinking of horse urine. As they approached the center of the city, huts and hovels and cottages began to crowd close to the sides of the track, and Stanley and Angie found themselves being suspiciously watched from almost every window and every door.

The denizens of Isabel Gowdie's dream-London were silent, mealy-faced, and surly. Almost all of them were misshapen or crippled or ugly. A boy with a huge encephalitic head watched them from an upstairs window. A woman with a raw cleft palate stood beside a fence, her front teeth and her nasal cavities exposed, whistling and dribbling. A large-nosed man with no arms or legs sat propped up on a filthy mud-caked cushion, his head protected from the rain by a huge drooping hat made out of whaleskin, watching them and singing to himself as they passed.

> *"Gut the pig and bite the toad,*
> *Kill the cat that crossed the road."*

Mangy and nasty-looking dogs roamed everywhere, and four or five of them began to follow Stanley and Angie as they penetrated deeper and deeper into this grotesque parody of seventeenth-century London. Stanley was amazed that Isabel Gowdie's dreaming imagination was so vivid and so detailed and so multilayered. But any woman who could work her influence across three and a half centuries must have an exceptional mind. And of course, she had the power of Satan on her side.

"We are going to be able to get back, aren't we?" asked Angie.

Stanley took hold of her hand and gave it a quick, reassuring squeeze. In truth, he had no idea whether they would ever be able to return to their own reality. They could be trapped here forever, like two ants underneath an overturned ashtray, walking around and around and never being able to find a way out. Maybe Isabel Gowdie would destroy them, the way that she had destroyed Stanley's ancestors.

His fear lay in the bottom of his stomach like cold soup. He had never been so frightened in his life, even when they were attacked by the boy-dogs at Tennyson. Here, in dream-London, he knew that they were entirely at the mercy of Isabel Gowdie's imagination; and that Isabel Gowdie, in her turn, was entirely at the mercy of the darkest and most terrible influence in the universe, the black thing that floated at the edge of human consciousness, the black thing that led people to kill, and torture, and rape, and in the end to deny their very humanity.

The street along which they were walking grew narrower and narrower, until the timbered houses overhung it on either side. The pavement was cobbled here, although it was greasy and slippery, and almost as hard to negotiate as the muddy tracks on the city's outskirts. After two or three hundred yards, Stanley found that his feet were bruised and that the backs of his calves ached. A gutter twisted down the middle of the street, but it was clogged with heaps of slippery entrails and horse manure and decaying cabbage leaves.

"Look," said Angie; but Stanley had already glimpsed the back of Knitted Hood's head, faintly distinguishable through the rain and the smoke. Knitted Hood was apparently guiding them onwards; because when they stopped, he stopped, too, although he didn't turn around. He waited until they started walking again and then led them further into the city.

Street after street was nothing but an acrid mountain range of wet black ashes and the skeletal remains of burned-down houses. Stanley saw weirdly-melted lumps of glass and lead, and an iron water pump that had turned by the heat into an extraordinary crucifix, with a melted-glass Jesus hanging from it.

They followed Knitted Hood's ever-receding back through a drowned and stinking market, where jostling crowds of hunchbacked people argued fiercely and viciously with each other about the price of damp-blackened turnips and slimy heaps of beige and purplish offal. At the opposite corner of the market, a handclapping circle had formed. A toothless man in a moth-eaten fur jacket and a bedraggled feather hat was playing a wild song on a hurdy-gurdy, and a cretinous-looking woman with a long blond pigtail had pulled down her rough brown dress to the waist, and was dancing an unbalanced hopping dance, her big white breasts bouncing up and down like two muslin bags full of cream cheese.

> *"Gut the pig and bite the toad,*
> *Kill the cat that crossed the road."*

Small hostile eyes followed them as they passed.

At last, they found themselves in a small dark courtyard, surrounded on all sides by houses with shuttered windows. Knitted Hood had disappeared, but Stanley had the feeling that they had arrived; that this was the place to which Knitted Hood had been guiding them. He walked slowly around the courtyard, with Angie watching him and shivering.

"Jacob Eisner was a ragpicker, that's what Madeleine Springer said. That means he probably had some kind of a shop, or a storehouse."

Angie said nothing, but shivered and waited. She looked exhausted after their walk through the rain all the way from Fulham.

Stanley tried knocking at two or three of the doors. There was no reply, not even an echo. He rattled one of the shutters. Still no response.

"They had a plague and a fire here," he remarked. "Maybe they all packed up and went to the country."

"Then why did Knitted Hood lead us 'ere?" asked Angie.

"Search me. That was only a guess."

"What do we now, if there's nobody 'ere?"

Stanley shook his head. "I don't know. We'll just have to go back and talk to Springer again."

"That's if we *can* get back."

They were just about to leave the courtyard when, without warning, one of the doors opened, and a young man stepped out. There was no doubt that he was Jewish. He wore a black cloak and a skullcap and his sidelocks had been grown into the long *payess* of the Orthodox Jew. Stanley's great-grandfather had cut off his *payess* when he left Hamburg for America, and his great-great-grandfather had refused even to speak his name for the rest of his life.

The young man glanced at them briefly and incuriously and began to walk away. But Stanley called, "Eisner?"

The young man stopped and turned. He had a pale, oval face, and he was much slighter than Stanley, but Stanley could see a faint family resemblance. Something about the eyes and the shape of the head.

"I'm Eisner, yes," the young man said. "What do you want? I have business."

His accent was an almost incomprehensible mixture of Yiddish and seventeenth-century East End. It took Stanley a moment to understand that he was speaking English at all.

Stanley took a step forward and held out his hand. "I'm Eisner, too. Stanley Eisner."

The young man frowned at Stanley and then at Angie. "*You* are Eisner, too?"

"It isn't easy to explain . . . but I have to talk to you."

"I have business. I cannot stop to talk."

"Please," said Stanley. It was growing very dark now, and he could scarcely see the young man's face. The last faint light of the day shone on the raindrops on the shoulder of his black cloak. "It's about Jacob and Joshua."

"My father Jacob is dead. My brother Joshua is dead, too."

"I know that," said Stanley. "I also know how they died, and why."

The young man narrowed his eyes. "How is it you know that?"

"Because I'm a Night Warrior, too; the same as your father. The same as your brother."

"And this girl?" asked the young man suspiciously.

"Effis the light-skater."

The young man looked at Stanley for a long time in silence. The rain whispered all around them and gurgled down unseen gutters and hidden drains. Stanley had a feeling of this old, burned, sagging city, with rainwater glistening on its rooftops and finding its way by millions of secret and complicated conduits to the Fleet and the Walbrook and the City Ditch, and down to the filthy dun-colored Thames, and out to Greenwich and the Thames Estuary, and the sea.

Stanley said, "We need help. Otherwise, believe me, we wouldn't have come. If you believe in Ashapola, if you believe in things that are good and things that are evil—then you'll talk to us, at the very least."

The young man looked away, looked back again, then held out his hand. "Solomon Eisner. If you are truly Night Warriors, I greet you."

They shook hands. Then Solomon took out a jingling bunch of keys and said, "Come inside. My business was not important. Only the sale of some woollen shoddy. It can wait until later.''

He unlocked the door. Stanley watched him in fascination. It was incredible to think that this man was an ancestor of his, that this man's children had given birth to succeeding generations of children, and that eventually one of his *ur-ay neklach*, his great-grandchildren, had given birth to Stanley himself.

Solomon led them into a small, low-ceilinged room, so dark that Stanley collided immediately with the heavy oak table in the middle of it and bruised his thigh.

''I'm sorry,'' Solomon told him. A small fire was still smoldering in the hearth, so Solomon took down a wax taper from the shelf beside it, poked it into the ashes to set it aflame, and used it to light a three-branched candelabrum. ''I have struck that table many times myself. I should know where it is by now!''

Although it was so small, the room was warm and stuffy and comfortable. There were three or four leather-bound books on the shelf next to the fire, including the Old Testament and the *Teitsh Chumash* and a dictionary; and if Stanley knew anything about the seventeenth century, it was that anybody who owned as many as three books was impressively literate. There were two woodcuts, too, in plain wooden frames, one of Moses and one of Jerusalem.

''Can I offer you something to drink?'' Solomon asked them. ''I have water, or I have wine. I know a wine merchant who gives me sack in return for sacking. Not that I drink myself.''

He set two roughly-molded green glasses on the table and poured them each a small measure of sack from a dark glass bottle. Stanley sipped his cautiously. Despite the fact that sack was *wyne seck*, or ''dry wine,'' he found it almost excruciatingly sweet to a palate that was accustomed to Pouilly-Fumés and Sancerres.

Angie said, ''You 'aven't got somewhere I could wash? I feel like I've been pulled through an 'edge backwards.''

Solomon looked perplexed. ''I have a bowl in the scullery,'' he told her.

''Oh, thanks,'' said Angie; and groped her way into the shadows of the next room. Stanley heard her say, ''Gordon Bennett,'' when she found the bowl. Then, ''Bloody 'ell.''

"You are strange people," said Solomon with unembarrassed frankness. "You are not like anybody I have ever met. Have you come very far?"

"I guess you could say that," Stanley replied. "Further than anybody else you ever met."

"But you are Night Warriors, and that makes you kin."

"I'm glad you think that way."

Solomon drew an invisible pattern on the bare tabletop with the end of his mittened finger, a Star of David, again and again. "I was the second son, so I was never chosen. But my father and Joshua were both ardent Night Warriors. They fought many, many battles; and then both would sit here in this room and tell me everything they had done in dreams. They would tell me about their fear, their danger, their moments of great excitement. Sometimes I felt jealous and wished that I could join them. But it was never to be. After what happened to both of them, I suppose that I should give thanks to God."

"Tell me about it," said Stanley softly.

"I knew that they had been searching for a long time for a witch-woman called Crowdie or Gowdie. She had given herself to the Devil, that is what my father told me, and the Devil had used her to turn the minds of hundreds of thousands of people against the Lord *Shaddai*."

Stanley, sipping his seventeenth-century sack, didn't fail to catch Solomon Eisner's use of the name *Shaddai* for God. It was a name which described God's satisfaction with the creation of the universe, rather than the essence of God Himself. Literally, it meant The One Who Has Said, Enough.

The Night Plague was the antithesis of God's satisfaction. The Night Plague was the sickness of the soul. The Night Plague was for those whose greed could never be satisfied—those for whom enough was *never* enough.

Solomon said, "They hunted her by day and they hunted her by night. They almost caught her one morning in the ribbon shop on London Bridge. There was a furious fight, and a chase, but she escaped. After that, she was careful to keep herself hidden, mostly in other people's dreams. But my father discovered that her favorite dreamer was a ratcatcher called Clark who lodged over a bakery in Pudding Lane. He had such fierce dreams, my father told me! Dreams of blood and teeth, and wading waist-deep through flooded cellars and stinking ditches.''

Solomon paused, his eyes unfocused, as if he could remember his father speaking as clearly as if he were still in the room with them. Then he said, "Early last September, as we ate our supper, my father told me that he was determined to find the Crowdie woman that night and destroy her. He said that it would be dangerous beyond all imagination and that it was possible that he might be hurt."

He swallowed. His eyes were brimming with tears. "If he was killed in the ratcatcher's dream, he said, his soul would die and his sleeping body would never wake up. I was to leave him sleeping for two days, shaking him from time to time; but if he didn't wake up after that time, I was to understand that he was dead, even though he was still breathing, and that I was to bury him.

"That same night—" He swallowed, and smeared his eyes with his fingers. "That same night, my beloved brother came to me and said the same. 'I will appear to be alive,' that is what he said. 'But my soul will have died, and you must bless me and bury me.' "

Solomon looked Stanley directly in the eyes. "I begged them not to do it. I fell on my knees and took hold of my father's hand and I pleaded with him. But he said, 'I am a ragpicker, and that is an honorable trade; but I am also a Night Warrior, and that means that I have been called by Ashapola to risk my life for the greater good of the whole world; and *that*, my son, is not just honorable. It is divine.' "

Angie came back from the scullery, and as she opened the door, the three candles dipped and sputtered in the draft. Solomon said, "That night they lay in wait for the Crowdie woman and a dozen other witches in the ratcatcher's dream, but somebody had warned her, and she surprised them. She set alight to the ratcatcher's dream; and his brain caught fire, too; and all of the Night Warriors died before they were able to escape. The ratcatcher burned, and the bakery burned, and most of London burned, too. They had to blow up buildings with gunpowder so that the fire couldn't spread any further."

Angie stood behind Stanley's chair and listened in silence as Solomon continued. "Every hour for three days, I shook my father and my brother with tears in my eyes and begged them to wake up. They breathed, their hearts were beating, but they had no life in them.

"In the end, I had to take their bodies by night and bury them. They were both heroes; and yet they have to lie in graves without monuments or markers; and nobody will ever know what they sacrificed."

Stanley said, "I'm sorry, Solomon. You can't even guess how sorry."

"Well, it's past now," Solomon told him. "I carry on the business, that's the best I can do. Old clothes, that's what I know best. It's a calling, rather than a trade."

"What happened to the witch-woman?" asked Stanley.

Solomon shrugged. "I never knew."

"You know what happened to your father and your brother. So somebody must have talked to you, after they were killed."

"There was a man called Joseph Springer," Solomon admitted. "A strange man, more like a woman than a man. He came to see me about a week after I had buried my father and my brother, and he told me that other Night Warriors had succeeded in catching Isabel Crowdie. He said that they had not been able to destroy her, because her Satanic power was far too great. But he wanted me to know that they had imprisoned her in a secret place, from which she could never escape, and so my father and my brother had been avenged."

"Do you have any idea where?" asked Stanley.

Solomon shook his head. "Places of imprisonment are never divulged, in case a Night Warrior is captured and forced to reveal where a demon or a witch is buried. But Joseph Springer did give me the tokens of imprisonment."

"The what?" asked Angie.

"The tokens of imprisonment. My father had several. Every time the Night Warriors imprisoned a devil or a witch, they took tokens from the place where they had buried them. They were tokens of honor, like commemorative medals. When they buried the demon Abrahel, my father brought back a sliver of marble and a branch from a yew tree from the place where they had buried him."

"What were the tokens that Joseph Springer gave you after Isabel Gowdie was imprisoned?" asked Stanley.

"I have never opened them. They are supposed to remain sealed forever."

"Solomon, it's very important that we take a look at them."

"I do not know whether that would be right."

"Solomon—we think that Isabel Gowdie has somehow gotten herself free, or partly free. Her Carriers are out again, spreading the Night Plague. It's absolutely critical that we find her."

"She's free?" Solomon frowned. "Joseph Springer said that she had been buried in solid rock."

"Please, Solomon. If we allow her to get away, then your father and your brother will have died for nothing."

Solomon hesitated for a moment. Then he took out his jangling bunch of keys, went over to the corner of the room, and unlocked a small metal-bound chest. He came back to the table with a soft gray leather pouch, tightly bound with waxed string, and sealed.

"Joseph Springer said that I was not to open it," he said.

"He didn't say that somebody else couldn't open it, though, did he? Especially if that somebody else happens to be a Night Warrior."

"I am still not sure that I should do this."

"Solomon . . . there's one thing more that I haven't told you. Both Angie and I have been infected by the Night Plague. If we don't find Isabel Gowdie pretty damn soon, then we won't even *want* to find her any more."

Solomon said, "*You* have the Night Plague? Both of you?"

"That's why we're here."

Without demurring any further, Solomon took out a sharp clobberer's knife and cut the string around the neck of the pouch. Carefully, he shook out on to the table a small fragment of pure white limestone and a handful of tiny seashells. One side of the limestone had been cut flat, polished, and then engraved with the picture of a bearded man with what looked like a ruff around his neck.

Stanley picked up the shells one by one and examined them.

"They must 'ave buried 'er on the beach," Angie suggested.

"But Joseph Springer mentioned solid rock, didn't he?" Stanley asked Solomon.

"That is quite right. 'We have buried her in solid rock, so

that in all eternity she will never escape.' Those were his very words to me.''

"So . . . they must have buried her in limestone, somewhere close to the sea.''

"White cliffs of Dover," put in Angie promptly. "Or somewhere along the South Coast, anyway. It's all chalk.''

Stanley nodded. "Dover, yes . . . that makes a lot of sense. She could have been trying to get away from England. Or maybe it was that fishwife ancestor of yours, what was her name? Elisabeth Pardoe. She lived in Dover. She would have known of a place where Isabel Gowdie could be buried.''

"We went to Dover on a school trip once," Angie added. "Those cliffs 'ave got thousands of 'oles in them—you know, what people dug during the war to make forts and that. They could 'ave buried 'er anywhere there.''

"Hey, you're not just a pretty face, are you?" said Stanley.

"I got me O-level in geography, if you don't mind.''

Stanley examined the piece of limestone. "I wonder whose face this is supposed to be. They obviously engraved it on here for a purpose.''

"Do you wish to borrow it?" asked Solomon.

"I don't know. I'm not too sure that I'll ever be able to find a way of giving it back to you.''

Solomon smiled and nodded. "You are a Night Warrior, sir. You will find a way. Now, I must leave you, to do some work. If I do not work, my family do not eat. And you—you have your witch to find, Mistress Crowdie.''

Stanley finished his wine, stood up, and clasped Solomon's hand. "I hope we don't fail you," he said.

"Do not think of failure," Solomon replied. "My father would never think of failure, not even in the smallest thing. A ragpicker learns that nothing need ever be wasted. Life is a dance that goes around and around, and what is failure to one man is success to another.''

"Well, I guess you're right," said Stanley. He was beginning to feel irritable and tired, and his stomach was knotting up again. He dreaded that feeling of sickness—especially after this morning's experience in the bathroom. God knows what abominations he was going to vomit up next.

Solomon said, as he opened the front door for them, "You

speak of failure? Everything has its place and its purpose. You see this black cloth cape? When it is worn out, it will be be patched and sewn by clobberers to make it look like new once again. Then, when it is very faded, it will be dyed by revivers, to restore its color. When it is both worn out and faded, the best pieces will be turned by translators into waistcoats, and smaller pieces will be sent to France and Russia and Poland, where the working people wear caps made out of black fabric. Any fragments will be ripped into shoddy, or mungo, which will be woven into new clothes. This can happen six or seven times to the same wool, until it is no longer fit for weaving. Then it is dug into the ground in hop fields, to fertilize the plants."

"Seems like even secondhand duds have their ecosystem," Stanley remarked.

Of course Solomon didn't understand what he meant, but he grasped his hand again, all the same, and said, "You will find the witch-woman, do not fear. When you do, promise me one thing, that you will speak my father's and my brother's names in her face before you destroy her. I would like her to know that she is being punished for taking them away from me."

"I won't forget," Stanley promised.

They were back outside in the dark, rainy courtyard. Although Stanley knew that this was only a dream, he was suddenly reluctant to see Solomon go. He yearned to be able to tell him who he really was, and to ask him about his family, and the way he made his living; and to explain to him what would happen to the Eisners in centuries to come.

It was impossible, of course. But he hugged Solomon in his arms and whispered *"Sholem aleichem, Solomon,"* and Solomon said, *"Aleichem sholem."* Then, without saying anything more, Solomon turned and walked off into the shadows, as black as his cloak, as black as his beard, as black as the thing that swam on the very edge of the human mind, the thing whose devouring hunger was never satisfied.

They stumbled their way back through Isabel Gowdie's dream-London in almost total darkness. Occasionally, a street corner would be fitfully illuminated by a tallow link, but most of London's twisting lanes and crowded courtyards remained unlit. It was easy to understand how cutpurses and murderers had thrived in a city like this.

Stanley tried to keep them headed westwards, but even in modern London, which was signposted and brightly lit, he frequently lost his way. By comparison, this illusion of seventeenth-century London was a wet, reeking, nightmarish maze. Several times they found themselves emerging from the streets on to the sagging wooden quays and piers that lined the Thames, and had to plunge back again into the inky-black alleys from which they had groped their way out, Idol Lane and Cloak Lane and Allhallows Lane.

They heard rats running through the fabric of the houses, and shutters opening and closing. They heard women screaming and men arguing, and the clatter of pewter tankards in a gin-house. They heard a man singing in a high, keening voice,

> *"Gut the pig and bite the toad,*
> *Kill the cat that crossed the road.*

> *"All those men and all those masks,*
> *All those evil deeds and tasks,*

> *"All that blood so needless spent,*
> *All those angels came and went.*

> *"Gut the pig and bite the toad,*
> *Kill the cat that crossed the road."*

Then they heard the plangent sound of a hurdy-gurdy, and the roar of lustful laughter. Stanley thought of the ugly, half-naked woman hopping in the rainy marketplace.

Stanley was exhausted and almost on the point of giving up when Angie gripped his hand more tightly and said, "Look! That's a torch, ain't it? That's somebody carrying a torch!"

At the very end of the lane along which they were walking, a tall hooded figure was standing in the shadows, waving a lighted link slowly from side to side. The flame made a soft flaring noise; and each time the link passed the figure's face, Stanley glimpsed the white chillingly-perfect features of Knitted Hood. *All those men and all those masks.*

"He's guiding us back to Fulham," said Stanley.

"Bleeding 'ell," Angie protested, hobbling on blistered feet. "If 'e wants to be so bleeding 'elpful, why didn't 'e just tell us where old Isabel Audi was in the first place, 'stead of making us walk all the way 'ere?"

"I don't think he *knows* where she is," Stanley replied. "And there was no way that Solomon would have told him, is there? Solomon was even more of a Night Warrior than me."

"I feel pukish," said Angie.

"The Night Plague," Stanley told her. "And, believe me, it gets a whole lot worse."

"It's all right," Angie said. "I'll manage. Let's just follow old Knitted 'Ood and get out of this stinking place."

It seemed to take them hours to walk out of the City of London and back through the muddy farmlands of Chelsea and Fulham. But the rain had died away, and although the wind was sharp, it had veered around the compass to the southwest, and it was far less cutting than it had been before. Knitted Hood stayed well ahead of them. Most of the time they could see nothing but his dipping, flickering link. But they followed because it was their destiny to follow, and because the only way that they would ever find Isabel Gowdie was to do what she wanted them to do.

Stanley thought: *She must know, too, that we want to kill her. She must be fearfully confident that we can't.*

Angie said, "Oh, God, Stan, I don't think I can walk any further." But at that moment, Stanley realized that they were passing the piggeries close to Langton Street; and the next thing he knew, Knitted Hood had stopped outside the front gate of his house, which rose like a mirage out of the marshy fields. Knitted Hood waved the link from side to side, as if he were beckoning them and challenging them, both at the same time.

Knitted Hood climbed the steps with an awkward, limping gait, and opened the front door. Before he went inside, he turned and tossed the blazing link as far as he could across the fields. It cartwheeled over and over, before landing in a shower of orange sparks in a nearby ditch.

" 'E's in the 'ouse," whispered Angie. "What are we going to do?"

"We don't have any choice. We have to go inside. Otherwise we're going to be trapped in this dream forever; or for as long

as it lasts. And God knows what will happen if we're still out
here when Isabel Gowdie wakes up. You heard what happened
to the Eisners.''

''I don't 'alf feel sick,'' Angie told him.

''Come on, let's risk it,'' Stanley encouraged her. ''Right
now, Isabel Gowdie wants to find us just as much as we want
to find her. That's my guess, anyway. Otherwise why would
that gook have guided us all the way to Whitechapel and back?''

''I think I'm going to throw up,'' said Angie.

Without warning, she bent double in front of the garden gate
and vomited. Out of her mouth poured hundreds of long white
slippery strings which at first Stanley thought were spaghetti.
Angie clung on to him and coughed and heaved and wept.

''Oh, Stanley, oh, God, Stanley I can't stand it. Oh, Stanley.
Oh, God.''

Stanley stood beside her until she finished. She retched again
and again, and spat, and spat, until finally she stood up straight
and clung to Stanley, quivering and sweating, her eyes filled
with tears.

''Oh, God, Stanley, we've got to find 'er. I can't take any
more of this.''

Stanley looked down at the coiled heaps of white spaghetti
that she had thrown up, and it was only then that he saw by
the light from the open door that they were *moving*, they were
alive. He closed his eyes and held her tight and almost vomited
himself. It wasn't spaghetti at all. It was a tangle of blind,
writhing tapeworms.

''Let's get inside,'' he said. His mouth felt as dry as cotton.
He helped her up the steps and in through the front door, and
closed the door firmly behind him. He didn't believe now that
Knitted Hood intended to harm him any more. He *did* believe
that if he closed the door, Isabel Gowdie's dream-London would
be shut away, at least for now.

They climbed the stairs to Stanley's apartment. The door was
ajar, and the lights were switched on, and all the drapes were
closed. Stanley ushered Angie through to the living room and
helped her to sit down. Her face was shiny and white; almost
as if she, too, were wearing a Mardi Gras mask, like Knitted
Hood. She couldn't stop shaking with disgust.

''I can still *taste* them, Stanley.''

He poured her a large vodka, no ice, and handed it to her. She took a huge mouthful, furiously rinsed her mouth with it, and then spat it back into the glass. He poured another glass. "This one you can take straight down. Right now it won't do you any harm to be a little drunk."

She swallowed, with difficulty, and then let her head fall back on the dark brown cushions. All the time, Stanley kept his eyes out for Knitted Hood. He had entered the house, but where was he?

"Wait here," he told Angie. "I'm just going to take a quick look around."

"Believe me, mate," Angie told him, "the state I'm in, I'm not going anywhere."

Stanley went through to the kitchen and cautiously reached his hand round the door to switch on the light. It was empty, everything just as he had left it. He checked the bathroom. That was empty, too, although it still smelled of burned plastic and some other unidentifiable but deeply offensive odor, like scorched fish skin.

He was about to open the bedroom door when he saw Knitted Hood standing at the opposite end of the hallway, close to the front door. Knitted Hood looked unusually tall: his hood seemed almost to touch the ceiling. His face was concealed in shadow.

"Do you know the place?" he asked in his deathly whisper.

"What place?" Stanley retorted. "I don't know what the hell you're talking about."

"Don't try to play games, Mr. Eisner, you know very well what place. The place where my mistress was imprisoned. The place where my mistress is still *imprisoned."*

"So what if I do know it?"

"You will have to release her. Otherwise, the pestilence will surely take your soul."

"Why didn't you just *tell* me where she is, instead of going through all of this rigmarole?"

"I do not know where she is; only that she awoke two years ago and that her awakening awoke me, too, and my fellow Carriers. She is still imprisoned; she is still unable to speak. All she can do is to dream."

"So you've been trying to find Night Warriors, to help you locate her, and to help you set her free?"

The choice is yours, my friend. Eternal damnation or eternal glory.

"Do you really think I'm going to tell you where she is?"

You will live in sickness and madness and agony for the rest of your life if you don't; and your soul will wander in despair for all eternity once you are dead. Those who have the Night Plague become the servants of Satan forever. The choice is yours.

"Not much of a choice, is it?" asked Stanley.

You disobeyed, you deserve no choice. I am the pestilence that was promised.

Stanley thought: *What now? If I tell Knitted Hood that Isabel Gowdie is probably in Dover, he may be able to find her; and if he finds her he may be able to set her free. On the other hand, he may not be able to. He may still need me, because I'm a Night Warrior, and the seals and bonds that keep her imprisoned were originally fastened by Night Warriors.*

"I must have time to think before I tell you where she is," Stanley replied.

You need no time to think. You must tell me now.

"And what if I decide not to?"

Then I will hurt the girl in ways that you cannot even think of.

"Supposing I don't mind if you hurt the girl in ways that I can't even think of? You gave me the Night Plague, after all. I'm beginning to get pretty interested in that kind of thing."

You are lying, my friend. I am a master of lies. I know when a man is lying.

"You lay one finger on that girl and I won't tell you anything."

Knitted Hood's white face gleamed in the lamplight. He still exuded that smell of cooking fat and sweat, and strong synthetic violets. *Perhaps the girl herself will tell me what you have learned; if I hurt you instead.*

He advanced on Stanley and Stanley, in spite of telling himself, *Stand up to him, stand up to him, don't let him see that you're afraid,* took two or three cautious steps back. As he approached, Knitted Hood seemed to defy perspective and grow surrealistically taller and taller.

"Don't you even *think* about it," Stanley began; but Knitted Hood gripped his shoulder with his gray-mittened hand and it was like being clamped in a metalworker's vise. He felt a surge of panic. He had managed to blot out of his mind the pain of being beaten and raped, but now the feeling came colliding back.

"I could break your collarbone with one squeeze," Knitted Hood whispered harshly. *"Or perhaps you prefer the same kind of pleasure that I gave you before?"*

He lunged his hand between Stanley's legs and painfully squeezed his testicles through his trousers. Stanley gasped in terror and tried to struggle away.

"Now will you tell me?" he demanded.

But Stanley didn't even get the chance to answer. At that instant, the front doorbell rang; and was immediately followed by a loud hammering.

"Mr. Eisner? Mr. Eisner! This is the police! Detective Sergeant Morris, Mr. Eisner."

Stanley was about to call back, but Knitted Hood hissed, *"Silence! Do you want me to crush your shoulder?"*

"Mr. Eisner? One of our patrol officers saw somebody suspicious entering the downstairs door. Can you just confirm that everything's all right?"

Knitted Hood's breath rasped in and out of his saintly mask. *"One word,"* he warned.

The doorbell rang yet again. "Mr. Eisner? Can you hear me, Mr. Eisner?"

There was silence. For a long moment, Stanley thought that Detective Sergeant Morris had given up and gone. Knitted Hood's grip gradually relaxed, although he still didn't take his hand away completely.

"Now speak," Knitted Hood insisted. But at that instant, the front door was kicked open with a shuddering bang, and Detective Sergeant Morris and two uniformed police officers came bursting into the hallway.

SEVEN
Golden Armor

KNITTED HOOD THREW STANLEY VIOLENTLY AGAINST THE wall, so that Stanley overbalanced, stumbled, and hit his ear against the kitchen door frame. Although his vision was jumbled, Stanley saw him whirl around and thrust his gray-mittened hand directly into Detective Sergeant Morris's face.

The force of his grip must have been devastating. His first and second fingers plunged straight into Brian Morris's eyes. Blood and optic fluid jetted out over Knitted Hood's shoulder.

Brian Morris didn't even have time to cry out. Knitted Hood gripped the detective's upper arm to give himself leverage and support, and then, with his other hand, *tore the whole of his face off*, with a terrible crackle of fat and flesh and tearing skin.

For a moment, Brian Morris stood upright, his hands half lifted like a dog begging for a bone. His face had been stripped right down to the naked cheekbones, and it hung down from his chin, inside out, a wet and bloody beard. He staggered, his jawbone slowly dropping open because there was no longer any muscle to support it. A large bubble of blood formed between his teeth, then silently burst. Without a sound, without any kind of a cry, he collapsed on to the floor.

The two other police officers stopped where they were, staring at Knitted Hood in disbelief. One of them reached behind him and drew out his truncheon. The other adopted a crouching pose which suggested that he was a weekend karate enthusiast.

Stanley called, "Don't go near him, there's nothing you can do!"

The karate officer glanced quickly at Stanley and said, "You all right, mate?"

"Leave him, back off!" Stanley told him.

On the carpet, Detective Sergeant Morris began to shudder, as if an electric current were being passed through his body. The karate officer obviously didn't know what to do—whether to risk a rush attack on Knitted Hood, or to call on his lapel radio for reinforcements, or to take Stanley's advice and beat a hurried retreat.

His hesitation was fatal. Knitted Hood rushed at both officers, like a great gray berserk scarecrow, and even though the policeman with the truncheon managed to strike a clumsy blow at the side of his arm, Knitted Hood snatched both of them fiercely around the neck and smashed their heads together with such force that Stanley heard their skulls break.

They must have died instantly. But Knitted Hood grasped each of their faces in turn, the way he had grasped Detective Sergeant Morris's face, and ripped them free from their cheekbones. Then he twisted the two torn-off faces together, so it was impossible to tell whose lips were which, and whose nose belonged to whom. The final grisly insult: in death, he had robbed them of their human identity.

Knitted Hood turned to Stanley, and his gray gaberdine raincoat was sprayed with blood. A single crimson drop slid down the side of his white celluloid mask.

He said nothing. He had no need to. Stanley, swallowing back his nausea, raised both hands in surrender and said, "It's all right. I'll tell you where Isabel Gowdie is."

"I thought that you would probably see reason."

"Reason?" said Stanley, almost hysterical. "For God's sake,

I don't want to wind up without a face, that's the only reason I need to see!''

There was no sound from the living room where Angie was sitting. Stanley suspected that she was probably hiding behind the sofa or trembling behind the drapes. He didn't blame her, either. Given half a chance, he would have joined her.

Knitted Hood came closer. The reek of synthetic violets was even stronger. His eyes gleamed dull and impenetrable like the wing cases of black beetles, but Stanley could tell that he was calmer now; that he was satisfied.

"She's somewhere in Dover, on the South Coast," Stanley blurted. "Buried in the chalk, probably. We're not completely sure yet."

Knitted Hood slowly nodded. *"You did well. My mistress will be pleased with you, and so will my Master."*

"What now?" asked Stanley.

"What now? We have to go to Dover now, and find my mistress, and break the seals that have imprisoned her for so many years."

"We?" Stanley was still frightened, but he was also hugely relieved. If Knitted Hood needed him to come to Dover, too, then his guess had been correct: without a Night Warrior or even Night *Warriors* to help him, Knitted Hood was incapable of breaking the seals that held Isabel Gowdie.

"You have no charge-keeper yet. You cannot become a Night Warrior until he joins you. But as soon as he does, we will go to Dover together."

"The charge-keeper is supposed to arrive tomorrow or the day after," said Stanley.

"Very well. You will see me again when he is here."

Knitted Hood stepped long-legged over the police officers' bodies and made for the door.

"Wait!" Stanley called after him, in desperation. "You can't leave three dead policemen in my hallway. I'll be arrested; and then I'll never be able to become a Night Warrior."

"You must go to the sanctuary of the one called Springer," said Knitted Hood. *"You shall hear from me again."*

"But—"

"Go now, and I will deal with these pitiful remains."

Stanley went into the living room. His knees would hardly

support him. He found Angie standing by the window, rigid with fear. "Is 'e gone yet?" she asked him. "I tried to come and 'elp you, but when I 'eard those policemen shouting out, I just couldn't make me legs move."

"It's okay," Stanley reassured her, although he felt as if his own perception of what was happening had been cracked like a greenhouse window. "But we have to leave. He's—he's killed all of them, all three of them. They're dead. We can't stay here."

Angie said wildly, "What are we going to *do*?"

"We'll have to go to Madeleine Springer's place. We can take Gordon's car, pick him up later. Give me a couple of minutes: I just have to throw some clothes in a bag."

He went through to the bedroom, threw open his closet, and dragged down his battered Vuitton suitcase. He opened it up and heaved as many coats and shirts and pants into it as he could manage. Then he came back into the living room and took a last look around. He threw his Filofax into the suitcase, as well as two bottles of Wyborowa. "That'll do it," he said. "Could you bring along my violin case?"

With the suitcase bumping against the door frame, Stanley led Angie out into the hallway. "You don't want to look at this," he told her. "Keep to the left-hand side."

They edged past the dead policemen. Stanley hadn't realized at first how much blood Knitted Hood had splattered around. The hallway looked as if somebody had fired a .357 into an economy-sized jar of Old El Paso taco sauce. They had almost reached the doorway when one of the policemen's radios suddenly crackled and a woman's voice said, "Oscar Bravo to 625, Oscar Bravo to 625, where are you now, Ted?" and Angie shouted out *"Ah!"* in terror.

"We'd better hurry," said Stanley as they made their way down the stairs. "They're going to start missing those cops in a couple of minutes."

"Where's Knitted 'Ood?" Angie asked anxiously.

"Oh, he's here someplace. You can bet on it."

They went out of the front door and down the steps. Isabel Gowdie's dream had evaporated now, and they were back in Langton Street, harsh and real and commonplace. Two cars were parked alongside Gordon's Montego: a dented blue Sierra, which must have belonged to Detective Sergeant Morris, and a police Metro, with its blue light still circling.

Stanley unlocked Gordon's car and threw his suitcase into the trunk. He laid his violin case more carefully beside it, although for all he knew it contained nothing but dust and maggots. Angie said, "I can't drive, Stan. I just can't. You'll 'ave to do it."

"All right, I'll give it a shot," said Stanley, and eased himself in behind the wheel. Across the street, gray and tall, he could just make out the figure of Knitted Hood waiting on the pavement: a figure that made him shudder now more than ever before. A figure to which he had already promised his help, and to which he may even have promised his life.

He started the engine. It sounded weak and rough. Angie said, "Okay now, press in the clutch pedal with your left foot, all the way down to the floor. Then wiggle it into first gear. That's right. Then ease your left foot up really smoothlike; and at the same time gently press the accelerator with your right foot."

"God Almighty, this is more difficult than skiing," Stanley complained.

He revved the engine wildly, pulled his left foot up off the clutch, and the Montego bucked forward and stalled.

"Kangaroo petrol," Angie remarked.

"What?"

"That's what we call it, when somebody jumps along like that. Kangaroo petrol."

"Listen, this is my first time, okay, and it isn't easy."

He started the engine again. The car was still in gear, and it jumped forward again.

"Neutral, Stan, neutral!" Angie admonished him.

He was opening his mouth to answer her when they heard a deafening, ear-compressing explosion. All three front windows of his upstairs flat burst out into the street, millions of fragments of glass tumbling and glittering into the night. Stanley and Angie heard it clattering on to the roof of their car. Immediately afterwards, three massive fireballs roared out of the empty window frames, momentarily lighting up the entire block.

Stanley stared at Knitted Hood. "My God, he must have planted a bomb. Or *something*. Look at it!"

The whole second floor of the house was burning fiercely; as fiercely as if it had been doused in gasoline. Even from the street, Stanley and Angie could see the brown velvet drapes burning, and the lampshade crumpling up like a dahlia dropped on to a bonfire.

"Come on, we have to get out of here," said Stanley. He wrestled the gearstick back into neutral, started the Montego's engine again, and then slowly managed to bunny-hop away from the curb. After a few yards' progress, the engine began to whine in protest.

"You've got to change up!" Angie told him.

"What?"

"You've got to change 'er into second! Press down the clutch again, ease your foot off of the accelerator, wiggle it into second, then lift up the clutch and press down the accelerator again."

Stanley stared at her. "You mean you have to do this *every* time you want to change gear? Every single time?"

"Course you do, silly. That's what driving's all about."

"It's so damned primitive."

He effected a grinding gear change, and they began to drive a little faster. As they turned into the King's Road (which was mercifully almost deserted, and so he didn't have to stop and change down to first again), he gave Langton Street a last quick glance in his rearview mirror. A crowd had already begun to gather in the road outside his blazing building, and burning tatters of material were flying up into the night.

He knew with terrible certainty that Knitted Hood hadn't really planted a bomb; or even splashed gasoline around. He hadn't had time, and he certainly hadn't been lugging a jerry-can around with him. He was sure that Knitted Hood had invoked the power of Isabel Gowdie, the woman who had been able to stir up storms by slapping a rock with a wet rag. If she had been able to drown shipfuls of fishermen all around the coast, setting fire to three dead policemen shouldn't have caused her too much trouble.

Fire burn, and cauldron bubble, he thought. *No wonder*

Shakespeare wrote about witches. He was afflicted himself by one of the very worst.

As they drove erratically westwards along the King's Road, they were passed by five fire engines speeding in the opposite direction, their sirens blaring. Two police cars followed.

"At least they ain't got time to worry about your driving," said Angie as Stanley catastrophically clashed the gears at the junction of Fulham Palace Road.

How he managed to drive Gordon's car all the way to Richmond, Stanley could never remember. They plodded over the Thames at Chiswick, then climbed at 20 mph with smoke pouring out of the exhaust pipe all the way up to the top of the hill where Madeleine Springer had first taken them. Stanley parked at an angle (no power steering) and climbed out of the car with his back drenched in sweat.

"Never again," he promised. "That was more difficult than playing Rimsky-Korsakov."

It was a still, black night. Below them, lights shimmered in the oil-black Thames. They crossed the slip road to Madeleine Springer's apartment building with the soles of their shoes scratching on the cobblestones. They rang the bell with the engraved card *Springer* beside it and waited shivering for her to reply. A TWA jet thundered overhead in the darkness, on its way to Heathrow. Stanley suddenly remembered that, tomorrow night, Leon would be crossing the Atlantic on his way here. *You'll know when they arrive, I promise you. You'll know for sure.*

Almost a minute passed before the intercom clicked, and a woman's voice said, "Who is it?"

"Madeleine? It's me, Stanley Eisner. And Angie, too."

"I've been expecting you."

The door lock buzzed, and they pushed their way in. Angie said, " 'Ow come she was expecting us? We didn't telephone 'er or nothing."

"I don't know," said Stanley as they rose in the elevator to the top floor. "There's a whole lot more to Madeleine Springer than meets the eye. And I don't just mean changing her sex in the middle of a conversation. Even oysters can do that."

"Oysters can't talk, stupid."

"How do you know? Have you ever given an oyster the chance?"

Their banter was a brittle attempt to conceal their shock and their nervousness. They were scared of Knitted Hood, but in another way they were equally scared of Madeleine Springer and everything that she represented. The armor, the weapons, the danger—and most of all the awesome responsibility of being the frontline troops in the battle against an evil which, up until now, they had believed to be nothing but allegorical.

Madeleine Springer was waiting for them in her open doorway when they stepped out of the elevator. She was wearing a black velvet skullcap embroidered with silver threads, and she had shaved off her eyebrows and covered her face in grayish foundation, with darker gray emphasis on her cheekbones. In spite of the nakedness and the severity of her makeup, her eyes were wide and luminous enough to give her face intense beauty and expression; and although her lipstick was gray, her mouth still looked sensual and desirable.

She wore a tight black velvet evening gown, with a deep V-shaped décolletage, and her shoulders had been covered in the same grayish foundation. She wore no shoes, and no jewelry.

"You're famous," she said as Stanley followed her into her sparsely-furnished flat. He looked around. Something had been changed: not the furniture, not the décor, but the shape of the room. The last time he was here, it was a long rectangle. Now it was almost exactly square. There was something else, too: a very fine-lined drawing on white handmade cartridge paper, of a shape that could have been a lily, or an ear of grass, or partly-opened lips.

Stanley sat down on the sofa. "You heard what happened?" he asked her.

Madeleine Springer closed her eyes momentarily to signify that she had. She walked across the room on her silent bare feet and closed the linen-slatted blinds. "There was a news flash on ITN. They think that it was Arab terrorists, blowing you up in revenge for Israeli shootings on the West Bank. After all, you are nearly the most famous Jew in London, give or take a Rothschild or a Seiff or a Barenboim or two."

Stanley said, "We went into the dream, Angie and me. We went right back into Isabel Gowdie's dream."

Madeleine Springer gave him a faint, knowing smile. "I thought you would. You're a lot more headstrong than you first appear. Underneath that mild-mannered musicianly exterior beats the heart of a true Night Warrior."

"Underneath this mild-mannered musicianly exterior beats the heart of somebody who's been infected with the Night Plague, and wants more than anything else to be cured."

Madeleine Springer went through to the kitchen, and Stanley heard her taking out glasses and pouring drinks. "Did you find what you were looking for?" she called.

"We found what Isabel Gowdie wanted us to find."

"We reckon she's in Dover, or somewhere like that," Angie put in. "Solomon Eisner give us this bit of chalk and all of these seashells."

"When the Night Warriors buried some demon called Abrahel, they brought back a piece of marble and a twig from a yew tree," Stanley added. "So it seemed to us that their tokens of imprisonment are always a piece of the rock in which the demon or witch was imprisoned, plus a small clue to the rock's location. In this case, we have the seashells, which tell us that Isabel Gowdie was imprisoned close to the ocean; and the limestone, which tells us that she was imprisoned in chalk. There's something else, too: Angie's ancestor Elisabeth Pardoe came from Dover, and she had probably suggested a place where the Night Warriors could bury Isabel Gowdie—even though Isabel Gowdie ended up killing her."

Madeleine Springer came back with a black lacquered Japanese tray and two large glasses of vodka and gin-and-orange.

"Are you hungry?" she asked them.

They both shook their heads. "We've been pretty damn sick," said Stanley. "The Night Plague's getting worse."

He looked at Madeleine Springer for a long time without saying anything. Then he added, "There's something else you have to know."

She remained silent, expressionless.

"Knitted Hood guided us through Isabel Gowdie's London. We couldn't have found our way if he hadn't. But he guided us back, too; and when we got there, he demanded to know where Isabel Gowdie was imprisoned.''

Madeleine Springer's face remained immobile, a face in polished gray wax.

Stanley went on, ''He must have been seen by a passing police patrol. They called Detective Sergeant Morris. Even if he was at home, he lives just over the river in Wandsworth, so it couldn't have taken him more than five or ten minutes to get there, at that time of night.''

He licked his lips, which were feeling dry and sore. ''They knocked; then they broke down the door. Knitted Hood killed all three of them, right in front of my eyes.''

''And that's when you told him where Isabel Gowdie was buried?'' asked Madeleine Springer, her voice distinct and cool.

Stanley said, ''Yes,'' so softly that Madeleine Springer obviously hadn't heard him at first. Then, ''Yes.''

''Well, I might have expected it,'' Madeleine Springer replied. ''But it won't make your task any simpler. You will have to work out a way of keeping Knitted Hood and the rest of his Carriers well away from you, while you deal with Isabel Gowdie herself. You may not find that particularly easy. You will certainly find it very much more dangerous.''

''I didn't consider that I had a choice,'' said Stanley, peeved that she hadn't appreciated how threatening Knitted Hood had been. ''I've always preferred my head with a face on the front.''

Madeleine Springer turned to Angie. ''Have you had any symptoms yet?'' she asked, completely changing the tack of the conversation.

Angie swallowed lumpily at the memory of the tapeworms. ''I've been sick,'' she said.

''You know that it's going to get worse?''

''Yes,'' said Angie.

''Right . . .'' Madeleine Springer told them. ''You can stay here for the time being . . . in fact, you'll have to. I'm expecting Kasyx and Zasta to arrive the day after tomorrow. Then we can really start fighting back.''

She turned to Angie. ''And if you start feeling sick again or if you're feeling any other symptoms of the Night Plague, tell me at once. I can't cure it, but at least I can help you."

"Thanks," said Angie unenthusiastically. "Can't I go back to me flat?"

"I don't advise it. Supposing you have an attack of sickness? Supposing you dream about one of your flatmates? You'd really be better off here."

"I ain't got none of me clothes with me, that's the trouble."

"Oh, don't you worry about that." Madeleine Springer smiled. "I have closets and closets and closets full of clothes. You're welcome to borrow whatever you wish."

Angie smiled; the first smile that Stanley had seen from her since they had begun to make their way through Isabel Gowdie's dream. *Riboyne Shel Olem*, give a woman clothes and you'll have her eating out of your hand. But he didn't feel very enthusiastic about staying here himself. It might be safe; it might be comfortable; but it still felt very much like being conscripted into the armed forces.

He took his drink and walked over to the window and parted the linen slats in the blind. Outside he could see nothing but the prickling lights of a cold night in southwest London.

"You're worried that you haven't done very well?" Madeleine Springer asked him.

Stanley didn't answer. If only Detective Sergeant Morris hadn't come blundering in like John Wayne—maybe he and his officers would still be alive, and Stanley would have been able to win a little time, work out some kind of a deal which didn't involve telling Knitted Hood where Isabel Gowdie was, at least not immediately, the way he had been forced to by Knitted Hood's face-ripping tactics.

Madeleine Springer came and stood close beside him. He was sure he could detect the very faintest hint of lily-of-the-valley.

"The judgment was yours," she told him gently. "You and your companions will have to deal with the consequences; but that is the way of wars. Sometimes a commander has to measure the cost of his mistakes in terms of other people's blood."

Stanley turned and looked at her. She really was exceptionally beautiful—elegant, overgroomed, strange; with eyes that were a journey in themselves.

"You will have your chance to vindicate yourself," she told him.

It was densely foggy at Heathrow Airport when flight PA 126 from San Francisco landed two and a half hours late. Stanley and Angie stood crushed against the barrier outside the customs hall, surrounded by Bangladeshis and Pakistanis and Tamils awaiting the arrival of their relatives from the east.

At last, Leon appeared, a skinny tousle-haired boy with dark circles under his eyes from trying to stay awake for most of the night. He wore a padded blue parka and jeans, and an extremely righteous pair of rainbow-colored sneakers.

Angie said, "That's 'im, ain't it? It must be! 'E looks just like you!"

She jumped up and down and shouted, "Leon! Leon" although there was far too much noise in the hall for Leon to be able to pick up anybody unfamiliar calling his name. Angie had done well out of Madeleine Springer's closet: today she was wearing a black square-shouldered fur jacket, with a matching fur hat, a yellow silk Jasper Conran blouse, and a black pencil skirt by Armani.

If only she could talk proper, she'd be stunning, thought Stanley.

Madeleine Springer had kept them apart for the last two nights. They had eyed each other with feelings of cruel lust over the breakfast table. They had dreamed about each other at night. Very early this morning, Stanley had looked quickly in Madeleine Springer's bedroom and seen that she was asleep. Then he had crossed silently to Angie's bedroom and eased the door open. She had been lying facedown on the white linen sheets, wearing nothing but a white silk slip. The slip had ridden up to expose her bare bottom.

Stanley had stood by the door staring at her for a long time; and had then taken a single step forward. He had been immediately confronted by Madeleine Springer, who must have been hiding behind the door. Although how? He had distinctly seen her sleeping in her own room, and there were no connecting doors.

"Not tonight," Madeleine Springer had cautioned him. "Tonight you must fight those feelings. Tomorrow night, you will become a Night Warrior, in all your glory. Like any knight, a vigil alone will help to purify you.''

He had felt a snap of angry resentment against Madeleine Springer. For an instant, he could have slapped her. But even his infected soul cautioned him against angering the messenger of Ashapola. The Night Plague had made him devious as well as quick-tempered. He had managed a sour-twisted smile, and returned to his room, where he had sat on the end of his bed for over an hour and wrestled with demons.

—*cut a cut a cut a cut a*—

''Leon!'' called Stanley. ''Leon!''

But to Stanley's surprise, before Leon could see where he was, an elderly man walking beside Leon took hold of the boy's hand and bent down to say something in his ear. Leon nodded, and then turned to look for his father. By the time they reached the end of the fenced-off area outside the customs hall, the elderly man and Leon were walking together hand in hand as if they were grandfather and grandson.

Stanley stepped forward and held out his arms. ''Hello, son,'' he said, and Leon came politely up to him and hugged him. ''Hi, Pop,'' he said in a rather formal voice. The grandfatherly man waited patiently beside them while they greeted each other, but he showed no signs at all of going away.

''Did this gentleman help you off the airplane?'' asked Stanley, stiffly rising to his feet.

Leon nodded. ''He flew with me all the way from San Francisco. We talked and we talked.''

''Didn't you get any sleep?''

''He got some sleep, don't worry.'' The grandfatherly man smiled. ''Leaned his head against my arm all the way from Nova Scotia to Glasgow.''

''Well, thanks very much, I appreciate it,'' said Stanley, holding out his hand. ''It isn't everybody these days who cares about kids.''

''Oh, Leon is no ordinary kid.'' The man smiled again.

''Sure, well, thanks. We'd better be going. This little guy looks like he could use some lying-down-type sleep.''

''I'm not tired at all,'' Leon announced.

Stanley took hold of Leon's bag and together they began to

walk out of Terminal 3 to the multistory parking lot. "Leon, this is Angie," said Stanley. "She's a real good friend of mine."

"Wotcha, Leon." Angie grinned. "I don't 'alf like your beetle-crushers."

Leon frowned up at his father. "She talks weird."

Angie laughed. "That ain't weird, that's proper English. Like, I called me skin and blister on the dog, and asked 'er to lend me a borrow of 'er jamjar."

"That's *weird*," said Leon.

"No, it ain't. Skin and blister is sister, get it? And dog is dog and bone, phone. And jamjar is car."

As they reached the door of the terminal, a voice right behind Stanley's right shoulder said, "Rhyming slang. The argot of the cockney thieving classes."

Stanley turned around and saw that the grandfatherly man was still close behind, listening to their conversation as if he had every right to. Stanley gave him a smile and a nod and said, "This is Leon's first time in Britain."

"Mine, too," the man told him.

"Well, I really hope you enjoy it," said Stanley. "It's kind of cold and damp this time of year, but there's a lot to see if you know where to look. Sussex is worth a visit."

The man smiled. "Oh, I won't have any time for that."

They continued to walk toward the multistory parking lot. They walked up the ramp to the second floor and made their way across to the other side where Gordon's car was parked.

"Is that your car?" Leon asked in amazement. "It's like a bumper car!"

"I borrowed it from a friend, okay?" replied Stanley testily.

"The steering wheel's on the wrong side!"

"It's a British car, Leon. In Britain they drive on the wrong side of the road."

"Don't they keep crashing into each other?"

While Angie got into the car, Stanley tossed Leon's bag into the Montego's rubbish-strewn trunk and was about to slam the lid when another bag was lowered into it. He looked around to see the grandfatherly man smiling at him.

"What's this?" he wanted to know.

"You mean you're not going to give me a ride?" the man asked him.

"Well, look, sir, I very much appreciate your talking to Leon on the way over, but I haven't seen my son in quite a while and we have a lot of private family matters to talk over. Besides, you don't even know where we're going."

"I assume that you're going to the same place that I am."

"Listen, I don't think so. I don't like to appear churlish, but—"

"Henry Watkins," the grandfatherly man announced, holding out his hand. "Your friend Springer might have mentioned me. Kasyx the charge-keeper."

Stanley stared at the grandfatherly man more closely. Sixty-six, maybe, sixty-seven. Maybe not as old as that. His hair was plumed with white, and it had been bleached by the California sun, but there were plenty of darker streaks over his ears. Stanley had seen an old-young face like that before: his own father, who had drunk a bottle and a half of Jack Daniel's every day for thirty years, and then stopped one Wednesday morning cold turkey because his doctor had told him he had only 120 more bottles to go before he would be discussing his bar bill with St. Peter.

Henry had a soft, withered neck, a very clean checkered sports shirt, and a good-quality green tweed jacket. He could have been any moderately-prosperous Californian geriatric making a cultural visit to Europe. But Stanley noticed something about his eyes. They had something of the same quality as Springer's. Clear, mystical, filled with evanescent light. They were the eyes of a man who had walked inside other men's minds; a man who had seen visions that no ordinary man could ever see.

"You'd better . . . get in the car," Stanley suggested. "You don't mind riding in back? It's kind of messy. Just push that stuffed animal out of the way. I borrowed it from—"

"Keldak, yes, I know." Henry smiled and settled himself down in the back of Gordon's car with his Burberry folded neatly on his lap. "Springer told me that your transportation was a little rudimentary."

Angie, who was jabbing the keys at the ignition lock, suddenly stopped and twisted around in her seat. "Springer?" she asked Stanley. " 'Ow does 'e know about Springer?"

"His daytime name is Henry Watkins," said Stanley. "But he has a nighttime name, too. Effis the light-skater, meet Kasyx the charge-keeper."

Angie was openmouthed. "*You're* Kasyx? I never would 'ave known! I didn't imagine nobody so—well, I thought you was going to be younger, know what I mean? You know, no offense meant, but it's not exactly a doddle, is it, being a—you know—"

Henry pursed his lips and flared his nostrils. "You make me sound as if I'm practically dead already. Well, maybe I am on the grave side of sixty. But you should see me when I transform. Eat your heart out, Arnold Schwartzenegger."

Stanley said, "That means that we're only one short now, Zasta. But we could still start without him, couldn't we? Four of us would be more than enough."

"No *way*," Leon protested.

"What's your problem, champ?" Stanley grinned, ruffling Leon's hair, and remembering (as soon as he had done it) that Leon loathed it. ("You make me feel like a Muppet.")

"I said no way is four of you enough."

Stanley laughed. "You don't even know what we're talking about."

"I do too know what you're talking about!"

"Leon, you've been in Britain ten minutes, and already you're starting to act like a brat!"

Henry laid a gentle hand on Stanley's arm and shook his head. "He's not behaving like a brat, Stanley. He's behaving like Zasta the knife-juggler."

Stanley was about to laugh again when he suddenly realized that Henry was totally serious. He stared at Henry and then he stared at Leon and then he stared back at Henry.

"*Him?* He's ten years old! *He's* Zasta the knife-juggler?"

"Does it surprise you? The Night Warriors are a hereditary line. The promises made by the forefathers have to be kept by their descendants."

"But Leon is just a kid!"

"Joshua was just a kid, too."

"But Joshua was—"

Henry looked grave. "Joshua was killed, along with his father, Jacob, yes. I have already told Leon about that. But Leon understands that all Night Warriors have to face unnatural dangers; and the choice is his."

"How can a ten-year-old kid have any choice? He doesn't even know what we're up against! These are creatures who tear people's faces off with their bare hands! You ever see anything like that? And you want the same thing to happen to my son? Well, you listen to me, Kasyx the charge-keeper, you've got another goddamn think coming right up next, after the break!"

Angie was driving them out of the airport now and eastwards along the M4 towards Brentford and Chiswick, over the ghostly sprawled-out encampment of the Great West Road and all its factories and warehouses, their lights gleaming dimly through the fog. She gave Stanley an occasional sideways flicker of her eyes, partly out of concern and partly out of conspiracy. She and Stanley shared something between them which Henry didn't share: they were both infected by the Night Plague. That gave their outlook on life an unpredictable perversity. They felt the same urgency to hunt down Isabel Gowdie as the rest of the Night Warriors, but their need was becoming disturbingly ambivalent. Did they want to find her to destroy her, or did they want to find her to set her free?

Henry said, "As he is now, I agree with you, Stanley. Leon is just an above-average grade-school kid. But in the form of Zasta the knife-juggler, believe me, you could never call him anything but a full-fledged Night Warrior. He's strong, he's fast, he's mature, he's quite capable of making his own decisions."

Stanley turned to Leon. "What did Henry tell you about being a Night Warrior?"

"I told him—" began Henry, but Stanley interrupted him. "Would you mind? I want to hear it from Leon."

Leon bit his lip. "He didn't just tell me, he *showed* me."

"What do you mean, he showed you?"

"On the plane, when it was dark, and nobody was watching. He put his hand on my shoulder and he showed me my armor. It was all shining and it was golden."

Stanley looked back at Henry. "You did that to my kid without asking me first?"

"Since when have you been so interested in your kid?" Henry retorted. "Besides, there was no time to waste."

Leon said, "Pop, I know all about it. I know who I am. It's something I have to do."

"You don't *have* to do it, that's the whole point," Stanley replied. "I know it seems like it's exciting and grown-up and thrilling. But that's only the half of it. It's very dangerous, too, and very scary, and a lot of it is pretty damn disgusting."

"And boring," Angie put in.

"That's right," Stanley agreed. "And boring. A lot of it is very boring. You know, like being a cop can be boring. You know, paperwork, stakeouts, court appearances."

Leon was silent for a short while, but he obviously had something to say, and in the end Henry nudged him and said, "Go ahead, say your piece."

"Well," said Leon, "I know that I don't *have* to do it. But the fact is that I *want* to do it. Jacob Eisner was killed by Isabel Gowdie; and he was Mol Besa, the same way that *you're* Mol Besa now, so you're going to hunt her down, right, and get your revenge? Well, Joshua Eisner was Zasta, the same way that I'm Zasta; and I think I have the right to get *my* revenge, too, if I want to."

"Now, wait up," Stanley began, but Leon interrupted him.

"You left me, Pop. You walked out on me. You weren't interested *then* if I was scared or disgusted or bored or in danger or anything. So why are you so interested now?"

"Leon, that is crap! That is complete crap! I might just as well be listening to your mother, or your mother's goddamned attorney! Of course I was interested in you. But your mom didn't make it very easy. In fact, she made it very difficult. In fact, she made it impossible. Your mom is one of those people who don't believe in other people having a point of view. Well, they *can* have a point of view, but it has to be hers."

"Pop, you're just the same."

"Well, then, damn it, that makes two of us."

"But, Pop, I really want to do this. I want to do this so bad that it hurts."

"And I don't want you even to *think* about doing it. Listen, Leon, you have no idea of how dangerous it is. How can I take the responsibility of exposing you to all those kinds of things you find in dreams? Rats, dogs, diseases, fires—God knows what else."

"Don't forget arrows and explosions and killer robots and guns that suck the muscles out of your legs," Henry added in a warm voice as he watched the industrial scenery going by.

"Oh, Pop, you're such a spoilsport," Leon protested.

"Oh, yes?" Stanley demanded. "If protecting the life of my only son is being a spoilsport, then I have no qualms at all about being a spoilsport."

"I'm not frightened, Pop," said Leon. "I was frightened when you walked out on Mom and me, and left us. But I'm not frightened of anything now. You went, and that made me brave."

Henry smiled to himself. "That's one spunky kid you have there, Stanley. You can't deny it."

Stanley turned around and sat bad-temperedly watching the traffic as Angie drove underneath the concrete piers of the M4 around the busy Chiswick roundabout and turned towards Kew and Richmond. He thought of Tennyson as they drove past the junction with Kew Gardens Road, although it was too foggy for him to be able to see the house. He thought of the chilling rain, pouring through the ceilings, and the dogs with the heads of half-mad children. He didn't want to risk Leon ending up like that. *On the other hand, it might serve the little shit right, talking back to his father in front of strangers. How did Leon dare to compare him with Eve? That neurotic, carping, tunnel-visioned, money-grubbing harridan. She'd fought him so viciously for custody. She'd produced an endless succession of unctuous walleyed attorneys and conniving feminist child psychiatrists. "If his father has custody, he'll treat him worse than the family dog." He'd like to see her face if he sent Leon back with the eyes of a lunatic and the body of a bull terrier.*

They drove up Richmond Hill and parked. Angie collided with the curb and said, "Sorry!" Stanley hefted both bags out of the Montego's trunk and carried them across to Springer's front door, while Henry climbed stiffly out of the back seat.

Before Stanley had reached the front steps, however, Henry called, "Stanley . . . just a word before we go in."

Stanley waited with closely-controlled impatience, without turning around. Henry came up close beside him and looked at him in a steady, fatherly way.

"Stanley, I know what kind of a battle you're fighting inside of yourself. I know it isn't at all easy for you. Springer isn't always sympathetic, either; because Springer's well . . . Springer's Springer. Not so much of a person as a singing telegram from God Almighty. But I want you to know that *I* care about you, and about Angie, too, and I want to assure you that whatever you say to me, whatever conflicts we have between us, all of the power that I have at my disposal is yours, too."

He hesitated, and then he added, "When I was first called to be a Night Warrior, I was as soft as sponge cake and green as grass. But I've fought some real big battles since then, and I've lived through some strange times and some strange places that most human beings wouldn't even think possible. I have experience, and knowledge, and I can tell you this much: this Night Plague may be the very worst threat we've ever had to deal with, but we're going to do our level best to lick it, and lick it good, and we're not just going to lick it for the sake of the human race, we're going to lick it for you personally. And for Angie, too."

Stanley said, "Thanks. I appreciate it."

"And, listen," said Henry, "don't be sore about Leon. He has to face up to his birthright one day. It might just as well be sooner, rather than later. I'll take care of him if things start getting out of hand."

"Meaning that I'm not capable of taking care of him?"

"Meaning that you have yourself to take care of, my friend; and we all need all the taking care of that we can get. We're not talking about Pazuzu, or Abrahel, or any of those minor-league demons. This isn't Jack Nicholson making suburban women fly in the air. This isn't Linda Blair with a revolving head. This is His Satanic Majesty, Stanley. This is Old Scratch. This is It with a capital *I*."

"What are you trying to do, scare me into being nice to you?"

"I hope you're scared already, and I really don't care if you're nice to me or not. Just remember what Stendhal said. 'If you know men thoroughly, and judge events sanely, that's the first step toward happiness.' "

"You sound like a goddamned philosopher," said Stanley.

"You got it in one." Henry smiled. "Did you ever read my paper on Voltaire and Rousseau, 'Sand Against the Wind?' University of California, San Diego, 1967."

"That's one I must have missed," said Stanley as Angie pressed Springer's doorbell.

Springer was eccentric and evasive this morning. He appeared as a willowy, wan, androgynous youth, in a black linen suit and a fine white cambric shirt, with dozens of expensive accessories: a gold fob-watch, an alligator-skin cigarette case with the initials *MS* on it, and a gold-topped walking cane from Swaine, Adeney, Brigg & Son, of Piccadilly. His hair was cut short and brushed back with hairdressing wax, and he wore wire-rimmed spectacles with dark crimson lenses, like two circular pools of congealed blood.

"So this is Leon," he said, taking hold of Leon's hand with fingers as cool and thin as diluted milk. "Welcome to England, Leon. May the fog be with you."

He said nothing at all to Henry, but Henry continued to smile as if he were used to being treated this way. Springer showed them through to their rooms: a large eastwards-facing bedroom for Henry, with an antique stained-pine bureau and a desk with a typewriter and a bottle of Malvern water on it, and a bed with a handmade patchwork quilt; and a smaller dormer room for Leon, right next door to Stanley's.

Leon's room was decorated in Chinese blue and white, and looked out over the ghostly leafless oaks of Terrace Gardens and the fog-white invisible Thames. A white bookcase contained copies of Kipling's *Just-So Stories* and *The War of the Worlds* and *Beano Annual, 1968.*

"Well, what do you think of it?" asked Stanley, walking over to the window and looking out.

"It's really neat," said Leon, bouncing on the checkered blue and white bedspread. "It's going to be radical here."

"Sure, it's neat." Stanley watched a flight of ducks winging through the fog towards Twickenham. Then he said, "How much did Henry tell you about the Night Plague?"

"I guess he told me everything that *he* knew."

"So you know what it does to people, this disease?"

"For sure. It's like AIDS, only you don't get it in your body, you get it in your soul. If you catch it, you don't know what's right and what's wrong any more, and you can never get to heaven when you die. He told me about the way they spread it around, too. The Carriers, and the witches, and everything."

"He told you that it comes from the Devil?"

Leon nodded, his eyes widening.

"Did you believe him?"

"Not at first, but after he showed me my armor."

"I see."

"It was neat, Pop. It was dark on the airplane and everybody was watching the movie, and he laid his hand on my shoulder and it was like *zzzz-zzzz-zzzz*, I got this kind of electric shock and I lifted up my arm and it had armor on it, golden armor."

"So you believed him?"

"I sure did."

Stanley said, "Did he tell you anything else about the Night Plague?"

"Like what?"

"I don't know . . . what *kind* of people get infected, and how?"

"Well, I know they get infected by doing it."

"What do you know about 'doing it'?"

"I know everything about doing it. We're always talking about doing it at school."

"At Napa County Grade School you spend all your time talking about doing it?"

"For sure. What else is there to talk about?"

Stanley blew out his cheeks. "I don't know. There's art, there's history, there's politics. The meaning of life. The kind of things that adults discuss."

"Oh, yes," said Leon with enormous scorn. "Uncle Mikey took me to the Silverado Country Club and the men in the locker room were *definitely* talking about the meaning of life."

"Who's Uncle Mikey?"

Leon gave him a quick sideways look. "Mom's new friend, that's all."

"Mom's new boyfriend?"

"Well, she has to have somebody. You're not there. And who's this Angie, anyway? She looks like she knows you pretty good."

Stanley's right arm jerked up. *You little punk, don't you talk to me like that. I ought to smack you right across the face, and then I ought to shake you and shake you and teach you some goddamned respect.* But he caught himself just in time, and his right hand curved around to smooth down his hair, and he stood up straight, and shrugged, and gave Leon a sloping grin.

"We're just good friends, that's all, Angie and me."

"Are we going to get something to eat soon?" asked Leon, instantly losing interest in the topic of his father's "friends." "I'm totally ravenooski."

"Sure," said Stanley. "How about a hamburger?"

He laid his arm around Leon's shoulders and gave him a squeeze. "Good to have you, champ," he told him. "Don't go forgetting that I love you."

"I love you, too, Pop. So does Mom. She doesn't say so, but she does."

"Let's leave Mom out of this, shall we? Wash up and change your clothes, and we'll go find some chow."

Springer took them to the Village Restaurant, just around the corner in Friar's Stile Road. They sat crowded together in two uncomfortable wooden booths, rather like a fourth-class Czechoslovakian railroad compartment, and ordered prawn cocktails and cheeseburgers.

Stanley could scarcely touch his cheeseburger. It was just another incarnation of that ubiquitous British "mince," with a half-melted Kraft cheese slice on top. But Leon was either too hungry to care or actually liked it. Stanley had always said that if you could eat a McDonald's you could eat anything.

Springer seemed unusually tense and fidgety. Henry on the other hand exuded tremendous calm, like a master craftsman brought in to finish a job at which he knows he excels. Stanley found it hard to believe that Henry had ever been as raw and as nervous as he was now. He seemed to have such power, such command.

Stanley was drinking too much, mainly because the Muscadet had been served at room temperature, and he hardly even noticed that it was going down. He was talking more loudly and more argumentatively than he ought to have been.

Springer took out a tightly-folded copy of the London *Daily Telegraph* and smoothed it out on the table. "There's no question at all that the Night Plague is spreading, and spreading very quickly. Look at this news item here: A lone gunman walked down the street of his home village in Lincolnshire yesterday and shot three innocent people dead and wounded seventeen others. When he was arrested he said that he simply didn't care about the people he had killed. 'They were nothing.' Then here's a case of a woman who set fire to her husband while he lay in bed because she suspected him of having an affair with another woman. 'He deserved to be hurt,' she told the judge, 'and if it was necessary I'd do it again.' And here: over a hundred and thirty drunken youths rampaged through the center of a market town in Hampshire, killing a police constable, disemboweling a police horse, and causing thousands of pounds' worth of injury and damage."

"But that sort of thing 'appens all the time," said Angie. " 'Ow do you know it's the Night Plague?"

Springer folded the paper. "Incidents like these may be common in Britain today, my dear, but only two or three years ago, they were almost completely unknown. There were no Rambo-style gunmen; no revenge burnings; no 'lager-louts,' as the British call them. And all of these incidents have something interesting in common. None of the perpetrators showed even the slightest degree of remorse.

"There have been attacks in New York that have been manifestations of the Night Plague, too. The 'wilders' in Central Park, who rape and bludgeon innocent women and then express amazement that anybody should care. The increasing number of meaningless assaults on the subway. 'They were nothing,' that's all they ever have to say about their victims. 'They were nothing.'

"One of the most evil symptoms of the Night Plague is a

total disregard for the lives of others; and, in the end, a total disregard for your own life, too.''

Stanley said, ''It's time we put a stop to it, then. Before—''

''Before it spreads all over Britain and Europe, and all across North America,'' Springer finished for him, ''and before you and Angie start exhibiting the same symptoms.''

It was then that Stanley realized that Leon was staring at him, a ketchup-dipped French fry forgotten in his fingers.

''Pop?'' he whispered hoarsely. ''Do you and Angie have the Night Plague?''

Stanley swallowed almost half a glass of warm white wine and then looked at Henry for moral support.

Henry shrugged. ''He has to know, Stanley. It's for his own protection; especially when he's a Night Warrior. There may be a time when he has to make a life-or-death decision whether to trust you or not.''

''Well, you've more or less told him now, haven't you?'' Stanley retorted.

''Leon—'' Henry began in a gentle voice, ''the fact of the matter is that—''

''The fact of the matter is that we do,'' Stanley interrupted him. ''Angie and I are both infected, and it's getting steadily worse. So if sometimes I start behaving like a different pop from the pop you knew—''

Leon said, ''I never knew you, anyway, Pop. Not that much.'' But he was only being defensive.

''Well, thanks a lot. But what I was trying to tell you is that we're fighting against it, and fighting against it very hard; and when we find Isabel Gowdie we'll get rid of it forever.''

Leon regarded his father with dark, unreadable eyes. ''After that,'' he asked, ''are we going to be happy ever after?''

Stanley didn't answer. Springer fished out his fob-watch and opened it. ''It's time we were getting back. Gordon is coming to the flat at three o'clock, and I think we need to make a few plans before we go out tonight.''

''We're going out *tonight*?'' asked Henry, wiping his mouth with his paper napkin. ''I haven't even had time to get myself acclimatized yet.''

''There won't be time for that, I'm afraid,'' Springer told him. ''Stanley and Angie will help you as much as they can.''

They paid the check and walked back along Friar's Stile Road, past art galleries with sporting paintings in the window, and video-rental stores, and handsome Victorian houses where televisions flickered.

Unconsciously, Stanley and Leon held hands; and then Angie came and held Leon's other hand, and somehow to Leon they were more of a family than he and his mom and Uncle Mikey had ever been; Uncle Mikey with his hairy chest and his loud laugh and his six-packs of Coors Lite; and Leon smiled to himself in a way that Stanley couldn't remember having seen him smile before.

Henry, standing in the middle of the living room, said, "The way you can see yourselves now, by daylight, is only the faintest reflection of what you will look like in dreams. In dreams, you will become god-warriors, immensely powerful, immensely responsive, and with accumulated knowledge and experience of seven centuries of Night Warriors at your disposal."

He beckoned to Springer and then added, "Mol Besa, Effis, Keldak—you've already been given some idea of what your armor and your weaponry will look like. Now I'm going to show you mine—and Zasta's, too."

Springer rested his hand on Henry's shoulder, and gradually they became aware of a low vibration in the room, and the pungent smell of burned electricity. Tiny blue sparks began to crawl around Springer's fingers, and to form an outline all around Henry's head and shoulders.

There was a ballooning sensation in the room, as if the room itself were a spaceship, about to detach itself from the building and rise up slowly into the fog, dripping down sparks as it went.

Henry closed his eyes. The air around him began to darken, to form itself into shadows and shapes.

Gordon, who was sitting cross-legged in the opposite corner of the room, looked over at Stanley and raised his eyebrows. Stanley nodded and tried unsuccessfully to smile. He was struggling with one of his attacks of irritability again, and an imaginary ticker tape of ceaseless insults about Henry and his pomposity had been chattering through his mind ever since they had returned to the flat. He didn't even dare to think too much about Gordon. Gordon's wrist was almost completely healed now, and he had regained his strength and his color, not to mention his strutting BBC-radio-show sauciness, and Stanley found it almost impossible to tolerate having him here.

So you helped me in hospital, you faggot, just to make yourself feel more saintly. But I don't want you around now, especially now that Leon's here. People like you are a plague on your own.

There was a low shuddering noise like somebody shaking a heavy antique closet. Then Henry turned around, and he was wearing the gleaming crimson armor of Kasyx the chargekeeper. Although Stanley didn't know it, Kasyx's armor had altered substantially since he had first become a Night Warrior. It was slabby and angular, as it had always been, but now every surface was covered with rows of radiatorlike fins, so that Kasyx could gather imaginary solar energy as he walked under the imaginary suns of other people's dreams. His helmet had been modified, too, to include a head-up visual display of the location of every Night Warrior within a particular dream.

Kasyx said, "You depend on me to replenish your weapons and your armor. As soon as you feel your power failing, you must return to me as soon as you can, for recharging. I myself have no weapons . . . only the ultimate sanction of discharging all my energy at once, which can create a devastating power wave, but which then makes it impossible for us to escape from whichever dream we happen to be fighting in. We would then be trapped in the dreamer's subconscious until our physical bodies died of malnutrition."

Stanley asked, "What happens if the dreamer wakes up while we're still inside his dream? Or *her* dream?"

"That's the time to bail out," said Kasyx. "But you usually get plenty of warning. The landscape starts to dissolve, the images become unstable. You get a feel for it . . . you sense a change in pressure, not unlike slowly rising to the surface of a swimming pool. It's possible to remain inside the imagination of a waking person, but it's like a totally gray limbo, until they go back to sleep again and start dreaming. The problem with allowing *that* to happen is that your physical body remains at the mercy of whoever might happen to find it. Some Night

Warriors have been killed during the day by demons who found their physical bodies sleeping.''

Kasyx beckoned Leon forward and laid his hand on his shoulder. "Now let's see what this young gentleman looks like as Zasta the knife-juggler."

Leon stood with his hands at his sides and closed his eyes. Kasyx said, "Relax, Leon . . . everything's going to be fine." Then he closed his own eyes, and energy began to hum through his fingers and etch a fine glowing gold outline all around Leon's head and body.

In less than a minute, Leon had been transformed into Zasta the knife-juggler. He wore a brilliant golden helmet in the style of a Spanish *conquistador*, but with a plain gold visor which completely covered his eyes. His breastplate was made of thin curves of golden armor, similar to the flow fences on the wings of airplanes, and he wore shining golden boots, as pliable and as well fitted as the best riding boots, but made of malleable metal.

Stanley asked, "Is that visor solid? How does he see?"

Kasyx said, "Zasta is as sensitive as a knife-thrower in a circus, who throws knives blindfolded at a woman spinning on a wheel. He 'sees' by psychic power, and when the time comes to use his knives, he 'sees' nothing but his target. Normal vision would be a distraction." He added, "Turn around, Zasta. Show them your weaponry."

Zasta did as he was told. On his back was an ingenious and complicated rack of dozens of knife scabbards; and each of these scabbards contained a differently-shaped blade. There were long thin throwing stilettos. There were massive saw-backed bowie knives. There were chivs and sticking knives and hook-bladed knives and gutting knives.

"How about a little demonstration?" Kasyx suggested.

"What can I use as a target?" asked Zasta. He spoke in Leon's voice, but with a new and quite formidable authority.

Springer looked around. "The lily picture, if you wish. I was tiring of it, anyway."

Zasta snapped his head sideways, sized up the lily drawing in less than two seconds, and then lifted his right hand. A gold-bladed throwing knife leapt out of its scabbard on its own and somersaulted over his shoulder into his hand. Without any hesitation, Zasta threw it at the picture, and it flashed across the room and hit the narrowest of pencil lines at the very top of the picture.

Before any of them had time to appreciate the accuracy of Zasta's throwing, however, another knife jumped over his shoulder like a goldfish skipping out of a pond, and he had thrown that, too, exactly an inch below the first knife and exactly on the pencil line. Without hesitation, a cascade of throwing knives followed, until the entire outline of the drawing had been embellished with golden blades.

"Looks like the right sort of chap to have on our side," said Gordon. "Bet he'd make a wonderful sushi chef."

The hum of psychic energy gradually died away, and Henry and Leon emerged from their armor. Now Springer came forward, fastidiously tugging at his white cambric French cuffs. He seemed distracted, and quite abrupt, but it occurred to Stanley that he was not so much irritated with them as worried about them. Ashapola cared for the least of His creatures, for all that He allowed them to choose their own destiny, and to believe in Him or not to believe in Him, whichever they wished. Ashapola was not an interfering God, but He cared about His creations.

"When you go to bed tonight, you will recite three times the sacred incantation of Ashapola," said Springer. "This will ensure that, when you fall asleep, your dreaming body will leave your physical body."

"What 'appens if I can't get off to sleep?" asked Angie.

"You will, once you have spoken the incantations and emptied your mind of all extraneous thoughts."

"What happens if somebody tries to wake me up while I'm away, so to speak?" said Gordon. "I mean, it's quite possible that Jeremy could come back, and fancy a cuddle."

"For God's sake," barked Stanley. "There's a ten-year-old boy here, in case you hadn't noticed."

"Hey, it's okay, Pop," said Leon. "I know all about gays. We had a gay awareness talk at school."

"There's a difference between being aware of them and having to listen to every sordid detail of their love lives," Stanley retorted. "And besides, what the hell is your mother doing, sending you to the kind of school where you talk about nothing but gays and doing it?''

"I think Gordon asked a perfectly reasonable question," put in Henry. "The answer is that once your dreaming personality has vacated it, your physical body cannot be woken. That is why it is advisable that you go to sleep in a place where you aren't likely to be disturbed. If you think your friend is going to try to wake you, Gordon, you should check in at a hotel tonight, or stay here, if you prefer it."

"I don't want him staying here," said Stanley. "Not so long as Leon's here, too."

"What the hell's got into you, all of a sudden?" Gordon demanded. "I practically saved your sanity, after you were attacked. I came and talked to you whenever you called me. I even lost my hand because of you!"

Stanley said nothing, but turned away. The bilious hostility which the Night Plague had aroused in him had begun to subside, and he felt ashamed of himself for what he had said. At the same time, he still wasn't prepared to apologize. He caught Angie looking at him with an expression of sympathy. *She* understood the struggle that was going on inside him, even if nobody else did.

Springer said, quite quietly, "We had better be aware that two of our number have been infected by the Night Plague. Both of them are essential to our task, but there may be times when their judgment and their motivation are not always what they ought to be."

He walked across to Stanley and Angie, and added, "Whenever you feel yourselves weakening, remember this: your mortal souls are at stake. You are as close as any human beings can ever be to true damnation."

"It depends what you mean by damnation," said Angie cockily.

Springer looked at her seriously. "You've seen those boy-dogs. You've seen a Carrier for yourself. You've seen the inside of Isabel Gowdie's dreams. Imagine living like that, forever and ever, without any hope of escaping it."

He turned back to the rest of the Night Warriors. "Our first task is to find where Isabel Gowdie is. Once we have done that, Stanley can be rid of his Night Plague, and we can hunt down her Carriers, and destroy them, too.''

"What about Angie, and everybody else who's already been infected?" asked Gordon. "There must be thousands already.''

Springer said, "To grow, and to take over an individual's whole personality, the Night Plague virus must be constantly fed by Satan's psychic energy. Satan created the virus, after all, and like any parent he must feed his children.

"He does this through the chain of infection and secondary infection. *He* feeds Isabel Gowdie, Isabel Gowdie feeds her Carriers, the Carriers feed their primary victims—like *you*, Stanley—and the primary victims pass on the psychic energy to the secondary victims—like *you*, Angie.

Springer paused, and then he said, "All we have to do is break the chain of infection. Destroy Isabel Gowdie, and that will starve the viruses of the energy they need to develop. They will eventually shrivel from sheer malnutrition, and die a natural death.''

"And that's going to put an end to all of this violence we've been seeing lately?" asked Stanley. "All these riots and random shootings and rapes?''

"Not altogether. Even when somebody has been cured of the Night Plague, his morality remains scarred, just as your face remains scarred after smallpox. But, yes, there should be some noticeable improvements. And it shouldn't spread any further.''

"So where do we start?" asked Stanley.

"We start in Isabel Gowdie's own dream. We have to. She's been bound in such a way by the Night Warriors who imprisoned her that she cannot escape from her own dreams into anybody else's dream. Obviously it will be much more dangerous, to fight a witch in her own dream, and she will have her Carriers to help her. But there is no alternative. In her own dream is where you will find her; and in her own dream is where you will have to destroy her.''

Gordon, rather sulkily, agreed to take a room at the Petersham Hotel, only a hundred yards away from Springer's apartment building, down a steeply-descending road called Nightingale Lane. Springer refused to involve himself in the conflict between Stanley and Gordon. When Gordon appealed to him to make Stanley see sense, he simply turned away and shrugged. He was nothing but a singing telegram from God Almighty, after all.

There was an atmosphere of high tension in the apartment that day. The Night Warriors scarcely spoke to each other, and at about four o'clock in the afternoon, as it was growing dark, Springer retired to his room and closed the door. Leon sprawled on the living room floor, drawing a large sprawling picture of Napa Airport with colored pencils, while Angie lay beside him and watched him.

"Here's Jonesy's famous hamburger restaurant," Leon explained, "and here's me coming out of it. Here's Bridgeford Flying Services . . . and here's me, getting into a plane for a flight to the Golden Gate . . . and here's me being airsick. Look, you can see all the half-chewed hamburger."

"Oh, that's nice," said Angie. She was wearing a very short black designer dress with buttons down the front, and black panty hose, and little black pixie boots, all borrowed from Springer's wardrobe. Although she was watching Leon draw, she kept glancing up at Stanley, who was sitting on the Chinese-French sofa, playing drafts with Henry. Stanley was aware that she kept looking at him, but he pretended not to notice. His blood was inflamed enough as it was, burning its way through his arteries as if it were alight. He didn't know whether he felt hot or cold, although his forehead was crowned with beads of perspiration.

He had seen Angie's breasts, pressed against the polished floor. He had seen the curve of her bottom, where she had lifted one leg. He was playing drafts with Henry to calm himself down, to keep his mind orderly, to stop himself from raging around the apartment in an explosion of frustrated lust and ungovernable hatred.

He had once wondered (in what now seemed like a life that he had never even lived) how muggers could approach total strangers and hit them or stab them without any hesitation and without any apparent qualms. He knew now. He was boiling with such utter contempt for everybody around him, such furious selfishness, that when Henry managed to crown his first draft, he had to clasp his hands tightly together to prevent himself from hurling the board across the room and hitting Henry in the face.

Henry glanced at him quickly. "If I win, you won't kill me, will you?"

"Are you psychic, too?"

Henry shook his head. "Just observant. Ever since I dried out, I started taking notice of the world around me. I couldn't believe how much of it I'd missed, in forty years of boozing." He crowned another draft. "I guess you could say that, these days, I see things the way that a small child sees them."

"What made you stop drinking?" asked Stanley.

"This did, being a Night Warrior. Understanding for the first time that other people relied on me. Drinking is a way of copping out; of failing to live up to your responsibilities. Being a Night Warrior is just about the direct opposite of that."

Stanley put down his glass of vodka.

"Oh, don't mind me." Henry smiled. "I'm just one of those guys who never knew when to stop."

"Maybe I should, too," said Stanley.

Henry said, "A little Dutch courage won't do you any harm, not tonight."

Later, Springer emerged from her room wearing a tight white woollen dress, her blond hair cropped in a shining crew cut. Without a word she went into the kitchen on very high-heeled white shoes and started to prepare them a meal. She didn't call any of them or even look at them, and they gathered that she wanted to be left alone.

"Never seen her so tense," Henry remarked, looking up from his newspaper.

Stanley said, "Do you think she has any cause to be?"

Henry shrugged. "We've never sailed quite so close to the wind before. Never come quite so near to Old Scratch himself. I should think that Springer's pretty worried about what kind of catastrophic wrath we're going to be stirring up, filling a contract on Satan's favorite domestic. Imagine what God would feel like if a couple of demons took out St. Ursula."

"Are you kidding me?" Stanley asked him.

"Only partly," said Henry. "This is pretty damned dangerous stuff, what we're expected to do tonight."

Stanley was silent for a moment. Then he said, "Henry . . . I want you to promise me something."

"Say the word."

"I want you to promise me that if I start doing something crazy . . . something that jeopardizes everybody else—well, I want you to promise that you'll deal with me. Do you understand what I mean?"

Henry stared back at him for a long time. "Yes, Stanley, I understand. I already made that promise to Springer."

Springer had made them a sparse and elegant Japanese meal, served in black lacquered *bento*, or lunch boxes, each with an open top shelf and two drawers underneath. On the top layer she had arranged a dried chrysanthemum leaf with a sliced clam on top and a skewer of ginkgo nuts and a bundle of spinach. In the second layer, there were two fish balls separated by a chrysanthemum leaf, glazed beans, one rice ball, and a knot of *wakame* seaweed. The bottom layer contained a cube of pickled pork, three flower-shaped slices of carrot, three shrimps alternated with slices of lemon, and a tiny mound of finely-shredded radish.

For Leon, she had prepared shrimp and sesame toast, which happened to be his favorite oriental food. She had invited Gordon to come from the hotel to join them, but in Angie's words Gordon had "got the 'ump," and said he would order something from room service, thank you very much.

Stanley appreciated the sparsity of Springer's meal. It felt more like a last supper than a warrior's breakfast. They spoke very little, except to compliment Springer with exaggerated politeness on her cooking. When it was over, and Leon had helped Springer to clear away, they sat around the living room for a quarter of an hour, until Henry stood up and cleared his throat and said, "This is my bedtime, folks."

He went around to each of them and shook their hands. "I'm

not going to make any speeches," he said. "But I want you
to know that what you're about to do is something brave and
noble; and that however it comes out, it will never be forgotten, not ever, not as long as there are Night Warriors to tell
the tale. Now, all I can say is—see you in the morning, I
hope."

EIGHT
Chalk Face

STANLEY CLIMBED INTO BED FEELING AS IF HIS BRAIN HAD been laid bare and lashed by armfuls of stinging nettles. He lay back in the darkness, staring up at the patterns of light on the ceiling, and took four or five slow, deep breaths to relax himself. But deep breathing did no good at all. It only made him feel hyperventilated and giddy, and his brain still throbbed with half-formed anxieties and misshapen terrors.

He licked his lips and haltingly recited the sacred incantation of Ashapola.

"Now when the face of the world is hidden in darkness, let us be conveyed to the place of our meeting, armed and armored; and let us be nourished by the power that is dedicated to the cleaving of darkness, the settling of all black matters, and the dissipation of evil, so be it."

He said it three times, as Springer had instructed them, but by the time he had finished he was no more sleepy than he was when he had first climbed into bed. A panicky thought came over him: supposing all the other Night Warriors fell asleep, and he didn't? Supposing they went in search of Isabel Gowdie and left him behind?

Knitted Hood wouldn't be very pleased with him then. *(Because there had to be a compromise, after all, a way of persuading Isabel Gowdie to cure him of the Night Plague, without actually having to destroy her, surely? And only he was capable of reaching such a compromise.)* He couldn't even imagine what revenge Knitted Hood would exact if things went wrong.

He switched on his bedside light. Ten after eleven. He never went to bed this early—or, even if he did, he never went to *sleep* this early. He picked up the book he had borrowed from Springer. *My Life*, by the artist and naturalist Thomas Bewick: "On setting out, I always waded through the first pool I met with and had sometimes the river to wade at the far end. I never changed my cloaths, however they might be soaked with wet and though they might be stiffened with frost on my returned home at night."

Stanley read five or six pages, then replaced the book on the bedside table and switched off the light. In spite of himself, he started to slip in and out of sleep, and had extraordinary dreams of Thomas Bewick crossing rivers on stilts, and of a hanged naval officer that Bewick had once come across, rotating on the end of his rope, while his dog sat below him and watched him spin.

He thought that he could hear voices, although he couldn't decide where they were coming from, whether they were near or far away. He sat up and listened. They seemed to be coming from the living room, and it occurred to him that everybody else must have fallen asleep and that they had already become Night Warriors.

He rose from his bed and moved silently across the room. As he did so, however, he realized that he was *gliding*, rather than walking. In fact, he didn't even have to move his legs. He raised one hand in front of his face and saw that it was transparent. He could see the outlines of the door right through his fingers.

In fear and fascination, he turned around and looked back towards his bed. He was still lying there, his eyes closed, his mouth slightly open, one arm resting outside the covers. He had left his body. He was nothing more than a dream self, a sleeping memory of what he was really like.

He passed through the wall of his bedroom into the living room. The molecules of the wall made a *ssshhh*ing noise against his ears as he penetrated it. He was right. All of the others had already left their sleeping bodies—including Gordon, who must have floated over through the night from the Petersham Hotel— and they were gathered in a circle waiting for him. Springer was standing a little way away from the Night Warriors. She wore a floor-length robe of pure white silk, rather like a priestess, and her hair was gathered in a silver-threaded snood.

"Your time has now come," she told them as Stanley joined them, standing right behind Leon. "You are Night Warriors now. You are members of that great and glorious host who captured and chained all nine hundred and ninety-nine manifestations of the Devil, and who earned for all time the gratitude of Ashapola and the Council of Messengers. You have dedicated your dream selves to the extinction of evil, and in particular to the pursuit and capture of Isabel Gowdie, the witch-woman, Satan's most favored servant, and all of her Carriers."

She raised both arms, closed her eyes, and lifted her face upwards. Around her slender wrists, five bangles of golden light materialized. She whispered, "Ashapola, lend your power to these your servants," and slowly and silently the bangles rose over her hands and floated across the room, so that each of the five Night Warriors was crowned by a golden halo.

Almost immediately, the haloes dissolved and disappeared; but as they did so, Stanley felt a huge surge of energy in every muscle. Around his head, his glass helmet appeared, with its contra-rotating metal circlets; his body was clad in dull bronze armor. He looked down at his chest and checked the mathematical calculators that winked and flashed on his instrument panel. To his surprise, he could read and interpret them easily, as easily as reading a music score or the page of a book.

In a fraction of a second, he calculated the temperature and air pressure in the room, the precise constituents of the air, the exact time, the phase of the moon, the velocity of the earth, and the angle and speed at which they would fly away from the earth's surface if the planet happened abruptly to stop rotating.

The other four Night Warriors were also fully dressed in their battle gear. Keldak in his green metallic armor; Effis in her masklike lacework helmet and endlessly-changing leotard of lights; Zasta in his golden armor, with his racks of shining knives; and Kasyx in his slabby metallic suit of darkly-gleaming crimson.

Kasyx was fully charged with energy—almost *over*charged, because dazzling blue lightning was crackling and snaking around his shoulders and along his arms, and every time he brought his hands close together, a zig-zag electrical discharge would leap from one to the other, like a Van de Graaff generator.

"Here, Mol Besa," he said, and Stanley stepped forward. Kasyx laid his hand on a special chrome-polished triangular plate on Stanley's left shoulder, and instantly Stanley felt a juddering surge of enormous power. Every nerve in his body fizzed and tingled, and he felt as if he were strong enough to fight anything and anyone, Knitted Hood included. He had *become* Mol Besa. He was no longer transparent. He appeared as solid as he did in reality. Although who was to say, now, what was reality and what was a dream? *Am I dreaming you or are you dreaming me?*

One by one, the Night Warriors stepped up to Kasyx and were charged up with power. Now they glittered and glowed, their lights and their dials and their instruments filling the living room with a firework display of celestial energy. White fire sparkled from Effis's body armor, and gradually her light-skates materialized from the soles of her boots—two blindingly-bright blades that were curved at the front and trailed behind her for almost a foot. From Keldak's left wrist, a dazzling hand appeared; a hand which he flexed, formed into a fist, and then proudly covered with a thin green metallic glove.

Zasta's knives shimmered; and the visor of his helmet gleamed. Mol Besa grasped his shoulder and said, "You look terrific. I'm proud of you. You're still sure you want to do this?"

Zasta nodded. "More than ever."

"All right, then," Mol Besa told him. "I can't say that I blame you. I don't know what your mother would say."

Springer said, "Listen to me, we have very little time to lose. Kasyx will tell you that, usually, when we wish to enter somebody's dream, we have to locate the dreamer, and to ap-

proach him as close as possible. Very few people have dreams
that radiate very far beyond their immediate surroundings. This
case, however, is completely different. We have no precise idea
of where Isabel Gowdie is . . . but her dreams are so strong
that they can manifest themselves miles and miles away from
her physical location.

"We will have to go to the house called Tennyson and enter
Isabel Gowdie's dream there. Once we are inside the dream,
we can hunt her down."

Mol Besa put in, "You realize that Knitted Hood will be
following us."

"Yes," said Springer. "But how you deal with Knitted
Hood, Mol Besa, is up to you. That is a difficulty that you have
created for yourself."

Mol Besa resented Springer's censorious remark, but said
nothing. *My time will come,* he thought to himself. *Then you'll
see who's the master around here.* He caught Effis looking at
him through the fire and flower patterns of her face mask; and
he knew that she knew what he was thinking.

Springer said, "I will take you as far as Tennyson. After
that, you must find Isabel Gowdie on your own."

"Very well, then," said Kasyx. "Let's do it. Mol Besa?
Shall we go?"

One by one, the Night Warriors rose through the ceiling of
Springer's living room, through the attic where the water tanks
gurgled, through the tiles of the roof, and out into the frosty
night. They flew silently, like kites, absorbed by the air, crys-
tallized by the frost, invisible except for the faintest of glitters
and the slightest distortion of the sky.

They circled over a cold and sleeping London; a London
through which the Thames lazily curved; a London of orange
streetlights and silent formal squares. From high above Richmond, looking towards the east, Mol Besa could see the wan
moonlike face of Big Ben and the secretive Gothic spires of
the Palace of Westminster. It was too foggy for him to be able
to see Nelson's Column or the dome of St. Paul's; but he was
strangely reassured by knowing that they were there, as they
always would be.

This was the London over which Peter Pan and Wendy had
flown; and there was still something childishly magical in the

way that the Night Warriors wheeled over Kew Gardens and descended towards Tennyson.

Mol Besa noticed that, as Springer flew through the night, she left behind her a trail of absolute darkness. No stars, no lights, nothing. A darkness of such intensity that nothing could penetrate it. He wondered if absolute darkness and absolute light were one and the same, perpetual, yin and yang; if Ashapola was Satan and Satan was Ashapola; and if, therefore, the Night Warriors were being asked to risk their lives for nothing more than the spinning of the same two-sided coin.

He could feel that same two-sidedness within his own personality. On one side, the calling to be selflessly heroic, to burst through the realms of darkness with a sword of righteous light. On the other side, the lust to damage and destroy.

—to cut a swathe through the—

The Night Warriors circled over Kew Gardens Road. Springer said, inside of their minds. *I must leave you now. This task is yours. May Ashapola keep you and bless you and may you all return safely from the realm of dreams.*

"I'll second that," said Mol Besa under his breath.

Kasyx led the way. In a diving, corkscrew motion, he descended through Tennyson's roof, through the ceiling, and into the upstairs bedroom. The rest of the Night Warriors followed him in quick succession.

"It's raining in here!" Kasyx exclaimed in astonishment.

The storm was dramatically worse than the first time that Stanley and Angie and Gordon had ventured into the house. The whole room shook with thunder, and the rain lashed down so hard that Mol Besa, in his glass helmet, was almost blinded.

"This is her dream!" Mol Besa shouted to Kasyx. "Her Carriers use this house as a way of escaping from the real world!"

"I'm soaking!" Effis complained.

Kasyx looked around the room. Then he nodded. "We should be able to enter this dream as easily as any other. The dream's pretty hostile, and the dreamer's a long ways off. But— why not? Let's give it a try. The quicker we get ourselves in, the quicker we'll be able to get ourselves out."

"I'm all for that," said Mol Besa.

"All right, then, stand close together," Kasyx ordered. The

five Night Warriors stood back-to-back in a circle, their hands clasped together. Zasta looked up at Mol Besa, his blind visor giving nothing away; but Mol Besa sensed his question in the angle he was holding his head.

"Everything's going to be fine," he told him. "We'll have this witch licked before you even know it."

"Pop—"Zasta began; but Mol Besa shook his head.

"I know, son. Believe me, I feel the same way." *In spite of everything, I love you.*

Kasyx lifted one hand and described an octagon in the air above their heads, in pure blue energy. The octagon hummed and trembled for a moment. Then slowly it began to widen and sink, until it shimmered on the floor all around them, as if they had been lassoed by vibrant blue light.

"Before, we were looking at the dream and experiencing it secondhand," Kasyx explained. "The moment we step out of this octagon, we will be *inside* the dream, living it."

"Just like it's real?" asked Effis.

Kasyx slowly shook his heavy-helmeted head. "It won't be *like* real. It will *be* real."

They stepped out of the octagon and found that they were stepping off sodden carpet on to muddy ground. The walls of the bedroom had vanished, and all they could see was a rain-swept landscape of low horizons and huddled huts. Mol Besa took two or three steps forward and then stopped, listening to the rain pattering on his helmet. In the distance, sheet lightning flickered fitfully behind the piggeries. He was back in Isabel Gowdie's seventeenth-century London; the London of rutted roads and mud and plague.

Gut the pig and bite the toad.

Kasyx came trudging up to him through the mire. "I hope you know the way to Dover," he complained, "because I sure as hell don't."

Mol Besa punched a series of small silver buttons on his holographic astrolabe. Immediately, a three-dimensional image of the southeast of England appeared on his instrument panel, with hills and forests and villages. A gold-glowing ribbon indicated the route they should take to Dover.

Keldak came up and peered over Mol Besa's shoulder. "That's over sixty miles away," he complained. "I couldn't walk sixty miles in a week, let alone a single night. Let *alone* arrive in a fit condition to do battle with a witch.''

"Don't worry about that," said Kasyx. "Mol Besa can formulate a way for us to get there.''

Mol Besa tapped two different programs into his instrument panel. The first program proposed converting the psychic tension they had created simply by trespassing in Isabel Gowdie's dream into kinetic energy. This energy would be more than enough to enable them to fly to Dover in the same way that they had flown over London. But Mol Besa was worried that depleting this tension might seriously reduce the validity of their physical presence in the dream, so that they would be wavering right on the very edge of dream and reality. Isabel Gowdie would then find it comparatively easy to expel them from her dream, if she wanted to.

The second program suggested time-compression: speeding up a twelve-hour walk to twelve seconds. The snag was that this program would use up most of their backup energy: they would be able to fight with the energy they had already, but there wouldn't be anything left in reserve.

"It's a hell of a risk," said Kasyx. "We could easily find ourselves in the position of having to choose between destroying Isabel Gowdie or escaping from out of the dream. In other words, this could be a kamikaze mission. Once our energy's gone, there's no way of getting back; not unless another charge-keeper comes in to rescue us.''

"Isn't there any other way of getting to Dover?" asked Keldak. It was raining hard now, and his green helmet was beaded with drops of water.

Mol Besa shook his head. "We could levitate in low-level orbit, and allow the world to pass under us; but that would take all of the energy in Kasyx's reserves.''

"What's it to be, then?" asked Kasyx.

Mol Besa said, "Time-compression, that's my personal choice. We can get to Dover in twelve seconds flat, which will make it much more difficult for Knitted Hood to follow us, and if we're fast enough, we might be able to locate Isabel Gowdie before he realizes where we are.''

"We can find her," put in Zasta. "We can find her easy.''

"Oh, yes?" asked Mol Besa. "And how're we going to do that?"

"Springer gave me this," said Zasta, and held out the talisman that Mol Besa had found in the drawer in Springer's kitchen, the rusted Celtic cross tied with rotten linen. "Springer said that it was torn from Isabel Gowdie's throat when she was condemned to be burned by the Scottish court. It's supposed to bring people back to life. But it would never work for anybody else, only Isabel Gowdie. When it gets close to Isabel Gowdie, it's supposed to sing. The judges in the Scottish court blindfolded it, because they thought it could see."

Mol Besa held out his hand, and hesitantly Zasta wound up the talisman's string and passed it over. Mol Besa pressed the talisman tightly against the palm of his hand. It was dead cold; and it was silent. "She's not here, she's nowhere near here. But if this really works—"

"Springer said she was sure that it works," Zasta insisted.

"Why did she give it to you, instead of directly to me?"

"She said you might not believe her."

"And what else?"

"She said that you might have argued against taking it into the dream. She said that half of you wants to find Isabel Gowdie and the other half doesn't."

"I see," said Mol Besa. "If that's the way she feels, then you'd better keep it, in case I accidentally on purpose lose it, or pretend that I can't hear it singing."

"It's all right," said Zasta. "*You* keep it. Springer said you should. It's kind of an act of faith. Something to help you to focus your belief."

It was extraordinary for Mol Besa to hear his ten-year-old son talking like this. But Kasyx had been right. As a Night Warrior, Zasta was far more mature, far more assured. As well as the education of a good modern grade school, he had the wisdom of the centuries and the inherited experience of scores of previous lives.

"Okay," said Mol Besa, and lowered Isabel Gowdie's talisman around his helmet. "Let's go witch-hunting."

The Night Warriors stood close together, their armor trickling with rain. Mol Besa punched into his instrument panel the full formula for time-compression, which was a fascinating re-working of Einstein's theory of relativity, formulated laterally rather than progressively.

As he completed the formula, Mol Besa saw a dark triangular shadow emerge from behind the piggeries. It remained motionless for a long while; then it moved slightly and he could see the pale oval of Knitted Hood's face. As he had promised, Knitted Hood was watching him, following him. Mol Besa smiled grimly to himself. He hoped for Knitted Hood's sake that he was capable of traveling at eighteen thousand miles an hour, because that was how fast the Night Warriors would be traveling on their way to Dover. He took a shining cartridge out of his ammunition belt and slotted it into the side of the instrument panel. There was a brief, high-pitched gabbling noise as the program was loaded into the cartridge. Then Mol Besa took the cartridge out, drew back the sliding chamber of his equation gun, and loaded it.

Knitted Hood watched him without moving. Acrid brown smoke drifted through the rain, carrying the smell of wet timber smoldering, and hessian, and human flesh. Isabel Gowdie's dream was a charnel house, a crematorium of the human spirit.

Mol Besa said, "Ready?" and prepared to fire. As he did so, however, the girl with the cart appeared, only fifty or sixty yards away, trundling another load of nodding white bodies along the rutted track. She turned her head to stare at them as she passed them by; and again Mol Besa had the nagging sensation that he knew her, that he had seen her somewhere before. Yet he couldn't place her; and before he could look at her more closely, she had turned her head away and continued along the track.

A dead arm swung from the side of her handcart, beckoning, beckoning. A child's body slipped sideways as she negotiated a particularly-deep rut; and stared at Mol Besa with bruised unseeing eyes.

"Some dream," Keldak remarked. "This is more like a nightmare."

"Life *was* a nightmare in those days," Kasyx commented. "Just think about it: we've only had antibiotics since World War II. If you caught anything serious in the seventeenth century . . . if you caught the *flu* in the seventeenth century, you'd be lucky to survive it."

"Come on, let's get it over with," urged Effis. "I 'ate this place. The sooner we're out of it, the better."

Mol Besa lifted his equation pistol and squeezed the double trigger. There was a sharp crackling noise, and a thin beam of red laserlike light came whipping out of the muzzle, curving around them. It spun faster and faster, around and around, until it had enclosed them in a basket of interlaced red light.

They could hear nothing but the laser's deafening crackle, like having an untuned radio pressed against each ear. Then there was a taut, deeply-pressurized implosion. Zasta shouted out loud. The world rushed in on them from all sides, like an avalanche, and they were buried in solid silence. They couldn't move, couldn't speak, couldn't see. All they had was the helpless understanding that they were compressing twelve hours of their lives into twelve seconds; that for each of those seconds they were hurtling towards Dover at an unimaginable velocity, disobeying the laws of time and space and gravity.

Twelve seconds seemed to last forever. But then Mol Besa heard rain prickling against his helmet again, and opened his eyes. The Night Warriors were standing together on the gray battlements of Dover Castle, overlooking the battleship-gray waves of the English channel.

The strange thing was that this was present-day Dover, with its customs sheds and warehouses and cross-Channel ferry terminals. Through the rain and the mist, Mol Besa could see a Sealink ferry disembarking trucks and cars, and a hovercraft leaving on its way to Boulogne.

"This isn't the seventeenth century," said Keldak. "We seem to have traveled in *time*, as well as space."

But Kasyx said, "No, no. We're in a dream, and dreams don't have any kind of logic like that. You can walk from one room to another in a dream, and jump three hundred years without even blinking."

Mol Besa clasped the talisman in his hand and looked around. "She's here somewhere. She must be. She knows present-day Dover because she's close; she can feel it. She may even be able to see it. But London looks like seventeenth-

century London because that's the only London she ever
knew.''

"Then she can't be very far away.''

Mol Besa held up the talisman in the flat of his hand. "If it
sings, then we'll know she's here for sure.

"Sing,'' he pleaded under his breath. "Come on, you have
to *sing.''* He turned the talisman one way, and then the other
way.

"It's not singing yet,'' said Effis dubiously.

"It will,'' Zasta retorted.

"Well, it might and it might not . . .'' said Kasyx. "There's
no harm in giving it a try.''

Mol Besa walked along the wet granite-gray stones of the
castle battlements, lifting the talisman this way and that, and
calling on Ashapola to help him. Kasyx would have been surprised if he hadn't. Entering a dream for the very first time
was wildly unbalancing and infuriatingly disconcerting; and it
was only after eight or nine dreams that Kasyx had eventually
acquired his "dream legs''—his ability to keep his balance and
his sanity, no matter how much the ground cracked open beneath his feet, no matter what imaginary monsters he had to
face.

Mol Besa stood facing the rain-ladén wind, looking around
him. The hovercraft had long disappeared towards France in a
fuming cloud of spray; the ferry stood empty, waiting for re-
fueling. Dover looked wet and dismal, all the way from
Cowgate Cemetery to East Cliff. Through the rain, Mol Besa
could see the tower of the Pharos, the lighthouse that the Romans had built to guide them towards Dover, and St. Mary's
Church. The Channel looked so realistic, with its mud-streaked
waters, that it was difficult to believe that this was somebody
else's dream.

Effis slid up to Mol Besa on her shimmering skates. "P'raps
we ought to take a look at the cliffs . . . she might be 'idden
in one of the tunnels.''

Mol Besa lowered the talisman and nodded. "Maybe you're
right. I just hope that Dover was the right guess. She could
have been buried anywhere from here to Brighton. It could take
us *years* to find her.''

Keldak came up, too. "No luck, my love?'' he asked.

Mol Besa shook his head.

"I'm sure she's here," said Keldak. "I can *smell* her, do you know what I mean? And I'm sure Kasyx is right . . . if she *weren't* here, she wouldn't know what present-day Dover looked like, would she?"

He nodded toward the talisman. "No joy with that?"

"Nothing."

"It's just an idea . . . but perhaps you should try taking off the strip of linen. I mean, if the Scottish court put it on because they thought the cross could *see* . . ."

"Maybe you've got something there." Mol Besa lifted the talisman, and Effis unpicked the tight linen knot with her fingernails. Soon the corroded Celtic cross was unbound, the way it had been when Isabel Gowdie wore it herself. Mol Besa held it up again and said, "Ashapola . . . guide us. Ashapola . . . help us to find the witch-woman."

There was a long moment when they heard nothing but the wind from the Channel buffeting in their ears, and the occasional clanging from the docks. The rain sprinkled against their helmets and dripped from their fins and their weapon racks and their power hookups. Then—very softly, very thinly—they heard a keening sound. It was like the squeal of wheels of a distant freight train, in a marshaling yard, squealing on and on and on.

Mol Besa lifted the talisman higher, and the keening grew sharper and louder. There was no question about it—it was Isabel Gowdie's talisman, calling to its mistress. *Mistress, I'm here! Mistress, I've found you at last!*

Mol Besa turned around in a circle. There was no question that the talisman keened more loudly when he held it towards the southwest.

"What's in that direction?" he asked Effis.

"Folkestone," said Effis. "The next port along."

"Anything else?"

"I dunno. I'm not a blinking geography expert, am I?"

"Tunnels! You mentioned tunnels!" Keldak said, his voice almost falsetto with excitement.

"That's right," said Effis. "They was always digging tunnels in these cliffs."

"But they've started digging another tunnel, much more recently! A tunnel that the Night Warriors in the seventeenth century couldn't possibly have imagined would ever be dug!''

Kasyx frowned behind his visor. "What are you getting at?''

"The Channel Tunnel, of course! They've started digging the Channel Tunnel just southwest of here! They're doing it from a place called Shakespeare Cliff!''

Shakespeare Cliff. The Bard's Disease. Suddenly, the reappearance of the Night Plague began to make an awful kind of sense. Mol Besa punched in the map inquiries to locate the English end of the Channel Tunnel working, and then overlaid the coordinates with the directional signal from Isabel Gowdie's talisman.

A three-dimensional image of Shakespeare Cliff and the tunnel that had been bored beneath it was created in scintillating light and color on his instrument panel. A hill, a cliff, an approach road. Even tiny moving images of the contractor's vehicles, crawling in and out of the tunnel entrance.

Across this image, a penetratingly thin green line passed from one side to the other—representing the exact direction in which the talisman keened the most loudly. The thin green line passed precisely through the eastern wall of the tunnel, 175 yards in.

"That's it," breathed Kasyx. "We've found her. She's there."

They left the castle and descended into the town. Although it was a sharp representation of modern-day Dover, almost unreal in its clarity and detail, the people who filled the streets were the same distorted cripples and plague victims who had populated Isabel Gowdie's dream-London. Suspicious eyes watched them from shops and cafés and garages. As they passed the offices of the National Union of Seamen, they saw blue-tinted lobsterlike faces pressed against the glass.

Some of the passersby were blurred and only half formed, as if they had been painted in oils and then smeared while the paint was still wet.

It took them nearly a half hour to reach the Channel Tunnel workings. A wide cutting had been hewn through the chalky downs, and earth-moving trucks toiled in and out of it, their wheels thick with whitish mud. The Night Warriors stood above the tunnel entrance for a while, the five of them silhouetted against the rainy sky, listening to the noise of drilling and blasting and the blaring of heavy vehicles.

"All right, then," said Kasyx at last, "let's take a look at this lady."

They descended the wet chalky slope. Mol Besa noticed that Zasta stayed close to him, and thought to himself: *He might be a Night Warrior, but he's still my son.* He turned around and saw that Effis was close behind him, too. Maybe he could still give people strength; maybe he could still give them guidance. The Night Plague hadn't yet overwhelmed him altogether.

They had almost reached the tunnel entrance when a heavily-built misshapen man appeared. He wore a builder's donkey jacket and chalk-filthy overalls, and he walked with a swiveling limp. He stood in front of them, leaning to one side, barring their way. His eyes were small and colorless and piggish, and the waxy skin of his face seemed to ripple and shift.

" 'Ere, you're trespassing," he told them. His voice was a treble-noted blare. "Don't you know it's dangerous?"

"We're inspectors," said Kasyx ambiguously.

"You can't come down 'ere," the misshapen man repeated.

"We have to," said Kasyx.

"You're not allowed to," the misshapen man insisted, taking a threatening step towards them.

Keldak started to peel off his left-hand glove; but Kasyx leaned towards Mol Besa and Keldak and whispered, "Remember—he's a figment of Isabel Gowdie's dream. She's checking us out, protecting herself."

He was right. The misshapen man circled around them, eyeing them up and down. His face constantly altered as he looked at them: his chin bulging, his cheeks sinking, his forehead sloping. But after he had completed a full circle, he said, in a peculiarly feminine voice, "All right. You can take a look around if you want to."

He stood aside, and one by one they walked past him and into the massive vestibule of the tunnel. There were lights and generators and trucks everywhere, and miles of snaking cable; and vast yellow-painted earth-boring machines bellowed past them on their way to the tunnel face.

The noise inside the tunnel was shattering. Mol Besa could hardly hear himself think. What Isabel Gowdie must have suffered when the Channel Tunnel company came boring into Shakespeare Cliff, he couldn't even imagine.

The five of them walked along the tunnel until Mol Besa's instrument panel told them that they had reached the precise point where the talisman's signal intersected with the holographic map of the Channel Tunnel. Mol Besa lifted his hand and shouted, "This is it! We're here! We've made it!"

The rest of the Night Warriors stopped and looked around. The tunnel walls were chalk-white and glossy with wet; white and glossy as Knitted Hood's mask. There were lights everywhere; working-lamps and halogen inspection lamps; so bright that Kasyx had darkened the glass of his visor; but no sign anywhere of Isabel Gowdie.

"You're sure this is the right place?" Kasyx bellowed at Mol Besa.

Mol Besa lifted the talisman up to the side of his helmet and he could hear it singing: a high-pitched screaming that tore through his ears like the blade of a tile-cutting saw.

"The cross seems to think that it is!" he shouted back. "And my instruments are absolutely sure of it!"

"Then where is she?" Kasyx demanded. "I don't see her anywhere!"

They prowled up and down, running their hands over the walls, kicking at the floor, staring up at the thirty-foot ceiling. All the time, compressors roared, drills hammered, and workmen shouted to each other.

"She's not here!" Keldak called out. "If you ask me, dear, she's been leading you all round the bushes!"

"She's here!" Mol Besa insisted, jabbing at his instrument panel. "Look at this image . . . this is the tunnel, and this is where the Celtic cross is creating the maximum signal. It's audiovisual mathematics, plain and simple. She's *here*!"

"All right, then, if she's here, where is she?" Keldak demanded. "If you're so incredibly clever, *where*?"

It was then that Zasta tugged at Mol Besa's arm. Mol Besa looked down at him and saw that Zasta was pointing halfway up the drilled-chalk tunnel wall. "What?" he said. "What is it?" But Zasta said simply, "Look."

Mol Besa peered up at the wall. At first he couldn't see anything at all. But gradually he realized what he was looking at. There were four small protrusions on the surface of the chalk, no larger than fingertips. And that is what they were, fingertips. The Channel Tunnel drilling machines had missed Isabel Gowdie's imprisoned body by less than twelve inches, although they had broken away just enough of the solid chalk to expose her fingertips.

Mol Besa stood for almost half a minute, staring at those fingertips. They belonged to a woman who had been incarcerated for over three centuries in solid white limestone: a woman whose evil had been so fearful that the Night Warriors had found it necessary to seal her and bind her and keep her imprisoned in the deepest cliff they could find. Only the unforeseeable progress of civil engineering had released Isabel Gowdie from her eternal bondage; only a circumstance which would have seemed beyond imagination in 1666—even to those who were used to running through the wildest imaginings of dreaming men and women.

Kasyx shouted, "She's still trapped! But all she needed was the smallest access to the outside world—that would have been more than enough for her to wake up her Carriers!"

"What do you suggest we do?" asked Mol Besa.

"We have to dig her out of there, first of all. Then you and she have to do the business . . . otherwise you're going to be stuck with that Night Plague for all eternity. Then we have to zap her."

"Easy, no problem," said Mol Besa with undisguised sarcasm.

"It won't be, believe me!" Kasyx yelled back. "Keldak! Effis! Zasta! Keep guard! I'm going to chisel this lady out of the rock!"

"But this is only a dream!" Mol Besa shouted.

"That's right! She was imprisoned in a dream, we can dig her out in a dream!"

"But if it's only a dream, how come she was freed by the *real* digging of the *real* Channel Tunnel?"

"Because, my friend, her body was buried in the waking world, while her soul was buried in the dream world. You can't bury a soul in the waking world, it will never rest . . . as anyone who has ever had a dream about a dead husband or a dead wife or a dead friend will tell you. By the same token, you can't bury somebody's fleshly body in the dream world, either. That's why people find it so important to *physically* bury their dead. The Night Warriors buried Isabel Gowdie in both waking and dreaming states . . . just to make absolutely sure that she could never escape, never again.''

''And now we're going to dig her out?'' asked Mol Besa, looking up at the wet chalk wall with awe.

Kasyx nodded. ''That's right, Mol Besa. Now we're going to dig her out.''

Mol Besa looked at him narrowly. ''Supposing I told you that I didn't want to do this? That I'd rather leave her where she is? I mean, surely we can cover up her fingers, and that'll seal her off again.''

''Mol Besa, you have the Night Plague,'' Kasyx shouted back. ''Thousands of British kids have the Night Plague, too. This woman is feeding it; this woman is Satan's soup kitchen. You have to get rid of your own infection; and then make sure that everybody else gets rid of it, too. You have to!''

Mol Besa nodded. He felt as if his head were bursting apart. Kasyx beckoned to Keldak and shouted in his ear, ''Target your fist to knock away the wall . . . a cuboid, okay? About that size. I don't want her injured. It looks like she's probably caught up in some kind of struggling posture . . . you see what I mean? One hand out in front of her, and the other one behind, like she's running through solid chalk.''

Keldak looked quickly at Kasyx and then said, ''Okay . . . I'll do what I can.''

The Night Warriors stood away from the limestone wall; all except Keldak, who approached it slowly, sizing it up with foxy, perceptive, calculating eyes. As he did so, he peeled off his left glove, and the well-lit tunnel workings were even more brightly lit by the beams of solid energy that radiated from his fist. His fist was so dazzling, in fact, that Mol Besa had to shield his eyes with his hand; and then, his eyes swimming with dozens of afterimages of Keldak's fingers, Mol Besa had to turn away as well.

The holographic satellite that floated in the air on the left side of Keldak's helmet orbited silently through ninety degrees until it was hovering in front of his facepiece. Keldak programmed it deftly and competently . . . creating within its target parameters a six-foot cuboid in the limestone wall in front of them . . . a block of chalk which would contain Isabel Gowdie, entire and unhurt.

"I hope this works," he told Kasyx nervously. "I've never done anything like this before."

Kasyx smiled. "Sure you've done it before. You've probably done it hundreds of times before. Keldak was mentioned in one of the earliest Night Warriors chronicles that I've ever seen . . . way back in the thirteenth century. Just because you've forgotten that you've done this before, that doesn't mean you can't remember how to do it."

"If you say so," Keldak replied without much conviction.

His holographic globe swung smoothly back to its "parked" position on the left side of his helmet. He slowly lifted his left arm, with its blindingly-bright fist, and for two or three seconds he closed his eyes tight, concentrating.

"Come on, Keldak, now's the time," Kasyx encouraged him.

Keldak arched his back, stiffened his arm, and shouted out, *"Ashapola!"*

His fist flew from his wrist with an ear-splitting rush like a subway train. It struck the curved chalk wall and hammered right into it, hosing a spray of pulverized limestone behind it. It disappeared completely into the rock, although flickering shafts of blinding white light played through the dust as it furiously chiseled out the cuboid that Keldak had programmed it to cut for him.

There was already so much noise in the tunnel that the hammering of Keldak's fist went unnoticed. But Effis and Zasta still kept watch on the tunnel entrance, where trucks and workmen came and went, and sheets of rain still poured steadily down from a gray and doleful sky.

More chalk dust spurted out of the groove that Keldak's fist had cut. Then, for a while, the light subsided, as the fist cut out the back of the cuboid, which would detach the block from the tunnel wall. Keldak raised his left arm, and already a second fist was forming on the stump of his wrist, to replace the one which was exhuming Isabel Gowdie.

"You ever deal with a witch before?" Mol Besa shouted.

Kasyx shook his head. "One or two demons. Never a witch."

"I'm scared," said Mol Besa.

"What of? Yourself or the witch?"

"Myself, mostly. I don't know what I might do."

"Just hang in there," Kasyx replied. "If you think you're going to need help, just don't hesitate to ask for it. Night Warriors work together, remember. We're a team."

Mol Besa nodded. But all the same, he was beginning to feel the stirrings of some extraordinary blackness inside him, like a stick stirring molasses. His blood jangled through his veins, and he was breathing in short, stressful gasps. *I've found her*, he thought. *I've found her at last. Now she can change the world in the way that she was always meant to change the world. Now she can spread the Night Plague from pole to pole.*

He swallowed dryly and glanced quickly at Keldak to make sure that Keldak hadn't picked up any psychic echoes. In dreams, you never knew what powers other people might have; what inspirations. Keldak, however, was much too busy watching his dazzling fist hammer out the last of the limestone block. His green armor was covered by a fine film of chalk dust, and he had raised his visor so that he could see better.

Mol Besa looked towards Effis. Behind her lacework mask, Effis's eyes appeared unusually dark, and when she realized that Mol Besa was watching her, she bared her teeth in the briefest of suggestive grins. It was a grin that said *I'll do things to you that you never imagined possible. I'll love you and I'll hurt you, you bastard. I'll love you till you bleed.* So she was being affected, too. The Night Plague had infected them both with the lust and cruelty and faithlessness of Satan; and here they were, only feet away from Satan's favorite servant. Their stomachs churned with nausea; their arteries were burning. The baleful influence of Isabel Gowdie grew stronger and stronger with every hammer of Keldak's fist.

There was a clattering tumble of rocks and heavy lurching noise. Keldak's fist had now smashed its way all around the limestone block. All that remained now was for the block to be forced out of the tunnel wall. Keldak swung his holographic globe around again and retargeted it. His second fist flashed from his wrist, *zwafffff!* blinding them all with its magnesium-bright flare. It vanished into the groove around the block in a brilliant interplay of dust and light. There was a second's pause, and then it detonated all of its energy at once, forcing the block to shudder two feet out of the rock face.

When the dust had settled, Kasyx stepped forward and laid his hand on the block. "Mol Besa, you and I can lift this out between us. If you can just give us a little mathematical assistance . . ."

Mol Besa punched three different equations into his instrument panel. The first postulated freezing the air just below the lower edge of the block, to form a ramp of ice down which they could slide the block with the minimum of effort. The second suggested sending this whole section of the tunnel wall far into the future, to a time when Shakespeare Cliff would have been worn away by natural erosion. The third was simply to create a localized vacuum just in front of the block, so that it would be forced out of the tunnel wall by the surrounding air pressure.

He checked the comparative energy levels which these differing solutions would require. The vacuum pull would be the noisiest and the most untidy, but by far the least extravagant. They needed to be thrifty with their power: especially if Knitted Hood caught up with them before they managed to destroy Isabel Gowdie.

"All right, let's stand clear," he said. "I'm going to evacuate a cuboid of air exactly equivalent to the size of the block, so the block will be pushed right out of the tunnel wall to fill it. Once it's out, it's going to drop two feet, and that's probably going to damage it. So watch out for flying debris."

"And watch out for Isabel Gowdie, too," warned Kasyx. "She's one powerful witch, and she's been imprisoned in this cliff for three hundred years, so she's going to be seriously pissed."

Mol Besa loaded his vacuum equation into a cartridge and then slotted the cartridge into his gun. "Are you ready?" he asked Kasyx.

Kasyx nodded. "Let's do it. Ms. Gowdie wants out, and out is what she's going to get. But let's just remember one thing, huh? This is *her* dream, she controls it, and we're just here under sufferance. If things look for a moment like they're going wrong, that's the moment we pull the plug and exit. We can always get her another day.''

"Says you," put in Effis.

Kasyx didn't quite know how to take that comment, but lifted his hand and said, "All right, Mol Besa. Let's get this block out of the wall, shall we?'' All the same, he kept his eyes on Effis. Behind the mask of a Night Warrior, he could detect the voice of somebody who was already half suborned to Satan.

As Kasyx turned away, something in Mol Besa's head whispered *SATAN*. He looked around, his hair prickling. He didn't realize that Isabel Gowdie had picked up the name of her Master from Kasyx's thoughts, and amplified them through solid limestone in a desperate *cri de coeur*.

SATAN, the voice echoed and reechoed, like the voice of somebody falling and falling down an endless nightmare well. *SATAN is the pestilence that was—*

"Promised," said Effis. The other Night Warriors stared at her; all except Mol Besa, who knew exactly what she meant. Without any further hesitation, he pulled the double triggers of his equation gun, and the cartridge flashed into the air and exploded right in front of the limestone block.

Mol Besa knew that he was converting mathematical formulae into pure energy, but he hadn't seen an equation cartridge explode before. Glittering numbers burst through the air like a napalmed bowl of alphabet soup, actual numbers and letters, $1/\sqrt{(1 - v2/c2)} \, m \, mo/\sqrt{(1 - v2/c2)}$. They tumbled and whirled, and then assembled themselves into thin sparkling lines of tingling incandescent energy.

"God Almighty," said Effis; and then the huge limestone block was wrenched out of the tunnel wall with a thunderous rush, and collapsed on to the tunnel floor, falling over on to its side and splitting from one corner to the other.

The Celtic cross around Mol Besa's neck shrieked so piercingly that it made his teeth ache. He tugged it away from him, breaking the string, and thrust it into one of the wallets around his waist.

There was a moment's pause, while the chalk dust gradually settled, and large pieces of limestone dropped off the sides of the block and fell clonking on to the tunnel floor. Mol Besa quickly looked around, but none of the workers in the tunnel appeared to be taking any notice of what they were doing . . . presumably because Isabel Gowdie didn't want them to. They were creations of *her* imagination; they would do whatever she wished.

Suddenly, a startling white light shone from the center of the broken block. It streamed out in all directions, like the sun rising over the Arctic, like a blinding welding torch, *white white totally white death white bone white eye-blinding white*. It was so brilliant that, by comparison, Keldak's fist looked like a dull light bulb.

Large rugged triangular lumps of chalk began to fall away. The block was disintegrating in front of their eyes. The dazzle from inside it was so intense that all of them darkened their visors or shielded their eyes. The energy was pure white but there was no question at all about its origins. It was the power of *total absolute* evil. It was Satan's power: relentlessly destructive, like unshielded radiation. The kind of power that could pass right through your body and phosphorize your bones and curse your family's genes for generation after generation, one distorted chromosome after another.

All the children down all the centuries to come, who would suffer pain because of this single blast of blinding power. *And we shall cut a swathe through the world.*

Mol Besa stepped back, tugging Zasta back at the same time. He had imagined Isabel Gowdie in dozens of different manifestations. A hag, a harpie, a blank-eyed siren. A seductive young woman with a bagful of spells. But he had never imagined that she would look like this; or that when she appeared, he would be so overawed.

The last fragments of chalk dropped aside, and Isabel Gowdie was free. She lay on her back on a bier of crumbled limestone, one hand still defiantly raised. It was that gesture of defiance that had led to her fingertips being exposed by the tunnel diggers; and to the Carriers waking up, after three hundred years, and to the renewed spreading of the Night Plague. Out of those four fingertips had passed the Satanic energy that had cursed England for the past two years with sickness and violence and tragedy—air disasters, rail crashes, prison riots, shootings, maimings, mindless murders, rapes, burnings—a sickness that would eventually spread dream by dream all over the world, if the Night Warriors didn't destroy Isabel Gowdie tonight and spread her ashes so widely that they could never be gathered together again.

Isabel Gowdie was tall and slender, emaciated by centuries of entombment. Her skin was white, her cheeks hollow, her jawline sharp. Her long white tangled hair rose into the air in a coruscating fan, giving off boundless energy and light. A white linen blindfold had been tied around her eyes, and her temples were studded with a coronet of seventeenth-century screws, which in those days had simply been twisted nails. The screws had been driven right into her skull, and Mol Besa intuitively knew that they were part of the Night Warriors' ritual of sealing a witch's mind, the Crown of Screws.

She was completely naked, with protuberant ribs and hook-like hipbones. Her breasts were small and slanted, and on each nipple the Night Warriors had placed their seal of black wax, imprinted with the double cross of Ashapola. More black-wax seals had been placed on her shoulders, on her knees, on her ankles, and on her wrists. It was only because the seal on her right wrist had cracked and split apart that she had been able to raise her hand while she was being buried in the limestone; a momentary gesture which, after more than three centuries, had at last assured her release.

Between the hairless lips of her sex, the shaft of a huge tarnished silver cross had been inserted; a last sacred gesture to ensure that—even if she were found—no demon or devil would be able to have intercourse with her, to reproduce their kind, and that even if Satan had made her pregnant before she was imprisoned, his offspring would never be able to leave her body.

Mol Besa slowly approached her. His emotions were churning wildly; his blood surged through his arteries; his brain boiled. She remained motionless and blindfolded, her one arm raised, with white light streaming in all directions. He felt her power. It was like standing in a hurricane-force wind, or opening a blast furnace, or falling a thousand feet into an icy Arctic lake. He felt wildly exhilarated, bursting with power. *This is what I've been searching for, all these years. This power, this influence. This, this, this! Now I'll be able to play the violin*

*again, and play not like Stanley Eisner, but like God Almighty!
Now they'll fall in front of me; now they'll weep!*

But there was something else, too. He was terrified of her.
She was sightless and naked and fastened with holy seals, but
he was terrified of her.

"What am I supposed to do?" he asked, turning to Kasyx.
His mouth felt as if it were stuffed with dry cotton wadding.

"You have to withdraw the cross; then you have to have sex
with her," Kasyx told him. "At the instant you ejaculate, the
Night Plague virus will rush back into her body."

"Why should it do that?" Mol Besa asked.

"Simple," Kasyx explained. "The virus is always vora-
ciously hungry. It's always trying to get back to its Maker, the
one who created it, the one from whom it derives its nourish-
ment. I mean, why should it put up with irregular supplies of
thinly-strained baby food, when it can suckle directly from
Satan's favorite servant? Or even, if it's lucky, from Satan himself?"

"What then?" asked Mol Besa numbly.

"That, my friend, is when we take her apart. That precise
instant. Effis will cut off her head, Zasta will cut her to pieces,
and Keldak will pulverize those pieces into dust, and then yours
truly will incinerate that dust into ash. Then all five of us will
scatter that ash as far apart as any ashes were ever scattered,
in the definite hope that Mistress Gowdie is lost and gone forever."

"Riboyne Shel Olem," Mol Besa whispered.

"Absolutely," Kasyx agreed. "Now you know why I gave
up drinking. The kick you get out of this makes Smirnoff seem
stupid."

Mol Besa stood as close to Isabel Gowdie as he dared. He
knew that she couldn't move; he knew that she was powerless,
except to direct her Carriers. All the same, he felt overwhelm-
ingly intimidated; and having sex with her seemed impossible.

Kasyx came up and stood beside him. "Mol Besa," he said,
"it's the only way. It's either this or damnation; and I've seen
a glimpse of damnation, and I'd rather have sex with Isabel
Gowdie every morning before breakfast for the rest of my life,
believe me, than be sent to hell. It's hell in hell. Take my word
for it."

"You've *seen* hell?" Mol Besa asked him. Anything to delay the moment when he would have to climb up on that bier of shattered chalk and—

Kasyx took hold of his elbow. "I've dealt with all kinds of demons, Mol Besa . . . and when you look a demon right in the eye, that's when you see hell. Believe me."

He was calm and reassuring and steadfast, but Mol Besa still felt rigid with panic. *He could have everything; everything he had ever craved. He could be wealthy, famous, Eve could be killed in an automobile accident. All he had to do was break those seals and take out that tarnished cross and—*

Kasyx said, "Come on, Mol Besa. We don't have too much time."

"I don't know," Mol Besa replied. "Maybe we should give her a chance."

"A *chance*? Look at her! Look at the power that's pouring out of her! That's devilry, Mol Besa. She gave up everything for that. Her humanity, her morality, her mortal soul. She was screwed by Satan, Mol Besa! Not just a nightmare! Not just a figment of anybody's imagination! That monster that floats around inside of our minds; that black thing inside of our joint imagination; that is what physically and actually had intercourse with this woman, Mol Besa, and what he passed on to her she passed on to *you*!"

"I know that," Mol Besa protested. "I know. It's just that—"

Kasyx looked away, making it obvious that he wasn't prepared even to listen.

Mol Besa hesitated, and then he said, "Okay. You win. If that's what I have to do. But do you mind if the others look the other way?"

As it happened, the other Night Warriors were already facing the other way. Not only was the light that Isabel Gowdie radiated too bright for anybody to look at for very long, but they were watching the tunnel workings, and the entrance to the tunnel, for any sign of trouble.

Mol Besa unlatched his belt and his instrument panel and handed them to Kasyx. Then he unclipped his bronze armored leggings, until he was wearing nothing but his helmet, his breastplate, and his boots.

It was damp and chilly in the tunnel. Mol Besa's breath steamed inside his helmet, partially fogging it up, so he took that off, too. The very last thing he felt like doing was having sex. He probably wouldn't be able to manage it, anyway. He was too cold and too frightened and Isabel Gowdie's fleshless body was shining at him as if it had been sculpted out of a winter moon.

Keldak turned around and gave Mol Besa a long, apprecia- tive stare, until Mol Besa grimaced and glared back at him. "Go on, lovey," challenged Keldak. "Do your worst. We're running out of time."

Effis looked at Mol Besa appealingly, eyes wide, although he didn't know whether she was appealing to him to finish off Isabel Gowdie, to give her back the filthy disease that had infected both of them, and then to chop her to bits and burn her; or whether she was appealing to him to forgive her and to let her go. Zasta didn't even turn around, but vigilantly watched the entrance to the tunnel. Perhaps Zasta didn't want to see the Night Warrior who was his father having sex with any other woman apart from his mother. Mol Besa didn't entirely blame him.

"Come on, Mol Besa," urged Kasyx. He was growing no- ticeably anxious now. "You have to."

With a sinking sensation of dread, Mol Besa climbed up the crumbling sides of the limestone bier on which Isabel Gowdie was lying. Chalk slid beneath his boot heels. Then, cautiously, he knelt astride her knees. It was so cold that his penis had shrunk to the size of a nine-year-old boy's, but he tried not to think about it, the way that he tried not to think about it when he had been unable to get it on with Eve. *Don't think about it, it'll come up when it wants to.* And sometimes it had.

Isabel Gowdie flared just as brightly. Her hair rose and fell as if she were floating in the sea, except that millions of tiny sparks flowed from the ends of her hair and sparkled out over the tunnel. Mol Besa laid one hand gently on her right thigh. It felt utterly chilled. He hadn't felt anything as cold as that since *(February, Chicago, when he and Eve had been walking together past Marshall Field, and Eve had pressed the palm of her hand against the window and her hand had frozen to the glass.)* He took hold of the tarnished silver cross and slowly withdrew it. There was the faintest tugging sensation as it came out, her pale vaginal lips peeled apart. It was an English altar cross, solid silver. It was untarnished where it had been buried inside her.

Mol Besa handed the cross to Kasyx, who laid it carefully on the ground. Then he shifted himself higher up on Isabel Gowdie's thighs, and took hold of his penis in his hand, and pressed it against her vulva. *This is ridiculous. I can't to it. It's cold and I'm half dressed in armor, and Kasyx and Keldak are watching me, and I'm supposed to be making love to a blindingly white witch with frozen-cold skin who scares me so much that all I want to do is vomit.*

At that moment, Zasta called, "There's somebody coming! Look, over there!"

Mol Besa frowned in the direction that Zasta was pointing. Zasta was right. There were four hooded figures marching down the wet chalk slopes that led to the tunnel entrance. They were difficult to distinguish through the rain, but they had a diseased and raggedy look that reminded Mol Besa of Knitted Hood. They were walking very fast, their coats flapping around their ankles. They were accompanied by six or seven huge dogs, who trotted close beside them, their spines protruding through their brindled rain-slicked skin, saliva swinging from their tongues.

"Carriers," warned Kasyx. "Somebody must have told them that we were here."

Mol Besa said, "What the hell do I do now?"

"Get on with it," Kasyx snapped at him. "The sooner you do it, the sooner we can finish her off."

"Kasyx, I can't!"

"What the hell's the matter with you? Think of something erotic! I don't know—Brigitte Bardot!"

"Brigitte Bardot's about a hundred!"

"Do it!" Kasyx yelled at him. "Whatever turns you on!"

Zasta and Keldak and Effis spread themselves defensively across the tunnel. The Carriers continued to hurry towards them at the same fast walking speed, their coattails flapping in the rain and the wind, their dogs trotting evilly beside them. They looked like the merciless villains in a spaghetti western—

faceless, relentless, fast. Their coats were spattered with white mud and their masks were as pale as death.

Mol Besa looked down at Isabel Gowdie. She hadn't moved. Her right arm was still raised, clawing for freedom the way it had clawed for freedom three hundred years ago. He jiggled his penis, but he knew that it wasn't going to rise. He was far too frightened; far too stressful; far too cold. *Perhaps if you take off her blindfold.*

He hesitated. He reached forward with a careful hand. He touched the soft old linen of her blindfold. *Perhaps if you take off her blindfold.*

Kasyx said, "The dogs! Look out for the dogs!"

As the dogs came nearer, closely followed by their bustling masters, the Night Warriors could see that they weren't ordinary dogs. Their faces were pale, their eyes were wide. They were Dobermans and German shepherds and half-breed weimaraners, but they had the heads of men. Men with staring, grotesque expressions, and lips stretched back across their gums. Men with bristling hair and madness in their eyes, but men all the same. As intelligent as men. As cruel as men. But quick, and vicious, and fearless as dogs.

Zasta tried a long shot, to give Mol Besa more time. He lifted his hand for a heavyweight long-distance throwing knife, and it cartwheeled, shining, over his shoulder. He caught it deftly. Then he aimed, reached back, and whipped the knife at dazzling speed straight towards the leading Carrier.

The knife hit the Carrier straight in the face. He clutched the knife handle with both hands, spun around, staggered, and then pulled the knife violently out of his hood. Along with it, he brought his white celluloid mask.

"Again!" said Kasyx, and Zasta tossed two more heavyweight knives. But the Carriers were still fifty yards away, and now that they were ready for them, they dodged the knives easily. They continued to hurry towards the Night Warriors with all the fussy haste of determined killers. They were afraid of nothing; not even death. Hadn't their mistress promised them life everlasting?

Mol Besa found the tightened knot of Isabel Gowdie's blindfold. He picked at it, failing to loosen it at first; but then he managed to pull out one end of it, taking all the tension from it. He hesitated, breathing hard. He glanced at Kasyx but Kasyx was too busy with the Carriers and the men-dogs. What he did now was up to him. What he did now was his decision; and his alone.

"Hurry," Kasyx urged.

Mol Besa tugged at Isabel Gowdie's blindfold. The fabric was rotten and began to tear; and through the separated weft he caught the pale glittering glimpse of an eye. He tugged harder and dragged the blindfold right off, setting off a shower of white sparks from her hair. And there she was staring at him, the witch-woman, the woman who had touched her foot with one hand and her head with the other, and promised everything in between to Satan.

Her eyes were the palest green, with whites that had the sticky consistency of scarcely-boiled eggs. They were pale, but they had an electrifying effect on him. He felt as if he had been abruptly gripped by the spine and jolted upright; as if every ganglion in his nervous system had been illuminated with cold white light.

The seals, she told him. He didn't know whether she had spoken out loud or not; but he had heard her distinctly. *You must break the seals, Mol Besa.*

Kasyx shouted at him, "Mol Besa? What's wrong?" But the Carriers were hustling even closer now, and the man-dogs had broken into a threatening lope. Kasyx was too busy directing Effis and Zasta and Keldak to be able to worry about Mol Besa.

Effis crouched low over her light-skates, her armor twinkling. The lenses on her skating boots revolved to catch the maximum brightness from the halogen lights in the tunnel; and almost at once her skate blades intensified to brilliant gold. She hesitated for a second, but then Kasyx shouted, *"Go!"* and she flashed across the floor of the tunnel at almost a hundred miles an hour.

She skimmed diagonally across the ground like the most elegant speed-skater there had ever been, building up velocity with easy flourishes of her skates. The man-dogs saw her coming and scattered, but she had targeted a heavy black and ginger German shepherd with a bristling head like Vincent van Gogh. Along the sides of her forearms, her razor-fans opened.

"Ash-a-pol-aaaaaahhh!" she screamed. She flashed past the

German shepherd as it tried to twist towards her and snatch at her arm. Her razor-fan sliced the side of his face right through to the bone, and all along the side of his body, cutting through fur, muscle, ribs, and internal organs. The man-dog collapsed sideways in a cascading splatter of blood. His tongue fell out of his cheek; his prune-black liver slipped on to the floor. Then, in a thrashing convulsion, stomach and intestines slithered in a heap out of his abdomen, leaving his body as empty as a fur sack.

A whirl of hot, pungent body steam was twisted away by the speed of Effis's passing.

One of the Carriers tried to catch Effis as she skated close by, but she turned a triple somersault in the air, skated around him in a quick, powerful circle, and then turned on him. She flurried her fists in the air like a boxer pummeling at a punching bag, and her razor-fans tore relentlessly into his coat in a whirlwind of sharpened steel. Shreds of fabric flew everywhere. Then the Carrier screamed, a chilling, whistling, high-pitched scream. Lumps of flesh began to burst through the air, then bone. Then his mask was sliced in half, revealing his face.

It was then that Effis stopped pummeling and quickly twisted away, pirouetting as she did so. The Carrier had been revealed for what he was, and as he stood on his feet dying, the other Carriers paused, although they didn't look at him. They kept their eyes on the Night Warriors; and on Isabel Gowdie.

Underneath the mask, the Carrier was exposed as a leper. He was in the last stages of lepromatous leprosy, and his nose and upper lip and most of his jaw had already been ulcerated. His blistered scalp had only a few diseased-looking tufts of hair, and his ears had long gone, leaving him with nothing but dark, encrusted holes.

The leper uttered a strange keening noise, *hoooo-eee-oop*, which was all that he could manage with his collapsed palate and eroded nasal cavity. It was both plaintive and disgusting. Then he dropped to his knees and fell forward. Chunks of gray fibrous flesh fell out of his coat and scattered across the chalky tunnel floor.

The other Carriers had already started to advance on the Night Warriors again; a little more cautiously than before, but still walking at a steady pace. The man-dogs began to fan out, with the obvious intention of circling around them.

Mol Besa meanwhile had done nothing to consummate the act of intercourse with Isabel Gowdie. He sat astride her still, his back rigidly upright, his teeth clenched, with sweat trickling coldly down his back. He was conscious, but he was powerless to move. He understood now why the Night Warriors had blindfolded the witch-woman before they entombed her. She had the Satanic power of hypnotism. The strength of her will streamed from her eyes like the exhaust from twin jet engines, rendering Mol Besa deafened and numb.

Break the seals, she commanded him.

He tried to shake his head. She had persuaded him to remove her blindfold and to lay himself open to a psychokinetic hammerlock, but he was still capable of willful thought; and he knew that if he broke her seals, that was the finish. The Night Warriors would have lost the war, and the Night Plague would sweep across the world in a massive tide of darkness.

Imagine a world without morals or pity. Imagine a world of drugs and cruelty and urban collapse.

Break the seals, Mol Besa, she repeated. Her green eyes widened slightly. *Use your mathematicks; and break the seals.*

Keldak was firing one dazzling first after another. He hit a man-Doberman straight in the face, and the creature's nosebone cracked and was punched right into his brain. For an instant, the magnesium-bright light from Keldak's fist flashed out of the man-dog's eyes, so that he looked like a hound straight out of hell.

Keldak hit another Carrier, too; a blindingly-bright punch which was swallowed up in the folds of the Carrier's coat. There was a noise like chair legs breaking; and then the Carrier fell to the ground in a flicker of light and a burst of powdery dust.

Zasta threw knives with laconic accuracy. He sent three whirling at one of the man-dogs as it tried to outflank them. The first hit the man-dog in the neck and pinned it against the tunnel wall. The second struck it in the spine; the third caught its back legs. It remained shuddering and shouting, half paralyzed and unable to move, until Zasta threw a heavy execution knife which hit it directly in the heart.

Mol Besa . . . you must break the seals . . . if you refuse to break them, you will surely die. My Lord and Master will see to that, no matter what happens to me.

Mol Besa squeezed his eyes tightly shut and tried to shake his head. It was then that he felt a cold clawed hand on his naked leg. He opened his eyes again and saw that Isabel Gowdie had managed to move her free right arm, and that her fingers were gradually inching their way up his thigh.

Break the seals, my darling Mol Besa.

"I can't—do that," he gasped. "I came here to—"

One sharp fingernail probed the division between his testicles; one sharp thumbnail scratched at his pubic hair.

I have been taken by the Lord and Master of the Whole World . . . surely you didn't think that you could satisfy me?

Slowly, her long chilled fingers began to massage his penis; slowly and erotically, an extraordinary mixture of fear and pleasure, irritation and arousal. As his penis swelled, she began to tug down harder on its outer skin and to dig her nails harder into his flesh.

Break the seals, Mol Besa . . . then perhaps I will let you take me.

"I can't," he replied, although it sounded more like a prayer than a denial.

She rubbed the swollen head of his penis up and down between the smooth cold lips of her sex, up an down, up and down, parting it but never quite penetrating it. *Don't you want me, Mol Besa? Don't you want me? Break the seals, Mol Besa, and you can have me!*

She continued to massage him, harder and harder, until he began to feel that tight knotting between his legs that told him a climax was imminent. If he could only force his way inside her. If he could only warn Kasyx. But Isabel Gowdie's grip on his mind was as uncompromising as the grip on his penis, and the tunnel all around them flashed and flickered with the light of battle, as Kasyx and the rest of the Night Warriors fought to keep the man-dogs and the Carriers at bay.

"Kasyx!" shouted Mol Besa.

Kasyx turned around, but at that instant a huge black shaggy wolflike man-dog sprang up on to his back and buried its teeth in his accumulator connections. The man-dog's teeth crackled with blue sparks. Electrical fireworks crawled across his eyebrows and poured out of his nose. The tunnel was filled with the reek of burned fur and frying human lips. The man-dog was being electrocuted but wouldn't or couldn't let go. Kasyx swung his shoulders, trying to shake the heavy man-dog loose, but it wouldn't relinquish its grip. All the time, pure energy was streaming out of Kasyx's accumulators, discharging itself in a frenzy of blue sparks from the bristling tips of the man-dog's fur.

God, thought Mol Besa, *we're down to the last of our energy in any case . . . we daren't lose any more.*

He tried to get up, to help Kasyx dislodge the man-dog. But Isabel Gowdie gripped his penis and his brain even tighter, and hissed at him ferociously, *Break the seals, Mol Besa, if you want to escape me. Break the seals, Mol Besa, if you want to be anything more than a eunuch, trapped forever in a witchwoman's dream.*

She gave his penis three harsh, triumphant rubs, and he ejaculated, pearl-white semen on pearl-white skin. He coughed, saw blackness, saw stars. But even as he softened, Isabel Gowdie still wouldn't let him go. *Break my seals, Mol Besa, you miserable wretch! Break my seals.*

Kasyx was roaring in desperation as his precious energy poured away through the burning, swinging body of the man-dog. Zasta, with only four knives left in his armory, began to edge backwards. Keldak needed more power: his fists were fading, and even though he was still hitting the man-dogs, there was so little force in his blows that the man-dogs did little more than flinch. All around them, fast as a flash, Effis was still skating and circling and slicing, but the Carriers were swinging balks of tunneling timber at her now, making it increasingly difficult for her to come close.

"Mol Besa!" Kasyx shouted. "Mol Besa, get this damn dog off me!"

Isabel Gowdie kept her grip. *Seals first, Mol Besa.*

He had no choice. He knew that he had no choice. "You witch," he mouthed at her. Then, without any further hesitation, he punched out a program which would liquidize the wax in the seals; and which would convert the religious energy with which the seals were invested into the briefest crackle of tame lightning.

Isabel Gowdie watched him with thinly-disguised greed as he loaded the program into a cartridge and slotted the cartridge into his equation pistol. He fired it, aiming upwards, and the cartridge ricocheted from one wax seal to the other—wrists, ankles, breasts, knees.

Each black seal sizzled for a split second and then vanished in a small puff of evaporated wax.

For a moment, Mol Besa and Isabel Gowdie were surrounded by curtains of white lightning. Then the lightning died, and the smoke cleared away, and the pale naked form of Isabel Gowdie was free. *You have done well,* she growled at him. Her voice was quite different now. Thicker, coarser.

"Then let me go, for God's sake," Mol Besa insisted. "It was part of the deal."

Deal? Do you think I make deals?

"Mol Besa! For God's sake!" Kasyx was clamoring. Two more man-dogs came running up to him. They had recognized now that he held all of the power. The Carriers, on the other hand, were keeping their distance, their faces expressionless, their faces perfect, probing and parrying, just to keep the Night Warriors occupied while Kasyx's energy slowly bled away.

—and we shall cut a swathe—

Isabel Gowdie rose from her bed of limestone. *I killed you before, Mol Besa. I'll kill you again.*

"But you promised—"

Do you really believe that a witch's word is worth anything? You're new, aren't you? Green as grass, soft as a baby's cheek. Come here, Mol Besa, let me show you what a witch's mouth is for; and it's not for making promises.

The witch-woman rose naked from her bed of limestone, with her eyes as green as soft-boiled death. Her hair floated white and sparkling all around her, her forehead still crowned with corroded screws. One by one, the screws unwound, until they dropped tinkling on to the chalk. Isabel Gowdie's temples were punctuated with rusty, oozing holes; but she was free of the mental bondage that the Night Warriors had once imposed on her, in the hope that she would never be able to think Satanic thoughts again.

Slowly, with a terrible stretching sound, her scalp parted, and her flying hair sank down to her shoulders. White skin peeled away from the top of her head layer by layer, fat was rolled back, hair roots dragged away.

When her scalp had completely opened up, Mol Besa saw to his horror that Isabel Gowdie had another face on top of her head, a cold white perfect face that exactly resembled the Mardi Gras masks of her Carriers. She was a woman inside another woman; and there could even have been more women concealed inside, layer by layer, sheath by sheath, a thousand evil personalities in one outwards manifestation.

The face on top of her head opened its glutinous eyes, as pale and as green as the first eyes that Mol Besa had encountered. It stared at him, and her other face stared at him, too, and both of them gave him the same mocking smile. Then she bent her head forward, and the face on top of her head whispered, with a string of glutinous liquid still clinging like a spiderweb from one lip to the other, *Kiss me.*

''Mol Besa!'' screamed Kasyx.

No choice. Mol Besa closed his eyes and leaned forward slightly and kissed her. The lips of the face on top of her head.

Instantly, her arm snaked around and grasped the back of his head and pressed his face against hers. A long cold fish-tasting tongue pushed its way up between his teeth and probed every crevice of his mouth. *A tongue that came out of the top of her head.*

Mol Besa gagged. His stomach convulsed. But still Isabel Gowdie licked his tongue, licked his teeth, thrust that long thick trout of a tongue all the way down his throat. *You're mine, you bugger. You set me free and I love you. You and I will always be one now, always be lovers, always be twined.*

Mol Besa! yelled Kasyx inside of his mind.

But Isabel Gowdie hadn't quite finished with him yet. While the face on top of her head watched him with sly satisfaction, licking her lips after their fishy kiss, her other face bent forward and took his penis between her tongue and the roof of her mouth. She sucked it slowly, quite hard, but very methodically, and then let it slip back out again.

He stared at her. At both of her faces. The tunnel was filled

with smoke, light, barking, and screams; and the endless grind
of tunneling machinery: drills, cutters, trucks.

*I have swallowed your seed, Mol Besa. Now I shall have
your baby.*

"What the hell are you talking about? You can't have a baby
by doing that!"

*Oh, yes, I can! And hell is exactly what I'm talking about!
There are no rules in hell, are there, my fine gentleman? No
one to say not, sir! No one to say, impossible! If you want to
have a baby by sucking seed, then you can have a baby by
sucking seed! It will grow in my stomach, along with my por-
ridge, along with my chops, and I shall give birth to it by
sicking it up! Then I shall suckle it and fatten it, but I won't
baptize it—because when it's fine and fat I shall kill it, and
boil it for fat—unbaptized fat!—and I shall mix that fat with
monkshood and henbane, deadly nightshade and mandrake;
and smear my body with it, and fly from one side of England
to the other, in the twinkling of an eye! Just imagine it! A witch
giving birth to a Night Warrior's baby! And making such a
flying ointment!*

Mol Besa had never encountered the real madness of Satan
before. Those New York muggers had been nothing, compared
with this. This was a world without any kind of order. This
was a world without any kind of moral structure whatsoever.
If you wanted to fly, what did you do? You killed unbaptized
babies, boiled them, mixed up their fat with witch's herbs, then
smeared it on your body and flew.

This was a world where dogs were men and men were living
corpses and women had secret faces under their hair.

Shaking, shocked, right on the brink of hysteria, Mol Besa
slid, half tumbled, down the chalky slope.

Kasyx reached out for him, with the man-dog still spitting
and crackling and burning on his back. "*Mol Besa!* Get this
thing off of me! We've got to get out of here fast!"

Mol Besa tried to grasp the fuming, spark-spitting body of
the man-dog, but he was given a jolt that made his teeth fizz
in their sockets.

He stumbled back and hurriedly punched out an equation
that would convert the man-dog into sound, rather than physical energy. He loaded the equation as quickly as he could,

aware that with every second, the Night Warriors' chances of returning to the real world were rapidly diminishing. As the cartridge loaded, he looked around and saw Isabel Gowdie standing on top of her bier of limestone, her hair flying with fire, naked and white, her arms crossed over her scrawny breasts. He had never seen a face so transfigured. Her eyes stared wide, her lips were drawn back over her teeth. She was evil incarnate; hatred incarnate; the Devil's domestic. It was scarcely possible to imagine that three hundred years ago, she had been born to some lowly mother as an ordinary child.

Now the Carriers and the man-dogs were closing in. Effis circled behind them, trying to dodge between them to rejoin the Night Warriors; but one of the Carriers had picked up a length of scaffolding and was swinging it over his head in a figure-eight pattern to keep her away.

Mol Besa's cartridge clicked. It was ready for firing. With fingers that would scarcely obey him, he loaded his equation pistol, then swung around to face Kasyx and the man-dog who smoldered on his back, and he fired.

There was a moment when he couldn't believe that his equation had worked. Then he heard an echoing sound like a terrible shout down a subway tunnel, and the man-dog vanished. Kasyx swayed for a moment, then dropped to his knees, weakened and shocked, his accumulator connections still discharging random bursts of energy.

Mol Besa knelt beside him. "We zapped the dog. Are you okay?"

"Get back," Kasyx insisted. "We have to get back."

"But I still have the Night Plague!" Mol Besa insisted.

Kasyx looked up at him. "If we don't get the Godfrey Daniels out of here now, then believe me, Night Plague will be the last of our worries."

With Mol Besa's help, he heaved himself up on to his feet. "Effis!" he called. "Keldak! Zasta! Come back here! Fast as you like!"

Effis dodged left, then right, then slalomed her way through the motley company of Carriers, scattering three or four snarling man-dogs, and pirouetted into position close beside Mol Besa, as if she had just successfully completed a winning round in an international ice-dancing contest. Keldak came back more slowly, followed by Zasta, who had only one knife remaining, a heavy throwing knife which he had been saving for his last defense. To cut his own throat, if necessary.

Mol Besa said, "It's not quite Alamo time yet, old buddy. Leastways, I hope not."

The dream was beginning to change. Having been released from her limestone tomb, Isabel Gowdie was waking up. The tunnel walls began to darken, the halogen lights began to fade. The cacophony of drilling began to take on a deep, rhythmic throbbing. As they came nearer, the man-dogs' flesh dwindled on their bones, until they were stalking across the floor of the tunnel as wolfish skeletons.

The Carriers, too, started to lose their substance, until they were scarcely more than stained gray sheets from a plague hospital, billowing in the wind.

Kasyx raised his hands above his head, and with the last of his power reserves, created the flickering blue octagon which was their portal back to the real world. He guided it slowly downwards, all around them, and the upstairs bedroom at Tennyson reappeared. The last they saw of Isabel Gowdie's Channel Tunnel was the slimy tunnel floor, which had now flushed a deep crimson color, a dream metaphor for Isabel Gowdie's sex.

Then the dream vanished, and they were back.

Wearily, they looked around. The room was the same as before, except that it had now stopped raining. The drapes were still sodden, and water dripped everywhere, but there was no wind, no storm, no feeling that Tennyson was two different locations at once.

"She's woken up, she's alive," said Kasyx.

"I thought if I took off the blindfold—" Mol Besa began. But then he admitted, "I don't know what I thought. She had me wrapped around her little finger."

"She takes her power directly from Satan," said Kasyx. "We didn't stand more than a one-in-ten chance of destroying her, anyway."

"Who said that?" asked Effis.

"Springer," Kasyx told her. "I know that she didn't tell

you, but then she didn't want to knock your confidence, first time out.''

"God Almighty, knock our confidence,'' Mol Besa retorted. He smeared sweat from his forehead with the back of his hand. ''We were an inch away from being massacred.''

"What do we do now?'' asked Zasta.

Kasyx said, ''We have to report back to Springer and recharge our energy. Then we have to go searching for Isabel Gowdie again.''

"But if she's escaped from the tunnel, how are we ever going to find her?'' Keldak wanted to know.

"Oh, we'll find her,'' said Kasyx. ''Whether we'll have the power to destroy her when we do . . . well, that's something else altogether.''

One by one, the Night Warriors rose into the air, their molecules absorbed through Tennyson's ceiling, and out through the roof. Outside, it was already morning. A sullen red sun shone through the freezing fog, and West London lay spread out beneath them like a deserted Macedonian battlefield after the Visigoths had stormed their way through.

They followed the curve of the Thames until they reached Richmond Hill, where they sank at last through the fog, and back through the roof of Springer's top-floor apartment. Mol Besa grasped Zasta's hand for one brief moment, and then they sank back into their sleeping bodies, as softly and silently as leaves falling on to the surface of a trout pool.

NINE
Frightening Child

STANLEY WAS WOKEN UP BY A VIOLENT SPASM IN HIS STOMACH. His whole abdomen was distended, churning in the throes of peristalsis. He tried to cry out, but his throat was dry and tightly constricted, and he could hardly draw breath.

God, I'm choking, he thought. *God help me, I'm choking.*

He pushed back his bedclothes and fell sideways out of bed on to the floor. His stomach heaved again, and the dryness in his mouth was suddenly awash with acid bile. He pressed his hand against his stomach and he could feel it heaving and twisting, almost as if there were some kind of living creature inside it, trying to struggle its way out. The last time he had felt anything remotely like it was when Eve had been expecting Leon, and Leon had kicked her as if he had an exercise cycle inside of her.

Stanley managed to drag in one long, thin, whining breath. He climbed up on to his knees and then heaved himself upright by hanging on to the side of the bed. He felt something in the back of his throat, something whiplike, and he retched explosively. Step by step, he staggered across to the door, opened it, and crossed the corridor to the bathroom.

He scarcely made it. He didn't have time to reach the toilet, so he dropped on to his knees next to the bathtub, and hung over the edge of it. The full force of the Night Plague stirred his stomach and convulsed his throat, and then he felt a thick greasy bulk forcing its way upwards, right up into the back of his throat, something that stank sweetly of decaying garbage.

He couldn't speak, couldn't cry out. He arched over the bathtub, and inch by inch, convulsion by convulsion, out it came. A huge tangled mass of rats, some of them fully grown, their eyes staring and their fur slick with stomach juices; some of them half grown; some of them embryonic, with pink mutated bodies and eyes like blood clots.

Stanley vomited and vomited, until the last tails and legs writhed out between his lips, and a three-foot mass of rats lay gray and shuddering in the bathtub. Stanley was too weak and disgusted to do anything but kneel by the tub with his forehead pressed against the cold metal, spitting and spitting in an attempt to rid his mouth of the foul taste of twenty or thirty rotting and partially-digested rats.

He could see that the rats' tails had become inextricably intertwined, which occasionally happens in an overcrowded nest. The more they try to pull away from each other, the tighter the knot becomes, until they form a ratking, from which they can never escape.

At last, Stanley was able to climb to his feet. He went to the basin and poured himself a large glass of water and swilled out his mouth. Then he squeezed toothpaste on to his tongue and sucked at it until his tongue and his cheeks burned with peppermint. He looked at himself in the mirror over the basin. His face was gray and waxy and he looked exhausted. *How long*, he thought, *before this Night Plague kills me? How long before I end up in hell, unredeemed, unredeemable, an outcast for all eternity? Poppa, Momma, was I born for this?*

He found a large gray dustbin bag in the kitchen, returned to the bathroom, and queasily swung the mass of rats out of the tub. He listened, but it didn't sound as if anybody else were awake yet. He dragged the bag into his bedroom and dressed. Then he quietly left the apartment with it.

The morning was very cold and ghostly. With the bag on his back, he walked down the hill and crossed the road to the banks of the Thames. The water was dull, like breathed-on steel. It even *smelled* cold. Through the fog, he could see the trees of Eel Pie Island and the outlines of moored boats.

He dropped the bag of rats into the water, and it swirled and bubbled and sank. *I'm going to beat you, Isabel Gowdie,* he swore to himself under his breath. *You can take anything you want from me; but not my soul. My soul is my own.*

He began to trudge slowly back up the hill. An invisible airliner thundered through the fog, somewhere above him, and it sounded as if the sky were splitting. He looked up toward the railings above the Terrace Gardens, and he could see Knitted Hood standing beside them, watching him, his face as white as candlewax.

For the first time, Stanley felt determined, rather than afraid. He carried on walking up the hill and passed within ten yards of Knitted Hood, on the opposite side of the road. Knitted Hood didn't turn as he passed; nor give any indication that he knew he was there. But Stanley wanted to show him that he didn't care, that he wasn't afraid, and that he was grimly confident that the Night Warriors would return Isabel Gowdie and all of her Carriers back to the earth to which his ancestors had once consigned them.

He went back up to Springer's apartment and rang the doorbell. Springer answered, a blond-haired woman of about twenty-five years old, wearing a white tubelike minidress and dozens of jingling silver bracelets.

"You've been sick," she remarked as Stanley stepped inside. The rest of the Night Warriors were up now—Leon in his Star Trek pajamas, Henry in a brown beach robe that had obviously seen more debonair times, and Angie in a Marks & Spencer nightshirt with a picture of Betty Boop on the front.

"Yes," Stanley replied, "I've been sick."

"Was it very bad?"

"It's not an experience I'm keen to repeat."

"Angie's been sick, too. Meat fat, heaps of it. With the Night Plague, you're always sick with the things that disgust you the most. It's intended to reduce your self-esteem to the lowest possible level."

Angie gave Stanley an unsteady smile, although there was nothing for either of them to smile about.

"There's something else, too," said Springer, walking through to the kitchen. "Angie had a dream of her own this morning, after you arrived back from Isabel Gowdie's dream, and before she woke up."

"I couldn't 'elp it," said Angie. "I tried not to 'ave it, but I couldn't stop myself."

Springer was making espresso coffee in a French *cafetière*. "She dreamed that she was having sex with her boyfriend Paul, and with Paul's best friend—"

"Mack," put in Angie. " 'Is real name's Kenneth, but 'e comes from Glasgow."

Springer said patiently, "Paul and Mack, yes. That means that both of them are now victims of a secondary infection of Night Plague. And only Ashapola knows how many girls they know between them, and how quickly the Night Plague will spread once *they* start dreaming."

Stanley stood close to Springer, watching her make the coffee. Although he had been so violently ill this morning, and his stomach still ached from all the muscular convulsions he had suffered, he found that she aroused him. Maybe she intended to arouse him. Maybe she was testing his licentiousness. Maybe she was seeing just how far his morals had decayed.

Her breasts swayed under the thin white wool of her dress; the curve of her bottom was clearly defined. But as he moved closer, she picked up two cups of coffee and deftly moved away.

"Remember," she said, arching one eyebrow. "I am nothing more than Ashapola's messenger."

He followed her into the sparsely-furnished living room. While they had been talking in the kitchen, Gordon had arrived from his hotel, wearing baggy green corduroy trousers and a floppy yellow sweater with stains on the front.

Springer said, "None of us are overjoyed at what happened last night. But you are Warriors, fighting a sacred war; and in this war like all others you will have to face up to serious setbacks."

"What do we do now?" asked Gordon. "If Isabel Gowdie can escape into other people's dreams, she could be anywhere."

"You can find her," Springer assured them. "The first thing to do is for you to travel to Dover and inspect the real workings for the Channel Tunnel. You will probably discover that when you dug Isabel Gowdie out of the chalk in her dream, there was a natural collapse of rock which released her body in reality, too. When you left her, she was waking up; and she will have left the tunnel as a real woman as well as a dream woman.

"Real people can be followed. Real people can be traced. She has no clothes, no money, and very little knowledge of modern Britain. If you can find where she went in reality, then you will have a much better chance of picking up the resonance of her dreams, too."

"So we're off to Dover again, are we?" asked Gordon.

"You can borrow my car." Springer smiled.

While Stanley was brushing his hair, Angie came into his room, still wearing her Betty Boop nightshirt. She stood beside him watching him for a while. Then she said, "Do you think we'll ever find 'er?"

Stanley put down his hairbrushes. "Oh, we'll find her all right. We have to. Otherwise you and I are going to wind up dead and damned."

She said nothing for a while. Stanley tugged a rust-colored sweater over his shirt and put on his Rolex, the one that the San Francisco Baroque Ensemble had given him after their performance of Frescobaldi's *Fiori Musicali* at Carnegie Hall, in New York. The New York *Times* music critic had described Stanley's playing as "sublime . . . the description 'baroque' may have been etymologically derived from the words for 'rough pearl,' but Eisner is the most polished pearl in an ensemble . . . that is a crown of polished pearls."

Angie said, "That dream I 'ad this morning . . . about Paul and Mack."

"What about it? It was only a dream."

"Yes, I know. But it was the same sort of dream I 'ad about you. I was all . . . well, I was all wet afterwards."

"What do you want me to say? That's I'm jealous? How can I be jealous of a dream?"

Angie came up close to him. "I shouldn't 'ave done it,

though, should I? It gave Paul the Night Plague, too, and Mack.''

"That's the nature of the Night Plague, sweetheart. That's how it spreads itself. It wasn't your fault."

"But I should be punished, shouldn't I?"

"Punished?"

She tugged up the front of her nightshirt, twisting it around in her hands. "You should beat me or something, for 'aving a dream like that, don't you think so?"

Stanley looked her up and down. He was about to say, *Beat you, of course not,* but then a small dark feeling uncurled itself inside of his mind, like a curled-up centipede. He came up to her and cupped his hand without any hesitation between her legs, and roughly kissed her forehead. "Maybe you're right. Maybe I should beat you."

She closed her eyes and offered her mouth. He kissed her lips and then clenched her tongue tightly and painfully between his teeth. He tasted blood. She winced and tried to cry out, but it was almost ten seconds before he let her go.

"When we get back from Dover," he told her, "I'm going to give you just what you deserve."

The fog cleared as they drove through Kent, and by midmorning the day was cold and golden. They stopped for lunch at the Bell, in a picturesque village called Smarden. Stanley was enchanted by the Bell. It had been built in the fifteenth century, with stone floors and open fireplaces. They sat together at an oak table, close to the fire, and ate huge steak-and-kidney pies and drank pints of Theakston's bitter. The winter sun shone through the woodsmoke; and for a while Stanley could understand how easy it was in England to pass in a dream from one century to another. Here, in Smarden, the centuries were layered one on top of the other like the pastry layers on top of his pie.

They drove on, until they were crossing the chalky Downs just above Dover, with the landscape already beginning to grow grainy and dark. None of them had spoken much during their drive. They were too anxious about how they were going to find Isabel Gowdie and what they could possibly do to deal with her when they did. Springer's old Humber was automatic,

so Stanley had been able to do most of the driving. Henry had
declined. He didn't like to drive, especially in a country where
nobody else on the road knew their left from their right, and
where they all drove so damned fast.

As they descended Jubilee Road, the curving ramp that led
them down toward the docks, the streetlights flickered on. The
English Channel was congealing in the gloom like cold gray
wallpaper paste. Gordon said, "I can't see how Ms. Gowdie
could have gone very far. Not without any clothes. Not without
money."

"Don't ever underestimate the servants of Satan," said
Henry. "She managed to survive a death sentence from the
Scottish court. She managed to survive three centuries buried
in solid limestone. She managed to get away from five of the
most powerful of all the Night Warriors. Finding herself some
clothes isn't going to present much of a problem to a lady of
that kind of determination."

They drove westwards from Dover until they reached the
Channel Tunnel workings. In Isabel Gowdie's dream, they had
been able to gain direct admission to the tunnel. In reality,
they were stopped at the high wire perimeter fence by a security officer with a beefy face and a blue paramilitary sweater.
He slid open the window of his prefabricated office, letting out
a strong smell of paraffin heaters.

"Can't let you in without proper authority," he announced.

"Actually, we're looking for somebody," put in Gordon,
winding down his window and sticking his head out.

"Who's that, then?" asked the security officer.

"A woman. Rather pale. We wondered if you might have
seen her."

"She belong to the company, then?"

"Well, not exactly. But we're certain she was here."

"What was her name, then?"

"Erm, Smith."

The security man slowly shook his head. He was obviously
beginning to think that he was dealing with a carload of fruit-
cakes. "Nobody like that around here, mate. Lost is she, or
what?"

"Sort of lost, yes," said Gordon.

"Police station's your best bet, then. She wouldn't be wandering around here. We've had to clear the site in any case."

"You had to clear the site, why?" asked Stanley.

"Didn't you hear it on the news? Had a bit of an accident last night, down in the tunnel. Whole load of Semtex went off. Side of the tunnel collapsed, two blokes killed, six injured. So there wasn't much chance of any woman wandering around."

"All right, Officer, thank you," Stanley told him.

They turned the car around and drove slowly back towards Dover. Stanley said, "So that was how she got out of the tunnel in real life. Once her dreaming self was released, she was able to arrange a little accident to release her real self. This is one magical woman."

"You sound almost *admiring*," Gordon remarked. "As far as I'm concerned, she's a total and absolute bitch."

"Whatever we think of her," said Henry, "the question is how do we find out where she's gone? She could still be in Dover; she could have gone anywhere."

"Maybe that security guard had the right idea," said Stanley. "Maybe we should try asking at the police station. If somebody's seen a naked woman walking around the streets of Dover, then they've probably reported it. Likewise, if Isabel Gowdie's stolen any money or any clothes."

It was dark by the time they found the Dover police station. The duty officer behind the counter was patient but unhelpful. No, he couldn't tell them if any thefts of women's clothing had been reported during the day. No, he couldn't tell them if a pale-faced woman had been seen stealing money. No, he couldn't possibly divulge if any naked women had been observed near the Channel Tunnel excavations. And why did they want to know?

They left Dover feeling despondent and drove back towards London on the main road. After they passed the first roundabout outside Dover, however, they came to a lengthy lay-by, where six or seven large trucks were parked, and tea and hamburgers were being sold from a small white-painted caravan with an awning in front of it.

Two girls in jeans and duffle coats were standing at the end of the lay-by, with rucksacks on their backs, thumbing for a ride.

Stanley pulled the Humber into the lay-by and switched off the engine.

"What are you doing?" asked Henry.

"Just trying something," said Stanley. He climbed out of the car and walked across to the tea caravan, smacking his hands together to warm them up. Two truck drivers were standing beside the caravan drinking huge mugs of tea and eating bacon sandwiches, and smoking at the same time.

Behind the counter, a fat woman in a pink gingham overall was wiping the work surfaces with a grayish cloth. Stanley momentarily prayed that the next time he was sick, he wouldn't puke up that cloth.

"Cuppa tea, dear?" she asked him.

"No—no thanks. I was just wondering if you'd seen a woman today, hitchhiking."

"We get loads of them, dear. Students, mainly."

"I don't think you could have missed this particular woman," Stanley told her. "She's real thin, with green eyes, and white, white hair. I don't know what she was wearing, but that's the way she looks."

The woman blasted steam out of her tea urn. "Oh, yes. She was here a little bit earlier on, as a matter of fact. She asked me for a cup of hot water, and when I gave it to her, she drank it straight off, even though it was practically boiling. I said, you'll scald your insides, doing that, but all she did was smile."

Stanley felt a burst of excitement. *Found you, you witch-woman!* he thought. *Tracked you down! Now we'll see who can manipulate whom!*

"Did you see which way she went?" he asked the tea lady.

"She got a lift," the tea lady sniffed.

"Gissa 'nother cuppa, Doris," said one of the truck drivers, banging his mug on the counter. "Oh, an' a packet of cheese-'n'-onion, too, would you?"

"Did you see who gave her the ride?" Stanley persisted. "Was it a truck or a car?"

"It was a lorry, I think," the tea lady told him. "One of them big foreign ones, Dutch or something. Blue and white, with a kind of a blue and white flag on the back."

"What time was this?"

"Oh, not all that long ago. About an hour, hour and a half, not much more."

"You're an angel," Stanley told her. Thinking: *Shit, we must have practically driven past her.*

One of the truck drivers gave a forced, hollow laugh. "If she's an angel, mate, then I think I'd rather go to hell."

Stanley gave him a tight smile. "Believe me, friend, you wouldn't. Not at any damned price."

He returned to the car and immediately started the engine. "She was there, only about an hour ago. She was given a ride in a blue and white truck. It was a big truck, so I guess the chances are that it's going to stay on the motorways. God, I wish I had a half-decent car, instead of this junker!"

They drove steadily through the darkness, mile after mile, checking out every single truck they passed. They flagged down one Danish truck, loaded with garden furniture, but the driver hadn't picked up any hitchers today. They gave him a pack of Benson & Hedges for his trouble, and drove on.

"This is like looking for a needle in a needle factory," Gordon complained. "They could have turned off anywhere."

"We'll find her, believe me," Stanley insisted. "I just have this feeling about it."

Sixty miles further on, however, when they crossed the Kent border on the M25 motorway and started to head westwards through Surrey, even Stanley was beginning to despair. There were no blue and white trucks anywhere, Dutch or Danish or domestic, and soon they would have to turn off toward Richmond and back to Springer.

They crossed the multilevel cloverleaf where the M25 intersected with the southbound M23, and it was then, toiling up the long slow hill ahead of them, that Stanley saw a blue and yellow truck, with a blue and yellow flag painted on the back of it, along with the words *Zwart-Wit Lithos, Mercurius Wormerveer, Leiden.*

"That's it, that has to be it!" said Stanley excitedly. He shifted the Humber down into second, and the old car's transmission whined and juddered in protest as it pursued the blue and yellow truck up the hill.

Gordon leaned out of the passenger window and waved his arm up and down to signal the truck to pull over on to the hard shoulder, which it eventually did, with an immense sighing and shuddering of air brakes. The denim-jacketed driver climbed down immediately and looked all around his truck, obviously thinking that they must have been warning him about an open rear door, a fuel leakage, or a punctured tire.

Stanley approached him as he came around the rear of his truck, a burned-down cigarette filter pinched between his lips.

"Pardon me, sir, I'm real sorry to stop you like this. But we're looking for a girl. A hitchhiker, very pale face, green eyes, white hair."

The truck driver nodded. "Yes," he said in a glottal Dutch accent.

"Have you seen her?" asked Gordon.

"Yes."

"Is she on board your rig now?"

"No."

"Do you happen to know where she went?"

"I let her off back there, on the motorway. She wanted to go to the sea."

"To Brighton?" asked Angie.

"Well, it was somewhere that sounded like Brighton, but, you know, not quite the same."

"Brighthelmstone?" suggested Gordon, as a sudden inspiration.

"That's right, that's the place," the truck driver agreed.

"Where's Brighthelmstone?" Stanley asked Gordon.

"It's the old eighteenth-century name for Brighton, before the Prince Regent discovered it and made it fashionable . . . back in the days when it was nothing but a fishing village. Isabel Gowdie would have called it that."

"That's great, what are we waiting for?"

They sped as fast as they could to the next exit, drove around the roundabout, and back toward the M23 and Brighton.

Although it was dark, Stanley was conscious of the shape and smell of the countryside through which they passed. In some ways, it reminded him of driving through Connecticut— less densely forested, less rural, but indescribably *older*. In Connecticut, there were plenty of ramshackle coaching inns down scarcely-used side roads, and some sad and abandoned country mansions. But here the coaching inns were lit up, ready for business, and lights shone across the fields from grand and distant houses.

"Why does this put me in mind of Transylvania?" he asked Angie. "I feel if we stop at one of these pubs, we're going to find everybody wearing garlic round their necks, and turning their backs on us when we ask for a pint of beer."

They inspected the passengers of every car and truck they overtook, but by the time they reached the South Downs they still hadn't caught sight of anybody who remotely resembled Isabel Gowdie.

"I don't think we have much chance of finding her this evening," said Henry. "But at least we're close. The best thing we can do is find ourselves someplace to stay for the night and go searching for her as Night Warriors."

"I'll second that," said Stanley. "I could use a drink."

The South Downs were vast and humped and shrouded in mist, a huge slumbering dinosaur sprawled across the landscape. Gordon guided them up a winding back road to Devil's Dyke, on the summit of the Downs. To the south, just below them, they could see the lights of Brighton glimmering across the horizon, and beyond Brighton the foggy darkness of the sea.

"This is a shortcut," Gordon told them. "We may even arrive in Brighton before Isabel Gowdie."

Brighton, to Stanley, looked like San Francisco's aged aunt. It was precipitously hilly, it was on the sea, and it was crammed with antique shops and fashion boutiques and shops selling 501s and studded motorcycle jackets. What impressed Stanley, however, was how much older it was than even the oldest quarters of San Francisco. As they passed a roundabout called Seven Dials, they passed the sweeping curve of a white-painted eighteenth-century terrace, and then they plunged downhill between rows and rows of small Regency houses towards the seafront.

Gordon guided them along the front until they reached the Palace Pier, a cast-iron Victorian pier strung with lights, with a funfair right at the very end of it, a half mile out to sea. Then he directed them further east, towards Kemp Town.

"I have a friend here, an artist. His house is absolutely vast.

Provided we cross his palm with silver, he'll put us up for the night."

Stanley parked the Humber in the private slip road in front of a huge flat-fronted Regency house. They climbed out stiffly, and Gordon went to ring at the doorbell. A foggy, briny wind blew off the sea, and Stanley could hear the ceaseless seething of the tide.

They waited for two or three minutes before the black-painted front door was opened, and a tall thin elderly man in a fez and a smoking jacket stood before them. Mounting the stone steps, Stanley could see that he was wearing dangling diamond earrings and purple eye shadow, and that his wrinkles were thickly powdered.

"Gordon, my dear boy! What on earth are you doing here? Who are all these people?"

"Hello, James, these are some friends of mine, over from America. I decided on the spur of the moment to show them the sights of Brighton."

James pursed his lips. "I didn't know that *I* was one of the sights of Brighton!" he replied in a tart Noël Cowardish voice.

"Well, actually, you're not," Gordon replied. "But we could do with somewhere to stay for the night."

"What's wrong with the Grand?"

"Somewhere quiet and private," said Gordon.

"You're not thinking of having an orgy, are you?" James demanded. He pronounced "orgy" with a hard *g*.

"James . . . we simply need somewhere to stay. Somewhere completely undisturbed."

James peered at them disapprovingly. "Well, I don't know, Gordon. It's scandalously short notice. And then there's—what—five of you, and that's five beds, unless you're all thinking of sleeping in the same bed, mind you. And that's five complete sets of bed linen that have to go to the laundry. Not to mention the general *disturbance*, and the use of electricity, and hot water, and wear and tear on the carpets, they're all original Tabriz carpets, you know, the *knotting* is superb!"

Henry stepped forward and opened up his billfold. "Would two hundred pounds cover it?"

James stared at him. "I think so, thank you," he said, obviously offended by Henry's abruptness, and turned and left them on the doorstep to make their own way in.

Gordon had been right: James's house was enormous. It was richly but fussily decorated with exquisite hand-printed wallpapers and gilded mirrors, and the walls were hung with hundreds of watercolors and oil paintings of the Sussex countryside. All of the furniture was antique, all of the drapes were velvet, with swags and ties and silk bows. In the main living room, a huge log fire was burning in an Adam fireplace, while two bulbous-eyed Boston terriers basked in front of it on a huge Chinese cushion.

"This stuff must be worth a fortune," breathed Henry.

"James inherited it all from his mother, Lady Hurstpierpoint," Gordon remarked. "God knows what's going to happen to it all when James passes on."

"Looks more like a museum than someone's 'ouse," Angie remarked.

Leon said, "I think it's neat. It's just like one of those old movies."

"You could only be American," James said to him, sweeping in from the opposite doorway. "Only an American child could be impressed by great art because it reminds him of a film. I suppose *I* remind you of Laurence Olivier."

"No, Roddy McDowall."

"Who?"

"You know, he was in *Planet of the Apes*."

James fixed Leon with a purple stare. "I think I'd better show you *folks* to your rooms, before you poison the air even further with your crassness."

The bedrooms were all furnished in the style of an English country house, with pale Regency stripes and mahogany four-poster beds. Angie took hold of Stanley's hand and squeezed it and said, "It's brilliant, isn't it? Only a pooftah could decorate a house like this."

It was well past eight o'clock, so they decided to go for dinner. There was a strange new camaraderie between them, partly because Stanley had been less cantankerous today. He still felt nauseous and headachy and irritable. He was still troubled by the blackest of momentary thoughts. Pain. Violence. Sadistic acts. But he felt more positive today. They were tracking down Isabel Gowdie, they were hunting down the very source of the Night Plague; and if they managed to find her and destroy her tonight, their achievement—although it would never be known, never be recognized—would affect the course of human history for centuries to come.

They would be saviors greater than any waking mind could ever imagine.

Henry had an appetite for Dover sole, so they went to Wheeler's in Market Street, a small crowded Victorian fish restaurant on three rickety floors, and ordered Colchester oysters and grilled sole, with a bottle of chilled white wine. They walked back to James's house feeling warm and well filled, and as relaxed as they possibly could be. Leon yawned and said, "I'm so tired, I could sleep for a week."

Leon went to bed while the rest of the Night Warriors sat in front of the dying fire with James, and shared a bottle of Fleurie.

James said, "I sense something peculiar about you, Gordon. You seemed to have changed a great deal since the last time you were here. You seem to have gone slightly mad, if you don't mind my saying so."

Gordon held up his left arm and tugged down his sleeve. "Not just mad, James."

James stared at his empty sleeve. "Is that a trick? Where's your hand?"

"Lost it," said Gordon. "Dog bit it off."

James was shocked. "A dog bit your hand off? I can scarcely believe it! Didn't it *hurt*?"

"Of course it hurt, you idiot."

"But don't you *mind*?"

"Too bad if I do, it won't grow back again. I didn't particularly want to be a professional juggler, in any case."

"My dear boy," said James, still shocked, but increasingly enthralled. "Do have another drink."

It was well past twelve o'clock before they went to bed. Not many hours of the night left for fighting. Stanley checked that Leon was asleep and then tiptoed along the board-creaking corridor to his own room.

In the large four-poster bed, Angie was waiting for him. She

was lying back on the plumped-up pillow, the silk-covered eiderdown drawn up to her waist, bare-breasted, her eyes misted
with the kind of desires that most girls could only guess at.

"We have to sleep," Stanley told her, unbuttoning his shirt.

"You promised to punish me."

"If you go to sleep now, I'll punish you twice as hard tomorrow."

"You promised." Her voice was congested with passion.

Stanley said nothing, but finished undressing. When he was
naked, he walked over to the bureau and picked up a silver-
backed hairbrush. Then he crossed over to the bed and dragged
back the eiderdown. Angie held out her arms for him.

"Oh, no. You wanted punishment. Punishment is what
you're going to get."

He seized Angie's wrist and tried to turn her over. But Angie
kicked and fought back, her breasts bouncing, her teeth
clenched. Stanley grabbed hold of her hair, twisted his fingers
into it, and forced her to turn over on to her stomach. She
screamed and wrestled, but he pulled her hair even harder.

"You bastard, that hurts, let go of me! You bastard, you
bastard, you bastard!"

He pulled her over his knee, still keeping his grip on her
hair, and smacked her hard on the bottom with the hairbrush,
bristle side down. Her white bottom flushed red. He smacked
her again, and then again, while she screamed and panted and
swore at him, and the scarlet flush spread wider and wider
across her cheeks.

He noticed, though, that she wasn't struggling any more;
not really struggling. He spanked her again, and again, and as
he did so he released his grip on her hair. Her panting grew
harsher and deeper, and she parted her legs wider and wider,
breathing, "Bastard, you bastard, you bastard!"

Her eyes tight shut, she raised herself up on her arms, her
back arched, her buttocks clenched, and then she gave a deep
suppressed shudder. Stanley couldn't tell how much self-control
it had taken for her to bury her orgasm so deeply, but when
she rolled off his knees and on to her back, her eyes were
completely unfocused, like the eyes of somebody concussed.

"You bastard," she whispered.

Stanley kissed her open lips. "We have to get to sleep now."

"Can't I sleep here?"

"No . . . just in case something goes wrong."

"You're not married any more."

"All the same, I have to think about Leon; and I have to think about my mother, too."

"You're too good to be evil."

"I'm fighting it, believe me."

Angie touched his bare shoulder, traced the line of his collarbone with her fingernails. "Do you think we're going to die tonight?"

He didn't smile. "Everybody has to die sometime."

She turned her head sideways and sank her teeth into the muscle of his forearm, so hard that she drew blood. Stanley winced and wrenched his arm away.

"Now you'll have to punish me again tomorrow," she whispered.

He half turned away, then he slapped her face with his open hand, once, and then again. Her cheeks flared scarlet.

"Get to bed, you bitch!" he snapped at her. "We're going after this goddamned witch."

Stanley lay back in bed with his mind a kaleidoscope of ideas, memories, voices; but there was scarcely any traffic passing through Brighton at this time of night, and the shushing of the breakers on the shingle beach was so repetitive and soothing that he soon began to feel calmer. He repeated the sacred incantation of the Night Warriors, but he was so dozy that he was scarcely able to finish it.

"Now when the face of the world is hidden in darkness, let us be conveyed to the place of our meeting, armed and armored; and let us be nourished by the power that is dedicated to the cleaving of darkness, the settling of all black matters, and the dissipation of evil, so be it."

After less than ten minutes, he was asleep. His consciousness sank deeper and deeper, like a jolly boat full of drowned sailors sinking and bumping down an ocean shelf, before plunging silently into the fathomless depths of sleep.

He rose from his sleeping body, and he could still hear the sea and the persistent rattling of his sash window. He moved across the carpet and was absorbed through the bedroom wall.

The Night Warriors had agreed to gather in James's living room. Kasyx was already there when Mol Besa arrived; Keldak and Effis arrived a few minutes afterwards. It was almost ten minutes later when Zasta appeared, rubbing his eyes. Mol Besa put his arm around his shoulders and said, "You're sure you want to come with us tonight? You don't have to if you don't want to."

"I have to come," Zasta told him.

"He has a right to," said Kasyx. "He may be your son, Mol Besa; but his vow to the Night Warriors comes first."

One by one, they stood next to Kasyx and were charged up with crackling, burned-smelling power. On their cushion beside the fire, James's Boston terriers awoke, and stared at the Night Warriors in alarm. One of them jumped down from the cushion and hid behind the sofa.

When all five of the Night Warriors were fully charged up, and clad in their armor, Kasyx said, "Let's go out on patrol. If Isabel Gowdie is anywhere in Brighton, we ought to be able to locate her."

They rose up through the several floors of James's house, through the attic, and out into the chilly, windy night. As they wheeled silently over the rooftops of Kemp Town, they could see the sea foaming in the darkness, and the spectral white cliffs of Rottingdean and Peacehaven. They turned over the town center, over the Steine, and glided over the extraordinary oriental domes and spires of the Brighton Pavilion. To Stanley, the Pavilion looked as if it had arrived by magic carpet straight out of the Arabian Nights; but inside of his mind, Keldak said, *Exterior by John Nash, early nineteenth century. Quaint, isn't it?*

Circling around the Pavilion, they crossed the Lanes, an enclave of eighteenth-century shops and houses built on a higgledy-piggledy medieval street pattern.

Kasyx said, "Let's circle again, I'm picking something up."

Silently, invisibly, like ink stains absorbed by darker paper, they turned over the Lanes for a second time. But Kasyx said, "It's still not too clear. Her body may be sleeping here—there are scores of pubs and hotels and boardinghouses—but her dreaming personality is somewhere else. Not too far away, though. I can sense it."

They widened the circle of their search. At last, Kasyx said, "It's stronger in this direction, on the seafront."

They began to sink lower. Mol Besa kept close to Zasta as they approached the shingled beach. But Kasyx was sure of his target now; the magnificent white-fronted Victorian façade of the Grand Hotel. "She's here . . . in one of the suites . . . that's where she's hiding tonight."

As they drifted towards the Grand, Zasta suddenly said, "Look! Look down there!"

They turned and looked downwards, and glimpsed a tall figure striding along King's Road, before turning suddenly into Ship Street, towards the Lanes, and disappearing. Knitted Hood, his gray gaberdine coat flying in the salty wind. Now they knew for certain that Isabel Gowdie was here in Brighton.

"What I want to know is, why did she come *here*, of all places?" Mol Besa asked.

"I don't know," Kasyx replied. "But I expect we'll find out. Satan never does anything without a very deliberate reason."

They sank through the roof of the Grand Hotel and into the suite where Kasyx's sensitivities had guided them. It was a large, lavishly-decorated suite, one of the most expensive. A cooler with two empty bottles of Moët champagne stood on the table in the living room, along with vases of roses and ashtrays crammed with burned-down cigar stubs. Evening clothes were strewn around the sofa. A lacy garter belt lay tangled beside the bedroom door.

In the bedroom, on a king-sized bed, a man and a woman lay heavily sleeping. The room smelled of stale alcohol and cigar smoke and sex. The man was in his early fifties, bulkily built, with a florid face and greased-back hair. The girl beside him couldn't have been older than twenty-five. She was a bubbly-permed blonde, with false eyelashes, one of which had partially come adrift.

The Night Warriors surrounded the bed. "Who's dreaming the dream that Isabel Gowdie's hiding herself in?" Mol Besa wanted to know.

Kasyx slid open an instrument panel on his wrist; a psychic DNA analyzer. Its principal purpose was the quick identification of friendly or hostile forces, but it had a data bank capable of identifying almost anyone.

"Isabel Gowdie's hiding herself in the girl's dream," said Kasyx. "She's a high-class prostitute. This man brought her down to Brighton from London, for a few illicit days together."

"But why would Isabel Gowdie want to hide inside somebody like 'er?" Effis asked.

Kasyx punched out some more data on his wrist. "I think I'm beginning to get the picture. He's a politician. A member of the Cabinet. The girl knows plenty more of them; and *sleeps* with plenty more of them. Isabel Gowdie's probably having sex with her, inside of her dream, to infect her with the Night Plague. Think of what could happen if half of Her Majesty's Government lost their souls to Satan."

"If you ask me, half of them have already," put in Keldak.

"This isn't a joke, Keldak," Kasyx told him, the dim light glinting on his crimson helmet. "We're talking about a whole nation here, ruled by men without any principles at all, except the principles of cruelty and mayhem and massacre. You've seen what the Night Plague's done to your country already. You've got riots in your country townships, looting and mugging in your urban ghettoes. The London subways used to be safe: now they're as dangerous as New York's. Now you're going to have *official* chaos. *Official* insurrection. You're going to go back to the Middle Ages, my friend, when nobody was safe."

Keldak said, "Let's just get after her, shall we?"

"You bet," Kasyx told him. "Now, stand close."

The Night Warriors stood shoulder-to-shoulder. Kasyx lifted his arms, and the brilliant blue octagon materialized above their heads. Slowly, it sank downwards to the floor, encircling them, reflecting from their visors and their armor plate.

Instantly, they were flooded with sunlight. They found themselves standing on the Brighton seafront on a warm midsummer day. The sky was bright blue, with tiny puffy clouds; the sea danced brightly on the shingle. Sea gulls swooped around them, catching the wind in their wings, crying like children.

The promenade was crowded. Not with the usual Brighton day-trippers, but with hundreds of the young prostitute's ac-

quaintances. Spivvy-looking Maltese men in white suits with
wide lapels; a harassed teacher in a green tweed sports coat;
crowds of jeering and shuffling boys; a frowning social worker.
A nun, in a wide white wimple, gliding past as calmly as a
ship.

Open-topped double-decker buses trundled up and down
King's Road, each of them crammed with silver-haired men in
three-piece suits and brassy women with scarlet lipstick and
clinging gold-lamé dresses. Rolls-Royces with ministerial
badges on them drove bumper-to-bumper with chugging 1960s
American cars with rebel flags and British number plates.
Somewhere, a maddening calliope was playing a screaming,
discordant version of "I Do Like to Be Beside the Seaside."

The Night Warriors pushed their way along the jostling
promenade, heading towards the Palace Pier. Kasyx said, "I
can sense something . . . Isabel Gowdie's here someplace. And
it wouldn't surprise me if some of her Carriers were, too."

"Knitted Hood's still awake," said Mol Besa.

Kasyx nodded. "He was probably going to the lodging where
Isabel Gowdie's hiding herself, just to make sure that nobody
disturbs her while she's asleep."

They passed fish-and-chip restaurants *(rock salmon & chips,
bread & butter & cup of tea, 7/6d)*; they passed sweetshops
crammed with candy walking canes and luridly pink Brighton
rock and sugar false teeth. Zasta picked up a stick of rock and
said, "Can you eat candy in a dream?"

Mol Besa smiled. "I don't know. Maybe you can in your
own dream."

Zasta said, "Look," and handed Mol Besa the stick of rock.
All the way through it ran the pink lettering *I am the pestilence
that was promised*.

"Maybe you'd better not eat it," Mol Besa suggested, looking around. The influence of Isabel Gowdie was closer than he
had first imagined.

They crossed the shingle, towards the pier. The people on
the beach were even stranger than the people on the promenade. Most of them were naked or dressed in their underwear.
A large-breasted girl in nothing but a lilac nylon G-string and
lilac stockings was trying to paddle through the foaming shallows in stiletto shoes. Not far away, a middle-aged man in

voluminous undershorts was watching her intently. He was still wearing his bowler hat and had a tightly-furled umbrella and a copy of the *Financial Times* under his arm.

Further along the beach, a ginger-headed man in a crumpled gray suit kept falling sideways into the surf, while his wife tried to snatch him upright. He fell again and again and again, like an endlessly-repeated newsreel. He was watched impassively by bulky blue-black lobsters, slow-moving, as big as sheep, and pale waiflike children with seaside buckets and spades.

The Night Warriors reached the entrance to the Palace Pier. Pierced cast-iron railings ran along each side of it, painted pale green, and below their feet was a boarded deck through which they could see the barnacle-encrusted pilings of the pier, and the crisscross support, from which hanks of seaweed waved like the hair of magical hags.

"She's here, she's real close," said Kasyx.

Their feet drummed on the boarded walkways as they advanced swiftly along the pier. Halfway along, three gray figures materialized in front of them out of the hot summer air. Carriers—probably the last three Carriers surviving, apart from Knitted Hood, although Isabel Gowdie would be able to infect many more, now that she had been freed from her imprisonment.

This time, the Carriers had only three man-dogs with them. They were all on leashes, but they were huge black shaggy beasts whose claws scratched and skidded on the deck boards, and flecks of rabid saliva flew from their stretched-open jaws. The Carriers wielded weapons, too, complicated pikestaffs with gleaming blades.

"Careful," warned Kasyx. "I've seen weapons like that before. Spirit spears."

Mol Besa said, "Spirit spears? What are spirit spears?"

"Each time one of those spears kills somebody, his spirit is trapped inside it. So the next time the owner wants to use the spear, he promises the spirit inside it that he can have the body of whoever he happens to hit, and live again . . . while the spirit of whoever he kills has to take his place inside the spear."

"Bloody 'ell," said Effis bluntly.

Kasyx nodded. "Believe me, the spirits inside of those spears

make absolutely certain that they hit their targets. Wouldn't
you?''

Mol Besa said, ''In that case, time to do a little mathematical
conversion.''

But there was no time to waste. The Carriers let slip the
leashes of the man-dogs, and the huge beasts came bounding
along the pier towards them, screeching and snarling and roaring in rage.

Keldak fired a fist at the leading dog. It exploded through
the man-dog's teeth and vanished with a hollow whistling noise
down his throat. The man-dog stopped short, shuddered, his
mouth a smashed-apart ruin. Then he blew up, and ribbons of
intestine and grisly fur sprayed in all directions, and the
fortune-telling booth close beside him was instantly painted
red.

Zasta reached his hand up, and a shining golden knife
jumped over his shoulder, followed by another, and another.
As each knife leapt into his hand, he turned it around, so that
the blades were interwoven together, and he was left with a
three-bladed throwing star made out of razor-sharp knives. He
flung it with a curving spin, the knife-thrower's equivalent of
a jughandle-pitch in baseball. The improvised throwing star
flashed in the sunlight for one split second, then sliced off each
of the man-dog's legs in turn, and the man-dog rolled screaming and limbless on to the boards.

It was left to Effis to deal with the third man-dog. She hopped
up on to the cast-iron railing, balancing for a moment on her
dazzling light-skates. Then she flashed away into the air, high
away from the pier, skating through the sky with an easy,
speedy style. She turned over the sea, against the sun, so that
Mol Besa could only see her by darkening his visor. For a
while he lost sight of her altogether. Then he heard a soft
rushing sound, and Effis reappeared, her light-leotard sparkling, crouching low, her skates leaving behind her a long twin
trail of iridescence.

She didn't attempt to use her razor-fans. Instead, she reached
down and snatched the dog's chain collar as she flashed past
him, heaving him high up into the air.

The man-dog roared in anger as Effis swept him out to sea,
hundreds of feet over the ocean. Then she let him drop, and

he turned over and over in the air before he hit the water with a faint, faraway splash.

As the other Night Warriors fought off the man-dogs, Mol Besa had been furiously busy with his keyboards. Using four-dimensional physics, he had formulated an equation for converting the spirits in the spirit spears into solid crystalline matter—an accurate and highly-stylized adaptation of the way in which mediums and psychics made spirits appear as ectoplasm. He loaded his equation pistol and aimed it at the three Carriers.

But before he could fire, one of the Carriers leaned back and launched his spirit spear. They could all see it coming. It flew through the sunshine with a faint sighing sound, more regretful than hostile. Kasyx shouted, "Look out!" and discharged a blast of pure energy from the ends of his fingertips, but there was nothing that any of them could do. The spirit spear struck Keldak's helmet and penetrated right through to the back of his head. Blood sprayed all over the deck boards.

For an instant, Mol Besa was stunned. Somehow, he had found it impossible to believe that any of them could be casualties. This was only a dream, wasn't it? This wasn't even real! But Keldak's left leg was kicking against the railings as he went through the last throes of brain death, and Mol Besa knew for certain that he was never going to wake up, never again.

"*Back!*" Mol Besa roared to the other Night Warriors, his voice strained with fury and grief. Then he fired his equation cartridge.

The cartridge had been programmed to seek out each spirit spear in turn, and it ricocheted from one side of the pier to the other, and then back to the spear that was embedded in Keldak's head.

Isabel Gowdie's dreams were different. With the influence of Satan behind her, she could dream dreams that obeyed no natural laws. But in this young prostitute's dream, the laws of matter still applied, even if they were distorted beyond recognition. One of the laws of matter was that no two objects could occupy the same space at the same time.

The first Carrier's spear exploded in a shattering blast of subnuclear fission. The Carrier was blown apart in a blizzard of ash and mold and tattered fabric. A second later, the second

Carrier exploded. His substance vanished across the sea like smoke. Then Keldak exploded, an instant cremation that left the shell of his green armor burning fiercely on the side of the pier, and destroyed the spirit who had been promised his body, too.

One Carrier was left. Unarmed, with no man-dogs to protect him, he began to edge away. But Zasta stepped quickly forward and singled out one enormous gold-bladed knife. He threw it diagonally across the pier, and it hit the Carrier with such force that the Carrier was nailed to the side of the amusement arcade. He hung there, twitching, while pieces of dry decayed flesh dropped from his empty sleeves, and dust sifted from his empty trousers. Eventually, the wind caught his perfect white mask and tossed it away; and as the Night Warriors passed him by, they saw nothing inside his hood but a blindly-staring skull, with turkey-leg skin stretched across it.

Mol Besa glanced back briefly at the smoldering remains of Keldak's armor. The calliope continued to pump out *"I Do Like to Be Beside the Seaside."* Mol Besa looked back at Kasyx and asked, "She's still here? Isabel Gowdie? You're still picking her up? I want her now, Kasyx. I want her real bad."

Effis was tearful. "Is 'e really dead?" she kept asking. "I mean, what's going to 'appen to 'is real body?"

"He won't wake up, that's all," Kasyx explained grimly. "We'll have to find some way of disposing of him."

The four of them spread out across the pier and made their way towards the funfair at the very end of it. The pier seemed like an isolated world of its own, out here, a half mile away from the shore. Looking back, they could see Brighton and the Downs and the sparkling shoreline. In front of them towered an old-fashioned Victorian helter-skelter, painted red and white, with a notice saying that you could see France from the top of it, on a bright day.

No sign of Isabel Gowdie. No sign of anybody. The dodgem cars stood abandoned; the candy-floss stall was empty. At the very end of the pier, however, stood a Hall of Mirrors.

"There," said Kasyx.

Without hesitation, the Night Warriors advanced on the Hall of Mirrors and went inside. The calliope played, *I do like to*

*stroll along the prom, prom, prom . . . with the brass band
playing tiddly-om-pom-pom . . .*

Mol Besa stopped for a moment and watched himself in one
of the tarnished mirrors as—in readiness for meeting Isabel
Gowdie—he punched out a program that would convert a human being into a Möbius strip of harshly-colliding atomic particles. In other words, he had decided to convert Isabel Gowdie
into an endless loop of agony . . . to give her pain everlasting,
amen.

It was sadistic, he knew that. But it was the Night Plague
that had made him sadistic. Isabel Gowdie would receive a
punishment which, without the infection that she had given
him, he would have been incapable of carrying out. He relished
the irony of that.

He shuffled further into the Hall of Mirrors. He saw Effis
passing in front of him, but obviously she couldn't see him.
He saw Zasta, turning this way and that, hurrying through the
mirror-maze in the frantic way that children always do. He
looked to his left and saw Kasyx, feeling his way with every
step.

The Hall of Mirrors was hot and stuffy and smelled as if it
hadn't been swept out for fifty years. Mol Besa kept going,
deeper and deeper, watching six of himself advancing towards
the end of a corridor, until he discovered that the corridor had
no end, but was a sharp left turning instead.

He turned again and shouted, *"Ah!"*

In the mirror facing him stood Isabel Gowdie, her face white,
her eyes milky-green, with white fire streaming from out of
her hair. She was wearing a garment like a white kaftan, embroidered with white, although one breast was exposed, baring
a nipple like a small curled-up mollusc.

You dare to pursue me, Mol Besa! she hissed in his head, in
a voice like a frying pan full of snakes. *I killed you once, I
will kill you again!*

"Not this time, Ms. Gowdie," Mol Besa told her, and
stepped cautiously forward lifting his equation pistol. "This
time, the Night Warriors get their revenge."

Isabel Gowdie's eyes brightened. *You threaten me with pain?
You threaten me with punishment? I am the Queen of Pain! I
am the Queen of Punishment!*

"Then, believe me," said Mol Besa, preparing to squeeze the equation pistol's double trigger, "this one you're really going to enjoy!"

You'd punish your children, too? Isabel Gowdie shrilled at him. *You'd sentence your children to eternal pain?*

Mol Besa hesitated. At that moment, he was joined by Kasyx, who said, "Mol Besa—whatever you do, don't fire yet."

"What's happened?" Mol Besa demanded. "What are you talking about? What children?"

Isabel Gowdie laughed shrilly. Then she dragged up her kaftan to expose her naked body. Her white stomach was hugely swollen and marbled with veins, as if she were seven or eight months' pregnant.

She grinned. *This is one of your children! You gave him to me only yesterday, don't you remember? Swallow him down, sick him up!*

"How can you have a baby in a day?" Mol Besa retorted.

You poor foolish Night Warrior! In a dream, you can have a baby in an hour! In a dream, you can have a baby in a minute!

Mol Besa tightened his finger on the trigger. "That's no baby; that's just a ploy."

Oh, it's a baby, all right. Our baby. The first unnatural union between a Night Warrior and a servant of Satan, and what a baby that will be! Brave, noble, powerful, and utterly corrupt! My Lord and Master will be delighted! And somebody will have to rule this world, when the Night Plague has cut such a swathe through all of you!

"That's it," Mol Besa told her. "I've heard enough."

You'd condemn your children? Isabel Gowdie grinned again.

"That child inside of you is no child of mine."

But what about this one? asked Isabel Gowdie. She reached out beside her, and to Mol Besa's horror she dragged Zasta into view. His knives had all been stripped from his back, and he was tightly bound with white-sparkling brambles.

"Let him go, you bitch!" Mol Besa bellowed at her. "Let him go!"

Why should I? He and his brother About-to-Be-Born will make good companions. Besides, he needs to learn a thing or two, does Zasta. Like the dangers of looking for witches in mirrors. Witches understand mirrors. Mirrors understand witches.

Zasta cried out, "Mol Besa! Kill her! Don't worry about me!"

For a chipped-off fraction of a second, Mol Besa was tempted to fire. But he could feel that it was the Night Plague tugging at his judgment. The black nudge of Satan. He slowly shook his head, backed away, and said, "No, Zasta. No way."

The mathematicks, ordered Isabel Gowdie. *Unload the mathematicks.*

Mol Besa slid back the breech of his equation pistol and removed the cartridge. "All right, are you satisfied now? Will you let Zasta go?"

Let him go? Are you mad? Never, as long as you come following me, Mol Besa! Never, never, never! He can be the best of my boy-dogs, the snappiest of all my slaves! You thought of it yourself, Mol Besa! You thought of it yourself!

In a fury, Mol Besa swung his armored fist at Isabel Gowdie's mirror image. It burst apart with a shattering crack, and thousands of laughing images of the witch-woman flew everywhere. Then, all around them, the Hall of Mirrors began to explode. Glass fountained up into the air and then showered down on their shoulders. Huge triangular shards of glass fell ringing to the floor.

Mol Besa smashed his way to the front of the Hall of Mirrors. The pier was deserted now; the sea was gray. The sky was beginning to cloud over, and lightning stilt-walked over the Downs.

"She's taken Zasta," Mol Besa told Kasyx with a dry mouth. "Kasyx, she's taken my son."

Effis said, "She won't kill 'im, will she? Or turn 'im into one of them dogs?"

"Wait," said Kasyx. "She hasn't gone far. It's almost morning now, she won't have wanted to travel too far away from her sleeping body."

Mol Besa looked frantically around, but the seafront was empty. A crumpled fish-and-chip wrapper was tossed over and over by the rising wind.

"Is she still in this dream?" asked Mol Besa.

Kasyx checked his wrist instruments. He waited for the holographic data to bleep back at him, then he shook his head. "She's left it. But she's still in a dream state, and she isn't far away."

"Then—?"

"The man in bed with her, the Cabinet Minister. She's gone into hiding in *his* dream now!"

They returned at a steady jog to the Grand Hotel. They were watched from the windows of cafés and pubs by creatures with faces like huge rodents. It began to rain, and the raindrops trembled on Mol Besa's visor. They pushed their way through the hotel's revolving door and took the stairs three at a time.

As soon as they were back in the dream location of the Cabinet Minister's bedroom, they gathered around his bed, and Kasyx held out his hands in front of him. With a soft sparkling sound, a thin blue line appeared, bisecting the air between his upraised thumbs. He plunged his fingers into the line as if it were the join between two curtains and stretched it apart. He was opening up the fabric of the prostitute's dream and letting them through to the Cabinet Minister's dream, like stepping from one room into the next. He passed through the opening he had created, and Effis and Mol Besa followed him.

They were swamped immediately in raging noise. They were inside the House of Commons, making their way along one of the back benches. The oak-paneled Gothic chamber was swarming with thousands of screeching and screaming creatures, all of them dressed as men, in black tailcoats and starched white collars, but all with the heads of diseased and misshapen beasts.

A creature like a vast cockroach sat in the speaker's chair, while the floor in front of him glistened with thousands of black beetles. A huge looming animal like a man-horse was standing on its hind legs, overshadowing every one of the animals around it, whinnying and screaming and pawing the air with its hoofs. Other creatures crawled and dropped from bench to bench and writhed down the gangways. Mol Besa saw massive slugs and huge translucent grubs and things like praying mantises that shivered and whined.

"A politician's nightmare!" Kasyx yelled, over the screaming and screeching and roaring. Wincing in concentration, he checked his instruments. "She's gone that way. See that open door!"

The three of them hurried out of the Chamber, Kasyx and Mol Besa at a steady trot, Effis sliding effortlessly behind them on shining light-skates. Mol Besa's boots crunched beetles underfoot. Outside the door, they found themselves back in the pouring rain, back in Isabel Gowdie's miserable and plague-ridden London of the 1660s.

Isabel Gowdie hadn't walked far. She probably hadn't expected Mol Besa to be foolhardy enough to follow her. They could see her sixty or seventy yards away, on the far side of the boggy straw-strewn tract that would one day be Parliament Square. Her white hair glittered in the rain, her kaftan flew and flapped. Beside her, with a fast obedient limp, walked Knitted Hood, and Knitted Hood was dragging along the reluctant but thorn-bound Zasta.

"What the hell are we going to do?" Mol Besa asked Kasyx. "If we try anything too threatening, she's going to kill him."

Kasyx looked serious. "That's the risk we all have to take. Zasta knew the dangers of what he was doing, just the same as you."

"Kasyx, he may be Zasta but he's still my son. And this time history isn't going to repeat itself."

Effis said, "You 'ave to give it a go, though, Mol Besa. You don't want 'im turned into one of them 'orrible dogs. 'E'd never forgive you for that."

Mol Besa closed his eyes. God, Ashapola, whoever you are, give me courage. With his eyes closed, he was conscious of that dark stingray that glides silently over the shoals of the human consciousness, Satan, with his smile and his dead expressionless eyes, and he thought to himself, with a nerve that only the Night Plague could have given him, *You can help me, too, my Lord and Master, Your Satanic Majesty, you unmitigated son of a bitch.*

He opened his eyes. Then he glanced at Kasyx and Effis and said, "Okay. Let's do it."

They marched steadily through the rain and the mud, following Isabel Gowdie and Knitted Hood with dogged determination. They hadn't gone far, however, when they heard the creaking of a handcart. From behind the low wall of a dripping ramshackle farmhouse, a girl appeared, the same girl that Mol Besa had seen so many times before, pushing a load of joggling, lifeless bodies.

She stopped when she saw them, and stared at them. Mol Besa stopped, too, and stared back at her. He had suddenly recognized her for who she was.

"Eve," he breathed in disbelief. "How can you be here?"

She was a younger Eve, a much younger Eve, the Eve when they had married. He was amazed that he hadn't recognized her before. The mud, and the poverty, and the strangeness of Isabel Gowdie's dream surroundings—they had all conspired to make her appear different. And there was something else, too. Over the past few months, his own rejection of her had changed his perception of what she really looked like. Litigation had made him remember her as ugly.

She tilted the handcart so that its shafts rested on the muddy ground. "We all have our different vows to attend to," she told him simply.

"Are you a Night Warrior, too?"

She smiled, shook her head. "My vows are much more important than that."

Kasyx touched Mol Besa's arm. "Look—they've stopped. They've seen us."

He was right. Through the driving rain, through the darkness, Mol Besa could see that Isabel Gowdie and Knitted Hood were standing quite still, waiting for them.

Kasyx said, "Time for a showdown, I believe."

They walked past the handcart and through the puddles and the clinging mud. Isabel Gowdie was soaked, her kaftan clinging to her pregnant belly. She stared at Mol Besa with a maddened smile on her face, the smile of Satan. Beside her, Knitted Hood remained silent, his exquisite white face watching the Night Warriors without expression.

So you decided to risk everything and follow me? Isabel Gowdie challenged them.

Mol Besa took two or three steps forward. "I want you to let my son go. If you like, you can take me instead. You've already infected my soul; there isn't any future for me, anyway. But his life is just beginning. His soul—well, *his* soul is young and pure, and I simply don't want you to have it."

Isabel Gowdie arched her head back and looked at Mol Besa under dripping eyelashes. She said nothing for a long time, then she slowly, slowly shook her head. *You can follow me through a million dreams, Mol Besa; from pole to pole; from Africa to South America. I will never give you back your son.*

Knitted Hood uttered a hollow, dry whistling laugh. *Hooooeeeee, oop.* Then he lifted Zasta up by one wrist, so that his feet were clear of the mud, and let him spin around. Zasta screamed in terror.

Mol Besa shouted, "Let him go! Haven't you had enough? Haven't you spread enough of your goddamned misery around?"

Oh, no, Mol Besa. Isabel Gowdie grinned. *Not by a long chalk.*

Kasyx stepped forward and laid his hand on Mol Besa's shoulder. "Mol Besa," he said, "come on. Leave it for tonight. This is one of those times when discretion is the better part of valor."

Mol Besa knew that he was right. He hesitated, with tears in his eyes, then he turned away. "If she so much as *touches* that boy . . ."

As he turned away, however, he was astonished to see Eve walking towards them, her arms by her sides, her face oddly illuminated. She passed between the Night Warriors and walked right up to Knitted Hood. She stood in front of him, the rain staining her linen bonnet and the plain brown shoulders of her dress. Then she said, quietly but clearly, "Let him go."

Isabel Gowdie glared at her in amazement and fury. *Let him go, you ugly sow? How dare you tell my Carrier to let him go?*

Eve turned to Isabel Gowdie and said, "Because I am Eve. Because I will always be Eve. Because ever since Eve, every mother has always had to undertake to love and protect her sons, no matter what the cost, forever. Sometimes we have had to weep for our sons. Sometimes we have had to bury them. But I shall not weep for my son; neither shall I bury him. You will let him go."

Knitted Hood stared at Eve, and then grasped Zasta around the neck and squeezed him. Zasta kicked and thrashed and cried out; but Eve unhesitatingly stepped forward and pointed one finger directly at Knitted Hood's face. *Let him go.*

There was a moment of total silence, except for the pattering rain. Then Knitted Hood's fingers gradually opened, and Zasta dropped down to the ground.

A split second later, the knitted hood that had given him his name burst silently apart. His head softly detonated, and his half-putrescent brains streamed upwards, into the sky, in a thick and poisonous rope. Right in front of their eyes, the contents of his body poured vertically out of his neck, hurtling faster and faster, lungs and spleen and bladder, a sudden liquid rush of intestines, until the gray gaberdine raincoat collapsed empty in front of them, and Knitted Hood vanished into the stormy sky.

Eve took Zasta's hand and stepped away from Isabel Gowdie. "Now," she said, "you will do what you have to do, to release my husband from the Night Plague, and all those you have infected through him."

You sanctimonious bitch! You daughter of a dog! And what if I won't?

"I can't harm you. I haven't the power. But I do have the power to protect the baby that has grown inside you."

What are you talking about, bitch? flared Isabel Gowdie.

"Your baby is my son's brother; and I am pledged to protect brothers down all the centuries of all mankind; as all mothers are; to atone for the crime of Cain, who killed his brother Abel."

I will boil this baby, you bitch!

"No. You cannot. If you so much as touch one hair of that baby's head, *then* I will have the power to punish you, beyond any punishment that you can imagine possible. You would be better advised to do what you have to do, to release my husband from the Night Plague, and to surrender your baby to whatever destiny lies in wait for it."

Isabel Gowdie's eyes narrowed. *You're lying.*

But Eve stepped forward, pointed her finger directly at Isabel Gowdie's forehead, and touched it, the lightest touch. Instantly, blood spurted from the screw wounds around Isabel Gowdie's temples. The witch let out a piercing shriek.

You're lying!

"You want more?" demanded Eve. "You want your brains to spew up into the sky, like those of your Carrier?"

Isabel Gowdie trembled. Sparks flew from her hair in all directions, her eyes blazed white. *I shall be revenged for this, Eve, daughter of a dog, wife of Adam.*

"Do what you have to do," Eve insisted.

The sparks in her hair subsided. Isabel Gowdie rubbed her left arm, and for a moment Mol Besa could see in her the thin unconventional Scottish girl she must have been so many centuries ago, before she had given herself to Satan.

We'd better be doing it, then, Mol Besa, she said. Staring at him proudly and defiantly, she lifted her kaftan up around her waist and knelt on the ground, with her forehead pressed deep into the mud. The rain fell on her bare white buttocks.

Mol Besa glanced at Kasyx, and Kasyx nodded his assent. Slowly, Mol Besa climbed down on to his knees behind Isabel Gowdie and opened his armor. Eve turned away, although Effis watched, her face curiously sad.

He was only just stiff enough to penetrate her. She was cold, but hot inside. He thrust at her in unsteady, jerky movements. His mouth was dry and it was hard to stop himself from shaking.

What was worse, as he coupled with her, the parting of her hair began to widen, and her scalp peeled apart, layer by layer, until the face on top of her head reappeared. One face, pressed against the ground, groaned in ecstasy. The other face, lifted to the rain, screamed in pain. Mol Besa felt Isabel Gowdie's thin rib cage convulse and convulse and tighten in spasm. Something pale slipped out of the mouth on top of her head, something which she caught in her upraised hands. At the same time, painfully, unpleasantly, Mol Besa ejaculated.

He stood up, rebuckling his armor. Isabel Gowdie lay where she was for a moment, while her hair closed over the face on top of her head.

She said softly, *It's done now. The plague is returned to me. You may have heaven, whatever heaven is worth.*

She stood up, muddied and wet, her white hair bedraggled but still twinkling with sparks. She was cupping something in the palms of her hands.

And this, she said, *this is what a servant of Satan and a Night Warrior can produce together, when good and evil reconcile their differences.*

She went from one to the other and showed them a tiny perfect baby, no longer than six or seven inches, a little boy, shining and naked. She kissed it, and then she lifted it up, and it floated out of her hand as if it were sparkling thistledown, as if it weighed nothing at all, and swirled around once, and vanished into the night.

That was when Mol Besa pulled the trigger of his equation pistol and turned the rest of Isabel Gowdie's infinity into an endless scream.

Stanley was leaning on the railing of the Embarcadero watching the docking of an Argentinian training ship, with all of its hands aloft in the rigging, when a slender young man in a white Armani suit came and stood close beside him.

San Francisco being San Francisco, Stanley edged a few inches away. It was only when the young man said, "How's life, Stanley?" that he looked up and realized that it was Springer.

"Life's fine," said Stanley guardedly. "You haven't come to offer me any more work have you?"

Springer smiled and shook his head. "Just came to see how you were. Warm today, isn't it?"

Stanley nodded, said nothing.

"How's Leon?" asked Springer.

"Leon's fine."

"And Eve?"

"We seem to be rubbing along okay. Time will tell."

"Henry sends his best," Springer told him. "Angie married that Paul of hers."

"Angie," Stanley repeated. It sounded like a name from another life.

"There's one more thing," said Springer. He fumbled in his pocket and produced a soft red velvet bag. "I kept this by me. Some people don't always have time to say goodbye."

He opened the drawstring and showed Stanley what was in it.

Stanley frowned. "Bones?'

"The bones of Gordon's left hand, to be precise," Springer explained.

He opened the bag wider, lifted it up, and without ceremony

shook the bones into the harbor. They fell with a light pattering splash.

Stanley looked down at them, watched them sink. "Good-bye, Gordon," he said. "It was pretty good to know you."

It may have been nothing more than a swirl in the water, a glint of the sun; but he was sure that he saw a hand rise out of the harbor for a moment and give him one last regretful wave.

If you ever hear the most elegant Baroque violin music on your stereo, then it will probably have been played by Stanley Eisner.

On the other hand, if you ever hear inexplicable screaming in the night, screaming that seems to come from nowhere at all, and goes on and on and on and on, then you will know that Isabel Gowdie has passed you by.

And if you ever hear a baby crying, plaintive and small, you will know that it is the Night Child, son of a witch and a Night Warrior, spurned by Satan, unloved by God, who can never, ever find his way home.